YUMMI YOGHURT

– A First Taste of Stock Market Investment!

by

John Lee
Lord Lee of Trafford DL FCA

Grosvenor House
Publishing Limited

This book is published by
Grosvenor House Publishing Ltd
Link House
140 The Broadway, Tolworth, Surrey, KT6 7HT.
www.grosvenorhousepublishing.co.uk

A CIP record for this book
is available from the British Library

ISBN 978-1-78623-520-6

"Bite-sized lessons in the art of Stock-picking from one of the UK's best-known Small Cap investors."

Claer Barrett, Personal Finance Editor,
Financial Times

"Most students when they leave school have little knowledge of the world of business - what's a dividend, a flotation, a takeover, a unit trust or 'going public'? So John Lee an experienced and successful investor who writes for *FT Money* has written a beginner's guide to the world of finance, business and investment. This is the chronicle of a family business which grows from a clever idea to a company with worldwide sales. It is a route that many have travelled and John Lee has created the signposts along the way for others to follow."

Lord Kenneth Baker, former Education Secretary

"An essential read for anyone who wants to understand the world of investments. Plain-talking in plain English. Devour and learn how to build long-term wealth."

Jeff Prestridge, Personal Finance Editor,
The Mail on Sunday

"To my knowledge, a first on Stock Market investment for teenagers. Investing in and supporting business growth is socially useful - helping to create jobs and wealth. Indeed "Yummi Yoghurt" is an excellent investment in itself!"

Gervais Williams, Managing Director, Miton Group

DEDICATION

To my Grandchildren,
Eli, Florence, Isaac and Ivan
Hoping that at least one of them will inherit my enthusiasm for
The Stock Market!

CONTENTS

ACKNOWLEDGEMENTS

With grateful thanks to:

Robbie Cathro for the cover illustration and
Kate Wakeham for her help with design and art direction

The Economics Department and Students of
Withington Girls' School

My secretary, Kathy Fogarty, for all secretarial back-up

The Team at Grosvenor House Publishing for
facilitating this publication

and finally, to the very many colleagues and friends,
and their families, who have offered guidance,
suggestions and support.

INTRODUCTION

I bought my first shares when I was fifteen – over sixty years ago – investing £45 in shipping company Aviation & Shipping who owned one ship. Sadly, the vessel foundered taking all my investment with it! Not the most auspicious start to my investing life!

Looking back, my early investment knowledge was almost literally gained on my medical father's shoulder as he sat crossed-legged on the floor in his library, smoking his favourite pipe, pouring over copies of the then-weekly publications *The Investor's Chronicle* (still going today) and *The Stock Exchange Gazette*. As I started to delve myself into these publications and talk with him I became increasingly fascinated and captivated by the Stock Market and the worlds of investment and public companies. Over the years investing became a core interest and activity of mine. I am passionate about encouraging people, particularly the young, to become investors themselves and to share the pleasure and hopefully the profitable experiences that I have had (we all make mistakes!). However, I have long felt that there was a need for a first-stage easy-to-read guide to Stock Market investment for beginners – I only wish there had been such a publication when I started all those years ago. Hence this book *Yummi Yoghurt* was conceived to fill the gap. It tells the story of a Devon farming family who started producing yoghurt to supplement their farm income, which developed into a very successful business ultimately becoming a publicly quoted company, and how the teenage children of another family made their first ever investments in Yummi, when it went public, using monies left to them by their grandfather.

What the Stock Exchange is, how to buy and sell shares, dividends, comparative valuations etc., are all covered, as are the reasons why shares may rise and fall. Yummi is not intended to be a comprehensive guide to Stock Market investment – what it is intended to do is to give the beginner a basic "feel" and understanding of investment – to whet the appetite – which should at the very least enable the reader to broadly understand city media articles and the language of stockbrokers, financial advisers and wealth-managers. In short, it introduces the reader to investment in a light, easy-to-read, undemanding way, and encouraging more people to save and invest surely has to be in our national interest as well.

THE STORY OF YUMMI YOGHURT
From Dairy Farm to Public Company

It had been a very happy day. The new purpose built Yummi Yoghurt factory had been officially opened by the Mayor, supported by the Member of Parliament. Regional TV and representatives from the two supermarket groups, on whose firm contracts the Baron family had felt confident enough to borrow from the bank to finance the new factory, had all been there. With the ceremony over, all present including the families of their 40 employees tucked into a lavish buffet. What had started out five years ago as a fun venture, utilising Tessa Baron's culinary skills, and as a way to diversify and supplement their modest Devon farm family income, had grown into a serious commercial venture. Husband Reg was now in charge of purchasing and transport, and daughter Fiona – who had just graduated in business administration – had control of the finances. The previous week they had met with their accountants to discuss results for the last financial year. After directors' salaries and all other costs they were showing a profit of just over £50,000! Yummi Yoghurt was really up and running – high quality, low fat fruit yoghurts from their West Country base.

Ten years later the business had gone from strength-to-strength. Turnover (sales) had soared to £9 million, their workforce was now 100 strong, a new factory extension had just been completed and they were supplying many of the country's major supermarket chains. Father Reg was now part-time Chairman, Mum Tessa a very hands-on Managing

Director, Fiona, now married, had moved to Marketing Director with her husband Jeremy (a chartered accountant) as Financial Director and Company Secretary.

In recent years they had received a number of takeover approaches from major national food manufacturing groups, but had rejected them all, wishing to remain independent, develop at their own pace, and above all maintain product quality. They believed that they had many years of growth still ahead. Yummi had now become quite a valuable business and on the advice of their accountants the family decided to consider their future options in conjunction with a recommended leading investment bank, Carstairs & Co.

Put very simply, the figures which they showed to the Carstairs team were:

Forecast sales:		£ 9,000,000
Less costs of sales, ingredients, packaging, staff wages etc.	£3,600,000	
Overheads, heat, light, transportation etc.	£ 900,000	£ 4,500,000
Profit before tax:		£ 4,500,000
Corporation Tax at 20%		£ 900,000
Net profit after tax:		£ 3,600,000

The Balance Sheet of Yummi was as follows:

Freehold property	£ 4,000,000	Yummi's factory in Devon
Plant equipment, vehicles	£ 1,500,000	
Stock	£ 500,000	Raw materials, packaging ingredients
Debtors	£ 2,000,000	Goods sold to customers e.g. supermarkets not yet paid for
Cash in the bank	£ 2,500,000	
Total Assets	£10,500,000	
Less Creditors	£ 500,000	Amounts Yummi owes
Net Assets	£10,000,000	

Represented by say 10,000,000 shares of £1 each £10,000,000
    The Net Asset Value is the difference between the total assets of £10,500,000 and the total liabilities of £500,000 = £10,000,000.
    Thus each share had a Net Asset Value of £1

Yummi was a cash-generative business, such that the Barons had more than repaid all the original money borrowed for a new factory five years ago, indeed they now had over £2 million in the bank!

So, the family were in a very comfortable financial position. However virtually all their wealth outside their original farm, which was now more of a hobby, was tied-up in the Yummi business. Having carefully considered matters Reg and Tessa felt that as they were 65 and 60 respectively, it would be nice if for the first time in their lives they could take some capital out of Yummi, and perhaps buy a holiday/retirement home in France which had always been a far-off dream. Having taken everything into account, Yummi's history, its accounts, its product reputation and future prospects, Carstairs recommended that the Barons should consider taking Yummi "public" i.e. selling a proportion of its share capital to outside investors while retaining control of the business. This course of action would allow Reg and Tessa to take some money out of the business – the proceeds of their shares they sold to the wider public.

Carstairs were now in the driving seat having been appointed by the family to handle and advise on the flotation. They recommended that Yummi should "go public" early next year giving eight months to prepare. On Carstairs advice, the Baron family decided to replace their West County solicitors and accountants with major national firms and also to appoint a financial public relations firm. They didn't find it easy to break the news to their local professional firms, but explained it was necessary, on the advice of Carstairs, to appoint firms better known and respected by potential new investors. However, the Barons assured them that they would continue to handle the family's personal taxation and legal affairs. It was explained to the Barons that although the financial PR firm was expensive it was important to plan a media campaign for the next few months – generating awareness of Yummi and its products, and its intention to obtain a public quotation – hopefully whetting potential investors' appetites to consider applying for Yummi shares when they become available.

During the year the family had a number of meetings with Carstairs, their new auditors and solicitors, and the financial PR firm together with their newly-appointed stockbrokers, all of whom would be involved in the flotation. Having discussed timing options with the Stock Exchange, the flotation was fixed for the last week of the following January. Immediately after Christmas Carstairs got down to deciding on the price that Yummi shares should be sold at, studying particularly the share prices of other quoted food manufacturing companies and also taking into account the general level of the Stock Market. Carstairs advised that there were two main options for Yummi to go public: there could either be an "Offer For Sale" with a prospectus in the national press, which would deliver the equivalent of a full-page advertisement setting out comprehensive details on Yummi – names of directors, professional advisers, financial history, the balance sheet, and a forecast of future turnover and profits, plus a projected dividend. A dividend is the amount of profits, after the payment of Corporation Tax, that the company's directors decide could and should be paid out to shareholders. In making this decision they would take into account the future financial needs of the business i.e. are they planning to buy new modern plant and equipment or perhaps, say, the next generation of computers or robots, to enable the business to become more efficient. The other option Carstairs explained is to go public by a "placing" whereby a company's shares are "placed" with investors i.e. institutions or private investors via Stockbrokers. A Stockbroking firm is one whose business is the buying and selling of shares – parts of companies – on behalf of institutions i.e. insurance companies, pension funds etc., and individual private investors.

The share capital of Yummi was now £10 million divided into 10 million shares of £1 each. It was decided that the Barons would sell 40% of their shares in the flotation leaving them with 60% – thus still firmly in control. It was jointly agreed after much discussion that they would go down the "Offer For Sale" route. Their thinking was that as Yummi was a consumer product, an Offer For Sale would provide much more publicity than a placing, so adding to customer awareness – hopefully resulting in even more sales of Yummi Yoghurt! It was also agreed that the shares should be attractively priced to generate significant public/investor interest. The last thing they wanted was a "flop" – all shares on offer not being applied for – which obviously would reflect badly on the company's image and reputation.

Having taken all factors into account, it was finally agreed that Yummi's shares should be offered for sale at a price for £3 for a £1 share, thus giving an overall valuation for Yummi of £30 million i.e. 10 million shares at £3 each. The Baron family's 60% holding would consequently be worth £18 million – making them multi-millionaires!

The Prospectus for the "Offer for Sale" would contain a forecast:

Sales	£10,000,000
Less cost of sales	£ 5,000,000
Profit before Tax	£ 5,000,000
Less 20% Corporation Tax	£ 1,000,000
Net Profit:	£ 4,000,000

It was decided that half of the profits should be retained in the business for further expansion and new automated production lines etc., leaving £2 million for dividends to shareholders. This would be the equivalent of a 20% dividend on each of the 10 million shares. Therefore, at the flotation price of £3 a share the dividend yield is calculated as follows:

$$\frac{\text{Nominal value of Yummi shares}}{\text{Market Price}} \times 20\%$$

$$\text{i.e. } \frac{£1}{£3} \times 20\% = 6.66\%$$

(Put another way, anyone investing £100 would be buying 33 shares at £3 each. Thus, with a 20% dividend they would receive £6.60.) Frequently a dividend is declared in pence per share, thus the 20% dividend could be expressed as 20p per £1 share. As can be seen, the £2 million cost of dividends is covered twice by the available £4 million of net profit.

At £3 per share the Price Earnings Ratio – a valuation for comparing share prices – was 7.5 calculated as follows:

Total Market Capitalisation: £30,000,000

$$\div \quad = 7.5$$

Post Tax Profits: £4,000,000

The Stock Exchange

The Stock Exchange is basically like any other market – an opportunity to buy or sell things or goods. Just as Smithfield is a market for meat and Billingsgate a market for fish, the Stock Exchange is a market where parts or shares of businesses are bought and sold on behalf of institutions or individuals by banks or stockbrokers. Essentially it provides a mechanism for businesses to raise money from shareholders for development and expansion. Most businesses in the UK are private companies i.e. owned privately by individuals or families. It is public companies – usually but not necessarily larger businesses – where the general public, you and me, can buy and sell shares. It is not only individuals who may own shares, they can also be held by institutions e.g. insurance companies or pension funds, or other funds. Many individuals instead of owning shares in their own right prefer to invest via funds i.e., Investment Trusts or Unit Trusts. These are essentially collective vehicles where the monies of private investors are blocked together, with the fund itself owning the shares in those public companies. There are a whole range of funds to invest in – many for example specialising in different parts of the world i.e. the First India Fund, as its name implies, only investing in companies quoted in India, while say the Blue Cross Health Fund might only invest in Healthcare businesses. Investing through such a fund helps to spread risk rather than the risk inherent in investing directly in a particular company.

The Jennings Family

Mark, a solicitor, and Lesley, a dentist, live just outside Bury, Lancashire, with their 18-year-old son Ben and twin 16-year-old daughters, Melanie and Helen. With both parents working professionally, the Jennings family are comfortably-off financially, with their house mortgage long since paid-off and having built-up a joint share portfolio – mainly "Large Cap" stocks i.e. shares in national or international companies. Father Mark had mentioned the Stock Market to his three children – none of them had so far shown much interest! However last Christmas their Grandfather – Lesley's father – died leaving £2,500 to each of his grandchildren. Ben decided to spend £1,000 on a second-hand car having just passed his test, but Melanie and Helen decided to save their windfall. Over the dinner table the family discussed their financial options – each child favoured Premium Bonds, but Mark was hoping to encourage them to think about the Stock Market. He had read newspaper reports that Yummi Yoghurt was "going public" and was aware that the whole family enjoyed their yoghurt brands. What better way to encourage the youngsters to invest than to point them towards acquiring a shareholding in Yummi!

On the Monday of the last week in January the prospectus (Offer for Sale) appeared in two national daily papers. 40% of the shares in Yummi were offered for sale at £3 per share. The minimum number that could be applied for was 100 – it was stated that if the offer was oversubscribed i.e. the public applied for more shares than were on offer – then those applying for a smaller number of shares would be favoured – those applying for larger numbers would be scaled back. The reasoning behind this was that with Yummi being a consumer product, the more shareholders there were the greater likelihood of developing awareness and loyalty of and to the Yummi brand.

Press comment on the Offer for Sale was universally favourable. Most commentators knew the product, there was no other sole UK yoghurt manufacturer in which one could invest, (most other quality yoghurt manufacturers being part of larger food manufacturing groups) and the terms – a PER of 7.5 and a dividend yield of 6.6% were considered very attractive. In addition, commentators agreed that Yummi offered considerable growth prospects – not only was the sale of yoghurt growing year-on-year, but Yummi had stated in their prospectus that they were developing a number of new related dairy products, some of which were to be launched in the New Year.

The Jennings family bought extra copies of the newspaper which contained the Yummi prospectus on the day it appeared. Ben, Melanie and Helen had all decided to apply for 200 shares each. Father Mark checked each of their application forms carefully, ensuring that the £600 cheques etc., (200 x £3 per share) were correctly filled-in. They all eagerly awaited Friday's announcement of the results of the Offer for Sale: Great News! A Huge Success – in total investors had applied for ten times the number of shares being sold – in City parlance it had been "over-subscribed" ten times.

It was announced that larger applications were being drastically scaled-down so that anyone applying for 500 shares or less would receive their full requirement. The three Jennings children were delighted – they would receive the 200 shares they had each applied for; Mark and Lesley breathed a joint sigh of relief that so far at least their attempt to encourage Stock Market investment by their offspring had gone smoothly.

Now on to the following Tuesday when dealings in Yummi shares were due to start on the Stock Exchange! The whole family was excited. Lesley checked at 8:00am – the moment of first dealings – a great "Yippee!" went up. Yummi shares had opened at £3.60 each, 20% higher than the £3 offer price. So, all three children each had £720 worth of Yummi shares – on paper a profit of £120 on their £600 outlay. This premium meant that the whole of Yummi was now valued at £36 million – a 20% rise on the original £30 million. This new valuation meant that the PE ratio which had been 7.5 i.e.:

$$£30,000,000 \div £4,000,000 \text{ after tax profits} = 7.5$$

Was now:

$$£36,000,000 \div £4,000,000 \text{ after tax profits} = 9$$

The dividend yield, which had been 6.66% at £3 per share was now down to:

$$\frac{£1}{£3.60} \times 20\% = 5.6\%$$

The Baron Family had given all their employees with over one year's service 250 shares each as a gift, so they were delighted too!

Ten Reasons Why Yummi shares might rise

1. Yummi delivers increased profits and dividends year-on-year.
2. Favourable press comment.
3. Other supermarkets etc., start taking Yummi products.
4. A general rise in most share prices on the Stock Market.
5. Yummi announce a new range of dairy products.
6. Rumours of a takeover bid for Yummi i.e. another company is suggested as being interested in buying them.
7. A well-regarded private investor or institution i.e. insurance company or pension fund buys a large number of shares.
8. Optimistic comment by Yummi directors on future prospects.
9. Yummi shares upwardly re-rated (see later explanation).
10. Statistical evidence of increased national sales of yoghurt.

Ten Reasons Why Yummi shares might fall

1. Yummi's profits fall.
2. Yummi reduces (cuts) its dividend.
3. A general fall in share prices because of world events.
4. The Baron Family sell a large percentage of their shares.
5. There is a contamination/health scare regarding Yummi's products.
6. A major supermarket chain delists (stops selling) Yummi products.
7. Unfavourable press comment.
8. Key executive(s) or professional advisors resign or are charged with an offence.
9. Significant rise in the cost of ingredients/cartons/packaging etc.
10. A substantial long-term Yummi shareholder sells all or part of their holding.

Price Earnings Ratios

In our story, at the time of the Offer for Sale, Yummi was valued on a PER of 7.5 i.e.

CAPITALISATION $\dfrac{£30,000,000}{£\ 4,000,000}$ ÷ = 7.5
AFTER TAX PROFITS (Earnings)

On the first day of dealings as a public company with the shares rising from £3 to £3.60, its PER had risen to 9 i.e.

CAPITALISATION $\dfrac{£36,000,000}{£\ 4,000,000}$ ÷ = 9
AFTER TAX PROFITS (Earnings)

Consequently the upward movement in Yummi's shares had delivered an increase in the Price Earnings Ratio from 7.5 to 9 i.e. valuing Yummi more highly (upwardly re-rating them).

If Yummi's shares were to rise to say £4 then the PER would go even higher:

CAPITALISATION £10,000,000 x 4 = $\dfrac{£40,000,000}{£\ 4,000,000}$ ÷ =10
AFTER TAX PROFITS (Earnings)

So the higher the Price Earnings Ratio, the more highly are investors valuing the business.

Some very highly valued shares can be on a PER of 50 plus i.e. where investors think that the growth prospects for rising profits etc., are outstandingly good.

Conversely other very lowly valued shares can be on a 5 PER or similar i.e. where investors think that profits have very limited growth prospects, or indeed might fall, or perhaps its dividend might be reduced, or borrowings (debt) dangerously high.

It can be seen that the PER, at any one time, is an indication of how investors assess a company's prospects – comparison being made between different companies on the basis of their Price Earnings Ratios. It is only one of a number of yardsticks which are used to compare the valuations of different public companies.

Ben Jennings recounted the story of his Yummi investment to his closest college friend, Sanjay Karim. He had never invested in shares before but had built up savings in his bank account. Following discussions at his bank branch, they indicated that they would be happy to introduce him to local Bury Stockbrokers James Sharp and Co. Sanjay decided to invest himself in Yummi even though the market price had risen from £3 to £3.60. The actual quote of Yummi shares was £3.50–£3.60 i.e. an investor could sell shares at £3.50 or buy at £3.60. The difference being the market-maker's 'turn' or profit. He decided to buy 100 shares and received a 'Bought' contract note as follows:

James Sharp & Co.
The Exchange
5 Bank Street
Bury Lancashire BL9 0DN

Tel : 0161 764 4043
Fax : 0161 764 1628
DX : 20536 Bury
E : mail@jamessharp.co.uk

WWW.JAMESSHARP.CO.UK

Partners
Ian Bolton Chartered FCSI
Michael Tulip ACA, Chartered FCSI
Martin Entwistle BA (Hons), Chartered FCSI

Associate
Stephen Ross Chartered FCSI

Authorised and regulated
by the Financial Conduct
Authority
Member of the
London Stock Exchange
Member of Nexexchange
Member of PIMFA

JAMES SHARP & Co.

Client Ref	S1234	
Contract No.	74B	
Date	28/03/2019	Time 10.00
Settlement Day	04/04/2019	
Stock Code	X775463	

Sanjay Karim
Hillside View
Bury
Lancashire
BY6 PQ

We thank you for your instructions and have this day | BOUGHT

Yummi Yoghurt Plc
£1 Ordinary Shares

Quantity	Price	Bargain Conditions	Amount
100	360p		360.00
		Commission	22.00
		Compliance Charge	10.00
		Total	392.00

Notes: Contract notes should be retained for tax purposes.
We have acted as agents on your behalf in this transaction unless otherwise specified.
This contract is issued subject to the Rules and Regulations of the London Stock Exchange and to our normal terms and conditions of business.
Any errors or omissions should be reported immediately to your Account Executive.
Best execution cannot be guaranteed for transactions effected outside official market hours.

IMPORTANT SETTLEMENT INSTRUCTIONS

Client Ref	Bargain Ref	Settlement Date	Total Consideration
S1234	74B	04/04/2019	392.00

PURCHASES   Please detach this slip and return it together with your cheque to be received by us no later than **three business days** prior to the settlement date indicated above. Alternatively, please make arrangements to transfer funds to the following account, quoting your client reference. James Sharp & Co Client Deposit, The Royal Bank Of Scotland, 40 The Rock, Bury, A/C No. 11175859, Sort Code 16-15-12, IBAN GB83RBOS16151211175859, SWIFT/BIC RBOSGB2L
PLEASE IGNORE SETTLEMENT REQUIREMENTS FOR ISA PURCHASES

SALES   Please detach this slip and return it together with the completed transfer form and relevant certificate to be received by us no later than **three business days** prior to the settlement date indicated above.

CP MAR 2018 Ref JSP

Thus Sanjay's total cost, after Broker's charges, was £392

At the end of each financial year every Public Company has to publish an 'Annual Report,' a copy of which must be sent to every shareholder, and should also be available on its website. Annual Reports contain a mass of detailed information e.g. names and backgrounds of directors, a list of its professional advisors, reports usually from the Chairman and Chief Executive covering the financial results for the past year, usually comments on current trading and future prospects, and what dividend (if any) is recommended. The report will also contain a Profit and Loss Account and Balance Sheet, certified and approved by the appointed Auditors (firms of accountants whose job it is to confirm the accuracy of the financial accounts). The Annual Report will also usually contain a formal notice of the company's Annual General Meeting, which public companies are required to hold each year. Twenty-one-days' notice has to be given of this meeting which is open to all shareholders to attend. This gives individual shareholders an opportunity to question Directors on the company's activities and results etc. and meet with them usually after the formal meeting has closed. Yummi always provided pots of yoghurt at their Annual General Meeting for shareholders to taste, plus a small pack to take away!

At the meeting a number of formal resolutions are usually put to shareholders:

1. To approve the Annual Report and Accounts.
2. To re-appoint certain Directors (Directors retire by rotation and have to be re-appointed by shareholders).
3. To confirm the re-appointment of X, Y, and Z Chartered Accountants as Auditors of the company for coming financial year.
4. To approve the dividend recommended by the Directors.

After the AGM dividend warrants (cheques) will be sent out to each qualifying shareholder – the amount they receive being obviously dependent on the number of shares they own and the rate of dividend paid per share.

Three years later Melanie, now 19-years-old, decided to use her gap year before starting a veterinary course to travel to the Far East. To finance her trip, she decided to sell half her Yummi holding. During these last years, Yummi had delivered outstanding growth – profits nearly doubling to £7 million after tax, and with the original 20% dividend now at a 40% level. Unsurprisingly the shares which she had bought at £3 had now risen to £8 reflecting this performance and were being valued more highly by investors. As a result the Price Earnings Ratio was:

Share Capital 10,000,000 x £8 = £80,000,000 (Capitalisation)

$$\div$$

£ 7,000,000 (after tax profits)
= 11.5 approx.

The Dividend Yield at £8, and with a 40% dividend, was now:

$\dfrac{£1}{£8} \times 40 = 5\%$ (i.e. anyone investing £100 in Yummi shares would receive a Dividend of £5)

Melanie contacted the family's Stockbrokers, James Sharp of Bury – her parents had been clients for many years, so she needed no real introduction, and instructed them to sell half of her holding – 100 shares at the best price. They first of all sent her a new client's application form to complete, and on its return duly signed, they carried out her instructions. The Stock Market quote for Yummi was £8 to sell. Melanie received a "Sale" contract note from the Stockbrokers as follows:

James Sharp & Co.
The Exchange
5 Bank Street
Bury Lancashire BL9 0DN

Tel : 0161 764 4043
Fax : 0161 764 1628
DX : 20536 Bury
E : mail@jamessharp.co.uk

WWW.JAMESSHARP.CO.UK

Partners
Ian Bolton Chartered FCSI
Michael Tulip ACA Chartered FCSI
Martin Entwistle BA (Hons), Chartered FCSI

Associate
Stephen Ross Chartered FCSI

Authorised and regulated
by the Financial Conduct
Authority

Member of the
London Stock Exchange

Member of Nexexchange

Member of PIMFA

JAMES SHARP & Co.

Ms Melanie Jennings	**Client Ref**	J1435		
'The Coppice'	**Contract No.**	100C		
Last Drop Road				
Bury	**Date**	21/01/2020	**Time**	11.00
Lancashire				
BY6 RT	**Settlement Day**	24/01/2020		
	Stock Code	X775463		

We thank you for your instructions and have this day	SOLD

Yummi Yoghurt Plc
£1 Ordinary Shares

Quantity	Price	Bargain Conditions	Amount
100	800p		800.00
		Commission	22.00
		Compliance Charge	10.00
		Total	768.00

Notes: Contract notes should be retained for tax purposes.
We have acted as agents on your behalf in this transaction unless otherwise specified.
This contract is issued subject to the Rules and Regulations of the London Stock Exchange and to our normal
terms and conditions of business.
Any errors or omissions should be reported immediately to your Account Executive.
Best execution cannot be guaranteed for transactions effected outside official market hours.

IMPORTANT SETTLEMENT INSTRUCTIONS

Client Ref	Bargain Ref	Settlement Date	Total Consideration
J1435	100C	24/01/2020	768.00

PURCHASES   Please detach this slip and return it together with your cheque to be received by us no later than **three business days**
prior to the settlement date indicated above. Alternatively, please make arrangements to transfer funds to the following
account, quoting your client reference. James Sharp & Co Client Deposit, The Royal Bank Of Scotland, 40 The Rock, Bury,
A/C No. 11175859, Sort Code 16-15-12, IBAN GB83RBOS161512111175859, SWIFT/BIC RBOSGB2L
PLEASE IGNORE SETTLEMENT REQUIREMENTS FOR ISA PURCHASES

SALES   Please detach this slip and return it together with the completed transfer form and relevant certificate to be
received by us no later than three business days prior to the settlement date indicated above.

CP MAR 2018 Ref JSP

So, after the Stockbroker's commission and their compliance charge Melanie received a cheque for £768 – more than the original total £600 cost for her 200 shares – and she still had 100 shares left! How grateful she was to Yummi and of course to her parents for encouraging her to invest! Without the money from the sale Melanie could not have afforded her Far Eastern trip – she would have had to rely on borrowing the cost from her parents or finding a part-time job.

Melanie had done well to sell at £8 because the following year Yummi suffered its first set-back since "going public." Tiny fragments of glass were found in one of their yoghurt cartons by an Aberdeen customer. She had bought the carton at a local major supermarket outlet who immediately notified Yummi. It was agreed that all Yummi products produced in that batch would be withdrawn, not only from the supermarket concerned, but from all other supermarket chains and independent outlets as well. Yummi undertook to reimburse any customers who had bought yoghurt provided they returned the cartons to their store of purchase for destruction. In addition, total production was shut-down while all machinery and packaging lines were cleaned and carefully checked. Fortunately, no other glass fragments were found nor was their source ever traced. It was calculated that the whole incident cost Yummi £1 million in production stoppage, compensation and loss of sales. Parallel to the public announcement Yummi also had to make a formal announcement to the Stock Market which caused their shares to fall from the then £8.50 to £7. Yummi forecast that their annual profits, which had been expected to rise from £7 million to £8 million would now mark time at the lower figure. With no more contamination discovered and optimistic comments about a return to profits the following year, the share price gradually recovered to £8 by the year end.

Two years later i.e. five years from going public, Yummi received a "Takeover Bid" from a large multi-million-pound international food group, Global Foods Inc – keen to buy

Yummi and its brand to add a new product range to their existing portfolio of brands. Their initial offer was £11 per share, valuing Yummi at £110 million. The Directors' of Yummi – the Baron Family members who still effectively owned 60% of the share capital and their two "Independent" i.e. non-family Directors immediately entered into discussions with advisors Carstairs & Co. While profits of Yummi had now risen to £10 million the prospects for further growth were looking more limited given that all the major supermarket chains were already stocking their yoghurt/dairy products. In addition, Reg and Tessa Baron had effectively reached retirement age, and Fiona and Jeremy were keen to spend more time with their young family so the feeling was that if Yummi could obtain a higher bid then they would accept it provided the bidder committed to retain both the Devon factory and all their employees.

Following further discussions and the provision of more detailed information to the prospective bidder, the bid level was raised to £13 a share valuing Yummi at £130 million. Terms were agreed and the Board of Yummi pledged to accept the offer and recommend it to outside shareholders. Formal documents were sent out in due course to all shareholders including the Jennings Family. So, Ben and Helen who had each retained their 200 shares were going to receive £2,600 compared with their original outlay of £600 and Melanie, with 100 shares left, should receive £1,300 – all making very sizeable profits on their original purchase. Ben's close friend, Sanjay, was also delighted – receiving £13 a share against his £3.60 purchase price. The documentation gave them the option of having their proceeds paid directly into their bank accounts rather than receiving a cheque.

So, for Ben, Melanie and Helen – and also Sanjay – their first foray into the Stock Market had been a huge success. They were all now looking for their next investment opportunity and had started to explore the financial columns of national papers, company websites etc., and happily to discuss ideas and opportunities with their parents and their Stockbroker – all having become clients of their local Bury firm of James Sharp. But they must be careful. Yes, Yummi had been a great investment but all investment in businesses – public or private – carries a degree of risk and they would be very fortunate to easily find another Yummi. Indeed perhaps it would be sensible to only consider reinvesting half their Yummi proceeds, keeping the other half in the Bank or perhaps something very safe like Premium Bonds. Rather than re-invest in the shares of just one company, they might consider buying shares in, say, three different ones, to spread the risk and increase their investment knowledge of companies and sectors. Crucially, they must remember that all investors make mistakes and lose money from time-to-time – but the aim is of course to generate more profits than losses!

On the final page I list twelve key recommendations which hopefully will help readers/investors to reduce risks and avoid losses.

To conclude our story the Baron Family – still owning their 60% of Yummi received a whopping £78 million for their holding i.e., six million shares at £13 following the takeover. Reg and Tessa happily retired to France, Fiona and Jeremy who stayed in post for six months to facilitate the physical and human aspects of the takeover, continued to manage the family farm and made generous donations to their local church and to West Country charities. They focussed their energies on charitable work with Fiona also becoming a Governor of their local primary school. Ben Jennings, who found his Yummi investing experience so rewarding and exciting resolved to become a Stockbroker, while Melanie, Helen and Sanjay built up very useful share portfolios over the years. Yummi – having become part of Global Foods Inc., developed a substantial export business, benefitting from the greater resources and connections of its new owner. The Baron Family were delighted with the onward progress and expansion of Yummi as its factory was subsequently doubled in size, becoming one of the largest employers in the West Country.

This story demonstrates how the development and growth of a business benefits not only the founders and its shareholders, but also employees and the local and regional community. In Yummi's case employment opportunities in a rural area would obviously be limited, so a new growing manufacturing business providing jobs nearer to home would be very welcomed. In addition, of course, a growing business provides a significant outlet for local tradespeople and suppliers – from builders and electricians to taxi drivers and catering vendors. Finally, the national Exchequer benefits from Corporation Tax paid by companies like Yummi out of its profits, and the tax deductions and NI etc., contributions from their employees. A happy story with everyone a winner!

SUMMARY OVER YUMMI'S FIVE YEARS PUBLIC COMPANY LIFE

	PROFITS AFTER TAX	SHARE PRICE	PE RATIO	RATE OF DIVIDEND PAID
On flotation	£4,000,000	£3	7.5	20%
1st day of dealings as a public company	£4,000,000	£3.60	9	20%
Melanie sells half her shareholding	£7,000,000	£8	11.5 approx.	40%
Takeover agreed five years after flotation	£10,000,000	£13	13	50%

GLOSSARY
(In alphabetical order)

AIM (Alternative Investment Market)	A junior Market to the main Stock Market, generally preferred by relatively new or smaller companies, where regulations are less stringent and costs of "going public" lower. Many AIM shares also currently qualify for Inheritance Tax relief if held for a certain number of years.
BALANCE SHEET	A summary of what a business owns and what is owes.
CAPITALISATION	The total number of shares in issue multiplied by the market price of those shares.
CREDITORS	Money owed by a business to third parties.
DEBTORS	Money owed to a business by third parties.
DIVIDEND	The income that a business pays to individual shareholders, from after tax profits, usually both as an "Interim" and a "Final" paid after the year-end, and having been approved by shareholders.
FLOTATION	The act of "going public".
FREEHOLD	Owned outright i.e. not rented or leased.
INSTITUTIONS	Insurance companies, pension funds etc., as distinct from individual private investors.

INVESTMENT BANK	A bank which provides advice to businesses or individuals and which may or may not lend or invest money.
INVESTMENT TRUST	A company which owns shares in other quoted companies.
ISA (Individual Savings Account)	Into which a person can put a certain amount of money each year, (the Government stipulates the annual maximum allowable), with any interest or dividend income generated, or any Capital Gains made, free of all taxation except Inheritance Tax on death.
MARKET-MAKER	A firm whose business is the making of a market in shares i.e. like a wholesaler or middle-man to whom a stockbroker or bank will go to, to actually buy or sell shares.
PRICE EARNINGS RATIO	A business's capitalisation divided by its after-tax profits.
PROFIT	The difference between total turnover (sales or revenues) and total costs.
PROFIT AND LOSS ACCOUNT	Effectively showing the difference between items of income and items of expenditure.
PUBLIC COMPANY	A business which the general public can buy shares in as distinct from a "private" business which is owned by individuals or a family, and in which the public cannot buy shares.
STOCKBROKER	A firm whose business is the buying and selling of shares for investors.
TAKEOVER	Where one business buys another.
TURNOVER	The total value of products sold.
UNIT TRUST	An open-ended fund which owns shares in quoted companies.

An Ever-Changing Economy

Opportunities and Risks for Investors

When I started investing over sixty years ago, the UK Stock Market scene was very different. Then there were any number of quoted small regional Brewers to invest in, Clothing and Textile Companies, and many others in Aircraft Production, Motor Car Manufacture, Shipping, together with Rubber and Tea Plantation stocks, plus of course the many other categories which currently still exist. Today there are very few opportunities to invest in these aforementioned sectors. Some were consolidated via takeovers and mergers, particularly in Brewing, with many Textile and Clothing businesses going under, succumbing to cheaper competition from Third World countries. There are now hardly any individual Aircraft, Motor-Manufacturing or Shipping companies in the UK to invest in – most of these sectors are now dominated by very large international groups, and all Plantation companies have gone, primarily into the ownership of indigenous families overseas.

Over the years, there has been a range of publicly quoted businesses which came and went: Mail Order companies, Holiday Camp operators, Furniture Manufacturers, Newspaper Publishers, all providing opportunities for the investor for a time. Those who invested early in Supermarkets were rewarded, but today they are seen as mature, extremely competitive, and with very limited opportunities for further growth. In the 1980s, the privatisations of the Thatcher Conservative government brought many new companies to the Stock Market which previously had been state-owned: British Telecom, British Gas,

BP, Electricity and Rail, Steel and Water companies, providing mixed fortunes for investors, albeit significantly increasing the number of individuals owning shares. However some of the smaller privatisations like Amersham and Associated British Ports delivered substantial profits for the shrewd and patient. Historically Banks and Insurance companies were seen as safe and reliable, but the financial crisis of 2008 ended all that, although more recently they have been rebuilding profitability and reputations.

In my early investing days there were numerous small public property companies, both residential and commercial, to invest in, but consolidation has seen most morph into today's much larger property groups, although new niche openings have arisen in Care Homes, Self-Storage and Student Accommodation.

If we look more globally we see a growing world population, rising standards of living, and most people particularly in the Western world living longer. Common sense tells us that large international Food, Drink and Household Products groups like the Swiss Nestlé, America's Coca-Cola, Colgate, and Procter & Gamble, the Anglo-Dutch Unilever, and the UK's Diageo should all progress. Healthcare is an obvious growth area – over the decades larger Drug manufacturers have prospered, handsomely rewarding investors, but their days of easy profits are long gone with new drug discoveries being very expensive and Governments taking a much tougher line on prices. The danger of smoking has changed the perception of Tobacco stocks from growth to slow decline. Expanding populations need more houses, but housebuilding in the UK has historically been very cyclical although in recent years Government incentives have brought increased profits for Housebuilders. The development of the Internet and that of mobile phones have led to profound changes to so many lives and businesses. Huge American companies like Apple, Facebook, Google, Microsoft, Netflix and more recently Uber have delivered multi-billion pound fortunes for their founders and big profits for early stage investors, and of course, the giant Amazon has transformed retailing for ever. Had one stood back and thought about the economic and commercial consequences of Amazon's growth (which I sadly did not!), one could have foreseen the obvious beneficiaries e.g. Packaging Manufacturers and Delivery Logistics, plus the associated massive warehousing complexes. But, on the negative side, the losers have been the traditional high street Retailers, as has been well publicised. The New World of the Internet/home computers/iPads/mobile phones and their related software technologies have spawned a plethora of new commercial activities in Banking, Gambling, Games, Media Downloading and Streaming, and Travel/Hotel booking, plus developments in Cyber Security to counter hacking and fraud.

For the next generation of investors there are certain to be new exciting opportunities ahead – in Renewable Energy and Climate Change as we focus on a cleaner and more environmentally friendly planet, in Artificial Intelligence, Healthcare, Robotics, and Space etc. Investment opportunities are ever changing with new businesses arising as others inevitably decline.

Twelve Recommendations to help you invest profitably and successfully, and to avoid losses

1. Endeavour to buy shares on modest valuations – hopefully with a reasonable dividend yield, single figure or low double figure Price Earnings Ratios and/or a discount to Net Asset Value.
2. Ignore the overall level of the Stock Market – avoid making judgements on the world macro outlook – leave that to commentators and economists (who are invariably wrong!) Focus on your own particular stock selection.
3. Be prepared to hold the shares you buy for a minimum of five years and ideally ten plus.
4. Try to understand the company' business – look it up on the web – perhaps ask the company registrars or the company secretary to send you a copy of the last Annual Report, as a prospective shareholder.
5. Ignore minor share price movements when deciding to buy. If you like the company don't be put off because the shares have risen a few pence more than when you first alighted upon them. Looking back, say five years hence, you will have either done very well or not, and if you have made a mistake hopefully you will have sold and taken a loss and moved on (see 11 Stop-losses).
6. Seek established companies with a record of making profits and paying dividends. Avoid "start-ups" or biotech and exploration/mining stocks, or construction businesses,

which are all inherently risky. Remember the secret of investment success is to avoid losses.

7. Look for moderately optimistic or better Chairman's/ Chief Executive's most recent comments.

8. Focus on conservative, cash-rich companies or those with a low level of debt (borrowings).

9. Ensure that the Directors have meaningful shareholdings in the companies they are managing i.e. you are making sure that they have faith and belief in the businesses they are running. The last Annual Report should contain a list Directors' holdings.

10. Look for a stable Board with infrequent directorate changes. Similarly, with professional advisors like auditors, solicitors, bankers and brokers etc.

11. Face-up to mistakes, perhaps apply a 20% "Stop-loss" i.e. if you buy a share for 100p and its falls to 80p sell it and re-invest elsewhere, unless there are extenuating circumstances. No one gets it right every time. However, if the overall level of the Stock Market falls ignore this "Stop-loss" rule.

12. Retain profitable shareholdings – hopefully to grow even more. Avoid the temptation to realise a quick profit. If you are invested in a good growing company which you like, which regularly increases its profits and dividends, stay aboard. The biggest mistake private investors make is too frequently chopping and changing – moving from share to share – stay put for bigger long-term profits!

TO LEARN MORE OR MAKE YOUR FIRST INVESTMENT

ASSOCIATION OF INVESTMENT COMPANIES – will provide details of all quoted Investment Trusts – www.theaic.co.uk

BANKS – most banks will undertake Stock Market transactions for their customers.

BOOKSHOPS – most bookshops will stock books on the Stock Market/Investment.

COMPANY'S ANNUAL REPORT – obtainable from its Company Secretary or Registrars.

COMPANY REFS – (Really Essential Financial Statistics) – online and hard copy information on all quoted companies via subscription – www.companyrefs.co.uk

IFA (Independent Financial Advisor) – a professionally qualified and regulated person who provides advice on a broad range of investments and on an individual's financial affairs

THE INVESTMENT ASSOCIATION – details of all Unit Trusts -www.theinvestmentassociation.org

MELLO – organises events/conferences/company presentations for private investors – www.melloevents.com

NEWSPAPERS – most have City/Business sections.

SHARESOC – the leading membership body for private investors (Information, campaigns, company visits etc.) – www.sharesoc.org

THE STOCK EXCHANGE – will provide a list of all Stockbrokers and their contact details and up-to-date share prices – mostly available online – www.londonstockexchange. com

STOCKOPEDIA – independent analysis of shares and data tools, via subscription – www.stockopedia.com

WEBSITES – all publicly quoted companies will have their own website, usually with a link to an "Investor Relations" section.

WEEKLY PUBLICATIONS – *The Investors Chronicle* (I have read for over 50 years!) - www.investorschronicle.co.uk; *Shares Magazine* also online - www.sharesmagazine.co.uk

BIONOTE

JOHN LEE is regarded as one of the UK's leading private investors having bought his first shares sixty years ago. He was one of the earliest to recognise the long-term potential of PEPs, the forerunner of ISAs when they were launched in 1987 and was judged to be the first ISA "millionaire" in 2003. He has written over 250 articles for *FT Money* and has given numerous lectures and interviews on his investment philosophy as a long-term "value" investor. In 2014 Pearsons published his well-received *How to Make a Million – Slowly: my guiding principles from a lifetime of successful investing*. He is a Chartered Accountant with a wide experience of investment banking and business and is Patron of ShareSoc, the leading body lobbying and campaigning on behalf of private investors. From 1979-92 he was a Member of Parliament, during this period he was both a Defence and Tourism Minister. A former High Sheriff of Greater Manchester, he sits as a member of the House of Lords as Lord Lee of Trafford and lives in Richmond, Surrey.

Printed in the USA
CPSIA information can be obtained
at www.ICGtesting.com
LVHW091259211123
764544LV00003B/4

Super Powereds: Year 1

By Drew Hayes

Foreword
(AKA: Skip this and the book will implode)

Okay, fine, so the book won't really implode. Well, probably. On second thought, I'm not going to make you any promises on what will or will not happen. However, I did want to draw your attention to these short paragraphs in order to explain the sizable length and chapter count of this novel.

Super Powereds began three years ago as a Webnovel over at my site: drewhayes.digitalnovelists.com. It is the first book in a series of four, and it was published chapter by chapter over the course of a year and a half. This explains the sheer number of chapters that are, admittedly, individually a bit shorter than what one would see in a classic novel. I debated rearranging them for this eBook; however, the chapter breaks often represented natural breaking points in the story, so in the end, I decided better to be a little odd than risk wrecking the book's flow.

I'll keep the rest of this short and sweet, since I know as well as anyone that so few people read the forewords. Thank you for purchasing (or sampling) this novel. It is the culmination of years of work, none of which would have been possible without the wonderful readers who offered me endless encouragement throughout the process. I sincerely hope you enjoy it, so I'll stop yammering and let you get on to reading.

Prologue

The two well-dressed men materialized outside of a small, white brick building. The taller of the two pulled out a miniature notepad, made an entry with the slash of a few pen strokes, and then stowed it away once more.

"Where are we, Mr. Transport?" The speaker was the shorter man, wearing a black suit with a black tie and presently putting on a pair of black sunglasses to fight back the sun's penetrating glare.

"Arizona, Mr. Numbers," replied the taller man (who, by elimination, could only be Mr. Transport), as he adjusted the sunglasses he had put on before they departed.

"I was under the impression our next case was in Colorado," commented Mr. Numbers.

"He was. However, there was an incident last week. Circumstances required that he be moved to a location able to accommodate his specific needs."

"I see," said Mr. Numbers. With that, the two of them walked around to the front of the building and proceeded inward. They were stopped as soon as they entered, not by the expected poorly-paid security guard, but rather by an elderly man wearing a white lab coat.

"Good morning, gentlemen. I've been expecting you," said the white-coated man. "My name is Dr. Hubert."

Mr. Numbers cocked his eyebrow slightly, and Mr. Transport replied with an almost imperceptible nod. This exchange took the place of the relevant conversation, which would consist of Mr. Numbers asking if the name and call-ahead had checked out, and Mr. Transport reporting that it had. This method was more efficient, though, and had the added benefit of allowing the duo to take people by surprise when things were not quite so congruent.

"We'd like to see the boy," said Mr. Numbers.

"Of course you would," Dr. Hubert agreed. "However, first, I'm afraid I must ask you to take off anything electrical. Watches, phones, anything with a battery must go. I do hope neither of you has a pacemaker."

Neither Mr. Numbers nor Mr. Transport had pacemakers. They did both carry expensive, high-powered phones, though, as well as top-of-the-line watches and a pair of taser guns. All of these were deposited into a small safe in the front lobby area with Dr. Hubert's adamant assurances that everything would be returned once they were done. Neither Mr. Numbers nor Mr. Transport showed any concern about the safety of their valuables.

Once that was completed, Dr. Hubert pulled out a small candle and lit it, then repeated the procedure twice more until all three men were equipped with a diminutive, wax lighting instrument. Dr. Hubert kept expecting one of the men to ask why they had

1

shed their electronics and were being handed candles in the middle of the day. They did not.

Dr. Hubert led them through the doors of the lobby, into a dimly-lit hallway covered in green tile. They made their way down it, coming to a solid steel door at the end. Dr. Hubert made a quick series of punches on the keypad and the door released, opening to reveal total darkness. As the trio stepped through, the door shut behind them, leaving them with only their candles to see by. Mr. Numbers and Mr. Transport paused to remove their sunglasses.

Their eyes adjusted, and they realized they had stepped into another hallway, this one formed of solid concrete. There were no doors to their sides, only another metal one at the end of the hallway. Dr. Hubert began the walk down, moving more briskly than he had before. Mr. Numbers observed that the deeper into this place they went, the more nervous Dr. Hubert became. He filed that away, and then began following a few paces behind.

They made their way down the hallway without incident, then stepped through the next metal door. Inside was what looked like a large, concrete bunker with a sizable glass window peering into the next room. Though both strained, they could not make out anything in the pitch black on the other side of the glass.

"He's normally more stable than this," Dr. Hubert said. "But, unfortunately, he was trying to fix his toaster a few days ago and received a nasty electrical shock."

"Ah," said Mr. Numbers. "So that's why a quarter of Colorado lost power last week."

"Yes," admitted Dr. Hubert. "Before he was able to sever the connection, he had drained his own city's power supply, along with that of all the areas surrounding it. We're trying to help him burn off all that electricity, but it comes in spurts and is almost impossible to predict."

"I see," said Mr. Transport.

"It's also affecting his natural abilities," continued Dr. Hubert. "That's why I had you remove all electrical devices and why we are keeping him out of the sunlight. He's been pulling from anything that gets even remotely close to him."

As if on cue, Mr. Number's candle jerked violently in the direction of the window and went dark.

"I'm sorry he's not more stable today," Dr. Hubert apologized again.

"If he were, he wouldn't be in consideration for our program," said Mr. Numbers, eyes still trained on his now dark candle.

"Oh, does that mean you're still counting him as a possibility?" Dr. Hubert asked.

"There will be some preliminary testing and an interview process," said Mr. Transport. "But if I were to offer my opinion, I would say we have a very viable candidate on the other side of that glass."

*   *   *

Mr. Numbers and Mr. Transport next materialized before a hospital in Nevada. Mr. Transport again produced his notepad, jotted down a few scribbles, and then put it back where it belonged.

"Another incident?" Mr. Numbers asked.

"Par for the course with this one, to my understanding," replied Mr. Transport.

The duo then entered the hospital. They spoke briefly to a nurse, producing badges that rendered her silent, procured the information they needed, and then headed upstairs. It was something of a walk to get where they were heading, and by the time they were done, they had crossed out of the main hospital and into a more run-down attachment wing. The doctors here were fewer and more haggard, and the walls looked worn-down and repainted. Hospitals were never what Mr. Transport thought of as cheerful, but this area was enough to inspire one to end it all. Which very well might have been the point.

Mr. Numbers stopped at the appropriate room, and the two entered. It was like the rest of the wing: worn-down, beat-up, and hopeless. This one had two unique additions, though: a young man lying in a hospital bed and a recently-exploded television that was still smoking.

"Mr. Campbell," greeted Mr. Transport. "A pleasure to meet you."

"Call me Nick," said the boy. He spoke with an easy tone that matched his overly-relaxed appearance. Despite the mandatory hospital gown, he had still taken the time to gel his thick hair. "And I take it you two are my interview committee?"

"Indeed," confirmed Mr. Transport. "What happened to the television?"

"Beats me. I went to turn the thing on and I guess the tubes overloaded or something," answered Nick.

"I see," said Mr. Transport skeptically.

Mr. Numbers had been browsing through Nick's chart during the exchange with Mr. Transport and chose this time to jump in. "So, according to the records, you won a ten thousand dollar scratch-off ticket, after which you were hit by a bus while celebrating in the street, which knocked you into a bounce house that had been set up nearby—a bounce house whose motor had the poor timing to overload and explode after your impact. Do I have everything correct?"

"You might want to tack on that my winnings just covered my hospital bill and damages owed to the bounce house owner," Nick added.

"You were held accountable for the damages," Mr. Transport said. It wasn't a question, but Nick chose to take it as one anyway.

3

"Well, you know how it is. People tend to blame my kind first and ask questions later," Nick said, not quite managing to mask the bitterness in his voice.

"We know, Mr. Campbell," said Mr. Numbers. "That's exactly what brought us here today."

Mr. Transport walked over to the room's entrance and shut the door firmly.

*   *   *

The two next appeared in a forest. This wasn't a forest in the sense of parks that can seem sprawling, or a cluster of spruces that can form on the side of an untended highway. This was a forest in an ancient and powerful sense, with trees that were massive and served as ecosystems within their ecosystem. This was a place untouched and unaware of all the progress *Homo sapiens* had made with their pitiful time upon the earth. Untouched, that is, with the exception of the trailer a few feet away from Mr. Numbers and Mr. Transport.

Sitting in a rocking chair, sipping a glass of lemonade, was a young girl whose file said seventeen, but whose face said fourteen. She was wiry and lean, with short hair that poked up in several different directions. She stared at the two of them unblinkingly, and the two stared right back at her.

The three of them stood in silence for several minutes like that—the girl's eyes flitting between the two of them; theirs remaining constant on her. At last, the girl took a long sip of her lemonade and said out loud, "That sounds lovely."

A simultaneous nod came from Mr. Numbers and Mr. Transport, and then they were gone.

*   *   *

"Hershel! Come downstairs. The nice men are here to see you." The speaker was a dowdy woman in her fifties who was setting down a kettle and cups in front of Mr. Numbers and Mr. Transport. "Are you sure I can't get you gentlemen anything to eat?"

"Thank you, Ms. Daniels, but we are quite comfortable," said Mr. Numbers.

"Oh, no need for that. Please, call me Sally," Ms. Daniels replied, her eyes lingering on Mr. Numbers and the strong figure housed beneath the covering of his black suit.

"Good morrow, my men," said Hershel as he descended the stairs into the yellow-painted kitchen. Hershel was a portly young man, with long, dirty-blond hair dribbling down to his chin and a forest-green shirt underneath the rich royal-purple of his cape.

"Why are you wearing a cape?" Mr. Transport was unable to suppress his own curiosity.

"It's a cloak," Hershel corrected. "After we partake in a large lunch, my men and I are taking the castle up at Rothring Peak and doing battle with a foul vampire lord."

4

"My little Hershel is a bit overly creative," Ms. Daniels commented. "He and his friends are active in the community's live-action role-playing club."

Mr. Numbers and Mr. Transport exchanged a look. There is no need for clarification on the meaning of this one.

"Well, we don't want to keep you," Mr. Numbers said honestly. "However, we were hoping to speak with Roy, if that's at all possible."

"Oh," said Hershel, disappointment sweeping across his face. "Of course. Everyone wants to talk to Roy."

"It's just that we have some things to discuss with him," Mr. Numbers attempted to clarify.

"I'm sorry," Hershel said. "I don't think he'll be around today. He went to a country bar last night and . . . well, he usually doesn't show up for a while after uproars like that."

"Ah," said Mr. Transport. "That does explain the cleanup crew that was dispatched this morning." Mr. Numbers shot Mr. Transport a look, but Mr. Transport merely shrugged, as if to say he didn't find it to be of any importance.

"If that's the case, then we will be on our way," said Mr. Numbers. "I don't want to keep you from your . . . activities. We will need to speak with Roy at a later date."

"Wait," Hershel said, jumping to his feet. "I know what you're here about, and I really want to get in. I'm tired of living like this. Never knowing when it will happen; never knowing where I'll wake up. Please, if you can really help me control it . . . please don't leave."

"It's okay, Hershel," Mr. Transport said as he patted the large boy on his shoulder. "We aren't giving up on you just because of a reschedule. You're a serious candidate for our program. I promise we'll be back once we can talk to Roy as well."

Hershel nodded his understanding, and then turned away quickly so the two men wouldn't see the tears forming in his eyes. He didn't know what his chances were at the moment, but he was smart enough to guess that crying in front of the agents wouldn't help things.

Mr. Numbers tapped impatiently on Mr. Transport's shoulder and gestured to his watch. Mr. Transport nodded, and then turned his head to Ms. Daniels.

"Thank you for the tea," said Mr. Transport just before they vanished.

*   *   *

The duo appeared in a sprawling garden, under a gazebo and next to a pair of wicker chairs. There was a small serving cart on the far side of a stone table. Sitting next to the cart and sipping on a cocktail was a man. He wore a white, open-throated shirt and a pair of khakis. This man was getting on in years, but wearing them unbelievably well.

It's not that the signs of age weren't present, but that they served to draw out and enhance his fine features rather than muddle them.

"I'm glad you could make it," greeted the man in a voice that made clear, without apology, that he had never considered their presence optional.

"Our pleasure, Mr. Adair," Mr. Numbers said hurriedly. For the first time all day (for the first time in years really), the pair was showing signs of nervousness. They had been told of their required presence for this meeting, but not about the subject matter it concerned. That left both of them feeling something they were not accustomed to: vulnerable.

"Sit, sit," said Mr. Adair. "Can I get you something to drink?"

"I'd like a gin and tonic, if it's no trouble, sir," said Mr. Transport. This was their final meeting of the day, so Mr. Transport didn't see the harm in indulging just a bit.

"Just water for me, thanks," said Mr. Numbers. Mr. Numbers was already writing out the riot act he was going to read Mr. Transport for asking for alcohol while on the job, but facially, he was working hard to keep everything upbeat and positive.

Mr. Adair pulled two glasses from the cart at his side, then a carafe from which he poured water into both. He handed the glass as it was to Mr. Numbers, but dipped his finger into Mr. Transport's. Immediately, the liquid bubbled and fizzed, stabilizing seconds later when Mr. Adair handed the glass to Mr. Transport.

Both drinks were delicious. Mr. Transport wished his had been made in the traditional way so he could have asked for a recipe.

"I know you boys are busy, so I won't mince words," said Mr. Adair. "You're here because you two are the admissions committee for the new program that is launching."

"Well, it isn't quite that simple," said Mr. Numbers. "There are evaluations and approvals and whatnot."

"Humility is wasted on the powerful, Mr. Numbers," said Mr. Adair. "You are two of the most trusted agents in your company, and with good reason. You both have abilities that could have made you well-known Heroes; instead, you chose to do the same work without the prestige. You are loyal, reliable, and dependable. Whomever you recommend for this program will be who gets in. You know it, I know it, and everyone who matters knows it." Mr. Adair punctuated his words by pouring himself a glass of water and swirling his finger about until the liquid turned a deep golden hue.

Mr. Numbers didn't have a reply for this one. He could already see any attempts to defer responsibility on that account were a lost cause.

"So, with that said, I asked you here to meet me because there will be one addition to the program that you will both endorse fully," said Mr. Adair, pausing to take a sip of his cocktail.

"And who would that be, sir?" Mr. Numbers asked.

"My daughter, Alice," said Mr. Adair. "She is a Powered, a person born with super human abilities, but unlike a Super, she lacks the capacity to freely control them. Though I'm sure your thorough friend here has already found that out." Mr. Adair gestured to Mr. Transport.

"My research said that she was in the non-lethal category," said Mr. Transport. "She flies, correct?"

"You are correct, Mr. Transport," said Mr. Adair. "My daughter's power is tethered to her emotions, so when she gets happy, she winds up bouncing off the ceiling. If we're lucky enough to have a ceiling over her at the time."

"Forgive me for saying this," said Mr. Numbers. "But the program's initial testing cases are supposed to be Powereds with desirable abilities that are currently a danger to themselves and others."

"I know," said Mr. Adair. "That's why I called you here to tell you that you would recommend her, instead of going through the channels to submit her as a viable specimen."

"With all due respect, Mr. Adair, that would compromise both our duties to the program and the company," said Mr. Transport.

Mr. Adair said nothing in response at first. He leaned back in his wicker chair and stirred his drink with his finger. As he stirred, the colors changed, going through a rainbow of shades and depths. Finally, it settled on a light pink, and Mr. Adair took a sip.

"Mr. Transport," Mr. Adair began. "You know what my code name is, correct?"

"The Alchemist," Mr. Transport answered readily.

"Right, and you know why I am called that, yes?"

"Because you have the ability to manipulate and change the properties of matter," said Mr. Transport.

"Correct again," Mr. Adair said. "So maybe, what you are missing is my role in this world. You see, while other Supers defend their homes or countries, I defend our economy. I turn radioactive sludge into oil, rocks into gold, worthlessness into pricelessness. Most Supers seek to garner favor from politicians and leaders. Leaders and politicians work to garner favor from me. I am one of the primary shareholders of the company you both work for, as well as several other powerful corporations. I am not going to threaten either of you, because we all know my abilities are ill-suited to a physical altercation. I am simply going to tell you that you will recommend my daughter for the first trial of the new program. End of story."

Mr. Numbers looked at Mr. Transport. They had been partners for many years and had learned to read each other's cues like a second language. There was no question for Mr. Transport as to what Mr. Numbers was telling him right then. Time to roll over.

"Yes, sir," said Mr. Numbers.

"Good, I'm glad we understand each other," said Mr. Adair. "So, when will things get started?"

1.

Six Months Later

Vince adjusted his backpack to put its weight on his other shoulder. Two months since the procedure had ended and he'd been put in recovery, and still his body felt like it was aching and healing. He never remembered feeling like this beforehand, but in all fairness, there were plenty of other things that hadn't existed beforehand either.

Today was an excellent example of what going through the program had yielded him: he was walking across the beautiful, sprawling college campus of Lander University, passing other kids his age and blending in like a normal person. Well, almost anyway. His damn hair still made him stand out. One of his biggest hopes had been that a side effect of the procedures would be his hair becoming a normal color, but no such luck. It was still silver like it had always been. And not old man silver, either: silver like moonbeams glinting off steel. It wasn't that it was unattractive; in fact, it accentuated Vince's bright blue eyes quite nicely. No, the problem was that his hair marked him as different, and, after all these years, Vince was yearning to be nothing more than a face in the crowd.

"At least we're in California," Vince mumbled under his breath as he quickened his steps. He was getting second glances from the other students, but not as many as he was used to. He also passed a few people whose looks made him do double takes of his own. It was comforting, in a mutual freak sort of way.

By the time Vince reached his dorm assignment, he was back on the positive side of things. After all, this was what he had worked for during those two months of recovery; studying and being tutored so that he could get his GED and come to this college. It had been hell to concentrate, especially with his body still adjusting to everything, but he had put in the time and pulled it off. It was an opportunity he couldn't let slip away. Besides, the nurses and technicians had told him the other people from the program would be given the option to come here, too.

The building Vince walked up to looked less like a dorm and more like a medium-sized house. He didn't see how it was possible to fit so many people into this one-story, brick home, but he trusted that whoever was managing housing had that in hand.

Vince walked through the front door and shifted his backpack once more. It bounced and landed on his shoulder lightly, betraying that it was far from stuffed to the brim with Vince's few articles of clothing and worldly possessions. One of the first things every wanderer lets go of is his unnecessary items. Travel light, move quick, stay alive. That was the code that kept Vince breathing and his abilities in check. But that was behind him.

9

In front of Vince was a cream-colored wall with a notice welcoming him to Melbrook Hall. There was another wall to his left and a hallway to his right. The notice had an arrow directing him to follow the foyer and then take a left. Vince did as he was told and found himself looking at a sturdy door with no window or discernible handle. There was only a small box jutting out with an oval-shaped green pad on top. Vince might not have been the most up-to-date with technology, but even he could figure this one out. He pressed his thumb to the oval, and after a minute, the door opened with a small beep.

Vince stepped out of the foyer and into what looked more like a living room than anything else. There were several couches and chairs set up, a metal coffee table in the center of the room, and a large, flat-screen television on the wall directly across from him. Everything was decorated in white and red and smelled like an odd combination of flowers and chemicals, which Vince could only assume meant they were using an artificial air freshener. He walked around the room, taking in the scene.

On each wall, perpendicular to the entrance, was another metal door and scanner, a sign above each. The one to the left of the entrance was "Boys," while the one to right said, predictably, "Girls." Vince went over to the television, only to notice that there were open doorways on either side that one could walk through. Vince did just that and found himself in a white-tiled kitchen. It had a large sink, a stove with multiple burners and a griddle, and all kind of cooking knickknacks that Vince had neither the knowledge nor the experience to make anything out of.

At the back of the kitchen, on the right, was a cupboard, which Vince opened to discover a fully-stocked pantry. On the left was another metal door. This one, however, had neither a sign above it nor a fingerprint scanner.

Vince walked out of the kitchen and back into the living room, then over to the boys' door. As he walked, he carefully skirted away from wall outlets whenever possible. He hadn't had an accident since the procedure, but that didn't mean he was eager to test his luck. Pressing his thumb to the scanner, the door opened and Vince walked into what he could only assume was the common room.

There was another television on the far end, along with pool and Ping-Pong tables. The other end held a set of dart boards and a wooden door with the word "Bathroom" on it. Opposite the entrance were three more metal doors. These had scanners clearly in place, but no signs, though they were numbered 1, 2, and 3. With a shrug and a heft of his pack, Vince walked over to the middle door. He pressed his thumb down and waited for the beep, but this time, all that came out was a harsh buzzer. He tried twice more before giving up and trying the room on the left, which was Room 1. This time, the door buzzed and opened, though Vince couldn't help noticing a chime that followed the usual opening sounds. He wasn't sure what that meant, and the sight before him left him little free brain space in which to contemplate it.

Saying his room was luxurious would be something of an overstatement, but it was definitely more opulent than a boy who was always on the run was accustomed to. There was a large bed in one corner, with a desk and computer set up in the other. Between the two was a large window, sunlight streaming through the blue curtains. The floor was carpeted, and as Vince walked across it, he saw that opposite the desk, there was a closet next to a chest of drawers. Slipping his pack off, Vince walked over and pulled open a drawer, trying to figure out if he had enough clothing to warrant any kind of organizational system.

He was shocked to see that the drawer he'd opened already contained many, many pairs of socks. Checking the next drawer, he found shorts, then T-shirts; he went back to the top and found boxers. He slammed that drawer shut more quickly than the others. Synapses flying, Vince came to the only logical conclusion:

"Crud. This is someone else's room."

It only made sense; this place was too nice and too well-furnished. Why had the door let him in, though? Vince brushed that thought out of his head quickly. It was faulty equipment, not intentional, but it wouldn't make it less awkward if this room's inhabitant came home to find an intruder. Vince turned on his heels, snatching up his backpack and bolting for the door.

All of which landed him face to face with a taller boy standing in the doorway, wearing sunglasses and running a comb through his sandy-brown hair.

2

Vince froze in place, staring at the room's owner and wondering how to explain the mix-up. It wasn't his fault, after all, but this still wasn't the first impression he'd wanted to make on his new dormmate. Vince groped around his head, looking for words to break the silence. Luckily, the boy in the door did it for him.

"Dude, that is some rocking hair," he said.

"Um, thank you," Vince replied softly. "I'm sorry I'm in your room. The door opened, and I didn't know . . ." Vince just trailed off, the look of confusion on the boy's face making him more unsure with each passing second.

"You're not in my room, neighbor. You're in your room. I'm in two," the boy told him. "I heard you trying to buzz into mine and realized someone else was here, so I came to say hi."

"But this can't be my room," Vince said, trying to explain. "It already has sheets and clothes and everything."

"Yeah, my guess is that's because they thought you needed those things," the boy with sunglasses explained. "The doors are keyed to us. They only open for the right person. If this room opened for you, then it's because it's your room. Did you even read the letter they gave you?"

"Letter?" Vince asked with a sense of dread. He did remember a slip of paper that had fallen out of his pack when the taxi had dropped him off, but he had just dismissed it as an old food wrapper or something.

"I'll get mine," said the boy. "Hang on a sec . . . um, what's your name?"

"Vince," said Vince.

"Nice. You can call me Nick," he said as he stepped out of the room. He came back mere moments later, holding a white piece of paper with fold lines across it.

"Here we go," Nick said. "'Rooms have been set up for each attending member by the program. These will be stocked for members as deemed necessary, and are keyed to each attendee's individual fingerprints. Communal areas are open to all, but will be under the jurisdiction of your administrators. You are expected to be in the central common room promptly at seven p.m. on move-in day to meet with your administrators and go over dorm rules.'"

"Huh," said Vince. "Lucky you held on to that, or I wouldn't have even known about the meeting, let alone about my room." Vince plunked down on his bed, shedding his pack at long last.

"Good choice of words," Nick commented, pulling out the chair from Vince's desk and helping himself to a seat.

"What do you mean?" Vince asked.

"Eh, it's nothing. Just . . . well, you said 'lucky,'" Nick said.

"And . . . what about it?" Vince kept prodding.

Instead of answering, Nick pulled a set of dice from his jeans. He closed his eyes (an act only visible despite the sunglasses due to the over-exaggerated scrunching of his face), breathed deeply for a moment, then tossed them onto the desk.

"Double sixes," Vince observed.

Nick nodded. He then took the dice, closed his eyes once more, and, a deep breath later, threw them on the table again.

"Double sixes. Again," Vince said. "So, you use trick dice?"

"Try them," Nick replied. He scooped up the dice and offered them to Vince. Vince got off the bed, took the dice from Nick's hand, and examined them. They had six different numbers on each side and felt as though they were weighted normally. Still, Vince wasn't sure enough in his tactile perception to trust merely holding them for an answer. He threw the dice on the desk for himself.

"Three and five," Vince said. "So, you know how to spin them?"

"Do it again," Nick told him. This time, he closed his eyes and didn't exhale until Vince's throw hit the table.

"Double ones," Vince noted. "So?"

"Again," Nick instructed him.

Vince repeated his throw three more times; each time, Nick closed his eyes and Vince wound up with double ones. After the third time, Vince let the dice rest on the table. He went back to his bed and sat on the edge.

"Are you telekinetic? Is that how you control the landing?" Vince asked.

Nick shook his head. "I can't move things with my mind, at least, not on purpose. My power is luck. It can be good or it can be bad, but if it's luck, then I've got some say over it."

"Luck? How does that work? Not to insult, I just tend to think of luck as more of an abstract concept than a viable ability," Vince said.

"No insult taken," Nick assured him. "I don't really know how it works. The docs tried to explain, something about quantum probabilities and minute alterations in the fabric of reality, but at the end of the day, all I know how to say is that it's luck. And mine is a lot better since I got it under control."

Vince winced inwardly. "That must have been pretty terrible. Before."

"It was and it wasn't," Nick said with a shrug. "At least my ability came in two flavors. You know I kissed a supermodel once? She was out with some friends and they played spin the bottle at the restaurant we were both at, and, well . . . it pointed to me. Of course, then I went outside to find my car had caught fire, but hey, you got to take the good with the bad."

"You're upbeat about this," Vince said.

"Sure am," Nick replied with a smile. "That's all in the past. We're not like that anymore. We're the first people in history to go from being Powered to being Super. I still don't understand what they did to us for those months, and I don't care. Far as I'm concerned, getting into that program was the best stroke of luck my ability ever gave me."

"So, why the sunglasses?" Vince said to change the subject. He didn't want to rain on Nick's parade, but he had been dealt too much disappointment in his life to just trust that his abilities were under control now and forever.

"If anyone in authority asks, it's because using my power can give me headaches that leave me sensitive to light," Nick explained. "But, between you and me, I just think they make me look cool. What about your hair? Natural?"

"Unfortunately," Vince replied. "One of those weird traits people with abilities sometimes get. The damn stuff basically drinks dye, too, so there's no way for me to change its color."

"You could shave it," Nick pointed out.

"Thanks, but no thanks," Vince countered. "I tried that once. Some guys can pull off the bald look. I am not one of those guys. I'd rather be the weirdo with silver hair than the freakish man-baby."

"An understandable choice," Nick conceded. "Well, with you here, that rounds out the boys' side. I wonder if any girls have gotten here yet."

"Wait, who's our third roommate?" Vince asked. "I haven't met anyone but you so far."

"Our third got here early and went out to explore the campus," Nick told him. "You'll see him tonight at the dorm meeting. He's an . . . interesting fellow."

"That doesn't sound good," Vince said.

"No, but it doesn't sound bad either," Nick pointed out. "Come on, you just arrived, and I'm famished. Let's go hit up a dining hall for lunch."

"Do you know where one is?" Vince asked.

"Not really," Nick admitted. "But I bet we get lucky."

3

Alice saw a pair of boys walking away from the building as she was heading toward it. They took no notice of her, clearly absorbed in their own conversation and playing catch with a pair of dice. Her new roommates, no doubt. Fantastic. At least the one with the brown hair was cute, or would be if he weren't wearing those ridiculous sunglasses in the shade. The other one, though . . . who was he trying to impress with that hair? Silver and spiky. Was he trying to flunk the secret identity challenge before the semester even started?

None of that was her concern, though. Daddy had been strangely unbending in denying her desire to dorm with the regular Supers, saying that she had to stay in the dorm set up for the "special cases" like herself. She didn't really see why she needed to be in the reinforced building; her ability was only flying, and she had suffered no uncontrolled attacks for over two months now. It was insufferable that she would have to . . . well, suffer through the group accommodations with a bunch of all-too-recently Powereds. Alice didn't want to find camaraderie in their shared former disability. She wanted to forget that part of her life had ever existed.

Still, no one could say that Alice Adair didn't make the best of a bad situation. She had taken a guiding hand in the construction of their dormitory, creating an environment that was spacious, desirable, and, above all else, elite.

She breezed through the hallway, disregarding the note that hung on the entrance. A quick thumb scan took her to the central common room. She surveyed the work of the decorators critically. Yes, it would do nicely. Now, at least, when the other students asked her why she was in this small dorm set off at the edge of campus, she could humbly explain that it was only available to those of sufficient means to afford such luxury and privacy. It wasn't her ideal situation, but it would work.

Alice moved briskly to the girls' side, anxious to get through lest the last boy be lounging about, hoping to sneak a peek at the other member of the fairer sex that would be sharing his roof space. The girls' side was identical to the boys', save that there were only two rooms, numbered 4 and 5 respectively. While group bathrooms were fine for males, Alice had been quite insistent with Daddy that she have her own private bathroom. The fact that this meant her fellow female received one as well was a very distant afterthought.

On that note, Alice realized her other roommate was sitting in one of the plush pink chairs Alice had picked out, watching the television on mute. It seemed to be a game show, and the girl was as silent as the screen, just watching and occasionally cocking her head to a different angle.

The girl was . . . "wild" seemed to be the word that popped into Alice's head first. Not wild in the sense of tequila, poor decisions, and eventual therapy, but wild in the way of the jungle. Her hair looked as though no one had even entertained the idea of touching it for years, sticking up at all angles willy-nilly. The girl's clothing was clean at least, though it had the look of something that had been worn for many years. Ironically, Alice's jeans had the same appearance, but hers had achieved the look through corporate innovation and the fashion demands of the public. The most disconcerting thing about the girl, though, was her eyes. While Alice had always considered her own green eyes (especially when paired with her platinum blonde hair), to be rather stunning, they held no candle to the amber irises that encircled this girl's pupils.

"Ahem," Alice said in her best impersonation of a throat clearing. "Good afternoon. I take it that you are my dormmate?"

The girl swiveled her head toward Alice in a motion that seemed more owl or hawk-like than human. She blinked those round, amber eyes twice, then gave an oddly-shaped grin.

"You snuck up on me," she said.

"Oh, well, I do apologize," Alice said formally. Just because the girl seemed uncouth didn't mean Alice could allow her own standards to lapse.

"Don't apologize," said the girl. "I just keep forgetting people can do that now. It's a pleasant surprise every time."

"All right, then," Alice said, shifting on her feet uncomfortably. She knew everyone staying here had an ability, but she had been unable to wheedle Daddy into telling her precisely what to expect. "My name is Alice. What do you go by?"

The girl blinked oddly once more, then cocked her head before answering. "I haven't had any need to go by anything in a long time. My given name is Mary, though it might take a few tries to get my attention with it. As I said, out of practice."

"I think Mary is a lovely name," Alice said politely. In truth, she didn't care one way or the other, but since she couldn't very well go around referring to the girl as Freak Eyes all year (at least, not out loud), Mary worked fine for her.

"I'll do my best to remember its mine," said the girl who was apparently Mary, turning her head back to the television and watching her show.

"Um, if you don't mind me asking, why are you watching that on mute?" Alice inquired.

"I used to always watch television like this," Mary replied without turning around. "I learned to read their lips. That way, if I wanted silence, all I had to do was shut my eyes. It was the only thing in my life where I could actually turn the voices off, so I relished it. I guess old habits die hard."

"Ah, well, I see," Alice said quickly, eyeing room number 4 and edging her way toward it. "Well, I'll leave you to that, then. See you tonight at the meeting."

With those words, Alice jammed her thumb on her door scanner and popped it open. She slammed the door immediately after and rested against her wall. It was strange

16

how uncomfortable that girl had made her, how it felt like, despite being so disconnected, Mary was looking right through her with those bright amber eyes. Alice had grown up wealthy and aristocratic, and if there was one thing she could not stand, it was the sensation that someone knew what she was really thinking.

Outside Alice's door, Mary sat in the chair, eyes still trained on her game show.

"That girl is more perceptive than she thinks," Mary whispered to a small stuffed bear that sat between her leg and the armrest of the chair.

4

"See, I told you we'd get lucky." Nick gloated as he munched on a thick hamburger.

"We didn't get lucky," Vince corrected. "We got lost. For half an hour. Until I went into a building and asked for directions."

"And wasn't it lucky I brought along a guy with no masculinity issues to ask for directions?" Nick pointed out.

"I think you're stretching on this one," Vince replied, picking at the basket of chicken fingers. Being a wanderer had given him a pretty ironclad stomach when it came to grease and taste, but he'd also always had to subsist on whatever was available at the time. As a result, he had a small appetite and an equally small percentage of body fat. He reflected ruefully that if he just had some muscle on his wiry frame, it would have been very pronounced.

"I might be," Nick admitted. "But, then again, you haven't even told me what you can do. Who knows if you're fit to judge the skills of others?"

"Shh," Vince hushed him quickly. "We're in public. You know we can't talk about that kind of stuff."

"Oh please," Nick said, taking another bite of his burger and then guzzling down soda. "We're at one of only five colleges in the nation that offer certification for Supers to become the government-approved responders known as Heroes. I'm sure, like, everyone in this cafeteria is a damn Super in disguise."

The young men paused for a moment and looked around. Besides themselves, there was a small group of ladies halfway across the dining hall, and a large table of boys and girls clear on the other end. There were also a few tables where, like Vince and Nick, only one or two occupants sat. No one in the room looked particularly Super, or even interesting for that matter. Except for the girl with short, pink and black hair sitting with her friend. Vince did notice her as he did his visual sweep. Even without the colored hair, something about her stood out.

"Okay, maybe half the people," Nick conceded as he finished looking around.

"According to the doctors who told me about this place, less than half of one percent of the student population is enrolled in the Hero Certification Program," Vince informed him. "So odds are pretty good you and I are the only people with abilities here."

Nick let out a low whistle. "Less than half of one percent? That seems really low."

Vince shrugged. "There are a lot more humans than Supers. Even if this is only one of five schools, Lander is still a big university. A lot of people are going to come here wanting a run-of-the-mill education."

"Poor bastards," Nick said, shaking his head. "All kinds of awesome stuff going on around them and they have no clue about it."

"They better not," Vince said. "I heard that keeping your abilities a secret is, like, half of your grade. They say if you're found out, you have to do some kind of awful makeup courses to graduate, and that's only an option if you're at the top of the class." Vince unthinkingly ran his hands through his hair. At least the campus was full of enough people with their own strange features that he might have half a chance of blending in.

"Don't worry about the 'do," Nick told him. "I didn't think it meant anything significant, and I already knew you had some sort of power when we met. Of course, I still don't know what the damn thing is . . . but hey, that's what friendships are built around, right? Secrets and mysteries."

"You're something of a drama queen, aren't you?" Vince asked.

"Gasp! A dagger, straight into my heart," Nick said, grasping his chest and leaning back in his chair. His breathing became labored and his hands slumped to the sides. He was dead, his life ended before its prime by the harsh words of someone he had thought of as a fast-growing friend. But hark! One of his hands lifted oh so slowly, making its way to the table and grappling the hamburger before raising it triumphantly to his open and waiting mouth.

"I don't even want to know what's going on in your head right now," Vince said to his slumped-back friend.

"Good call," Nick assured him.

Vince sighed and pushed away his now-forgotten chicken strips. Nick was loud, indiscreet as could be, and showy every chance he got. But he was also the only person to try to be Vince's friend in years, and he knew what it had been like for Vince before. Those two qualities alone made him someone Vince knew he'd need to keep around.

"Get a book of matches and meet me back at the dorm," Vince told Nick. His words seemed to bring some life back into Nick's hamburger-munching corpse.

"You're supposed to wait until midterms before you go all pyro on shit," Nick chided him.

"I'm not going pyro! I just . . . look, you said you wanted to know what I can do, right?" Vince asked him.

"Why yes, yes I do," Nick said with a series of enthusiastic nods.

"Then get a book of matches and meet me in the dorm," Vince repeated, pulling up the remainder of his food and walking away from the table. He dumped his refuse in the bin and made his way to the exit. He was relatively certain it would take Nick at least a few minutes to find some matches, plus a few extra to finish his burger. Vince was counting on those precious extra moments, because, if he was going to try and do something with his power, he needed to get prepared and focus.

And, just to be on the safe side, pray.

19

5

Vince had been in his room for only a few minutes when he heard a knocking at the door.

"No way he's that fast," Vince muttered to himself as he hopped up from his bed and opened the door. As it turned out, yes, there was a way that Nick was that fast.

"Hey, I grot mamfes," Nick mumbled through a mouthful of burger. In all of the scenarios that had run through Vince's head of how Nick would finish his meal and get matches, the possibility of Nick's curiosity overwhelming his desire to eat while stationary was one that had not occurred.

"How did you find matches so quickly?" Vince asked as he gestured for Nick to sit in the computer chair again. Mercifully, this time, Nick swallowed the food in his mouth before answering.

"They were lying on the ground by the door when I left the dining hall," Nick explained.

"Let me guess, you used your power?" Vince asked rhetorically.

"Sure did," Nick replied with a grin. "I wanted to get this show on the road."

"Fantastic," Vince said dejectedly. "Just what I needed."

"Okay, see, now I'm confused. You're the one who volunteered to show me what you can do. What's the problem?" Nick asked.

"It's . . . I guess it's nothing, really. I just get nervous about using my ability," Vince admitted.

"Still? Didn't you go through the two months of therapy to get used to controlling it?" Nick took another bite of burger after his question, clearly banking on Vince to do some explaining.

"Yes, and I can control it . . . mostly. It's just there are some aspects to it I'm still working on. Look, it should be fine. If we use matches, then everything will be okay," Vince said reassuringly, though he never could have admitted who he actually was trying to reassure.

"Sweet," Nick said as he polished off his lunch. "So, what do I do?"

"Just face me and light a match, then hold it up in front of you," Vince said. He sat down on the edge of the bed so that he was only a few feet from Nick.

"Can do," Nick said, pulling a book of matches from his pocket and carefully extracting one from the end. Vince noticed the matchbook had a few missing from it already. It was a pretty decent guess that Nick had focused his luck and some poor smoker had dropped their matches without noticing. Much as he was hesitant to view luck as an ability, Vince had to admit it definitely had its uses.

Meanwhile, Nick had plucked his match and was trying to light it with all the skill of a drunken hobo. On his fourth try, he finally got the match head to ignite and was so surprised he nearly dropped the small flame onto Vince's carpet. He was able to keep his hold, though, and slowly moved the burning match so it was directly between himself and Vince.

Vince's eyes were locked on the flame, focusing on it with all of his concentration. Ever so gently, Vince raised his hand and opened it so that his palm was level with the match. For a few seconds, nothing happened. Then, the flame began to lean toward Vince's palm. A moment later, there was a small burst of heat and Nick was pinching only a tiny piece of ash between his fingers.

"Whoa," Nick exclaimed. "What did you do?"

"I absorbed the energy of the flame," Vince explained. "That's my ability: I can absorb energy and store it for later."

"What do you mean 'for later'?" Nick said, already pulling another match from the book.

In response, Vince held up the index finger on his right hand. A small flame appeared at the tip of his finger; a flame about the same size and intensity as the one he had just vanquished. It burned for almost ten seconds, then vanished just as quickly as it had appeared.

"I can use the energy I absorb any time I want," Vince continued once his finger was out. "I can use it slowly, like I did just now, or release it in controlled bursts. In this case, it would have made a tiny fireball. I don't have the ability to extend or increase it, though. However much energy I have absorbed is what I have to work with."

"Awesome," Nick said, nodding his head. "Now, do this one."

Vince sighed, but he couldn't deny this was good practice, so he accommodated his dormmate's demands for entertainment and absorbed the rest of the matches one by one.

"I have another question for you," Nick said as Vince snuffed out the final match from the book.

"Shoot," Vince replied. His mind had wandered off near the end of their practice session, focusing instead on how the aching weariness he had been fending off seemed to be decreasing a bit in his absorbing hand. He wondered if using a part of his body as an absorption point had pain-fighting properties.

"I get that you absorb the flame as it exists, but why is it every time you use your power, I wind up holding nothing but a fleck of ash? Does stealing the energy destroy the matchstick?" Nick was poking at the small piece of ash Vince's last absorption had left on his fingernail.

"Yes and no," Vince said, turning his attention back to his dormmate. "Remember when I said I was still getting the hang of some stuff? Well, that's what I meant. See, I don't just absorb the existing energy. I absorb the potential energy as well. At least, I do if I don't sever the connection."

21

"Yeah, I've really got no idea what you're talking about," Nick said, flicking off the piece of ash and checking the matchbook to see if he had missed any.

"Okay . . . how to explain this? Look, let's pretend that you have another match and you light it, okay?" Vince said.

"Sure, why not," Nick agreed.

"Now, if you leave the match be, the fire will eventually consume all of the wood," Vince said. "However, if you were to lick your fingers and put it out halfway through, then you would still have some of the matchstick left. With me so far?"

"Mostly," Nick said.

"Good," Vince said, choosing to plow ahead and hope for the best. "Well, obviously, the match that is allowed to burn all the way down produces more fire, and therefore more energy. See, that's why the match disintegrates in your hand. When I steal the energy of the flame, I don't just take all the energy that's there, I also take all of the energy that has the potential to be there."

"I don't suppose you could break that down a little easier, could you?" Nick asked, pulling out his dice and fiddling with them. Vince took a deep breath and tried to hold his patience. This could be a confusing concept if someone wasn't used to it; Vince needed to keep that in the front of his mind.

"Think of it like this," Vince tried again. "There is only ash in your hand because, in the fraction of a second where I begin drawing on the energy of the match, the whole thing burns up in a flash and is taken into my body. That make sense?"

"Actually, yeah," Nick said. "But, if it burns all at once, then why aren't my fingers singed? I mean, if I'm holding it and it burns, it should hurt."

"You're not totally wrong," Vince said. "Normally, that would still burn you. But heat is a form of energy, and I'm taking everything the match has to give. So, while it might flash-burn in your fingers, all of the heat flows into me."

"Dude," Nick said. "I get it, but your power is fucking complicated."

"This from the guy whose ability works on quantum probabilities," Vince pointed out.

"I don't know what you're talking about," Nick said. "I just control luck. Nothing complicated about that."

"Right," Vince said sarcastically. "Nothing complicated at all."

6.

Mr. Numbers and Mr. Transport sat at a small café in Paris, sipping their respective coffees. They had been saddled with a busy day so far; however, they were provided with a nice gap at lunch time, so Mr. Transport had suggested they adjourn to one of their favorite dining establishments. Mr. Numbers had concurred, and they had left the sweltering plains of Africa for a more tranquil and enjoyable environment in which to dine.

As was their custom, they were reviewing the particulars of their next assignment before departing. Mr. Transport had been somewhat surprised to see that it was classified as "long term." Those assignments were quite rare, given his and Mr. Numbers's capabilities for handling things in a prompt and efficient manner. The deeper he read into the dossier, though, the more concerned Mr. Transport grew.

"Mr. Numbers," Mr. Transport ventured tentatively.

"Yes, Mr. Transport?" Mr. Numbers replied without looking up from his own copy of the assignment file.

"Do you feel that perhaps there was a misfile, and we were given someone else's assignment?" Mr. Transport asked, trying desperately to keep any hope out of his voice. It was very bad for one's job (and health) to be heard questioning the wisdom of the company they worked for.

"The possibility crossed my mind," Mr. Numbers admitted. "However, if you read on, you will see certain accommodations at the target's place of employment have been made specifically for us. It even references us by name several times."

Mr. Transport flipped a few pages ahead, and sure enough, Mr. Numbers had been correct. "Very well," Mr. Transport said carefully. "Just wanted to be certain we were deployed to the right area."

"Quite understandable," Mr. Numbers agreed. "It would be irresponsible of us as agents to allow time and resources to be wasted on a clerical error. Since that is not the case, though, it seems we have a few more hours until we begin our new assignment."

"That it does. Perhaps we should use that time to pack and prepare, so we are properly equipped for the full term of the assignment," Mr. Transport suggested.

"Excellent idea," said Mr. Numbers. "Would you mind depositing me first, then swinging back by in an hour or so to pick me up?"

"Not at all," assured Mr. Transport. He reached into his wallet and pulled out a few bills. Mr. Transport kept a variety of currency for almost every country in the world available at his apartment. It was much faster than trying to haggle or work out an exchange rate every time; plus, it allowed him and his partner to stay in the background, the area in which they were most comfortable. Mr. Transport set the money on the table, careful to tip generously. A moment later, he and Mr. Numbers were gone.

23

Across the café, an elderly gentleman glanced at their table and noticed their absence. He nonchalantly folded his paper, set some money on his own table, and headed off to make a phone call. The elderly gentleman did not tip nearly as well as Mr. Transport.

*   *   *

Several thousand miles away, in the middle of the Arctic tundra, Mr. Transport and Mr. Numbers reappeared. Both began shivering almost immediately.

"How long?" Mr. Transport asked, willing his teeth to keep from chattering.

"Three minutes fourteen seconds until health problems begin to set in," Mr. Numbers replied automatically as he felt the temperature around him, tested the speed of the wind, and added in the meager protection his black suit offered him.

"Watch is set for three minutes," Mr. Transport said, quickly fiddling with the high-priced device on his wrist. Mr. Numbers and Mr. Transport were very careful when they wanted to talk openly. They always selected areas with no possible people to surround them, and abstract locales with ample background noise so that listening devices and GPS would be rendered ineffective. They never used the same place twice and always kept their conversations under five minutes. Say what you will about Mr. Numbers, he was a very calculating man. No pun intended.

"Now then, what do you actually make of our new assignment? Are we being punished?"

"For what?" Mr. Numbers shot back. "Our success rate is ninety-eight percent. We finish our missions in the fastest time of any team, and we have had no recorded insubordination in the history of our career."

"Then what would make them do this to us?" Mr. Transport asked, allowing the uncertainty and fear he had kept hidden away since he saw the document flood into his voice.

"We mustn't assume the worse," said Mr. Numbers. "Many of the reasons they had for putting us on this job are actually quite sound. They expect me to see any problems coming before they reach a critical point, and you'll be necessary in the event we need to evacuate ourselves and any others involved."

"I don't imagine that's really all there is to it," Mr. Transport said flatly.

"Nor do I," said Mr. Numbers. "Unfortunately, with the data I have, I don't yet know what the ulterior motive of placing us in this position is. The only option we have is the same one we've always had: do our jobs, stick to the books, and give me enough time to see what's happening behind the scenes."

"Do you think you'll be able to figure it out before we're stuck in whatever trap someone is planning?" Mr. Transport asked.

"I always have. Of course, that doesn't mean I always will, but I don't really see any other options available to us, let alone any better ones," said Mr. Numbers.

24

"Agreed," said Mr. Transport. A loud beeping began emanating from his wrist. Mr. Transport raised his watch and promptly turned it off. Without another word said, he and Mr. Numbers were gone from the sprawling white mounds of snow.

They reappeared in the apartment Mr. Numbers was currently renting under the name Mr. Digit. Mr. Transport tipped his head to Mr. Numbers, then vanished to go pack his own bags. Mr. Numbers moved about his home, carefully controlling his movements so as not to show his body's relief at entering the heat by shivering from the residual cold still clinging to him. Instead, he packed up his clothes (which consisted predominantly of suits), gathered his very few personal effects, and then bagged up the remainder of his possessions, which were his toiletries. The room would need to be cleaned of all traces of him, but the company had a department for that. They would also take care of settling up the rent and making sure no one asked questions about Mr. Digit's sudden departure.

Mr. Numbers took a moment to go to his window and pull back the thick, black curtain. Looking out, he sighed as his eyes took in the splendor of Rome. From his vantage point, he had an excellent view of the Coliseum. That was why he had chosen this apartment in the first place. Mr. Numbers was not the type to get caught up in sentimentality or nostalgia, but as he sat on his window sill looking out, he had to admit that he was going to miss this view. He wished he could rent this place again once his assignment was over; however, that was against protocol. Once an agent had left a place, he could never return.

Mr. Transport reappeared some time later, carrying a large, brown tweed suitcase and a black duffel bag. As Mr. Transport walked toward the window, Mr. Numbers noticed a slight clinking sound coming from Mr. Transport's bag. Mr. Numbers bit back his desire to chastise Mr. Transport for bringing along alcohol. Given what the duo would soon be doing, there was a very strong possibility that Mr. Numbers would be seeking a nip of the hard stuff himself.

"Ready?" Mr. Transport asked as he reached the window and joined Mr. Numbers.

"Of course," Mr. Numbers replied on cue, holding his own baggage firmly so it wouldn't be left behind.

And then the room was empty, only the slight echo of a voice filled with duty and the warm Roman sunlight left to fill it.

7

The silver-haired boy was fidgeting nervously. Alice noted that in the back of her mind, not particularly intrigued, but not ambivalent either. Every little detail added up to the sum of who a person was, and that was information worth having if she was going to be dealing with these people on a regular basis.

The five students were assembled in the central common room, scattered among various seats. Mary was off to the side on her own, save for the stuffed bear she kept perched carefully in her lap. Alice had been tempted to ask why Mary had a stuffed animal, but the moment she had looked into those amber eyes, all desire had melted away in the face of the overwhelming certainty that talking to Mary was a bad idea.

The boys were clustered together for the most part. Silver Hair and Sunglasses were lounging on the white couch, with the third boy in the chair to their side. He was a husky one, wearing a shirt that had strangely shaped dice on the front. Alice deduced within a few moments of hearing him speak that the boy was lacking the basic set of social skills. Then again, given who she was surrounded by, she could hardly say that he didn't fit in.

Alice, herself, had taken a center position in the room, eager to appear eager for whatever authority figure Daddy had managed to wrangle into this babysitting job. Alice didn't expect whoever showed up to pose any real problem for her (after all, they would obviously know who her father was), but she still preferred to get her way through charm and cunning, rather than threats and force. It was the way a proper lady got things done.

As the clock struck seven (a bit too loudly, Alice noted with a grimace), a pair of men appeared in front of the group of students. They were dressed almost the same, save that the shorter of the two wore a tie, while the taller one did not. They wore black suits and white shirts, and both kept their dark hair trimmed. But while the short one had bright blue eyes, the larger one had muddy-brown ones.

"Hello, students," said the shorter of the pair. "You may call me Mr. Numbers. My friend, Mr. Transport, and I are here to oversee and assist you in your academic endeavors. Our apartment is what lies behind the steel door in the kitchen. You will not be permitted access. However, an intercom is on the counter next to the pantry for emergency contact. Do we have any questions so far?"

Alice glanced around to test the temperature of the room. It seemed everyone but she and Mary were struck dumb by the appearance and promptness of the two men who had materialized in front of them. Alice suppressed the urge to scoff. Of course these poor dregs were surprised; their only experience with people who had abilities was undoubtedly others like themselves. The sight of someone using precision teleportation would be truly alien to them. Alice wasn't quite sure why Mary wasn't more taken aback, but she readily chalked that up to just another aspect of the girl's strangeness.

"I take your silence to mean we are on the same page," Mr. Numbers continued. "Now, I want to be clear here. We've met most of you already, when we were selecting people appropriate for the program you all participated in. We were nice and friendly then. We will continue to maintain that same level of friendliness during our tenure as your house administrators. However, please do not misinterpret my good nature as weakness. Mr. Transport and I are here to enforce the rules, and you will find we are both excellent at our jobs."

"Um, what rules are you talking about?" The question came timidly from the silver-haired boy.

"A full copy will be issued before the week is over," Mr. Numbers replied. "I will touch briefly on the main three, though. First, you are to keep your identities secret at all times. This is a requirement of all those who participate in the Hero Certification Program, or HCP as we call it around here, and it is the duty of the administrators to observe who has broken it, intentionally or otherwise. That will be covered in more depth tomorrow during your first class. Secondly, there is to be no fighting with other Supers or with regular humans outside the confines of the classroom."

"Wait," the silver-haired boy said again. "We're going to be fighting in class?"

"Of course," said Mr. Numbers. "You are training to be a Hero. This means you must learn to fight against time, villains, and environmental conditions to save as many people as possible in any given scenario. Combat training will be a very important part of that."

"Don't worry," Mr. Transport broke in, speaking for the first time. "All fights are strictly monitored, and there is always someone with a healing power on hand to tend to both parties afterward."

"Mr. Transport is correct, though both he and you could stand to take a course in not interrupting," Mr. Numbers said, staring at the silver-haired boy. "Now then, the third rule is the most important for all of you. Your powers must stay within your control at all times. This is a rule specific to your situation and certainly doesn't need explanation. Be aware that this is the primary reason Mr. Transport and myself were selected for this assignment. Should any of you lose control, we will act quickly and decisively to ensure the safety of those around, while simultaneously shutting down the problematic party."

"Wait, I thought we all had control of our abilities. That's why they let us enroll here." This time, the speaker was the dark-haired boy wearing sunglasses. Alice noticed he spoke with a strange accent. Not quite northern, but not quite southern, either. It seemed to be a hint of dialect from a region all its own.

"You all do have control of your abilities. Currently," said Mr. Numbers. "The procedure you underwent was experimental, though. Those who created and performed it are certain you will remain as Supers and not drift back to your previous uncontrollable states. However, there are those who remain skeptical such a thing is possible, and the

27

positioning of Mr. Transport and myself as overseers is a compromise to assure the safety of the regular student body."

"So, what happens if someone loses control?" Alice was shocked to realize this question had come from her own mouth. It wasn't as if she was a danger to anyone if she began floating around again, but she was concerned that the slip-ups of some of these cretins could affect her college career. At least, that's how she rationalized the sudden nagging fear that had formed in her stomach.

"Testing," Mr. Numbers replied simply.

"What Mr. Numbers means to say," Mr. Transport said, jumping in as he saw the looks of distress cross his charges' faces, "is that we will test and investigate the reason why control was lost. Maybe there was a psychological component, and it doesn't mean things failed. Maybe it's an individual case, or maybe it just means that person will need another round of treatment. We don't anticipate anything going wrong with any of you, but if it does, we'll be there to find out exactly why it happened."

"I feel testing was an adequate answer," Mr. Numbers said. "Now, do any of you have any questions about the rules I have set down so far?"

There was silence, though this time, it was less motivated by being dumbstruck at the dramatic entrance and more motivated by the sudden fear they had all presumably acquired of someone losing control and screwing the deal for everyone.

"Excellent," Mr. Numbers said. "Then I will turn the floor over to Mr. Transport for some 'getting to know our dormmates' activities." With that, Mr. Numbers sat down in the chair directly opposite Alice. Alice, for her part, worked very hard to avoid his observant blue eyes and focus on the tall Mr. Transport. It seemed that everyone was following her lead on that account; everyone, that is, except for Mary.

Mary was staring directly into Mr. Numbers's big, blue eyes, meeting his gaze with her own amber orbs. Since everyone was gazing intently at Mr. Transport, no one noticed the two looking at each other. If they did, though, certainly no one noticed as Mary brought both of her hands up and began clapping them together softly, engaging in a very gentle, very silent, session of applause.

8

"Well then," Mr. Transport said as the eyes of his charges fell curiously upon him. He was glad Mr. Numbers had allowed him to be the "good cop" in their interaction with the students, but he still felt a bit awkward dealing with a group of eighteen-year-olds. After all, Mr. Transport could scarcely remember a time when he'd shared the worries and concerns of an everyday teen. Of course, the reason Mr. Transport had trouble finding those memories was because they didn't exist. Being able to pop out of nearly every situation had a profound impact on diminishing the amount of things he'd had to worry about in his formative years. "Why don't we do an exercise to get to know one another better?"

Mr. Transport waited for some sign of agreement or excitement from the students. Instead, he got back blank stares. So after a moment, he elected to take that as the sign of their agreement. "Okay," Mr. Transport continued. "Here is how it works. I want everyone to stand up, say their full name, what their ability is, where they are from, what their cover major is, and one interesting fact about themselves."

Again, Mr. Transport was met with silence; having settled on choosing to perceive that in the positive, though, Mr. Transport was able to keep right on trucking. "I'll begin. My name is Mr. Transport. My power is teleportation of myself and others. My birth location is considered classified. I am not currently enrolled in Lander University, so I lack a major, and my interesting fact is that I collect bottle caps from sodas all over the world."

"They still make soda in bottles?" Nick asked skeptically.

"Yes, they do, in other countries as well as in America," Mr. Transport answered, grateful to have anyone say anything. "Why don't you pick up the ball and tell us about yourself now?" Mr. Transport had something that almost seemed like conversation momentum and he would be damned if he was going to lose it.

"No prob," said Nick, standing from the couch. "Nick Campbell, and I've got the power of creating and controlling luck. I'm from Sin City itself, good old Vegas. I'm majoring in business while at Lander. My interesting fact is that I've been punched in the mouth by a senator." With that, Nick plopped back down on the sofa and threw out a big, broad smile.

"Punched by a senator? Would you care to elaborate on that story, Mr. Campbell?" Mr. Transport asked.

"You're not the only one with shit that's classified," Nick answered.

"Okay then," Mr. Transport said quickly. "Who would like to go next?"

Before the word "next" was fully out of his mouth, the blonde girl sitting directly opposite him and Mr. Numbers had popped up from her chair like there was a spring loaded in it. He hadn't yet had the pleasure of meeting this young lady, but, by process of elimination, he knew who she was before she began to speak.

"My name is Alice Adair, and I have the power of flight. I'm from Los Angeles, California. While at Lander, I will be enrolled in the communications program. An interesting fact about me is that I have been riding horses since I was five and have won several championships," Alice said with a firm tone and a confident aura. She was a bit agitated that the sunglasses boy, or Nick as it were, had beaten her to being the first to speak, but she kept that annoyance off of her face as she returned to her seat and smiled placidly.

"Very nice to meet you, Alice," said Mr. Transport. "Who wants to go next?" He braced, waiting for another student to pop up, but it became all too apparent he had already worked his way through the confident public speakers in the group. Well, no matter; Mr. Transport knew the default solution for problems like this.

"Well, since no one wants to volunteer anymore, how about we just start at this end of the room," he said, pointing to Hershel, "and we'll work our way down."

There were some mumbling and dissatisfied tones, but slowly, Hershel rose to his feet. The boy looked a bit better than when Mr. Transport had last seen him. The months of therapy and procedures had shrunken him from round to a wide husky, though the confidence of an elf lord about to siege a castle was strangely gone from his eyes and body language. Now that Mr. Transport thought about it, Hershel and that small girl, Mary, were the only two who hadn't spoken a word since he and Mr. Numbers appeared in the room.

"My name is Hershel Daniels, and I'm from Chicago. I'm majoring in creative writing, and an interesting fact about me . . . is . . . um . . . well, I won a couple of writing competitions for my fantasy short stories," Hershel said in soft tones. He moved to sit down, but Nick stopped him.

"You forgot to tell us what your power is," Nick pointed out.

"Oh," Hershel said. "Um . . . well, I guess that's because I don't really have any powers. I mean . . . I do, but . . . it's complicated."

"How complicated can it be?" Nick kept pressing. "You can either do something superhuman, or you can't."

"Well, it's more that I do something, and then I can do something super. Does that make sense?" Hershel asked timidly.

"He's a shifter," Mary said from her chair on the end.

"Oh, why didn't you say so? So, you turn into some other form that has the powers, right?" Nick asked.

"Yes," Hershel said, nodding emphatically. "That's how it works."

30

"No shame in that," Nick said reassuringly. "Some of the best Heroes on the record books had to go through a transformation before they were ready for business. It makes keeping your secret identity and Hero identity separate all the easier, too."

"I guess it does," Hershel agreed, looking thoughtful about the benefit Nick had brought up. He sat down in his chair successfully at last, the burden of speech passed off of him and on to the next poor sap.

Since the person to Hershel's right was Nick, who had already gone, the turn skipped to Vince. It wasn't really that Vince was scared to talk in public; it was just that everything in him was ingrained to go against the idea of volunteering. In his world, volunteering drew attention, and attention made people notice he was different. Once people noticed that, well . . . things always had a tendency to get far too interesting for Vince's tastes.

Vince rose to his feet and addressed the room. "My name is Vince Reynolds. My power is the absorption, storage, and redistribution of energy. I'm from New York . . . originally. I'm enrolled as undecided as far as my major goes. My interesting fact is that I've been in forty of our fifty states." Vince sat back down on the couch quietly.

"I have to ask, how do you get your hair that color?" Alice said once Vince had hit the couch. She didn't really care about who his stylist was, but she was curious. The strong tone and voice that had come from Vince didn't match up with the skittish body language she had seen all night. She wanted to hear more from him to try and reconcile that personality discrepancy.

"I don't," Vince said, this time a bit sheepishly. "My hair is naturally this color, and for some reason, I can't get dye to stick in it."

"Oh," Alice said. "I'm sorry, I didn't know." That was unfortunate; she had been planning on getting a full course of dialogue from him, but if it was natural and a feature he was clearly embarrassed about, then there was no way for her to press onward from her present position.

"Don't worry about it," Vince said quickly. "Nick more or less asked the same thing when he first met me. It's good that people think I dye it this way; it makes it easier to blend in as a human."

"Very positive attitude, Vince," Mr. Transport said. "Now then, shall we hear from our last student?"

All eyes turned to the short, wiry girl who had thus far only spoken once, on Hershel's behalf at that, in the course of the night. Unlike the others, Mary didn't stand. She delivered her introduction from a cross-legged, sitting position in her chair.

"My name is Mary," she began. "And my power is an advanced brain which gives me telekinesis and telepathy. I was born in Louisiana, but I've been in the forests of Colorado for about eight years now. I'm double majoring in psychology and biology, and an interesting fact about me is that I know how to turn beavers into hats."

31

"What's your last name?" Hershel asked.

Mary blinked several times, then let her gaze move around the room. She unconsciously let her hands pet the head of the stuffed bear in the lap. A few seconds of silence passed, and Mary looked back at her fellow dormmates.

"I don't really remember. Like I told Alice, I haven't had any need for names in a very long time," Mary said.

"Thankfully, we had ample need," Mr. Numbers interjected. "Your last name is Smith. You may check the releases your parents signed if you need confirmation."

"I have no reason to doubt you," Mary said graciously.

"Thank you, Mary," Mr. Transport said. "Tell me, does your bear have a name?" He was fairly certain girls who were Mary's age didn't name their stuffed animals, but then, his understanding was that eighteen-year-olds didn't normally keep their stuffed animals with them out in the open anyway, so he'd opted to ask in the hopes of seeming friendly.

"No," Mary said bluntly.

"I see. That was a silly question," Mr. Transport said hurriedly.

"Why do you think that?" Mary asked him.

"Well, because you're obviously old enough that you wouldn't be naming your bear," Mr. Transport said.

"You misunderstand," Mary told him. "I did name my bear. His name is No."

"Huh," said Mr. Transport. "Why did you name him No?"

"Why not name him No?" Mary responded.

"Yes, well." Mr. Transport paused and resisted the urge to press his fingers to his temples. He didn't need the children seeing that he could be annoyed, gotten to, or given a headache. It was best to just get things back to business. "Since Mr. Numbers already introduced himself, that takes care of the meeting agenda for tonight. But there's one last thing before Mr. Numbers and I retire. As you were all told, classes for Lander take place on the ground level, while classes for the Hero Certification Program take place in a special underground campus. Now, other dorms that house Supers have special elevators to convey their students between campuses. However, since ours is new and it is not yet hooked up to the network, I will be your method of travel between these two schools."

"Why couldn't we just get clearance to use an elevator at a nearby dorm?" Nick asked.

"Too much paperwork," Mr. Transport said with what he hoped was a believable grin. "No, in reality it is simply that getting approval takes months and months, and since we weren't sure if any of you would be able to attend this year, we were unable to secure that approval in time. Fear not, though, for I know all of your class schedules, and I will always be around to teleport you as needed."

32

"How do we get back up?" Nick said, asking yet another question.

"You can call for me on my phone, or you can ride the elevator. Getting up doesn't require clearance. Only going down. Now, I'm sure you all know there is a meeting welcoming you all tomorrow at eight in the morning, so I expect to see each of you here ready to go promptly at seven forty-five. Aside from that, please intermingle, get to know one another, and have a great night."

Mr. Transport gently kicked Mr. Numbers, who said something that might or might not have resembled "good night," depending on the language one was using as well as the level of sarcasm tolerated before the meaning of a word was reversed.

With a nod and a smile, Mr. Transport vanished, presumably taking Mr. Numbers with him, since the chair Mr. Numbers had occupied now sat empty. The students were overtaken with surprise at their disappearance, though this time, the spectacle wore off much more quickly. The vanishing administrators left behind a vacuum in conversation, rendering the five gifted individuals with no idea what to say to one another. This vacuum was broken quickly by Nick, whose powers evidently included a need for attention and an utter lack of social insecurity.

"Okay," Nick said. "I'm now officially taking bets. Gay couple or just a pair of best friends who secretly wish they were a gay couple?"

9

The first thing Nick did, once he had secured his door tightly shut behind him, was to shed those idiotic sunglasses. He blinked several times as his eyes readjusted, then strolled over to his desk and turned on his computer. He opened a word processing program and immediately began writing down the day's events with as much detail as he could remember. It was a very minor challenge for him. There had been times before he had gained control of his power when he would go weeks between note-taking sessions, and he had still managed to glean information from those.

Nick made no motion to save his file as he typed. He had procured a surge protector that doubled as a battery in case of a power outage, so he was relatively certain nothing would interrupt his process or destroy his work thus far. It was probably redundant in a place like this, with safeguards on top of the safeguards, but Nick hadn't survived eighteen years of bipolar luck without learning to be a little redundant in his safety measures.

It took him only a few minutes to finish—Nick had shockingly quick hands—and then he leaned back in his chair and began reviewing the day's events. He had done quite well and had adhered to the primary tenants of survival in a new area: speak much, say little, and see all. The glasses had been a good addition; he needed to thank Ms. Pips for that suggestion next time he was in Vegas. They kept anyone from reading what was on his face effectively, and they made him look like something of a jackass.

That suited Nick's needs just fine. People overlooked and underestimated those they thought of as stupid, which was precisely what he wanted. Nick was a boy who could affect the outcomes of dice throws in a school for people who could lift cars and eat fire. He was going to need every advantage he could get, and surprise was an excellent one to have.

Nick continued scrolling down, rereading his recent notes. He had befriended Vince easily enough, and Hershel was socially ignorant, so getting on his good side had only required minor encouragement. Mary was a lost cause; Nick needed a telepath hanging around him like he needed a bullet to the head. Alice, on the other hand, was a whole different story. She had some skill in reading people, but her subtlety and manipulation skills were amateurish at best. The way her eyes had been darting about during the meeting, how she'd tilted her head when she was trying to figure out a new aspect to someone, the clumsy way she had tried to lead a conversation with Vince, all of those had been tells of a novice. Nick estimated he could get her to trust him within the span of a month. After all, there were few things as vulnerable as someone with just a little bit of knowledge.

The two agents he had babysitting him were going to be simple to get around. They had run a classic "good cop, bad cop" routine to categorize their interactions with the students. As long as he created some personal problems to ask Mr. Transport for help with, and let Mr. Numbers yell at him occasionally for minor discipline issues, neither one would think to wonder what was going on behind those sunglasses.

Nick finished reading his notes, then went through them twice more. After the final pass, Nick deleted every word he had written and closed the file without saving, making sure to purge the autosave function as he did so. That done, he undressed and got into bed. He would plan for how to handle the next day for only an hour, then allow himself to get some sleep. He needed to be in top form when he met the other students, after all.

*   *   *

Mr. Transport and Mr. Numbers sat at the dining table in their new apartment. It was a spacious two-bedroom that existed behind the door in the kitchen. They would, of course, be sharing the cooking area with the children, but since the kids had meal plans and little practical experience in taking care of themselves, neither Mr. Transport nor Mr. Numbers anticipated battling with them for space on the stove.

They had also been provided with their own mini-fridge, which Mr. Numbers took as a negative sign, indicating some higher-up was aware of Mr. Transport's penchant for beer and liquor. Still, the fridge was there, so Mr. Transport had put his beer and a bottle of gin in it as they unpacked. Now, the two sat, still clad in their suits, going over their assignment folders one last time before the mandatory destruction of them.

"Do you think it went well?" Mr. Transport asked from his seat.

"Exceedingly," Mr. Numbers said. "We made them perceive us in the way they were supposed to. The only exception, of course, is the telepath."

"She shouldn't pose a problem for us, though," Mr. Transport said. "Remember your training. Telepaths can only read what is going through your mind at that moment. Just be careful and remember to control your thoughts around her."

"I'm aware of the necessary techniques," Mr. Numbers said with a slight edge to his voice. "I'm just not certain it holds true with that one. There's something about her, something different. I worry she might be able to go deeper than most telepaths."

"I'm sure the doctors or nurses would have made note of it in the file. Besides, why would a telepath who has spent her life without control of her ability be more adept with it than those who have honed it through a lifetime of practice?" Mr. Transport asked.

Mr. Numbers let out a small sigh. "I suppose you're right. Still, we'll have to stay on our toes around her. Heaven knows we have secrets we can't afford to let some eighteen-year-old girl in on."

"I thought she was seventeen," said Mr. Transport.

"She was when we met her, but she had her birthday while she was undergoing treatment," said Mr. Numbers.

"Oh. I do hope they did some sort of celebration for her," said Mr. Transport.

"It is my understanding that there was cake," assured Mr. Numbers.

"Very good then," said Mr. Transport. "Well, I'm ready when you are."

"Let's get the lighter and the bucket," said Mr. Numbers.

* * *

Alice tossed and turned sleeplessly in her bed. A telepath! What had her father been thinking, allowing a telepath to be her dormmate? He knew how much she valued her privacy. At least, she had thought he knew. What was she going to do? That Mary girl could be listening to her at that very moment. She would never know a moment's peace; never know a good sleep again.

Alice had always been excellent at reading others, a skill she had first learned from watching her Daddy interact with other people. Now, she was stuck with a dormmate who had been living in the damn forest for the last few years, and who was a mind reader to boot. All of Mary's social habits had been scrubbed clean by the wilderness and the solitude, so Alice had no idea what was going on in her head. On top of that, Mary could see Alice's thoughts plain as day.

Never had the tables been turned on Alice like this, never had she felt so exposed, so vulnerable. Her only consolation was that the others would be simple to deal with. Hershel was a big, insecure geek, Nick was a tongue-wagging idiot, and Vince was uncomfortable with his own uniqueness. They had all shown weaknesses to capitalize on for her own gain, so she was comfortable with them. As for the agents, Alice barely spared a thought for them. They worked for Daddy, because, whether they knew it or not, everyone worked for Daddy in some way. She would be polite, and if they crossed her, she would handle them.

No, there was no problem with anyone else. Alice flipped over in her bed for the thousandth time, trying to figure out how to handle Mary.

* * *

Hershel was also thinking about Mary, though he and Alice had very different problems with the girl.

"She was so pretty," Hershel said to no one. He used to have friends, back before Roy had begun popping up more frequently, and had even managed to hang on to some personal connections through his LARP group. Those were gone now, back in Chicago, while he lay in bed alone. He desperately wished he still had them so he could tell them about his day, about how he had gotten Roy under control, and about the beautiful girl with the amber-colored eyes he had met on his first day at college.

Hershel could do none of those, though, so instead, he was talking to an empty room. He wished he could have talked to her after the meeting was over, but she went back to the girls' side almost as soon as the two administrators were gone. Did she know he was going to talk to her, and that's why she ran? A wave of insecurity washed over

Hershel, one that he was more than accustomed to. Hershel was pudgy, shy, and unremarkable. He had spent his whole life feeling those waves of insecurity crash against him. The only times they weren't there was when he was dressed up in costume pretending to be someone else. Then, he was brave, strong, and confident. Then, he was someone worth being.

Hershel felt something stir in his mind. He realized he had been calling out to Roy without noticing. That seemed to happen at his lowest points, when he wanted to be anyone else in the world besides Hershel Daniels. If not for the treatment, Roy would probably have appeared already. Fortunately, that was no longer the case. Hershel could call to him all night, but until he used the trigger that had been created, Roy would stay nothing more than a tickle in the back of his head.

Still, it was hard enough to get to sleep alone. Hershel didn't want to try and pass out with both of them stirring, so he decided to think of something besides Mary and how insecure she made him feel.

"She really is so pretty," Hershel said once more. He rolled over and tried to visualize anything besides Mary's amber eyes.

*   *   *

In her own room, Mary blushed.

"Yes, I think he's very sweet, No," she said to her bear. "I just think he needs a little more time to acclimate to college on his own. This is a big, new environment, and if I were to be with him, I'd become nothing more than a security blanket."

The bear stared back at her from his resting place on the bed.

"Okay, you got me. I also want to see what his other side is like," Mary admitted. "Besides, there are much more interesting thoughts going on right now, don't you agree?"

No said nothing.

"So many people thinking of little old me," said Mary. "I feel like this is going to be a very interesting year."

No still said nothing.

"Oh, you rascal," Mary laughed. "Maybe after a few weeks. Right now, we need to get to bed. It's going to be very loud tomorrow unless we're rested and in control."

Mary scooped No up and got under the covers with him. Like turning off a light switch, Mary banished away the voices in her head. And just like that, it was as though she were back in the forest, communing with the quiet. The ability to have silence on demand, that was something she would never grow tired of.

*   *   *

Vince was asleep. Unlike the others, he hadn't had any large revelations about his roommates or sudden fears about the day to grapple with. Vince had merely come in, undressed, and gotten into bed.

37

Of course, before he slept, Vince had tenderly removed a gold pocket watch from his backpack and gently wound it as he did every night. He then checked the time and made sure the watch was running right before he set it down in a place of honor on his bedside table.

Then he had gotten into bed himself, pausing on his direct flight toward the land of slumber only long enough to run a finger along the watch and softly whisper, "Goodnight, Father."

After that, he was gone into a dream that seemed to feature fire more heavily than the ones he had regularly.

10.

"Welcome, freshmen!" The speaker was a tall man with glasses, black hair, and a charcoal-colored suit. He cut an impressive figure even from behind his podium, looking around the room, emanating confidence and ease, as though he had made this speech dozens of times before. Which, coincidentally, he had.

"It is my pleasure as Dean of the Hero Certification Program to be the first to congratulate you on making the cut and being enrolled in our very elite little academy," the dean continued. "My full name is Blaine Geffries. However, I want you all to just call me Dean Blaine. It is my hope that each and every one of you grow stronger in the years ahead, and that the best of you graduate from here with full certifications, and go on to become acclaimed Heroes. I want to watch all of you find the lessons you need to succeed!"

"Of course he does," Nick muttered to Vince quietly from his seat in the middle of the auditorium. "The more prestige a Hero has, the better it looks on the school that trained them."

"I didn't think the five universities that ran this program were in competition," Vince said curiously.

"Where there is money, there is competition, and these bad boys are government-funded," Nick replied.

"Now, I know all of you are a little nervous," Dean Blaine said in an understanding voice. "After all, most of you are from schools, if not towns, where you were the only Super present. Having peers around you who can understand and relate to what you're going through is a new experience, and I'm here to tell you that it will be a wonderful one. You're going to have friendships, support, and respect all built on the mutual understanding that only fellow Supers can share."

"Is being a Super hard?" Vince whispered to Nick. "I knew a few of them, and by comparison to . . . everyone else, it seemed like they had it pretty easy." Vince chastised himself internally. He had just referenced himself as something other than a Super, a taboo Mr. Transport had advised them against committing before he'd brought them down that morning. It wasn't just that the program that had created them was classified, which it was, the problem was that if the other students knew that Vince and his group had once been Powereds, they were almost sure to face harassment and discrimination. Of course, in a school where there were telepaths, any secret was inevitably going to come out. The goal was merely to avoid that day for as long as possible.

"It isn't really hard, per se," Nick responded, breezing over Vince's near screw-up. "It's just different. I know you were on your own most of the time, but for those of us around people, it was an odd experience, always knowing you were the one who was different." Nick was careful to try and cover for Vince, not out of friendship, but out of necessity. Nick wanted every advantage he could get his hands on, and being targeted as a freak among freaks would rob him of too many opportunities for him to permit it.

"You're going to need that support network, too," Dean Blaine continued. "As all of you should know, becoming a Hero is a grueling task. You'll be taking combat classes, training your tactical skills, learning to think around corners, and—possibly most importantly of all—you'll be learning about the ethics behind having and using abilities. And, of course, you'll be doing all of that while maintaining your secret identity up top."

The sound of groans permeated the audience, which was about fifty people strong. Dean Blaine only gave this talk to freshmen, and despite what many conspiracy theorists believed, the portion of the population that were Supers was still remarkably small. Of course, the percentage jumped considerably if one were to include Powereds as well, but no one did.

"Now, now, none of that," said Dean Blaine without breaking his smile. "I know many of you have lived out in the open with your abilities for years, but this is how we do things at Lander. Learning to protect a secret identity helps you hone a lot of the skills a Hero will need. Ingenuity, thinking on your feet, and planning are all major elements of keeping your secret safe. Those of you who fail at keeping your secret . . . well, let's just say that fail was the operative word there."

There was no laughter at Dean Blaine's joke, not that he had expected any. That was a joke just for him.

"Of course, there are always extenuating circumstances, but let's just say you should do your best to keep the fact that you're a Super close to the vest. If you need to show off, work out, or just get the powers pumping, then you are always welcome down here, where you can be the Super we all know you are," Dean Blaine reassured them.

"Lovely," Alice said to no one in particular. She had opted to sit alone near the top of the tiered auditorium. She loved that sort of spot because it allowed her a vantage point above all the others, observing and noting their behavior. She had also chosen it because Mary, and for some reason Hershel, had both sat near the bottom. Alice was not about to give that girl any more time staring into her mind than she had to.

"With that settled, let's go over today's activities, shall we?" Dean Blaine asked rhetorically. "Since above-ground classes don't start until tomorrow, we'll be using today to do our combat ranking. For those of you who don't know, we do rankings among the classes at the beginning of this and end of every other year. This is so we can get a sense of where you're starting from based on the previous test, and how much you've grown by the end. We won't just be taking into account who wins each fight; we'll be looking at how they use their abilities, bodies, and brains to make the most of every situation. Today's will be a single elimination tournament, so the more you win, the more you fight, and the better chance you have to showcase what you can do."

Vince felt his heart sink. All he had for energy was the half a book of matches he had absorbed yesterday while showing off for Nick. Unless he fought someone with electrical or fire abilities, he was going to be working at a big disadvantage. It was really his own fault; Mr. Numbers had warned them there would be combat. He'd even had a passing thought of trying to find a place to absorb energy, but he couldn't bring himself to do it. There was still a nagging voice in the back of his brain telling him that he would lose control and drain the whole school. Or town. Or state.

"I'd like all of you to come down now and meet the professors who will be overseeing the first battle of your college careers, the freshmen combat coaches: Coach George and Coach Persephone!" Dean Blaine announced, gesturing to the side of the stage where a pair of people, both wearing sweats, walked on and joined up with the dean in the center.

The man was dark-haired, tall and muscular. The woman, on the other hand, was blonde, lean, curvy, and just plain sexy. She looked like she wouldn't be able to take on a sack of potatoes, let alone watch over Supers in combat. Not that that really mattered to the men in the audience, who were staring unabashedly, with only a few exceptions.

Nick was certainly not one of those exceptions. "Look at the tits on her," he said as he and Vince rose from their seats and began making their way to the stage with the rest of their class.

"You better hope she doesn't have enhanced hearing," Vince warned as they descended.

"What? Like she doesn't know she has amazing tits? I mean, we can see them through a sweatshirt. I seriously doubt me saying this would result in a groundbreaking realization for her," Nick defended.

"No, but it could be a skull-breaking one for you. The woman teaches Supers how to fight. I can't imagine she's as frail as her form looks," Vince said.

"You have a point," Nick agreed. "On the other hand, though . . . yowza."

Fortunately for Vince, they reached the stage, and even Nick wasn't dumb enough to keep chatting about their coach's breasts with her in human earshot. At least, Vince hoped Nick wasn't that dumb.

Once all the students were together, Coach George stepped forward and addressed them.

"Good morning, new meat," he said with a grin that was far more believable than the one the dean still had shellacked onto his face. "To the upper classman, I'm a professor, but you haven't earned that right yet, so to you, my name is Coach George, and by the end of the year, you are going to curse me, my mother for birthing me, and God for allowing me to exist. I am going to work every last one of you down to the bone. I am going to break you apart until you have no concept of what you can or can't do, because I want each of you to end this year doing things you never thought possible. You will all hate me for the rest of your life, but if you are very skilled and very lucky, you will live long enough to come back here and thank me one day. You will thank me for making you strong enough to survive."

Coach George stepped back, and Coach Persephone stepped forward. "First off, yes, eyes up at my face, gentlemen. Secondly, I'm going to be training you as well, though, while my brutish counterpart will be teaching your bodies how to endure combat, I will be educating your minds. You will use your powers in new ways you never would have imagined before, and you will do it because the only options I am going to hand you are to find a way or suffer bodily harm. You should know that Coach George and I are the harshest instructors in this academy, because we have to be. This is where you are torn down and built up correctly with the building blocks that will enable you to survive the years to follow. If we do not think you can survive, we will fail you. So work hard and learn fast, or you'll wash out and be no better than a Powered."

The students winced visibly at that, the idea of being compared to a Powered kicking them into gear and setting their determination not to wash out firmly into place. Which, of course, was exactly what Coach Persephone had been aiming for.

"All right," said Dean Blaine. "So, before we pair off for the first round of combat, does anyone have any questions so far?" No hands came up, so Dean Blaine continued. "Fantastic. Then I want the girls to go to Coach Persephone and the boys to go to Coach George so they can pair you up."

"Isn't that sexist?" The question came from a girl near the front of the crowd with dirty-blonde hair. Vince looked at her, and realized with pleasant surprise that the girl with the pink-streaked, short hair from the dining hall yesterday was standing next to the question asker.

"And what is your name, miss?" Dean Blaine asked in response.

"Julia," the girl replied.

"Let me guess, Julia, you're a women's studies major, right?" Dean Blaine asked.

"Um . . . yes," Julia replied.

"There's always one," Dean Blaine said with a sigh. "We go over this every year, so I'll tell you the same thing, Julia. The point of this test is to get an idea of how you fight against an opponent when you are at relatively equal footing. Both you and your opponent will have an ability, so the only other difference is your physique, and sadly, boys are usually stronger than girls. This means that getting an accurate assessment requires us to pair you with people who have similar body types. If it makes you feel better, though, this is only the case for freshman year. Once you become sophomores and have been trained by George here, we'll be setting you against anyone, regardless of sex."

"I guess that makes sense," Julia conceded.

42

"Great," Dean Blaine said. "Okay, everyone, report to your respective coach and get ready for a good old-fashioned tussle."

11

Vince was impressed at the combat cells Lander possessed. Seventy feet by seventy feet in size, they were made of reinforced concrete that was several inches thick, with five-inch plastic serving as a window and a triple-locked door as the only entrance and exit. What was truly amazing, though, was that there were so many of them. Right now, each member of the freshman class was standing in a cell just like Vince's, staring across at some other student they would soon be facing off against.

In Vince's case, the boy who had entered was a few inches taller, a few muscles broader, and a multitude of follicles shorter. His head was perfectly bald, drawing more attention to his striking face and frost-blue eyes. The only other person near them was a girl wearing a white uniform, staring down at them through the glass. She was one of the senior class, doing her duty by watching over the new recruits to make sure no one was killed. Serious injury wasn't a concern since there were healers on hand, but no one could bring back the dead. At least, no one employed by Lander.

Vince and his opponent were both wearing black uniforms of a style similar to the girl's. It seemed the hierarchy at Lander was that freshmen wore black uniforms, sophomores and juniors wore grey, and the few seniors that managed to stay in class were issued white. This supposedly represented the students growing closer to the goodness and purity that all Heroes were meant to represent. Vince thought it was just that there was more training and fighting in the lower years and black didn't stain as easily, but he kept that particular theory to himself.

"Introduce yourselves," came a female voice from a speaker hidden somewhere in the concrete around them. It took Vince a moment, but he realized it had come from their overseer. Apparently, there was some sort of intercom system set up for the rooms. It made sense; how else was someone going to talk to them through solid walls?

"My name is Michael Clark," Vince's opponent said, a broad and confident smile smearing across his face.

"Vince Reynolds," said Vince.

"I like your hair," Michael commented.

"I like your . . . style," Vince reciprocated as best he could.

Michael laughed. "I know it's a bit odd, but you know how that goes, right? What can I say? I just love feeling the cold air against my head."

Vince said nothing, merely kept sweeping his eyes over Michael, trying to get some sense of what the boy would be doing once the metaphorical bell sounded. He didn't have to wait long to find out.

"Begin," said the same, crackling intercom-voice. Vince resisted the urge to look around for the speaker again, and that discipline was all that saved him. Before the word was even done being spoken, Michael had reared his right arm back and was punching in Vince's direction. Granted, since there was forty feet between the two of them, it was a ridiculous gesture that shouldn't have endangered Vince in the slightest. Vince leapt to the side anyway.

A flash of blue light roared past him, striking the wall where he had been standing only moments before. A quick peek back showed that a long chunk of the wall was now coated in ice. Someone who had cold-based powers. Freaking perfect.

"I'm impressed," Michael complimented. "Not many people think to get out of the way of a punch from across the room."

"I try to prepare for the worst case scenario," Vince admitted.

"Let me know if that helps you," Michael said as he balled up both of his fists. "Because, to be honest, fighting me in the first round is the worst case scenario for anyone."

Vince didn't respond this time. Instead, he took off running. Michael was a good shot with those freezing punches of his, but he was still shooting from forty feet away. Vince was quick on his feet, and more importantly, he'd had a lot of practice at running away, so he was able to stay a few steps ahead of each punch as it went out.

Michael was no slouch either, though; he began looking to where Vince was running and firing ahead of him. More than once, Vince was only saved by a quick roll to the side or a slide underneath. The upside was that the more Michael fired, the more Vince began to get his timing down. Michael needed to take a deep breath between every two punches, though whether it was part of his fighting style or just a necessary moment to recharge Vince was unsure. The good thing was that every time he took that breath, Vince had a moment to pause and see where Michael's eyes were aiming. The only real chance Vince had was to wear Michael down slowly until his endurance was thin. Using powers still seemed to require him to use physical actions, so if Vince could get Michael gasping for air, then he might have a chance at getting close to him.

Unfortunately, it seemed Michael had figured that out, too.

"What the hell is your power?" Michael asked as he threw two more freezing punches that Vince leapt over. "Running away?"

Vince said nothing, conserving his air for movement, not talking.

"If this is all you can do, then you should just give up," Michael chastised him. "So you've got a weak power. That doesn't mean you should jump around and make an ass of yourself because you're up against a real opponent." To punctuate his words, Michael let loose another flurry that crashed at Vince's feet.

Vince hurdled over the fast-forming ice and kept moving. He realized the problem with his strategy the moment he was away from the slicked ground behind him. The more punches Michael threw, the more ice formed around the room, which made running away increasingly difficult. Already, small pillars and blocks of ice were forming where more than one punch had landed. If Vince didn't bring this to a conclusion soon, he was going to run out of room to dodge.

"Damn it," Michael cursed. "I don't care if you can't fight. Just give up so I can move onto an opponent with some skill."

Michael threw another blast of ice right at Vince's feet, forcing him up into the air, then threw a left punch toward Vince, who was suspended in mid-jump. On instinct, Vince hurled his upper body forward, turning a midair somersault and dodging the blue blast that would be blaring down below him in mere instants. But the blast didn't come. Vince crooked his eye back to Michael to see him standing there with an extended left fist and a pulled back right one.

Michael hadn't used a blast out of his left hand; it had been a feint, which meant he still had one to throw. Michael's right arm shot back out just before Vince's feet touched the ground. The concrete below was instantly frozen, impossible to get traction on. Vince was on it only for a moment before his leftover momentum sent him flying onto and across the concrete. As he skidded along the hard surface, Vince tried to think. Michael would have to take a breath now, which meant Vince had maybe an extra second to get to safety. There was no way Vince could scramble up in time; he'd be a sitting target. What other options did that leave him?

As he rolled along the ground, he noticed he was near a moderate-sized block of ice that had been built up by Michael's attacks. It wouldn't be much in the way of cover, but it was a better option than anything else Vince had. Rather than trying to get up, Vince used his window to keep rolling, picking up speed and veering his course so that he was able to stop himself directly behind the ice block.

The crashing sound of energy accompanied by the cracking sound of growing ice told Vince he had made it just in time. Several more crashes followed, ironically building more ice and reinforcing Vince's defensive wall. Moments later, the sounds stopped.

"So, you've resorted to hiding now? Is this the best you've got? You must have some kind of ability, or you wouldn't be here. How about you try using it?" Michael taunted. "What is it, then, are you just scared of fighting?"

Vince let Michael talk; it bought him precious time. He checked his body and found that aside from a bloody lip, the fall had given him minimal damage. Vince knew he couldn't stay like this for long; it left him utterly vulnerable if Michael were to come around to this side. Michael was still being a bit cautious because he didn't know what Vince's power was, but that wouldn't last forever. The wear-down approach wouldn't work; Michael could destroy the terrain before he got tired. So, lacking any sort of reliable defense, Vince decided to use the next best thing:

Pure. Offense.

"You seem to be mistaken," Vince said as he pulled himself up carefully from behind the ice block. "Our powers work in contrast to each other, that's why I've been taking the defensive. It was the smart move until I understood your tactics. Let me assure of one thing right now, though."

Vince slowly, deliberately, wiped the blood from his mouth with the back of his fist. "I know how to fight."

12.

"Gaaaaah!" Vince cried as he was knocked back across the field, his small body rolling in the grass before coming to a stop.

"How many times do I have to tell you? Learn their timing and adjust your own to fit into their defensive gaps. Most people fight with patterns, and that's all they know. If you can flow through those patterns, they won't even be able to see how you're hitting them, let alone find a way to block you," said a tall, dark-haired man in a tattered, red coat.

"Sorry . . . Father," Vince squeezed out as he gasped for air. His father's last punch had knocked the breath out of him. He was used to it, though, and would recover quickly. Father didn't hold back when teaching him how to fight, because no one Vince ever went up against would be holding back either.

"You're getting better, Vince," Father encouraged. "You landed two punches on my arms that time before you fell into your own rhythm."

Vince managed to pull himself to his feet. Small and slight at eight years old and wearing ragged clothing, the only thing remarkable about him was his tousled, silver hair. That, and the look of determination screaming out of his soft, blue eyes.

"How do I keep from falling into my rhythm?" Vince asked.

"Simple," Father replied. "Don't have one."

"I don't know how," Vince admitted. Father never chastised him for admitting ignorance, saying it was the only way for Vince to find his weak spots and grow stronger.

"It's not something that's easy," Father explained. "You have to be able to adapt to your opponent's style, to work in a way that is the most detrimental to them. The only way to achieve it is through proper training and a variety of skilled opponents. However, you have a slight advantage in this area."

"What's that?" Vince asked.

"Your power is that of absorption. You can deal in all different types of energies. That means your core nature is an adaptive one," Father said. "You were built to handle all kinds of different challenges, so I have faith you'll be able to learn how to fight without a form."

"How does my ability factor in?" Vince asked harshly. "I can't even control it unless you're around."

"Just because you can't control it doesn't mean it doesn't say a lot about you," Father pointed out. "Now, the train will be pulling out in two hours, so if we want to jump on a car, we only have an hour and a half left. Do you want to spend it whining, or do you want to spend it training?"

Vince took a deep breath, making sure he had fully recovered from the blow to his stomach and losing his wind. He hadn't, but it was good enough for the moment.

"Training," Vince said with a grin.

*   *   *

Ten years later found Vince charging across partially-frozen concrete, ducking blue blast blows as they flew toward him, making a beeline for his enemy as he put all of Father's training into use. Vince knew Michael's pattern, and knew that any freezing attack would have to be concluded in a two-punch combo. More than that and Michael needed a breath. Vince also knew that, while Michael's style so far had been long range, the way he held himself and threw his blasts were indicative of someone comfortable with close-range fighting. Michael definitely had training, and from the way he had been attacking, Vince was betting it was in boxing.

Vince sidestepped another blast as he circled, closing the gap between himself and Michael. It was harder to dodge the closer Vince got, but he'd learned to dodge boxing blows at close combat range; there was no way a punch with a lag time was going to hit him. The problem would be that once Vince closed the gap entirely, he wouldn't be able to take a single one of Michael's punches, or this match would be all over. Normally, he could just count on his practice taking blows to let him work through the pain, but getting frozen solid wasn't something you could grit your teeth and push through.

Then, all at once, Vince realized he was in range to actually strike back and every cohesive thought was gone from his mind. All he saw were his opponent's movements, feeling the pattern that Michael wove to take down his prey. Vince flowed around Michael, using footwork to keep Michael from being able to get off a clean shot. At the same time, Vince began lightly throwing his own punches. Mere taps at first, easy to recover from for both parties. Vince wasn't trying to do damage: he was trying to see how Michael blocked. The more soft blows Michael avoided, the surer Vince was that Michael's training was in boxing, which told Vince exactly how to take him off guard.

Vince slid to Michael's side and threw a left directly at Michael's face. Michael blocked it immediately, rearing back his own left to deliver an ice-punch to Vince's face. He never got the chance, though, as Vince followed the momentum of his punch through with a hard knee to Michael's ribs. Without stopping, Vince used the force to spin himself around Michael's back, out of range of his frozen fists, and delivered a right-handed blow to the same spot on the ribs he had struck with his knee. Vince was preparing to let fly a punch to the back of Michael's head when the ground beneath his feet suddenly went slick.

Vince backed away quickly, getting onto a part of the concrete that offered more traction at the sacrifice of his position behind Michael. This had obviously been Michael's plan—he must have punched the ground to steal Vince's footing—but Vince had no other option besides playing into it.

49

"I can't believe it," Michael said. "All that fucking running, and it turns out you have some decent hand-to-hand skills. I'll admit, I did not see that coming."

Vince noticed Michael was talking, but not punching. Maybe he was foggy from the blows, but Vince doubted it. More likely, he had either realized he couldn't hit Vince at this range, or he was trying to lure Vince into relaxing and letting his guard down.

"Of all the things I expected today, using this on someone who hasn't even shown me their power wasn't one of them," Michael said. His tone was casual, but his eyes were hard. Vince had embarrassed him, and it was very clear Michael did not take kindly to that. "You got in some good shots, Vince, but that won't work on me anymore."

As he spoke, Michael's body seemed to turn blue. After a second, Vince realized that ice was forming over Michael's frame, cracking and fissuring as it went to allow movement, while thickening to protect what was underneath. It seemed to take no time at all before Michael was almost totally covered in ice armor. Vince could still make out his eyes through a pair of slits, but there was no way he was going to find a vulnerable chunk of Michael's flesh to pound on this time.

"You did pretty good for being as weak as you are," Michael goaded. "But I want you to see what a real warrior looks like. I'm going to be the number one ranked in this class, because no one is as powerful as me!" Michael tilted back his armored head and laughed, unconcerned about his worthless opponent as he stood in the invincible protection his ice offered him.

The moment Michael's head was back, Vince began charging forward. He'd made it halfway there when Michael noticed his headlong sprint.

"You think this is for show? Or are you so dumb you really think you can punch through several inches of ice?" Michael asked, taking his stance once again as Vince drew closer.

Vince never slowed down for an instant, running right up to Michael and stopping on his left foot, letting the speed carry his right forward into a powerful round kick. Michael moved to block it, but the foot drew back a few inches before it would have struck the armor around his arm. Vince kept spinning, though, pulling off a complete three-sixty before planting his right foot down and launching forward on it. Michael realized that Vince was still carrying most of the momentum from the run in his body, and that he was cocked back to throw a punch right at Michael's face. It took everything Michael had not to laugh at this sad, determined idiot. So Vince wanted to break his own hand just trying to land a blow on him? Well, that was just fine by Michael's standards; he knew how powerful his ice was. He didn't even make a motion to block. Let Vince give it his all and fail miserably.

Vince kept moving forward, stopping just short of bouncing into Michael's chest and throwing the rest of his momentum into his right fist, just as Michael had expected. Vince furrowed his brow in concentration; he would have to time this just right. Vince's punch soared upward, on a dead track for Michael's jaw. A fraction of a second before it hit, though, to Michael's tremendous surprise, a fireball roared forth from the clenched fist, striking the icy covering an instant before Vince's flesh did.

Black and white spots flashed in front of Michael's eyes as he landed on his back. He couldn't understand it. Vince had hurled a fireball to melt and weaken his armor before the punch connected, that much was obvious. But if Vince had that sort of power, why had he played defensive for so long? One thing was certain; Michael was done taking it easy on this kid.

Michael rose to his feet, reinforcing the area around his chin that Vince's fire had melted. Michael had no banter or sass this time, only unadulterated hatred in his eyes for the boy who had put him on his back.

"Crap," Vince said from the same spot he had knocked Michael back. "I was really hoping that would put you down for the count."

"It didn't," Michael replied.

13

Vince woke up an hour or so later in the healing clinic. He blinked as his eyes adjusted to the lighting and stretched slowly to banish the discomfort that had accumulated in his back after sleeping on the hard bed.

"Oh, thank God, you're finally awake," said a female voice to his right.

Vince pulled himself up to a sitting position and looked over. Resting on an identical bed was a tall girl wearing a black uniform similar to his. She had the lean, firm look of a track star and held herself, even while sitting, with a sense of poise and control. The most striking feature about her, though, were the bright pink streaks running through her otherwise dark hair.

"Was I out long?" Vince asked.

"Given that you were pretty much a hunk of solid ice when they brought you in, no, I'd say you slept an appropriate amount," the girl replied as she smirked.

"Solid ice, huh?" Vince said. "I seem to have recovered pretty nicely."

"Heat lamp and some healing. It's a dynamite combo," the girl quipped. "I guess sleep is part of it, too, but damn it was boring having no one to talk to."

"Sorry about that," Vince apologized without being sure why. "Why are you hanging around here, though? Didn't they heal you already?"

"Yeah," the girl said. "But they told me I had to rest in here until this afternoon at least."

"Why?" Vince asked.

"Some bullshit about fifteen broken bones needing to rest for a few hours even with healing," the girl explained. "I'm Sasha, by the way. And before you say anything, I know it's an old-woman name, so keep the jokes to a minimum."

"I wouldn't have dreamed of it," Vince lied. "My name is Vince. How'd you break fifteen bones?"

"I lost my fight," Sasha replied with a shrug.

"Well, that does make a certain amount of sense," Vince said agreeably. "What type of ability were you fighting?"

"Some chick that can turn into solid steel," Sasha said.

Vince let out a low whistle. "That's a good one."

"Yup, especially when she waited until I was charging her at with super speed to do her little shift. Kicking steel at a few hundred miles an hour . . . yeah, it kind of sucks," Sasha said. "So, how about you? I know you were fighting an ice dude, but what do you do? And while we're not on the subject, but I'm still going to ask anyway, who does your hair?"

"I absorb and redistribute energy, like absorbing the flame from a match and then shooting it out of my thumb. As for the hair, my genetics are my stylist," Vince said.

"Sweet ass," Sasha said. "If you can pack away fire, it must have been one hell of a fight with you and Frosty."

"Um, sort of," Vince said awkwardly. "I kind of forgot to charge up before coming in today, so I was working with less than I would have liked."

"Hey, no need for excuses. We're both losers here," Sasha said. She pulled out a lighter from the back pocket on her uniform and tossed it over to Vince.

"I don't smoke," Vince said.

"Which makes you look way less cool when standing around outside, but I didn't give it to you so you could light up," Sasha said.

"Then, what's it for?" Vince asked.

"You used all your energy in the fight, right?" Sasha said right back.

"Well, yeah. Did I tell you that?" Vince was growing more confused.

"No, but I figured you wouldn't have been a guysicle if you had any juice left. So, I thought you might need a recharge," Sasha explained through her transparent exasperation.

"Oh, I couldn't," Vince said quickly. "I usually drain all the energy and fuel when I do it, so your lighter would be useless."

"It came in a pack of twenty for five bucks. I'll be okay with the loss. Besides, I've never seen that ability before. I'll trade a lighter for a show," Sasha said.

Vince wanted to protest more, but the truth was he did feel stiff and listless. He remembered how draining the matches had made him feel a bit better the day before, and his aching muscles throbbed again. Vince had spent nearly all of his life with at least a little energy stored up. He was beginning to wonder if the recent constant fatigue had not been a side effect of the experiments done to him, but rather a side effect from constantly running on empty.

With only slight trepidation, Vince flicked the lighter on with his left hand. With his right, he reached out to it, forging a connection to the energy leaking out from the metal-topped, plastic container. The flame jerked toward him and began flowing in. The lighter had far more potential energy than a single match, so it took a few seconds before it ran dry and the light of the flame vanished. Vince stretched again, noting that the soreness had definitely decreased. He also felt a bit more awake and alert. The lighter had packed significantly more juice than half a pack of matches.

"That was pretty cool looking, I have to admit," Sasha commented.

"Thanks," Vince said. "I think I needed that more than I thought. You want the lighter back?"

"Keep it," Sasha said. "Dead lighter isn't much use to me, you know?"

"That I do," Vince agreed. "So, are they going to tell us when everyone is done fighting, or do we just rest until we feel like we should go?"

"Oh, you're free to go anytime," Sasha told him. "If you hurry, you might still catch the last of the boys' matches."

"What about the girls?" Vince asked.

"Those wrapped up, like, half an hour ago. My roommate already texted me some of the rankings," Sasha said.

"How'd you do?" Vince couldn't imagine a girl with super speed had faired too poorly.

"Nineteen out of twenty-two," Sasha said glumly. "That steel bitch took me down in the first round. Even Julia did better than me."

"That sucks," Vince said. "Is Julia your roommate?"

"Yeah, and number fourteen in the ranking," Sasha said. "She made it to the second round, but then she got put down hard. They couldn't really dock her too many points for it, though. I mean, the broad who beat her did wind up ranked number one for the girls."

"Who was that?" Vince asked out of curiosity.

"I haven't met her yet," Sasha said. "But Julia told me it was some telekinetic girl named Mary."

14.

Mr. Numbers and Mr. Transport sat at Dean Blaine's desk, looking across the sleek mahogany surface at his unapologetic scowl. The lights in Dean Blaine's office were fluorescent and bright, like a compromise between high beams and lamps. The décor was stark, with little more than a diploma and a few awards adorning the four walls around them. Mr. Transport had a vaguely uncomfortable feeling, but was unsure how to place it. Mr. Numbers, on the other hand, had been something of a hellion during his younger days and knew immediately why this sensation was both unenjoyable and familiar. It felt almost exactly as if he was once again fourteen years old and sitting in the principal's office, trying desperately to figure which crime he had been discovered at.

"When I agreed to host your students," Dean Blaine began at last. "I did so with the understanding that these were unfortunate children who were being provided with an opportunity to get some measure of control in their otherwise hectic lives. These were Powereds that had been spurned by fate and society alike, and now that they could actually use their abilities, they wanted to become Heroes, give something back to the world. That was the way your organization pitched them, correct?"

Mr. Numbers cleared his throat. "Well, we aren't really consulted in matters of marketing and diplomacy, but I will admit that does sound like something our company would say."

"Regardless of who said it, you two are the representatives that I have at hand, so you are going to have to be answerable for your company as a whole," Dean Blaine said. "Which brings me to why I called you down here to my office." He slid a piece of paper onto the smooth, polished surface of his desk. "Would one of you like to guess what that is?"

Mr. Transport took the paper first, since he had the longer arms and could reach. "It appears to be a ranking of the freshman female students entering your program," Mr. Transport said after a quick glance.

"Correct," Dean Blaine agreed. "Now, will you read for me the first name on that list?"

"Mary Smith," Mr. Transport said. He was very thankful he had worked so hard for so long at keeping all emotions, including surprise, out of his voice when needed.

"You nailed it," Dean Blaine said with a very out-of-place smile. "Now, for the last question. Can you please explain to me how a girl who had almost no control over her abilities until a few months ago managed to wipe the floor with every other freshman we put her up against?"

"In all fairness, just because she won doesn't mean she wiped the floor with them," Mr. Numbers jumped in.

"I saw her last fight, which was, coincidentally, her longest, myself," Dean Blaine said. "It lasted all of twenty two seconds and was against a girl who transformed into solid steel."

"How did Mary beat that?" Mr. Numbers asked with genuine interest.

"She forced her opponent halfway through the concrete wall, face first. We were forced to remove the girl before she suffocated," Dean Blaine explained.

"Given their respective powers, that seems like the best method she had," Mr. Transport said.

"Oh, the strategy was sound, no one could question that," Dean Blaine acknowledged. "The problem is that no girl her age should be able to generate that much telekinetic force, let alone one whose abilities have been fully-functioning for only a few months. Forcing a human being made of steel through several inches of concrete at point-blank range is a feat that only those who have been training for decades are able to pull off. There are certified Heroes that couldn't have managed to accomplish that so effortlessly."

"So, if I am to understand you, you're concerned about why Mary is so much stronger than she should be," Mr. Numbers said carefully. He desperately wished he had his usual calculations running through his head so he could jump ahead of the conversation, but unfortunately, around Dean Blaine that was impossible.

"I am concerned that you did more than just *help* these children!" Dean Blaine exclaimed as he rose from his seat. "I am concerned that perhaps your company, under the guise of feeling sorry for these dregs of the world, decided that they wouldn't just give the kids control, they would amplify the children's powers a bit. After all, they've already agreed to be guinea pigs, why not run them through every experimental procedure you've got?"

From the way the dean was panting and gesturing, it was very apparent to both Mr. Numbers and Mr. Transport how much harm the dean believed a little extra testing could do.

"I can assure you, that is not the case," Mr. Numbers said. "Even if the doctors and nurses were not heavily monitored during the children's treatment, which they were, the company has never successfully found a way to amplify a person's natural abilities, Super or Powered."

"Until a few months ago, I was under the impression that no one had ever found a way to turn Powereds into Supers, so you'll forgive me if I'm a bit skeptical of your assurances on the lack of existing technology," Dean Blaine said. He did seem a bit pacified, though, at least enough to retake his seat.

"Be that as it may, it is the truth," Mr. Numbers said. "All our company did was give Mary the ability to control the power she already had. Perhaps it is just that she was born with a very strong ability, and is only now learning to use it."

"It is . . . possible," Dean Blaine conceded. "And for the girl's sake, I hope that's the truth of it."

"What do you mean?" Mr. Transport said, a bit more harshness to his voice than he wanted. The dean wouldn't notice, but Mr. Numbers would scold him for tipping his hand even slightly, though he couldn't help it. Mr. Transport had been put here to control, but also to protect, the students in his dorm. Responding with harshness to a perceived threat was a natural reaction. As it turned out, though, it was an unwarranted one.

"I mean that for a girl that young to be that powerful there are only two options . . . if one discounts the possibility of outside enhancers," Dean Blaine said, not without some suspicion lingering in his voice.

"Which we are," Mr. Numbers replied without missing a beat.

"Yes . . . anyway, the only ways she could be that strong are if she was born with a tremendous gift, or if she put herself through an unimaginably hellish training," Dean Blaine said.

"What sort of training?" Mr. Transport asked.

"Well, most telekinetics are also telepaths. Something to do with the part of the brain that gets the power," Dean Blaine said. "Anyway, many of those with the advanced mind ability train up their telekinesis by learning to sharpen their focus. The better they can focus, the more power they can use and the faster it comes. One of the more popular methods of training is to open up their telepathy as much as they can bear and try to function constantly under the barrage of voices. It helps them learn to focus on tasks at hand and blot out the ambient noise that's always assaulting them."

"Interesting," Mr. Numbers said, praying silently that Mr. Transport wasn't giving anything away on his face. "I had never heard of that."

"You wouldn't have," Dean Blaine said. "It's really only something you know of if your job is training Supers day in and day out."

"So, some of the more powerful ones must be able to blot out a lot of noise," Mr. Numbers said casually. "What's the most you've heard of someone being able to function with?"

"Well, of course, I don't know what all of them do, but the best I've personally witnessed was a Hero who could still function while hearing all the thoughts around him in a three mile radius," Dean Blaine said. "He's a top notch one, too, can do some amazing things with that brain of his."

Neither Mr. Transport nor Mr. Numbers responded. At that moment, they had glanced at each other and were having another of their standard silent conversations. There wasn't much to say in the way of details, merely a subtle sense of panic and surprise. Unbeknownst to Dean Blaine, the company Mr. Numbers and Mr. Transport worked for had done a similar radius test on Mary in their pre-program evaluation.

Mary's range was five miles, and she was able to function perfectly normally while listening to all of that in a populated city.

Mr. Numbers and Mr. Transport quickly excused themselves.

15.

"You're sure it's okay for you to be walking?" Vince asked as they made their way down the steel and concrete hall.

"No, but I think they were mainly worried about me breaking the sound barrier, not going to the main hall to check the results," Sasha replied. Julia had texted her that the boys' fights were finished, but rather than getting the results from her roommate, Sasha had cajoled Vince into seeing for himself.

"Well . . . okay," Vince said reluctantly. "Just let me know if you need to lean on me or something."

"I bet you say that to all the mending girls with super speed," Sasha said.

"Only the ones with pink and black hair," Vince shot back.

"Good answer, Silver. Good answer." Sasha might have continued their verbal dance, but at that point, they stepped out of the tunnel and into the main hall. It was really more of an entrance foyer than anything else. Conveyor systems that ran to the respective dorms were on one side, while an enormous screen was perched overhead on the opposite end of the room. There were various hallways like the one Vince and Sasha were emerging from, and at the moment, there was a tremendous cluster of black-uniformed freshmen under the screen, looking eagerly for their name in the listings.

The screen was split into two sections currently, the boys' list and girls' list. Most of the attention was geared toward the boys' listings, but in fairness, the girls had been finished for at least an hour or so. Vince and Sasha made their way into the rabble of freshman and began their short search of the boys' list. It took Vince a few minutes to find his name, not because the list was enormous or complicated, but because he was looking in the wrong part of it. When he couldn't find himself in the bottom section, he finally looked to the higher rankings, though he was utterly unprepared for what awaited him there.

"Eighth?" Vince exclaimed. "How the hell am I eighth? There are, like, thirty guys, and I went down in the first round. Was there a mistake?"

"It isn't just about how many fights you were in," Sasha said soothingly. "They were also evaluating how you used your abilities against the ones you were fighting, how you dealt with their techniques, and how well you thought on your feet. If you were fighting a really lopsided battle and still managed to show solid skills, then that was factored in."

"Yeah, but still . . . eighth?" Vince sighed and tried to relax. It was a good thing; a high ranking was something he should be proud of. He'd been a Powered until two months ago and here he'd managed to show up twenty-two Supers by outdoing them. It was an accomplishment. Vince just wished it was one he felt like he had earned.

"Didn't you say the guy you fought was named Michael?" Sasha asked.

"Yeah."

"Looks like he made it to number three," Sasha said, pointing up at the list. Vince checked for himself and, sure enough, she was right. Michael Clark was the third strongest male there, below the number one slot, Chad Taylor, and the number two slot, Shane Desoto. Vince was about to look away when the name in the number five slot caught his eye.

"Who is Roy Daniels?" Vince asked.

"According to Julia, the sexiest man she's seen in years," Sasha said. "She keeps texting my ass about him. Also, he's number five."

"I wonder if he has a brother," Vince speculated. "One of my dormmates is named Hershel Daniels."

"Hershel, huh? I don't see him up there," Sasha said.

It was true. Vince looked and looked, but Hershel's name didn't appear anywhere on either list. Nick was listed at number thirty on the boys' side, and Alice had come in just below Sasha at twentieth on the girls', but try as they might, the only Daniels they could find on the board was Roy.

"Weird," Sasha said at last. "Do you think Roy is Hershel, but they messed up his name?"

"I somehow doubt it," Vince said. "Nothing against Hershel, he seems like a really nice guy, but he isn't the type that your roommate would be constantly texting about."

"How do you know? Maybe he's Julia's type," Sasha said, a glimmer of antagonism in her voice.

"Does she like LARP and tabletop games? Because that's what Hershel told us he loves to do in his free time," Vince countered.

"Oh. No. Totally a different dude," Sasha agreed quickly. "Well, whatever. Just ask him about it when you get back to your dorm."

"I'll have to," Vince said. "Especially since none of my fellow Melbrook residents seem to have hung out after they saw their ranks."

"No worries. I bet they lick their wounds in time for Casino Night," Sasha said optimistically.

"Casino Night?" Vince asked.

"There are flyers up all over the dorms," Sasha said.

"Must have missed them," Vince said, doing his best to sound casual in the deflection.

"It's in the student union tonight, at seven," Sasha explained. "Free food, fake gambling with free chips you can use for raffles, and all the karaoke you can handle. Supers and Normals are both invited."

"That sort of sounds like fun," Vince said.

"Yeah, we can meet more fellow freshman. Maybe we'll even make a friend or two that can't lift a bus or melt steel," Sasha said.

"Very true," Vince agreed. "I don't really know anyone here except my dormmates. Oh, and now you, too."

"Same boat," Sasha said. "I met Julia because she's my roommate, but you're the only other friend I've made so far. Combat doesn't really engender communal feelings on the first day."

"Maybe that's why they do it," Vince speculated.

"Point," Sasha said. "Well, I'm going to head back up to the dorm. Seven is only a few hours away, and I am desperate for a shower. You think you'll go to Casino Night?"

"Positive."

"Sweet," Sasha said, pulling out the "e" sound a bit. "Want to meet up at the entrance and then lose all our fake money together?"

"Absolutely," Vince said. "I'll see if I can talk any of my dormmates into coming along."

16.

Nick was already seated comfortably at a blackjack table when he noticed Vince and some pink-haired girl walk into the garishly decorated student union. The event planner had obviously been trying for an over-the-top, Vegas-style décor with the gold banners and fake statues, but what the decorator had failed to realize was that Vegas's brilliance was in the subtlety beneath the glamour. Nick took no offense to it, though; that was the signature appeal of his home town. Often imitated, never duplicated.

Nick was grateful that Vince had told him about the event. Throwing his first fight to stay off anyone's radar had left an unpleasant taste in his mouth. Tactics and stealth were all well and good, but there was something so viscerally wrong about losing in any way. It had been necessary, though, and, as Nick pulled a few more additions in to his pile of chips, he felt the sourness ease from his taste buds. It didn't matter that the chips were worthless: it only mattered that he was winning.

"Hit," said a female voice next to him. Nick had been seated and working up a hot streak when Mary had plunked herself down next to him. He didn't want to be rude, but he didn't want a mind reader so close to him, either. He had waffled for a few moments, then let it be. The girl could follow him even if he did get up; besides, he had no idea how good her range was. Even being in the same building might give her free access to his head. Better to stay put and keep up the appearance of friendliness toward his dormmates. It wouldn't fool her, but that was a lost cause, anyway.

"Good play," Nick complimented her as a ten was laid onto her queen, giving her twenty.

"The advice helps," Mary replied without looking at him. This was the first time they had spoken all night. He took her meaning quite clearly.

"Glad to help," Nick lied, turning his attention back to the game. He was almost immediately interrupted again.

"Whoa," Vince said as he came up to the table. "That's quite a stack you've accumulated."

"Well, I am from Vegas, after all," Nick said.

"And eighteen," Vince countered. "So you couldn't have hit the casinos. How'd you get so good at blackjack?"

"Chill, Vince, it's a game of luck," the pink-haired girl interrupted. There was a beat of silence as Nick watched the word "luck" leave her lips and enter Vince's head. Once there, it plunked around a few times before finally coming to rest in a spot labeled "natural conclusion."

"Yeah," Vince said as his eyes narrowed. "You're right, Sasha. It is a game of luck." The sense of accusation wasn't precisely dripping from Vince's words, but there was definitely some accusatory condensation on them.

"So, it's Sasha? I'm Nick, and this is Mary. We're both in Melbrook with Vince. I do apologize for my good friend's poor manners in not introducing us," Nick said, switching into his usual affable mode and swinging the focus away from his blackjack success.

"Nice to meet you two," Sasha said, giving a slight incline of her head.

"Sasha, would you mind grabbing us a seat at the craps table? I know we wanted to roll some dice, I just need to have a quick word with my dormmate," Vince said.

Sasha looked at the two of them for a moment, then shrugged and said, "Okay." She wandered off toward the craps area, but not without keeping an eye on them. That girl was sharper than she wanted to let on. Nick could respect that.

"Nick," Vince whispered harshly as soon as Sasha was gone. "Do you really think it's a good idea to be doing . . . what you're doing out in the open like this?"

"You mean winning?" Nick asked innocently.

"I mean using an unfair advantage."

"Hold your horses there, hoss," Nick said in equally low tones. "First off, this isn't even real money, so stay off the soapbox. Secondly, I'm not doing what you think I'm doing. I'm winning because I know how to play blackjack well. There are some basic strategies any kid who grew up around a city of gambling knows. So re-fucking-lax and go worry about your date, instead of your dormmate."

"It isn't a date," Vince snapped immediately. "And . . . I'm sorry. You're right. I guess I was just worried because . . . well, the whole 'secret being a big portion of your grade' thing. You really haven't been using?"

"Ask Mary," Nick replied. "See if I've focused or breathed deep even once tonight."

Vince looked at Mary, who didn't turn toward him, but shook her head to the negative anyway. "Sorry," Vince said once more. "I guess that whole speech and a day of fighting has gotten me paranoid."

"Don't worry about it," Nick assured him. "If I were you, I'd think the same thing. Now go catch up to your girl before someone else does."

"She's not my girl," Vince said, but he departed from their table and made his way over to Sasha and the craps game. Nick turned back to the blackjack table, annoyed that he had missed several hands while talking to Vince and had now lost track of the cards.

"I notice you didn't bother mentioning to him that you don't actually need to breathe deep or close your eyes to use your talent," Mary said softly.

"It wasn't pertinent," Nick defended. "After all, I'm really not doing anything."

"You don't consider counting cards doing anything?" Mary asked.

"Fine. I'm not doing anything that others couldn't do with skill and practice. Besides, for all you know, I do need to shut my eyes to use my talent. Maybe that's why I wear the sunglasses."

"No, it isn't," Mary said with unfaltering certainty.

Nick was ruffled by how sure she was. It was unnerving, talking to someone he couldn't bluff. He wanted to know more about what she could see, but was afraid of how much he would be exposing of himself. He shrugged off the fear. In for a dime, in for a dollar.

"How much do you know?" Nick asked flatly as he slid several chips out to place a bet.

"Enough," Mary replied as she followed suit and put her own chips into play. "More than you want me to, which isn't saying much, but less than you're scared I do, which also isn't saying much."

The dealer put two cards in front of each of them, so they each paused to do a quick spot of mental math.

"Have you told anyone?" Nick asked.

"No," Mary replied. "And I won't, either. I've been hearing stuff I wasn't supposed to all my life. I learned a long time ago that it's best if I treat it like a therapist or an attorney, with ironclad confidentiality."

"Is that supposed to reassure me?" Nick asked as he rapped knuckles against the green velvet and the dealer handed him another card. An almost instantaneous calculation flew through his head and he waved off to show he was staying.

"It's supposed to let you know where I stand," Mary replied, tapping her own hand as well. She went for another hit after the first, then elected to stay.

"And where is that?" Nick asked as the dealer began hitting his own stack, stopping once he struck eighteen.

"As your friend," Mary replied. "Someone you can talk to and trust. Someone who understands some of the things you've gone through."

"Table has eighteen," the deal announced. The girl to Nick's right had already busted, so Nick was first to be compared to the dealer's numbers.

"Nineteen," Nick announced. To Mary, he resumed his whispering tone. "You'll forgive me if I'm a bit reluctant to take you up on that. I've got trust issues."

"No problem," Mary whispered back. "Twenty," she announced happily, smiling at all the other players at the table. Both of them pulled in the chips they had won and pushed a few more out for the next round.

"I'm just saying," Mary resumed in her soft tones. "I'm going to be in on just about everything you do anyway. I thought that since there is finally someone you can't lie to, maybe you'd like to try talking to them. It's not as if you have to worry about giving away something I don't already know."

64

Nick couldn't think of a snappy comeback for that one, so instead, he just checked his cards. He hated himself for realizing that Mary was right, and he hated her even more because the moment he thought it, a small smirk crept onto her face.

17

Alice was bored. She had come along to Casino Night with the rest of her dorm (with the exception of Hershel, whom no one had seen since the beginning of the day), but the truth was, she had little taste or stomach for craps. There was no nuance to it: just chunk the dice and pray for the best. Alice preferred her games more . . . strategic.

She stood next to Vince and the pink-haired girl he seemed to be getting along with so well—Sasha was her name, if Alice recalled correctly—as they all watched and occasionally participated in the craps game. Her poor luck on her few attempts had hardly endeared her to the game, and that, coupled with the events of the day, were all contributing to her increasingly sour mood.

Alice tried to smile and keep her facade plastered up by focusing on the positive. It wasn't as if she had really expected to fare well in the combat trials in the first place. She could only fly, while a significant majority of the girls here had abilities that were far more fighting-based. Still, she had been downed in her first round in less than a minute by some girl with sonic blasting powers. It had hurt, and despite all the preparation she had given herself to brace for the inevitable loss, Alice had found that once the match was done, her pride was stinging a bit as well. It certainly hadn't helped matters when she learned Mary had come out as top of the class. Still, Alice was an academic at heart, and being a Hero wasn't just about how many cars you could throw in a minute. It was also about wit, resourcefulness, and intelligence, all of which Alice was confident she could use to elevate her own status. Eventually.

Alice abandoned the craps table when she heard Vince and Sasha making plans to meet for breakfast the next morning before heading off to class. They would all be spending their mornings attending their aboveground classes, but the afternoon would find them all down in the secret levels, training up on the things that really mattered. Vince and Sasha both seemed excited about what the next day would hold, which told Alice that they knew nothing of what was actually in store. She did, and she had the good sense to dread it. Alice left the two to their slowly-blooming, obvious romance and wandered across the room to find some entertainment of her own.

She passed Nick and Mary, whispering in hushed tones at the blackjack table. If it had been anyone else but Mary, Alice might have lingered to see what they were discussing. With a telepath, though, there was too much risk of giving away more information than she gained. Instead, Alice trudged across the room, passing by the happy faces while wearing one of her own. Eventually, she found herself at the only part of the student union that allowed for seating without participation: the karaoke stage. Some blonde girl Alice recognized from the program was wailing her way through a pop song as Alice gently plunked down in the back. Ignoring the warbling, Alice pulled out her phone and began checking her email. It was bad form to appear so antisocial in a public place, but she needed a moment to gather her thoughts and get into the right frame of mind. A few minutes by herself would be a relatively small concession for being able to mingle and socialize the rest of the night.

Alice was so caught up in actively ignoring the poor blonde on stage that she didn't even notice when the song ended. She didn't notice the mild applause or the announcement of the next song either. What she, along with everyone else in range of the speakers, did notice was what followed. A husky, male voice vibrated across the room, breaking into the deep, opening chords of a country song. Alice didn't listen to country, and for the life of her, couldn't have told you what the song was. At that moment, though, she couldn't hear anything else in the room. Shoving the phone hastily back into her pocket, Alice turned all of her attention to the boy—no, the man—who had pulled a stool on stage and was seated on it as he crooned into the microphone.

He was tall (that was apparent even though he was sitting) and wore a plaid, button-down shirt, a small, grey cowboy hat, and a pair of clearly worn-in jeans. There was something oddly familiar about his face, though, Alice noted, and his body was hard and lean. He was well-muscled (as his half-open shirt proudly displayed), but with the flat muscle of an athlete rather than the bulky and superficial kind that body builders acquire. If Alice had to guess, which she was actively doing, she would say he was a quarterback in high school, given his physique and frame. Alice's eyes danced around the crowd, noting their reactions to the clear improvement in entertainment.

A large chunk of the women in the audience were staring at this mystery man with unabashed interest, the most fervent being the blonde who had sung before him. Many of the men were trying to seem unimpressed by him and his performance, though a few who must have recognized the song were happily enjoying his rendition. As he sang, the man's own hazel eyes swept the crowd, lingering ever-so-intentionally on the women eagerly looking up at him. They came to rest on his blonde predecessor, who looked as though she was applying all her self-control toward not letting out a squeal.

The song finished, and the man stood from his stool and took a wide bow. There was blatantly more applause than there had been for the girl, yet, as the man walked down from the small platform that was serving as a stage and tipped his hat at the blonde by way of introduction, it seemed like she neither noticed nor cared.

For her part, Alice felt a bit better. Watching a gorgeous man sing had really done nothing for her, except that it had pulled her mind out of its funk and forced her to focus on something else for a while. Settling back in, she felt her problems were somewhat less pressing than they had been before, as was usually the case, and decided she would take a cue from the singing cowboy. This was an event to meet people and make connections: in other words, a social activity. That made it Alice's home turf. She might not be able to beat everyone in combat, but there were few who could work a room like Alice Adair.

Alice rose from her seat and set off.

18

Vince had some trouble finding Hughes Hall the next morning. In his defense, Lander was a very large campus, and he had hardly had free time to explore it. He might have gotten up a bit earlier if he had been thinking ahead, but Casino Night had gone on a lot longer than he'd expected, and it turned out being frozen solid had left him drained by the day's end. On the plus side, he had won enough chips to put his name in a few raffles. He had even managed to win a clock radio. It wasn't quite as nice as the two hundred dollar gift card Nick had won, but it was something to be happy about.

If Vince had been a bit pettier, he might have accused Nick of rigging the raffle, but given the amount of chips his sunglasses-wearing friend had turned in, it didn't really surprise anyone when Nick's name was drawn. That boy was either cheating up a storm or really knew how to play blackjack. Since he was one of Vince's few friends, Vince was opting to give him the benefit of the doubt. Had Vince been a bit more experienced in the ways of the world, it might have dawned on him that the two options were not mutually exclusive.

Vince was in a good mood, even as he scrambled to find Sasha's dormitory. It was his second day attending Lander and the first day of real classes. He had basic math and literature classes in the morning, followed by gym and Ethics of Heroism in the afternoon. He still wasn't sure why gym was ascribed a three-hour chunk of his time every day, but he assumed there would be a logical explanation when he got there. Besides, he and Sasha were getting breakfast before their morning classes together, which made him just a bit happier than he would admit to anyone who was asking. He did enjoy women with multi-colored hair.

Vince had been polite enough to invite his fellow dormmates to come along. Nick had said no due to an early class, Mary had politely declined without explanation, and Alice had informed him that she would be avoiding the dorm food as much as was humanly possible. Vince had looked for Hershel as well, but to no avail. It seemed their friend hadn't even come home last night. Vince was beginning to get worried, but he was trying to hope for the best. If he didn't see his portly dormmate soon, though, Vince was planning on finding Mr. Numbers or Mr. Transport.

Vince saw the bell tower and finally got a sense of where he was. With its lush foliage, sprawling campus, and large buildings, Lander was one of the largest and most scenic colleges in California. All of which sounded great on the brochure, but was somewhat less charming when trying to hustle between locations across campus. Vince was really hoping he didn't have any classes that were too far apart when he finally saw a sign on a multistoried building that read "Hughes."

He walked into the lobby quickly, checking the wall clock and realizing with a twinge that he was late. It wasn't by much, but it was enough to irk him. He had been taught that punctuality was one of the most important virtues to have. He made his way through the white-tiled entryway and past the door leading into the dorm area itself. Some of the dorms were segregated into male and female, his own being one of them, but Hughes had alternating floors. The rooms were done in suites, with two rooms sharing a common living room area. It engendered a sense of community, or so Sasha had told him, since people could leave their living room doors open and still preserve a getaway in their bedroom. It occurred to Vince that whoever had built Melbrook for him and the others had clearly taken some cues from the Hughes dormitory set up.

In fact, Vince was right. Alice had toured the Lander campus (along with several others) before talking with the architects who would ultimately design Melbrook. She had found the Hughes design an excellent integration of privacy and community, though her original designs had her room set off in a separate area. Specifically, it was in an entirely separate building on the opposite campus and utterly unaffiliated with Melbrook in any way. That attempt had failed, but she'd considered it something of a long shot anyway.

Vince bounded up the stairs to the second floor and began moving down the hallway. Since the rooms were arranged sequentially, it didn't take him much time at all to find Sasha's room: 216. He was about to knock when he heard shouting from the other side of the door. Vince couldn't quite make out the words, but they definitely sounded angry. There were several voices, at least two female with one probably male. Vince was still standing there, debating on whether he should knock or wait a few moments for things to calm down, when he heard an object land heavily against the door. All thoughts of tact aside, Vince jerked the doorknob, which was fortunately unlocked, and burst into the room.

"Is everyone okay?" Vince yelled before he could take in the scene around him. As the sights the room held registered into his mind one by one, it became clear that things were undoubtedly not okay.

There were two girls and a boy, all right. The most attention-grabbing one was the blonde that Sasha had pointed out as her roommate Julia yesterday, who was a few steps outside of her bedroom and into the living room. She was rearing back a large, black pump, clearing intending to send it flying. If Vince had bothered to look down he would have noticed its twin resting by his feet, the obvious culprit in the case of the mysterious thudding noise against the door. Julia was wearing a sizable plaid shirt, though. with her arm reared back and pulling the fabric up, it was evident that the shirt wasn't quite sizable enough.

Standing between Julia and the guy, looking haggard and unhappy, but playing the referee, was Sasha, wearing a tight, pink shirt and grey sleep shorts. Ordinarily, Vince would have savored this image a bit more than he did. Unfortunately, his attention couldn't help but be captured somewhat by the other male in the room. He was a heavy guy, wrapped poorly in a towel, and was hunched over in a submissive position. He was clearly trying to defend himself verbally, but from the look on Julia's face, Vince had a feeling the boy hadn't gotten that far.

Leaping into this chaotic scene, as all three pairs of eyes turned on him in surprise, Vince tried to look on the bright side. At least he had found Hershel.

19

"Who the fuck are you?" Julia screeched at Vince.

"Um, I'm Vince," he said lamely. "Sasha and I were meeting to go get breakfast."

"Vince, thank God," Hershel cried, dashing over to his dormmate's side and all but cowering. "This woman has gone mad, she won't listen to anything."

"Why are you in a blanket?" Vince asked.

"Why do you know this guy?" Sasha said.

"WHY WERE *YOU* IN MY BED?" Julia thundered. Vince was impressed, he would have never thought a girl her size would have pipes like that.

"I keep trying to tell you that. You fell asleep with me," Hershel said with as much projection as he had. It turns out that wasn't much, but Julia's eruption had silenced the room pretty effectively.

"Bullshit I did," Julia denied. "I was . . . with . . . Roy last night. You know, the tall, hard-bodied man that you definitely are not!"

"Can someone please tell me what the hell is going on?" Vince tossed out, hoping to get some sense of what was happening around him.

"I've been listening to them for a while," Sasha said. "I think I understand the gist of it. If you two don't mind, I'll recap and we can see where the disagreement is." Both Hershel and Julia nodded their agreement, though Hershel did so with gratitude and Julia with barely-suppressed rage.

"Thanks," Sasha continued. "So, Julia met Roy last night at the karaoke part of Casino Night. They came home and got busy—"

"Got busy? That's presumptuous," Julia butted in.

"There was a tie on the door, I slept on the living room couch, and these walls are a lot thinner than you seem to think they are," Sasha replied succinctly.

"Oh," Julia said, a bit of the wind leaking out of her sails.

"Whatever, I don't give a damn, I was just recapping," Sasha said. "So, they were at it for a few hours, kudos to Roy, by the way, then finally passed out and we all got some sleep. I wake up this morning to her throwing a hissy fit and beating the shit out of the guy in the towel. It seems she and sex-man passed out last night, but she and that guy were the ones that woke up together."

"Which I can explain," Hershel interjected before Julia could build up to another tirade. "If Vince would please shut the door." Vince complied and Hershel continued. "I am Roy . . . technically. He's the version of me with powers."

"I thought you were a shifter," Vince said.

"I am. I shift into Roy. He's the part of me with abilities. Also, charm and confidence," Hershel admitted a bit sadly.

"And looks," Julia spat out.

"Hey, now," Vince said. "There's no need for that. Hershel didn't sneak into your room and crawl into your bed. You took him home, and he turned back in his sleep."

"He couldn't have warned me?" Julia asked.

"Roy was a bit . . . preoccupied," Hershel said, blushing freely.

"Wait, so Roy is a hot, Super version of you?" Sasha asked. "I'm just trying to get a grip on this."

"Yes and no," Hershel said. "Same body, with the obvious alterations, but we have entirely different personalities. Roy tends to be . . . easily distracted."

"So I was a distraction? Well, why the hell isn't Roy here explaining all of this?" Julia asked.

"Roy is rarely inclined toward dealing with the morning after," Hershel said. Without warning, Julia whipped the shoe in a straight path for his head. Sasha knocked it away faster than Vince could see, literally, and Hershel desperately tried to cool the blonde. "It wasn't just that! There's a certain trigger that brings Roy out and when it wears off, I go back to being me. It was an unavoidable change. I know that Roy liked you very much!"

"He did?" Julia suddenly seemed to calm exponentially. "How do you know? What did he say about me?"

"Well, we don't talk . . . not really. But we have access to each other's memories and what we were thinking or feeling at any given time," Hershel explained.

"Oh," Julia said. "Wait, does that mean you remember everything from last night?"

"Well . . . yes," Hershel said, bracing himself for assault. This time though, it was Julia's turn to go red.

"Ummmmm, well, this clearly seems like just a giant misunderstanding," Julia said quickly. Her next words bounded out her mouth so fast they nearly fell on top of one another. "Hershel, I'm sorry I threw things at you why don't you grab your pants I'm going to be in the shower I'll see you all later." Without a pause or a breath, Julia snatched up a towel from inside her room and bolted out of the living room, on a beeline toward the showers and away from the remaining three.

"Huh," Sasha said. "That must have been some kinky shit."

"I'd really like not to comment," Hershel said as he gathered up his clothes from Sasha and Julia's bedroom floor.

"Hershel, it doesn't look like those really fit you," Vince pointed out.

"They don't," he said. "I'll be able to get home in them, though. Besides, we make it a rule to take care of the other's clothing whenever possible. It's a consideration that keeps both of our wardrobes intact."

"So . . . you still haven't told me how you know each other," Sasha pointed out.

73

"Remember when we saw the name Roy on the boards yesterday and I told you about my dormmate, Hershel?" Vince asked.

"Ohhh," Sasha said. "Well, that explains why Hershel wasn't up there at least."

Hershel had shut the door to the bedroom and was presumably getting dressed.

"Poor guy," Vince said. "I can't imagine this was how he wanted to start his career at Lander."

"I wouldn't feel too bad for them. I got a front audio seat for last night's show, and I have a feeling the memories of that experience were worth it," Sasha said.

"You think your roommate is that good?" Vince asked.

"Maybe, but I also know something you don't," Sasha said.

"Do tell."

"I know that Julia's power is to make duplicates of herself," Sasha said.

"Like, illusions or dummies?" Vince asked.

"Like real live, walking, talking, capable of independent action duplicates," Sasha elaborated.

"Well . . . imagine that," Vince said.

"No need," Hershel replied as he stepped out of the bedroom. It was an awkward ensemble that adorned his body, since Roy was clearly taller and leaner, but nothing was bursting, so it seemed Hershel was right and he would be able to get back to Melbrook. "I'm afraid I'll have to apologize, but knowing she has that ability means I'm almost positive Roy will be calling on her again."

"Just spare me the morning fiasco next time," Sasha said. "And, if possible, keep Silver here awake instead of me. Melbrook is probably just as nice a place to get it on."

"I'll keep that in mind, but sadly, I can make no promises," Hershel said. "I'll see you at Melbrook, Vince. Sasha, thank you for your understanding."

"No worries," Sasha said with a wave. "I sort of expected this. It is college, after all."

With a nod, Hershel stepped out the door, keeping his eyes peeled for fear of running into Julia, leaving Vince and Sasha alone in the living room area.

"So," Sasha said after a moment, "you wishing you had talked to the girl that's a walking orgy instead of the chick with the colored hair?"

"Nah," Vince replied. "I've got a thing for girls in grey workout shorts, so you're still narrowly in the lead."

Sasha laughed, then looked at what she was wearing. For the first time all morning, she became all too aware of just how well her shorts lived up to their name, and the fact that her tight, pink shirt wasn't being hampered by the presence of a bra. The thought riding on the coattails of the previous two was the realization that Vince must be just as aware of these things.

"Ready for food in five!" Sasha yelped as she moved past Vince in a blur and slammed the door to her bedroom behind her. Vince wished he could have seen her mad dash for cover, but that was the sacrifice you made when you hit on a girl with super speed.

20

Nick had never suspected he would be grateful for assigned seating, but as he took his desk at the end of the row next to a short boy with messy hair, Nick did take a moment to thank his lucky stars. It wasn't that he preferred aisle seats—he had a feeling that no position in the room would liven up Ethics of Heroism—but it did make things a bit easier on him. Nick had known when he chose the cover persona of a happy-go-lucky, chatter-happy dimwit that there would be certain concessions involved. One that he hadn't counted on grating as much as it did was the need to be around his fellow dormmates constantly, seeking them out and keeping conversations aloft. He'd vested ample time with Vince, but the others were a bit more difficult to wrangle, and of course, Mary was a lost cause. Thus, if he had been able to choose his own seat, he would have been forced by his own sense of commitment to take one near his fellow Melbrook residents. Being placed on the end, away from them, allowed him a measure of alone time without offending his actor's sensibilities.

Nick extracted a binder and a pen from his bag and turned to an untouched section. He already had notes from his economics and accounting classes that morning, so this was his last mind-stretcher of the day. Afterwards came gym, whatever that entailed, and then he would be done with his first day of college. It was pleasant of them to have put it on a Friday at least, allowing the students a chance to acclimate to the town around Lander.

Nick perused the room, taking cursory notes and finding the positions of the others from his dorm. Hershel had finally popped back up that morning, and he was easy to spot as he waded through the rows, awkwardly trying to find his spot. The others took a few minutes to locate since the room was full of the freshman class, all clad in their black uniforms. He managed to locate the final one, Mary, just as the door opened and Dean Blaine walked into the front of the room.

"Good morning, class," Dean Blaine said with a large smile. "As all of you will hopefully remember, my name is Dean Blaine, and I will be your teacher for Ethics of Heroism. And before anyone asks, no, you aren't getting special treatment. I consider it my personal pleasure to instruct the new freshmen every year, helping them to understand not just what we do, but why it is so important that we do it."

A hand went up quickly. The class's suck-up, no doubt. Nick knew there would be one: there always was, and of course, they couldn't wait to identify themselves by asking the first question. There was no surprise in Nick that someone was already drawing attention to themselves. What did surprise him was the voice of the question asker. He chided himself for not having anticipated someone that obvious.

"Does that mean you and the two coaches make up the entirety of the Hero Certification Program's staff?" Alice asked once Dean Blaine pointed to her.

"Certainly not," Dean Blaine assured her. "There are several more professors on staff here, though you won't be working under any of them until sophomore year."

"Why not?" This time the question came from a tall girl with her hair pulled back tightly into a braid. She didn't bother to raise her hand.

"Well, simply put, you wouldn't gain anything from them yet," Dean Blaine explained. "You see, freshman year of this program is the year that we ready your minds and bodies for what is to come over the following three. This is the year that you get the basics, and it's the year we see how many of you have the determination to see our program through to the end. The other professors will be working with you on more specialized programs, programs that you don't have the groundwork for yet."

"See it through?" Alice shot the tall girl, who apparently didn't believe in the courtesy of the hand raise, a dirty look.

"Yes," said Dean Blaine. "The training here is rather grueling, and many who think they want to pursue this line of work soon change their minds once they experience it. The dropout rate of the Hero Certification Program is approximately sixty-five percent. That does not include students who are cut by the staff, either. That number only represents voluntary departures."

The tall girl let out a low whistle, but ceased her questioning of the dean.

"Anyway," Dean Blaine continued. "As all of you should know, this will be the only Friday that we meet. Normally, this class will be on Tuesdays and Thursdays, with the other three days allotted for personal study. I'm sure most of you are counting on that as a free period, but I assure you, it is time you should cherish. That is a boon we only provide to the freshmen, to help ease the transition. Now then, on to the syllabus."

There was a collective sigh that rippled through the class. No one groaned, but it was close.

Dean Blaine laughed. "Same reaction every year. Forgive my little joke, but there won't be a syllabus. This is a discussion class, one for which you will be graded on participation and attendance, but written work doesn't really mesh with the subject matter we're covering. If I asked you for a paper on why Heroes give themselves and their careers to protecting the safety of the people, you'd just be up all night writing words. When I ask you that question, which I will, incidentally, I want to look you in the eye and hear what you really think. So come prepared to talk and think, but otherwise, you won't need anything but your wit."

That was a relief to almost everyone else in the class. Nick swore inwardly. Now he'd have to bluff the dean at least twice a week. Of course, he could always answer honestly, but Nick was smarter than he appeared; at least, smart enough to know that was a dumb idea. The views Nick had been raised with didn't correlate so well with the rest of society's values. The truth had its place, and it was called a deathbed.

77

"That brings us to the matter of today. I'm sure many of you are anxious to be off to the next class and find out what gym is all about," Dean Blaine said. There were a few enthusiastic nods around the room; clearly the idea of training openly with their abilities appealed to many of the students. "Well, I commend your curiosity, and I'm going to reward it. Today, we will be dismissing Ethics of Heroism early to give you all an extra half hour of gym. I think it will give you a proper appreciation."

The rest of the class seemed upbeat as they stowed their binders and began rising from their seats. Nick was a bit more apprehensive. Among all of them, he seemed to be one of the few who noticed that Dean Blaine hadn't told them what, exactly, they would be getting a proper appreciation of. He tried to assure himself that he was just reading too much into things.

Several hours later, when he finally had the energy to, he admonished himself for not trusting his instincts.

21

"Two-minute break," Coach George shouted to the freshmen.

"Oh, thank you, dear and sweet merciful Lord of heaven," Hershel gasped. Vince and Nick had a similar sentiment, but lacked the breath to express it.

What the course schedule had referred to as "gym" was, in fact, a tortuous, living hell. For the past three hours, there had been nothing but nonstop physical exertion. Pushups, sit-ups, weight training, resistance training, all with running in between. There had been a total of five two-minute breaks, counting this one, and the rest of the time had been spent constantly active.

Hershel cursed himself for showing up to gym. He knew it had been a stupid idea when he did it, but after the morning's incident, he couldn't bear being Roy again so soon. He had imagined that he would be able to handle whatever physical activities were thrust upon him for at least one day. He had been wrong. He had been oh-so-very wrong.

The only upside was that almost no one was faring well throughout this training. Vince and Nick were both gasping for air beside him as they stopped running, and across the track he could see the girls leaning against the wall, resting with as much vigor as possible. The coaches had separated the boys and girls into two herds at opposite ends of the track, warning that dire consequences would occur if anyone fell so far behind that they wound up in the other sex's herd. A young-looking boy with messy, brown hair had been the only one so far, and Coach Persephone had swept him off to another area. No one wanted to know what he had to do.

Truthfully, though, Hershel wasn't sure how long it would be before others followed suit. The only reason more hadn't lagged behind was that both groups were losing speed and stamina at similar rates. Near the head of the boys' group, a bald guy was holding it together pretty well, and next to him was a boy with short, blond hair who didn't even seem to be sweating or breathing hard. Those with physical-based powers were kicking ass at life today. Hershel cursed himself again. If Roy were doing this, he wouldn't need a rest at all.

"Why . . . why did we let Dean Blaine dismiss us early?" Vince asked as he sucked in air.

"We're idiots," Nick responded instantly. "He was right, though. I now have a profound appreciation for Ethics of Heroism."

Vince and Hershel nodded their agreement. Neither would be fantasizing about another early release any time soon. Or ever, for that matter.

"Time's up, you over-confident wimps," Coach George yelled. It couldn't have been two minutes. There was no way it was two minutes. Hershel felt tears welling up inside him; he couldn't take any more of this. He was out of shape to begin with; at least the others had some semblance of stamina. Before he could actually lose control, though, Coach George hollered once more.

"Everyone run over here and take a knee." They followed his instructions quickly, never more happy in their entire lives to sit down on the hard, wooden floor than they were at that precious moment. Coach George stood in front of them; Coach Persephone came up next to him. Somewhere inside, Hershel felt Roy stir at the sight of her. Hershel shoved him down immediately. It was bad enough he'd been getting dirty looks from Julia all day. The last thing he needed was to be labeled as the student who tried to bang a coach, even if it wasn't really him that was doing it.

"You did piss poorly today," Coach George began. "That amount of exercise shouldn't even faze a Hero, but you all were struggling just to make it to the end. With precious few exceptions, I daresay none of you would have finished if we kept going for the extra thirty minutes."

Hershel certainly wasn't going to argue that point, and he suspected none of the other freshmen would either.

"When this year is over, you're going to look back on today with a sense of nostalgia for how light the workouts were. You're going to have fantasies that when you come into class, we just tell you to run most of the time. This will be the happiest day of your career in gym, because, from here on out, it only gets worse," Coach George said. The scariest part of his mini-speech was that he wasn't yelling or trying to put fear into them. He seemed to be sincerely warning them, which made it all the more terrifying.

"Now, before I hand things off to Coach Persephone to talk about how the rest of this year will work, there are two people I want to see up front. Chad Taylor and Mary Smith, get up here."

Mary made her way slowly to the front. She was dripping with sweat and still breathing hard, but she seemed to have held together better than many of the others, Hershel included. The boy who rose was the short-haired blond who seemed perfectly at ease. It was as though he had been sitting in air conditioning all day; not even his hair was too ruffled. Hershel didn't know what his ability was, but in this situation, it was an awesome boon. It was humorous to see the two standing next to each other, Chad with his height and broad shoulders next to Mary's slim frame and understated smile. If someone was looking in from the outside, they would have never guessed what those two had in common.

"Okay, class, I want you to take a good look at these two. Before, they were just names, but now, you've seen their faces. These are the two freshmen standing at the top of the heap. They are the number one ranks from both sexes, and I have to tell you, there is a large gap between them and the rest of you. So burn these faces into your minds, because from now until the end of the year, your only real goal is to beat them. You have one year to get stronger, get faster, get better, and take another shot at the combat trials.

80

In the world of Heroes, if you aren't the strongest, you're just next in line to die. Work hard," Coach George said. He dismissed Mary and Chad to go sit down, then took a step back as Coach Persephone came to the front.

"I want to speak briefly with you about the year to come," Coach Persephone said. "For the first semester, we will be spending all three hours as we have today, only with gradually increasing intensity. This is done to give you the base endurance and strength that every Hero needs to function. After winter break, however, the format will change. We will still be spending the first two hours with physical training, but afterward, we will be splitting you into two classes. They will be combat training and alternative training."

There was a murmur among the students. What kind of training was there besides combat? Coach Persephone ignored the commotion and went straight to answering the implied question.

"Alternative training is where we will help those of you with skills ill-suited to fighting learn to use them effectively in the field. Though some of you will no doubt think that this is inferior to combat training, let me assure you that there are ways to protect the innocent for those of us who can't throw a tank."

She paused for a moment, and Hershel thought he saw her dart a glance at Coach George. But as she resumed a moment later, he assured himself it must have been imaginary.

"As for who will go in to what class, the top five ranked students from each sex will automatically be in combat training, while the bottom five will automatically be in alternative training. The rest of you will be evaluated by Coach George and me to determine where your talents lie," Coach Persephone explained.

A hand went up shockingly fast. Hershel recognized the question asker as Sasha from his morning misadventure.

"Yes, Ms. Foster?" Coach Persephone said, pointing to Sasha.

"What if we are in the bottom five, but really want to do combat training? Is there any way for us to prove we can handle it?"

"Actually, yes," Coach Persephone said. "You can challenge another student for their rank. The two of you will be assigned a supervisor, a combat room, and a healer on hand. Then, you will duke it out, and whoever is standing at the end keeps the higher rank."

"But why would people with higher ranks agree to a challenge? All they can do is lose," Sasha pointed out.

"They very well might deny you the right to challenge. Of course, this is a graded class that requires a passing grade to continue with the Hero Certification Program, and you will find nearly all of you lack the physical strength to pass it on merit alone. Fighting in challenges earns you bonus points, and successfully defending your rank earns you significantly more points. On the other hand, declining challenges will take points off of your grade, so sitting pretty on your rank is a dangerous move to make unless you are confident that you're strong enough to handle every hurdle Coach George and I will put before you," Coach Persephone said.

Hershel felt his heart sink. He had been certain that the fighting was behind them until the end of the year. Hershel comforted himself by trying to remember that he wouldn't actually have to fight anyone: Roy was the one with the ranking.

"There are rules for the challenging process, though," Coach Persephone continued. "The main one is the rule of five. You can only challenge someone within five ranks of you. If you want someone higher, you'll have to climb your way to them challenge by challenge. Additionally, the top five on either side cannot be challenged by anyone lower. So rank six cannot go after rank five even though they are one rank apart. This is due to the difference in ability that the top five have compared to the rest of the class. They may challenge within their ranks, but otherwise, none of you can fight them until the end of the year. Aside from that, make sure all fights are registered and monitored. Otherwise, they don't count, and, in fact, will be punished severely. Everyone understand?"

The class nodded collectively.

"Good. Now go hit the showers. You all stink to hell. Oh, and enjoy the weekend. It's the last one you'll have for months with only minor soreness," Coach Persephone said.

22

"Mary Smith, daughter of William and Rebecca Smith. Diagnosed with abilities at age two when she was discovered telepathically lifting her blocks. Confirmed to be Powered at age five when training and coaching left her unable to block out others' thoughts. Several more years of attempts to gain control ended in failure and validated the diagnosis. Left home at the age of ten to live in the woodlands her grandfather had willed her mother. Maintains contact with family when she goes into town for supplies, usually semi-annually," Mr. Transport read from the top paper stuffed into the manila folder.

"If she still sees her parents, shouldn't she remember her name?" Mr. Numbers pointed out.

"Apparently, she never really learned it," Mr. Transport explained as he flipped through her file. "Since her telepathy was always active, she could sense when people's thoughts were directed at her. The name wasn't reinforced and eventually the few people who interacted with her lost the habit of using it."

"That makes sense, I suppose. What it doesn't do, though, is explain why she can tolerate a range of five miles if she's been out of civilization for seven years. Her focus should have atrophied, not evolved," Mr. Numbers said nervously. He rose from the table in the living room of his and Mr. Transport's apartment and went to the fridge to get a bottle of water.

"I've been digging into that," Mr. Transport replied. "It seems that even in the forest, she never got silence. Animals still have thoughts; they're just more primordial than humans. From the telepaths I've talked with, they describe it as hearing a conversation in a foreign language. It might be loud, but because it's gibberish, it's easier to ignore. That's why she was able to live there and hold on to at least some of her sanity."

"Some of her sanity," Mr. Numbers mumbled. "For all the pity people keep showing her, the girl seems to be adjusting fine. The bear thing is a bit odd, but otherwise, she's doing as well as the others and better than some."

"She's a telepath. She knows what normal people are thinking, so she emulates those thoughts and the actions that follow. Just because she can fake societal adaptation doesn't mean there aren't some scars on her from her years as a Powered," Mr. Transport said.

"Yes, except those scars have turned out to be riverbeds that send her abilities gushing forth in blasts far beyond what her experience should warrant," Mr. Numbers said.

"I don't know about that," Mr. Transport retorted. "What is experience if not the accumulation of scars and lessons that allow us to use our mind, bodies, and powers more effectively?"

"I'm not getting into a philosophy or semantics argument with you. I'm just laying the facts out on the table. You and I recommended a girl whose experience as a Powered has likely made her one of the strongest, if not *the* strongest, Supers of her generation," Mr. Numbers said with as much control as he had available at hand. Opening his water, he retook his seat and began looking through the files on his side of the table.

"You're worrying too much," Mr. Transport said. "The only reason the dean even looked twice at her is because he knew about her past, which is why I lobbied not to divulge that information to staff. Aside from that, we both know she isn't the strongest. You watched the combat tapes with me and read the files."

"True," Mr. Numbers agreed. "I daresay the only reason this hasn't fallen down on our heads is because, compared to that boy, even Mary would have one hell of a fight."

"Exactly. It doesn't matter if she is near the top. Hell, Roy was fifth and Vince was eighth, so she has company. The only thing that cannot happen is Mary becoming the undisputed strongest in her grade. It would be troublesome with any of them, really, but with her, we would have to own up to the oversight," Mr. Transport said.

"Who would have ever thought spending all those years without any control would actually *help* her so much?" Mr. Numbers asked with no expectation of an answer.

"It's my fault," Mr. Transport said. "I handle research. If I had only looked into telepathic training methods, I might have discovered this."

"It's no one's fault, or it's both of our's fault. Neither of us goes down alone, you know that," Mr. Numbers corrected immediately. "Besides which, I think it might be a good thing in the long run."

"How do you mean?" Mr. Transport asked.

"What would be worse to deal with: a tremendously powerful telepath who can control her abilities, or one that has no say whatsoever in what she does?" Mr. Numbers asked.

Mr. Transport was silent for a few moments, imagining each encounter realistically rather than snapping off the obvious acceptable answer. There were several things about Mr. Transport that Mr. Numbers didn't always care for, but his tendency to take each question posed to him with seriousness and analysis was not one of them.

"Well," Mr. Transport said at last. "I think that would depend on the context of dealing with them. If they are on our side, then control is preferable. However, if they've gone rogue, then I'd rather have them lacking any real influence on what their power does."

"A good answer," Mr. Numbers said honestly. "So, that means we should worry less about precisely where we might have gone wrong, and focus on ensuring that Mary Smith and every other subject we recommended into the program stays on the straight and narrow path. That's the best way we demonstrate the sound judgment of our selections."

"Very good plan," Mr. Transport commented. "But that leaves us with the meat of the matter. How exactly do we do that?"

23

Logically speaking, there had to be a part of Alice that didn't hurt. She comprehended that in a rational, understanding-of-biology sort of way. Unfortunately, all that knowledge couldn't convince her body to find a position that didn't provoke spasms of soreness coursing through her nerves. Never in her life did she suspect she would ever look back on her one-on-one sessions with her personal trainer as such a light, peaceful workout. Yet here she was.

"Here," in this case, was sprawled out on the sofa in the communal area, watching TV and trying desperately to get comfortable. She would have much preferred to be in her own room, or even in just the girls' lobby, but returning home had led to the discovery that the cable had only been hooked up to the common room so far. The other rooms only had access to basic channels, and subpar entertainment wasn't going to do much to take her mind off of what today's workout had done to her.

Unfortunately, the others seemed to have had the same idea, as they were slumped over and groaning in the chairs and loveseats scattered throughout the room. Everyone was there except Hershel, who had excused himself a few minutes ago to change. Alice couldn't really imagine he owned more comfortable clothing than the sweat pants and Star Wars t-shirt he had been wearing, but she supposed anything was possible. The rest of them were watching a sitcom, shifting occasionally and presumably trying not to think about how they had an entire week of this starting on Monday. Even Mary's presence didn't take the top spot of worry in Alice's mind for the moment. The only thing the telepath was going to pick up from her was: "Ow. Ouch. Ugh. Why did I sign up for this?"

Alice's forced focus on the flat-screen was interrupted by a bottle of water bumping gently against her head.

"What the hell!" Alice exclaimed. She relaxed as she noticed the bottle was not alone. It seemed to have come with an assortment of friends who were hovering a few inches from the faces of Vince and Nick. Mary was already sipping on hers. Alice may have been weary, but she wasn't so tired she couldn't put this simple puzzle together.

"Oh. Thank you for the water, Mary," Alice said as she took the bottle and twisted off the cap.

"No trouble," Mary replied honestly. It wasn't as though the bottles were heavy or hard to maneuver. The four weary, would-be warriors sat in suffering silence after that, the only punctuation aside from groans and television banter being the occasional sip from a bottle of water.

"Well, well, you ladies sure can't handle your exercise," said a deep voice from the side of the room. Standing in the doorway to the boys' side, wearing a different shirt and jeans, but sporting the same cowboy hat, stood the man from the karaoke platform last night. For a moment, Alice thought she had certainly slipped off to sleep in her fugue of pain and gladly welcomed the dream that was beginning. That delusion was quickly shattered by Vince.

"Who are you, and how did you get in here?" Vince cried, pulling himself halfway from his chair. It would have been a grander gesture if he had made it all the way out, but given his current physical condition, it was still somewhat impressive.

"Now, come on, Vince, is that any way to talk to the man whose mess you cleaned up this morning?" the tall man asked, waltzing over to the chair Hershel had been sitting in and plopping down forcefully. Alice had no idea what he was talking about, but now that she knew it wasn't a dream, she was beginning to feel concern gnaw at her. She had been privy to the designs of this place. There should be no way he could have come in through the boys' side. The only entrance was the front one. So, how had this cowboy broken into their home?

"Roy?" Vince asked skeptically.

"Sure as shit in an outhouse," Roy replied. "Pleasure to finally meet you in the flesh." Roy leaned over from his chair and grasped Vince's hand, giving it a hearty shake.

"Hey, that's cool that you guys know each other," Nick said. "Maybe now you explain why there's a stranger sitting in our home? Who else thinks that would be awesome? Just me? Come on, show of hands, people." Nick threw up his own hand and Mary followed suit.

"Um," Vince began awkwardly. "This is Roy. He's Hershel . . . kind of."

"How can he be Hershel?" Alice asked incredulously.

"Well, you see, my beautiful blonde cohabitant, I'm the form the fatty turns into when he can't take it anymore," Roy explained. "Not only does he get stronger, faster, leaner, and all around sexier, but he also gets a pair of testicles and a shot of social sense."

"Wait, when Hershel said he was going to change earlier" . . ." Alice let her thought die out as she put the pieces together.

"Tubbo was hurting, and he doesn't cope so well with pain, especially from a workout, so he went to his room and invited me to handle things. I don't suffer from shit like pain or fatigue," Roy said as he flashed a set of pearly-white teeth around the room.

"Stop calling him fat," Vince said. "It isn't nice. Hershel is our friend, and he's just a little out of shape."

"An action figure in the microwave is a little out of shape," Roy said. "Hershel is a doughy chickenshit. Besides, I can talk all the trash I damn well please. I *am* Hershel, after all."

"No, you aren't," Vince disagreed. "Hershel might be awkward, but at least he has always been kind to everyone. You're not."

87

"It might not be a fun truth, but that doesn't make it not real. Just deal with it, Freak Hair, me and Husky are the same person," Roy said.

"No, you're not!" Vince said, his voice rising noticeably.

"Yes, I am," Roy reinforced.

"Yes, he is," Mary said softly. Both of the battling boys looked at her. She was sitting in her chair, petting No on his head and not meeting either of their eyes. There was something about her that seemed . . . sad. Just a few moments ago, she had been the same old Mary, with the wild hair and the unreadable eyes. But now, in the time that Roy had come in the room, it was like some of the light had left her somehow. It was impossible to put a finger on what was different, but it was equally impossible to ignore the change.

"Well," Roy said after a pause. "If the telepath agrees with me, it must be true. I'll see you girls later on." Roy's eyes stared right at Vince and Nick, making certain they knew he wasn't just referring to the actual women.

"Where are you going?" Vince asked, an undisguised tint of suspicion in his voice.

"Whiskey Shallows," Roy replied. "It's a popular club around here. I told a few of the admirers I met last night that I'd stop by. You girls are welcome to come, if you think you can peel yourselves out of your chairs." With that, Roy tipped his hat to Mary and Alice, and then strode out the front door.

"Wasn't he just a ray of sunshine?" Nick quipped. Alice chuckled politely, but Mary just stayed quiet, while Vince seemed to be rolling something around in his head. Slowly, but forcefully, Vince uprooted himself from his sitting position and got on his feet.

"I'm going with him," Vince said simply.

"The word 'why' comes to mind," Nick said. "Are you in the mood for more narcissism and ego?"

"Not even remotely," Vince replied. "But I was there this morning when Hershel had to try and explain himself out of the situation Roy had left him in. The worst part of it wasn't watching him run, or panic, or take that girl's insults and accusations in stride. It was how resigned he was to it. Like he had done this countless times before and expected to be doing it for a long time after."

"What do you think you can do?" Alice asked.

"Not sure," Vince replied. "Maybe I can at least keep tabs on Roy, and help Hershel with whatever mess he wakes up in."

"I'm sure Hershel is used to dealing with these things alone," Alice said, a trace of bitterness clinging to her words.

"I'm sure he is. But Hershel doesn't have to be alone anymore. I want to go show him that," Vince said.

"Very noble," Nick said sarcastically. "I expect you'll expect us to rally to your words and leap up to join the cause?"

"No. I expect you all to do what you need to do. I'm sure some of you need to rest. I need to do this," Vince countered. "I'm changing clothes and leaving in twenty minutes. If you want to come, then come. If not, then I'll see you in the morning."

It was an idiotic idea. They were all sore and tired, and it was evident that Vince was on a fool's errand. Roy was three ranks higher, so even if Vince wanted to, he wouldn't be able to do anything to stop him. There was literally no point to anything that silver-haired moron was doing. So why did Alice . . . care?

24

"Well," Nick said at a volume higher than normal. "This seems like a lovely, cultured establishment."

Vince, Alice, and Nick all stood in the entryway of Whiskey Shallows, a club with a country theme and a powerfully pumping stereo system. It had taken Vince a few minutes to look up the address and he cursed himself for having wasted the time. They could have found their way using the tacky neon glow and the ridiculously loud music, both of which were detectable from blocks away. He was happy Nick and Alice had decided to join him, though. Nick, he'd been only moderately surprised by; after all, his sandy-haired friend did seem to enjoy getting out of the dorm at any chance presented. Alice, on the other hand, had been a huge surprise when she emerged from her room in a fashionable top and tailored blue jeans.

It had been a very fortunate surprise, though, because, in the haste of his bravado, Vince had utterly forgotten that he didn't own a car. Neither did Nick, since before the procedure they'd had a tendency to blow up around him, so it fell on Alice to cram the two boys into her BMW and chauffer them to the club. Vince had been very tempted to ask why she was tagging along, but had decided against it. It wasn't as though she had been unfriendly at all; he had merely thought she would see herself above coming to a place like this. It was his own fault for making such assumptions about her simply because she projected a confident and put-together aura.

As the out-of-place trio maneuvered through the robust crowd, Vince was surprised by how many people his age seemed to be in attendance. Most of them had large, black Xs on their hands like he and his friends, so they were old enough to get in, but too young to drink. He looked around more and realized that none of the faces looked familiar. It made more sense, though: only the Supers would be reeling after today's workout. The rest of the college would be out celebrating their return to school and the first Friday of the year. This place was close to Lander, so even if the younger students couldn't drink, it was still a good place to get off campus and meet new people.

Vince passed a pair of girls in a corner taking shots behind a potted plant while trying to keep their hands out of sight and re-evaluated the possible reasons the underage students would come. Vince was tempted to yell at Nick and Alice to split up and cover more ground looking for Roy, but he wasn't confident he would hear or feel the cell phone in his pocket with all the bass and noise surrounding them.

That was a shame, because he could have used a way to cover more ground. The club was huge, with three bars on the first floor and two more on the second. An enormous dance floor sat a few inches higher on the first floor, making sure everyone could have a good view of the people shaking their stuff. It seemed oddly like a way to window shop to Vince. After a moment, he realized that's exactly what it was.

"I think we're doing this wrong!" Alice yelled, getting Vince and Nick's attention and dragging them near a set of restrooms where things were marginally quieter.

"How so?" Vince asked.

"We're looking for one person in a giant club. That could take forever. We should be looking for a group instead," Alice explained.

"Why a group? All we want is Roy," Vince pointed out.

"Yes, but Roy said he was meeting people here," Alice explained.

"If he was telling the truth," Vince said.

"Yeah, but if we're going to question his truthfulness then we have to ask ourselves if we're even at the right club. Why don't we just work under the assumption he was honest for now?" Nick said.

"Right. So, if Roy is meeting people, then we need to look for a cluster of people, probably ones that are our age if he met them last night on campus," Alice said.

"Cluster of people our age," Vince agreed. He turned his head back toward the club and tried to count how many clusters of people he saw in the college-aged range. Once he passed thirty, he turned back around to Alice. "I don't suppose there's anything else that would narrow it down?"

"It'll be almost, if not completely, made up of girls," Alice replied.

"How do you know that?" Nick asked.

"I saw him last night. Trust me, that boy only has one thing on his mind and definitely isn't just sitting on a stool all night," Alice said.

"Gotcha," Vince said quickly, closing off the subject. "Okay, let's scout for groups of girls our age with a cowboy hat poking out from the middle."

"You know, I'm a little surprised there's such a massive country bar out here," Nick said as they started back into the main area of the club.

"There's everything around Lander. There's a gay club, a techno club, a dance club, and a bunch of bars," Alice said. "Lander is a pretty huge school and people come from all over America, so local business owners found a niche for just about every kind of way to drink and meet new copulation partners."

Nick laughed loudly. "I've never heard picking up bar skanks put in such a classy way."

"It's a gift," Alice replied.

"Speaking of gifts, I think we just got handed one," Vince said, pointing to the dance floor. Standing a few yards away from them, dancing simultaneously with three girls, was Roy. He was moving smoothly to the beat while holding a drink in his left hand. Periodically, he would take sips, usually while executing spin maneuvers. Not one drop of the brown liquid was spilled; in fact, none of it looked like it dared summon up the nerve to even approach the rim of the glass, unless, of course, it was making a direct beeline for Roy's mouth.

Vince noticed Roy's hands weren't stamped and wondered how he managed to pull that off. It wasn't really relevant, so he pushed the thought aside. What mattered now was keeping an eye on Roy, and, if possible, dissuading him from abandoning Hershel in an awkward situation. If Roy wasn't willing to play along, at least Vince might be able to explain things to the girl so she didn't freak out whenever Roy changed back. He didn't have much of a plan, but then, Vince had never been great at strategy. He set a goal and he found a way. That style had always worked out before, so he set his shoulders and prepared to shadow Roy for the rest of the night.

That plan was almost immediately interrupted by a familiar voice behind him.

"Hello again, Sucker Punch."

25

Vince turned around and found himself face to face with his former opponent. "Michael, right?" Vince asked.

"Damn right," Michael replied. Michael was a touch out of place, wardrobe-wise, having chosen to wear only a black tank top that drew attention to the impressive arms and shoulders his practice at boxing had wrought him. Combined with the steel-toed boots on his feet and the unpleasant sneer on his face, it made for an appearance that was anything but warm or friendly.

"You decided to come out tonight too, I guess," Vince said.

"*We* did indeed," Michael corrected him. A quick glance behind Michael revealed two other males standing in proximity to him. One was tall with ink-black hair and the other was strikingly familiar. It only took Vince a moment to place him; after all, Coach George had been adamant about searing that face into his mind.

"You're Chad, aren't you?" Vince asked. Nick jerked visibly and Alice suddenly seemed uncomfortable. From the rumors that were floating around, Chad had dominated every opponent he went up against except the number two rank. Even then, it hadn't really been a close fight: just a minute or so longer than the others.

"I am," Chad confirmed. "You're Vince Reynolds, the girl to your side is Alice Adair, and the boy slowly edging his way behind you is Nicholas Campbell."

"Wow," Vince said. "That's really impressive. How'd you do that?"

"Student directory and an eidetic memory," Chad replied with a bored shrug.

"Awesome. Well, it was cool running into you, Michael, but we're sort of in the middle of something," Vince said as he delicately tried to extricate his group from Michael's and go back to keeping an eye on Roy.

"Hold up there, Silver," Michael said, placing a hand firmly on Vince's shoulder. "I owe you some payback for the cheap shot you pulled on me the other day."

"You mean where I used my talent against yours in a perfectly acceptable and legal way during a recorded and observed fight? Is that how you define a cheap shot?" Vince asked.

"You lured me in to thinking you couldn't do anything but run, then you cracked me in the jaw. You tricked me," Michael said, his hand tightening its grip.

"It's called strategy, and I suggest you adapt to it quickly in this school. Isn't this moot anyway, though? You won, you beat me, you proved you're the better fighter between us," Vince tried to pacify him.

"Maybe I feel like I deserve a little more payback for that crack across the jaw," Michael replied, flexing his impressive arms.

"Okay," Vince said simply. In a motion like flowing mercury, Vince snagged Michael's carelessly exposed arm, gripped his shoulder, and applied pressure above and below the elbow. "If that's the case, then maybe you should keep in mind that I'm better than you when we take out any extraordinary advantages."

"Gaah," Michael grunted as Vince intensified the pressure. He was holding Michael close so that anyone that happened to glance over might think they were still merely talking. He had come here to observe Roy under the radar; the last thing he needed was the bouncers noticing what was going on.

"I'm going to have to ask you to release him," Chad said as he moved slowly up to Michael's side. "As you recall, those beneath the top five ranks may not challenge us formally, or otherwise."

"Wasn't really looking for a challenge, I just wanted to come out with my friends. Michael here is the one who had a problem with mutual coexistence," Vince replied.

"Noted, but you're the one who took it from verbal to physical," Chad countered. "It was a nice grab, by the way, but from the way his face is contorting, I'd say you have only a few more seconds to release it before Michael makes this situation worse and escalates things."

Vince looked at Chad, and then felt the shaking in Michael's muscles. If it had been anything else, Vince might have been able to absorb Michael's energy and keep him restrained. With cold, though, that just wasn't an option. Making a snap decision, Vince released his hold and quickly took a step back.

Michael wheeled around, eyes wide and a long vein bulging noticeably on the top of this head. He shook out the arm that Vince had been holding and then curled his hand into a fist.

"If you do this, you know there will be severe consequences, right?" Chad asked in his same detached tone.

"Fuck 'em," Michael replied tersely. Vince shifted his footing slightly, readying himself to dodge Michael's blows.

"You girls take all the fun out of being at a club, you know that?" The voice was Roy's; he swaggered up to the tense zone that surrounded Vince and Michael. "I mean, really, you were doing good at staying covert for a while, but taking a fighting stance? Now everybody is paying attention to you shitheads instead of me."

"Not your fight," Michael grunted, his eyes never wavering from Vince's waiting form.

"No, but it is my night. So now, instead of drinking and playing with my girls, I had to take time out to come make sure you morons don't go trashing the club," Roy countered.

"I don't need your help, Roy," Vince said as he measured Michael's breathing and line of sight.

"I didn't come to help you. I came to help me. Now both of you, calm your asses down so I can have fun, or I'll take you out back and make sure neither of you can so much as move, let alone fight," Roy said calmly.

"I'm ranked higher than you, dipshit," Michael spat at him.

"Well then, here are two things to think about. First, you never fought me, so that ranking is arbitrary. Second, Hershel is the one on the admittance slip, so he's the one who can't be uncovered as a Super. As far as any regulations are concerned, I'm nothing more than a public persona," Roy said, a big grin spreading across his face as he took a sip of his drink.

"Hold on," Nick said, jumping in from the sidelines. "You're saying that you could tear this club down around us and they couldn't touch Hershel for exposing his identity?"

"You're a touch smarter than those glasses make you look," Roy answered. "Now then, girls, what do we do? Do both of you walk away right now, or do I beat you both like red-headed stepchildren?"

"I don't need to fight," Vince said honestly.

Michael's response took a touch longer. His eyes lingered on Vince, then glanced at Roy, and finally, took in all of the people who were casting sidelong glances at him in the area around them. Vince was better than him without abilities, and if he used them, he'd be exposed. He took a long breath and lowered his arms.

"Another time, Vince," Michael said, before turning and walking back in the direction of the entrance. The tall, dark-haired boy accompanied him. Chad, however, lingered for a moment.

"Nice job, Roy," Chad said. "It would have been problematic to deal with the fallout from that. And as for you, Mr. Reynolds, it would be wise to remember your place at this school."

"What's that supposed to mean?" Vince asked, his voice still a hair on edge from the almost-confrontation.

"It means you are weak. You have no right to things such as pride and aggression when dealing with those more powerful than you. You would be better served to bow your head and avoid conflict," Chad explained.

"That's not really my strong point," Vince shot back.

"If it were, I wouldn't have needed to tell you that, now would I? Think about it, because the next time Michael catches up to you, he will likely be smart enough to do it without a crowd present," Chad said. He turned and moved to catch up with the other two, sliding easily through the crowd at an oddly brisk speed.

"What a cock," Roy said simply. "Anyway, that was fun, but time to go tell my prospects for the night about how I stopped a bar fight. Later, bitches."

"Wait," Vince said. "Um . . . thank you. For keeping Michael and me out of trouble."

"Don't thank me," Roy said in a more serious tone than he had shown all night. "I wasn't lying; I only came over because your little show was distracting my girls. If it hadn't had a direct impact on me, I would have watched him beat you right off your high horse and never lifted a finger. We share a dorm, but we're not friends. Remember that." Roy turned away from them and began heading back to the dance floor.

"I don't know about you two," Nick said as Roy walked further from them. "But personally, I'm seriously beginning to think that he might not be the best candidate for our BFF for Life club. Just me talking out loud, though. Totally open to other opinions."

"Shut up, Nick," Vince and Alice said in unison.

26

"Good afternoon, class. I trust everyone had a fun weekend," Dean Blaine said as he breezed into the classroom. It was Tuesday, and all of the freshmen were gathered in his lecture hall for their first real session of Ethics of Heroism. Well, almost all of them. As Nick did his customary sweep of the room, he noticed three of the seats now stood out as empty. There had been two students in Monday's gym who had broken down crying, and one who had simply collapsed. As he stared at the cheap, plastic chairs left vacant, the fact that there was no possibility these two things weren't related gnawed at the back of his mind.

In fact, what were the odds that this lecture hall would have had precisely the correct number of seats for this class size? Nick realized these empty seats were meant to be noticed, meant to remind them that some of the class hadn't been able to cut it. And if they were using a method like this, then it could only mean they expected many more chairs to be ownerless before the year was through.

"Now then, I'm sure some of you are wondering how we will be discussing such a complicated and tangled topic as ethics, and how it pertains to Supers. We're going to start by defining who Supers are. And that, my students, begins with an understanding of where they come from. Can anyone tell me who the first officially documented Super was, and in what year they revealed themselves?"

Several hands shot up, and Dean Blaine pointed to a boy in the front. "Mr. Desoto, please enlighten us."

"The first documented Super was Captain Starlight, a former World War Two pilot who approached the government about working with people like him, the so-called extraordinary individuals that would eventually be known as Supers. This took place in 1957, and was caused by Captain Starlight's frustration with returning to civilian life after having achieved a sense of purpose defending his country during the war," the boy in front said. Nick realized with a start that it was the other guy they had dealt with on Friday, Shane Desoto. His voice hadn't sounded familiar; but, then again, Shane hadn't spoken once the entire night.

"You're close, Shane. Speculations about motivations aside, it was indeed Captain Starlight who approached the government, but that took place in 1959," Dean Blaine corrected.

"Actually, the government officially announced that the meeting took place then, but it really happened two years prior. It took two years of testing, trials, and Captain Starlight bringing in other Supers for them to see before the politicians were able to accept that there were such things as Supers. They changed the date because they felt taking two years to confirm things that could plainly be seen might read as incompetence to the voters," Shane corrected right back.

"An interesting hypothesis," Dean Blaine said. "May I ask where you heard this theory?"

"My grandfather told me," Shane replied.

"Wise as I'm sure your grandfather is, I'd wager he wasn't necessarily privy to every detail of Captain Starlight's life and rise to fame," Dean Blaine said.

"Would you, now?" Shane said simply, crossing his arms.

"Thank you, Shane, let's move on. Now, can anyone tell me what important events came about as a result of Captain Starlight's revelation to the government?" Dean Blaine asked. This time, he pointed at a hand in the air that was familiar to Nick.

"Because of Captain Starlight's brave actions revealing the existence of Supers, the government made the rest of the country aware of them, setting up special laws to protect aspects of their lives, and ultimately, setting up the Hero Certification Program so that Supers who had undergone proper training and qualification would be able to protect our country without being held liable for incidental damages caused in the process," Alice said rapidly.

"Very nice, Ms. Adair," Dean Blaine complimented. "Those are all correct, though there were, of course, many more ramifications to Captain Starlight's revelation than that. But we will get into those at a later date. For now, we know that Captain Starlight was the first officially documented Super. Does that mean he was the first in existence? Please tell us, Mr. Campbell."

"No," Nick responded immediately. The dean had been scanning his eyes across the class during the discussion thus far. Nick had noticed those eyes hesitate for an instant on him seconds before the question came, so he had been ready for it. Nick noted that he needed to look just a dash more interested in discussions. The goal was to draw no attention, either from being too observant or too apathetic. Clearly, he had fumbled and fallen below the acceptable apathy line.

"How do you know that?" Dean Blaine continued pressing.

"I don't," Nick said honestly. "But nobody does. Since there are no records, we can't really say for certain one way or the other if Captain Starlight was the first Super. The popular consensus leans toward the negative, though."

"Correct, Mr. Campbell. Without documentation, no one can prove or disprove the existence of previous Supers," Dean Blaine said. "Of course, the odds of an entire genetic offshoot beginning with one man and then continuing to appear at a steady rate for half a century afterwards are ludicrously low. This means that most likely Captain Starlight was nowhere near the first. Again, though, we don't know, and this lack of knowledge has led to many controversies and theories. Who can name one?"

Dean Blaine pointed to a young man wearing glasses in the front row.

"My mom used to say that the stories of the Greek gods were really about Supers, people just didn't know it then."

"A popular theory indeed," Dean Blaine said. "And this led to one of the greatest controversies that our existence has caused in this century. Who would like to venture a guess on what that was? Mr. Reynolds, give it a go."

"Religion," Vince said awkwardly. It was an interesting paradox that Vince could be so self-assured and insecure simultaneously. Nick already had a few ideas at how that tendency could work in his own favor, though.

"Please elaborate," Dean Blaine told him.

"People pretty much all agreed that the Greek gods were just Supers in disguise, so it was only a matter of time until they began speculating about whether other iconic figures from the past had really just been people with powers. The most obvious ones were all those tied to magical events. Prophets, saviors, warriors of their lord, everything was thrown into even more speculation that it had been," Vince explained.

"Very good, Mr. Reynolds," Dean Blaine said. "The addition of Supers to our world meant the opening of new possibilities. Events that had been mentioned in religious texts could now be challenged not only on historical accuracy, but also the possibility that if they had occurred, then perhaps it wasn't a divine hand that had guided them. The truly devout had to defend their faith on a whole other level, and it was not well-received. Now then: we know who the first Super was, can anyone tell me the name of the first documented Powered?"

"Who cares?" yelled out the braided blonde from the back. The rest of class laughed and echoed sentiment.

"I'd wager the Powereds care," Dean Blaine said seriously.

"Yeah, but they don't count. I mean, this is a class about heroism and Supers, not malfunctioning humans. Why would we need to know anything about the first of a thousand gears to break?" the girl shot back.

"You wouldn't," Dean Blaine said. "Unless you were the one trying to put the machine those gears had supported back together. I want you to think about that, because Powereds will be coming up over the course of this class. Their history and ours are more closely intertwined than you all might realize. Still, since no one seems to be informed enough to discuss their origins today, we can skip ahead to how Captain Starlight helped create special criminal classifications for Supers gone awry."

Nick cursed under his breath. Dean Blaine's eyes had hesitated on him again when he mentioned Powereds. Of course the dean of the college would know about him and the others, but little tics like that would give them away if anyone ever suspected. Nick took a deep breath. No one had any reason to think they were any different from every other Super in attendance. He just had to keep it that way.

27

Roy was acclimating well to gym. After the first day of trying, Hershel had wimped out and left the physical exertion to his bigger, stronger, better half. Hershel handled the ethics class, and then made the change before even setting foot in front of the coaches, all of which suited Roy just fine. Hershel got to sit through the boring stuff, while Roy was free to show all these pansies what a real Super could do.

Roy lapped the majority of the freshman boys once again as he breezed past them on the track. While every day was sprinkled with different exercises, running was a constant. It seemed that whatever curriculum Coach George had in mind factored heavily on cardio and endurance. For most of the class it was a grueling, daily struggle just to keep up and not give in. For Roy, and a few other notable adversaries, it was a time to get in a light jog and simmer in the envy of others. On that note, Roy noticed Vince giving him a dirty look as he breezed by. Vince had been cold to him since that night in the club. It probably hadn't helped matters that Roy had shaken his dormmates off and left Hershel alone to wake up in a downtown alleyway. Normally, he and his fat body-based roommate shared a more cordial relationship, but Roy had felt the need to make a point.

A little fallout from a cohabitant didn't even qualify as a blip on Roy's radar. The idiot in sunglasses had been just as chatty since that night, and of course, Alice was practically drooling every time he walked in a room, so that made Vince the only one with an open grudge against him. It was possible Mary didn't like him either, but she seemed to always avoid him, so who could tell? Besides, that one was off limits. He could push Fatty around a lot, but slipping the sausage to a chick he liked would be like declaring open war. Roy felt that would cut into a lot of his time and fun, so it was easier to give the chubby dipshit a little bit of accommodation.

"Time!" Coach George yelled from across the gym. "Line up!"

The boys and girls filtered from their opposite sides of the track to the center of the gym where George and Persephone stood waiting. The rule of staying on opposite sides had stayed in effect since day one, and though lapping was permitted, falling behind was never tolerated. So far every student who had fallen back into the other sex's group had been taken out and not seen again. It seemed they were playing hardball. Roy was almost entertained.

"Well," Coach George said once they had all fallen into line. "It seems you survived another day. I'm a touch surprised. I was sure we'd be kicking another couple of you out today."

Panicked looks fleetingly leapt across the faces of some of the slower students. Personally, Roy felt it was warranted. Even Fatty had kept up with his group for one day. If he could do it, then the only excuse for failing was laziness.

"I was wrong," Coach George continued. "If I were you, I'd savor those words, because you won't be hearing them very often. I'm a man, though, and I'll own up to my mistakes. I was wrong, and today every one of you managed to keep up and stay in the program. So the question I find myself asking is this: are you all just that much better than I thought, or are you all so weak and worthless that it's impossible to tell which piece of shit has sunk to the bottom of the toilet?"

No one said anything. The weaker students were struck dumb with fear and the stronger ones were arrogantly self-assured that this conversation wasn't for them.

"I think it might be the latter," Coach George said. "So I want you all to think about something. There are only so many spots for advancement out of this year into the next. Just passing isn't enough. We're only taking the best. Next time you're slowing down to stay with your group, instead of driving harder to leave them behind and knock some slow shit out of the running, I want you to think about that. Think real hard about whether you want to be a nice guy who helps everyone squeak by with mediocrity, or if you want to be a Hero. Because I promise you, a mediocre Hero is just a corpse that's a week behind schedule. Get out of my sight."

The line broke and students began moving quickly toward the showers. Roy began swaggering, but felt a firm hand grip him on the shoulder.

"Daniels," Coach George said. "I think you and I need to talk for a minute."

"Sure, Coach," Roy said with his patented smile flashing. "Want me to run faster and drive a few more people out of the running?"

"Actually, Daniels, I'd like you to take note of something," Coach George said.

"What's that?" Roy asked.

"In this class there are several students with physical gifts well-suited to endurance or running. Yet you lap the other groups more times than anyone else," Coach George explained. "Why do you think that is?"

"I guess I just want it more," Roy replied, chuckling at his own wit.

"Try again, jackass. It's because everyone else is taking this time and training seriously. Ms. Foster alone could have passed everyone several thousand times during that run. But she didn't, because she was running without using her abilities as much as possible," Coach George said.

"Sounds pretty dumb to me," Roy replied. "I mean, if she's that good at running, then why practice it so much?"

"Because she wants to get stronger. As does Mr. Taylor, who shares your limitless endurance, yet maintained a constant pace during today's run," Coach George said without an inkling of a smile in his eyes.

"You just told everyone to work harder in order to knock each other out, now you're getting on my ass for doing well and applauding others for sandbagging it," Roy said, shaking Coach George's hand loose. The gym had emptied entirely by this point, only the two of them left in its large interior.

"I'm 'getting on your ass' because you accomplished nothing today, or yesterday, or really any day except the one where you came in human form. This is training, Daniels, it's designed to make you stronger, better, and more able to endure the toll that being a Hero will put on you. This is the foundation of being a Hero, and you're pissing it away," Coach George said.

"Thanks for the lecture," Roy shot back. "But in case you forgot, I'm in the top five of this 'hard-working class,' and I would have been number one if I hadn't fought that stupid psychic guy."

"No, you wouldn't have," Coach George said simply. "You're the weakest of the strong, Daniels, and if you don't start putting in the effort, you won't even hold on to that title for more than a year."

"Okay, how am I supposed to do that, then? I don't get tired. I don't get sore. I don't even get short of breath," Roy countered. "I'm super strong, super durable, and have super endurance. Now, please tell me how to get any benefit out of lifting a few weights and jogging around a track."

"Sorry, Daniels," Coach George said with a shake of his head. "That's not my job. Heroes are supposed to be creative and show ingenuity. If I were you, I'd get cracking on that, before the rest of the class leaves you behind."

Roy scoffed. "It hasn't even been a week yet."

"Time flies, Daniels," Coach George said as he turned and headed toward the exit. "And at this level, so will the progress of your competition."

28

As the days turned into weeks, Vince noticed a funny thing: he was getting used to his new life at Lander. He was slowly growing accustomed to sleeping in the same bed, under the same roof, every night. He was growing tolerant of Nick's flapping gums and Roy's douchebag demeanor. His body was even beginning to get used to the five-times-a-week workouts from hell. It was strange, but each day that passed found him more comfortable with his life here. He was beginning to feel like he might finally have a shred of normalcy in life, with his powers under control and his wandering suspended. On the day he truly became certain of this, he reached an important decision.

"Sasha, would you like to go out with me tonight?" Vince asked stiffly. It wasn't that he wasn't comfortable around his speedy friend, but the life he'd had before Lander had hardly equipped him with much experience in the realm of a social life. This deficiency was one of the reasons he was determined to stop dallying and make up for lost time.

"Sure," Sasha replied offhandedly. The two were eating breakfast on this Friday morning as was their routine, so she sipped her orange juice before continuing. "I think Julia is going out tonight, and the other two never stay in on a Friday, so we can hang out and watch a movie."

"Yes . . . well, that does sound fun," Vince fumbled. "But . . . you see, I meant would you join me tonight . . . in a romantic capacity? As in a date."

"Yeah, I know," Sasha said. "Took you long enough. Why do you think I invited you to come watch a movie in my *empty* dorm?"

"Oh," Vince said. Then, realization dawned. "Oooh. I was thinking something a bit more traditional for our first date."

"You got a car?" Sasha interrupted.

"Um . . . no," Vince admitted.

"Me neither, and while I can get anywhere in town in under ten seconds, it sort of takes the fun out of it if you can't join me," Sasha pointed out. "So our options are a romantic candlelit dinner in the dining hall, or watching a movie."

"How's seven work for you?" Vince asked.

"Better make it seven thirty. We do still have to grab a shitty dinner here after all," Sasha said.

"Point well made," Vince agreed.

*　　　*　　　*

"I still can't believe you finally grew a pair," Nick commented as he reclined on the couch in the boys' lounge and flipped through the television stations.

"I always had a pair," Vince said defensively. "I was just getting settled in to my new surroundings. What do you think?"

"You look dumb," Nick replied, barely glancing at Vince's outfit.

"How is a button-down shirt and slacks considered dumb?" Vince asked.

"It's not, if you're going on a job interview. For going to a dorm to watch a movie, though . . . little dumb," Nick replied.

"I think it looks nice," Hershel chimed in softly.

Vince stood in the lounge area with his open bedroom door behind him. Nick and Hershel were sitting on the couch, killing time and offering him advice on what outfit to wear. Inside Vince's room loomed an ever-rising stack of rejected combinations. In all the years Vince was a wanderer, he had never needed to worry about fashion. After thirty minutes of trying on clothes, he was beginning to suspect that he should have relished that time a touch more than he had.

"No, Nick's right," Vince said. "This is too formal. I'll try again." Vince turned around and went back into his room, shutting the door while he changed.

"Nick," Hershel said shyly. "Not that I don't appreciate him wanting our input, but why isn't he asking the girls what he should wear on a date? You know, since it's a girl he's trying to impress and all."

"Because, my dear boy, he's an idiot. Plus, I may have convinced him I'm something of a fashion expert," Nick said, not quite hiding the chuckle in his voice.

"That's mean! You shouldn't trick him like that. He seems to really be into this girl," Hershel said.

Nick cocked an eyebrow and stared at Hershel. Of course, as far as Hershel could tell, Nick had simply put his eyebrow up and pointed his sunglasses right at him, but the general effect was still the same. Sort of. "I don't remember saying I tricked him at any point in that statement."

"So . . . wait . . . you really are a fashion expert?" Hershel asked, confused.

"I feel like my wardrobe answers that question all on its own," Nick replied. At that moment, Nick was wearing carpenter's pants and a green tank top. Not knowing what to say, Hershel did the next best thing: he changed the subject.

"If you have time tonight, do me a favor," Hershel said. "When you see Roy, please tell him he has to stop skipping gym. He's missed three classes already in the past few weeks, and we only get four per semester. I don't want to get drummed out just because my alter ego is throwing a hissy fit."

"He has seemed a bit more on edge," Nick agreed. "I mean, even when he comes to class, he always looks a bit pissed. That first week he was pretty cheerful when he was lapping us in typical asshole form. What happened?"

Hershel let out a sigh. "Coach George called him out on not trying and told him if he doesn't work harder, the other Supers will leave him behind."

"And he felt the appropriate response was to change nothing except his consistent attendance?" Nick asked.

"He doesn't like it when people imply there might be others stronger than he is, and he handles it like a child," Hershel said. "I think he wants George to admit he was wrong and that Roy could skip the whole semester and still come out on top."

"Could he?" Nick asked, a slight twinge of true curiosity creeping into his voice.

"Maybe," Hershel said. "The only person who's ever been able to beat him was our dad, so I know it can be done, but other than that, no one has ever really gotten the better of him in a fight."

"What about during the opening combat trials? I mean, if he came in fifth, he must have lost to someone," Nick pointed out.

"He lost to rank number four: Rich Weaver. Rich has the ability to trap your mind in a fantasy, leaving you utterly unable to move or even perceive what's happening around you. He locked Roy down in the first five seconds, then just walked out of the room. Twenty minutes later, they declared him the winner and he let Roy free," Hershel explained.

Nick let out a whistle. "Hard to believe someone that powerful only made it to rank four."

"Apparently, he fought Chad after that," Hershel noted.

"That does explain a bit of it," Nick agreed. "I have got to find out what that guy's ability is." Nick's speculations were interrupted by the sound of Vince's door opening again.

"Okay, this had better be good, because if I don't leave soon, I'm going to be late!" Vince declared as he stepped out of his room.

Nick looked him carefully up and down this time. Vince was wearing black jeans and a pair of flip flops, along with a blue collared-shirt. The dark tones worked well with his hair, yet didn't clash noticeably with the striking blue of his eyes. Vince had accidently assembled a truly well-planned outfit that highlighted the best parts of himself.

"Adequate," Nick said simply.

"I'll take it," Vince said with a smile, shutting his room's door and dashing out the exit.

"Ahh, young love," Nick said to no one in particular.

"I should probably go change, too," Hershel said, pulling himself up from the chair.

"Big plans tonight?" Nick asked.

"Not that I know of," Hershel replied. "But I can feel Roy stirring around in my head, and he's pretty anxious to get going. I guess he's got something planned."

"Cool," Nick said. "You two have fun."

"Will do," Hershel assured.

Roy did indeed have something big planned, and at that moment, it was unfortunate that Hershel only had access to Roy's thoughts from when he was out.

105

Hershel couldn't see any of the things going on in Roy's consciousness when Roy was nothing more than a presence in the brain. If Hershel had been able to, though, he undoubtedly would have refused to change and thwarted Roy's scheme before it even began.

That, however, was not the case.

29

Vince arrived at Sasha's dorm and paused before knocking. He checked his breath, made sure his clothes were fitting well, and ran his fingers through his silver hair. Vince was nervous, almost pathetically so. It wasn't that he had never had any romantic interaction with a lady, but a real date, possibly the beginning of a real relationship? That was something he'd always considered impossible until the procedure. Vince took a deep breath to steady himself. Sasha liked him, obviously, and they'd been getting to know each other for weeks. It was never going to be any easier than this.

Vince finally pulled back his hand and knocked on Sasha's door.

"Took you long enough," Sasha said as she pulled the door open. "Come on in, I've got popcorn in the microwave."

"You look nice," Vince said sheepishly as he stepped into her room.

"You, too," Sasha said with a smile. "Who helped dress you?"

*   *   *

"Yeah, baby, I'll meet you by the Science building and then we can head on back to your place," Roy said into his phone as he entered the Melbrook common room. He snapped his cell shut and surveyed the area. No one was around; it seemed even the losers he was bunking with had things to do on a Friday night. Roy had half expected to run into Nick when he left his room, but the sunglass-wearing fashion boy had left the area while Roy was busy changing. Alice was a pretty little dish; not surprising she would have places to be. As for Mary . . . well, who knew what telepaths did for fun? The only other member of Melbrook missing was Vince, and Roy knew very well where that dick was.

Roy Daniels was many things: lover, fighter, drinker, warrior. One of the many things Roy didn't consider himself, though, was the type of man who let someone else interfere in his business. Vince had spearheaded that little campaign to follow him around the club and try to cockblock, and now that he had a date, Roy was finally going to be able to return the favor. The key difference was, of course, that Roy wasn't going to *try* anything. Roy was going to *do*, and succeed, because Roy was a winner. And that's how the world worked for winners.

Adjusting his hat, Roy strode though the common room, down the hall, and stepped out into the brisk night air. He paused to admire the stars in the sky, thinking he might try fucking a broad outside tonight to savor nature's beauty. About that time, he felt a tremendous force smash across the back of his head and hoist him into the air.

*   *   *

"Is ninja a type of power?" Vince asked as the black-clad warrior on the screen leapt into the air, hovered, and dropped down, depositing his fist in some unwitting minion's fragile skull. "I mean, sticking someone with the title of ninja seems to convey all kinds of ridiculous abilities. I almost wonder if there's a real world variation of this somewhere."

"Plenty of people have enhanced physical abilities," Sasha pointed out. "I suppose doing a couple of these moves would be possible for a chunk of the Super population. I don't think that's so much the point of these films, though. It's about learning a martial art and training yourself into being above normal."

"I guess you're right," Vince agreed.

"Personally, I think it's almost sad. All those normal people out there, desperate for any avenue to make themselves extraordinary. I see why so many people follow that path," Sasha commented as she munched on popcorn.

"What about people who learn martial arts for exercise, or self-defense, or to gain better control over their bodies and minds? I don't think everyone who learns a martial art is trying to somehow become one of us," Vince countered.

Sasha shrugged. "People can say whatever they want about their reasons, it doesn't make it the truth. I developed at an early age, so I have almost no memories of not being a Super, and let me tell you something: no matter how nice someone is, no matter how respectful they are, no matter what they say, every powerless human you meet is thinking the same thing when they meet you."

"And what's that?" Vince asked.

"They're thinking: 'Why not me?' They think they should have been born special, been made powerful, been gifted," Sasha said. "I might just be a cynic, but it's what I believe. And I'd bet dollars to donuts that any telepath would back me up."

"I could always ask Mary," Vince said.

"You should. I bet she'd have some interesting input on it," Sasha said.

"Maybe," Vince said. "I doubt I will, though. She's sort of quiet and doesn't hang around us too much. I think she might just like keeping to herself, and I don't want to interfere with that too much."

*   *   *

Roy began kicking and punching as soon he felt himself hoisted. He wasn't sure who the dumbass with the big balls and the death wish was, but he was going to pound into their head what a stupid fucking idea jumping Roy Daniels had been.

"That won't do any good," said a small voice from behind him.

Roy kicked a few more times, but the voice was right. He wasn't hitting anyone or anything, just flailing about in air. Slowly, he let his limbs relax and felt his body rotate around until he was looking at the source of the small voice.

"You know, if you wanted me that bad, you should have just bought me a bottle of whiskey," Roy spat out.

"It's almost cute how you default to your enormous ego when you don't know what to do," said Mary, leaning, relaxed, against the outer wall of the dorm, effortlessly holding Roy ten feet above the ground.

"So, if you didn't want to flirt, why'd you sucker punch me?" Roy asked.

"The blast was to distract you while I put you in the air," Mary explained. "You've a very strong person, but this situation renders you essentially powerless."

"Oh yeah?" Roy let a wild grin slide across his face, then began flexing and kicking with all his might. He twisted his hips, slammed his fists together, and jerked his body in every conceivable direction to rip himself free of her grip.

"Yes, actually," Mary said with a smile of her own. Roy's wild tantrum had moved him not one iota closer to the ground or away from his starting position. "I'm holding you by the torso in midair. You have no ground to push off against, so no way to generate significant force. Hercules himself wouldn't be able to break free of me once he was suspended."

Roy's motions slowly subsided. "I totally thought that would work."

"You watch too many movies," Mary chided him. "Do yourself a favor, pick up a physics book. Even you'll find a little use in it."

"Noted," Roy said. "Why are you hanging me up here like laundry, anyway?"

"We need to talk," Mary replied.

"We can't talk on the ground?" Roy asked.

"We could, but both of us know that would be me talking and you not listening. I like this situation better," Mary said.

Roy automatically started to lie and tell her that of course he would be listening when she talked to him, but then his brain kicked in and he remembered what type of Super he was talking to. "Okay, fine," Roy said instead. "I would have ignored you. Now, what's so damn important you needed to shanghai me?"

"A couple of things," Mary said, walking slowly around Roy. He noticed that he was being turned as she moved, so that they were always face to face. "First off, I'm not letting you ruin Vince's date tonight."

"Oh, it wouldn't have been ruined," Roy tried to explain.

"You planned on barging in with Julia and having loud, raucous sex in her and Sasha's room to ruin any romance their date might have held," Mary said.

"Right . . . but that doesn't mean it would have worked," Roy said.

"What it would have done is piss Vince off, especially when he realized that you knew about the date because he told Hershel. That would cause him to pull back from dealing with your other persona, robbing Hershel of one of the very few friends he has here," Mary elaborated.

"Yeah, well, Fatty can always stick to his usual friends, pie and fried chicken," Roy snapped.

109

He might have said more, but he was too busy suddenly being violently shaken like a soda in a paint mixer. "That," Mary said in a much more strained voice, "is the other thing you and I are going to talk about."

*   *   *

"Do you ever shut up?" Sasha asked.

"Huh?" Vince squawked, caught unaware.

"Seriously, the movie has gone to the end credits, we're sitting here in a barely lit room with only a few inches between us, and you are still trying to talk about plot validity," Sasha said.

"I'm . . . sorry," Vince said. "I haven't really been on a lot of dates."

"Surely you jest," Sasha said. "It's okay. I knew you were a noob when I met you. Might even be why I kind of like you."

"Kind of like me, eh?" Vince said with a slowly-spreading smile, barely visible in the television's fading glow.

"A little. But it's diminishing the more you talk," Sasha replied.

"Gotcha," Vince said. He leaned forward and wrapped his arms around Sasha, pulling her close to him. His lips quickly sought hers and found them with only minimal searching. The kiss was awkward at first, but as the intensity grew, both lost their sense of self-consciousness and became immersed in the task at hand. When they finally parted to take a breath, it was Sasha whose words filled the electrified silence.

"Not bad for a virgin," she mused.

"Stop talking so much," Vince shot back. She did, and they sank down onto the couch, movie, popcorn, and the rest of the world soon utterly forgotten.

*   *   *

"You're going to stop talking badly about Hershel, you're going to stop making it a point to be a raging dick to his friends, and most importantly of all, you're going to start going to every one of your classes and actually try to get stronger," Mary said as she slowly twirled Roy around.

"That's an awful lot of demands for a girl with no leverage," Roy replied.

Mary snorted out a small laugh. "Sorry, it's just funny because in this situation, you're the one with no leverage. And I mean that in a literal sense, not the slang kind. Never mind. Hershel will get it tomorrow."

"Nice to know Tubbo is good for something," Roy said.

"You think I'm kidding, don't you?" Mary asked. "Or that you can play along and once you're on the ground, never listen to me again. You don't even perceive me as a threat, despite the fact that I've rendered you helpless."

"Truth be told, I see this more as a Mexican standoff," Roy said. "I can't hurt you, but you can't really hurt me, either. All you can do is inconvenience me. Thing is,

110

me not being able to hurt you is only applicable right now. Once I'm set down, that limitation is no longer in place."

"A Mexican standoff is when both parties are able to kill each other, not unable to hurt one another," Mary pointed out.

"You know a lot of slang for a wilderness dweller," Roy commented.

"I'm a telepath. We learn things quickly," Mary said. She stopped turning Roy and began walking toward him. "In fact, I've learned so many things about my roommates that aren't to be believed. Take you, for example. I learned something very interesting about you." Mary stopped just short of Roy, only a few inches out of his reach. Then she took three steps forward. He began to coil and leap for her, but her next words froze him in his tracks.

"I know you have a weakness, invulnerable cowboy."

Roy was very, very still. "Okay, so I'm only resistant to damage, not invulnerable to it. No one is truly invulnerable. Supers might be able to shrug off a lot, but there are always limits. That doesn't make it a weakness."

Mary shook her head. "That's not what I'm talking about and you know it. I've already gotten the phone number. I'll use it."

They stared at each other in silence for a few moments, thoughts racing through Roy's head while Mary calmly observed them.

"What do you want?" Roy asked at last.

"I already told you," Mary said. "Be nice to Hershel's friends, don't be mean to Hershel, and start showing up and working in class."

"I can do the first two, but the last is out of my hands," Roy explained. "I'm beyond human limits in physical power. What the fuck is running around a gym going to do for me?"

"You know, I think this might be my fault," Mary said. "I'm trying to force you into something without giving you motivation. I apologize."

Roy felt himself lowering and his feet hit the ground. He and Mary were now only inches apart. It was well within his ability to crush her like a grape. Yet, staring into those amber eyes, Roy felt something he wasn't accustomed to: a sense of hesitation. This girl had been ready for him entirely. He would be a damn fool to assume she didn't have some sort of ace in the hole if he made a move. Aside from the one she had already alluded to.

"I'm going to offer you a deal," Mary said.

"Listening," Roy shot back, then thought back to their conversation. "I mean, really listening this time."

"So, you do learn," Mary quipped. "Here is my proposition: go challenge Chad tomorrow for his ranked spot. You're in the top five as well, so it should be allowed. If

111

you can take that spot, then you can forget all of my other demands, and I promise to neither use nor divulge what I know about your weakness."

"Pssh, is that it? Shit, I was planning on beating him up for that spot soon, anyway. All that does is make my Saturday fun. So, what's the catch?" Roy asked.

"The catch is that if you lose, you have to do all the things I asked of you, without back talk or me constantly threatening you. Essentially, if you lose, I own your ass until the end of the year," Mary explained.

"That's it?" Roy tried to confirm.

"That's it." Mary nodded.

"Deal," Roy said. "I'll do it around one, so make sure you don't miss the show tomorrow." Roy began striding off toward the west of campus.

"Oh, Roy," Mary called out.

"Yeah?" Roy asked without turning his head.

"You haven't won your freedom yet, so if you ruin Vince's date, you do know I'll bring hell crashing down upon you, right?" Mary asked.

Roy nodded briskly, then, as casually as he could possibly manage, changed his direction toward the north of campus, where his car was parked.

*　　　*　　　*

Julia stood outside the Science building, pink heels and low-cut shirt giving away that her plans for the night involved the attentions of a male. She checked her watch for the tenth time that minute and muttered under her breath.

"Where the fuck is Roy?"

30

Alice was bored . . . again. As she sauntered into the dorm lobby, laden with bags and well-lit by the morning sun, she began to entertain the possibility that the reason she was bored might be because she was lonely. Yesterday had left her feeling restless, so she'd jumped in her car, taken a firm grip on Daddy's credit cards, and burned up the town. Her dinner had been at an upscale restaurant that none of the rest of her class would even be able to pronounce, let alone gain entrance to. She'd even spent the night in a posh hotel room rather than trudge back across town to her comparatively squalid little dorm room. She had spoiled and pampered herself rotten to lift her ever-falling spirits.

And yet . . . and yet she still felt off somehow. It couldn't be loneliness, not logically. Alice had always been alone. Certainly Daddy had kept a devoted staff at the house, but they had never been people to her, let alone friends. Daddy's schedule had always kept him busy, and her mother had passed away when Alice was just a girl, so she had grown up entertaining herself.

Of course, her play had to be within limits, lest she grow too joyful and lift off the ground. It was a hard lesson Alice had learned at a very early age: joy that lets you walk on air is always followed by the misery of crashing to the ground. It was why Alice had learned to grow so careful in her emotions, so reserved in her feelings. Being alone all the time had actually been a boon there; she had suffered through fewer stimuli and gained a greater sense of control.

She walked into the girls' side of the dorm, then into her room, where she deposited her bags. Perhaps it was loneliness after all, only it was affecting her for the first time because her nose was constantly being shoved in it. All around, the other students were meeting people and forging friendships. Yet Alice, for all her social grace and tact, had spent yet another Friday night by herself. Well, it wasn't as though she'd ever had to make friends before. She could always manage a conversation with surgical precision, but when it came to taking that leap, she found herself unable to plunge. She realized it was a somewhat ironic way to think of her dilemma, given that her own ability left her nothing to fear from gravity, though since that was only a recent development, perhaps it make a sad sort of sense.

Alice began putting her new purchases into her closet. Maybe she would try reaching out to her dormmates tonight. It was Saturday, after all; one had to assume they were planning something. They were idiots, and of course Mary was an enormous hazard, but they knew what it had been like to grow up as a Powered, and that should provide them with at least a bit of common ground.

Besides, if she spent too many more Friday nights alone she'd have to hire a contractor to widen her closet.

*   *   *

"They don't seem to be bonding well," Mr. Numbers noted as he and Mr. Transport dined on breakfast in their apartment.

"Is that problematic to our plan?" Mr. Transport inquired.

"Not problematic per se; however, it does lower our chances of success," Mr. Numbers replied.

"Do tell," Mr. Transport encouraged.

"We need to keep them on the straight and narrow. Peer pressure is a tool that could work for or against us in the long run, but it is not even on our thin list of options until they are moving and thinking as some semblance of a collective," Mr. Numbers explained.

Mr. Transport took a bite of eggs and mulled over Mr. Numbers's point. "You're proposing that it would be easier for us to manage them as a herd than as individuals."

"Correct," Mr. Numbers confirmed. "It does put all of our eggs in one basket; however, given that the loss of even one student to the side of villainy will result in our termination, it could be said that all the eggs are in that basket anyway."

"I see what you mean," Mr. Transport agreed. "Do you have a solution?"

"Not a solution, but a possibility. One of the greatest ways to bind people together is through necessity," Mr. Numbers said.

"Ah, such as how you and I didn't care for each other when we were first paired, yet trusting our lives to one another forged a powerful bond," Mr. Transport commented.

"Precisely," Mr. Numbers said.

"We can't put their lives in constant danger without arousing suspicion, though," Mr. Transport pointed out. "What do they value with similar or equal intensity?"

"Their grades," Mr. Numbers replied succinctly.

With that, the conversational portion of breakfast was done.

*   *   *

Hershel's eyes snapped open, and he leapt out of bed. He couldn't believe the memories Roy had bequeathed him from last night. Fighting the number one rank? And Mary . . . he was both floored and amazed by her. To handle Roy with such total control . . . it was unreal. She'd even exploited his weakness for betting. Fortunately, Hershel had no such weakness, nor did he have any desire to see his alter ego be singled out as the top rank. Roy was already unbearable lately; winning this fight would validate his arrogance and leave him unwilling to listen to another word from anyone. Hershel threw on some pants and a wrinkled shirt. He was getting off campus, walking to a coffee shop, and keeping Roy caged all day long.

"No, you're not," said a familiar voice as he stepped into the common room. Mary was waiting for him, sitting on a couch facing the boys' side and sipping on a bottle of water.

114

"I most certainly am," Hershel replied with more force than he meant to. "Do you have any idea what you did? Once Roy beats Chad there won't even be the possibility of getting through to him. You should have just hung the weakness over his head if you wanted to stop him."

Mary shook her head. "Roy would never have obeyed, no matter what it cost him. You and I both know that. The only real chance of controlling Roy is through his own pride. He made a bet on his own strength. He'll honor it when he loses."

"*When* he loses?" Hershel said, stepping toward Mary and sitting down on the couch. "Do you know who you're talking about? I've barely seen any Super even damage Roy. The only person who ever beat him in combat was our dad, and he's the one who taught Roy how to fight. He won't lose, Mary. He never loses, on anything, or to anyone."

"That's why I told him to fight Chad," Mary explained. "Roy needs to be beaten. He needs a dose of humility, and you need to stop thinking of him as this unstoppable force. You're just as strong as he is, and after today's fight I hope you'll be one step closer to believing that."

Hershel paused. His initial fear and hesitation was waning as the girl he had been unable to stop thinking about was finally talking to him and looking at him. A part of him wanted to believe she was right, and that Roy could lose. The only hurdle was the decade of experience that said otherwise. Still, as he looked into her strong, amber eyes, his resolve weakened, and he did what men have been doing for women they admired for centuries.

He caved.

"You really think Chad might be able to beat him?" Hershel asked.

"I know he can," Mary responded. "Unlike the rest of you, I've actually seen Chad fight."

Hershel snorted. "You know Roy will remember this whole conversation when he comes out."

"Will it change his mind?"

Hershel shook his head. "Roy could hear a direct message from God saying he'd lose and still show up ready to go."

"Exactly," Mary said. "So have breakfast and relax for a bit, then go change into Roy. Let this day run its course and have a little faith."

"I'll try," Hershel said. "Why are you so sure Roy will lose, though?"

"For one thing, he already fought a number one ranked student last night, and you saw how well he did there," Mary countered.

"You didn't hurt him though," Hershel pointed out.

"See if you still say that to me tonight," Mary said.

115

31

Mr. Numbers and Mr. Transport were interrupted from washing their breakfast dishes by the sound of the intercom in the kitchen sounding.

"Mary and Roy here. Roy would like to be taken down to the underground levels for some special training," came Mary's voice through the speakers. "Would Mr. Transport be on hand to assist us?"

Mr. Numbers and Mr. Transport looked at each other and gave a nod. Mr. Transport went to the door and swung it open.

"Good morning, students," Mr. Transport declared. "So, you wish to put in some training time on the weekend? Well, kudos for the determination."

"Actually," Roy said from just outside the doorframe, beyond where Mr. Numbers could see from his vantage point. "I'm the only one going down, and I'd appreciate it if you hung close by. I don't think my business down there will take too long."

"You can always take the lift back up if you like," Mr. Transport tried to deflect.

"Please go with him," said Mary. "I think it will prove to be necessary."

"Very well," Mr. Transport said with a sigh. "Let's keep it brisk if at all possible, though. I do have things to do today."

"No problem," Mary assured him. "Roy will be done in no time at all, won't you, Roy?"

"Damn straight," Roy agreed.

"Well then, off we go," said Mr. Transport. A moment later the door began to swing shut as Mr. Transport's body was no longer there to wedge it open. It stopped before locking, pushed open by the small hand of Mary Smith, who poked her head into the room and locked eyes with Mr. Numbers.

"While they're gone, what do you say to a game of chess?" Mary asked.

"Hardly seems like much of a game with a telepath," Mr. Numbers replied gruffly.

"No powers, I promise," Mary countered with a quick grin.

"Fine," Mr. Numbers conceded. The girl was clearly up to something, and if he wanted to know what it was, he needed more data.

*   *   *

"What exercise are you looking to practice?" Mr. Transport asked Roy as they arrived in the underground area.

"Combat," Roy replied briskly, striding off toward the gym. Mr. Transport had never seen Roy so focused on anything. He was in his combat uniform, had left his silly little hat back above ground, and seemed to be dead set on whatever he was doing. It was more progress than Mr. Transport had dared hope to see from the narcissist in the entirety of the year, let alone in the span of a few days.

Mr. Transport set off at a brisk stride, not quite catching up to Roy, but never losing sight of him, either. They emerged in the weight room, where several grey uniforms were getting some exercise and a pair of black uniforms stood near the free weights at the back. It seemed the two other freshmen were stretching near the weights, rather than lifting them. Mr. Transport was about to conclude they must be too intimidated by the older students to work out around them when he suddenly realized who those two students were.

"Chad!" Roy bellowed from across the room, drawing the attention of everyone there, including the intended party. "I've come to challenge you for your rank of number one," Roy declared, cocky smirk twitching at the edges of his mouth.

Chad seemed oddly nonplussed, giving Roy a shrug and then turning to the other freshman. "Shane," Chad said to his friend, "would you be so kind as to get a referee and a healer so that we may count this as a sanctioned match?"

The other freshman, Shane one could easily conclude, gave a nod of his head and set off toward the offices. Chad finished his stretches and walked calmly over to Roy.

"You're in the top five, so I won't be taking it as easy on you," Chad said simply.

"Taking it easy? You're better off worrying how you'll find the strength to last five minutes against the powerhouse you're facing," Roy shot back.

"So be it," Chad replied. "Let's select a room."

*   *   *

"First move goes to the lady," Mr. Numbers said as he gazed at the chessboard.

"Let me guess: from my opening move, you can deduce my strategy, my personality type, and my favorite food?" Mary asked.

"I thought you promised no powers."

"I didn't need my powers to know that about you," Mary answered, moving a pawn forward. Before her finger had even left the piece, Mr. Numbers had run the simulations and knew how he would win this game.

Mr. Numbers made his move, then Mary, and so on for several turns. Eventually, Mr. Numbers made a striking observation.

"You have no idea how to play chess, do you?" Mr. Numbers asked.

"I don't know much about strategy," Mary admitted. "I do know how the pieces move, though."

"Are you sure? Because your moves say otherwise. The only ones you're using to their full potential are the pawns and the king," Mr. Numbers pointed out.

"Sometimes, a piece must make some bad moves in order to make good ones," Mary said.

117

"I presume you have an explanation to go with that statement. By all means, proceed."

"All right," Mary said, picking up a piece. "Take this rook for example. It's quite the powerhouse when you think about it: unstoppable, yet limited in its movements. All it can do is charge blindly forward or to the side."

"Correct," Mr. Numbers said.

"But what if this rook were defective somehow? What if it could only move forward, if it didn't have the ability to go side to side? That weakness would limit its movements tremendously, leaving the rest of my army vulnerable and exposed."

"That is true, but only in a purely academic sense. A rook is used by the player wielding it, so it cannot be defective. Your rook can move side to side, and is not broken, so start using it correctly," Mr. Numbers retorted.

"Let's say that it was," Mary continued. "Just for the sake of argument. Now, as the person controlling this army, should my first priority be charging blindly forward despite my weakness, or would it be fixing my rook?"

Mr. Numbers said nothing for a moment, then moved his knight and took another of Mary's pawns.

"You know an oddly large amount about human psychology for a girl who has lived in the woods," Mr. Numbers observed.

"Maybe," Mary acquiesced. "But have you ever wondered what I did out there in the silence?"

"Ate gophers?"

"Actually yes, but that's not what I meant," Mary said. "I spent those years growing up, and sorting through all the thoughts and things I'd been exposed to. I read psychology books and watched television, all to put the various and often horrible things I had grown up hearing leak from people's minds into perspective. Think of it as intensive training in dealing with humanity."

"An interesting pastime," Mr. Numbers said. "Also, checkmate."

"Good game," Mary said with a smile. "We should play again next weekend. Maybe I'll learn a little about strategy from battling you."

"I don't think you'll improve that much playing only one game a week," Mr. Numbers told her.

"Probably not, but at least by next week my rook should be in working order."

*   *   *

"This is a match for ranking," said the crackling pre-recorded voice of Dean Blaine through the speaker box. "As such, the only ways to win are to incapacitate your opponent or force him to give up. Should serious injury occur, the match will be stopped while the injury is reviewed and it is determined if the student can continue. Everyone do your best!"

118

The last line felt a touch out of place as Roy and Chad stared at each other from across their combat cell. The referee was watching from his post through the thickened window, along with Mr. Transport, a girl in grey who was presumably a healer, and Shane. For Roy, though, none of those people mattered. The only one of consequence was looking unconcerned and removing the jacket from his uniform, revealing a tank top scarcely hiding the chiseled physique underneath it. Chad let his arms dangle at his sides, then gave the referee the nod that he was ready. Roy followed suit, and a husky, male voice bellowed through the speaker.

"Begin!"

Roy took off charging. There was no need to draw this out: he was going to crush this blond pansy and take that number one rank as soon as possible. In a way, he felt a touch of gratitude to Mary. If she hadn't given him the idea, he might have forgotten all about the rankings in lieu of the fine tail that was wandering the campus. This was good, though. He'd win the fight, show everyone he was the best, and let Coach George know he could shove that smug concern right up his ass.

Roy didn't even slow down as he neared Chad, rearing back and clocking him with a right hook that would knock a train off course.

At least, that was what he'd planned to do.

Roy's fist whistled powerfully through the air, connecting with nothing and jerking Roy slightly off balance. Before he could recover, an open palm crashed into his jaw, sending him stumbling back and leaving stars in his eyes.

"Fuck," Roy swore. That had hurt. It had been a long time since anything had hurt, which meant that Chad wasn't all apathy and confidence. That kid had to be swinging with some significant power to make Roy feel his blows.

"This is pointless," Chad said, seemingly unmoved from the position he'd been in when Roy charged him. That was impossible, though; Roy knew he'd been dead on with his punch. Unless Chad had an ability that let them pass through him . . . "I'm sorry, but you aren't strong enough for me to waste my time fighting. I won't learn anything from beating you."

"Giving up already?" Roy asked as he drew himself to his feet.

"Walk away, Mr. Daniels," Chad said. "You've stepped into a league you're not ready for."

"Fuck you, I'm not!" Roy yelled, swinging his huge fists for Chad's midsection as he rushed forward once more. Roy missed again, but this time, he saw what happened. Chad wasn't teleporting or going insubstantial: he simply avoided the blows by a fraction of an inch, gauging the punches perfectly and placing his body in the areas where they were not. Another palm struck Roy's ear and he felt his vision blur for a moment.

"You are a mess. You telegraph your movements so clearly that anyone with a bit of training can read them. You swing wild, focusing on power instead of precision,

119

and you have literally no guard nor reflexes designed to block. You fight like what you are: an overly-strong fool who never learned how to focus his power," Chad said as Roy blinked and cleared his eyes.

"I don't need to guard from sissy shit like that," Roy spat back. "Or didn't you know? I'm tougher than a three dollar steak, Blondie."

"Spoken like a true idiot," Chad sighed. "I'll bet you didn't even bother to research my power before challenging me, did you?"

"Yeah, I know what it is," Roy responded. "You suck dick like a Hoover."

"I'm afraid not. My power is total control of my body, from the muscles that I move all the way down to my cells and the chemical composition of my skin," Chad explained.

"That's a pretty weak-ass power," Roy chuckled.

Chad's eyes narrowed slightly. "Most people would agree. Of course, most people wouldn't think of ingesting carbon and other minerals daily to make their muscles as strong as interwoven steel cables and their bones harder than diamonds. Most people underestimate how useful full control of one's mind is, of the power in being able to instantly train reflexes and increase the speed of one's perception. I assure you, it is not a weak power, and if you come at me one more time, I'll illustrate that to you personally."

Roy pulled himself up and blinked one last time to clear his eyes. "Bring it on, babycakes." Roy charged forward once more, but this time, didn't get a chance to swing his fists. Roy had barely realized it before Chad was suddenly beneath him, driving his own fist into Roy's stomach. Before the pain could fully register, Chad had taken Roy's left arm and spun it around behind him, cracking and breaking the arm loudly. Roy's feet went out from under him as Chad's hand wrapped around Roy's head and drove it crashing into the concrete. The snap of a kick was all the warning he had before he felt impact and the sensation of broken ribs. In what seemed like less than a second, Chad had utterly destroyed him.

"One last thing about my 'weak' power," Chad hissed down at Roy. "It is an inheritance from my father." Chad raised his leg until his foot was over his shoulder, then brought it crashing down on Roy's head.

32

"I must admit, I did not see this coming," Mr. Transport remarked.

"I did, eventually," Mr. Numbers admitted. "Though this is far sooner than I expected."

The duo was standing outside of the recovery ward where Roy was asleep. Mr. Transport had gone and fetched Mr. Numbers while Roy was being tended to by the healer on duty. Thanks to Roy's natural toughness and swift healing, he would be fine. Truthfully, this was, to someone with his power, the equivalent of stubbing a toe. It hurt badly when it happened, but there was relatively little actual damage done. The only concern anyone had was a fear that he would revert back to Hershel before the wounds could be treated fully.

"So Mary coaxed him into it somehow," Mr. Transport said in curiosity. Mr. Numbers had filled in Mr. Transport on the game of chess they had played during Roy's fight and the conversation that had occurred within it.

"It would appear that way," Mr. Numbers confirmed. "In all fairness, Roy is hardly the most difficult member of our dormitory to manipulate."

"Agreed," Mr. Transport said. "Still, she did an excellent job of tearing down his pride. She talked him into fighting one of the few students in the class who could utterly trounce him."

Mr. Numbers nodded his agreement. "Roy would never accept his loss in the ranking matches as a genuine failure on his part, since his opponent used mental abilities and dealt no actual damage to him. This time, though . . . this time he lost on his home turf, in the area where he was certain he reigned supreme."

"I imagine there is another stage to this plan," Mr. Transport speculated.

"Certainly," Mr. Numbers confirmed. "But it's time for us to start moving proactively on our own. Contact the dean and humbly request to put our new idea into action. Much as I may dislike the way she did it, Mary was correct in what she told me. Right now, we're dealing with pieces that don't yet see their full potential. They're reined in by their own perceived limitations."

"How do we help them with those?" Mr. Transport asked.

"For now, we delegate and see how the telepath does at handling it. If she proves unable, we will step in as needed. Our concern is not to help them with their personal demons right now, it's to get them to start looking at each other as a team, or at least as mutual assets," Mr. Numbers answered. "We need them to have a group mentality, and the sooner we achieve that, the more effective it will be."

"You're right," Mr. Transport agreed. "I do wonder if this incident will sow any dissent in the group, though. After all, Mary did essentially trick one of the team into being mercilessly beaten."

"Yes, but it was the member no one liked," Mr. Numbers pointed out. "How this is perceived by the group depends on her actions and their effects from this point on. Hopefully, she has a good plan in place."

*   *   *

"I feel achy," Hershel said as he stirred in one of the oh-so-very uncomfortable recovery room beds.

"Roy was beaten pretty severely," Mary said from her vigilant perch on a stool next to the bed. She had never left Roy's side since he was brought here, and when he shifted back into Hershel, she had stayed by his side as well.

"I remember," Hershel said, pulling himself up to a sitting position. "That last kick was a doozy."

"Yes indeed," Mary agreed. "They removed all the physical damage, though. What you're feeling now is essentially residual impulses from the nerves that know there should be pain and recovery in a certain area, even though there isn't."

"Hey, I'm not complaining," Hershel said quickly. "Compared to what he did to Roy, this is some pretty minor soreness."

"Yes . . . well . . . I'm sorry about that," Mary said slowly. "I knew it would be rough, but it was the only way."

Hershel leaned forward a bit, wishing he was the sort of person who was confident enough to rest a hand on her shoulder when trying to reassure her. "None of that. You gave both Roy and me ample warning about what would happen. Roy was too stubborn to listen, and this is what I was hoping for. I mean, he was pretty groggy at the end, but I could already feel the hammer blow to his pride from that fight. Plus, he lost the bet. You did the right thing."

"I know," Mary said with a small nod of the head. "That doesn't always make it the easy thing, though. I hate seeing people get hurt."

"Well, then, let's make sure it wasn't in vain," Hershel replied. "I assume you have some sort of plan now that Roy has to listen to you?"

"Oh yes, indeed I do," Mary said, a small grin tugging at the corner of her mouth. "Roy will remember this conversation, correct?"

"Yup. We share memories of when the other is in control," Hershel confirmed.

"Good," Mary said. "Then listen well, you arrogant moron, because as of now, you belong to me. So let's go over just what you'll be doing for the rest of the year."

Even though Hershel knew she was no longer speaking directly to him, the tone of her voice and the glint in her eye compelled him to gulp. Later on, when Roy woke up and remembered the conversation, he would reflect that for once he and Hershel were in agreement.

33

"Welcome, class. If you would take your seats quickly, we have much to cover today," Dean Blaine said as the students filed into Tuesday's Ethics of Heroism class. Nick moved briskly, taking his seat and sliding into his usual defensive posture. It said that he was bored, but not so much so that he wasn't paying attention. It conveyed respect without conveying interest, and all in all, served the purpose of making him blend into the sea of faces. Nick might have been considered lacking by some in the power department, but the skills he did possess were honed and polished.

Sitting comfortably in his cocoon of apathetic camouflage, Nick allowed his eyes to wander around the room. He hadn't seen much of his dormmates this weekend, but then again, he'd spent a lot of time working on a business model for one of his real life classes. Of course, he had heard about Roy's sounding defeat at Chad's hands—that one had spread like wildfire—but he hadn't had a chance to catch up on the nitty-gritty details with Hershel. As for Vince, he hadn't come home until Sunday night, and despite Nick's respectable arsenal of wheedling techniques, he had refused to divulge any details of his weekend. Not that Nick couldn't string things together on his own, but it was always so much more satisfying to coax a secret from someone's lips.

"Class," Dean Blaine said once everyone was sitting in their chairs. "Today, I introduce you to what will ultimately culminate in the grade for your mid-term exam." Nick could actually hear necks pop as they swiveled forward in a sudden burst of attention. "You will all be participating in research projects, and in one month you will make a presentation to the class as well as turn in a twenty-page paper."

"I thought we weren't going to have papers in this class?" The speaker was the girl with tightly pulled-back braids, or Stella Hawkins, as Nick had learned since the first day of class. In all the weeks since then, she had never raised her hand once when asking a question, driving Alice to grind her teeth, but not even denting Dean Blaine's plastered-on grin.

Well, that was usually the case at any rate. Today, Stella's question triggered a slight twitch in Dean Blaine's right cheek. Nick was confident no one else would have noticed it, but to him, it was plain as day. That meant he wasn't as sure-footed on the topic of this project, or that there was something about it that made him uncomfortable. It wasn't much, and Nick wasn't sure what to do with it, but it was something, and something didn't mean nothing. Nick trained his complete attention on the now-speaking dean.

"That is generally the policy," Dean Blaine replied, no trace of the tremor from his face audible in his voice. "However, this is something of a special project. It will be a team project, one to help you all branch out and better get to know your fellow classmates. It will be on the full career of a Hero from the list I'll be hanging on the board. I want you to trace them from their training, their career path, and their retirement. Yes, Miss Adair?"

Alice's hand had been up since halfway through the dean's explanation, and it seemed she was a few seconds short of waving it around like an elementary school student to demand his attention. "How is this applicable from an ethics standpoint? This seems more like a history project."

"As I was explaining before you put your hand up," Dean Blaine replied curtly, "this project will trace the life of a famous Hero. While I do want you to spend some time discussing the major events in their life, the real purpose of this project is to look over some of their exploits from a more personal level. Look at some of the foes they dealt with and some of the battles they lost. Your goal is to help me, and the rest of your class, understand the motivations and complications of the person behind the mask."

"How does that help us with ethics?" Stella belted from the back of the room.

"Think of it as advanced preparation. I want you to see what these people went through, because a Hero's life is often fraught with hard choices and living with the consequences of them. By digging deep and understanding choices that past Heroes have made, I hope you will ask yourself what decisions you would have made in similar circumstances," Dean Blaine explained. "Because one day, those life and death decisions could be on your shoulders, and it's best to start preparing for them sooner, rather than later."

Dean Blaine braced himself for more questions as his explanation finished, but the somber subject matter seemed to have cowed even Stella. It wasn't surprising; after all, when one thought about becoming a Hero, one usually focused on the glory and pride that came with defending the innocent. Rarely did people stop and consider the responsibility that came along with the job, where the direction in which to punch a villain could result in a building full of people losing their lives.

"Okay then," Dean Blaine said, making a snap judgment to steer the thoughts of his class toward less chilling waters. "I'll now announce the pairs for the projects. You will have the rest of the class to discuss possible Heroes from the list I'll be posting in a minute, and the two of you have until the end of the week to let me know your pick. Don't hesitate, though. They are first come, first serve, and each Hero may only be done by one team."

Dean Blaine produced a piece of paper and began calling out pairs of students. As each team was named, the duo would rise from their seats and flag each other down from their respective positions, stopping only when one relocated to the other's area. Nick tried not to center too much on disappointment. If the list was already chosen, then he couldn't use his power to affect the outcome. If he had known and had blasted out some luck during its creation, the situation would have been different, but luck was only applicable to objects in motion. No amount of luck changed the dice roll once the results were written down. It would have been beneficial for Nick to land on Hershel or Vince's team and solidify the sense of friendship he had been crafting with them, but as Hershel was announced to be paired with someone named Alex, and Vince was put with Will Murray, it became clear that Nick would be expanding his social circle. It could be worse, though; increased connections were rarely a bad thing.

"Next team," Dean Blaine announced. "Nicholas Campbell and Alice Adair."

"At least it's not the telepath," Nick mumbled under his breath. Humorously enough, Alice was muttering approximately the same thing from her own desk across the room. The two began the dance of waving, determining who would move over to the other's area, neither one particularly excited about their partner, but each confident they hadn't gotten the shortest stick in the room.

Many might have believed that dubious honor went to Hershel, who drew up a seat next to his new partner.

"Hi," Hershel said. "I'm Hershel Daniels."

"Oh, I know," said the sandy-haired boy. "I heard all about the fight this weekend. I'm Alex, though. Alex Griffen."

"Nice to meet you, Alex," Hershel said. "So, I guess you already know about Roy then?"

"Totally," Alex said, nodding enthusiastically. "Seems like an awesome ability, turning into someone crazy strong and tough."

"It's . . . not as great as one might suspect," Hershel said delicately. He was hesitant to badmouth Roy at the moment. Roy had attended gym the day before, but he'd been different from usual: less proud, certainly, but less sure of himself as well. Hershel knew better than most what that was like, so the last thing he wanted to do was pile abuse onto his recovering alter ego. "It can be fun, though, and it's rarely boring. What about you, Alex? What's your power?"

"Nothing too exciting," Alex replied. "I'm basically a Jedi."

125

34

"Looks like we got Everest," Vince said, striding into the library and depositing his books on a small table occupied by a short boy wearing glasses.

"That's great!" Will, also known as the short boy wearing glasses, exclaimed. "I thought for sure someone would have beaten us to him."

"When I spoke with the dean, he told me we were the third team to make our selection," Vince replied, taking his seat and spreading out the books. "I guess the others are taking their sweet time in picking a subject."

"Who else had been chosen?" Will asked as he unloaded the contents of his own backpack onto the table, cluttering it even further.

"Apparently Shane and some Amber girl took Captain Starlight, and Doc Nominal was chosen by guys named Gilbert and Adam," Vince recounted. Fortunately, there hadn't been many names on the sign-up sheet, so the few that were present were easy to recall.

"Oh, I know Gilbert," Will said. "He and I are in the same physics class together above ground. Good guy, if a bit of a slacker on studying. No one else though, huh? I was sure that Alice girl who is always asking questions would be first in line."

"That's not an unfair assumption," Vince admitted. "She's working with Nick, though. I don't think they exactly dislike one another, but they never seem to talk much. Then again, I don't think any of us really talk a lot with Alice, except in passing."

"She doesn't seem like she would lack social skills," Will observed.

"No, she doesn't. Really the opposite," Vince said thoughtfully. "She's always polite and composed. I guess in the whirlwind of the first few weeks, we just haven't had time to get to know one another."

"I imagine that's the case with many of us," Will said. "In fact, it's possible that's why Dean Blaine gave us this project in the first place. It does force us to expand our social circles a bit."

"You might be right," Vince agreed. "Though, that still doesn't explain what's holding up Alice and Nick on choosing a Hero for their project."

*　　　*　　　*

"I respectfully disagree," Alice said through a thin mask of patience. "I think Lord Pholos will make an excellent case of study for our project, and is not a 'bore in a cape' at all."

"Oh, come on," Nick replied, spinning his chair in a circle and staring up at the ceiling. "Do you know what Lord Pholos was before he got into the game? A manager for a paper clip company. Seriously, how could he possibly be more boring?"

"Maybe the fact that he was one of the few older men who became certified as a Hero is, in itself, an interesting story," Alice retorted.

126

"Great story, that one. He was born in a family that had religious disagreements with the existence of Supers, so he was raised to pretend he was human. Then his wife leaves him at thirty, his normal world falls apart, and he escapes into a new one, one where he can use his powers to have the fame and respect that eluded him in his younger years," Nick returned.

"That's . . . well . . . it's still . . . fine," Alice spat out bitterly.

The two of them had been at it for some time now, camped out in the common room of Melbrook, Alice making suggestions and Nick spearing holes in them. He had to admit, she'd picked a few that would have actually made exceptional projects, and that was the problem. Nick didn't want to be exceptional; he wanted to coast though this presentation with a middle-of-the-pack Hero that would earn him a middle-of-the-pack grade. Since Alice didn't know this, though, he was forced to play his character in an alternate direction. Instead of showing that he wanted an average presentation and grade, Nick was making himself out to be a perfectionist and knocking down any Hero suggestion that wasn't "good enough" for him and Alice to work on.

Nick was also finding a slight bit of amusement in watching Alice vainly try to conceal her mounting frustration. How this girl had ever gotten the impression she was skilled in hiding her emotions and manipulating people was beyond Nick's impressive comprehension.

"Okay," Alice said after a moment to gather her composure. "Let's see what other options there are." She pulled out the Xeroxed list that Dean Blaine had provided each group, showing which Heroes were available for them to choose from. "How about The K?"

"Retired too young."

"Alphablaster?"

"Honestly? You want us to do a report on someone with vocabulary based powers?"

Alice had to admit, even to her, that one seemed pretty bad. "Well, what about Everest?" Alice asked.

"Perfect," Nick replied.

"Really?"

"Totally," Nick confirmed. "But Vince already texted me and told me that's the one he and his partner got approved to do."

"But . . . then, why didn't you . . ." Alice began to stammer.

"Oh, relax," Nick assured her. "We'll find someone good."

"Well . . . well, I'm done!" Alice declared, dumping the pages in Nick's lap and stopping his slow, circular turning. "You pick the next one and let's see if I think *your* choice is good enough."

Nick scooped up the pages and pretended to look through them. The truth was, he had memorized this list before he and Alice had even left Dean Blaine's classroom for gym. It had taken Alice a bit longer to break than he'd expected, but the disintegration of one's pride was always difficult to apply a realistic time frame to. She'd finally defaulted to the princess he knew lurked inside that socialite facade, though, and that meant he could get a topic chosen and be done with it.

"Ozarell lived an interesting life," Nick remarked offhandedly.

"Interesting enough?" Alice asked, crossing her arms and setting her jaw.

"There's always Lickotaur," Nick ventured once more.

Alice did nothing but raise an eyebrow.

"Okay, look," Nick said in his best I'm-being-humbled-by-this-experience voice. "It seems like you and I both have different ideas on who we should pick for this project. Agreed?"

Alice slowly nodded her head.

"But the one thing we can both agree on is that if we don't pick someone soon, we're likely to end up with nothing but the dregs left as our options," Nick continued the train of thought.

"That's not entirely impossible," Alice acquiesced.

"So, rather than bickering back and forth all day, why don't we try a different method to pick our subject?" Nick asked.

"Just a wild guess here, you already have such a method in mind?" Alice asked, not bothering to mask her sarcasm.

"That I do," Nick said, breezing right past the accusation in her words. Instead, he set the list down on the coffee table and produced a penny from his pocket. "Let's flip a coin on it."

"Like what, heads or tails on each name systematically as a veto system until we narrow it down to one name?"

"No, that would take forever," Nick chided. "I mean literally. I'll flip the penny and whatever name it lands on is the one we use."

"That is utterly ridiculous," Alice replied without hesitation.

"But more productive than fighting all afternoon," Nick pointed out. "Besides, it isn't as dumb as it seems. Remember, my power is controlling luck. If I max out my good luck in this situation, then the penny should land on the best option for us."

"Uh huh," Alice scoffed skeptically. "And after less than a year of control, you think you can use your abilities for something that abstract?"

"Well, I haven't tested it," Nick lied, "but theoretically, it should be possible. What's it hurt to try at least?"

"Fine," Alice said, after a calculating pause. "I reserve the right to veto whoever it lands on if I don't like it, though."

"I'll agree to that, as long as we look them up and give them a thorough once-over," Nick said. Alice gave him a nod, and with sudden dexterity, he flipped the small, copper coin into the air. As soon as it was out of his hand, he focused himself and poured his luck into the coin, willing it to come down on the best possible result. He was careful to breathe deep and do other mild physical gestures that the others hadn't picked up on yet. Nick had spent weeks before coming here creating fake tells that would crop up whenever he used his powers. The only real tell was difficult to miss, so he'd been fastidious in drawing attention away with the decoys.

The penny tumbled down onto the list, landing squarely on a single name. Alice and Nick both leaned over and looked down at the printed page tucked beneath the coin.

Nick let out a low whistle. "Man, talk about the dregs."

*   *   *

"So, you're a telepath?" Hershel asked.

"Nah, man. Jedi," Alex said once more. "You know, like the order of space knights created in films by the great George Lucas." The two of them were in a cafeteria getting dinner and discussing options for their project. In the course of the day, Hershel had found that he had a surprising amount in common with his new project partner, including a love of sci-fi, video games, and vintage comic books. The one sticking point he kept coming back to was Alex's power, or at least, Alex's description of the power.

"You can move things with your mind, and pick up thoughts and emotions, right?" Hershel asked.

"I know this sounds crazy, but to me, it feels like I move things with the Force, not my mind. Other than that, you're pretty close," Alex agreed with a cheerful head nod. "Plus, I can sort of do the mind trick."

"The one where you put thoughts into weak or unfocused minds? That's the Jedi mind trick you're talking about?" Hershel tried to clarify.

"Yeah. I can make it work about ten percent of the time," Alex confirmed.

"So, one out of ten times you try to tell someone to do something and they do it?"

"Eventually," Alex said.

"You do realize that sounds a lot like a telepath and telekinetic," Hershel said carefully. "Not like the abilities of practitioners of a religion from a science fiction movie."

"Yeah, but it's not," Alex said simply. "I know what you're thinking, I've heard it since I was a kid. Every teacher and coach my parents hired to help me hone my powers tried to convince me it was my mind doing this stuff, not the Force."

"And they were unsuccessful, I take it," Hershel noted.

"They were unsuccessful because they were wrong. If I try to focus my mind and make even a pencil move, nothing happens. But if I reach out to it with the Force, I

129

can juggle weights and golf carts. I know myself, and I know my power. Maybe it's because I've always seen it a certain way and it's too late to change, but in my head, I'm a Jedi," Alex said once more, not forcefully, but with a sense of deep conviction and confidence.

So, there it was. Alex considered his powers to work as though he were a Jedi and would not budge one bit on the topic. It was an oddity, but then again, Hershel loved dressing up like an elf lord and defending his castle. If anyone should be able to understand sculpting one's own reality, it was him. Besides, it seemed likely that state of mind and perception were important for someone whose powers were linked to their brain.

"A real Jedi, huh? That's pretty cool," Hershel said, smiling and picking up the ketchup for his fries. "Anyway, who do you think we should do our project on?"

35

"Oh dear," Will said, gazing at the glowing screen of his cell phone. "It seems I'll have to cut our study session short today."

"That's fine," Vince assured him. "I think we got a lot of good material for the project so far. We can pick up here tomorrow."

"I appreciate your understanding," Will said with a smile. He reached across the table and began scooping books and notes into his backpack.

"Did something come up?" Vince asked.

"You could say that. It seems my sister has been challenged to a ranking match, so I feel a bit compelled to be there in support," Will explained.

"I didn't know you had a sister," Vince commented, packing away his own things. If Will was heading out, Vince felt he may as well do the same. He could get back above ground, grab some dinner, maybe even see Sasha for a bit before he tackled the rest of his work for the evening.

"Her name is Jill. It is purely speculation, but I've always believed our parents must have been sadists to give twins rhyming names," Will said.

"It's not really that bad," Vince lied. Will stopped packing, looked Vince in the eyes, and stared. "Okay, it's pretty bad," Vince said, breaking after mere seconds.

"I know," Will said simply, readying himself to leave. Vince was about finished as well, so they exited the library together and began walking toward the lifts and combat cells. The two had been holed up in the underground library, which was similar to the one on the regular campus, but stocked with a somewhat different selection of reading material. Very few normal Lander students found themselves in need of books on how to deal with radioactive fallout, or the study of ancient war formation techniques. In the HCP, though, such things were considered required reading.

"Sooo," Vince said, awkwardness and a poor understanding of social convention forcing him to make small talk. "What are your sister's abilities?"

"She manipulates technology," Will answered.

"Like, she can turn on cars, or like she can become the Internet?"

"Somewhere in between," Will chuckled. "She can interface with software, but only to a limited point. If you asked her to type on a computer without her hands, or drive a car from a block away, those things would be in her arsenal. Asking her to hack into the Pentagon would be well out of her reach, though. It's like she talks to the machines and asks them nicely to cooperate."

"That seems pretty useful," Vince said. "As long as you have plenty of tech around."

"At that point, having a brother whose power is mechanical genius comes in rather handy," Will said.

"Yeah, I've seen some of the stuff you use in class. The self-writing pen seemed pretty awesome," Vince said.

Will shrugged. "It frees up my hands and lets me get written notes. The hardest part was designing it so it could balance continuously on the tip while moving."

"I bet," Vince agreed. "With you building her gadgets, and her being able to use them with a thought, I bet your sister is one dynamite fighter."

"She's good, but there are plenty better," Will admitted. "She only came in fourteenth in the initial ranking. Of course, as the gear I build for her improves, and she learns to fight more effectively, I expect to see a significant rise in her ranks over the years."

"I'm sure you will," Vince encouraged. "What about your rank, though?"

"I'm not combat compatible," Will replied with open honesty. "I can build things ahead of the technological curve. There are some who don't even believe that should count me as a Super. I'll certainly never be able to match what the others can do on the front line of battle. I'll have my uses, though. They just won't be gauged on how well I throw a punch."

"If you're focused on the rhino charging at you, you're likely to miss the panther sneaking up on your rear," Vince said.

Will raised his eyebrows curiously.

"It's something my father used to say. It meant I should learn to use misdirection and keep myself aware at all times, but it seemed sort of applicable to your situation," Vince explained. "Just because you aren't a thick-skinned, muscle-bound monster doesn't mean you aren't dangerous."

"True," Will said slowly. "Although, I still feel my place on the battlefield is supporting others in the background."

"Maybe it is," Vince agreed. "All that really matters is that you're happy with what you're doing and where you're going."

"And I am," Will said as they walked into the central hall. Vince saw the lifts at the south end and readied himself to head back above ground. Before he left, though, a question struck him.

"I hope your sister does well today," Vince said. "Who is she fighting, anyway?"

"One of the girls she shares a suite with. A friend named Sasha," Will told him. "She has pink streaks in her hair and super speed. Very difficult to miss."

Vince was in whole-hearted agreement as he changed his direction and began walking next to Will once more, mind already racing ahead of him to the fight that was beginning in the combat cells.

36

Ever since Vince had first met Sasha that first day in the infirmary, she had been perpetually light-hearted. Her emotional range seemed to consist of sassy, flirty, and spunky. This wasn't to say she never had her down moments, just that she seemed to carry everything, even sadness, with a strange sense of cheerful apathy, as though nothing mattered too much, like none of it could really touch her.

The girl Vince was gazing at through the observation window looked nothing like the one he had grown close to over the previous weeks. Oh, her face and hair were the same, as was her uniform, but the girl herself was utterly different. Gone was the smirk hidden in the angles of her face, the carefree posture, and the easy manner with which she moved. Her eyes were hard now, and focused. Every step she took as she and her opponent positioned themselves for the fight to come was calculated, careful, and delicate. It struck a memory within Vince of when he and his father had snuck into a zoo, and Vince had gotten to see a pair of tigers. Sasha shared their same rippling gait, smooth and deliberate, but able to attack at any moment.

The other girl in the cell, Jill, didn't seem to be taking things any lighter. She was a girl of medium height with chopped-short, dirty-blonde hair. Instead of the standard uniform, Jill was sporting something that looked a lot like a one-piece flight suit, except with baubles and electronics bulging out at random intervals. As the girls moved to their starting sides of the cell, Jill took a helmet she had carried in her arms and slipped it over her head, obscuring any sign of her face behind a black visor. Outside gear had to approved, but so long as it corresponded to your power, it was permitted in official matches.

"I see they're taking each other quite seriously," Will commented. He and Vince were standing together to watch the fight, making sure to give the referee and a small girl who was presumably the healer ample room in which to act if necessary.

"Yeah," Vince agreed. "They are."

"Is Sasha your girlfriend?" Will asked bluntly. If either one had been paying more attention, they might have noticed the sudden swivel of the small girl's head toward their direction. Both had eyes only for what was on the other side of the glass, though, so her action went unobserved.

"Sort of. We haven't really talked about it or anything, but . . . yeah, pretty much," Vince said.

"I hope that we can maintain our affable partnership, regardless of the outcome of this fight," Will said.

Vince hesitated before he answered, "You think Jill's going to win, don't you?"

"I don't know," Will replied. "I built the suit she's wearing, and I am very well-informed of my sister's capabilities in combat, but when dealing with super speed, nothing is written in stone."

As the girls readied themselves, waiting for the referee's signal to start, Vince silently agreed with Will. Both of them seemed intensely focused on this match, and he didn't know which of them would be walking away from it. He doubted they did either.

"I don't have to take this personally, if you don't," Vince said. "After all, this isn't a squabble. They're trying themselves against one another as warriors. Whoever loses, there's no shame here."

"Agreed," Will said. "Though, I'd keep that little theory away from whichever actually does lose."

"Duh," Vince said with a nod of his head. Vince was young, foolhardy, and ambitious. That didn't make him utterly idiotic, though.

The referee pressed a small button and the dean's recorded voice began to play from within the cell. When it concluded, their match would begin. "Be ready," he said to the small girl at his side. "This one could easily end messy."

*   *   *

Sasha adjusted her footing without taking her eyes off Jill. The proverbial bell had been rung, yet both of them stood steady, neither rushing forward to make the first move. Sasha adjusted again, wishing dearly that Jill's head wasn't hidden behind a helmet and visor. It wasn't that Sasha was so cutthroat that she would have gone for the face or eyes (not to say that she wouldn't, though), it was that blocking the face took away a lot of unconscious tells. Eye movements, facial tics, even nostril flaring could often be that little extra advantage that meant the difference between a win and a loss.

Sasha took a step forward, then one back, gauging Jill's reaction. Her opponent moved back a hair, but otherwise, kept her same stance. So that meant Jill was playing defensive, waiting for Sasha to make the first move. It was the smart play, the one Sasha would have made if the roles were reversed. Charging someone with super speed was a good way to go down fast. You fully commit to an attack, and before you realize it, they've moved out of the way and turned your own momentum against you.

It seemed Sasha was stuck on the offensive. That was okay, though; it was the area Sasha was the most comfortable in anyway. Choosing an angle, Sasha accelerated into a blur and demolished the gap between her and Jill. She didn't make contact with her, though, instead, opting to ring around her twice before coming to a stop at her rear. Jill was half turned when Sasha halted. Sasha spat a curse under her breath. Jill's reaction time was good, and that meant once she attacked, there was a possibility Jill could counter with whatever gizmos were hidden up her sleeves. Super speed was a wonderful gift, but its weakness was that it was hard to aim precisely when going several hundred miles an hour. Sure, Sasha's perceptions were sped up somewhat—otherwise, she'd

134

never be able to maneuver with her talent—but there were limits. They increased proportionally: in the same way that it would be hard for a regular person to do something precise while he or she was running full speed, Sasha was bound by the same obstacle. If she wanted to do more than swing wild, she'd need to slow down significantly when she made her attack.

It wasn't ideal, but Sasha had picked this partner. She'd issued this challenge. It would move her up five ranks, into the range where she'd be eligible for combat. She narrowed her eyes slightly, clearly betraying her intention to attack. It didn't matter. If Jill could keep up, then she would; if she couldn't, then no amount of warning from Sasha would make the difference. It escaped her own thoughts that mere moments earlier she had been thinking about the advantages of reading facial tics, but before that realization could bob to the surface of her mind, she was already running again.

Sasha didn't bolt in directly; that would have been ludicrous. Instead, she circled Jill, drawing progressively closer, then pulling back. She pulled a few feints, seeing how quickly Jill reacted to her advances. The closer she got, though, the more confident Sasha grew. Jill was close on her blocks, but not quite there. If Sasha had followed through on one of her punches, she would have definitely made contact. Sasha looped around again, this time, committing to her attack mentally. She would pull up short and let loose a flurry of super-fast punches. Even if Jill did manage to block one, the other fist would gain momentum and connect at least five times before Jill would be able to react. Sasha put in one last bolt forward, then pulled back on the metaphorical throttle and let fly at Jill with both hands.

Those who were blessed with super speed had been given a significant measure of durability along with that gift. As such, their bodies could withstand moving and stopping at such high speeds. It meant that Sasha could punch flesh and bone with tremendous momentum and only suffer minimal damage herself. While it didn't work against harder materials, steel for example, she could easily handle regular combat. So when Sasha's fists connected with Jill's ribs, she felt a sense of elation that she'd gotten her blows through without Jill even coming close to blocking either hand. A millisecond after that, it dawned on her that Jill hadn't even tried to block. She might have speculated more about why as she continued to punch Jill if that had been an option, but unfortunately, that's when Sasha's time ran out.

That next millisecond, you see, was when the pain started.

*   *   *

"What happened?" Vince cried as Sasha violently flew back from Jill and into the concrete wall.

"She electrified her suit at the moment of impact, giving your girl a devastating shock," Will said, his voice even, but his tone not entirely hiding the distress he felt in his own stomach.

135

"She can do that?" Vince asked, eyes on Sasha's crumpled, twitching form.

"It was the only option she ever really had," Will confirmed. "Sasha was too fast for Jill to have a hope of hitting her with any other kind of weapon. The best bet she had was to use herself as bait and strike when Sasha made contact. It was a good idea, but it wasn't without its risks."

For the first time, Vince let his eyes move away from Sasha and back to her opponent. Jill was hunched over; he could tell from the movement of her back that she was breathing with arduous labor.

"My sister put all of the suit's power into that jolt," Will continued. "That means the electronic shields and dampeners were shut down. She took Sasha's blows full on and left herself completely vulnerable."

"I think her ribs are broken," Vince noted, a fresh note of empathic concern in his voice.

"At the least. She has no physical powers, so those blows affected her just like any other human. She should be okay for now, but I'd be distressed if the end of this match weren't in sight," Will admitted, gesturing to the referee.

Vince looked over, and realized the referee was methodically counting down from ten, eyes locked on Sasha's fallen form. If she couldn't get up before zero, this bout would be over and the girls could get healed. Vince actually felt a rush of relief as the referee dropped past the count of three. It sucked that Sasha lost, but right now, his mind was solely fixated on getting to her and making sure she was okay. When the referee's hand struck the number two, though, the counting stopped. If that hadn't told him enough, the gasp from Will made the picture clear before Vince could turn to the window and see it.

Sure enough, Sasha was clawing her way up the concrete wall with one hand, slowly dragging herself vertical. The significance of this wasn't lost on anyone watching, least of all her opponent. Without hesitation, Jill threw her hands up, signaling her surrender and the end of the match. With twin sighs of relief, Vince and Will bounded down the stairs to the door, eager to make sure everyone was all right.

136

37

"I heard through the grapevine that Ms. Foster advanced her ranking this week," Mr. Numbers said as he moved his knight.

"Are we calling the weekly logs you get of all combat trials 'the grapevine' now?" Mary asked as she began contemplating her next move.

"Touché," Mr. Numbers replied. The two were sitting in the common room early Saturday morning. Thus far, they were the only two up and around, save for Mr. Transport, who was off running errands. As soon as Mr. Numbers had stepped out of his room, Mary had been waiting, chessboard in hand. So, after a cup of coffee, Mr. Numbers had accepted her challenge and the duo had begun their second game of chess. Mr. Numbers took a sip of his coffee as Mary made her next move.

"I notice you're using both rooks normally this time," he commented.

"He's been fixed," Mary answered to the unasked question.

"Has he now," Mr. Numbers mumbled, measuring the board to plan his retaliation. "I also heard through the grapevine that Mr. Daniels's attitude has improved tremendously since his bout with Mr. Taylor. It seems he is punctual when attending gym and attentive to everything Coach George says to him. The only curious habit is that whenever he is running, he makes strange hand motions."

"Motions similar to the ones learned in the foundation of a martial art? Say, ones that a person might work on constantly if they were trying to ingrain the movements as reflex in their brain, for example?" Mary asked.

"Precisely those," Mr. Numbers confirmed.

"How odd," Mary said neutrally. "It's your move."

"I'm aware," Mr. Numbers said, shifting one of his pawns. "I take it you and your dormmates will be meeting up with your partners to work on your projects today?"

"Hershel might. He and Alex have been eating together ever since they were paired up," Mary said. "If I recall correctly, Vince and Nick are spending the day watching a movie marathon in the boys' lounge, then Vince is celebrating Sasha's victory with her tonight."

"You seem very well-informed of your dormmates' plans. And Alice?"

"Alice is going to contemplate many options, then ultimately spend her day sulking over the fact that she has no one to spend time with, despite the fact that her own fear of intimacy with others is the driving force behind that," Mary told him, moving her queen.

"You could always try to break through that fear and befriend her," Mr. Numbers pointed out.

137

"Others could. I'm too much, too soon for her—like dropping an aqua-phobic in the middle of the ocean. Befriending a telepath won't challenge her personal limitations and obsession for privacy, it will shatter them. Maybe one day, though. I think I would like that," Mary said.

"I see," Mr. Numbers said, moving his knight once more in order to set a trap. "So, which chess piece will you be fixing next?"

"Well, the others are a bit more complicated," Mary responded. "The bishop is easily as strong as the rook, albeit in a different way, but, unlike the rook, he's afraid of his own strength. The knight doesn't understand that just because she isn't as outwardly dangerous as the other pieces, doesn't mean she is useless. And, of course, the king doesn't see that his role is as a strategist, maybe even a leader. Instead, he is stuck on the perception of himself as vulnerable and weaker than anyone else on the board." Mary moved her king to illustrate the point, going back and forth along the rear row as she had throughout the entire game.

"And the queen?" Mr. Numbers asked as he repressed at smile at Mary moving directly into his trap. She was an utter amateur, but a part of him still took a beat of pride away from every victory, regardless of its challenge or relevance.

"The queen is a very powerful piece," Mary said. "But she's not so strong that she can stand against the other army by herself."

"Indeed," Mr. Numbers agreed. "Checkmate."

"So it is," Mary noted. "Next week?"

"Not in the mood for another?"

"One total loss a week is all I can handle, I'm afraid," Mary said with a soft smile. "Besides, I think the rest of my day just became a lot fuller."

*   *   *

Alice didn't hear Mary's declaration; she had already stormed off to her room. Having woken earlier than usual, Alice was on her way into the common room so she could get water from the kitchen when she realized she could vaguely overhear Mr. Numbers and Mary having a conversation. Never one to pass up the opportunity to gather information, Alice had planted herself on the other side of the wall and strained to catch every word. When talk had turned to her, though, and Mary had called out—so perfectly—exactly what her plans were and why they involved no other people, Alice had all but stomped back into her bedroom, slamming the door and sitting down on her bed. She had been fuming ever since, her pride battling against her rationale as she tried to make peace with the things Mary had said, a mental tornado that could only settle down on the trailer of one logical conclusion.

By the time Alice reached it, Mary had been waiting for nearly half an hour.

38

Two crisp knocks signaled Alice's arrival at Mary's door. Mary got up from her bed slowly and walked over to answer it. Of course, she could have just waited outside in the girls' lobby, or been waiting by the door when Alice knocked, but that would have made her foreknowledge of the arrival just a bit too apparent. While Alice was by no means simple enough to think Mary didn't have some inclination she was coming, she didn't want to talk about or acknowledge it. And Mary was respecting those wishes; after all, Alice was here to offer something of an olive branch, so it was the least Mary could do.

"Yes?" Mary said as she pulled open her door.

"I'm heading into town today for some light shopping and lunch. Would you like to come along?" Alice asked, not without some stiffness in her voice.

"I'd love to," Mary replied with a warm grin. She stepped out and closed the door firmly behind her. "When do we leave?"

"Immediately," Alice said, glossing over the fact that Mary had physically responded to the answer before even asking the question. It was to be expected with a telepath. She'd known this when she decided to invite Mary along. It was part of the package, part of spending a day with a girl who could read her thoughts. Mary had been right about Alice avoiding her, and about her having trouble connecting with people at college, but Mary had taken it too far when she said that Alice would be unable to make friends with a mind reader. The fact that Mary had been basing her deduction on Alice's actions, and that it was a completely logical conclusion, became utterly irrelevant in the face of one all-consuming truth that had burned its way through Alice's wounded pride and hidden shame:

No one told Alice Adair what she was or wasn't able to do.

"Let's hurry," Alice said. "The restaurant I'd like to visit fills up early for lunch, so it's best if we're there as soon as possible."

"Of course," Mary nodded in agreement.

*   *   *

"What's on the docket?" Vince asked as he stepped into the boys' lounge, fresh bowl of popcorn in one hand and a pair of sodas in the other.

"*Zombie Prince 4, War Zombies 2, Hellsong: The Rise of the Zombie King,* and *How to Lose a Guy in 10 Days,*" Nick said from his perch in a recliner, remote in hand and eyes fixed on the slowly loading screen.

"Should I even ask about the last one?"

"Hey man, that's a good film, and it provides excellent insight into the female perception of romance," Nick defended.

Vince sat down in the recliner next to Nick's and put the popcorn on a table between them, sliding over one soda as well. "I'm not buying it."

"Okay, fine. The girl at the video store was hot, and I didn't want her to think my cinematic taste was one-dimensional," Nick sighed.

"Despite the fact that it clearly is," Vince pointed out.

"Hey man, you don't know me entirely. Maybe I like romantic comedies. I could be very multi-layered," Nick said.

Vince crunched a kernel of popcorn and kicked his seat into the reclined position. "I'll believe it when I see it. So, where's Hershel, anyway?"

Nick shrugged. "I think he and his project partner were grabbing lunch after doing some work this morning. They said they might stop in."

"Those guys are really determined to do well on that assignment, aren't they?" Vince asked.

"That, or they have nothing better to do," Nick said. "Though, I don't see the rush. We've still got weeks left. We should be spending more time thinking about which Halloween costumes we should be saving for or working on."

Vince snorted. "We're in college. You really think anyone actually cares about Halloween, let alone puts in effort on a costume?"

*   *   *

"I'm leaning toward Cleopatra," Alice said as she sipped her espresso delicately. "Of course, there are a few famous Victorian characters I would enjoy portraying as well, but the drawing point is also the problem. Those gowns are so complex and elegant, and while they would be fun to wear, it would hardly be in the spirit of the holiday at our age."

"How so?" Mary asked politely. It had been a bit of a straining day for her so far. The lunch had been delicious and Alice was enjoyable enough company, but Mary wasn't used to asking clarifying questions or pretending she didn't already know the answers to things she might idly wonder. This habit of feigning ignorance was helping Alice feel more at ease with their time together, but it was at the cost of Mary's nerves.

"For girls our age attending a university, the accepted societal convention is that our costumes should be somewhat more . . . sensual than they were in our younger years," Alice replied.

"So we're supposed to dress slutty?"

"I prefer to think of it as we can get away with doing so judgment free," Alice said, a blatant smirk creeping across the side of her mouth.

"That is a good point," Mary agreed. "Although, I don't know if it would fit my style. I was thinking I'd just be a mummy or something."

Alice looked at the girl sitting across the table from her, slowly working her way through a piece of cheesecake, and realized something that had never entered her mind before. Mary was insecure about the way she looked. She'd always been so cheerily bizarre, so oddly confident, and seemed to be three steps ahead of everyone else that it had never occurred to Alice that a girl like Mary might suffer from something as mundane as a poor body image. It wasn't that she was unattractive, either: her amber eyes were striking, and her wild hair actually seemed to compliment her face. She was petite, too. It was easy to forget with the powerful energy Mary seemed to exude, but she was only about five foot two, with a lithe body that matched. In that moment, discovering her terrifying, invincible, telepathic neighbor had a weakness, Alice felt something she had never genuinely expected. She felt a spark of a connection to Mary.

"A mummy might be fun," Alice said kindly. "I bet we can find something that flatters you more than that, though."

Mary raised an eyebrow. "You want to go costume shopping?"

"Why not? I said we would go shopping anyway, and besides, it's early October, so the stores should be open. We'll have fun." Alice gave Mary a sincere smile, and with a crash, Mary realized she had just maneuvered herself into spending a Saturday being dressed up like Alice's personal doll.

Mary was a firm believer that necessity and duty should trump one's own desires. That said, she still found herself thankful that Alice didn't have telepathy as well, otherwise, all the cursing going on in Mary's head might have been a tad difficult to explain.

39

"Well, gory as that was, I think this is where I bail out for the day," Vince said, rising from his chair and stretching deeply while the ending credits for the previous movie rolled across the screen.

"Ah, come on, we've still got like two more!" Nick protested.

"Yeah," Hershel agreed. Hershel and Alex had joined up with them halfway through the first movie, finding the siren song of slacking while watching slasher cinema too alluring to resist in favor of homework.

"And I'm certain they'll be wonderful movies," Vince placated. "I've got to get heading over to Sasha's, though, remember? We're celebrating her rise in rank."

"So bring her back," Nick countered. "What better way to celebrate life than to observe those lacking in it?"

"You want me to congratulate the girl I'm dating on a serious accomplishment by making her watch bad zombie movies?"

"Vince," Nick began in an offputtingly serious tone, "a woman who won't celebrate with zombie movies isn't a woman you want to keep around. Trust me, that's gospel truth right there."

"Amen," Alex chimed in.

Vince stared into the sleek lenses of his friend's glasses for a moment, then shook his head and barked out a laugh. "Okay, okay. You guys win. I'll bring it up to her as an option. But if she says no, consider me gone for the night."

"That seems fair," Hershel said.

"Yeah, yeah, fair schmare," Nick said with a wave as he dragged himself out of his own chair. "We may as well get some dinner ourselves while Vince is applying the zombie barometer to his relationship."

"Zombie barometer? Really?" Vince asked as the other two stood from their reclined positions to join them.

Nick simply gave a small nod and replied with two words: "Gospel. Truth."

The four hungry young Supers headed out of the boys' lounge and made a path for the entrance hall, nearly plowing right into Mary and Alice as the two girls entered the common room.

"Oh good," Alice said briskly. "I'm glad you're all here. I have something we need to talk about. Just let me go put away our packages." With that, Alice scooped up Mary's bags, along with her own, and moved with surprising swiftness into the girls' lounge.

"Actually, we were sort of heading out," Vince began calling after her.

"You're staying," said Mary with a thou-shalt-not-question-me-for-I've-been-stuck-trying-on-clothes-all-day-and-I-am-desperate-to-share-the-pain tone. Okay, Vince

142

may not have picked up on all of the subtlety contained in her words, but the gist of it came through.

"I guess we have a few minutes to spare," Vince acquiesced. Hershel and Nick might have had fleeting thoughts of protesting on their own, but one look from Mary's weary yet scorching eyes told them quite clearly that they'd be better off minding their own business.

"Um, well, I guess I'll go head over to the dining hall and grab us a table," Alex offered.

"I'm sure you're welcome to stay," Nick assured him. "I'm equally sure that being able to leave is the privilege in this case, though, so do what you want."

"Yeah, I'll just meet up with you guys after," Alex said, taking in a long stare at Mary's haggard stance and making a (wise) snap decision. "Give me a call."

"Will do," Hershel assured him, although he wondered how much longer he would be able to stay out. Weekends were historically Roy's turf, but he hadn't been lobbying for them nearly as hard since his bout with Chad. In fact, Roy hadn't been doing much of anything besides working on the training Mary had given him. It was beginning to concern Hershel a bit, but for the moment, he was grateful to have been handed the chance for a sense of normalcy, regardless of how fleeting it might turn out to be.

Alice emerged a few moments after Alex departed, taking a position at the front of the room and gesturing for the others to sit down around her. She made no comment on Alex leaving, taking it on faith that they had ushered him out the door in a properly diplomatic fashion. Interestingly enough, it never occurred to her that their method had been forewarning him so he could escape to freedom.

"Now then, I want to talk to you all about Halloween," Alice began once everyone had awkwardly settled in. "Mary and I were looking at some costume options today, and it occurred to me that there aren't many celebration options for people in our position."

"Wait, the two of you went shopping? When did I miss that turn in the road?" Nick interrupted.

"Annnnnyway," Alice continued. "My point is that we aren't old enough to drink at the bars, and it's not like the school has many fun activities. I thought we should talk about some possible options."

"Um, well, I hate to say it, but I think my plans for Halloween are already set," Hershel said. "Roy has been looking forward to that for months, and it's really always been his favorite holiday."

"That seems like something of an odd choice," Vince commented.

"He gets to walk around in a costume lacking a shirt and hit on women dressed in far more appealing clothing than they would normally wear, all while hopping from bar to bar finding an endless supply of co-eds," Hershel explained.

143

"That does make a lot more sense," Nick agreed.

"Yeah," Vince said, distracted. The mention of Roy in a bar had reminded him of something he'd been curious about the night they had gone to Whiskey Shallows. "Hey, Hershel, how come Roy can drink out in public like that? He's the same age as you, so shouldn't that be illegal?"

"Oh, Roy has a fake ID. Given how mature he looks, no one ever really questions it when he goes out," Hershel explained.

"Ahem," Alice said, clearing her throat purposefully. "If we're quite done discussing yet another way that Roy is violating rules, perhaps we can move back to my original point and discuss what we might want to do for Halloween?"

"I've got a better question," Nick said. "Why are you assuming we'll all want to do something together? I mean, we've all done our own thing for the past few weeks and that's been working out pretty well. How about we all just do whatever we want for Halloween?"

There was a beat of silence as Alice used every drop of self-control she had to keep from blushing. She'd gotten so wrapped up in shopping with Mary today, she had managed to forget that the rest of her dormmates were her cohabitants, not really her friends. With a swift and disproportionate sense of embarrassment, she imagined how silly she must seem, suddenly trying to rally everyone together out of the blue. Urgently, she grasped for anything she could say to gracefully exit the conversation and retreat to her room, where she could forget all about this little foray in social expansion.

"We've all been 'doing our own thing' because we were getting acclimated to the campus and the program. That doesn't mean we shouldn't consider each other friends and ignore our sense of unity. We're the only people on this entire campus that know what kind of horror it is to have powers and not be able to control them. We all lived through that, we all dealt with that, and right now, we're all doing our best to make sure no one else ever knows about that part of our past. If that doesn't make us at least connected enough to consult together on holiday plans, then I don't think we'll be bonded to anyone. Ever," Mary said sternly.

Nick stared across at her, and Mary matched his gaze. Many people would have been subtly intimidated by not being able to see Nick's eyes, but for Mary, it was no concern at all. She didn't need to look into his eyes to see into his head. And Nick knew it.

"Okay, okay," Nick said with a shrug. "It was just a question. So, Alice, I assume you had some ideas for what we could do?"

"Oh, um, yes," Alice said, recovering quickly. Outwardly, she went through the few options she'd compiled thus far, gauging everyone's reactions to the possible celebrations. Inwardly, though, she was dealing with the sense of shock and overwhelming gratitude she felt for Mary. In all of her life, Alice couldn't think of one

144

time anyone else had stood up for her like that. It was a very novel, very nice sensation. And somewhere, in the deepest parts of her mind, the mask of friendship she had worn toward the tiny telepath became just a few degrees closer to reality.

40

"You have got to be kidding me! More books? Where are you even finding these things?" Nick wailed as Alice walked into the common room with a pile of books bundled in her arms.

"Yeah, that's the appropriate reaction here, bitch about me finding more resources. Don't even pause for a minute to consider helping the lady in need," Alice snapped.

"I'm a proponent of gender equality," Nick shot back. The duo was meeting to work on their group project yet again, though in this case, "work" might have been a somewhat loose definition. It more often consisted of Nick finding ways to occupy himself outside of the subject at hand, and Alice berating him for it as her method of research avoidance. Neither appeared particularly adept at knuckling down for hard work, but as the due date drew closer, Alice found her stress level rising in proportion, and she was determined they make headway with what time they had left.

"Such a gentleman," Alice mumbled as she set the books down and took her seat. She'd tried to maintain her implacably polite demeanor for the first week or so, but something about Nick seemed to render her usual defense inaccessible.

"Hey, you're the one that campaigned for it. I'm just respecting your wishes."

"If you're granting wishes, I'd love for you to pick up a damn book and help me with this. Our presentation is in two weeks!" Alice said through gritted teeth.

"Yeah, but Halloween is in a week and a half, so shouldn't we really be focusing more on what we're going to do costume-wise?" Nick replied.

Alice took a deep breath. "I've already gotten mine prepared, because, unlike you, I plan ahead of time. By that same token, I'd also like to plan ahead for what we're going to say when standing in front of the entire freshman class, presenting the life of a superhero we know next to nothing about."

"What's to know? I mean, the guy is pretty infamous as is. He was part of the world's most respected team of Heroes, then one day, out of the blue, he goes rogue, kills his partner, and gets taken down by the rest of his team. It's one of the most famous stories of any Hero. Do you really think we're going to shed any new light or insight into one of the most speculated-on events of the past century?" Nick asked.

"I think we'd damn sure better try," Alice responded. "We picked this topic. We told Dean Blaine this was the guy we wanted. If we go in there with this report half-assed, it reflects horribly on us. Besides, he can't be all that infamous. I've never heard of him."

"Tell me you're joking," Nick said. "You've never heard of Globe the Traitor? He's, like, the favorite cautionary tale of everyone in the Super community. 'Don't grow too full of yourself, or you'll end up like Globe.' Your parents never told you about him?"

"I was raised with other educational goals. Besides, since it was never even considered that I might one day gain control and become a Super, such cautionary tales would hardly have been necessary. What happened with him, anyway?" Alice asked.

"I thought you'd been researching him."

"I have," she said defensively. "I simply started with his early life, which was oddly difficult to find information on. I haven't gotten to him joining a team of Heroes yet, let alone betraying them."

"I can try to fill you in," Nick said. "You have to understand that not a whole lot is really known about the details, though. It was a pretty big PR mess for the Super community, and I think a lot of the records were sealed and information was hidden away."

"That might explain why I'm having such trouble finding anything about his early life."

"True point," Nick agreed. "Anyway, from what I know, Globe was part of a team of Heroes around fifteen years ago, give or take a few. They were really powerful— I mean, out of the five members, two were considered so strong that it was thought they might grow into Armageddon Class."

"Those are the ones who could actually destroy the world if left unchecked, correct?"

"Bingo," Nick confirmed. "Globe was one of those two, and the story is that he got a little too full of himself. He felt like he was doing all of the work and carrying his team. Those feelings snowballed over time, and eventually, he decided he didn't need them anymore."

"So he quit the team," Alice surmised.

"That's one way to put it. Another would be to say that he murdered Intra, one of his teammates, and tried to kill the other three as well before they were eventually able to kill him instead. It was one hell of a resignation letter."

"That's awful," Alice gasped. "He turned on his own team?"

"Even worse, Intra was apparently his best friend. The two of them were partners before they joined up with the other three members," Nick added.

"It seems odd, though," Alice remarked. "I mean, I guess I can see growing unhappy with a team, but why not just leave? Why end your relationship in murder?"

"Hence why I said this is one of the most speculated-on events in modern history. It doesn't really make sense. There must have been some other motivation going on behind the scenes. We don't know what they were, though, so the whole thing just ends up being one big, head-scratching mystery," Nick said.

147

"Hmm," Alice said, the wheels turning in her head. "Maybe we can take an angle of looking at it from the point of view of the rest of the team. My father is well-connected. It's possible he could pull some strings and line up a few interviews for it."

"He'd have to be *really* well connected."

"Just tell me the name of the other team members," Alice said, a twitch too quickly to pass over Nick's comment nonchalantly.

"We only have their code names, of course," Nick said. "Even in death, the identity of a Hero is protected. If memory serves, though, the other team members were Intra, the one who was killed, as well as Black Hole and Shimmerpath. There was one more, too."

"We know of two. Is the last one terribly important?" Alice asked.

"Couldn't hurt," Nick replied. "Let me think a second. He had something to do with changing the composition of things."

Alice felt her stomach take a very abrupt and deliberate trip in the southern direction. "You know, Nick, I think we're fine with just these two—"

"The Alchemist!" Nick declared triumphantly. "The fifth member was a man by the name of The Alchemist. Anyway, after Globe went nuts, the team was disbanded and everyone left alive disappeared from the world of Heroes. Think your dad would be able to find them?"

"I'm unfortunately certain of it," Alice said through gritted teeth. "My father is Charles Adair, but back in his Hero days, he went by the code name The Alchemist."

"Ohhh," Nick said as understanding seemed to dawn on him. "Awkwaaaard."

41

"Still no answer." Alice all but swore as she paced the room, snapping her cell phone shut.

"Ain't that always the way? Parents are always calling when you're busy, but the minute you actually need to talk, they're nowhere to be found," Nick commented from his sprawled out position on the couch.

"Oh, this is just so . . . so *him*!" Alice spat out, dropping into a chair with a huff.

"In all fairness to your dad, it's not like he knows you're trying to reach him this hard," Nick said.

"Not that. I mean . . . well, yes, him being busy and unavailable is classic, too, but I meant the thing with his old teammate. That is just so Daddy," Alice grumbled.

"He makes a habit of helping to kill murderous teammates, huh?"

"Don't be a jackass," Alice snapped. "It's so like him to have this huge part of his life and tell me nothing about it. I mean, I can sort of understand why he might not want to tell me about what happened with Globe: I'm sure that was really traumatic. But I never even knew he belonged to a team. I thought he just got his certification and did a little Hero work to help his career. Now, it turns out there's yet another part of his life he didn't bother to share with me. The funniest part about this is that as much as I want to feel mad, I can't. I can't, because I don't even feel surprised by it anymore." Alice let out a long, slow breath, deflating as it exited her lungs.

"I, um, actually sort of know what you mean," Nick ventured cautiously. "Ms. Pips isn't really big on sharing either."

"I thought your last name was Campbell?" Alice asked.

"It is," Nick confirmed. "It was my parents' last name. The woman who raised me is named Ms. Pips, though."

"Oh," Alice said simply, grabbing the implication immediately.

"Yeah," Nick said, glossing onward. "I mean, don't get me wrong, I love Ms. Pips and she loves me. A guy couldn't ask for a better godmother. She's just not the type that gushes anything. Feelings, personal history, dreams . . . really, any of that crap is kept close to the vest. You know, kind of like your dad, or that's how it seems at least."

"It seems right," Alice agreed. "He's a better dad when he's around, but you don't build a multi-billion dollar lifestyle by having lots of free time to hang out with your defective daughter."

"Defective?"

"Not anymore, I guess. Just still sort of think of myself that way. From ages three to eighteen, I was damaged goods. That sort of mindset takes a little time to fade," Alice admitted.

"It really does," Nick concurred. "What about your mom? Is she around more?"

149

"I never actually met my mom," Alice said softly. "She passed away giving birth to me."

"I'm sorry," Nick said reflexively.

"It's okay. It was a long time ago. Besides, I never met her, so it's hard to miss her," Alice reassured him.

Nick pulled himself to a more upright sitting position on the couch and looked across at Alice. "You're a terrible liar," he said.

"I beg your pardon?" Alice wasn't able to keep the surprise off of her face.

"My parents died in a car accident when I was a few months old. I might have met them, but I have no memory of them at all. I've spent my entire life being raised by Ms. Pips without ever knowing my birth parents. I know too well how easy it is to miss someone you've never met," Nick said.

Alice didn't have a response for that, so instead, she fiddled with her phone.

"Going to try your dad again?"

"Doesn't seem like much point to it," Alice replied. "I guess we might as well go back to me nagging and you slacking off."

"Do we have to? I thought we were bonding there for a moment," Nick whined.

"We were, which is why I'm nipping it in the bud," Alice countered. She picked up one of her books and tossed another at Nick. To her credit, she didn't aim too directly for his head, which might have been taken as a sign of fondness.

"Ouch!" Nick yelped.

Then again, maybe not.

*   *   *

"How did I never realize you two were suitemates?" Vince asked as he plugged in the movie and rejoined Sasha and Jill on their couch.

"I do spend a lot of time downstairs training," Jill said, handing a bowl of popcorn to Sasha so it was accessible to everyone on the couch.

"Still seems odd. Then again, I still don't know who shares a room with you, so I guess I can't be that surprised," Vince noted.

"My roommate is a girl named Amber. She has an older boyfriend who lives off campus, so she spends most of her free time with him," Jill answered. "It's nice, actually, a bit like having a single room."

"Wait, so the other girl, Amber, is she like us?"

"Of course, Vince. They almost always room Supers together," Jill giggled. Vince had been surprised by her bubbly nature when they'd actually gotten to talk after her and Sasha's fight. She'd been so cold and hard when in combat; but, then again, the same could be said for Sasha. More than anything, he was glad the two girls had been able to shake hands and continue on with their apparent friendship after the bout had been decided. He wondered how many other Supers were able to maintain such amiable relationships after challenges. His suspicion was very few.

"Okay, it's set up," Will called from behind the television.

"Sweet," Sasha said. "And you're sure this won't fry our TV, right?"

"Ninety-three percent sure," Will answered as he emerged from the tangled depths of the mythical land known as "Behind the TV."

"That still seems like a pretty significant margin of error," Sasha said.

"Relax. If my brother designed it, it won't blow anything up. Unless it's supposed to blow something up. Anyway, the point is, even if it doesn't work, it won't be destructive. He's religious about using safeguards," Jill assured Sasha.

"What do you mean 'even if it doesn't work'?" Will asked as he plunked down in a chair next to the couch.

"Nobody bats a thousand, little brother."

"We're twins," Will pointed out.

"Yes, but I'm older by two minutes," Jill replied, sticking out her tongue.

"Stupid sister, rushing out the birth canal," Will grumbled. "Anyway, what cinematic masterpiece are we using to test my new device?"

"*Flesh Reaper 4: Hell's Reaping*," Vince told him.

There was a beat of silence before Will's strangled voice managed to eke out one lone word: "*Really?*"

"Hey, it's like a week and a half before Halloween, the video store was pretty heavily favoring the horror section. I did the best I could," Vince defended.

"You understand what I built, right? It's a three dimensional immersion device. We're not just talking about pictures standing off the screen, we're talking about being in the center of the film. We're talking about seeing the landscape of it in every direction, of sitting on this couch underwater, or in space, or on Mount Fuji. We're going to be utterly, visually submerged in this world, and the world you chose for that is *Flesh Reaper 3*?" Will asked.

"*Flesh Reaper 4*," Vince corrected him. "Besides, it'll be fun to have something a little scary. All I'm doing for the real Halloween is going to some party that Alice found."

"That doesn't sound so bad," Jill said.

"Maybe not. I don't know, I've never to been to one of these before. Apparently, it's hosted by one of the local frats, but everyone is welcome. You just have to be in costume and pay the five-buck entry charge," Vince said with a shrug.

"Are you going?" Jill asked Sasha.

"Already working on my costume," Sasha said with a naughty smirk.

"You two are more than welcome," Vince said. "Again, I don't know if it will be worth the five bucks, but if you've got nothing else to do, it might be fun."

151

"We will certainly keep that in mind," Will said. "At any rate, I think it's time to put my new invention through a test drive."

"Woo!" Sasha yelled.

"Do it!" Vince joined in.

"Um, go, bro?" Jill said, less enthusiastically.

"Ladies and gentleman, I present to you an entirely new way to watch movies, a way that is closer to living them than merely observing the pictures pass before your eyes," Will said, firing up the remote. "Years from now, when everyone is using these devices, tonight will be a historic night, the night when the first lucky viewers were given the privilege of experiencing a new level of glory in the film . . . *Flesh Reaper*." Will's steam died off noticeably when he got to the movie title.

"*Flesh Reaper 4*," Vince corrected.

42.

A week and change later found the male Melbrook residents, along with a few additions, gathering in the common room for one last wardrobe check before venturing off into the haunted night.

"Okay, pilgrims, y'all about ready to get on the trail?" The questions came from a cowboy standing toward the center of the room. He wore faded jeans, a white linen shirt, and a brown duster along with a matching cowboy hat. Slung low across his waist was a pair of gun belts with a plastic six-shooter tucked into each side. He had a three-day scruff on his face and a casual posture, adding a sense of realism to the costume. The whole thing was marred, though, by the presence of a pair of black sunglasses across his eyes.

"Seriously, Nick?" Vince said, adjusting his chainmail. Vince was dressed as a knight, complete with plastic sword, plastic chainmail, and a plastic helmet, all spray-painted grey to look like metal. The effect was not altogether successful. "If you're going to all the trouble of using an accent, would it be so bad to take off the glasses?"

"Yes," Nick said quickly. "Plus, they add to the effect. Pardner."

"It does add a touch of dashing," Will commented from his seat on the couch. Will was wearing a tailored, black tuxedo, complimented with an array of hi-tech gadgets tucked away within its folds and pockets, for his costume as a spy.

"I don't think anyone will notice," Roy tossed in, flexing his pecks. Roy was dressed as what one could only assume was either some sort of ancient gladiator, or a male escort that catered to a very specific fetish. He wore little more than an expanded loin cloth and sandals, leaving the rest of his muscled body intentionally exposed. At present, he was oiling up his chest before moving on to his arms.

Vince bit back a remark that wanted to snake out. Roy was still an annoying cock-bag, but he had toned it down tremendously since his fight with Chad. They rarely saw him anymore; he was almost always training when he was in control of the body. When he was around, though, he seemed to make a genuine effort not to verbally abuse those around him directly. Indirectly, it still seemed a free-for-all, but progress was progress.

"What's taking the girls so long?" Alex asked. He was standing near the hallway, wearing a white tunic with black pants underneath a brown robe. A familiar, tubular metal device was fashioned to his hip, and anyone who wasn't utterly ignorant of classic sci-fi cinema was able to recognize his costume in a heartbeat.

"Is that a real question?" Roy asked. "I mean, you have met women at some point in your life, right?"

"I'm sure they just want everything to look perfect," Vince cut in. "I know Sasha spent a lot of time on her costume, and I'm sure the others did as well."

153

"That we did," Mary said as the door to the girls' side opened and the women began trickling out from their lounge. Mary was dressed as a gypsy, wearing long, flowing garments, a scarf, and rings of coins that jingled when she walked. After her was Alice, who sported a nun's habit and dress, though it fit her form in ways the sisterhood would surely not have approved of, given that there was a slit up the side and the bottom of it was not even near her knees.

"Wow, someone jumped whole hog onto the slutty train," Nick observed when Alice came into his field of vision.

Alice merely gave a shrug. "It is Halloween, after all."

"True. Why a nun, though? Pardner," Nick asked.

"It's kind of an inside joke. Think about it for a while," Alice replied.

"I sincerely hope my sister showed a touch more prudence in selecting her ensemble," Will commented.

"Not that it's any of your business, little brother, but I think I walked a nice line," Jill said as she emerged through the door. Jill was decked out in what appeared to be a torn, orange, prisoner's jumpsuit. While select parts of it were shredded or removed to create an aesthetical appeal given Jill's slender frame, it was definitely more conservative than Alice's, while not being quite as covering as Mary's.

Sasha came out last, wearing a jumpsuit as well. Hers was in one piece, and unlike Jill's, it was definitely sewn to fit her figure. In fact, a phrase like "skin-tight" would not have found itself out of place in describing her ensemble. It was decorated with checkered flags and logos of various products. Aside from that, her hair was flared out as though the wind had been blowing through it, and she sported a pair of aviator sunglasses across her face.

"Hey, the glasses thing is sort of my shtick," Nick said.

"And when you make them look this good, you can have that shtick back," Sasha rebutted.

"Touché," Nick said, then hastily added, "Pardner."

"That's not getting old," Vince sighed, then turned his attention to Sasha. "You look fantastic."

"Thanks. I thought fast girl, racecar driver, there's something of a connection there," she said. "Plus, I had it down to two options, and this was the one I could do and be sexy."

"What was the other?" Vince asked.

"I was going to wear a football helmet, drag along a bunch of broken things, and tell everyone I was a Powered," Sasha said, all but cackling at her own humor. The others joined in, though not quite so enthusiastically, and it should be noted that Alex didn't laugh at all. As for the Melbrook residents . . . well, they were working very hard to fit in. Let us say that in their defense and leave it there.

"Yeah, that would have been a good one," Alice lied. "Anyway, let's get going. How are we doing cars?"

The group then began the sizeable chore that is transporting many people in limited vehicles to the same location. It was solved in relatively short order, and the freshmen departed to the raucous Halloween party. Their spirits were high, but five of them were a bit lower than they had been. On a day of costumes and pretend, they'd been reminded that their outfits were a touch redundant, because they were already lying to everyone about who they really were.

43

The warehouse that the fraternity had rented was . . . well, just that. It was a warehouse in the industrial district of Lander that someone had clearly deemed unfit for use, but that someone else (likely someone well-compensated) deemed more than adequate to house hundreds of young, bright minds and extensive musical equipment.

Still, none of the partygoers paid much attention to lack of structural integrity. Instead, they lined up outside, allowing local police to check their IDs and mark their hands appropriately, then depositing five dollars with the doorman and entering the bass-thumping building already nearly crushed with bodies.

Once inside, the aesthetics were slightly better, in the same sense that being chased by a cheetah is slightly better than being chased by a bear, because at least you won't have to run for long from the cheetah. The walls were multi-colored tones of grey and faded white that might as well have been grey, and the concrete floors provided poor acoustical absorption from the massive sound system set up near the rear of the building. Overpriced drink and food carts littered the walls, with a few selling alcoholic beverages to those with unmarked hands, as well as those with marked hands who were willing to pay double under the table. Near these concession areas stood a smattering of tables and chairs, though most of the warehouse was dedicated to room for the young ones to dance and mingle. It was a scene that anyone with culture and sense would dub a new level of hell.

"This place is awesome!" Vince cried out, the others nodding in agreement as they holed up at one of the few open tables and took a moment to collect their bearings. "I can't believe they can finance this whole party with just five bucks per person. That's really nice of them."

"I'd say less nice, more intelligent," Will corrected.

"How so?" Vince asked.

In response, Will pointed to an area of the warehouse where a small section of couches had been set up and roped off. Sitting on these plush seats were a collection of males in costume, as well as a rotating selection of females entering and leaving.

"This is the best place to go for all of us underage students, and they know it. So now, they've got access to hundreds of young girls, away from home for the first time and looking to spread their wings of experimentation. On top of that, they're in positions of power in this small, one-building kingdom, able to expel people at will. It's a sweet setup when you think about it," Will explained.

"That seems a bit underhanded when you point it out," Vince said.

"War is hell, and mating is the greatest war any man will ever fight," Will shot back.

"Besides, what do you care who gets first crack at the girls with self-esteem and daddy issues? You've got your own dysfunctional lady right here," Sasha jumped in, putting her hand on Vince's knee and squeezing gently.

"That's great for you two, but some of us need to work a room to know who we're taking home tonight," Roy said, rising from the table and locating the nearest vendor with alcohol. It might have been Vince's imagination, but he could have sworn Roy shot Mary a questioning look before setting out on his own. Even stranger, though, was that he was almost positive she responded to his gaze with a small, affirmative nod. He shook it off as a mere misinterpretation as Roy began weaving his way through the crowd, not unsurprisingly drawing looks of admiration from many of the female attendees.

"I hate to say it, but he has a point," Alex said. "This seems like a great opportunity to meet some new girls. Hell, that's part of why I came. I just wish Hershel were here, too."

"Trust me, he wouldn't be much help in that department," Nick told him. "Besides, I'll come wing for you. Chicks totally dig the shades."

"Thanks," Alex said sincerely. "I've had a little trouble getting into my groove up here. It's harder to snag a date than it was in high school."

"You just gotta get confident, buddy," Nick assured. "That's all any lady wants."

"You're probably right," Alex agreed, rising to his feet with Nick following suit. "I guess the biggest difference is I never had to try before. I mean, back then, everyone knew about my
. . . extraordinary talents, so most of the girls were always hitting on me."

"Being regular sucks," Nick agreed, throwing an arm around Alex's shoulders and dragging him off into the crowd. "Let's try my extraordinary talent. I call it 'lying.'"

"What about you guys?" Vince asked the remainder of the table once Nick and Alex had departed.

"I have a girlfriend back home," Will told him. "And my understanding of college courtship says it is traditional for the women to wait for a man to make the first move on them."

"Shitty, but true," Jill confirmed. "So you two are just stuck with us."

"Oh, assballs," Sasha swore.

"Geez, did you want to be alone that bad?" Alice asked.

"Huh? Oh, no, no. Not that. Sorry," Sasha said. "I just realized I forgot my chapstick in Alice's car."

"I'll go get it," Vince volunteered. "Alice, you want to come with, or just have me use the keys?"

157

In response, Alice pulled out her keys and slid them across the table with a light jingling sound. "I understand the need for protected lips, but my ass is settled and getting up in this outfit is an ordeal just to keep myself covered."

"Thanks, Alice," Sasha said, snagging the keys and handing them to Vince. "And thank you, my big, strong knight."

Vince accepted the keys and her praise with a sheepish grin, then got up and began fighting his way against the current to exit the building. It took some doing, but he finally reached the other side of the entrance, confirmed with the doorman he would just be exiting to retrieve something from the car, and made his way into the parking lot.

The October air was surprisingly refreshing after the small amount of time he'd spent sweltering inside the warehouse. He made his way down the street, savoring the sweet crispness and realizing how much he missed being outdoors on nights like these. He'd adapted so quickly to living in one place and sleeping indoors all the time, yet, as his feet slapped against the pavement, a small wave of nostalgia crashed against him. Maybe he would see what sort of camping options Lander had nearby. He was sure at least a few of his friends would be interested in spending a night among the trees.

If Vince had been a bit more focused on the task at hand, and a bit less lost in his haze of memories and potential plans for the future, it's entirely possible he would have heard the figure sneaking up behind him in time to react. That was not the case, however, and so, as Vince rounded the side-street to the parking lot where Alice's car was located, he felt a blast of freezing energy smash against his lower back, frosting over his legs and sticking him in place. The next blast hit his upper back, locking his arms and reinforcing the restriction on his torso.

"You'd think a guy like you would learn to watch his back," said Michael's all-too-familiar-by-this-point voice.

"S-S-S-orry," Vince chattered though his rapidly cooling jaw. "I d-d-on't think lik-k-ke a c-c-coward."

"I've gotten really sick of that mouth of yours, Sucker Punch," Michael sneered as he circled around to Vince's front. Vince snorted a laugh out through the cold and Michael's eyes narrowed. "What's so funny?"

"Ir-rony," Vince answered, slowly letting his reserve of heat pour out all over his body, melting the ice on contact with his skin.

"I'm glad you got a good chuckle," Michael taunted. "See, I figured something out about you. You might be a good fighter, but you're weak as shit. All you had was one punch when we fought. Even if you've got a little fire in you tonight, I'm betting if I wrap you in ice ten inches thick, you won't be able to burn your way out of it."

"You b-b-bet wrong," Vince lied, trying valiantly to keep the rush of fear off of his face.

"Could be," Michael agreed. "Let's find out."

44

Most eighteen-year-old men would feel at least a bit self-conscious to be eighty percent uncovered and coated in oil at a crowded, costumed social event. Then again, Roy Daniels had never been especially similar to other people his age. Perhaps that was why, as he took a tour around the dance floor, sipping on a beer, he savored all the looks and glances people were throwing his way. At no point did the idea that anyone found his costume, or the large amount of well-muscled body that it exposed, to be in any way unattractive cross his mind. Roy's ego had undoubtedly taken a hit at his loss to Chad some weeks earlier, but that was only the part of his esteem tethered to fighting. When it came to his looks, that mountain of security was still utterly unmoved.

Roy pulled up to new vendor in order to refresh his beer supply. He'd done a few tours of the room now, and had selected the five women that he felt were at the top of the attractiveness scale. Roy had shown patience, and it had paid off, because three of those women had arrived after he had. It was always important to make sure you waited to find the best, because if something better came along and you were already mid-game, it was a huge pain in the ass to start over. Roy was willing to do a fair few things for new tail, but working harder than he absolutely had to was not one of those things.

"I totally thought that line would work," Nick's familiar voice complained as he and Alex joined in the line behind Roy to purchase drinks.

"Traditionally 'nice shoes, want to fuck?' is used as a joke, not a real line," Alex explained to him.

"Still, I felt the slap was a bit much," Nick added, rubbing his cheek.

"I take it you girls . . . er, that you're striking out with the girls?" Roy asked with a half-turn, catching himself mid-sentence with the belittling terminology he was accustomed to using. Mary had left no wiggle room for that one; it was fully off-limits.

"Striking out is such vulgar terminology," Nick replied. "It implies that we're playing a game, which would make these women prizes to be won. I think we can all agree they're intelligent, independent beings who deserve to be held in higher esteem than that."

"You do realize there aren't any girls in earshot, don't you?" Roy asked.

"Oh. Yeah, them hoes be shutting us down," Nick shrugged.

"Word," Alex seconded.

"I can't say I'm surprised. Nick, you're wearing sunglasses at night in a party, and Alex is dressed up like someone from a sci-fi movie," Roy pointed out.

"Chicks dig the shades," Nick shot back.

"That's why you're standing in line with another guy right now?" Roy countered.

"I don't see you doing much better, Romeo," Nick said. "You're waiting in line by yourself."

"I'm choosing my target carefully," Roy told him. "There's a lot of talent here tonight. I want to make sure I'm getting the biggest piece of chicken on the table."

Nick and Alex responded with very questioning, very confused looks.

"It's a southern metaphor," Roy explained.

"Dude. You're from Chicago," Nick said.

"Hershel is from Chicago. I'm from the deep south."

"That makes, quite literally, no sense at all," Nick said.

"Word," Alex seconded again.

"Look, I don't have to explain myself to you guys. The point is I'm picking the best girl here to go home with. That's the only reason I'm solo right now," Roy said, stepping forward as the boy in front of him finished setting his money on the counter.

"So, that's it, huh? You'll just pick the best one and, of course, she'll go home with you?" Alex asked.

"Yup," Roy said as he selected his beer.

"This I've got to see," Nick said.

"Feel free," Roy agreed. "Just keep your distance while the master works. As for me, I've picked my target, so it's go time."

*   *   *

"Looks like I wasn't so wrong, after all," Michael chuckled. Vince couldn't reply, unfortunately, since Michael had frozen him almost totally solid. The only part of his body still exposed was the top half of his head, allowing him to breathe. And, of course, to stay conscious and suffer. The rest of his body was caked in inches of ice. The only thing keeping him from hypothermia was the slow pulse of heat he was releasing all across his body intermittently. Vince only had a few lighters' worth of fire in him, though, and his reserves were running dangerously low.

"You look kind of silly," Michael commented as he surveyed his work. "I think it suits you, though. It's like a living piece of art, a testament to what happens when you take on Michael Clark. I feel like you've learned your lesson tonight, haven't you?"

Vince stared at his bald tormentor, unsure of exactly how Michael was expecting him to convey surrender.

"Oh, right, froze your jaw there. Okay, I'll make it simple. Just blink twice to show me you understand, and I think we can finally be done with this."

Vince locked eyes with Michael. The smart thing was to blink twice, get free, and come at Michael again on another day. A day when he wasn't totally helpless and fast running out of energy, a day when he had a real chance at taking this cock-bag down. It was the most basic strategic decision he could have been presented with.

Vince didn't blink. His eyelid didn't even twitch.

160

"That's a shame, Vince. I really thought you and I had come to an understanding. I guess we need to continue the education, though," Michael sighed. He pulled back his fist and focused his energy.

"I have severe doubts that this is a sanctioned match," said a deep, male voice from behind Michael. Before Michael was able to turn and see who the speaker was, two beams of orange energy had snared him. One wrapped around his forearm and the other grabbed his torso, yanking him up into the air.

"Who the fuck are you?" Michael spit, jerking and twisting his arm to get free.

"My friends call me Thomas," the speaker said, stepping into Vince's view. "I have a feeling you won't be counting yourself as one of those, though." Thomas was a dark-skinned male, one Vince recognized from gym and their Ethics class. He was dressed as a Native American, and both of his hands were outstretched, a beam of orange energy emanating from each one.

"I've got him restrained," Thomas called out. "You guys check on his victim."

Vince heard three people approaching behind him. He would have turned to look if he'd possessed a full range of motion. As it was, all he could do was listen.

"He's not a victim," Michael yelled. "We were just having a fight."

"An unsanctioned fight, in the middle of an alleyway where anyone could have seen you using your powers, and where it looks like you're tormenting him after having won a long time ago. Yeah, this seems real legit," Thomas said calmly

"I think he's okay," called out a deep, female voice. "Violet's going to weaken the ice so we can pull him out."

"I wouldn't be averse to a little help here," Thomas called back. "He's still struggling, and this guy isn't the number three rank for nothing."

"I've got to work on the ice, and we'll need Camille as soon as I'm done," said a new female voice, presumably Violet.

"That just leaves me," said the original female voice. She walked past Vince as she approached Michael. It was a girl he easily recognized from class. Though she was dressed as some sort of Viking woman, the tightly braided, pulled-back hair gave her away as Stella, the girl that always asked questions without raising her hand. She strode right over to where Michael was struggling a foot or so off the ground and punched him in the throat. His twisting and jerking was immediately replaced by rasping and choking for air.

"That was excessive force," Thomas chided her.

"No, it was the best solution," Stella argued. "If I'd said to let him down, and we'd fought him all honorably, then he would have used his full power, so we would have had to do the same, and it would have caused a lot of property damage, as well as creating a damn good chance we'd all be outed as Supers. Sometimes, the only option is a quick punch to the throat."

161

"I've almost got him over here," said Violet, still behind Vince. He wasn't sure what she was doing, but he could feel the ice behind him cracking apart and giving way. All at once, a chunk of it fell off and Vince felt himself tipping backward. Two pairs of arms caught him and laid him down on the pavement. His energy almost completely depleted and his life out of danger, Vince did the only thing he was capable of at that point.

"Thank you," Vince mumbled weakly, and then passed out into sweet oblivion.

45

Vince came around a few minutes later, shivering slightly, and pulled himself up off the concrete.

"Whoa there, buddy, I'd go slow if I were you. Camille patched you up, but cold has a way of seeping in on people," said the dark-skinned boy dressed as a Native American.

"I'm getting used to it," Vince said. "Sadly."

"I take it you and Baldy have a history?"

"Only in his sad, angry little cue ball of a head," Vince said. "Thanks for saving me, by the way."

"Of course," Thomas said. "It was an illegal match, and you were down. There was nothing else to do."

"Well, I'm still glad you wandered by. My name is Vince, by the way."

"Thomas," Thomas replied, extending a hand. Vince accepted and shook it.

"So I heard," Vince said. "Where are the rest of your friends?"

"Camille went to get some help, and Violet and Stella are escorting Frosty back to campus," Thomas told him. "He'll be less of an ass after he sleeps off the alcohol . . . we hope."

"Michael was drunk?" Vince said in surprise.

"My understanding is that most students have a pre-party a bit before these events, especially the underage ones who can't buy anything during. It seems he went a little overboard," Thomas said.

"I guess I feel a little bit better," Vince said. "Also, you should call your friend Camille. I'm going to be fine. I don't need any more help, and I really don't want to cause a fuss."

"You sure about that? You took a pretty nasty beating there."

"I'm sure," Vince confirmed. "Your healer took care of nearly everything except the exhaustion. Right now, all I want to do is catch a bus home and sleep for a day."

"Your call, I guess," Thomas shrugged.

"That it is," Vince agreed. "Thanks again for saving me, though. I can't express how glad I am you guys stopped him."

"A person was in need," Thomas replied. "That's the exact reason we're going through this training anyway, right? Besides, once we report him on Monday, I'm pretty sure you won't have to worry about Michael anymore."

"Report him?" Vince asked.

"Of course. He broke the rules," Thomas answered.

"Sure, but I mean, I'm okay and everything. Like I said, I'd rather avoid a fuss," Vince said.

163

"He broke the rules," Thomas said again. "That means he has to be reported, so he can face the consequences."

"Yes . . . yes, you're right, of course," Vince agreed. "By all means, make the report on Monday. If you'll excuse me, though, I really am feeling drained from my ordeal."

"Of course. Go home and rest. Are you sure you don't need any more help?"

"I'm positive," Vince reassured him. "But tell your friends thanks as well from me."

"Will do," Thomas agreed.

*   *   *

"Mr. Reynolds," Dean Blaine called as Vince entered Ethics of Heroism on Tuesday. "May I speak with you a moment?"

"Um, sure," Vince said awkwardly. He had a pretty good inclination what this was going to be about, and it was something he'd been hoping dearly would slide by unnoticed.

"It seems Coach George would like you to go to the gym today, instead of attending my class," Dean Blaine said, any possible resentment at his class being snubbed hidden artfully in the smile that stretched across his face.

"Is that okay?" Vince asked. "I mean, we start presentations today."

"You and Mr. Murray are scheduled for Thursday since, as you know, we weren't able to fit all of them into just one class. I do hope you'll hurry back to watch the others if possible, but if Coach George feels this is important enough to pull you from class, then you should make sure to give him your full attention," Dean Blaine assured him.

No other option coming to mind, Vince waded against the incoming crowd and made his way to the gymnasium. Nick noticed idly that Vince was exiting instead of entering, but he'd been suspecting something was up since Saturday, anyway. Vince wasn't the kind of guy to flake out, so when he'd vanished early in the night, only to text Sasha that he'd gotten suddenly ill and had caught a bus home, it was obvious he was lying. Inconvenient, too, since he'd had Alice's keys when he ditched. Fortunately, Sasha was able to dash over and recover them, so the pilgrimage home had been possible.

Whatever Vince was dealing with was obviously tethered to what had happened Saturday, but Nick's attention was focused on his task at hand for the day. He and Alice were scheduled to present, and he had a bad feeling he knew exactly the spot they were going in. Sure enough, as the class settled into their seats, Alice's tall frame remained standing, speaking hurriedly to Dean Blaine and gesturing to the mountain of poster-board she had dragged along with her. One might think she hadn't heard of a slideshow program, but one would be wrong. The posters were supplemental to the slide show. She'd worked extra hard to get them done in time. As she motioned for him to come up

164

to the front, Nick groaned inwardly. He should have picked a worse subject to do the report over. Not even Globe was going to drag them down enough with her putting out this kind of effort.

"Class, it seems one of today's teams brought along some materials that would be inconvenient to store, so they've kindly volunteered to start us off today," Dean Blaine told the students as Alice ordered Nick around behind him, the duo quickly setting up their posters and loading the presentation onto the computer. "I'm sure all of you feel just devastated by this loss of opportunity, but please try to keep your disappointment to yourself."

A polite chuckle rippled through the class. People learn early on to laugh at the jokes of those in charge, and that goes for Supers just as much as humans. Dean Blaine cast a glance back at Alice, who flashed him a grin and a thumbs-up, so he continued. "It seems our group is ready. I urge you to give them your full attention and ask any relevant questions once they are finished. Remember, participation is a vital part of my class."

With that, Dean Blaine took a seat at a desk formerly occupied by one of the ever-mounting number of students who had washed out. Nick cleared his throat and stepped to the center of the classroom. He'd managed to talk Alice into letting him speak on the grounds that he had more practice at it than she (truth), and that he would give a better presentation overall because of that (lie). The reality was that he wanted to control the flow of the presentation, hindering where he could and helping it if he had to. Nick was determined to squeak out of this incident as nothing more than an afterthought in the minds of the class, no matter how much effort it took.

"Alice and I chose something of a controversial Hero for our presentation," Nick began. "In fact, I think many would argue whether he should still even be rightly categorized as one. Certainly, there have been outcries by some to strip him of any semblance of that title, even in reference to the years he served dutifully as one. There is some validity to those opinions, just as there is some in the beliefs of a few people that this Hero was a victim of some deeper problem, or that his fall from grace was orchestrated. Today, we are going to look over the known life, and ultimately, the demise, of a Hero with the code name Globe."

Nick's monologue was interrupted by a loud CRACK that echoed through the room. The source was immediately visible, as a part of Chad's desk fell heavily to the floor. Chad hastily rose from his seat.

"I'm so sorry about the interruption," Chad apologized to Nick. "My hand slipped while I was resting it on the corner of my desk. I think I must be feeling ill, so I'll excuse myself to the infirmary and let you get back to your work. Again, very sorry." Without so much as a glance for confirmation to Dean Blaine, Chad strode out of the room.

"Okay . . . right then," Nick said, damning that blond bastard for making sure this presentation would stick in the mind of every single person in attendance. "Anyway, Globe first appeared as the top graduate in his year of the Hero Certification Program . . ."

46

"I assume you know why you're here, Vince," Coach George said as the silver-haired youth entered his sparse office and took a seat down on the opposite end of George's considerably wide desk.

"No, sir," Vince lied.

"Good boy," Coach George complimented him. "Never give away more information than you have to. No sense in confessing to a crime I might not know about."

Vince blinked in surprise, unsure of how to react to such a statement.

"It's the right strategy," Coach George continued. "Unfortunately for you, it's not any good in this case. You're here because of the fight you and Michael had on Saturday night."

"I'm not sure what you mean," Vince said.

"The point at which a lie is exposed is when you give it up for a better one. You don't cling on to the one that's no good anymore. Now, I've got a full report from Thomas Castillo about how he and some friends pulled your ass out of a mini-glacier. Let's be clear here: I didn't call you in to dock you or punish you for having an unsanctioned fight," Coach George informed him.

"I . . . I wouldn't really call a jumping much of a fight," Vince admitted, taking the coach's advice and giving up on denial.

"Get in enough of them and you will," Coach George assured him. "Now, I don't really care that much about the fighting. I know we make a big deal in the beginning, but that's mostly just to cover our own asses legally. My concern is about what I read in this report."

"What do you mean?" Vince asked.

"I mean, Michael had you dead to rights. It didn't sound like there was any real struggle between you two from how unharmed Michael was. I know what your power is, kid, and I know they never successfully found a limit on how much energy you can absorb. You should have at least given that little nutjob a run for his money. So, I want to know how much power you had stored up when that guy surprised you," Coach George demanded.

"Enough," Vince said, crossing him arms and sitting back in the chair.

"See, that's the one amount we know you didn't have. Enough," Coach George shot back. "You threw one fire punch in your ranking matches, and this time, I'm guessing you only had enough heat stored up to fight hypothermia while you got the shit knocked out of you. We both know you can do a lot more than this, so I want an answer. Why are you trying to scrape by on the bare minimum with your power?"

"I'm not," Vince replied. "I work as hard as anyone out there. I run, I lift, I train, I do everything you ask to get stronger and prepare myself for combat."

"You do," Coach George agreed. "That's why I'm taking time out of my day to have this conversation, rather than just drumming you out of the program immediately."

Vince's eyes widened slightly. He'd been expecting a lot of things, but expulsion from the program had seemed too extreme for just one fight.

"I have . . . issues with my power sometimes," Vince said carefully.

Coach George looked at him for a moment, then spoke again in a lower tone. "Look, kid, let's just put our cards on the table here. I know about you and the rest of your petri dish dorm. Of course, they were going to tell the people who were supposed to help teach you." The last part was proactive, accurately anticipating the question Vince had been about to interrupt him with. "You say you've got issues with your power? Well, I've got issues with people who can't use the very thing that qualifies them for this course in the first place. This is your only chance. If I were you, I'd try really hard to convince me there's some reason you should stay."

George had expected another snappy comeback, but to his surprise, the kid lowered his head a bit and seemed to genuinely think. Most men his age would have assumed that it was a bluff and made up some crap to throw back as an answer, but the kid with the goofy, silver hair was being rational about it. George readied himself to actually listen to what Vince would say, a courtesy he wouldn't have normally extended.

"If the procedure isn't permanent, and Alice loses control, what happens?" Vince asked at last.

"She starts free-floating around the place again," Coach George replied.

"And Mary?"

"She won't be able to block out the voices."

"What about Nick and Hershel?" Vince asked again.

"Nick, god only knows what, and Hershel would start shifting uncontrollably to Roy again," Coach George answered. "I assume you're building toward a point here?"

"I am," Vince answered. "And this is it: if the procedure isn't permanent, if I lose control again like I did before, what happens?"

"You have an entire faculty of capable Supers to keep you in check," Coach George told him.

"A faculty that can only react," Vince pointed out. "You can't anticipate. That means, for you to contain me, something has to have already happened. If it happens when I'm down here, then it's probably no big deal. But I have normal classes, too, and I eat lunch in the dining halls, and that's time I spend with regular humans. Humans who wouldn't be able to survive a sudden wildfire or a lightning bolt to the chest."

"You're scared of hurting other people?" Coach George asked.

"Yes. I'm terrified of it," Vince said. "I want to be a Hero to help people, to use my abilities the way my dad always told me I should. I want it more than I've wanted anything in my life, aside from control of my powers. I will work hard, and I will do what you say, but I won't absorb more energy than I have to until I'm positive that I won't lose that control. If you have to kick me out, then you have to kick me out. I'm not endangering innocent people for the sake of my own ambition, though."

George stared down at the skinny boy sitting across from him. All the training had stacked a little muscle on his shoulders, but he still gave off a lean, almost shrimpy impression. Physically, this kid was nothing worth taking a second look at. His eyes, though, that was a whole other story. George had seen a lot of tough talk in his years of dealing with kids who grew up stronger than everyone else. What he hadn't seen near enough was eyes filled with determination and integrity, eyes like the blue set that were meeting his gaze from across the table.

"I'll give you one year," Coach George said eventually. "You can keep up this tentative crap until the end of your freshman year. As long as you keep up the work in gym and the start of combat training, I think you can keep pace with the slower half of the class."

"Really?" Vince asked dumbly, unable to disguise the shock in his voice.

"Yeah, really," Coach George confirmed. "Be warned, though, this is all you get. At the end of this year, you either make peace with the necessity of using your power, or don't bother coming back. Starting second year with that attitude won't just put you at risk, but people who'll be depending on you as well."

"I understand," Vince nodded.

"Good. Now get out of here. You've still got a few minutes before gym," Coach George said, gesturing to the door.

"I will. Um, thanks," Vince said lamely.

"Thank me by working hard," Coach George told him, and Vince exited his office with a quick nod of agreement. George, on the other hand, leaned back in his chair and savored the few moments of solitude he had left before he'd have to ride and demean the remainder of the freshman class. He reflected back on his talk with Vince, going through the boy's logic and motivation in his head once more.

"I'll say this for him," Coach George mumbled out loud. "That kid has the same brass balls as his dad."

47

"How are the presentations going?" Mr. Numbers asked as he entered Dean Blaine's office.

"Fine, save for one student having a very bad reaction to the name Globe," Dean Blaine replied. "Where's your other half? I asked to see both of you."

"He's in Moscow, tending to some company business," Mr. Numbers lied. Mr. Transport was actually in Kenya, but Dean Blaine didn't need to know that.

"I suppose the job must come first," Dean Blaine acknowledged. "Still, I assume you'll provide him with a full record of our conversation?"

"Of course."

"Excellent. I really wanted you down here to touch base on your charges and see how they're adapting outside of my class," Dean Blaine said.

"They're doing better," Mr. Numbers replied. "Mary and Alice seem to be pursuing a friendship with one another, albeit at a halting pace. The others are growing more interconnected as well, and even Roy has been on better behavior. Of course, the project helped them with branching out their social circle quite a bit. Thank you again for that."

"It was a small concession to assist my students," Dean Blaine said, waving it off. "It was a good idea, too. I might actually continue using it in years to come. It gave a lot of the remaining students an excuse to get to know one another."

"On that note, how many do we have left?"

"We're down to approximately forty students. I suspect, by the time George finishes, the number will be closer to thirty-five. Usually, those who can survive the first semester make it to the end of freshman year," Dean Blaine said.

"Fifty percent left? That's a pretty high rate for a freshman class. Is George going easy on them?" Mr. Numbers asked.

"Quite the contrary: he seems to get harsher as the years go by, and Persephone hardly tempers him at all anymore," Dean Blaine commented.

"That's good, though," Mr. Numbers said. "Anyone who can't even make it through this will have a breakdown two weeks into being a Hero."

"Agreed," Dean Blaine said. "It's a very difficult job. I was quite thrilled to leave the combat field once this administration position became available."

"I'm surprised they don't try to bring you back. Your power is so unique, it made the difference in a lot of fights," Mr. Numbers said.

"Well, thank you, but now, I'm sure there's another Hero with a unique power to make that difference. Times change, and we must change with them. Those of us not blessed with enhanced physical attributes are lucky if we can make it to thirty as a Hero.

There were some good times, but this is where I do my good now. To that effect, is there any other assistance you require from my end to help bond the students?"

"I think the project accomplished what we needed," Mr. Numbers told him. "Besides, Mary is doing an excellent job bringing them together on her own, and Mr. Transport and I have a few activities planned to strengthen their unity."

"I do hope one of those activities will get Mr. Reynolds to begin using his powers," Dean Blaine commented.

"Ah yes, Vince. We're unsure what to do about him. He's clearly afraid of his own abilities, or afraid the treatment will prove to be temporary," Mr. Numbers said.

"That would match well with the report I received from George," Dean Blaine agreed.

"Normally, we would have him work through those fears, but in this case, they're actually very realistic things to be scared of. This will be something he either finds a way through, or he doesn't," Mr. Numbers said.

"It would be a shame to lose a Super with such potential, but that is the way things go," Dean Blaine said. "At any rate, I thank you for your time, and tell Mr. Transport that the next time I schedule a meeting, I expect him to make time for it."

"Of course, Dean," Mr. Numbers said respectfully. "Oh, one quick question. You said one of the students had a bad reaction to the name Globe. Which student?"

"Chad Taylor, the number one male rank."

"Very odd," Mr. Numbers agreed. "I just wanted to be sure it wasn't one of our charges. I'll leave you to your work. Have a good day, Dean Blaine."

"And you, Mr. Numbers," Dean Blaine echoed.

Mr. Numbers stepped out of the office and made his way through the underground area toward the lifts. Finally away from the dean, his mind was kicking back into its regular gear. Just as well, too; Mr. Numbers now had some additional research on his plate.

First and foremost, though, Mr. Numbers needed to get their plans for winter break squared away. He and Mr. Transport had hatched a lovely scheme to bond their students together, but it was taking far more prep work than originally expected. If it worked, though, then it would be well worth the effort. Unfortunately, that effort was eating what little free time he possessed. He hadn't even had time to pop by town and pick up more puzzles. It was frustrating to be a man as brilliant as Mr. Numbers, with nothing to take his mind off of that brilliance.

48

"Because there are certain things about my life you just don't need to know," said the exasperated voice from the other end of the cell phone.

"But, Daddy, don't you think the fact that you were part of a really famous team of Heroes might have been something your daughter would have wanted to know about?" Alice shot back. After weeks of trying, she had finally managed to track down her father and get him on the phone, though the results weren't panning out exactly as lucratively as she'd expected.

"Given what we were famous for, no. I felt it was something better left in the past," Charles told her. "And given that many of the records about the incident were sealed, and we agreed to keep it confidential, that only added to my motivation. Now, I'm in the middle of a very important meeting here, so was there anything else you needed?"

"No, Daddy. That was it," Alice said stiffly.

"Good, then. Study hard, finals are right around the corner."

"I will, Daddy."

"Of course. I love you, Alice. I'll call you soon," Charles said.

"Love you, too," Alice all but mumbled. There was the click of disconnection and then Alice was just sitting in her room holding a cell phone. She wasn't sure why she felt any surprise: it had always been like this. He was a kind father, and he was good to her when he was around, but he was always so sectioned off, so sealed away. Alice often wondered what it was like to have warmth in a person's life. Not just tolerance or caring, but genuine joy at someone's company. She wasn't sure, but she suspected she was getting closer to it here than she ever had at home, and as bad her phone call had been, that thought cheered her slightly. Well, that and the fact that she was still riding high on getting the best grade in the class so far for their presentation. Nick had seemed oddly unexcited by it, but it felt good knowing she had set the bar for the others to follow. There were still more presentations on Thursday, but she was confident that they would not be easily dethroned.

A soft knock rapped at the door.

"Come in, Mary," Alice called. The boys couldn't get into the girls' lounge area unless they were let in, so the only person who could be knocking on her door was her fellow Melbrook female.

The door was pushed open and Mary entered. "Hey, the guys are going to the dining hall in, like, ten minutes. I thought I'd see if you wanted to come," Mary offered.

Alice did her best to keep a sneer of disgust from rippling across her face. Her little understanding of dormitory food held it in the esteem of old vomit and fresh excrement. Still, it was nearing the end of the first semester, and she'd yet to set foot in one of these establishments. Not to mention it was where the rest of her . . . maybe not yet friends, but associates, gathered to dine, so if she was serious about trying to get closer to people, this was one of her best opportunities.

"I think I would like that very much," Alice lied.

Mary chuckled. "You know, it really isn't that bad."

"We shall see," Alice said skeptically, rising from her bed and sliding on her shoes.

In truth, the food wasn't that bad. And what was lacking in culinary refinement was made up for with the experience of sitting around with people Alice was growing ever more comfortable with, complaining and laughing about their classes and day-to-day lives. It would have been an overall positive experience except for the fact that a girl who has been raised with dieticians and organic diets most of her life has a very poor tolerance for things deep fried in grease.

Alice would never admit it, but as she spent the next few hours unwillingly regurgitating her last meal (along with a few others), she still felt like it had been an overall good idea to eat with the others. She also made a mental note that, from here on out, she would be bringing her own damn food.

*   *   *

"Thank you for that wonderful presentation on Lord Pholos, Mr. Riley and Ms. Dixon," Dean Blaine said as the two students bowed to polite applause from the class. Eventually, they collected their materials and went to their seats, so Dean Blaine retook his customary spot at the front of the classroom.

"That concludes our presentations, and I do hope you all got a lot out of doing them," Dean Blaine said, addressing the class.

"Actually, yeah," Stella interrupted in her usual style. "It put things in a new perspective to actually see some of the hard calls our guy had to make in his career. Even though they worked out, they might not have. That's some crazy kind of pressure."

"Precisely what I wanted you to realize," Dean Blaine said with a smile. "We have a tremendous program here for getting your bodies in the condition necessary to be Heroes. The harder part, in my opinion, is training your minds to understand what a Hero is, and what they should strive for. It's a lot of responsibility, and the stress from it has broken more than one Super with awe-inspiring abilities.

"Now, we've put a lot of time into this project, but after today, we'll be easing up on the throttle a bit," Dean Blaine continued. "We'll still be having our discussions, of course, but I understand you all have finals in your other classes to prepare for. Since this course runs for two semesters, what you just did counts as the mid-term for the class. But you can think of it as the final for this semester."

There wasn't quite cheering from the class, but there was a noticeable elevation of everyone's mood. Finding out they could cross a class off of their finals list early was welcome news to any student. Ever.

173

"I'll still expect you to all show up and participate, of course," Dean Blaine clarified. "I just want you to know there won't be any other projects this semester. There is one particularly important class you'll need to attend, though. I've lined up a guest speaker for next Tuesday's class, and I expect full attendance. That means mental and physical. This will be an important step in developing a Hero's mindset, so I want you to come sharp and ready to listen."

"Who's the speaker?" Stella asked.

"If I were going to tell you, don't you think I would have mentioned it in that extensive preamble?" Dean Blaine retorted.

"Point," Stella said, leaning back in her chair.

"The speaker is a surprise, but I hope you will take my word that their words will be worth hearing. Grade-shatteringly worth hearing, in fact," Dean Blaine said, adding no inflection to his voice. The meaning came through loud and clear, though. Miss this class, and find a new reason to be at Lander.

49

"What do you think he's got planned for Tuesday?" Vince asked Nick as the two flopped down in the boys' lounge after gym.

"Hookers," Nick replied without a pause.

"You think the dean is going to bring hookers to a class centered on ethics?"

"A man can dream," Nick sighed longingly.

Vince shook his head, a habit that was growing more and more frequent the longer he knew Nick. "I'm just glad we're done with the graded work in his class for the semester. My other classes are starting to seem a lot scarier now that it's almost finals time."

"I know what you mean," Nick half-lied. He did understand Vince's plight from an objective standpoint, it was just one that he had never found himself in.

"I think most of my weekend will be spent meeting up with others in the class and getting a study group organized," Vince speculated. "Hopefully, if we share knowledge, I can cram enough between now and then to scrape through."

"Don't worry too much about that," Nick told him.

"You think it'll be okay?"

"I have no idea. I just think you should be worrying more about whatever test they'll give us in gym and less about ones with the highest danger potential of a paper cut," Nick explained.

"Why would gym do a test? The combat matches are at the end of the year," Vince pointed out. "We're only halfway there."

Nick could have pointed out that after the break was when the class format would change and students would no longer be able to battle to change their ranks, so it was only logical that the coaches would utilize one last testing activity before deciding who would be combat and who wouldn't. He didn't, though. Instead, he just said, "It's a chance to torture us. You see them just letting that pass by?"

"I hate to say it, but you make a point," Vince admitted. "Thanks for that, by the way. Now, I'm even more stressed."

"Always here to help," Nick chuckled.

"At least you have an ace in the hole," Vince said. "I mean, worst case scenario, you can crank up your luck and just fill in test answers randomly. I bet that power comes in really handy."

*　　　*　　　*

The ten-year-old boy sitting at the blackjack table took a sip of his soda, but otherwise kept his eyes intent on the game. He had sandy hair and was a little tall for his age, though it was clear he still had ample growing left to do. The boy wore a striped collared shirt and jeans, along with a pair of black-framed glasses he had to keep pushing up onto the bridge of his nose. The only other people at the table were the dealer, a woman who had money but not much sense or sobriety, and a well-built, balding man wearing a black suit.

"Why exactly is your son sitting at a blackjack table in the middle of the day?" Ms. Anders asked. She was nervous, but doing her best not to show it. She was new to the Las Vegas branch of Child Protective Services, so of course, when the time for Ms. Pips's yearly review had come around, it was Ms. Anders who'd been handed the job. Unfortunately, Ms. Anders wasn't quite new enough not to have heard any rumors, so while she'd been willing to come, it hadn't been without a large sense of hesitation that was now slowly eroding into fear. The two women were sitting at a small table a few feet away from where the boy was watching the blackjack game.

"Because I have to work," Ms. Pips answered. "And unless you've found a reliable sitter service in this town, I think you answered your own question."

"I more meant why is Nick not in school today? It's April, so summer break isn't for another month," Ms. Anders clarified.

"I take it you didn't read his full history before our meeting," Ms. Pips deduced. "My son has to be home-schooled because of his condition. The public school system declared him too dangerous to attend with the other children. Since I can't take off every day to teach him, I hired a tutor. I'm not sure what he's learning right now, but I trust the man's teaching methods implicitly."

"I see," Ms. Anders said. "And, just to be clear, when you say condition . . ."

"Nick is a Powered. He has uncontrollable luck, good and bad. After the day he found a thousand dollars on the playground and was in the bathroom when all of the toilets exploded due to a plumbing mishap, he was officially deemed unacceptable at any institution of learning," Ms. Pips said matter-of-factly.

"Yes, of course. My apologies for bringing that up." Ms. Anders was trying very hard to act less flustered than she was feeling. "Now, you've had Nick for nine years now, correct?"

"Ever since my sister and her husband had their car accident, Lord rest her soul."

"And, in those years, how do you feel that Nick has developed, emotionally? I mean, living with a Vegas casino owner must be a unique childhood," Ms. Anders said.

"Nick walks around every day with the knowledge that, because of a fluke of birth, he could die at any minute. A plane could fall from the sky, or a truck could hit him while he's in the shower. He has to deal with his mortality in a much more real way than the rest of us ever have. I don't think my son ever had a chance at an existence that wasn't unique," Ms. Pips answered.

"An excellent point," Ms. Anders said. "That takes care of the preliminary work. I just wanted to introduce myself and get some initial information. As you know, in the next few weeks, I'll speak with you and Nick, both together and separately, just to make sure he's adapting well to his environment."

"I'm familiar with the process by this point," Ms. Pips said with a surprisingly reassuring smile. "Though, to my knowledge, I'm also the only foster parent in this city with no complaints or reports who still receives yearly check-ups."

"Standard procedure, I assure you," Ms. Anders lied, gathering her notes and hastily rising from the table. "I'll give you a call to set up another appointment."

"I'll look forward to it," Ms. Pips replied, rising as well. "It was a pleasure meeting you, Ms. Anders. Enrique will escort you out."

As if by magic, a muscular man stepped into view and waited patiently as Ms. Anders finished grabbing her things, then quietly followed her as she found her way to the door. Only after Enrique had returned and confirmed that she was in her car and out of earshot did Ms. Pips make her way over to the blackjack table where the boy was sitting.

"So sorry, dear, but I have to speak with my dealer for a moment. Please feel free to try your luck at another table, and tell them to get you something top shelf on me for the inconvenience," Ms. Pips said to the woman still tossing away her cash in the vain hopes of getting twenty-one.

"'S okay," she slurred. "Needed to change anyway. Got no luck at this table." With that, she stumbled away in search of another place to settle down and piss away time and funds.

"Okay, Nick," Ms. Pips said as soon as the woman was gone, "what's the count?"

"Deck's almost done," Nick replied, adjusting his glasses once more and double checking his numbers. "There should still be two threes, a four, two fives, three sevens, an eight, a nine, two jacks, and a king."

"Gerry?" Ms. Pips asked.

"Spot on, by my count," said the large, balding man in the suit.

"Good job," Ms. Pips praised him. She then turned her attention on the dealer. "Tom, was he showing any tells you noticed?"

"He fiddles with his glasses when he's adding and scratches the velvet with his right index finger when he's mentally removing cards from what's left in the deck," Tom replied quickly.

"Nice observations, Tom," Ms. Pips said. "Thanks for helping out today. Go ahead and get lunch at the restaurant on me."

"Thank you, Ms. Pips," the dealer said respectfully. He knew when he was being hustled off, and he had been at the casino long enough to know he should take the free lunch and get out of the way.

177

"Impressive," Ms. Pips said, patting Nick on the head. "You tricked one of our better dealers with both fake tells, plus, he didn't even catch on that the glasses were fake."

"They aren't," Nick replied.

Ms. Pips raised an eyebrow. "Excuse me?"

"They aren't fake," Nick repeated. "When Gerry took me to get some, I realized that without a distortion it would be obvious to anyone observant that the lenses weren't real. I knew that would bust me off the bat, so instead, I had Gerry forge a prescription that would show distortion, but wouldn't mess up my near-sight so much that I couldn't see that cards."

"That true, Gerry?"

"Yes, ma'am," Gerry replied. "Nick saw the hole in the plan and told me how he wanted it filled."

"Ha!" Ms. Pips barked a laugh. "And here I thought Tom was losing his touch. That was smart, Nick. I didn't think you'd find that one so easily."

"You'll have to do better next time," Nick said with a genuine smile.

"And so will you, my little con man, so will you," Ms. Pips said, smiling back. "Okay, Gerry, let's get the glasses off of him before he damages his sight for real. After that, take him over to Fleece and have Nick work on his hand skills."

"Um, Ms. Pips, I feel I would be remiss if I did not inform you that Fleece is set up over at The Bare Back this week," Gerry brought up.

"So?" Ms. Pips asked.

"Given the mature nature of that club, I feel Nick might be too young to visit Fleece at that location," Gerry said.

"He's ten years old, Gerry, and it's just a strip club. He nursed from tits when he was a baby, it's not like they've changed a lot in the last decade," Ms. Pips said.

"Yes, ma'am," Gerry said obediently. His tenure and loyalty to Ms. Pips had earned him the right to bring possible problems and objections to her attention when it seemed necessary; Ms. Pips trusted he had the best interests of the family at heart. But no one had the right to argue back with her once she had laid down her decision.

"One more thing. Do some digging on our new CPS rep. I don't think she'll be much of a problem, but she's got an idealistic streak in her, and I'd rather be prepared," Ms. Pips said.

"Yes, ma'am," Gerry repeated.

"Okay, Nick, you work hard for Fleece today," Ms. Pips said, turning her attention back to the boy.

"Yes, Ms. Pips," Nick said respectfully.

"I'll check with Fleece after. If you can get three solid pulls today, I'll let Gerry do some work on misdirection with you later tonight."

178

"Thank you, Ms. Pips," Nick replied. He loved working with Gerry, and misdirection was one of his favorite subjects, so he knew he'd have to really try and get those pulls this afternoon.

"Be good," Ms. Pips told him with a kiss on the cheek. "And always remember: luck is for tourists and losers."

"Winners cheat," she and Nick finished together in unison, as they had since she'd taught him the motto when he was first diagnosed as a Powered all those years ago.

*   *   *

"I bet that power comes in really handy."

"Hell yeah, it does," Nick replied. "Who knows how I'd get by without it?"

50

"Anything good going on this weekend?" Alex asked as he and Hershel sat down in the dining hall.

"Not that I've heard of. I think most people are freaking out about finals on the horizon and speculating on Tuesday's mystery speaker," Hershel replied.

"Yeah, that's about what I've come up with, too. That sucks. There's usually a video game tournament or some other dorm-sponsored event on any given weekend," Alex complained, adjusting his tray to try and find a point of attack on the noodle surprise he had been served.

"Don't you hate when class messes with college?" Hershel joked.

"That I do," Alex said. "On the plus side, I heard there's a big party going on next weekend held by one of the upperclassmen. Every Su . . . person in our class is invited."

Hershel held his breath and tried to covertly scout the room to see if anyone was paying the pair attention. Not seeing any turned heads or huddled groups whispering, he decided to breeze over Alex's almost fuck-up and hope no one had heard.

"Sounds fun," Hershel said. "Nice of them to invite us freshmen."

"Apparently, it's a tradition to let those of us who haven't dropped out by this point participate. Plus, from what I've heard, our gym final is going to be brutal, so the experienced ones are showing us a bit more kindness," Alex explained.

"No idea what that's going to be yet, huh?" Hershel asked.

"No more than you. It's a pretty tightly-guarded secret. The only thing I've been able to uncover is that it's really intense."

"That part I could have guessed," Hershel commented. "Oh well, a party sounds fun. Roy's been good lately, so it'll be nice for him to blow off some steam."

"Ah. So you're going as Roy, then?" Alex asked.

"Well, yeah. Parties are kind of his bread and butter," Hershel said.

"No, I understand and all. It's just that . . . well, I haven't made a whole lot of friends at Lander besides you, so I was kind of hoping I'd have someone there I already knew. And Roy is cool and all, but he and I don't get along quite the same," Alex said, working to avoid meeting Hershel's eyes as he spoke.

Hershel gave thought to his words before answering. He hadn't seen Alex really hang out with anyone besides him and his roommates, and given what he believed his power to be, it made a certain amount of sense. Most of the other Supers probably thought of him as idiotic or deranged.

"It might be nice to actually get to go out for once," Hershel said tentatively.

"You sure that's okay? I don't want to accidently cause problems for you two."

"I'm not, but now that we've talked about it, Roy will remember the conversation next time he comes around, and I can see how he feels about it. He's been really focused ever since his fight with Chad. He doesn't even go out too much anymore. I'd say there's a decent chance he'll let me have this one without objection, or at least agree to change halfway through," Hershel said.

"That'd be cool," Alex said.

"Yeah. You know, I think this would make the first party since I changed that I actually go as Hershel instead of Roy."

"Better hope it's a good one then," Alex chuckled.

"Better hope it's not too good, or Roy's gonna be pissed he missed," Hershel pointed out.

"Agreed. We will hope for a good party, but not a great one," Alex said, lifting his soda in toast.

"Here's to a lackluster, but still entertaining party," Hershel said, lifting his own in suit. Glancing around, he realized that while Alex's earlier comment may have passed unnoticed, their impromptu toasting was definitely gathering a few odd stares from throughout the cafeteria.

Hershel felt less bothered by it than he would have expected.

51

"Good afternoon, class," Dean Blaine greeted his students Tuesday morning, entering the already-full classroom with a slightly shorter, far more nervous man in tow. "I'm glad to see all of you could make it to listen to today's guest speaker. Your commitment to learning has been noted."

Nick was staring at the man who had come with Dean Blaine, clearly their guest speaker. He was twitchy, obviously uncomfortable with crowds, and his appearance was slightly unkempt. Nick could only guess what status this man must have to have garnered the podium away from Dean Blaine.

"Now, I'm sure you're all curious to hear from today's speaker, so I'll turn things over to him in just a moment. Before he begins, though, I would like you all to realize that this man has come as a personal favor, and I expect him to be treated with the same respect you would show to me. I'll consider anything less than that as a very personal offense," Dean Blaine spelled out clearly. "With that said, I give you Jacob Stuart."

The shorter man, Jacob, moved from behind Dean Blaine and took the dean's usual spot at the front of the room. He glanced around uncertainly and fiddled with his hands. After a few seconds of fumbling, Jacob took a deep breath and composed himself before he began to speak.

"As your dean said, my name is Jacob Stuart. What he didn't mention is that I'm a Powered."

To say a ripple of surprise went through the class would be like saying that fish are somewhat inclined toward water over land, when handed a choice. It was kept in check, though, and it became immediately clear exactly why Dean Blaine had put such emphasis on respecting their speaker.

"Your dean felt that you would all benefit from hearing about things from the perspective of someone who can't control their abilities," Jacob continued, blowing past the ripple of shock because . . . because, well, he had already been expecting it. "I think he is either an optimist to the point of idiocy, or you must be the most open-minded class of Supers in the history of the world. From the looks on your faces, though, I'm sad to say it's seeming closer to the former than the latter."

Scowls and sneers were pulled up short as some Supers realized they were showing too much on their face. Nick continued a steady leer, not so angry as to draw attention, but unhappy enough that anyone who glanced at him wouldn't mistake him as sympathetic to the plight of a Powered.

"My ability is teleportation, and it activates every time I sneeze," Jacob said. "I can't control where I go, or how far away I land from where I started out. I seem to have some natural sense of preservation, though, because I never teleport into an object or five miles up in the air. I'm always safe, just horribly inconvenienced. That's more or less all you need to know about me, so why don't we go ahead and let you ask any questions you might have? I'm sure most of you have never had occasion to talk to a Powered, after all."

"If you accidentally teleport when you sneeze, why don't you just teleport back afterward?" Stella blurted out in typical fashion.

"Because I can't," Jacob replied.

"But you just said you had the ability of teleportation," Stella kept probing.

"Yes. When I sneeze, I teleport uncontrollably. And that's the only time I can do it. Unless I'm sneezing, I can't teleport any more than I can turn lead into gold," Jacob explained.

"I get that you have the accidental thing," Stella continued. "I'm just asking why you never learned to use your power outside of the trigger, so you could do it whenever you wanted?"

"Let me ask you something, young lady, what's your power?" Jacob asked in response.

"I turn into steel."

"That sounds like a good one," Jacob complimented her. "But why don't you ever try flying instead?"

"Because that's not my power," Stella said slowly. "I told you, I turn into steel."

"And I told you, I teleport when I sneeze. I don't have the power to teleport at will any more than you have the power to fly. There's a common misconception that Powereds are too lazy or stupid to master our gifts, when the reality is that we just don't have that ability. Trust me, this isn't a lifestyle choice."

A well-manicured hand near the front raised slowly in the air.

"Yes?" Jacob said, gesturing to the girl asking the question.

"Do you hate Supers?" Alice asked. The class reacted visibly, and Nick nearly fell out of his chair. What was that crazy bitch doing, drawing attention to herself in this kind of discussion? They needed to slide by and pray for class to end swiftly.

"I'm sorry, I think I misheard you," Jacob said.

"You didn't," Alice said. "I asked if you hated Supers. Your ability must make having any kind of normal life nearly impossible, yet when you look around, there are people with all of the gift and none of the burden being idolized and worshiped by society. If not for a variant in your genetic coding, that might very well have been you. So, do you hate us?"

"Of course I do," Jacob told her. "Every Powered hates Supers, and not just for the reasons you listed. While you are elite and special, we're looked at as a type of disabled person. We're considered lesser citizens, a social burden that people have to put up with. Most people think of us as nothing more than the price they pay for having

Supers and Heroes. So of course, I hate you, but not violently, just achingly. Aching for what might have been.

"I've got one for you now. Do you hate Powereds?"

"Of course I do," Alice echoed.

"And why is that?"

"Same reason. Because, when I look at you, I see what might have been if not for a twist of fate," Alice elaborated.

"Wow," Jacob said. "You're a lot more honest with yourself than most Supers."

"Thank you," Alice accepted gracefully.

Another hand rose a few rows over from Alice, this one male.

"Is there any hope for your kind?" Chad asked without waiting to be called on.

"There's always hope, kid. If you take nothing else from this, then please take that," Jacob answered. "No, there's no science, or miracle cure in the works that will make me more like you. No one has even been able to figure what the difference between Supers and Powereds is. As far as modern science can tell, we're genetically identical. So I'm not expecting some breaking news tomorrow announcing that we can become Supers, or even that we can just become human. But I have hope, because if I didn't, then I don't know how I would be able to keep pressing on. And besides, in a world where people can dance on the clouds, it isn't so crazy to hope for the impossible."

Chad accepted this explanation with a silent nod.

"Is it true no one knows what causes Powereds?" a dark-haired boy in the front called out.

"We don't even have a clue. Powereds can be born from Supers, regular humans, or other Powereds. The stats are across the board, and no one combination has been proven more likely," Jacob said.

"How did your parents take it?" Vince asked quietly. Nick made a note to whip up some cyanide punch and kill everyone he shared that damned dorm with. Two of them had called attention to themselves. Two!

"My parents?"

"Yeah. I mean, most parents are overjoyed to have a kid who is a Super. What's it like telling them that you're a Powered?" Vince elaborated.

"If you're able to tell them, then you're one of the lucky few," Jacob said. "Most of us get outed by the powers themselves. I sneezed myself right out of a birthday party when I was a kid. When I couldn't do it again by focusing, my secret was pretty much out. As for how they took it . . . well, I was fortunate. They loved me and tried to be supportive of me. It was hard, though, because every time I came back after I vanished, I could see the disappointment they were hiding. Disappointed that they had almost sired greatness, but instead. all they got was me. It's such a thin line between Powered and Super, yet that line may as well be a ravine from how separated we are."

184

Undoubtedly, some students wanted to chime in with how they wished that line was bigger so they wouldn't have to talk to or deal with Powereds anymore. One didn't qualify for the HCP by being stupid, though, even if they could make it in despite ignorance. Dean Blaine had laid it clearly on the table before the talk began. This was to be constructive questions only: anything else would piss off the man who could boot them from the program with nothing more than a word.

"We won't be able to go on much longer," Dean Blaine interrupted from his seat. "Mr. Stuart has an engagement to which I have agreed to accompany him in fulfillment of our bargain. Let's take one more question, and then, you will be dismissed early."

Several hands went up this time; some were last minute flurries of determination for the dean to see their participation and up their grade, others were genuine probes of curiosity. Jacob scanned the crowd and selected one hand a few rows up.

"Okay, you, in the sunglasses," Jacob announced, pointing up at Nick.

"Do you have any pepper?" Nick asked.

"Pepper?"

"Or a feather, or a thin line of cloth. Really anything along those lines," Nick said, half of him cursing himself for being the third Melbrook member to ask a question, and half trusting in himself and his gambit.

Ever so slowly, a smile crept across Jacob's face. He reached into his pants pocket and pulled out a long case. He popped it open and delicately removed a slender, white feather. It was sturdy as well as slim, and it looked very well cared for.

"Smart kid," Jacob commented.

"What the hell? How did he know you had a feather?" Stella blurted out.

"Because he's putting himself in my shoes," Jacob replied. "He's wondering, if he were in my situation, how would he use it to his advantage? And he came to the same conclusion I did. You see, teleporting randomly can still be pretty useful for snapping yourself out of dangerous situations, and just because I can't make myself teleport, doesn't mean I can't make myself sneeze."

"Crafty," Stella complimented.

"Dangerous," Nick corrected. "It's easy to get caught up in the pity party of what it must be like to be a Powered, but we're idiots if we forget that they aren't always helpless. Sometimes, a power that can't be controlled is even more hazardous to fight than one that can be."

"Mr. Campbell," Dean Blaine cautioned, raising his voice in warning.

"No, it's okay," Jacob said. "The boy is right. You are a fool if you forget that the key word of Powered is power. We have it, and some of us have stretched our resourcefulness to its limit for even a shred of more control. If you become Heroes, you'll have to deal with Powereds sometimes. Never underestimate them or make assumptions.

185

Always be ready to ask yourself, if you had their condition, how would you try to utilize it? Sometimes, answering that question will be the difference between winning and losing."

"On that note, I'd like to hear a round of applause to thank our guest for taking time out of his day to speak with us," Dean Blaine said. There was a lukewarm sound of clapping that faded away quickly.

"You can take your time in going to gym," Dean Blaine said as the last, lone clapper gave up the fight. "The coaches won't be expecting you until your regular time. I thought you might like to take these extra minutes to talk amongst yourselves about what we covered today. That is your choice, though. Just be at gym when the hour arrives." With that, he and Jacob exited the room, and after a minute or two of waiting to make sure he wouldn't come back, the rest of the class began flowing toward the door as well.

Nick gathered up his own things and sighed inwardly. He'd managed to diffuse a lot of the sympathy the class had been building toward Jacob, and in doing so had marked himself as someone with no compassion for Powereds. It was a bit paranoid, admittedly, to worry that someone would make such a leap from Melbrook students being sympathetic toward Powereds to suspecting they had once been Powereds themselves, but Nick often thought of paranoia as nothing more than extreme preparedness. He had done what he had to do, even if it was built on a very unlikely fear. Unlikely was something you learned to account for when you grew up with bipolar luck, though, so Nick reaffirmed that it was necessary to shift the pity toward Jacob partially into suspicion and fear.

Knowing all that, he still felt a sense of guilt rising in his stomach. That, at least, he knew exactly how to deal with.

52

"What. The Fuck. Was that?" These were the words that greeted Dean Blaine as he returned to his office some hours after the class and his errand with Jacob had been finished.

"Mr. Campbell," Dean Blaine said graciously. "My secretary informed me you'd been waiting in my office for some time. I must say, I'm impressed at your patience."

Nick stared back at him stonily. There might have been some emotion in the eyes hidden away by those sunglasses, but the face was an absolute blank. No feeling, no sentiment, no expectation, only an unending resolve in waiting for his answer.

"Fine, then. 'That,' as you put it, was my attempt to develop some semblance of humane feelings toward Powereds," Dean Blaine said.

"Have you ever done it before?" Nick asked.

"Well, no," Dean Blaine admitted.

"Then why, in God's sweet name, would you do it this time?" Nick asked, rising to his feet.

"Because it's more relevant," Dean Blaine replied.

"No, it isn't," Nick corrected him. "There is no relevance to it at all. Powereds are broken products, lesser Supers, a group with an unfortunate disability, and not one person in that class needs to think any differently. We're all Supers, after all. So who is going to get offended?"

"Mr. Campbell, if you're afraid that my experiment will compromise your secret, I can assure you—"

"Stop," Nick said, holding up his hand. The gesture was unnecessary: the tone of his voice alone would have frozen water. "Do you fully understand how tenuous our position here is? Do you realize what a ridiculous stroke of luck it is that the only real telepath in our class is one of us? Do you think for one moment that you really understand what it will be like if our secret gets out? Let me assure you of something, Dean Blaine. I'm certain your heart is in the right place, but don't you ever fucking dare believe for an instant you know what it's like growing up as a Powered. Until you've seen the looks of disgust and disappointment on people's faces, until you've been literally terrified out of your mind about what you'll cause to happen next, and until you've seen that same fear in the eyes of those you love, only then can you talk to me about how you're doing your best to keep our secret."

"Feel better?" Dean Blaine asked. "That was quite the little monologue."

"It needed to be said," Nick replied. "You're too careless, and I understand today was about trying to help us, but honestly, the best thing you can do to help us is treat us like everyone else."

"In that case, I should probably kick you out since you've sworn at the dean of your program twice in last few minutes," Dean Blaine said.

"Do what you've got to do," Nick shot back. "Just understand that while Mary and Roy, and maybe even Vince, could still hang on if we got outed, Alice and I wouldn't last a week. We're not the combat type. The only thing that lets us fly through here is being part of the community of Supers. If we were targeted, or different, there's no way we'd be able to hold on."

"I take it that's why you consistently make grades at almost exactly the median of the class," Dean Blaine speculated.

"On my best day, it's still tenuous that my power should have gotten me in here," Nick said. "Not making waves is the best strategy I've got."

"Very well, Mr. Campbell," Dean Blaine said. "I'll take what you've said under advisement for my future lessons. I'll do this, because this is the first time you've actually talked to me as yourself, the bright observant boy we both know you to be, rather than that insipid character you've concocted."

"It made more sense to abandon the pretense, otherwise, I couldn't have had this discussion with you," Nick confessed.

"A wise choice. Though I'm sure you'll be playing the same part in our future classroom interactions," Dean Blaine said.

"Of course," Nick confirmed.

"I can accept that. I do hope you realize my door is always open to you, not just when you wish to go on a tirade. Since you've already shown your true self to me, there's no harm in dropping by to talk. If you would like," Dean Blaine offered.

"I'll keep that in mind."

"Good. I think we're done then, Mr. Campbell, unless there was something else?"

"No. As long as there are no more stunts like today, we should be fine," Nick said, turning to go.

"Oh, and I should point out that there were two problems with your argument," Dean Blaine said. "Firstly, Ms. Smith is not the only telepath in your year, as you should know from having met Mr. Griffen."

"Alex is a nice guy, but he's closer to an empath than a telepath. He rarely gets thoughts, mostly emotions," Nick said.

"As far as you know," Dean Blaine pointed out. "It would be wise not to underestimate anyone who has made it into my program. That brings up the second problem. Your 'tenuous power,' as you described it, is not what elevated you into the HCP."

"Oh?" Nick asked without turning around. He was confident his face was still controlled, but there was no reason to risk giving anything away when it was avoidable.

188

"Indeed. The power qualifies you as a Super, but in your evaluation, it was your intelligence and strategic thinking that made you Hero material," Dean Blaine said.

"Good to know," Nick said, walking to the door and swiftly exiting the dean's office. Somewhere in the course of that conversation, he'd lost his power and momentum, but he'd gained insight into how the dean worked, and that might prove to be invaluable. Aside from that, he'd gotten a slight idea at what Dean Blaine's power might be, and that information he *knew* would be useful. Now, he just had to think of a way to test his hypothesis.

After finals, though. Even Nick wasn't confident enough to try and take on more projects before the semester ended.

53

"I'm glad you talked us into coming out," Hershel told Alex as they entered the living room of a two-story house. The couches were wrapped in plastic, and it seemed someone had laid a blue tarp down on top of most of the carpet. The house was full, though not bursting like the other clubs and parties they had been to. It was loud enough to see that people were having fun, but it hadn't crossed the line into utter pandemonium yet.

"I think we all needed it after that bummer of a presentation on Tuesday," Alex said. "I mean, I agree with what Dean Blaine was trying to do, but he should have known most people weren't ever going to be sympathetic toward some Powered."

"You are," Vince pointed out.

Alex shrugged. "Nearly everyone thinks I'm crazy or delusional. It's hard for me to get up on my high horse about how I'm so much better than someone else. Besides, that's not the Jedi way."

"The Jedi had better get out of my way," Nick said, shouldering into the room. He and Alice were the last of the group, Mary having opted to stay in and the rest of their friends studying for finals already. In truth, Nick was tempted to use the same excuse; however, after letting himself go and tearing into Dean Blaine, he felt like he needed to recenter his character. Sadly, a social environment full of Supers was the best place for that.

"Welcome, Fish," said a tall, blonde girl holding a red plastic cup. She and Alice had a slight similarity, in the way that a dog and a wolf can look the same if one isn't paying attention. She wasn't imposing, per se, but the way she walked, smiled, and even tossed her hair left no doubt in anyone's mind that this woman was a warrior. "I'm glad you guys made it out. My name is Angela, and this is my house."

"Thank you for inviting us," Vince said politely.

"No worries. It's a tradition to invite those of you who last this long to join us. It's our way of saying good job on getting this far, and that we're welcoming you into the Super community at Lander," Angela replied.

"This party is all Supers?" Alex asked.

"You got it," Angela confirmed. "Feel free to let down your hair and be yourself. Tonight, your secret identity is safe with us."

"We really appreciate it," Alice said, using all of her willpower not to curtsy. She had been rapidly realizing that the stiff formality she had learned at Daddy's functions were not suited to the college environment. Plus, she was wearing slacks, so she would have looked ridiculous.

"Like I said, no big deal," Angela assured. "Besides, you had the balls to come. That means you belong here. You'd be amazed how many people who are here to learn

190

about fighting life and death battles are too squeamish to come out to a party with older students."

"That, and it is the beginning of finals," Hershel pointed out.

"Which is why this also shows us who the irresponsible crowd is," Angela said with a wink. "Anyway, the keg is in the garage, and we have some liquor on the counter. Help yourself to whatever you want; buying for the freshmen is also part of the tradition."

"Um, we're under age," Vince said.

"As am I. As are most of us here, in fact. I recommend you enjoy it while you can, though. Apparently, once you hit junior year there isn't enough free time for a beer or a party," Angela said. "Your call, though. Drink or don't, but mingle and have some fun either way." With that, Angela sauntered back off into the shapeless blob of people.

"Sasha's going to be pissed she missed a chance to be irresponsible," Vince commented once she was gone.

"So's Roy," Hershel added.

"Think he'll want to come out?" Alex asked.

"Absolutely. Now, ask me if I care," Hershel said with a sideways grin. "Come on, guys, let's mingle."

A bit surprised at being led by the most socially awkward of the group, everyone followed Hershel as he led them into the kitchen, where most people were gathered. Given that the kitchen was where the liquor was kept, as well as the cups, not to mention that it was only a door away from the keg in the garage, it was the logical gathering place for the attendees. What seemed illogical, though, was the ease with which Hershel was navigating them through it. He was greeting people, shaking hands, getting names, and moving onward. It was oddly mind-blowing, though it shouldn't have been. After all, Hershel was a role-player, and with Roy's memories, this was a role he knew by heart. If the others were surprised by his rapport with the older students, they were flabbergasted when Hershel finally reached the cups and plucked a few from the top.

"What does everybody want?" Hershel asked, turning his attention to the liquor selection.

"Are you serious?" Vince asked in a nearly strangled voice. "You know we can't drink."

"No, I know that we legally *shouldn't* drink. I also know that since I didn't drive here, I feel like seeing what it's like firsthand for once, and it seems like these first two years are going to be the only chance we'll get. More importantly, I don't want to go through college with my alter ego as the only one doing stupid crap and trying new things," Hershel said, not without conviction. He didn't feel quite as certain as he sounded, but he was determined to make some memories of his own. His talk with Alex had made him realize how easily he defaulted to letting Roy be the one to go party or chase the girl. This was his life too, damn it.

191

"Spoken like a man after my own heart," Nick said, stepping to Hershel's side. "Let me try . . . the gin."

"And?" Hershel asked.

"Um . . . ice?"

"You want straight gin for your first taste of alcohol," Hershel said incredulously.

"I thought that's how you were supposed to take it," Nick lied.

"Never mind, I'll make you something myself. Roy's tried tons of drinks," Hershel said, waving off Nick. "Anyone else?"

Alice cautiously raised her hand, and Alex joined more enthusiastically.

"Guess that makes me the designated driver," Vince grumbled.

"Aw, cheer up, Silver," Nick consoled him. "At least you can see things better than us from up on your moral high ground."

"I'm not on the high ground. I get why you guys want to try it. That's just not my thing," Vince defended.

"Well, bottoms up to Vince for being our reliable driver then," Nick said, accepting a drink from Hershel and toasting with it. He took a sip and was pleasantly surprised. Nick had been drinking since childhood and actually did prefer straight gin, but for a mixed drink, Hershel's concoction was pretty good. The smiles and smacks of the rest of the group confirmed his opinion.

"That's tasty, Hershel," Alice complimented. "All I've had is wine with dinner once or twice, and this is way better."

"I do what I can," Hershel said modestly.

"What are you drinking?" Alex asked, noting Hershel's liquid was a different color.

"Screwdriver," Hershel replied. "Your drinks have whiskey in them, and I don't drink whiskey."

"Much as I love your same old faces, let's get out of this corner, and go get our mingle on," Nick said, gesturing grandly. He began wading back into the crowd, the others following with far less grandeur. Not without any, mind you; just with less.

54

Walking around the party was a somewhat surreal experience. Sure, it was a new environment to most of them, but that, in itself, wasn't overpowering. The odd part was just how normal everything seemed . . . until it didn't. Seeing a guy talking to a hot girl at a party: normal. Seeing that same guy produce a rose made of perfect glass from nowhere: significantly less normal. It wasn't the extraordinary parts that seemed out of place, though; it was seeing them used so casually in a place like this. Slowly, it was dawning on the Lander freshmen just how paranoid the secret identity had made them over the semester. Hiding their nature was hardly a new experience for some, but it struck Alice that she hadn't gone flying since she'd first learned she was able to. Sure, she'd used it here and there in training, but that wasn't the same thing as soaring above world. Alex, too, was missing the days when he didn't have to keep his nature hidden away under lock and key.

As the group maneuvered the party, they saw mostly unfamiliar faces. Occasionally, a member would recognize a sophomore that they'd seen in the hall a few times; however, that can hardly be considered the same as seeing a friend. Gradually, though, more small, huddled groups of freshmen joined the party. They moved in packs, unconsciously fearful that they would be picked off should they separate from the herd. Such fears seemed baseless, as all the older students went out of their way to show kindness and a welcoming attitude to the freshmen. Still, the small groups maintained their tight formations.

It was in one other such group that Vince finally saw someone he knew outside of his own social circle.

"Hey!" Vince called out. "Thomas, right?"

"Right," Thomas answered, leading his own small circle toward Vince's. Smacked over the head with a sudden realization of potential unwanted conversation topics, Vince detached himself from his friends and intercepted Thomas on the premise of a friendly handshake.

"Didn't expect to see you here," Vince said with a large smile, squeezing and pumping Thomas's hand.

"Ditto," Thomas echoed. "I thought you'd have had your fill of parties."

"Eh heh. No, you know me, social butterfly. Anyway, who are your friends?" Vince asked hastily.

"Oh, this is Stella and Violet," Thomas said, taking a step to the side and indicating each girl in turn. Vince already knew Stella on sight, but Violet turned out to be an almost unremarkable girl from their class. Average height, cute without being eye-catching, but with hair dyed a shade of purple so deep, it was almost black (hence the almost quantifier).

"Nice to meet you both," Vince said, resisting the urge to look over his shoulder and see if the others were still hovering in the area. "I never got a chance to say it in person, but thank you again."

"No prob," Stella quipped. "So, you don't want your buddies to know you got your ass kicked, huh?"

"Beg pardon?" Vince nearly choked on his words.

"What Stella is trying to say is that it's clear you wanted to greet us before this conversation was in earshot of your friends, and we'll, of course, respect your wish for privacy," Violet said, a lilting and slightly high-pitched voice piping out of her.

"Oh, um . . . yes," Vince admitted. "I appreciate what you did, but I haven't really told them about what happened."

"There is no shame in what happened to you," Thomas assured him. "We will, as Violet said, of course, respect your wishes."

"Sort of a moot point, anyway. Looks like they wandered off," Stella pointed out.

"Huh," Vince noticed. "That they did."

"Well, now we get to talk to you outside of a combat situation, so all the better for us," Violet said cheerfully.

"Thank you," Vince said again, unsure of how to respond to such a statement. An honest thought and change of subject both occurred to him at once. "Wasn't there someone else with you that night?"

"Oh, that was my roommate, Camille," Violet explained. "She's not big on parties. I pretty much had to drag her out of the house that night."

"Too bad, I would have liked to thank her in person," Vince said.

"Do it Monday, then," Stella said. "In the meantime, how about showing us where the beer in this joint is?"

*   *   *

"Why are we leaving Vince?" Alex asked as Nick herded the group away, after a minute or so of standing around.

"Because it's a party, and the point is to meet new people, not feel guilted into sticking with the ones you already know," Nick explained.

"Still, it seems like we should have said something," Alex objected again.

"I'm actually with Nick on this one," Hershel agreed. "He was mingling with new people. Us hanging around wasn't going to help him with that. Besides, it's a small house, he can find us when he's ready. In the meantime, we can do some mingling of our own, and I think I see the perfect opportunity now." Hershel picked up his pace, leading the others to a ping-pong table on which cups were being arranged in a triangular formation and beer was being poured into them.

"Anyone got the next game?" Hershel asked.

194

"Nah," replied a tall boy with black hair who was setting up the cups on one side. "You want in?"

"Sure," Hershel replied. He turned back to look at the others. "Who wants to play with me?"

"I'll watch and learn the game first," Alice said.

"Still working on my first drink. I'm out," Alex said.

"Guess that leaves me," Nick shrugged, stepping up and taking his place on one side of the table.

The other team took their place, and the dark-haired boy laid down the rules. "One bounce is allowed: any more and you can smack it away. Distractions and trash talk are fine, as long as you don't touch the ball. Game can't be won until one team misses and another scores in the same round, so if we keep scoring, neither cup gets removed. Powers are fair game."

Nick raised an eyebrow. "You sure about that?"

"Totally," the boy confirmed. "It makes these games a lot more fun. Besides, how often do we get to just let go and use them? They're only allowed on your turn, though, and no deflecting with it unless your opponent has bounced more than once."

"Fair enough," Hershel agreed. "I'm Hershel, and this is Nick."

"Ben and Chris," said the dark-haired boy, gesturing first to himself, then to his darker-skinned companion. "You need a warm-up round?"

"Nah," Hershel said. "Let's do this."

55

"How do you guys know each other?" Vince asked once the ladies had gotten their cups and beer to fill them. Thomas, like Vince, had found the idea of underage drinking unbecoming of one reaching for the goal of being a Hero.

"Thomas and I dated for a bit in the first month," Violet said. "It didn't work out too well, but we stayed friends. I met Stella at the gym one day, when I was looking for a sparring partner. We gave each other a good workout and decided to do it again the next day. We kept fighting, and somewhere along the way, started doing stuff outside of beating each other senseless."

"Wow," Vince said. "You must be pretty tough if you can fight someone who can turn into solid steel."

"Sort of," Violet admitted, blushing slightly. "I manipulate density. So I can make myself denser than titanium, or so insubstantial that I pass through walls. I can do it in objects, too. That's how I weakened the ice and popped you out that night."

"She's a handful when you get her in the fighting mood," Stella complimented. "She's only one rank behind me at three."

"Impressive," Vince agreed. "And, Thomas, you have some sort of energy beams? I saw them when you grabbed Michael."

"Essentially," Thomas nodded. "I command my inner energy outward of my body. It shapes according to my will, though the dimensions are limited by the amount I can summon. In my time at Lander, it has grown significantly stronger, though."

"Really? Just from extreme exercise?" Vince asked.

"The exercise certainly helps, but I attribute it more to the constant training I do in my off time. Having a variety of skilled opponents forced me to learn new styles of fighting, and that helped me grow as a warrior," Thomas explained.

"I see," Vince said. "It sounds like you spend a lot of time training outside of class."

"We all do," Violet chirped in. "Everyone higher up says it's crazy easy to go from the top to the bottom in your first year if you don't work hard."

"It is especially important in cases like my own," Thomas pointed out. "I am ranked as seven, but my power could easily be viewed as ancillary, more useful as support than combat. I have to work very hard to demonstrate otherwise."

"You've got a leg up on me," Vince said with a smile he didn't feel. "I'm only at eight."

"I'd heard about how you were ranked that high after losing your first bout. You must have put on a hell of a show," Thomas said.

"He took on that douche we pulled off of him. Guess that counts for something," Stella said.

"Not to mention Michael is the worst type of opponent for me," Vince said, only half-defensively. This whole line of conversation was making him realize just how little effort he was putting in compared to some of the other students. He'd been avoiding additional conflict for fear of having to charge up his powers more. That might be a reality he'd have to face sooner than expected if he wanted to keep up with people this determined, though.

"Why is he your worst type?" Violet asked.

"I absorb energy," Vince explained. "Michael's power is cold-based. Cold is literally the absence of energy, so he can come at me all day, and I can't absorb anything he throws."

"Cool power, though," Stella said. "What all can you absorb?"

"Oh, you know, just the basics," Vince deflected. "Hey, what's going on over there?"

*   *   *

What was going on over there was a surprisingly close battle of beer pong with both teams down to a single cup. As it turned out, Ben was a shifter like Hershel, so his powers were out of commission until he decided to make the change. So far, he was doing well enough in normal form. Hershel was keeping up decently, but it was really Nick and Chris that were the juggernauts of the game. Chris, it turned out, had the power to teleport objects he touched. This made his style of play less bouncing-based and more just teleporting directly over the cup he wanted. That should have sealed the game, save only for the Nick factor.

With his honed dexterity and power over luck, Nick was tearing up the table on par with his opponent. Sure, he should have been laying low, squeezing by without drawing attention, staying in the middle ground, but damn it, this was fun! He'd been in such a secondary position at Lander, so accustomed to the idea that everyone around him was better at everything. They were stronger, they were faster, a few of them were even smarter. For the first time in months, though, he was doing something he could win at. It felt good to be a winner; it reminded him of who he really was under his ridiculous facade. Besides, it wasn't like people didn't already know what his power was. It would have been more suspicious if he hadn't been running the table. At least, that's what he told himself as he dunked yet another ball into a red cup.

"Fucker," Ben swore, chugging down the contents.

"You're good, Sunglasses. You're real good," Chris told him, picking up the ball for his turn. "But me, I don't miss." The ball vanished from Chris's hand and reappeared a few inches over one of the remaining cups on Hershel and Nick's side.

Nick threw Hershel a glance and the heavier boy took the cup and guzzled. He was beginning to feel all the alcohol, and far sooner than he'd expected. Roy always had such insane tolerance that Hershel had forgotten somewhere along the way that it didn't extend to him. He needed to finish this game soon if they were going to have a chance.

"Come on, Hershel!" Alice cheered in spite of herself. "Sink it to keep the pressure on."

Hershel drew in a breath and took his aim. He released the ball, and it flew almost true. As it landed for its first bounce, it veered ever so slightly off course, sending it into the cup's rim instead of the bitter beer inside.

"Oooh, so sorry there, freshman," Ben taunted. "Looks like you just don't know how to push through in the clutch. Don't worry, though, that comes with experience." On the word "experience" Ben tossed his own ball. It arced gracefully through the air, hopping once and depositing itself in the lone remaining cup in front of Nick. Without a second glance, Nick scooped up the red cup of failure and did his duty.

"Ah, well. Win some, lose some," Hershel said, trying to stay steady in spite of a slowly mounting urge to slur.

"You fought a good game," Ben said sportingly. "Chris and I haven't had anyone go that long with us in a long time. Up for another?"

"Not sure about Nick, but I'm going to pass," Hershel replied.

"I can keep going," Nick said with a smile. Unlike Hershel, Nick had earned his tolerance for alcohol the hard way and was nowhere near hitting his limits.

"Sad to see you go, big boy," Chris said. "You were the weak link in the team, anyway."

"Dude," Ben snapped at his friend. "Be nice."

"Fuck you, I've never been on board with this 'coddle the freshmen' idea," Chris shot back.

"It's fine," Hershel said with a grin. "I was the weak link. It's true, so how bad could it be that he said it?"

"I'm sorry," Ben apologized. "My friend can be an asshole when he's competing and drinking."

"Like I said, it's fine," Hershel shrugged.

"Yeah, Ben, it's fine. He knows he can't drink. Next game, I say we take on the broad and the pussy who wanted to watch," Chris said with a snicker.

"Hey!" This was actually snapped by Alice, Alex, and Nick simultaneously. In addition to yelling, Alex was searching for something not too property damaging to throw at Chris. Alice, unfortunately, lacked such means of recourse, but was unhappy nonetheless. Before any of them could take any action, though, Hershel acted first. He held up his right hand in a swift, stopping motion honed from years of commanding troops. Elf troops battling an orc invasion admittedly, but command skills were command skills, regardless of the venue in which they were acquired.

"Alex," Hershel said in an oddly still voice. "May I have your drink, please?"

198

"Um, sure," Alex said, handing Hershel his cup and the remaining liquid inside.

"Thank you," Hershel replied, swallowing the last of it in one gulp. He handed the cup back to Alex and walked back over to the table.

"I thought you didn't drink whiskey," Alex commented.

"He doesn't," came a deeper, rougher voice from Hershel's throat. A slow ripple seemed to move across Hershel's body, giving him an amorphous appearance. His torso and limbs lengthened, muscles emerged where only fat had been, and his face became leaner and more chiseled. It happened in a matter of seconds, and then someone totally different was standing where Hershel had been.

"I do," said Roy, his eyes hard and a smile that seemed more dangerous than joyful slicing across his face. "Now, I'm going to show you what happens to the poor bastards who question the drinking skills of a Daniels man."

56

Roy had changed the game, and not in a figurative sense.

"Whiskey," Roy reiterated.

"Excuse me?" Ben asked, trying to understand.

"Your boy called me out, so I'm upping the stakes. We play with half cups of whiskey instead of beer, unless you girls think you can handle full ones," Roy replied. Mary might bitch him out for being condescending, but given the circumstances, he was confident he could talk his way out of too much earache.

"Half is fine," Chris said, answering for his partner. "Mind if Ben changes first?"

"Be my guest," Roy replied with a generous smile. Ben's features melded together, his skin becoming scaly and thick, while his hair retreated into his head. His pupils became vertical slits and small, dagger-like claws grew out from his hand. "Snakeman?" Roy asked when Ben's transformation was done.

"Closer to lizard, actually," Ben corrected with a shrug. His voice sounded a bit more like sandpaper rubbing together than it had before, but there weren't any of the drawn out "S" sounds that one might have expected from his appearance.

"Hope that form comes with improved aim," Roy said.

Ben grinned, an act which had become several degrees more disturbing. "It does."

"Good. You won the last game, so you shoot first once the cups are filled," Roy said.

"Agreed," Chris said. "We'll get the whiskey."

"Fine by me," Roy said. Once the two had ventured off to the kitchen, though, Roy immediately turned his attention on Nick. "Please, please, *please* tell me you can at least halfway hold your liquor."

*   *   *

"This took an interesting turn somewhere," Vince said as he sidled up to Alice and Alex, joining in the slowly-growing crowd watching the cups be filled.

"I feel like we should have expected it somehow," Alex replied. "So, who are your friends?"

"Oh, right," Vince said, reddening at his blunder. A quick round of introductions later and everyone was gathered to observe the beginning of the rematch.

"I get Roy doing this, but why is Nick going along with it?" Alice wondered aloud.

"Because it's fun," Alex answered automatically. The other threw him a speculative look, so he clarified. "I sense thoughts and emotions too, remember? Just

200

because I don't pick up with the clarity of Mary, doesn't mean I can't feel the waves of enjoyment flooding off of Nick."

"He does love being the center of attention," Vince pointed out.

"No, the kid who wears sunglasses all the time likes people looking at him? I never would have put that one together," Stella snickered.

"Hush, you," Violet chided her. "It can't be easy to have a power like luck. I mean, how are you even sure when it's working, or if it's just coincidence? That has to make it difficult staying afloat in the HCP."

"Knowing Nick, I think he just assumes everything good is his power at work," Alice said.

"Knowing Nick, I'm not so sure that it isn't," Vince countered.

Alice opened her mouth to say otherwise, then thought better of it. "I hope luck powers come packaged with a new liver, or the ability to turn alcohol into water, otherwise, we'll be carting him out of here if they lose."

"I guess that means we're hoping they win," Alex said.

"Of course," Vince said automatically.

"Then shut up and cheer, because they're starting."

*   *   *

Roy's powers didn't actually make him any better at beer pong than Hershel. Sure, his senses were a little sharper, and of course, he had strength and endurance far beyond the human threshold; however, none of that made bouncing a ping-pong ball into a cup an easier task. What did help, though, was a wealth of experience playing drinking games, a nearly endless alcohol tolerance, and more confidence than a rooster in a hen house.

"Suck it," Roy called as the ball left his hand, hurtling through the air and landing deftly in one of the few remaining cups on the other side of the table. Chris's hand hesitantly picked up said cup, removed the ball, and choked down the contents. He and Ben were veteran beer pong players, using his power and Ben's skill to triumph over nearly every opponent. Since they usually won, though, they had to drink less, and as they worked their way through an ocean of whiskey, it had begun to dawn on the duo that this had a significant disadvantage at times. Ben was holding up well thanks to his own enhanced endurance, but Chris's awareness and focus were deteriorating by the minute.

"Your shot," Nick said cheerily. Chris nodded in acknowledgment and took several deep breaths. He cleared his mind and held the ball firmly. His eyes locked on the area over one of the remaining cups on Nick and Roy's side, and with a burst of energy, the ball snapped out of his hand in a puff of smoke. It reappeared almost instantaneously, dropping straight down toward the cup. Chris's aim had been off though, and the ball struck the cup's rim rather than the brown liquid below. It took a bad hop and struck the table once before landing on the carpet.

"And that's the game," Roy announced, plucking the ball from the ground and dousing it in a cup of water.

"You think you've won just because I missed once?" Chris challenged.

"I know we've won, because you've hit the point where you can't focus properly. Ben is good, but not good enough to take on both of us, and my money says you've always used your power, so you don't have any real skills at this game," Roy explained.

"I'm fine," Chris spit back defiantly. "I just slipped."

"Right, and as more alcohol is digested and enters the blood stream, you're going to find it easier to teleport things precisely," Nick said. "Never thought I'd say this, but Roy is right. Out of respect for your partner, we'll let you take the remaining cups and walk away from the game so you don't have to slam them down."

"Fuck you, take your shot," Chris replied.

"Now, hold on, man," Ben said, butting in. "I'm not staying in shifted form all night, and when I go back, there will still be a lot of alcohol in my system to process. They're actually being nice and letting us call it here, so I say we take them up on it. They upped the stakes and played better, no big deal. It's just a stupid game of beer pong."

"I am not giving up," Chris said. "And I am not losing to a damn freshman."

"So be it," Nick said, shrugging. He took the ball from Roy and tossed it casually into the air. It sailed effortlessly into one of the remaining three cups.

"I'm not drinking anymore," Ben declared as Chris's eyes fell on him. "I told you I wanted to be done."

"Fine, I'll do it myself then," Chris countered, snagging the cup and forcing it all down in one swallow. "Your shot," he said, wiping his mouth and handing the ball to Ben. In response, Ben's skin grew pink as he shifted back to his regular form.

"I told you, I'm out. And you should be, too. You're going to be sick as a dog."

"Who gives a shit?" Chris said, weaving his body back to facing the table.

"Me." The voice that made that declaration was very calm, very relaxed, and contained not so much as an iota of threat in its tone. At the same time, everyone in range discerned a simple truth from that voice, something that radiated down and registered on a primal level:

The owner of that voice was not to be fucked with.

"Now, Chris," Angela continued, walking up to him as the crowd parted before her. "We know that you're an asshole, but you're our asshole. We put up with your crap out of love and camaraderie. I'm going to be feeling a lot less love if you start throwing up in my house."

Chris's gaze locked on the tall girl in front of him. She was smiling placidly and had open, caring body language. Physically, she seemed the opposite of daunting. It was

202

more like a gentle kitten asking a favor. Chris had been in class with her for a year and a half, though. He was intoxicated and rapidly getting worse. But he wasn't drunk enough to make the mistake of crossing her. It was hard to imagine the poor bastard who ever had been that drunk.

"Good game, guys," Chris said, stumbling away from the table. "Sorry, I got a little too competitive there."

"No problem," Nick said graciously.

"Come again anytime," Roy sniped as Ben led Chris away, presumably to the bushes or an unoccupied toilet to try and forcibly reduce the amount of alcohol assaulting his system.

"Now, as for you two," Angela said, turning her attention to the winners. "Nice game. Try to keep the pissing matches to a minimum in the future, though. If someone gets angry and a fight starts, all of our identities are in danger. Not to mention, two Supers can tear up a house in no time flat."

"My apologies," Nick said. "Things got a bit out of hand, and our drive to win got the better of us."

"You're fine, Chris's liver will recover, and you provided some excellent entertainment. I'm just saying, be careful who you challenge around here. Looks can be very deceiving."

Roy and Nick nodded agreement, and if Mary were there, she would have heard all four of her dormmates sharing almost the exact same thought simultaneously. There were variations of course, with Roy's being a bit more racy and Vince's leaning more toward a guilty self-admission, but the overall wording was inherently similar:

"Lady, you don't know the half of it."

*   *   *

"Surely, there must be something more interesting to do on a Saturday night than playing chess," Mr. Numbers commented while Mary was pondering her next move.

"Nah, I'm not much of a party girl. Besides, they can't get into that much trouble without me," she said.

57.

The days on the Lander campus slipped by and finals season went into full swing. Students in the HCP were expected to maintain at least a C average in their normal courses, so even though many would have preferred to let schoolwork fall by the wayside, the Super community found itself stressed out and studying hard. Adding to the anxiety of the freshman class was fear of the unknown, manifesting in terror and rumors regarding their end of semester exam in gym. Coach George had announced it would take place on December 17, the day after all normal finals were wrapped. Anyone who didn't show up was assumed to be dropping out of the program. Different students were dealing with this looming challenge in different ways. Some were hoarding information, rumor-mongering in a desperate attempt to find anything that would give them an edge. Others were throwing themselves into their other classes, working hard in a sort of cosmic trade-out for the class they wished they could be preparing for. Some, though, had altogether unique coping methods.

"I really don't see how having a *Quantum Leap* marathon is an appropriate way to spend the last Saturday we have for studying," Vince said as Nick rearranged the furniture to allow for more viewers.

"I still have a math final. Isn't quantum a mathy word?"

"Seriously, Nick."

"Look, people need to chill out today," Nick explained. "Research shows that relaxed people test better than stressed out ones. I'm offering that opportunity in the form of classic sci-fi television. No one is making you partake in it."

"Except that you commandeered the boy's lounge," Vince pointed out.

"You've got a room and a library left," Nick countered. "Though you, more than any of us, could use a day to do nothing. You're worrying so much, I think your hair has started to shift in hue from silver to white."

"Funny," Vince said. "How can you be so calm about all this? In four days, we have to take our semester final for gym, a test that's going to determine if we're still in the program after Christmas, and no one has any idea what it entails."

"Oh, plenty of people know what it is. They just aren't telling us freshmen. I can only assume it's what constitutes hazing around here. Psychological torture, if you will," Nick said. "Besides, every test we take will be determining if we're still in the program. Better to learn how to go with the flow now and save yourself from an ulcer by the time we're juniors."

"We could be spending this time studying for our other tests at least," Vince said.

"Buddy, this whole last month has been almost nothing but study group and reviews. I don't know about you, but I am burned out. Me rereading the same crap today

204

isn't going to do a lick of good. Spending some time with my friends, though, that one might have some positive effects. Given the two choices, I'm going with the one that involves time travel and popcorn," Nick said.

Vince laughed a bit in spite of himself. "I don't know how you do it, Nick. You're the only person here who can just roll through things so carefree. I'm seriously beginning to believe that's your actual power."

"Just an easygoing guy, I guess," Nick lied. "Let things fall where they may and do the best you can. Take our gym final, for example. Sure, I don't know what's coming, but neither did any other class before me, and they still seem to have students graduating."

"Far fewer than we do currently, though," Vince said.

"So maybe this will weed out a few more of ours. And maybe I'll be one of them. If I thought spending the day holed up in my room agonizing over the possibilities would help, then I'd . . . no, even then, I still probably wouldn't do it. That's beside the point, though, since it doesn't help," Nick said.

"Too bad. I've logged some serious hours pursuing that strategy," Vince quipped.

"Never too late to change horses," Nick said.

"Until the race starts," Vince replied.

"You'd be surprised some of the things I've seen happen on a race track," Nick said. "That will have to wait for another day, though, because I need to finish moving all this crap before the others arrive."

"Who all is joining in your little festivity, anyway?"

"Mary took her last final yesterday, so she's down. Hershel, Alex, and Will all said they'd be coming. Alice has said she will 'stop by' but wouldn't commit to any more than that. Oh, and I think Will's sister might come," Nick said, ticking off the attendants on his fingers.

"Her name is Jill. It's one letter off from Will. Why is it you can't ever seem to remember that?" Vince asked.

"Because my brain is just too damn chocked full of knowledge to take on anything new at this point. See what I mean about needing a day off?"

Vince raised his hands in surrender. "Okay, okay, you win. Put me on the list, I'll spend my day watching television with you guys instead of expanding my mind."

"If you're looking for mind expansion, I'm pretty sure those guys who play Ultimate Frisbee on the lawn and listen to indie music keep some on them," Nick informed him.

"Huh?"

"Never mind. Should have known you wouldn't get that joke, Boy Scout," Nick said. "So, you going to invite your woman?"

"Nah, she's visiting her parents this weekend," Vince said.

"Oh, that's cool that they live close by," Nick commented.

"They live in Seattle," Vince said.

"Right. Forgot to adjust normal expectations. My mistake," Nick said. "Well, if you're staying, then you can help me with the couch."

"Sure," Vince agreed. They went to each end of the couch and hefted it up. As they were inching around the room, a thought struck Vince.

"If everyone is coming, why aren't we doing this in the main common room?"

"Because Mr. Numbers and Mr. Transport occasionally come through there, and I thought they might be a bit of a buzzkill on our day," Nick said in a strained voice.

"Hey, they aren't that bad. They've always been really nice to us," Vince said.

"Not denying that, but they're adults. Today, we're blowing off legitimate work to piss the day away having fun. That is most definitely adolescent behavior, and I feel it will be more enjoyable without any judgmental gazes being cast our way from the kitchen."

"I thought you said this was a valid stress management technique to improve test performances."

"Oh, Vince, you can't believe everything you hear these days. Now, let's get to the video store before someone steals my idea and checks out the first season."

58

"I must say, it warms my heart as an educator to see such a robust turnout this morning," Coach George announced as he paced along the line of skittish students. "How about you, Persephone?"

"Heart thoroughly warmed," Coach Persephone answered.

"Glad to hear it. I must say, I thought more of you would break by now. I was certain some would take this opportunity to drop out of the program, rather than face today's exam. You've proven me wrong so far, but then, the day is just beginning," Coach George said.

It was indeed just beginning. The students had been told to be lined up in the gym on exam day at seven in the morning, sharp. Most, if not all, had arrived early, rather than risk seeing what happened to those who strolled in minutes after the deadline. Many of them were still blinking the sleep out of their eyes, but they were in attendance and paying attention with the vigor that only fear can provide.

"I'm sure many of you are wondering what today's test is. Well, as most of you know, this is the last chance any of you will have to show us which training course you'll be placed in next semester. As such, the only way we felt we could accurately measure your abilities was to pit you against one another," Coach George continued.

Some of the higher ranked students perked up. If it was just going to be fighting, they were confident they would sail through this day easily.

"Now, before anyone gets too excited, this won't be like your first day. I don't just want to see who can kick the shit out of each other. I want to see who can think on their feet, adapt to a changing environment, and yes, a little bit of shit kicking will be in there too. You see, my little freshmen, today, you enter the labyrinth."

The students glanced at one another with confused stares.

"As you all know, we're located underneath the actual Lander campus. What most of you don't know, though, is that this is the top level of our subterranean stronghold. Farther down are other levels, whole environments designed to simulate real-life situations for training purposes. At the very bottom is a level we call the labyrinth. Constantly moving, always shifting, it's a maze that would make you go crazy if you were abandoned there. Today, it will also be your battleground," Coach George said.

Coach Persephone stepped forward, holding two boxes. She began at one end of the line, fitting small bracelets on each student and handing out what looked like tasers that had been dipped in paint.

"My colleague is equipping you with the tools for your exam. Each of you will be given a bracelet and a weapon that is color coded. The bracelets will turn yellow on those of you who can be injured by mundane means, while they will be red for those who are only susceptible to more extreme forms of damage. By the same token, if you have a power that allows you to deal out tremendous damage, you get a red weapon, and if you lack that skill, you get a yellow one. How the game works from here is simple. The weapons generate a specifically calibrated electrical pulse that reacts with the bracelets, so if someone strikes you, it will deactivate your bracelet. Once you're deactivated, you're out," Coach George explained.

Coach Persephone was making her way down the line quickly; nearly half the students had already been outfitted. Those that had received their new equipment quickly took the time advantage to familiarize themselves with it. It didn't take long: there was no interface for the bracelets and only a single button on the tasers. Some of the smarter ones began to idly wonder just how the bracelet knew what color to turn once it was attached to them.

"Now, that should be simple enough to understand, but in the interests of realism, we added the color coding system. Those with red bracelets can only be taken down with shocks from red weapons, while those with yellow bracelets are susceptible to both kinds. Additionally, since some of you folks change form in the course of a fight, the bracelets use a very complex sensor system to determine which category you fall into. That means if you're only extra durable when you're composed of steel, your bracelet will only be red when you fit that requirement."

There was a sound like a sword being pulled across an anvil and suddenly, Stella was silver all over. The bracelet on her wrist flashed three times, then turned red.

"You now know how the game is played. Next comes the question of winning. That is the easy part. You win by surviving and destroying. The three who stay in the game the longest, and the three who deactivate the most other students all get the best scores. Everyone else gets evaluated on an individual performance basis. That's pretty much it. Use your powers as needed, but remember that unless your weapon connects with the other person, no amount of damage counts as a win for you."

"This sounds fun," Nick whispered to Vince.

"Really?"

"Are you out of your mind? We're about to trapped in a maze with over thirty other people who are all much stronger than I am. Most of whom are stronger than you, as well. We're going to get the hell beaten out of us," Nick whispered furiously.

"At least we can all work together," Vince pointed out.

"To start you all off we'll be using a random drop chamber so that you'll all be placed at different locations throughout the labyrinth. You'll be totally on your own and surrounded by potential enemies. Once you've been knocked out of the game, a guide function on your bracelets will activate and take you to the nearest exit. I suggest you don't dawdle, because, while you might be out, the others will still be looking for blood," Coach George continued.

"We are so going to die," Vince amended.

208

"Yup," Nick agreed.

"That pretty much sums it up," Coach George said. "I could take questions, but I'd rather see you find your answers in the field. When we call your name, follow Persephone to the drop chamber. Once you arrive, consider the game started. Remember, we'll be watching all the moves you make, so be smart in your strategies. Oh, and one more thing."

Coach George faced them, and a broad grin broke across his face. Many of the students involuntarily shuddered. More would have if they'd been perceptive.

"Have fun down there!"

59

"Pitch black. Of course, it's pitch black. Why would I hope for anything different?" Alice grumbled as she was dropped into a room within the labyrinth. She groped around the walls slowly, finding that the room was blocked off from every direction except for a single exit in the form of an open archway. She floated up a few feet and checked the ceiling too. Whatever opening had allowed her entrance had sealed up immediately afterward. On the plus side, though, the ceilings were high. Alice was estimating around ten feet. The doorway didn't extend all the way to the ceiling, but if she only had to lower herself to pass through doors that still might work out to be a pretty good deal.

"Yellow weapon and yellow bracelet. Yeah, I'll be out of here in time to get breakfast," she said, talking to herself in an effort to keep focused. It was disorienting to be in this much darkness. Not even her bracelet gave off any light, which, given that it had a glow system incorporated, was odd. Still, she should probably be thankful that it wasn't exuding light. It would have stood out like a beacon in this environment. At least now, she could hug the ceiling and have a fighting chance of lasting.

*   *   *

Mary wasn't all that put out by the darkness. As soon as she landed, she opened her mind, stretching her perception until she could hear the thoughts of nearly every other student in the labyrinth with her. After a few moments of careful hunting, she located the thoughts of the person she was looking for and began making her way to him. It was slow going without any source of light, but Mary could feel his direction. Plus, she was well aware of any others that were approaching, so she steered clear of them.

It wasn't that Mary didn't plan on fighting; it merely wasn't beneficial for her, yet. She moved quickly and carefully through the corridors, feeling the occasional student grow close to her and listening to the grinding shifts as new doors opened while others closed. She was still listening to everyone's thoughts and was accumulating some very useful facts about how the labyrinth functioned; however, at no point did she deviate from her plan or alter the goal of her path.

At long last, she reached a closed door. She felt around the side and located the switch. As the door slid open, she was temporarily blinded by the deluge of light assaulting her eyes. After a few seconds to adjust and a myriad of blinks, she was finally able to see again.

"Hey there, stranger," she said, greeting the room's other inhabitant. "Need a hand?"

*   *   *

Roy was on a one-man rampage. So far, he'd taken down a stretchy guy and some weird chick with dolls. Now, he was hot on the trail of someone else, though whom was anyone's guess in the damn darkness. He'd been lucky and found a lighted room to fight the first two in, but after twenty minutes of waiting, he'd given it up and started roaming the corridors, looking for more prey.

Roy could hear the footsteps ahead of him and didn't bother to disguise his own. If whoever was in front of him was lucky enough to have a red taser, they still wouldn't be able to pinpoint his location fast enough to stop him. Instead, he barreled forward, forgoing all manner of stealth in favor of a full-on charge. He heard the steps in front of him quicken as well, and the chase was on.

Roy's senses were above a normal human's range, but they were far from the most powerful thing about him. Still, it was enough to keep track of the person running away from him. They were crafty, moving around corners and doubling back down corridors, but they weren't good enough to beat Roy. As far as Roy was concerned, no one held that distinct honor. With each turn, he was drawing closer and closer, and as he rounded one last corner, he was positive he was almost right on top of his prey.

As Roy swung around the corner, a blast hit him square in the chest, slamming him back against the wall. His head swam, and he saw stars as he tried to pull himself back up. His efforts were interrupted by a small jolt to his neck. It wasn't enough to incapacitate or even annoy him. It was only enough to cause his bracelet to glow white in the darkness and emit a small, sad beep.

"And another one bites the dust," said a cheery female voice at his side.

"You ambushed me," Roy said accusingly.

"Don't be silly. I trapped you. That's way more effort that a simple ambush. Thanks for playing, though."

A small, green arrow appeared on the bracelet, pointing to the left. As Roy stood and angled himself in that direction, the arrow moved as well, turning until it was facing forward.

"What's your name?" Roy asked.

"Amber," said the voice in the darkness.

"Amber," Roy said, tasting the name and memorizing its flavor. "That was a hell of shot. You and I will have to spar one day, when this is all over."

"Sounds fun. You bring the muscles, I'll bring the concussions," Amber said.

*　　　*　　　*

Vince turned another corner and entered into a new room. It was as dark as the others, but this one had the added adornment of muffled breathing in the corner. Vince's hand tightened around his weapon. He had a red taser, so theoretically, he could take down anyone here, but if it was someone with real combat skill, he'd be at a disadvantage if he gave his location away. Never in his life did Vince suspect he would be so thankful to all the times he and his father had snuck aboard a train at night or crept through town silently. Those experiences had taught him to shroud the sounds of his movements, and right now, that was likely the only thing keeping the other person in the room from leaping.

Vince readied himself to take the offensive; he'd prepared an attack plan as soon as he'd arrived in this endless, black environment. Before he could strike, though, the other person took him completely by surprise.

"Vince?" The voice was very familiar, it only took Vince a moment to realize who he'd been on the brink of battling.

"Alex? Is that you?" Vince asked.

"Yeah, it's me," Alex confirmed.

"How did you know who I was?"

"Man, you guys always forget my power lets me sense others' minds. We've hung out enough to where yours is familiar," Alex explained.

"That's . . . cool," Vince said, only barely stopping himself from using the word "creepy" instead.

"Comes in handy," Alex replied. "So . . . how are things?"

It dawned on Vince that neither of them were sure how to proceed from here. Yes, they had run into a friend, but this was still their test. They both needed to take down others while simultaneously surviving. Still, Vince didn't know if he had it in him to just coldly attack someone he considered a friend.

"Hey, Alex," Vince said. "In all of Coach George's ranting, did he ever say we couldn't work together? I mean, if you and I wanted to team up with someone we trusted on the hopes of increasing our score, I don't think that violates any of the test rules."

"That's true. He said survive and destroy. He never got specific about how we do it," Alex agreed.

"I like that solution a lot better than us duking it out in the dark," Vince said.

"You and me both. So, we work together until we're the only two left?"

"I think that would be a beautiful problem to encounter," Vince said cheerfully. "Let's get moving."

*   *   *

Nick was the only one of the five to be dropped into a room that was lit when he arrived. Rather than leaving his cocoon of light, though, he sat down in the center of the room and began concentrating. Nick had known his plan the minute Coach George had explained the game to them. Nick was going to do nothing.

Well, nothing physically, anyway. Nick's strategy was a focused, steady stream of luck that he hoped would keep him hidden. People were wandering around a maze with no sense of direction or idea where they were going. They were depending almost entirely on luck to guide them, and since Nick happened to hold some sway in that department, it should be guiding them anywhere else but to him.

212

Admittedly, it wasn't the most ambitious of plans, but given the circumstances, it would ideally ensure that he lasted into the final three survivors. The top head-hunting positions were all still open, though Nick was under no disillusions that he'd ever had a shot at claiming one of those. Instead, he put his efforts and power into making sure he stayed all alone in his little room for as long as possible.

It seemed to be working for a while, but then, all at once, the door in front of Nick slid open. It was difficult to see outside; apparently, it was pitch black in the next room over. Nick made no movement to get up from his seat. If someone had found him, then they had found him, and if it was just the labyrinth being weird, then he wasn't going to interrupt his concentration. A few seconds after the door opened, though, a familiar voice came wafting in from the darkness.

"Hey there, stranger. Need a hand?"

60

"Not even a little bit," Nick replied. "Thanks for the offer, though. Try not to give away my position on your way out of here."

"Really? Just kicking me out? Where's that legendary Nick wit and chatty nature?" Mary asked.

"Seen any good movies lately? How's the folks? Cold enough for you these days? Get the hell out of here."

"Now, that wasn't so hard," Mary said, walking fully into the room. The door swooshed shut automatically as she left its proximity.

"Yet you're still coming in. For a telepath, you sure can't take a hint," Nick sighed, rising to his feet. "Or maybe you're thinking of zapping me and upping your stats."

"Or, and this is just a crazy idea, I want us to help each other so we can do better in this trial," Mary said.

"Who needs help here? I had a perfectly good plan, and you're the number one rank on the girls' side. Pretty sure we'll be just fine on our own," Nick said.

"You know Nick, the word 'us' can mean more than just the two people currently standing in a room together," Mary pointed out.

"Let me get this straight: you want me to abandon my safe little hidey hole so that I can go with you, charging through a labyrinth, all in the name of helping our dormmates?" Nick asked.

"Everyone except Roy. He's already out of the game," Mary confirmed.

"Oh, well, that changes everything," Nick said, throwing his hands up dramatically. "They'll be fine. I mean, they'll lose, and quickly, but they'll be fine in the long run."

"Are you sure about that? You know this test is going to determine who moves on to next semester. What if they do so badly they get cut from the program?" Mary asked.

"Then we buy them a conciliatory fruit basket and move on with our lives," Nick said.

"You can act as blasé as you want about this, Nick, but don't forget, I peek inside your head more than occasionally. You and I both know that you've put in a ton of time working this group, creating just the right persona and positioning yourself precisely where you want to be in the group dynamic."

"And your point here is?" Nick asked.

"You aren't the kind of guy who will let all that hard work go down the drain if it's avoidable. The best way to make sure your efforts bear fruit is to keep the group the way it is, and that means everyone advancing to next semester," Mary explained.

"See, this . . . this is why I hate telepaths." Nick all but swore. "Fine. Lead on, oh champion of the misfit Supers."

"I think I'll do just that," Mary said with a smile, opening the door once more and stepping out into the unknown.

*   *   *

Alice's strategy was panning out well so far. She'd heard more than a couple fellow students padding beneath her, but thus far, none of them had discerned the floating blonde over their heads. Once or twice, she'd briefly entertained the idea of dropping on top of them in surprise and trying to shock them out of the game. Common sense and awareness that her weapon was only effective on a select few had ultimately prevailed and helped her adhere to her hiding strategy.

As time ticked away, Alice noticed fewer and fewer students passing beneath her. Of course, some were being eliminated, but it seemed to be happening with alarming frequency. It began to occur to her that she might just have a shot at being one of the last people standing—as long as she kept herself hidden, of course. It was this need that kept her moving, carefully crossing doorways only when she was positive there was no one else waiting on the other side. She could have stayed still in one room, and in fact, tried to at one point, but standing alone in utter darkness and silence is far more terrifying than moving through it with a purpose.

Alice tried to keep her method of movement simple. She alternated left and right turns, not really caring about tracking her own movements, only wanting to avoid back-tracking if possible. She also noticed occasionally, that when she was in a room, the door she entered through would close and two others would open. If she'd been hoping to get a sense of where she was, this might have been discouraging. As it was, being lost suited her just fine.

As she navigated through the catacombs of darkness, she ultimately came upon a room with something unique in it: a door that required being physically opened. If there had been another way out of the room, she likely would have taken it, but the curiosity was her only option for pressing forward, so Alice groped around until her hand struck a small switch.

The first thing that struck Alice was the overwhelming brightness of the light that assaulted her eyes as the door slid open. The second was the ridiculous amount of wind that smashed against her. For a few brief and very confusing seconds, Alice truly believed she had somehow opened up a door leading into a hurricane. Then her eyes adjusted and things made both more and less sense.

Dashing around the room in combat was Sasha, recognizable only when she slowed down enough to change direction or when she clashed with her enemy. The enemy Sasha was fighting was . . . also Sasha. The duo were duking it out, fighting at insane speeds that were generating the winds Alice had felt.

Alice blinked her eyes to make sure she was seeing things correctly, then very seriously considered flipping that switch again to see if it would make the door close. Unfortunately, before her thoughts could solidify into action, the pair of Sashas noticed her and shouted in unison.

"Alice! Give me a hand with this imposter!"

*   *   *

At first, Vince was convinced he was hallucinating, but then Alex's question confirmed what he was seeing.

"Is someone using an orange flashlight?"

Both of them had noticed an orange beam glowing lightly from a few rooms down. It was sweeping erratically, as if wielded by someone trying desperately to make sense of their surroundings.

"Looks that way," Vince whispered.

"So, do we run away?" Alex asked.

Vince shook his head, then realized Alex could no more see him than vice versa. "No," Vince said. "There are other people who are too good at moving with stealth for us to have a chance at being the last two standing. Our best chance is to start taking down others when we can find them."

"Best defense is a good offense," Alex echoed.

"More or less. Though, to be honest, I'd feel better if I had a red bracelet to go with my red weapon. Equal out the offense and defense," Vince whispered back.

"Hey, at least you have one red item. I'm yellow on both accounts," Alex complained.

"That doesn't seem right. I mean, I saw them give Mary a red weapon," Vince said.

"Hey, Vince, I think we're kind of stalling here," Alex pointed out.

"Oh . . . yeah, you're right. We should get moving," Vince said.

"You should also realize that, in total silence, the sound of a whisper carries far," said a familiar voice from one room over. While Vince and Alex had been talking, the orange light had gone out and its owner had made his way much closer to the duo. He now stepped through the doorway and reignited his light source, which turned out to be his left hand.

"Thomas!" Vince said happily. "I thought that shade of orange looked familiar. I didn't know you could use your energy like a light."

"I can do a lot of things with it," Thomas replied.

"Man, Nick must have put a whammy of good luck on me before we came down because I keep running into friends," Vince said, relief evident in his voice. He hadn't been looking forward to trying to take down another student, no matter how necessary it was.

216

"I don't know that I would go that far," Thomas said, and without another word, his right hand burst into orange light as well. Instead of a dim glow, this light arced out and spilt into two beams, one each slamming into Vince and Alex and wrapping around their torsos. Their arms were pinned to their sides immediately, and as soon as they were encased, they felt themselves lift several feet in the air.

"It's nothing personal," Thomas said as he used his left hand to pluck out his own red weapon. The flashlight-like glow vanished, but the pulsating energy emitting from his right hand kept the room amply lit. "It's as you said, some of us are lacking in the skills to succeed at the stealth portion of this exam. That only leaves bringing down other students."

"A little warning might have been appreciated," Vince said, struggling to push against the orange energy enveloping him.

"Appreciated and ill-advised," Thomas replied. "You are both strong opponents. Without surprise, I doubt I could have taken you both. Such tactics would never be acceptable in a man-to-man fight. However, the environment here seems to suggest it is well within the rules, if not expected."

"Surprising us was the right idea," Alex said, an odd smile dancing on his face in the orange light. "Explaining why you did it and giving us time was wrong."

"My apologies if I gave you hope, but I did so because my abilities have already been tested against telepaths. Your kind deal in moving only solid matter with your minds, and energy is far less dense than that," Thomas said.

"I'm only going to say this one more time," Alex said, taking in a deep breath. A vein in his forehead bulged and sweat materialized on his forehead. "I am not a *fucking telepath!*"

61

Vince had to admit, he didn't think Alex was going to be able to do anything to Thomas's energy . . . right up until Alex yelled and the circle binding him was forced apart. Without pause, Alex dropped to the ground, made a quick motion with his hand and flung Thomas across the room. Now, in the time it took Alex to land and attack, Thomas could have easily struck again, or made some move to defend himself. The trouble was that while Vince was slightly surprised by Alex's ability to push away energy, Thomas was absolutely flabbergasted. He stood in dumb shock as Alex's force gripped him and sent him crashing into the wall. When he struck, his concentration faltered, and the energy binding Vince dissipated.

"That was pretty cool," Vince said as he landed carefully on the hard stone below.

"Thanks," Alex said. "Sorry about the yelling. It just gets frustrating sometimes."

Vince made a very precise mental note to never question the origins of Alex's power to his face. "I hope you didn't hurt him too badly."

"I am fine," Thomas answered, rising to his feet. "I'd like to know what trick you used, though. You should not be able to stop energy. How did you do it?"

Alex shrugged. "Nothing is beyond the Force."

"Very well, then," Thomas replied. "It seems I will have to fight you both head-to-head. I had hoped to avoid that, but if it must be, then it must be." He lit up again, this time both hands glowing bright orange. Without warning, five beams from each hand lanced out directly at Vince and Alex. They were ready this time, though; Vince rolled to the side and Alex held up a hand, knocking the beams away. As Vince pulled himself back up, he pinned his attention on Thomas, readying himself for the next volley. He noticed that Thomas's hands still showed ten beams extended. Vince put it all together just in time, leaping forward and narrowly missing the five that slammed down in the spot where he had been.

"What the hell?" Vince cried out, ducking to the side as the five orange strands snaked out, each one trying to snare him.

"I told you: my energy moves like an appendage, taking whatever shape I require," Thomas explained from his spot near the wall. "All of them move independently, and if one of them touches you, then you are as good as restrained."

Vince snuck a glance at Alex, only to see his friend working double time to try and deflect the beams from all angles. While Vince's five were staying fairly closely-knit, the ones battling Alex were spread out, forcing him to block them at random intervals from every direction. At the rate things were going, Vince and Alex would lose, and soon. All it took was one beam getting through to snare them once more, and even if

Alex could get himself free, one had to wonder how many times that trick would work. As for Vince, if he was caught, that was probably the end of things.

In a moment of desperation, a plan formed in Vince's head. It was stupid and more than likely wouldn't work at all. Still, it was a way to lose proactively, and Vince preferred that to just jumping around, waiting to be picked off.

"Alex!" Vince called. "I need you to buy me thirty seconds. Can you do that?"

"No idea," Alex replied. "Guess we'll find out." With that, Alex stepped forward and brought to bear all that he had. Thomas's orange beams were slammed backward against the sheer might of Alex's will. Try as he might to move them forward, Thomas kept striking an invisible wall, one that didn't seem to be yielding one bit.

As soon as the beams were restrained, Vince stopped running and bent over. His breathing intensified, indicating he was trying to get his breath back before he tried whatever was to come next. He placed his hands on top of his pockets and stared at the ground. He was about to do something crazy. He should be scared, he should be wary, he should be worried. Instead, he was exhilarated.

*   *   *

Before either Sasha could say another word, Alice bounded through the door and flew up to the ceiling. It was higher in this room, at least fifteen feet down to the floor, and Alice hugged it as closely as she could, desperate for every inch she could put between herself and the two women beneath her.

"Someone want to explain what the hell?" Alice called down.

"He's a mimic!" Sasha yelled.

"No, he is," the other Sasha countered. "He snuck up on me and grabbed my hand."

"Okay, so we're all agreeing that one of you is a mimic at least, right?" Alice asked.

"Yes!" This was yelled in unison by both Sashas. "He can copy your appearance and powers if he touches you," one of the Sashas elaborated.

"But it isn't as strong as the original," the other one chimed in.

"Well, sounds like a good show for me then," Alice said, crossing her arms.

"Huh?" Technically, this wasn't done in unison, nor was the wording exactly the same, but there are certain gut-generated noises that have a universal meaning, regardless of the particular syllables used to create them.

"The real Sasha is faster, so she'll win," Alice said simply. "Seems like this will sort itself out."

"It isn't that simple," Sasha informed her. "I'm not used to fighting someone who can keep up with me."

"Yeah," Sasha agreed. "He's used to dealing with all kinds of powers, so even if I'm a little faster, he's still got enough combat experience to give me hell."

"Then what do you want me to do? In case you didn't notice, I'm not exactly king of the combat hill myself," Alice retorted.

"Just come lend a hand," Sasha said.

"With two of us, it'll be that much harder for him," Sasha pointed out.

Alice paused and gave it some thought, then pulled out her own yellow weapon. "Okay, Sashas, one question before I decide who to help. Your boyfriend is Vince, so you've spent a lot of time with us in Melbrook throughout the semester. So, then, who is Mary's best friend?"

"You," said one of the Sashas.

"Hershel," said the other.

"Bingo," Alice said, dropping down next to the girl who had answered "Hershel" and putting her weapon at the ready. "Let's get this faker," she said, smiling at the Sasha next to her and glaring at the one across from them.

"You got it—OW!" The Sasha responding was the one next to her. Coincidently, it was also the one Alice had slammed her weapon into the neck of as soon as she had looked across at her identical counterpart. The bracelet on her wrist flashed yellow, then turned clear as a small green arrow appeared in one spot.

"Damn it," Sasha swore, and as Alice watched in fascination, her features seemed to melt together, shifting and squirming until Alice found herself staring at a boy shorter than she with light hair buzzed close to the head. "I'm impressed. I didn't think you were planning the double cross. See you girls back up top." With that, he made his way to the exit indicated by the arrow and stepped out of the room.

"That was amazing!" Sasha squealed. She walked over to Alice and gave her a hug. "How did you know he was the fake one just by that?"

"I didn't," Alice replied.

"You . . . wait what?" Before the words were fully formed, Sasha felt Alice's weapon dig into her side, sending its charge into her and eliminating her from the test.

"I said I didn't know. I just asked a generic question you'd both answer. The one I picked to surprise was random," Alice explained.

"But . . . you just eliminated the real me, too," Sasha said in a hurt voice, still holding on to Alice in their now very-awkward hug.

"Yes, I did. And I'd feel a lot worse about it if I hadn't noticed you adjust your grip on your weapon before coming in for this hug," Alice replied.

"Touché, my fellow crafty lady," Sasha said, releasing the hug and checking her bracelet. "You're more dangerous than you look. What would you have done if you'd taken out the real me first, though?"

"Been eliminated, but done so with at least one win under my belt," Alice answered.

"Not a bad plan. Good luck with the rest of the test. The longer you're in here the tougher the remaining opponents will be," Sasha informed her.

Alice nodded her understanding, then made a dash to get back into the relative safety offered by darkness. Also, she made a note not to go into any more of these damn lit rooms.

*   *   *

"Fudge," Mary said as she and Nick rounded a corner.

"What?" he asked.

"Someone heard us. Someone tough. Hurry, and follow me quickly. There's a lit room nearby, and we have to get there," Mary said, quickening her speed to a run.

"Why is it so important we get there?"

"Because I have no idea how to fight this guy in the dark," Mary replied.

"Do you know how to do it in the light?"

"Not really," she answered.

"Peachy," Nick sighed, turning up the speed and following his diminutive guide as fast as he could.

62

The door opened, showing only darkness outside of the well-lit room Nick and Mary had entered only moments before. There was a slight whooshing sound, and then another student was standing in front of them, yellow weapon ready at hand. Small wisps of smoke curled in the air for less than a second around the area in which he had appeared. The boy himself wasn't too impressive: short in stature and excessively lean. He had a wide grin on his face, though, one that left Nick feeling disconcerted, given that he and Mary had the advantage in numbers.

"Who's this guy?" Nick asked, plucking out his own weapon and standing ready.

"His name is Gilbert, and he's a teleporter," Mary informed him, her red weapon already drawn.

"He also has perfectly good hearing and doesn't necessarily like being talked about as though he weren't in the room," Gilbert added. "Also, come on, there's only like forty of us left, you couldn't be bothered to learn everyone's name?"

"I've got a shitty memory, so sue me," Nick quipped.

"Better idea," Gilbert replied, vanishing from his spot and reappearing behind Nick, lunging forward with his weapon. Nick slid to the side as soon he saw Gilbert disappear, though, so Gilbert's sneak attack cleaved nothing but air. Before Nick could try a thrust of his own, Gilbert was standing on the other side of the room.

"I see how this guy could be problematic," Nick admitted, reorienting himself to face his opponent's new position.

"Exactly," Mary agreed.

*   *   *

"Any time now!" Alex announced, sweat dripping off his forehead in intense concentration.

Vince took one last deep breath and stood. Everything had worked so far; that in itself was a victory. Now, came the hardest part. Vince put his hand into his left pocket and produced his weapon, the red coloring tinted a sickly shade from Thomas's orange light. Vince felt a rush of adrenaline crash over him, elation not far on its heels. Do or die time. Vince couldn't stop the grin that crept into the corners of his mouth.

"Clear me a path!" Vince yelled, charging forward without waiting for confirmation. If Alex could still do it, then he would; if not, then this wasn't going to work anyway. As Vince pumped his legs, a part of his mind realized that this was only his second real fight since coming to Lander, and once again, he was betting heavily on a suicidal charge right at his opponent. He really needed to learn another way to problem solve.

As his heart raced and his feet slapped the concrete floor, Vince noticed he was in Thomas's range. He hadn't been snagged yet, though, so that meant Alex was still keeping the energy at bay. There were still several more feet to cover, and as Vince drew closer, he realized Thomas's tendrils were bonding together, striking back with more power. Each attempt seemed to get closer to landing on Vince's fast-moving form. It was going to be a photo finish.

In the end, Vince very nearly pulled it off. His finger was on the button, and his arm almost completely extended when he felt his legs go out from under him. A few inches more and he would have driven his weapon into Thomas's shoulder. That was simply not the case, though, as Vince was once more jerked into the air, his arms pinned to his torso. Without pause, Thomas lanced a shot of energy over at Alex, easily snaring and capturing him once more. From the way Alex was panting wearily, Vince had a sinking suspicion that he wouldn't be able to break free this time.

"Well now," Thomas said, a little short of breath himself. "That was an impressive move. Marshal all your forces into one all-out attack. Risky, but very nearly effective."

"Thanks," Vince said, resisting the temptation to kick his legs futilely. "You were wearing us down the other way, so I figured why not give it a shot."

"If your partner had been a hair stronger, or if you had been just a bit faster . . . despite all our power, it often seems these fights come down to a very narrow margin of victory," Thomas said as he lowered Vince to only a few inches off the ground. At the same time, an orange tendril emerged and nimbly plucked an object from Thomas's back pocket. It was his own yellow weapon, and the tendril was soon shaped into a hand holding the device, a finger carefully placed on the button to activate it.

"That really is neat how you can do that," Vince said, watching the show.

"Thank you. I've found it useful. Hands, beams, shields, even needles. My energy takes any form I can think of and stays just as powerful regardless," Thomas said.

"Very adaptive," Vince complimented.

"Much appreciated. I am sorry yours was so limiting in this environment," Thomas said graciously. He maneuvered the weapon upward. There was only a foot or so between himself and Vince, but he was still keeping that buffer, just in case. This silver-haired boy had shown himself occasionally unpredictable.

"I don't know about that," Vince said. "I mean, it's limiting in some senses, but with a little creative risk-taking, it can actually be pretty useful."

A "How so?" died on Thomas's tongue, the victim of a sudden case of shock in multiple senses. Before the innocent words had a chance to be born and greet the world, Vince's eyes crackled with red lighting, which leapt out and struck Thomas in the chest. The voltage shattered his concentration, as well as temporarily disabling his motor skills. It also hurt like hell.

223

As Thomas felt the twitching in his muscles subside, and his vision slowly come back into focus, he noticed his bracelet was now glowing clear with a green arrow. The "How so?" was gone, off to wherever unspoken words go when they are truly forgotten. A new combination was being assembled, though, and this phrase burst into the world unhindered by any outside influences.

"What in the hell was that?"

Vince was standing over him, having been freed when Thomas's concentration was shattered. He looked vaguely different, and Thomas realized it was because they were being lit only by the meager light from his now clear bracelet.

A clattering sound reached Thomas's ears, and after bathing the area once more in orange light, he could see that Vince had tossed him his weapon.

"Try it out," Vince said. "I think you'll understand then."

Obediently, Thomas picked up the red device and pressed its button. There was nothing, no arc of light from one metal point to the other, no soft hum of electricity, no difference of any kind.

"You drained it," Thomas mumbled, his tongue still shaking off the after effects of voltage overload. "Shouldn't that have set off your own bracelet?"

"I thought it might," Vince admitted. "That's why I didn't do it when I first got down here. Once you were hammering away at us, though, it was obvious we were going to lose eventually. So I decided to give it a whirl."

"You weren't catching your breath for the charge," Thomas said, more to himself than to Vince as understanding set in.

"I was drinking the whole battery down to empty. It was a big risk, because they told us the electricity was calibrated to react specifically with the bracelets. I wasn't sure if my draining it would alter it anyway, so even when I took the shot, I didn't know if it would work," Vince explained.

"And if it didn't, then you'd be stuck down here with no way to eliminate other students," Alex concluded, wobbling his way over and joining them.

"Pretty much," Vince said. "So I just wanted you to know, the only way I was able to beat you was by taking several gambles that very easily could have totally knocked me out of commission."

"I appreciate the attempts to spare my ego," Thomas said, slowly rising to his feet. "They are unnecessary, though. I lost in fair battle to strong opponents. I feel no shame in this fight."

"No hard feelings?" Vince asked, extending his hand.

"It is the nature of the exam," Thomas said, accepting and shaking back. "You might want to get moving, though. This room has been visibly lit up for some time now. Other students are bound to have noticed."

224

"Crap," Vince said, realization slowly dawning on his face. "Good call. Alex, you okay to move?"

"Winded," Alex admitted. "I should be fine after a few minutes of rest, though."

"Good luck," Thomas told them. "Do well today. I would not want the men who were able to defeat me to be taken down easily."

"Of course," Vince said, trying to hide the first trembles in his hands as the adrenaline wore off. He and Alex had pushed themselves to their limits to take down one other competent student. Vince wondered how much more they had left in them to deal with the next challenge.

63

The last five minutes had unveiled some unfortunate truths. The first was that Gilbert could teleport faster than Mary was able to read his mind and anticipate the movement. The second was that while she could grab him, he could easily teleport out of her telekinetic grip. The last was that Gilbert clearly had some gymnastics experience.

"Were your parents monkeys or something?" Nick yelled as he ducked away from one of Gilbert's attacks. Without missing a beat, Gilbert vanished, reappearing at the other end of the room, doing a flip off the wall and landing perfectly.

"My parents put me in tumbling at an early age. Turns out, short guys have an advantage in that field," Gilbert explained.

"Good for you," Nick grumbled, pulling himself to his feet, but keeping his eyes trained on Gilbert. "I don't suppose you've thought of a plan yet," he said to Mary out of the side of his mouth.

"Right now, all I'm hoping for is that all that jumping around wears him down faster than dodging winds us," she replied. Her breath was a little short, and Nick had noticed her movements were slowing ever so slightly. Gilbert, on the other hand, was getting faster, if anything. He was clearly in better shape than they were, not to mention, he was able to conserve energy by using only the most necessary movements. Running out the clock clearly wasn't going to work.

"Incoming," Nick announced as Gilbert disappeared. Trusting his instincts, Nick tumbled to the side, popping up with his weapon at the ready. This time, Gilbert had gone for Mary, though; fortunately, she had ducked down in time and smacked him away with a mental punch. He flew back, vanishing from sight, then reappearing for a few wall rebounds before coming to rest delicately on his nimble feet.

They were going to lose soon, Nick realized. His own body was beginning to show the first symptoms of wear; from this point, it was a steady downhill slide. Gilbert had them in endurance and mobility, so the only chance left was strategy. Unlike Vince, though, Nick wasn't a fan of all or nothing tactics.

Mary! Nick thought forcefully. He needed to talk to her, but giving Gilbert any more information than he had was too risky. Hopefully, the girl was still listening to minds around her and would pick up his call.

Hope panned out as Mary jerked her head in Nick's direction and angled her head curiously. Good, she was listening.

Mary, I need your help to beat this guy. Take both of our weapons with your mind and start attacking with them using the patterns I'll be thinking of. Dodge as necessary, but make sure to follow my patterns perfectly.

Mary gave a small, almost imperceptible nod, and Nick released his weapon. It dropped by maybe three inches before jerking to a stop and zipping away into the air.

Nick barely had time to think of the first pattern before Gilbert was on them again. They managed to avoid him, but neither weapon struck during his brief tenure in their vicinity. This time, when he reappeared across the room, though, there was no temporary ceasefire. Nick directed Mary to press the attack, making minor alterations on the pattern's trajectories, but continuing without pause. Gilbert had to teleport away, and Nick felt a thin smile appear on his face. They were finally making him reactive instead of proactive, and that was exactly where Nick needed him to be.

It wasn't a perfect system. Gilbert began attacking more frequently, avoiding their weapons and coming at them with a single jump. He stayed longer, too, until Mary knocked him back or the weapons flew over. With each disappearance, Nick saw a little bit more. Finally, just when he was growing sincerely worried about his own stamina, Nick found the opportunity he had been waiting for.

Nick concentrated on a new pattern for Mary to attack with and simultaneously began edging away from her. The margin for error on the timing of what he was about to do would be razor thin. As he'd anticipated, Gilbert ducked and flipped away from the weapons buzzing and circling him. He was clearly about to teleport, merely picking his destination. Just before he made the jump, though, his dodging forced him to turn his back on Nick and Mary for half a second. Nick took off from his spot, dashing with all the speed his storky legs could afford him.

Mid-run, it occurred to him that moments like this were probably why so much of the time in gym class was spent conditioning their capacity to run. Gilbert had already teleported out of range of the weapons, but Nick didn't see that. He didn't need to. Nick had been watching and analyzing Gilbert's movements with each jump out of danger. The good thing about using the same pattern when evading was that it made such movements second nature, allowing for faster reaction time. The bad thing was that, if your opponent was observant enough, they could use those same habits to predict your movements before you made them. Nick was exceptionally observant.

There was a very small lag between Gilbert disappearing and reappearing, but there was one, and that, coupled with the half second he was turned away, proved to be just enough for Nick's run. Gilbert appeared directly in front of Nick, his eyes widening in surprise at another person being in a spot he'd clearly anticipated as being empty. Before he could react any more than that, Nick reared back and punched him directly in the side of his head. Gilbert dropped like a politician's approval when raising taxes, smacking the ground and twitching slightly.

Without looking, Nick held out his left hand and felt a small smack as his weapon landed in it. The press of a button and a flick of the wrist later, found Gilbert with a bracelet that had become clear save only for a small, green arrow.

"Think he'll be okay?" Mary asked.

"Nope. But that's why we've got healers," Nick replied, taking a deep breath and getting his bearings.

"You throw a hell of a punch," Mary complimented as she ambled over to him.

"That's the problem with the overly combative types like you and him. You guys forget that just because I wield a metaphysical thing like luck, it doesn't mean I can't clean a clock on occasion," Nick said.

"I suppose there's some truth to that," Mary admitted. "You know, if I wasn't in your head, I would have never believed you pulled that off without using any luck."

"Then things are exactly as they should be," Nick said. "I suppose you still want to keep looking for our dormmates."

"You could have said our friends," Mary pointed out.

"Yes, that was also a verbal option. Not the one I elected to use, though."

"Nick, Nick, Nick," Mary said with a shake of her head. "You still have so far to come."

"Emotional growth can wait for later. Right now, let's just get this test over with," Nick said.

*　　　*　　　*

"Do you hear something?" Alex whispered as he and Vince crept through the dark.

"Kind of," Vince whispered back. He wasn't quite sure what was reaching his ears. It wasn't the scrape of shoes against the concrete beneath them, or the hurried hustle of a fellow student moving to a new location. It was softer and slightly harmonic. As he and Alex stepped into a new room, the sound bounced off a nearby wall and magnified significantly. Only then did the two finally realizing what they were hearing.

"Someone is singing," Alex said, his voice not as hushed as it should have been.

"Mmhmm," Vince replied. He should have been more worried about Alex not hiding his voice, or more curious about what would cause someone to be giving away their position by singing. These were thoughts that might have been scrambling around in his mind, but if such thoughts existed, they were lost in a fog, growing thick within his brain. Without wondering why, Vince began moving toward the sound of the song. A part of him dimly registered Alex coming as well. It was noted, in a very abstract sort of fashion, and then promptly forgotten.

The two students moved more swiftly through the dark halls, the song bouncing off the walls and guiding them clearly. At last, they came to a halt in a dark room like any other, save for the fact that, in this one, dwelled the singer who had brought them there. Vince raised his hand, and a small flame burned in the center, illuminating the room around them.

It was a bare, concrete room with only one other person. Sitting cross-legged in the center of the floor was a girl Vince barely recognized from class. She had long, dark

228

hair and olive skin. He remembered thinking she was pretty looking at one point. Now, he was transfixed by her beauty, amazed he had ever found the strength to tear his eyes from her. He kneeled down in front of her, bringing out more fire so he could see her better. This time, he didn't even notice that Alex was following suit. There was no room in his mind for anything else. The test, the program, the world all paled in comparison. There was only her. Her, and the song.

She never stopped singing, not as she reached into her pocket and produced an oddly familiar yellow device, not as she pressed it to Alex's temple and he collapsed to the ground, not even as she held it against Vince's eager skin.

It was only when Vince came back around that the song had stopped, and by then, his bracelet was clear, and it was far too late to matter.

64

"Stella?"

"Nope," Nick replied.

"Will?"

"Totally," Nick said.

"Alice?"

"No doubt," Nick told her.

"Really?" Mary said uncertainly. "She's so pretty, and I've heard her thoughts wander in that direction several times before. You sure?"

"Daddy issues with an overprotective, emotionally distant father. Not saying she won't be busting wild in days to come, but as of now, I'm positive she's a virgin," Nick said.

"I really have trouble believing you can deduce whether someone has had sex just by briefly meeting them," Mary said.

"You can see in my head. Am I lying?"

"I said I have trouble believing, not that I didn't believe," Mary pointed out.

The two were trekking through the darkness of the halls, still in search of their fellow companions. Mary's mental eavesdropping had steered them away from more potential fights, but they'd been forced to take some twists and turns that took them farther from their goal. The tension had culminated in boredom, which had led to conversation and had ultimately found them having the current conversation. Adrenaline and fear are powerful silencers; however, even sneaking through a pitch black labyrinth can grow tedious after enough time.

"So, what about Hershel?" Mary asked.

"Oh, come on, as much as he moons over you, there is no way his brain hasn't given that one away," Nick said.

"I try not to listen. It didn't seem polite," Mary explained.

"Not polite? You dig through my head like a hobo scrounging for food outside a restaurant dumpster, but he's a no-fly zone?" Nick said, his voice rising octaves in mock-outrage.

"He doesn't have anything to hide, nor does he need the advanced levels of therapy you do. Besides, he's romantically interested in me. It seemed like a poor idea to listen to the thoughts of someone I might end up dating," Mary said.

"Hrumph," Nick hrumphed. "Yes, by the way. Still pure as the driven snow."

"That's nice," Mary said, grateful that Nick couldn't see her smile in the darkness.

"Advanced therapy, huh?"

"You've got some issues."

"National Geographic has issues," Nick said. "I have personality."

"You have a complete inability to trust anyone," Mary pointed out. "I mean, you don't even trust Vince, and that kid thinks of you as his best friend."

"Friends stab you in the front," Nick mumbled.

"Real cute. On that note, Vince?"

"Surprisingly, no. And before you ask, not with Sasha. She's not either, but the two of them haven't knocked boots. Not with each other, I mean," Nick said.

"Wow. They've been dating for months now. Wonder what's holding them back," Mary speculated.

"He's a gentlemen, and she thinks he's a virgin and doesn't want him to think she's a slut," Nick answered.

"I thought I was the telepath," Mary said.

"Please," Nick scoffed. "Nothing new in that story. Admittedly, usually the guy is only pretending to be a gentleman, but the context is the same."

"Shut up," Mary said quickly. Had Nick been a bit dumber or a touch more sensitive, he might have thought she was silencing him after his last comment. Instead, he merely shut his yapper. Moments later, he heard footsteps echoing toward them. The intruder came close, then turned away a few rooms later. The steps faded away quickly, but he stayed quiet until Mary signaled the all clear.

"We're okay now," she told him finally. "Also, that is terribly jaded view of the courting process."

"Funny how 'reality' and 'jaded' seem to mean the same thing at the end of the day," Nick shot back.

"Whatever, Mr. Sad Sack. You know what I find to be 'reality'? That you've been here as long as we have, experienced this new environment, and started acting like a real Super just like we four. But you haven't grown or changed one bit. Hershel's popping out of his shell, Roy's calming down and getting focused, Alice is letting herself make connections to people, and Vince is getting used to having structure. Not Nick, though. You're the same guy today, as you were when we first met," Mary said.

"I grew up a long time ago," Nick said, a few strands of bitterness snaking into his voice. "Besides, I notice you weren't on that list either, Miss High and Mighty."

"Of course I'm growing. I'm learning to play chess," Mary corrected him.

"Oh, well then, my mistake," Nick said.

"Apology accepted," Mary said. "Alex?"

"Nope," Nick told her. "But then, no surprise there. Super in a small town is bound to have some fans."

"I suppose you have a point," Mary admitted. "We're almost there, by the way."

"About time," Nick complained as they loped carefully through the darkness. "Who is it?"

"Why? Hoping for someone in particular?"

"Yes: Roy. We need another heavy hitter. Too bad he's out of the game."

"You're lying," Mary informed him. "Why don't you want to admit that you'd prefer we find Vince? You and he hang out plenty. There's nothing wrong with wanting your friend to help during a stressful situation."

"I don't have friends. Just assets," Nick told her.

"I ought to knock you on your asset," Mary snapped. "Anyway, you'll see who it is in a minute or two."

"Fine," Nick snapped. He needed to get his game face back on. Soon, they'd have company, and that meant Nick the quip-filled chatterbox, not Nick the conniver. He couldn't hide things from Mary; however, that was no excuse to let himself get sloppy in front of others.

"You're really pathetic sometimes," Mary scolded. Nick blinked, then realized she was rebuking him for his thoughts, rather than any recent words.

"I gotta be me," Nick told her. He hesitated for a minute as a question popped into his head. He was about to stifle it, then realized Mary had heard it already so he might as well ask. "Does Vince really think of me as his best friend?"

"And trusts you without hesitation," Mary assured him. "Kind of sad, knowing the man you really are."

"Yeah yeah yeah, be careful you don't fall off that soapbox."

The two stepped through a series of arches rapidly and stopped in a dark room like many of the others they'd been in over the last hour.

"Speaking of being elevated . . . ahoy up there!" Mary called, her voice echoing off the ceiling.

"Mary?" Alice's tentative voice drifted down.

"And Nick," Nick tossed in.

"Oh, great," Alice groaned from her vantage point on the ceiling. "You had to be tagging along."

"You know me, Princess, one for all and all for one. We're passing this test as a team," Nick lied.

"Well, to be technical, we're the last of the team," Mary said. "Vince and Alex went down about fifteen minutes ago."

Nick whistled. "Who took those two out?"

"Let's just say if you hear someone singing, run like hell," Mary told him.

"Um, guys, not that I'm not thankful to have company, but I'm guessing you two have some sort of plan?" Alice asked.

"My plan was to round up as many of us as I could," Mary said. "As of now, I'm officially open to suggestions."

"Might I recommend surrender," said a new voice in the room, one that didn't immediately register to its other inhabitants. Nick wasn't the only one with decent deductive skills, though; it only took Mary a moment to confirm her fears and the mystery voice's owner.

"Hi, Chad," she said weakly.

65

"You sure it's him?" Nick half-whispered.

"Seeing as he's the only student in our class whose thoughts I can't hear, yeah, I'm pretty sure," Mary confirmed.

"Ahem. It's dark, I get that. I am still standing right here, though," Chad called out.

"Oh no, we've offended him. Now he'll easily beat us and knock us out of the test. A totally different outcome than what he was already planning," Nick said.

"Actually, I was planning to let you and Alice go," Chad corrected. "Neither of you pose a good fight for me."

"Really?" Alice asked from overhead.

"Yes. Mary stays, though. I imagine she will make an interesting opponent," Chad informed them.

"Cool by me!" Nick declared. "Alice, fly your ass down here and let's book."

"But . . . what about Mary?" Alice asked hesitantly.

"I appreciate the sentiment, Alice, but you should go. Chad is a strong Super, so fighting him is likely to cause a lot of collateral damage. It will be easier if I don't have to worry about hitting either of you in this darkness," Mary told her.

"You're sure?"

"Of course. I'll catch up with you two later. Now, hurry up," Mary instructed her.

"You heard the girl, time for us to exit, stage right," Nick told her.

Without any more coaxing, Alice floated down to Nick's side and the two slowly made their way into another room. They stumbled along into another hallway and were lost once more in the endless twists of the labyrinth. Neither Chad nor Mary said anything until their footsteps had totally faded away.

"You lied to your friend," Chad said matter-of-factly.

"Yes, I did," Mary admitted.

"That was very kind of you," he complimented.

"It was kind of you to let them go," she returned.

Mary heard something that sounded suspiciously like a shrug. "I meant what I said. Their powers aren't suited for combat. I won't learn anything from them or be suitably challenged. I gain no satisfaction from defeating weaker opponents."

"You and me both," Mary said. "Though, I don't think that's applicable to either of us in this case."

"No, it is certainly not," Chad agreed. With that, he rushed forward.

*　　*　　*

"Holy crap!" Nick exclaimed as they heard a tremendous smashing sound some yards behind them.

"Ditto," Alice seconded. "Do you think she's okay?"

"I'm sure she's fine," Nick lied hurriedly. "We should be moving faster."

"You think Chad will change his mind?"

"I think there is a metric fuckton of power being flexed uncomfortably close to my proximity, and I'd like to increase that meager bit of distance," Nick clarified, quickening his pace.

"You make a compelling case," Alice agreed, matching his speed. "This doesn't seem a little wrong to you, though? I mean, we're here learning to be Heroes. Doesn't running away go counter to that?"

"Only if your definition of a Hero is someone who gets needlessly pummeled," Nick replied. "You and I have precise, useful talents. Kicking ass isn't in either of our repertoires, though."

"Maybe if we teamed up—" Alice began.

"We could hamstring the only one of the three of us with an outside shot of winning," Nick finished. "Moments like this are exactly why I'd guess they're splitting us into combat and alternative training. To illustrate when a strategic removal of forces is more beneficial than a grand last stand."

"You sure jazzed up the concept of running away there," Alice said.

"Why thank you, Princess, I consider it my gift. Since when are you so concerned about Mary's well-being, anyway?"

"She came looking for me. Both of you did. Something sits wrong with me, hightailing it away from her now that things are rough," Alice justified.

"And here, I just thought you were growing chummy with our diminutive mind-reader," Nick said.

Alice tried to brush off his comment; however, she discovered that it didn't brush quite so easily. She wasn't just worried about getting away, and she didn't feel guilty purely because she was leaving someone behind. These feelings were more persistent because it was Mary she was running from, and Mary who was in danger. At some point in their living situation, tolerance had transitioned into fondness. Alice stopped running.

"I'm going back," she declared, turning around.

"No, you're not," Nick told her, pulling himself up short as well. He strode back over to her, groping a bit before finding her precise location in the darkness. "I get it. She's our friend, we care, we want her to be okay, and it seems like making a grand stand will facilitate that outcome."

"We'll think of something," Alice said stubbornly.

"We'll distract her, we'll get in the way, and it's possible we'll get hurt or killed. Accidents happen, even with the safety measures the HCP takes. And Mary will blame herself for not being able to protect us. You want to toss in the fact that we're learning to be Heroes? Then remember this: a Hero's first priority is the greater good. You feel inadequate and guilty, so you want to ameliorate those feelings by trying to help. That's selfish, though. It puts your need to feel good about yourself over Mary's need to stay safe and win," Nick lectured her.

"I still feel like shit," Alice admitted, something she didn't think she could have said if she'd been able to see Nick's face.

"Sometimes, doing the right thing leaves you feeling like an asshole," Nick told her. "Now move."

*   *   *

"You're amazing," Chad complimented her. "You can't see me or sense my thoughts, yet you've still managed to last this long. I'm sincerely impressed."

Mary wheezed in a breath and blinked sweat from her eyes. She appreciated the sentiment, but she didn't feel particularly amazing. Fighting Chad was hell. He was fast, strong, had ridiculous endurance, and worst of all, he didn't seem remotely fazed by not being able to see. She'd been generating what was essentially a bubble of telekinetic power to stop him, but he'd already broken through twice. She'd released a massive burst and driven him back, but he'd landed glancing blows each time. Not to mention the fact that those massive blasts took a lot out of her. She could feel her mental reserves slipping and her bubble weakening.

""Why . . . can't I read . . . your thoughts?" Mary rasped out between ragged breaths. She needed him to talk, to buy even a few extra seconds if she could.

"Brains work on certain frequencies through electrical impulses. I've done some extensive remodeling of how mine functions to maximize potential. You could think of it as you pick up FM, but I'm broadcasting on AM," Chad explained.

"Impossible," Mary said.

"No such word. Think of any wonder or miracle in this world and sooner or later, you'll find someone with that power. It's just a matter of perseverance. Speaking of, while I admire your attempt to stall in hopes of a better outcome, don't you think it's time we let this dance come to its inevitable conclusion?" Chad asked.

"I suppose," Mary agreed. With one last push of effort, she slammed an area nowhere near the last spot Chad's voice had come from, striking in a wide area, rather than focusing on a more central point. Mary had tried several attacks already, but no matter how fast she'd been, Chad was always gone by the time her blast hit the area he'd last been. She let her bubble drop and put that energy into the strike as well. This was a last shot gambit, one depending almost entirely on luck. Chad wouldn't be where she'd heard his voice, so the only choice left was to pick a totally different spot and pray for the best. There was a smashing sound as her force struck empty wall, and she knew it was over.

"Well done," Chad's voice said from behind her. "A foot over and you would have hit me. I'd love to fight you again when we're on a more equal ground."

"Sure," Mary agreed. "After break, though. I need a long rest after this."

"Of course," Chad agreed, delicately placing his weapon against her shoulder and giving it a quick pulse.

*   *   *

"Finally, sweet light," Nick said as the door slid open and he stumbled into the lit room. Alice followed suit, though more cautiously. Her last light-room encounter was a bit too fresh in her mind to leave her at ease.

"The loud noises have stopped," Alice pointed out as Nick walked to the center of the room and dropped to a sitting position.

"I noticed. We'll wait here for five minutes to see if Mary joins us," Nick told her.

"And if she doesn't?"

"More wandering in the dark. Staying mobile and hidden are our best bets at that point," Nick said.

"You say that like there was a point when that wasn't our only option," Alice pointed out.

"Well, with Mary, we could have pulled off a little magic. Just you and me, though, we're less useful. Have to face facts: this challenge was designed to favor combat types," Nick sighed.

Nick waited for a reply, but when one didn't come, he turned around to face Alice. He'd expected to see her lost in thought or worry, annoyed at being stuck with him again. Instead, what greeted his eyes was her collapsed form and a barely noticeable pale glow from her wrist.

"Shit," Nick swore, scrambling to get on his feet. He reacted quickly, but not quickly enough. A sharp pain emanated from his gut and dropped him right back to the floor. As his vision cleared, he saw a female figure ripple into view. She was a fellow student, of course, one with short, mousy hair and a cocky grin.

"I don't know," she said, jumping into the conversation. "I find that a power is as useful as the person wielding it."

"Well, crap," Alice said weakly from her spot on the floor. Nick felt that summed it up nicely.

66

Hershel tossed another shirt into his suitcase while Nick and Vince lounged about, watching TV. Hershel had decided to do his packing in the boys' lounge to spend a little more time with his dormmates before the trek home. It was the day after the exam, and the mood was surprisingly upbeat.

"I still can't believe everyone passed," Vince declared yet again. It was a bit of a surprise that all of the students had been told they would be returning next semester, and from Vince's reaction, he must have been placing himself as a particularly high candidate for elimination.

"I still can't believe we all got beaten by girls," Nick chimed in, folding his arms bitterly.

"What are you, five? Who cares if we lost to girls, I'm just happy we get to keep going," Vince said, switching the channel to some competitive cooking show.

"It's a point of manly pride," Nick said defensively. "Though I have to admit, yours had a pretty awesome power."

"Enchanting people through song," Vince said with a shake of his head. "I talked to her afterward. Apparently, she can make people feel all sorts of stuff with her singing. Adoration was just the easiest."

"I'm glad it was you and not Roy. Heaven knows how he would have reacted if he actually liked a girl," Hershel laughed.

"What about Julia? I thought those two hooked up fairly consistently?" Vince asked.

"They do, but that's only because of how . . . unique her power makes her," Hershel said, opting to skip over the more lurid details.

"Very diplomatic way of saying she's her own gang bang," Nick said.

"Right . . . anyway, Selena, the girl who can sing, told me she snared a bunch of others before and after me. I wouldn't be surprised if she's toward the top in knocking out other players," Vince said.

"So nice of them to tell us we're all coming back, but then hide our scores and which training we'll be going into," Nick said.

"Oh, come on, it's not as if anyone would stay for the results, anyway," Hershel pointed out. "Alex, Will, and Jill already left town yesterday."

"Sasha, too," Vince pointed out. "Though she does that with more ease than most, so I'm not sure if that counts."

"I don't blame them," Hershel said with a sigh. "I miss my mom and my town. I can't wait to get home and sleep in my own bed."

"It will be nice to get some real food," Nick agreed. "Hey, Vince, where are you going for the holidays, anyway?"

Vince was spared from having to answer by the door to the boys' lounge opening to reveal Mr. Numbers.

"Before anyone leaves, Mr. Transport and I would like to see you all in the common room," Mr. Numbers said briskly, turning around and walking right back out.

"That wasn't creepy at all," Nick said once Mr. Numbers was out of earshot.

"I'm sure they just want to wish us safe travels over the holidays," Hershel said optimistically.

"Sure. That, or the order came down to terminate their little project and bury us in shallow graves," Nick replied.

"Let's be realistic. It'd be much easier for Mr. Transport to just ditch us in a volcano or something," Vince said.

"Point conceded," Nick said as they walked out into the lounge. Alice and Mary were already there, and of course, the two men wearing suits were standing in the center, just like they had that first day they'd popped in and scared the crap out of everyone.

"So, what's this about?" Hershel whispered to Mary as the boys ambled over and stood near the girls.

"Let's call it a surprise," Mary whispered back, her tone saying quite clearly that that was the end of the subject.

"Thank you all for coming," Mr. Transport announced with a big smile. "Mr. Numbers and I wanted to take a moment to congratulate you on making it an entire semester. As you know all too well by now, this program is grueling physically as well as mentally, so we are very proud that one hundred percent of Melbrook students have lasted into the second semester."

"And surprised," Mr. Numbers tossed in.

"Well, yes, statistically, this does count as an unexpected outcome," Mr. Transport tried to recover. "We know, though, that you've all made it this far through determination and hard work. You five are doing an excellent job in showing that years of practice with one's abilities don't matter nearly as much as heart."

"We are very happy to have done so," Alice said, all but beaming. The girl devoured praise and accolades.

"That's good," Mr. Transport said. "Because there is one more small task we need to take care of before you're released for Winter Break."

It wasn't the change in scenery that registered first with the five young students: it was the sudden slice of freezing wind ripping across their bodies. The shivers started immediately, as well as a reflexive search for shelter from the scouring wind and the white snow that was dumping down upon them. Everywhere they looked, there was only more snow. Everywhere, except up, where a huge peak loomed overhead, lost at the top amidst the clouds.

"I hope you've all still got a little bit of gusto left," Mr. Transport yelled over the wind's howl. "I brought you here for what you can think of as a final exam for Mr. Numbers and me."

He really didn't have to elaborate. Given the surroundings, there was only one logical conclusion. Giving words to it only served the purpose of hammering that unavoidable truth fiercely into their minds, which would be almost cruel given the circumstances. Mr. Transport didn't have any need to elaborate . . . but he did anyway.

"You five are going to climb a mountain."

67

"Bullshit," Nick replied, only pure willpower keeping his teeth from chattering.

"Not at all, I assure you," Mr. Numbers confirmed. "Your parents have all been made aware that you'll be detained for a few more days. No one is expecting you."

"But . . . why?" Alice asked, perplexity and cold slowing her words.

"Because you were all admitted as part of a very special program, one that is being measured in different ways than just your grades. Think of this as an extracurricular activity mandated by your scholarship," Mr. Numbers explained.

"This is crazy. We'll freeze to death," Vince pointed out. While Vince was admittedly cold, being trapped in a one-man tundra a few months back made it seem more bearable by comparison.

"Now, don't be silly," Mr. Transport said. "We've left you packs filled with supplies and winter wear. You'll find everything you need to reach the top safely."

"That's it? We just climb up?" Nick asked, probing for potential pitfalls.

"Well, there are two caveats. You have to reach the summit together, and you need to do it in six days," Mr. Transport admitted.

"Why six days?" Hershel asked.

"Because that's how much food we gave you," Mr. Numbers said. "There's a phone at the top with a pre-programed number. Call us once you make it, and we'll come pick you up."

"Wait, you're leaving us?" Alice all but squawked with incredulity.

"Yes," Mr. Numbers said.

"You're Supers now. Supers find a way," Mr. Transport said, and then both men were gone.

"Motherfuckers." Everyone turned in surprise, because that vulgarity was spat out from the mouth of Mary.

*　　　*　　　*

Ten miserable minutes of trudging forward had revealed a set of five oversized backpacks waiting in the snow. Each was a different color and labeled with a name. Nick's was golden, Alice's pink, Hershel's a dark green, Mary's red, and Vince's blue. It should be noted that none of them gave a shit about that, though; instead, they tore into the bags savagely and began piling on clothing. Only after everyone was coated, booted, and gloved did they begin to contemplate a strategy.

"Figures the one time I'd have an advantage, they'd screw me over," Alice complained. "I mean, come on, it's a damn climbing challenge! It was basically made for people with flight. But no, we all have to make it up there together or it doesn't count."

"Forgive my impudence here, but how the hell will they know? They left, remember?" Nick reminded her.

"They'll know," Mary assured them. "They went to all the trouble of setting this up, they'll make sure we follow the rules."

"Speaking of, how did you not see this coming, telepathic girl?" Nick asked.

"I did. I just hoped they would change their minds," Mary explained.

"Nice strategy, that one," Nick scoffed.

"It could be worse," Hershel said optimistically. "At least I have my emergency flask on me. This way Roy can help if we need him."

"Why do you keep an emergency flask of whiskey?" Vince asked him.

"Pretty much for situations exactly like this one," Hershel replied.

Vince placed his fingers on the bridge of his nose and sighed. "It saddens me how much sense that makes in this context. Okay: we know what we have to do, so how are we going to do it?"

"They gave us climbing gear, food, Sterno, flashlights, and water," Alice said as she rifled through her bag to take inventory.

"Aside from which, we have a flier who isn't allowed to fly, an energy absorber in an environment with nothing he can absorb, enough whiskey for a few appearances of the one person who could do this easily, me, and Mary, the marvelous brain girl," Nick said. "If we're going to build a strategy around someone's powers, it looks like Mary is our number one candidate."

"He has a point," Vince agreed. "Could you just lift all of us up to the peak?"

"No," Mary said sadly. "Grabbing hold of a person is a delicate procedure. It isn't like throwing objects. I have to worry about pressure and rupturing organs, that sort of thing. I can do it if I have to with one person, maybe two for short bursts, but I'm not confident I could get us far at all. Certainly not safely. Not to mention that I can't really lift myself."

"Why not?" Hershel asked.

"It's a jarring experience, being dangled in mid-air. It makes my stomach queasy and messes up my concentration, which just makes things less stable in a terrible cycle," Mary said.

"So then, what's our strategy?" Vince asked.

In response, Nick rose to his feet, dusted off the snow, and produced a pick, along with a section of rope from his bag. "I'd say our strategy is climb like motherfuckers in hopes of making it home before Christmas."

After a moment of staring at each other, the rest of the group pulled out their instruments and followed suit.

*　　　*　　　*

To say the act of climbing a mountain was grueling would be like saying Genghis Khan had a mild penchant for empire expansion. It was cold, hellish, and hard. But as the five struggled up the mountain, they found it was doable. For the first time,

242

they were thankful for the months they had spent in gym. Without Coach George's constant conditioning they would have never had a chance at making viable progress. Proof of this was Hershel, who was forced to use some of his whiskey in the first half hour for fear his muscles would give out and he would go tumbling down. Each of them held this fear, but luckily, it wasn't too steep at the mountain's base, and there were plateaus where rest could be acquired. On one such plateau, they stopped midway through the day for a lunch of water, jerky, and despair. There was nowhere to go but up, though, so they bucked up and began climbing once more.

Even Alice found herself hugging the side of the mountain as they climbed higher. With each bit of escalation, the wind grew stronger and colder. Gliding next to the rocks at least gave her some refuge from the wind's chilling bite. Admittedly, she could have flown up to their next logical break stop and waited, but she wasn't confident they would find her once she departed. Besides, even if it wasn't steep, accidents could happen, and she wanted to be close by, just in case.

The day wore on and progress grew slower. The mountain was getting steeper, and their muscles were growing colder. There was a brief huddle, during which they agreed to camp on the next viable rest stop they reached, since it would be madness to try and keep going in the dark. Unfortunately, that spot was farther up than they'd expected, and by the time Roy hauled himself over an icy cliff, nearly everyone else was ready to collapse. Mary followed after him, then Vince. Alice floated over to stand with them, trying not to shiver despite herself. Nick was the last man to scale the side, rolling over and resting for a moment before pulling himself to his feet.

"Well," Vince said. "That sure suc—" A loud cracking sound interrupted Vince, coming from the edge they had just scaled. There was a moment of realization as Nick looked down to the source of the noise and saw it was coming from directly under his feet.

"Shit!" Nick managed to say as the ice they had mistaken for rock gave way and he went him tumbling back into the open air.

68

There are certain things a person is programmed to expect when falling to their death. Fear, of course. Also a bit of nausea as your stomach rises up. Some of the more metaphysically-inclined believers tell us to expect our lives to flash before our lives. The one thing no one is ever really expecting, though, is what happened Nick. To be more precise, a pink-clad missile dropped from the heavens and sacked him in the gut.

"Ooof," Nick grunted as he was swung upward onto the same thin shoulder that had just lodged itself in his intestines.

"Not exactly a picnic for me, either," Alice replied, slowing her decent gently.

"Good hit," Nick cracked out, trying to right his perceptions in the blitz of snow and wind assaulting his senses.

"Not going to lie, I enjoyed the hell out of it," Alice chuckled. "Now, give me your sunglasses."

"Why?"

"Why? Because I can't see shit, and I'm the one driving. Oh, and you aren't getting any lighter, if you were wondering." Their progress downward had come to a stop, and Alice was now pushing them upward with increasing momentum.

"Excellent point," Nick agreed, whipping off his shades and placing them in her hand. He would have been more contrary in different circumstances, but being fireman-carried in mid-air was enough to make even him agreeable.

"You might want to hold on," Alice cautioned him. "I've never tried to fly with two people before."

"What's wrong with a slow, safe rise?"

"I can't hold you that long. My grip is already slipping," Alice admitted.

Nick reached down and grabbed her belt firmly without another word.

"Watch the hands," Alice snapped and then, they were off. Nick might have described the feeling as exhilarating had his life not been in jeopardy. Instead, the only words that came to mind were "hellish," "wild," and "horrifying." It turned out Alice didn't just float like an abandoned balloon; she cut through the air with shocking speed and hurtled toward her objective. An objective that was difficult to see even with eye protection, primarily due to her cargo severely compromising her maneuverability. Her grip was steadily deteriorating, but she didn't even dream of readjusting. This was all she had; if she couldn't find a place to land, then Nick was going to fall.

Then, mercifully, something pierced the white world surrounding them. A bright burst of flame from thirty feet up and to their left. Alice never hesitated, adjusting her course and barreling toward it. She had no hope of sticking a safe landing with both herself and Nick, so she slowed down as much as she could before arriving, then yelled at the top of her lungs:

"CATCH!"

"What!" Nick shrieked as she flipped him over her shoulder and left him falling through the air once more. This drop was shorter, as he felt an invisible force wrap around him and control his descent. Despite the wind and his naked eyes, he saw Alice pull up short a few feet away, plowing into the snow-covered ground with her feet, but managing to stop before she hit the mountain's side. As his own feet finally made contact with the sweet, sweet ground, he turned to face his second savior.

"I thought you couldn't lift people."

"I said it's hard, not impossible," Mary corrected.

"Holy crap, are you okay?" Vince asked, fumbling over to check on his friend. He paused when he arrived, then cocked his head quizzically.

"Huh. I never knew you had brown eyes."

*   *   *

"I am going to cut those two into pieces while they sleep," Nick grumbled as they huddled around the heat provided by a small can of Sterno.

"Good to see that Ethics class really paying off," Vince quipped.

"At least they gave us tents," Hershel said optimistically. Roy had turned back into Hershel a few minutes after Nick and Alice's spectacular air show. They'd taken the time to pull out the pop tents, anchor them down, and then break into the jerky and gather by the small can of heat.

"I don't think they'll let us die out here," Alice said.

"Because they're such awesome guys?" Nick asked.

"No, because my dad has more money and political influence than some countries, and I'm his only child," Alice explained.

"You never mentioned that before," Vince said.

"It was never a comforting thought before," Alice pointed out. "If I'd said it at a different time, it would have just sounded bitchy."

"It still sounded a little bitchy," Nick said.

Alice punched him in the arm in response. "Next time, I'm letting you fall."

"Yeesh, okay, I'm sorry, I'm sorry. Thought a little levity could lighten the mood."

"Well, it is making me laugh," Mary said, giggling softly. "Bodily harm to Nick is always good humor."

"Huzzah, I've finally found my role in the group," Nick said.

"I thought you had smart-ass pretty much on lockdown since day one," Hershel told him.

"Seconded," Vince agreed.

"That went without saying," Nick added. "Anyway, enough about me. Let's get back to Alice being a secret millionaire."

245

"It wasn't really a secret," Alice defended. "I told you about him a little when we did our project. It just isn't something I wanted to bring up. I mean, come on, except for Nick, I don't know anything about your families, either. Maybe you're secret millionaires too."

"My parents are optometrists," Mary said. "They're well off, but hardly millionaires."

"So neither of them had any abilities?" Hershel asked.

"Only a talent for asking people to read off charts. Me being a Powered was a total shocker for them."

"How'd they take it?" Vince asked.

"Not bad. Better than when I decided to live in the woods by myself," Mary said.

"My mom rolled with it really well," Hershel said. "She took to it like she found out she had another son. She never batted an eye about the fact that I couldn't control when I changed."

"How about your dad?" Nick probed.

"He . . . well, he left a few years ago, but it wasn't because of me or Roy. Hell, he's the one who taught Roy how to fight. Roy got a lot more unruly after Dad was gone, though. He used to be kind of nice." Hershel cleared his throat and Vince took the cue to pull attention away from his friend.

"What about you, Nick? Alice said she knew about your family, but we don't."

"My parents died when I was a baby. I was raised by my mom's sister, Ms. Pips. Not much else to tell. You?"

"I never met my biological parents," Vince said. "I was given up for adoption at birth. Things went okay for a little while, then my power showed up and . . . well, there aren't a lot of foster families out there who can cope with someone as 'special needs' as I was. So when I was six, I gave up and ran away."

"Wait, I've heard you talk about your dad before," Hershel said skeptically.

Vince nodded. "I call him my dad, because he was. Just not biologically. He found me that first week. I doubt I would have made it without his help. He was a vagrant, too, so he took me in and showed me the ropes. For some reason, my power never flared out of control around him. I wondered if he had an ability of his own, but he always denied it. He taught me about life, taught me how to fight even though he only had his right arm, and helped me learn to live on the rails. He died in an explosion when I was thirteen."

"I'm so sorry," Alice said.

"It's okay. It was five years ago. I've made peace with it," Vince assured her.

"But . . . wait, that was when you were thirteen. You joined us when you were eighteen. What did you do in between?" Hershel asked.

246

"I kept wandering. Dad taught me how, and it seemed safer than staying in one place, or getting too close to people. With him gone, it was too dangerous," Vince explained.

"So, you've been alone for five years?" Alice asked, hoping to be corrected.

"I wouldn't say alone. I met people, even made friends here and there. But in the way you mean it, yeah, I guess I was," Vince told her.

"Okay, I think the rough childhood award definitely goes to Vince," Nick said, breaking the dark mood that had slipped over them.

Alice rewarded him with another punch for his efforts. "Be sensitive, you dick."

"It's fine," Vince said, waving her off. "Ancient history. Besides, I think it's safe to say we all went through our tough spots."

"I'm inclined to count this as one of them," Mary noted.

"Agreed," Vince said. "We should get some sleep now that it's dark, though. No sense in wasting any daylight tomorrow. Does anyone know how to turn off the fire?"

"More trouble than it's worth to try and relight it," Mary said. "Just absorb it so we can use the heat later."

"Can do," Vince said, draining the can of the remaining fire. "See you guys in the morning."

69

The thing about climbing mountains is that the first day is pretty much the easiest. From then on, you're dealing with sore muscles, thinning air, and often-increasing steepness. The five of them made it to the third day with their free-climbing strategy, but a couple of close calls forced them to regroup and examine their options. None of them had any experience on a mountain; however, they did grasp the basic concepts of ropes and hooks, so after some debate and the working out of a few details, the strategy was officially changed.

Now, they had Alice fly up ahead of them and secure several hooks, linking the rope and then attaching it to her friends at the lower altitude. It took several tries for her to get the hang of it, but by the time they stopped to rest at the end of day four, she was able to work reliably and with increasing speed. That was good, because communication was breaking down.

After that first night, they'd been too tired to really converse when they camped. It had turned into slinging out the tents, stuffing down some food, and collapsing within. If the day had been particularly hellish, they might eat around a can of Sterno, but those were limited and it was mutually understood that they were to be used sparingly. Vince was another asset they tapped for warmth, huddling around him on breaks for a quick wave of precious, precious heat.

They were cold, they were miserable, and they were tired. They were making progress, though. On the fifth day, Hershel drank the last of his whiskey for Roy's final appearance. Vince developed a nosebleed midway through the day, and Alice's head began to throb in pain. They pressed as far as they could, but they could feel themselves slowing down. When the light began to fade, they were forced to camp, though they hadn't gotten as far as on previous days.

"So, I hate to be the buzzkill," Nick said as they huddled around the final can of Sterno. "But what happens if we miss the deadline tomorrow?"

"I don't think they'll let us die, but . . . I guess, maybe we fail?" Alice said uncertainly, her fingers gently rubbing her temples.

"Which entails . . . what, exactly?" Hershel interjected.

"I think it means we're done," Vince replied somberly. "They're testing us, just like George and Persephone. I imagine failure here has the same result."

"But that's not fair! We've passed all the same standards as everyone else. Why would they hold us to some ridiculously higher standard?" Hershel asked.

"Because we're different," Nick replied automatically. "We're not like everyone else, so it makes sense that we have different criteria to fulfill."

"They warned me to expect it when I took them up on the offer to enroll in Lander," Mary agreed.

"Me too," Vince said.

"Ditto," Alice chimed in.

"Roy and me, too," Hershel said, dejectedly. "I just never thought they meant this."

"Wish you hadn't taken the offer for Lander?" Alice asked him.

"Not even a little bit. Yeah, this sucks, but I've had so much fun these last few months. I never knew what it was like to feel normal in any group of people. With Alex and you guys, though, I'm not the freak. I'm just another Super," Hershel admitted.

"There are days I think that's the real reason they gave us the offer," Vince speculated. "They wanted us to have a chance to see what regular Supers felt like, so we could blend in later on."

"Maybe so," Mary agreed.

"Not that it will matter much if we can't finish this mountain tomorrow," Nick pointed out.

"We don't know that," Alice countered.

"But we have excellent grounds to suspect it," Nick shot back.

"Then, there's only one option," Vince said, a surprising resolve echoing through his voice. "We don't fail."

The others were silent for a moment. Vince was so cheerful and easygoing that they often let it slip their mind how determined he could be when the occasion demanded it. It could take them back a step.

"I hate to point this out, but you guys realize that tomorrow, all you'll have is me, right? And I doubt I can climb as fast as Roy," Hershel said.

"Maybe not, but you're fresh," Mary said encouragingly. "Roy's done all the labor, so I bet you can easily keep up with our worn-out bodies."

Hershel was about to voice his own lack of surety in just that subject, but the looks on his ragged friends' faces made him think better of it. Instead, he took a cue from Vince and mustered up his resolve.

"I will."

*   *   *

If the other days were hard, the sixth day was impossible. They had to move fast to make up for lost time, and as such, didn't permit themselves as much time for breaks. That strategy showed its downside within the first three hours, as sore hands struggled to hold grips and weakening spirits began to falter. Each of them wanted nothing more than to slide down the mountain and collapse into a pile of sweet, exhausted sleep. Instead, they kept going up. They halted briefly for lunch and a Vince warm-up, then got right back at it. The day wore on, and as the sun began to descend, hope trickled out of them. If it was dark, they were done. The cold and wind made it too dangerous, and that's

249

ignoring the problem of seeing their way without light. With Alice placing hooks, there were no free hands to hold flashlights.

Hershel was puffing hard as the shadows grew longer. He hadn't been given several months of intense conditioning; he'd let Roy handle that. The only thing that kept him moving was the knowledge that this was only a sixth of the torture the others had endured. As he cursed under his breath and hoisted himself another few inches, Hershel made two promises to himself. The first was that he was going to start getting himself into passable shape, and the other was that he was going to start carrying a bigger emergency flask of whiskey.

Vince's nose was bleeding freely again, so he tore off a few scraps of cloth, stuffed them in his nostrils, and let it be. At this altitude, there was nothing else to be done; the only way out was at the top.

Mary and Nick were holding together okay, though Nick had several close calls and was able to save himself only because of his excellent reflexes. Mary was able to press herself close to the rocky surface of the mountain and a few times, actually held herself up telepathically so she could rest her aching hands. It was dizzying and dangerous, but an assessed risk she deemed to be worth it.

Alice's head was still pounding, but she did her best not to show it. She pulled free some hooks from below her team and flew up higher to reattach them. They were coming up on a cliff that jutted out slightly, blocking the view above. It would be tricky to climb, so Alice decided to attach the hooks on the plateau the cliff would be concealing. She floated up past the side, blinked, and moved up several more feet to confirm what she was seeing. When she was absolutely sure, she dropped back down and yelled to the others.

"The top! We're almost at the top!" With her news delivered, Alice flew back up to re-secure the hooks.

As for the other four, while weariness and fear can do a lot to drag down the human spirit, suddenly finding out your goal is in sight can kick the shit out of nearly every negative feeling you've got. Such was the case as the cries from their aching muscles and cold bodies were no longer nearly as relevant as the sense of almost being done. They hurled themselves upward with the last of their strength, leaving nothing behind in their quest to finish. Within half an hour, the last of them, Hershel, was pulling himself over the side and flopping onto the cold, but level, ground.

They rested for a brief moment before dragging themselves vertical to complete the final task. It was Nick who found the phone, using his power and picking a direction randomly. He pulled the device from the snow and removed its waterproof cover. He glanced at his teammates and waited. Then, he stepped forward and handed the phone to Alice.

"Make the call," Nick told her.

"Why me?"

"Because I'd be dead, and none of us would be up here, without you. Now, call those bastards and let's go home," Nick said.

Alice nodded and accepted the phone. She punched a few buttons, and in mere seconds, a familiar voice greeted her.

"Hello," Mr. Transport said placidly.

"We did it," Alice said, her voice weary and cracked, but her tone full of pride.

70

"We should all pitch in, pool our money, and have those two killed," Nick suggested, soaking in the heat and the comfort of the common room couch.

"Nick, I'm right here," Mr. Transport said. All five students had been given a chance to take hot showers and unwind a bit; now, they were meeting to talk about the test at Mr. Transport's request.

"I know," Nick said happily, not even bothering to glance at him. "I believe in fair warning."

"Now look, I know it wasn't an enjoyable experience, but it was necessary," Mr. Transport explained. He was met with dark glares and grumbling. "Listen, it's Christmas Eve, and I'm sure you all want to get home to your families, so we don't have to talk about this now. Just promise you'll take the rest of the break to really think about what you learned on that mountain. About yourself, about each other, about everything."

"I promise," Mary said, not quite enthusiastically. The others merely nodded in agreement.

"Non-verbal is good enough for me. Whenever you're ready, go get your stuff and I'll drop you off at home," Mr. Transport offered.

"Pass," Alice said, waving him off. "I'll take my car. I'm only two hours up the road."

"I can take both you and your car in a span of seconds," Mr. Transport pointed out.

"Still no. I just spent six days on a damn mountain, I'm looking forward to a nice, relaxing drive," Alice reiterated.

"Fair enough," Mr. Transport said, putting up his hands. "When anyone else is ready, I'll be waiting in here."

*   *   *

"Hershel!" Mrs. Daniels yelled, flying out of her house to meet her son walking up the driveway. "It's been too long, dear," she said, giving him a strong hug.

"I missed you, too, Mom," Hershel managed to squeak out as she squeezed his lungs.

"My, look at you," she said, releasing her death grip and taking a step back. "You must be at least two inches taller than when you left."

"You think?"

"I know my son, don't I? Come on inside. I'll fix up some dinner and afterward, we can get the tape measure if you don't believe me."

"Sounds like a plan," Hershel agreed, dragging his bag inside and depositing it by the door. He'd unpack later; for now, he was just happy to be home.

The house seemed just as he remembered it, though now, there was a Christmas tree by the fireplace. Underneath were several presents, some wrapped in green paper and others wrapped in red. The red would be for Roy, the green for him, same as it had been for years and years. A spicy scent wafted through the house. His mom would be working on several dishes for lunch tomorrow. On Christmas, they went to Hershel's grandmother's house and met up with the rest of his family. Hershel realized that this was the first year he would be able to enjoy himself at that gathering and not worry about Roy butting in. Still, he might change later in the day. It was Christmas for Roy, too, after all.

"So," his mother said, interrupting Hershel's internal reverie. "Tell me about college. Have you met any nice girls?"

Hershel smiled in spite of himself and went over to the kitchen table. He took a seat in his usual spot and basked in the familiarity for a moment before dealing with his mother's question.

"Well, there is this girl in my dorm . . ."

*   *   *

Vegas was cold, but that could hardly be blamed on the season. It was a desert: those were hot in the day and cold in the evening. Nick walked up the familiar landscape of the strip and picked out the lighted monstrosity he called home. One good thing about this town: an unaccompanied minor with a suitcase didn't even draw a second glance as he walked into the lobby of a casino/hotel and strode right past the reception desk. Nick would greet everyone soon, but first, he wanted to go up to his room and change. He was still dressed as a Lander student, and that wasn't an image that belonged here. His only hope was that the sunglasses and different wardrobe would keep anyone from recognizing him. He should have known better.

Nick made it to the elevators and punched the up button. The elevators were gold in color, and the hall was faux marble. It was ostentatious, but with a touch of class, just like the rest of Ms. Pips's establishment. It didn't quite give him a sense of being at home; however, it was an environment he was comfortable in. For Nick, that was more or less the same thing. There was an audible ding as the doors swooshed open and Nick took a step back to accommodate anyone exiting. The elevator turned out to hold only one other occupant, a bald man wearing a dark suit. Nick sighed and stepped on board. He knew perfectly well this man wasn't planning to get off.

"Good to see you, Gerry," Nick said evenly. He would greet his former wrangler more enthusiastically later in the evening. For now, though, there were cameras everywhere, and it was a poor habit indeed to start showing fondness to anyone.

"You look good, Campbell," Gerry replied. He leaned forward and punched a few buttons on the pad. The elevator began rising to a floor inaccessible to regular guests.

"I wanted to let you know that Ms. Pips is currently overseeing a high-stakes poker game, but she should be on hand for lunch tomorrow."

"They do put on a hell of a spread for Christmas," Nick recalled.

"Of course. We can't have any of our clients regretting their decision to spend the holidays handing us their money," Gerry said. "Anyway, she'll be around tomorrow. You're on your own tonight, though. I had a couple of your suits cleaned and pressed, and I alerted the staff to expect your return."

"I have missed the people," Nick said.

"You've missed the girls," Gerry shot, a bit of slyness in his voice.

"Never as much as they miss me," Nick said with a smile.

The elevator dinged and opened on a plush hallway. The carpet was red, and the trim of the walls was gold. There were very few rooms in this hallway, because up here, the designers hadn't been concerned with cramming in as many as they could fit. This was the level that few would ever see and fewer would ever stay in. Nick stepped off and began heading down to his room. He stopped after a few steps, noting Gerry hadn't exited with him.

"I've got some things to do," Gerry said in response to Nick's glance backward. "If you'd like me to catch you up on things, we can meet in the usual place around two."

"Sounds good," Nick agreed. The usual place would be a restaurant a few streets over from the strip where he and Gerry had hamburgers and hung out. It was one of the few places away from Ms. Pips's direct area of influence, and likely, Nick's favorite spot in the world.

Nick swiped a card at the door and entered his suite. Sure enough, Gerry had laid out a couple of suits on the bed. He always remembered every detail, a habit he had worked very hard to ingrain in Nick as well. Still, Nick's first concern wasn't just with changing his clothes. He whipped off his sunglasses and tossed them on a dresser. He then shed the rest of his Lander ensemble and hopped over to the shower. Admittedly, he had taken a shower less than an hour before, but that had been all about heat and necessity. This was about re-centering. Nick always found a shower the best tool for wiping away a character and coming back to himself.

Half an hour later, Nicholas Campbell emerged. He promptly dressed, wearing a deep purple, button-down shirt with no tie beneath a perfectly tailored black suit. He styled his sandy hair with a tussled look and adorned himself with only one piece of jewelry, a silver wristwatch. He frowned slightly when he noticed there were tan lines on his face from those ridiculous glasses and made a mental note to visit a spray bed as soon as possible. All decoration and preparation complete, Nicholas paused only to give the sunglasses a dirty look before striding out the door.

*　　　*　　　*

"You're sure you want me to drop you here?" Mr. Transport asked again, just to be certain.

"Positive," Mary assured him, enjoying the sound of leaves crunching beneath her feet and the sticky smell of pine in the air.

"Don't you want to see your family?"

"I'll see them tomorrow," Mary told him. "I wanted to spend one night at home, though." She was already walking toward her trailer, small bag swinging in hand as she surveyed the spots that could use repair.

"Whatever makes you happy, I suppose. Merry Christmas," Mr. Transport wished her. Then he was gone.

Mary finished her tour of the trailer, coming back to its entrance and unlocking the door. It was cold inside, but a few minutes after she turned on the generator, the whole place would be thoroughly warmed. Besides, in comparison to her past week, she could barely classify it as chilly. Mary carefully opened her bag and tenderly removed a small, brown bear, setting him on the counter.

"It's good to be home, don't you think, No?"

No was his usual, stoically silent self.

*   *   *

"So good to have you home, Ms. Adair," the maid said, greeting Alice at the door and taking her bag.

"Thank you, Greta. Tell Francis the rest of my luggage is in the car. Is my father home?"

"He'll be in China until the end of the week," Greta told her. "But he's promised to come home in time to see you before you go back to school."

"Of course he will," Alice sighed, knowing it was fifty/fifty at best that she would see her father during this break. That might have been for the best, though; she wasn't sure what she would say to him. She'd never really had a grasp of what to talk about with him anyway, but at least before, she'd known the right steps and decorum. After her semester at Lander, though, she didn't find the prospect as appealing. Alice had slowly been dropping out of the habit of shying away from real interaction and using polite falsities. She was finding she liked the life she led this way far more than the other. Daddy wouldn't approve, though.

Alice made her way up the marble staircase to her wing of the house. Most of the servants were off for the holiday, so she'd have the house more or less to herself, with the exception of Greta, Francis, a few chefs, and some additional support staff. Normally, she preferred it this way: it was less lonely to be actually alone than to be surrounded by people and still be by one's self. As her steps echoed down the empty hallway and she pushed open the oak doors to her pink-themed bedroom, it occurred to her that she'd become far more accustomed to the bustle of Melbrook.

255

Alice laid down on her bed and stared up at the ceiling. There were paintings adorning her walls, along with a picture or two of her father. The only real photograph she held dear was on her bedside table, though: a photo of a beautiful, blonde woman with an infectious smile. Alice had digital copies of it, of course, but there was still something special about the original. Alice rolled over on her side and stared at the woman for a few minutes, wondering for the billionth time how different this moment in her life would be if that woman were still a part of it. There would be someone waiting for her, certainly. A hug, some conversation, and possibly even a meal prepared out of love rather than obligation. Perhaps Daddy would even be here as well, if that woman was around to wrangle him in.

Alice had long ago mastered the art of crying silently, so not one sob echoed through the empty catacombs of her mansion.

*   *   *

"Thanks again for bringing me out here," Vince said as he and Mr. Transport walked along a snow-covered dirt path.

"I'm not exactly certain where 'here' is. We've walked a good way from the city," Mr. Transport pointed out.

"We're almost there," Vince assured him.

For a few brief moments, Mr. Transport thought back to Nick's death threat jokes and wondered just how much Vince had disliked the mountain test. Then he mentally snapped himself back to reality and realized that, while one of his charges might eventually kill him, Vince was easily the least likely candidate on that list. Well, after Hershel.

They turned down another path and pushed their way through some brush. This time, though, the scenery opened up and Mr. Transport found himself staring at a set of lightly snow-dusted train tracks. In front of him was a sheer cliff about sixty feet high that looked down on the scene. The tracks seemed to run back in the direction of town, though they were clearly a long time out of use. Mr. Transport was about to question (once again) precisely where they were; however, the sight of Vince's face paused his words. It wasn't sad, per se. Exposed would be a better word. Soundlessly, Vince reached into his pocket and pulled out a small, gold watch. He begin winding it carefully, a few clicks at a time.

"My dad gave me this watch for my thirteenth foundday. He said I never had to worry about stealing power from it, because it relied on being wound," Vince said, his voice somewhere far away.

"Foundday?" Mr. Transport asked.

"I didn't know my real birthday, since I ran away at such a young age, so we just celebrated the day he found me instead," Vince explained.

"That sounds very . . . festive," Mr. Transport said uncertainly.

256

"It was. I know how bad it sounds, living on the rail, scrounging for food, but it was fun. It was nice to have somewhere I belonged," Vince said.

"Not to overstep my bounds, but it seems to me you have found that once more. And I don't think any of your fellow Melbrook residents would disagree with me."

Vince let out a small laugh. "I guess you have a point. I think that would make my dad happy."

"I'm sure it would," Mr. Transport agreed.

There was a gust of wind across the tracks and the sedentary snowflakes bounded about for a few elegant swirls before settling back onto the cold, rusted steel.

"This is where he died," Vince said, not as much to Mr. Transport, but to the world at large. "I try to come by here at least once a year. Usually around Christmas, if I can. There weren't any recognizable remains of anyone from the explosion, so there's no grave. Just . . . this spot."

Mr. Transport stayed silent. A few minutes passed by and Vince finished winding his watch. He flipped open the cover, checked the time, then snapped it shut.

"Thank you, Mr. Transport. I know it's cold and wet out here. We can go back to Melbrook now."

"There's no hurry. I'm not expected anywhere until a few hours from now," Mr. Transport told him.

Vince nodded his understanding. A fresh crop of snow was beginning to drift down upon them, some of it clinging to his hair, changing its appearance to more white than silver. Mr. Transport resisted the urge to shiver. He wouldn't be showing any discomfort until Vince was ready to leave on his own.

"Merry Christmas, Mr. Transport," Vince said over the soft winds.

"Merry Christmas, Vince."

71

"So, I'm the last one then?" Hershel asked.

"Correct," Mr. Transport confirmed. "Alice again elected to drive back, Nick did the same, Vince never left, and Mary requested pickup yesterday."

"Nick drove back? He doesn't have a car."

"I suspect that changed over the break," Mr. Transport said. "Are you ready to go?"

"Almost. I just have to run upstairs and grab one thing," Hershel said, darting up those steps with vigor.

Hershel and Mr. Transport had been sitting in the Daniels' living room. Christmas break would be over in a few days, and this was the date Hershel had submitted to be picked up. He was excited and nervous. It would be great to be back at Lander, but time spent there could hardly be considered relaxing or predictable. A few weeks at home had left him restless, though, and he was anxious to see his friends once more.

"Thank you for bringing back Hershel," Mrs. Daniels said, walking into the room and setting down a tray of cookies. "It saves us quite a bit on airfare."

"Glad to do it," Mr. Transport said politely.

"Well, please help yourself to some sweets, anyway. I appreciate what you and the other man have done for my boys all year," Mrs. Daniels said with a smile. She proffered her hand and Mr. Transport willingly accepted. He was surprised, though; he had expected a delicate shake, but instead, was treated to a surprisingly firm grip choking his fingers.

"Um, Mrs. Daniels," Mr. Transport tried to begin.

"I'd also like you to know Hershel told me about your little extracurricular test on the mountain, and I am not altogether pleased with my children being put in danger," Mrs. Daniels said, cutting him off.

"I can assure you they were always under observation and never in any real danger," Mr. Transport explained hastily.

"And I can assure you that had better be the case. I accept that there is some risk of injury when entering the HCP, but I find abandoning five children on a mountain very unacceptable," Mrs. Daniels said in a calm, even tone.

"Noted," Mr. Transport said, trying in vain to wriggle his fingers free.

"Please do," Mrs. Daniels said, releasing her grip. "I may be a normal person. But trust me when I say that being a mother is a power all its own. I think we understand one another now, don't we, Mr. Transport?"

"Implicitly."

"Sorry it took a few minutes," Hershel said, descending the staircase with a duffel bag slung over his shoulder.

"Nothing to worry about, sweetie," Mrs. Daniels said in a cheerful tone. "Mr. Transport and I were just discussing how happy you seem to be at Lander."

"I really am," Hershel said. "I miss you, though, Mom."

"Oooh, that's my boy," Mrs. Daniels said, wrapping her son in a tight hug. "You don't worry about me, though. You go on and have a great time. I'll see you in a month at Parents' Weekend."

"Awesome," Hershel said, finishing the hug and walking over to Mr. Transport. "Well, I'm ready when you are."

"Take care, dear," Mrs. Daniels told him. "And Mr. Transport, be sure to take of my sons."

Mr. Transport nodded his understanding and, to his credit, managed not to gulp. It took some effort, though, which, considering he was looking at a middle-aged woman a good foot shorter than he, made him feel not so masculine. He didn't really rush off, but he didn't dawdle either, as he thought of their destination and activated his power.

*   *   *

"I still feel like it's stealing," Vince's voice said as Mr. Transport and Hershel materialized in front of them. Vince and Nick were in the common lounge, watching television and clearly having some sort of debate.

"It isn't stealing. They offered it up to someone who could fulfill a set of specified conditions. I fulfilled those conditions, so everybody wins," Nick defended. His had just finished his sentence when he became aware the room had suddenly doubled its occupants in the span of less than a second. "Oh, hey, Hershel."

"Hershel!" Vince said, jumping up from the couch and greeting his friend with a hug. "It's good to see you, man. How was your break?"

"Lots of fun," Hershel replied, setting down his bag. "I saw some old friends, got to eat home-cooking, and just freaking relax. Yours?"

"Not bad. I stayed here for the most part. Tried to keep the same training schedule so the first day back wouldn't destroy me. Not much else, really," Vince said.

"I did something cool," Nick volunteered.

"It wasn't cool," Vince corrected him. "It was immoral and unethical."

"What'd you do?" Hershel asked.

"I won a car," Nick said with a dopey grin.

"You didn't 'win' a car. You used your power on a slot machine to make the right combination come up. You cheated and stole a car," Vince shot back.

"Also, I did this," Nick said. "Pretty much for the last few days. Turns out, Vince will hang on to shit like this tighter than a miser to his last dollar bill."

"Because you haven't made it right," Vince pointed out.

259

"Hate to break it to you, buddy, but there isn't really a process for giving back a car you won off a slot machine. Want to know why? Because it would be batshit insane," Nick told him.

"Glad to see nothing has changed," Hershel laughed with a shake of his head. "So, we've still got a couple of days off left. Any big plans?"

"Tomorrow, we go see which class we qualified for and what the rankings for the finals were," Vince said. "Nothing on the docket today, though."

"Actually, that is incorrect," Mr. Numbers said, stepping into the room from the kitchen. "Now that you have all returned, we need to discuss your test."

Mr. Transport's fingers involuntarily twinged with pain.

"Killjoy," Nick said.

"It shouldn't take all day," Mr. Transport said encouragingly. "Plus, once it's over, you still have a day left for fun."

"Or for plotting your eventual murder in the event we don't find your reasoning for that whole stunt satisfactory," Nick tossed out.

"You'd need far more than a day to conceive a plan with any chance of working," Mr. Numbers informed him.

"Heard and remembered," Nick replied.

"Don't be such a drama queen," Mary said as the door to the girls' side opened, allowing her and Alice to emerge. "I could hear your squabbling all the way in my room."

"Hey, Mary. Hey, Alice," Hershel greeted them.

"Hi, Hershel," Mary said with a soft smile. Alice merely greeted him with a directed nod.

"Now that we're all here, let's get started," Mr. Numbers told them.

72

"I learned never to stand too close to Mr. Transport," Nick said, kicking things off.

"I'm actually going to second that one," Alice agreed.

"Very funny," Mr. Transport said. "Be serious, though. What you took from the test is almost as important as the test itself."

There was a pause of silence before Mary's voice spoke up.

"I learned that being Super doesn't mean I can do *anything*," she admitted. "I've been able to handle everything so easily now that I can control my power, but none of it really helped me on the mountain."

"You helped save me," Nick pointed out.

"And Alice helped save us all by securing the ropes as we scaled the mountain," Mary replied. "My point was that, when I was Powered, I always assumed Supers could just do anything. I was wrong."

"Yeah," Vince agreed. "The only people with really useful powers were Alice and Roy."

"That's because of the environment, though," Alice said. "If we'd been stuck in a volcano, then your absorption ability would have been indispensable."

"Which brings up another point," Hershel said. "None of us is the best in every situation. In fact, there are probably situations where four of us would be totally screwed without our fifth friend."

"I guess that's why so many Heroes form teams," Vince speculated.

"Which, for those of you still wondering, is the realization we were supposed to come to, right?" Nick asked, looking over at Mr. Numbers.

"No comment," Mr. Numbers answered.

"We were supposed to realize why it's useful for established Heroes to form teams?" Hershel asked uncertainly.

"We were supposed to realize that we are a team," Vince explained to him, catching on. "They wanted us to depend on one another, to lean on one another, and to save one another. They wanted us to work as a unit rather than a set of individuals."

"But why? I mean, we more or less did our own thing last semester and got through without issues," Alice said.

"Because it's going to get harder," Mary told her. "We've done well so far, yes. However, we all are about ten to fifteen years behind everyone else in this program. They've spent a lifetime learning to use and control their powers, while we're just scratching the surface."

"Funny thing for the number one rank on the girls' side to say," Nick pointed out.

"Yes, I did well. A lot of that was by surprise and luck, though. You were with me in the labyrinth fighting Gilbert. Did it seem like I would have won by myself?" Mary asked.

"Fair enough," Nick agreed.

"So what's the point here?" Vince asked. "That we suck alone?"

"That we should work together more, I think," Alice said. "That we're facing a very difficult obstacle, not unlike climbing a mountain, and that the only way we'll make it is if we work together and are ready to help and save one another."

Nick and Mary glanced at one another from their respective positions. They alone knew that, while Alice was close, there was a whole other reason their caretakers had wanted to instill that team mentality. This was the point where they could steer the conversation to that logical conclusion, or cut things off and let the others believe it was done solely out of concern for their progress in the program.

"I think you're right, Alice," Mary agreed. "It makes the most sense. And it's true. We've got a long way left to go before we're Heroes. We'll need to start leaning on each other more as things get harder."

"It's a valid point," Vince concurred.

"True," Hershel said with a nod.

"Personally, I think they did it to kill us and cut open our bodies for science," Nick said. "But I guess encouraging us to work together is a possibility."

"Were we right?" Alice asked Mr. Transport.

"You took the lesson you took," Mr. Numbers said, answering before Mr. Transport had a chance to try. "Mr. Transport told you, the lesson you take is as important as the test itself. There wasn't a right or wrong one, only the one you arrived at. I'll say this, though: you five turned a difficult experience into a positive learning opportunity."

"That makes my frostbite all the more bearable, thank you," Nick quipped.

"Don't be such a baby," Alice scolded him.

"I'm pretty sure of all the situations in life I get to bitch about, being abandoned in the freezing snow and told to climb a mountain is right up near the top," Nick shot back. "It's over, though, so can we finish this meeting already? I want to swing by the video store and see if they still have Christmas-themed horror movies out."

"Nice to know nothing changed over the holidays," Vince said with a finger pressed to his temple.

"I think we've got a good sense of what you took from our lesson," Mr. Transport said. "Enjoy the rest of your day. Don't forget to meet me here at ten tomorrow, though. I'm sure you'll all want to see which class you wound up in and how you did on the final."

"And now, that will hang over my head all day," Alice said.

262

"You know what's good for that?" Nick asked.

"We all know you're going to say bad horror movies," Hershel told him.

"No, I wasn't," Nick told him.

"Fine, what then?" Hershel asked.

"Awesomely bad horror movies," Nick replied with a wide grin.

"You kids have fun," Mr. Transport said, rising to his feet. "We're going . . . anywhere that isn't here."

He and Mr. Numbers vanished, leaving the students finally alone and back together for the first time in several weeks.

"So, what kind of car did you win, anyway?" Hershel asked.

"Beetle," Nick told him.

"Stole," Vince corrected.

"Damn it," Alice groaned.

"Seriously, Hershel? They've been like this for days. Please don't reignite this crap when it dies," Mary said.

"My bad," Hershel said, putting up his hands.

"Okay look, Vince, you've been plugging away at me on this relentlessly, and I haven't caved. Now, it's apparent we're bothering those around us. So how about we say that this is in an area of murky morality and just agree to disagree. You think I'm wrong, I think I'm right, and neither of us seems to have a shot at changing the other's mind," Nick said.

"Agreed," Vince said after a brief pause. "I still think you should give it back, though."

"I'm well aware," Nick told him. "Now, who wants to ride in my ill-gotten gains to the video store?"

73

"Welcome to the halls of horror!" Nick declared as the guests walked into Melbrook.

"Good to see you, too, Weirdo," Sasha said, giving him a quick hug. Greetings were exchanged all around as Will, Jill, Julia, and Alex followed suit. After procuring a few choice cinematic classics, the Melbrook students had decided to see how many of their friends were back from break. As it turned out, the answer was all of them.

Vince appeared from the boys' side lounge, dragging in some extra chairs. Since there were so many people, they'd elected to hold the movie marathon in the common room and thus, needed to increase seating. He stopped and set down the four-legged burdens, then noticed everyone else had arrived. It was good to see them, with one being a bit more warmly appreciated than the others.

"Hey," Vince said, walking up to Sasha.

"Hey yourself," she replied.

"You look nice," he told her.

"Missed you, too," Sasha said with a slowly spreading smile.

"Yeah, this is totally comfortable for everyone else watching, if you were wondering," Julia tossed out.

"Sorry," Vince said, blushing rapidly.

"Speak for yourself," Sasha said. "I'm not ashamed to say I missed my man."

"That's okay, we're ashamed enough for you," Nick tossed out. Alice punched him in the arm reflexively. "Damn it!" he swore.

"You'd think a guy as smart as you could handle a little pattern recognition," Mary pointed out.

"Real funny," Nick said, rubbing his arm. "I'm going to go set up the movie."

"Good timing," Hershel said. "The popcorn will be done in a couple of minutes. Anybody want a soda before we start?" A few people raised their hands, so Hershel bustled off to the kitchen.

Julia let out a sad sigh. "I was really hoping Roy would be around my first night back."

"Take a cold shower," Jill chided her. "I'm sure he'll show in a day or so."

"But I haven't seen him in weeks," Julia continued complaining.

"Man, you really don't get the point of a booty-call buddy, do you?" Sasha asked.

"Psh, with Amber spending all her time out with her boyfriend and you two being prudes, someone has to be getting a little in that dorm," Julia said. "And it might as well be a little that is toned, fit, handsome, and skilled."

"I'm literally begging you here, please stop talking," Mary jumped in. "This is leading to mental images I'd really rather not have to deal with."

"Fine," Julia said, crossing her arms. "But I'm still hoping he shows up."

"That's your prerogative, I suppose," Mary said. "Though personally, I'm glad we get to spend some time with Hershel."

Vince had a feeling Hershel would very much wish he had been present for that particular statement.

"I've got the drinks," Hershel said, walking back into the room. "Popcorn will be done in thirty seconds."

"Which will be just in time, because we're about to watch *Mad Santa Massacre*," Nick said, twirling the remote in his hand.

"Joy. It'll be just like our Halloween movie session all over again," Will said, speaking for the first time.

"Except this time, it might be someone else who screams like a girl," Jill chuckled, throwing her arm around her twin.

"My device was more realistic than even I expected," Will said defensively. "Which is why it is being redesigned."

"Only you could take something back to the drawing board because it was *too* good," Jill told him.

A loud ding echoed through the room.

"And that's the popcorn," Hershel said. "Okay folks, time to get started."

*   *   *

"It sounds as though they're hosting a kegger out there," Mr. Numbers noted as he and Mr. Transport sat at their kitchen table.

"They just got back from break. It is completely natural for them to rejoice in seeing their friends," Mr. Transport said.

"I never said it was unnatural. I merely insinuated it was annoying," Mr. Numbers pointed out. He took a long sip of tea from the steaming cup in front of him.

"You seem edgy," Mr. Transport noted.

"I just spent a full week with my mother," Mr. Numbers told him. "You'd find your nerves diminished in tolerance as well."

"I suppose that's fair," Mr. Transport acquiesced. "How do you think they'll take discovering their classes tomorrow?"

"Perfectly well," Mr. Numbers said. "There aren't any big surprises, after all. It's been clear from the beginning who had the talent for combat and whose skills lay in other areas."

"You're right. I'm just a little worried. There's always been a stigma of the combat Supers being more elite, more valuable. I'd hate for our students in alternative training to feel like they somehow failed to measure up."

265

"Be reasonable, Mr. Transport. They're just thankful not to be destroying buildings or drowning in a sea of errant thoughts. I sincerely doubt any of them will care if they are perceived as 'less cool' than their peers."

"My understanding is these programs are exceptionally competitive," Mr. Transport said. "It's not unreasonable to worry about how they'll cope with additional social pressure."

"We left them on a mountain in the middle of December. I'm confident they can handle quite a bit of pressure," Mr. Numbers said.

"True," Mr. Transport agreed. "I was impressed by the lessons they took from it. I thought for sure some would go down a negative path."

"I was more impressed that Mary and Nick decided not to reveal the whole reason we did it," Mr. Numbers said.

"Do you think that means they trust us?"

"I think it means they are giving us some metaphorical rope, to see where our loyalties lie and what we do with our position over the group," Mr. Numbers informed him.

"Let's hope we live up to their standards," Mr. Transport commented.

"I'm less concerned with their standards and more concerned with the school's," said Mr. Numbers. "Things grow increasingly more difficult from this point on."

"Still, it would be nice if they knew we had their best interests at heart," Mr. Transport said.

Mr. Numbers resisted the urge to point out that this statement would be easier to demonstrate if it were actually true. Despite years of service, Mr. Transport still had a streak of idealism in him, and it was a trait Mr. Numbers had resolved to foster in his companion for as long as he could. He was amazed it had endured for these many years, though each year seemed to edge it closer toward its inevitable destruction.

"Indeed," Mr. Numbers said simply, turning his attention back to his tea.

*   *   *

The lone figure stood outside the Melbrook dorm, obscured by darkness and hidden behind a tree. In the abundance of shadow, it was difficult to make out a definite shape or the sex of the figure, only that it was watching the flicking lights from within intently. The figure stood there, unwavering, confident its hiding place wouldn't be discovered. It waited for hours, watching until the hour grew late, and the guests emptied out and returned to their respective dorms. It lingered on even after that, seemingly unwilling to abandon its place quite yet. Eventually, it left its obscured position and moved quickly across the campus, sticking to the darkest patches to maintain its anonymity.

74

"As I call your name and say your new training program, line up on the appropriate side of the gym," Coach George bellowed. "Combat training to the right, alternative training to the left. Those of you with ranks that predetermine your class, please take your places now." There was a soft scuffle as ten boys and ten girls took their appropriate positions at the right and left of the gym.

"Nervous?" Vince asked Alex as they milled together with the remainder of the freshman class. There were only eleven students left after the twenty predetermined ones had taken their spots.

"Very," Alex admitted. "I mean, we fought hard, but then again, we went down so easily against Selena."

"You have nothing to be ashamed of," Thomas said, joining the conversation. "You put forth a tremendous effort in our battle. It would be pure folly not to place you in combat training."

"Castillo, Thomas. Combat," Coach George's booming voice announced to the gym.

"See you on the right," Thomas said reassuringly before jogging over to take his side.

"Hunt, Tiffani. Alternative." A girl with short blonde hair flipped out at the ends walked over to the left side of the gym.

"Riley, Adam. Combat."

"Wells, Allen. Combat."

"Belden, Camille. Alternative." Vince perked up at this name, recognizing it as one of his saviors from Halloween, the one he still hadn't managed to thank. She was difficult to notice in the crowd, but when she broke out to walk to the left side, Vince wondered how he'd missed her before. She was diminutive, even shorter than Mary, with shoulder-length hair so blonde it bordered on white. There was something familiar about her as well, though Vince couldn't put his finger on it. He resolved himself to seek her out after this was over and thank her for the healing help.

"Reid, Gilbert. Combat."

"Wilkins, Selena. Alternative."

"Murray, Jill. Combat."

Vince took a deep breath to settle his stomach. He and Alex were the only two left.

"Griffen, Alex. Combat." Alex flashed Vince a thumbs up before heading over and joining the line on the right.

"And lastly, Reynolds, Vincent. Combat," Coach George declared.

Vince let out a sigh and threw a smile on his face, heading over to the right side of the gym. Inside though, he felt a ball of worry knot itself tighter. A part of him had been hoping he would end up in alternative training, so he wouldn't have to keep fighting people. Now, he had several years filled with fisticuffs to look forward to.

"We'll be giving all of you your mid-term grades today in private. However, as promised, we're now going to announce the top three longest survivors and the top three killers from the exam," Coach George began. "The number three killer was Chad Taylor. Number two was Britney Fletcher, and number one was Selena Wilkins."

There was a mumbling of confusion. Everyone knew who Chad was, but the other two weren't prominent warriors, though Vince and Alex felt a bit better in knowing the girl who'd taken them out was the best on the field.

"As for survivors, number three was Tiffani Hunt. Number two was Shane DeSoto. As for number one, well, she was the only person to make it on both lists: Britney Fletcher." Nick noticed the girl who'd taken out himself and Alice blushing slightly. Well, at least he knew the invisible girl's name now.

"I'm sure some of you are looking up and down the combat row, trying to place the names other than Shane and Chad," Coach George said to the assembled class. "Well, you'd better turn your heads to the left side of the gym, because that's where you'll find them. You see, those people who captured the top spots in both categories, they're in alternative training. And they kicked ninety percent of your asses."

Coach Persephone took a step forward. "There is a perception among many that Heroes specializing in combat are the best. That's true, in that they are the best at combat. Keep in mind, though, that few criminals are so thoughtful as to arrange a bare-knuckle brawl in a secluded location where you can prove to them your superiority. More often than not, skills like stealth, planning, and improvisation are far more useful. To those of you on the combat side of the room, most of you were likely hoping to end up in this training course. You feel it's the better option, and in certain cases, you're correct. Don't forget this lesson, though: just because someone is physically weaker than you, doesn't mean they aren't a very real threat. You're dismissed for today. We'll see you in class tomorrow."

The lines broke as students began scattering in their own directions. Vince began crossing the gym to thank Camille, but his arm was grabbed halfway there.

"Reynolds," Coach George said, holding him in place. "You need to come by my office sometime before gym tomorrow."

"For what?" Vince asked.

"Let's call it part of your probationary requirement for half-assing it with your power," Coach George told him. George released Vince's arm, and the silver-haired youth headed off in his original direction. Unfortunately, Camille had vanished during the brief discussion. Vince knew what she looked like now at least, so he was confident he could thank her next time.

Vince headed off to the changing room, wondering what requirement Coach George was going to give him. Since the last time a subject had taken him down this path had resulted in he and his friends being stuck on a mountain, he was understandably concerned. Still, it couldn't be that bad, could it?

"Hey man, what's with the long face?" Nick asked as he emerged from the locker area in his above-ground clothes.

"Nothing," Vince said, shaking off his concern. "So, what are we doing with our last day of pre-class freedom?"

"Cocaine and strippers," Nick replied. Vince simply raised an eyebrow in response. "Fine, fine. We'll think of something else. Let's go rally the troops. Buzzkill."

Vince nodded his agreement, and the two set off to actively waste some time.

75

Vince knocked hesitantly on Coach George's office door. It was during his visiting hours, so he should be there, but Vince still felt a bit out of place. Nick was organizing a putt-putt outing for the group to do on its last day of break, but it would be another few hours before they departed, and Vince had ultimately decided he would rather find out what Coach George wanted now, rather than put it off for a day.

"Come in," Coach George hollered from the other side.

Vince turned the handle and walked in, taking in a more comprehensive view of the small office than last time. There were various degrees along the walls, as well as a multitude of pictures. Some were very old, but many seemed recent. The contents of these photographs were completely varied, with no common theme or person spanning them all.

The actual desk took up a significant portion of the room, and it was literally covered in papers. Vince wasn't sure how anyone could find anything in that enormous sprawl of pages. Sitting atop that mess, though, was something even more surprising: a car battery.

"Reynolds, glad you made it early," Coach George said from behind the desk. "Take a seat."

"Um, okay," Vince said uncertainly. "Why did you want to see me?"

"Because I'm adding something to your diet," Coach George told him.

"I'm not sure I understand."

"You keep yourself stocked with a little fire by draining lighters, right?" Coach George asked.

"Yes, sir."

"Well, I saw what you did during the mid-term, when you drained your weapon and blasted Castillo with electricity. That was impressive."

"Thank you," Vince said, struggling for a moment to figure out who Castillo was before remembering that was Thomas's last name.

"So impressive, in fact, that I decided you need to add it to your training regiment," Coach George continued. "Hence, I brought you a snack." He patted the car battery.

"You want me to drain the battery? But I already keep some fire in reserve," Vince said.

"So you can't hold more than one form of energy at a time?" Coach George asked.

"No, I can hold as many as I want. At least, that's been my experience so far. I was referring to the talk we had last semester, about me not wanting to have too much in case I lost control," Vince explained.

"Listen, Reynolds, I'm more than meeting you halfway here. I'm cutting you more slack than I've given anyone in a very long time. I'm still your teacher, though, and I would be remiss in my duties if I let you get by without mastering all the weapons at your disposal. So here's the deal: you're going to keep up your fire reserves, and in addition, you're going to drain this car battery every day before class."

"But—"

"And before you object, let me make this clear, I'm not making a request. You're going into combat training. That means you're going to learn how to fight with both types of energy," Coach George finished, cutting Vince off.

Vince took a deep breath and considered the situation. A car battery wasn't all that much power in the grand scheme of things, but then again, with electricity, a little went a long way. Still, it could be manageable, with the right precautions.

"I have to drain it every day before class. If I have any left over when gym is finished, do I have to keep it with me?" Vince asked.

"I don't care what you do after," Coach George told him. "As long as you start my class each day with a full battery's worth of power, you can discharge the rest down here when we're done."

Vince nodded. "I can work with that."

"So glad to hear it," Coach George said. "Now, get out of here, kid, I've got work to do."

Vince scrambled up and headed out the door. He made his way to the lifts, thankful he'd faced his problem today instead of waiting and worrying. It hadn't been nearly as bad as he'd expected. He just had to start using another type of energy. In fighting. Which he would apparently be doing every day there was class.

As the lift began to rise, Vince felt his stomach begin to drop.

*   *   *

"Your move," Mary said, setting her pawn down. Nick was rounding up people for putt-putt, Vince had gone to see Coach George about something, Alice was getting herself dolled up, and Hershel had gone to get lunch, leaving her the perfect opportunity for a match with Mr. Numbers.

"Indeed it is," he said, quickly analyzing the board. "I find it interesting that you wish to continue these games, even after our disagreement over the mountain test." He moved his knight.

"We have the same objective, we're just going after it in different ways. I disagreed with your methods, not the results," Mary said, positioning her rook.

"I see. And do you feel our tactic has borne fruit?"

"Everyone is a little bit closer after the experience, I'll give you that. Not to mention, for the first time, Alice got to see how her power can be useful, even lifesaving," Mary said.

271

"Ah yes, is that why you claimed you had trouble lifting people with your gift?" Mr. Numbers asked.

Mary blinked in surprise. "That was true," she told him.

"Then what about when you plucked the fit version of Mr. Daniels off the ground and held him restrained in mid-air while threatening him?" Mr. Numbers pointed out, shifting his knight once more.

"Roy is incredibly resistant to damage. That means I can hold him in the air indefinitely and not worry about crushing him. Other people aren't quite as durable," Mary replied.

It was Mr. Numbers's turn to be surprised. He'd assumed she was lying in order to elevate Alice's need and usefulness within the group. He had been wrong, though; she truly did possess that limitation. He mentally adjusted several calculations, then turned his focus back to the game.

"So the mountain was a success, then," he said.

"It bonded us, yes. It also made the stronger of us realize our limitations, which is somewhat counterproductive to my work with Vince, Nick, and Alice," Mary informed him, moving another pawn.

"Such endeavors must invariably suffer small setbacks on occasion," Mr. Numbers commented.

"Agreed, but let's try to keep those to a minimum in the future. It will be better for everyone. Especially Mr. Transport," Mary chuckled.

"What do you mean?"

"Ask him about when he went to pick up Hershel. I'll let him explain the rest," Mary said, a small grin still stuck to her face.

"I will," Mr. Numbers agreed. He took the game in three more moves.

76

The next day was a hectic one. Book bags were packed, breakfasts were scarfed, and new classes were attended. The time above ground passed more or less the same for everyone, getting the syllabi for their new courses and hurriedly finding the locations of their classrooms. There were lectures on attendance requirements and expectations for the year, but they may as well have been monologues about ham versus bacon on eggs benedict for all the HCP students could tell. Each one was focused on the coming afternoon and the final hour of gym when they would at last begin a new regimen of training. Alternative and combat alike were excited, scared, and awash with the curiosity for something new. The morning flew by. However, there was still one roadblock before the new classes in gym could begin.

"Welcome back, everyone," Dean Blaine greeted them as the freshmen wandered into his classroom. "I hope you all had an enjoyable vacation." There was a grumbling of answers that seemed to lean slightly toward the affirmative. "Glad to hear it."

As Nick took his usual seat near the middle row, he noticed something. The extraneous chairs appeared to be gone. He kept watch as the remaining ones filled up and confirmed his suspicions. There were exactly enough chairs for the current number of freshmen attending the class.

"Now, as I'm sure some of you have noticed, we've scaled back the clutter of extra seats over the break," Dean Blaine said once everyone was seated.

"Took you long enough," Stella called out.

"So pleasant to hear your voice again, Ms. Hawkins," Dean Blaine said with his usual unwavering smile. "I assure you, we had our reasons for waiting, as well as for removing them over break. Would anyone care to take a stab at what those might have been?"

Alice's hand shot up in the air as usual. Dean Blaine pointed at her out of habit, only doing so after realizing that her hand had, in fact, been up.

"You wanted us to look at the empty seats and be reminded that those were students like us who didn't cut it. And to remind us that if we didn't do our best, our seat could be empty too."

"Very good, Ms. Adair. So, why did we remove them?"

"Because . . . because we're starting a new semester, so you wanted the empty chairs to be fresh examples?"

"Not quite, no. Anyone else?" Dean Blaine asked. This time, a black-haired boy with a thin goatee raised his hand.

"Mr. Weaver," Dean Blaine said, pointing at him.

"You took the chairs away because you're finished cutting people with that system," he said.

"Correct, Mr. Weaver. All of which leads us into what I'd like to talk with you all about today. I think it's time we discussed how the remainder of the Hero Certification Program will work as far as continuation and admittance," Dean Blaine said.

"Admittance? We're already in the program," Stella pointed out.

"You're in this year's program, yes. I'm talking about the years to follow, though," Dean Blaine told her. There was a ripple of stillness as the implications of his phrase settled in the minds of the class.

"Allow me to clarify before anyone asks further questions on the topic," Dean Blaine said; years of giving this speech had left him well-prepared to avoid the tidal wave of panicked queries that would strike if he didn't take charge. "Each year, we take a small number of promising Supers and admit them to the freshman course of the program, the one you are all currently enrolled in. The first semester of that time is used to trim the fat in multiple ways, both by beginning the basic necessary physical conditioning and eliminating those who lack the qualities to move onward. The second semester is spent continuing to lay the groundwork for continuing in the program, giving you training a bit more specialized to your particular talents. Near the finale of the second semester, we hold another battle session to assess your combat abilities, as well as looking at your other skills through various tests to see how much you have grown, and how much further we think you can grow. At the end of this year, you all have the option of applying for the next year's program. I should caution you, however. There are only twenty-eight spots available."

A few of the mentally swifter students reach the conclusion first, but it was, of course, Stella who voiced it:

"So, three of us will be gone?"

"Correct," Dean Blaine confirmed. "While you are, of course, welcome and encouraged to continue pursuing a degree at Lander, you will no longer be part of the Hero Certification Program. I should tell you that, generally speaking, we have cut the class down to much fewer than thirty-one by now, so feel proud that you are part of such a talented group."

Vince raised his hand hesitantly.

"I believe I said no questions, Mr. Reynolds; however, since I just took one from Ms. Hawkins, I will make one more exception for fairness before I expect that rule to be followed once again," Dean Blaine said.

"Thank you, sir. I was just wondering, if it's usually a lot lower than this, and there are twenty-eight spots, does that mean the sophomore year generally has unfilled spots?" Vince asked.

"An astute and fair question, and actually my next point," Dean Blaine replied. "No, the classes are always filled and many are turned away. Let us say, hypothetically of course, that you don't make the cut this year and are removed from the program, Mr. Reynolds. In the duration of next year, you work hard and improve your abilities. When the year's end comes around, you apply for the sophomore training once more. You are tested, measured, and found to be one of the twenty-eight most deserving candidates. You would then be accepted and placed into the next year's course."

"Wait, wait a second. You mean we're not just competing with ourselves, we're competing with everyone who ever completed their freshman year in the HCP and wants back in?" Stella asked.

"I'm going to choose to interpret that as a statement, rather than a question, since I feel I've been quite clear about my negative feelings toward those right now," Dean Blaine said stonily. "That would be a correct summation of the situation, though. You should also note that the twenty-eight spot limitation is only for the sophomore year."

The class relaxed a little bit. It was scary to have to jump through another hoop, but if it was only one time, they each felt like they could make the cut.

"Junior year, we only accept twenty students, and senior year, it will be a paltry fifteen," Dean Blaine continued. "Of course, the process will be the same each time, as will the existence of an outside pool of competition. And I suppose I should mention that of the fifteen accepted senior year, only ten will graduate and become fully licensed Heroes. You may now ask any additional questions you may have."

"Why limit the number of Heroes out there?" Alex asked immediately.

"Because Heroes must be the best. They are tasked with dealing with Supers, Powereds, and all manner of natural disasters, along with everyday problems. Just completing the course isn't enough. You have to prove you're better than everyone else. Because you'll have to be," Dean Blaine explained.

"What if there are more than ten capable Supers in the senior year class, one or two who would make awesome Heroes and are just below the cutoff point?" Gilbert tossed out.

"They are welcome to apply for the year once more and try again. Perhaps with another year of training, they will rise in standing and make it out. If not, though, well, then, they weren't the best, were they?" Dean Blaine queried back at him.

The class lapsed into a stunned silence, taking in everything that Dean Blaine had explained to them and trying to mentally assess their current standing.

"The ultimate thing to remember here is to work hard, try your best, and never forget that just getting by is not an option for students who want to be trusted with the lives of the weak and innocent," Dean Blaine advised them. "I know this system seems harsh, because it is. When Heroes fail, people die. That isn't a responsibility that can be trusted to just anyone. Keep that firmly in mind as you learn this semester, and I'm sure you'll find the gumption to push yourself just that little bit harder."

77

"Rule number one is that you're stronger than you think you are," Coach Persephone said as she walked down the line of students before her. The two hours of conditioning were over and they had finally arrived at a more specialized training. She was handling her kids in the regular gym, while George had taken his down a floor to a combat field. The faces staring back at her were uncertain and timid. She knew these expressions well: every year, she was surrounded with the same looks on different faces. It was an arrangement of features that told the familiar story of someone who was powerful, yet mortal, a Super who had to fear the mundane. She knew these expressions very well—she'd seen one in the mirror all her childhood, after all—and she took a particular joy in wiping them off any student in her charge.

"That isn't just pretty talk, either. I'm not encouraging you, or trying to build your self-esteem. I'm being literal. Each of you is more powerful than you believe. Alice Adair, for example, can fly. Now, how useful would you rate that skill in combat, Mr. Weaver?"

"Not very," said Rich, body language solid, but voice hesitant.

"You'd be right much of the time," Coach Persephone agreed. "In circumstances where battle is taking place in an elevated location, or the enemy has the high ground, or even mid-air, though, you would be very incorrect. The ability to move freely through the air is a very rare talent among Supers, and one that has turned the tide of many battles. What about Tiffani Hunt's ability to create illusions? Any thoughts on its battle worthiness, Mr. Murray?"

"Well," Will began thoughtfully. "Normally, no, it wouldn't be useful in a one-on-one battle. However, if it were able to alter the opponent's perception of their environment, it could be downright deadly. If used properly."

"Mr. Murray has hit upon the magic phrase," Coach Persephone praised. "And that is 'if used properly.' You see, none of you are a tremendous threat in a regular fistfight, but we don't deal with those situations. We deal with criminals and villains that are clever as well as powerful. Being a Hero very rarely boils down to something as simple as a fistfight. So while you are under my care, it is important that you understand the purpose of this course. I'm not trying to teach you how to fight like the students in the combat course. I'm teaching you how to find the right scenarios where you are deadly, and then, how to orchestrate them in a field of battle. She paused for a moment, seeming to collect her thoughts. In reality, she had given this speech many times and found a small break here drove home her next words well.

"To put it more concisely: Coach George is turning your fellow classmates into tanks. But, as for me, I'm building snipers."

*   *   *

277

"Rule number one is that you're weaker than you think you are," Coach George said, pacing the line with a half snarl plastered to his face. He knew all too well the faces that stood before him in the sparse, concrete combat area under the glaring fluorescent lights; they were same cocky stares that met him every year at this time. These were the kids who grew up unstoppable. They didn't understand fear or insecurity. Sure, some of them knew what the words meant, but they didn't *know* the horror of wondering if you'll be able to walk out of a bad situation alive. They weren't picked on or made to eat dirt, though plenty of them had done the picking. These were the expressions of arrogant idiots who'd never known what it was to really lose—George had worn one himself for longer than he cared to admit—and he took a special joy in smashing it off the face of any student in his care.

"I know you all grew up powerful, the baddest-ass kid on the block," Coach George continued. "I'll bet, with the exception of you who had Supers for teachers, none of you has even lost a fight before Lander. Hope you enjoyed it, kids, because that ride of luxury stopped the minute you stepped into my gym. This course is designed to show you just how weak you all really are, so that I can teach you how to be strong. Reynolds, punch Castillo in the mouth."

"What?" Vince asked, making no move to strike Thomas, who was standing next to him. "Why would I do that?"

"Wrong answer, Reynolds. Fifty push-ups. Now," Coach George ordered.

Vince looked at him uncertainly, then got down to the floor and began his penance.

"You see, this is not playtime. I'm going to be teaching you how to fight with the intent of taking an opponent down for the count. Me giving an order should be met with instant obedience, because there will be times when that order will save the life of you or another. Foster, punch Griffen in the mouth."

Alex never even had a chance to react before Sasha's fist buried itself in his unsuspecting jaw. The impact knocked him to the ground.

"Good job, Foster. The sound of flesh on flesh impact was the only acceptable answer there. Griffen, fifty push-ups," Coach George said.

"But you told her to hit me!" Alex pointed out from his prone position as he rubbed his jaw.

"And if I'd told you not to dodge, then you'd get a 'good job,' too. But you didn't duck a fist flying at your face. That shit doesn't float in combat training," Coach George explained.

Alex groaned, but he flipped over and began doing his own push-ups.

"Now, I'm sure, at this moment, Persephone is giving her kids a pep talk about how to use their special talents to be better Heroes. You lot don't have special talents, though. You only have the one: kicking ass. Sure, it comes in different flavors, but at the end of the day, that's what it all boils down to. I'm going to tear you down and then build you up again, but this time, the right way," Coach George declared.

The gym was silent save for the soft grunts of Vince and Alex still doing their push-ups. That was fine; George didn't have to hear the grumbles and the 'yeah, rights' to know they were there. Kids like these didn't take anyone's authority on words.

"I know each of you is thinking that this speech doesn't apply to you. That you're the exception to the rule, a true warrior in every way, and that I don't know a damn thing about combat. I know, because I've been you, and I'm going to do with you what my coach did to us. I'm going to establish, right here and now, who the authority on the subject of winning fights is."

Coach George shrugged off the jacket of his uniform and cracked his knuckles for show. "Anyone who wants to see where they stack against the old timer can step up now. One by one, I'll be glad to knock you down."

Smarter students of this age, ones who had been on the losing end of a few fights, might have suspected that Coach George wouldn't make an offer like this unless he was able to follow through on it. Unfortunately, for a large portion of the class, they didn't fall into that demographic, and as such, hadn't learned just how humiliating and devastating a loss can be.

Yet.

78

"This is some kind of trick, right?" Roy asked as the rest of the students stared uncertainly at Coach George.

"Not at all, Daniels. This is part of the learning experience," Coach George said.

"What exactly are we supposed to learn?" Sasha ventured to ask.

"Respect. Not the kind that makes you say 'sir' and 'ma'am,' the kind that lets you trust implicitly that I know what I'm doing. This class will be far more lucrative for you all if you do as I tell you, when I tell you."

"Of course we will, you're our teacher," Jill assured him.

"Some of you will," Coach George agreed. "Some of you need to really know you should, though. Need to know it in a visceral way, a way that can only come by having the man you're learning from best you in a fight. I'm not condemning that fact, I'm acknowledging it for what it is and getting it addressed right here and now. Nobody has to fight me, and there won't be punishment for anyone who does. Just ask yourself this simple question: can you one hundred percent trust the battle instructions of a teacher you haven't tested firsthand? If so, then fine. If not, then let's fix that problem."

There was a brief silence after Coach George finished, broken almost immediately by Roy's deep, confident voice.

"Oh, I have so got dibs on first."

*   *   *

"The first step is understanding exactly what it is your power does," Coach Persephone instructed her students. "This is also the last step, because it is a step that never truly becomes accomplished. Trying to define the miraculous is a capital enterprise in futility. Still, we can improve our understanding, and from there, we gain strength."

Nick leaned over and whispered to Alice, "If I cough the words 'hippie bullshit,' you think anyone will notice?"

"Shush!" Alice snapped at him.

"Nick Campbell," Coach Persephone said without turning to face him. "Do you have a problem with my instructions?"

"Yeah, look, not to stir the pot or anything, but what about people like me? I mean, hell, I don't even know how my power works, let alone have a clue on how to understand it," Nick told her, stepping forward from the line.

"You manipulate probability," Coach Persephone said.

"Probabilily," Nick said, grinning slightly.

"That is somewhat abstract, I'll give you that. If you want my honest advice, though, and not just an opportunity to show the class how you can make a bad joke from a common word, I would tell you experimentation is the key," Coach Persephone said. "Start trying to do things with your power you haven't done before. As you find things that work and things that don't, you will grow closer to understanding the mechanics behind your ability."

"Ah, great idea. Thanks, teach," Nick said, retaking his place beside Alice.

"Nick Campbell, walk over here right now," Coach Persephone told him.

"What'd I do? I asked a question," Nick began protesting.

"Just walk over here, young man," she reiterated.

Nick let out an exaggerated sigh and began slowly schlepping toward his teacher. It wasn't far, maybe thirty feet at the max, and yet he only made it halfway. Once there, Nick proceeded to jerk his head back, twitch slightly, and collapse onto the ground.

*   *   *

"Anyone else?" Coach George asked. Scattered around him were the bruised and often unconscious figures of several freshmen students—Roy, Stella, Michael, and Sasha among them. The ground in the area was now cracked, and in several places, there were scorch marks burned into the surface. Most changed of all in the scenery, though, was Coach George himself. Coach George was a shifter it seemed, one of the more common types of Supers, especially of those who specialized in combat. Coach George was a bit extra special, though, for while shifters like Hershel turned into Roy, or the sophomore Ben had turned into a lizardman, Coach George turned into something different.

"So, is he technically a robot or a cyborg?" Vince asked Jill, one of the evidently more intelligent students who had opted to decline Coach George's challenge.

"You'd probably have to ask my brother on that one. I can't really connect with him the way I do other machines, though, so my money is for cyborg," Jill replied.

Coach George had shifted into a man of metal, but unlike Stella, he was a more functional model. His eyes seemed to act as scanners, and several times, he had blasted a charging student with a weapon from his body. His favorites seemed to be the energy guns that came out of his forearms.

"It looks like we're done here then," Coach George told them, turning back into his human form. His pants and shirt were ripped and singed in a few places, but the skin he showed had no injury of any kind.

"When we're done, someone go grab the healer girl to clean up in here. But first, I want to say something. Pay attention, those of you on the floor who can still hear. Today was an important lesson: it taught you what failure is, some of you for the first time. For others, it was one you've had before, but could stand a little repeating. I meant what I said, though: I don't hold it against you that you needed to test my mettle. I did the same thing to my coach when I was in your spot, and my ass wound up on that same floor. So listen close, kiddos, because this is the part that matters. Today, I taught you how to lose, so that starting Monday, I can teach you how to win. Come ready to hurt and ready to learn. Class dismissed."

281

"Well, that was pretty horrifying to watch," Thomas said, walking over to Vince and Alex.

"Agreed," Alex said. "I say we hit the showers, go get dinner, and try very hard to forget what we're coming back to on Monday."

"I'll catch up with you guys," Vince said. "Somebody still needs to go get Camille."

"I can do that. We're friends, after all," Thomas volunteered.

Vince waved him off. "Don't worry about it. I still owe her a thanks from Halloween, anyway."

"Very well," Thomas said. "At least she should be free. It's not like anyone in the alternative training class will need healing."

*　　　*　　　*

"If you're wondering why you can't move, it's because I've scrambled the receptors to your nervous system," Coach Persephone explained to Nick's twitching, collapsed form. "I'm not targeting any of the automated parts like heart and breathing, so you'll be fine when I stop. Although, you might be a bit twitchy for a few hours."

"How are you doing that?" Tiffani Hunt asked from the line.

"As a child, I always seemed to be able to turn people's moods with ease. Eventually, it was diagnosed that I was a Super, though at the time, we all believed I had a minor ability to influence people's minds. In an effort to understand my power, I did exactly what I told Nick here to do: I experimented with new things I'd never tried before. Most failed, but some didn't, and eventually, I made a fascinating discovery," Coach Persephone said, walking the rest of the way over to Nick and staring down at him.

"I learned I didn't have power over the mind. I had the ability to, at will, create, emit, and direct pheromones of all types. At first, I was disappointed, thinking the mind power to be more useful. My time at Lander taught me otherwise, though. I learned there are all sorts of things that pheromones influence and control. Did you know there are even some that can disrupt the nervous system?"

Nick made a slight gurgling sound from his place on the floor.

"Your homework over the weekend is to try one new way to use your power. Failure or success is irrelevant, I only demand that you try. Dismissed," Coach Persephone told them. With that, she turned and began heading toward the exit.

Camille began moving toward Nick's pitiful form to administer some help, but the sound of her name being called in a familiar voice pulled her attention away rapidly.

"Hey, Camille!" Vince yelled, jogging over from the entrance to the gym.

Camille took very deep, very rapid, very unsuccessful steadying breaths. She'd known this was going to happen eventually. It was unavoidable: he was just the kind of guy who had to thank anyone who'd given him aid.

282

"Coach George sent me up here," Vince explained once he reached her. "He did kind of a number on our combat clas,s and a lot of the guys could use some healing. Do you mind?"

Camille shook her head no and began to hurry past him toward where she was needed, but he stepped in front of her before she made it.

"One more thing. I just wanted to say thank you for helping me on Halloween. You guys really pulled me out of a tight spot there, and I don't know what I would have done without you. So thank you, a lot."

"No problem," Camille squeaked, flushing bright red and bustling past him toward the door. To her credit, she didn't break into a full-on sprint until she was out of the gym and on her way to the lower floor. Her heart was racing and her breathing was more erratic than a drunken bull-runner's, but she slowly got both back under control. It looked like he didn't remember, and she wasn't sure how she felt about that. It made things easier, though, and that was something.

Upstairs, Vince was quite uncertain how, but he had a strange feeling he'd offended the girl he meant to thank. Added onto the tingle in his brain that there was something familiar about her, Vince had no idea what to make of the small female. Instead, he wandered over to the circle of fellow students watching with amusement as Nick slowly regained control of his limbs.

79

"How you feeling, buddy?" Vince asked, handing Nick a glass of water. They were back in Melbrook, lounging the common room with Alice, Mary, and Hershel. It had taken Nick twenty minutes before he could effectively coordinate his movements, and even then, he'd needed help making it to the dorm.

"Glitchy," Nick replied, sipping the water carefully. "That woman is a nutjob. Who just attacks a student on the first day?"

"Coach George attacked around eight, but they sort of volunteered for it," Hershel commented. Roy had shifted back not long after being healed, happy to fade away after another trouncing. He wasn't used to losing, especially not this often.

"'Volunteered' is the key word there. I just asked a simple question," Nick said.

"You were being an asinine smartass, no surprise," Alice corrected. "Just be glad I don't have her power."

"At this particular moment, I'm more wishing no one had her power," Nick replied. "Let's just grab some dinner, rent some movies, and spend the rest of the night relaxing."

"Actually, if you guys are interested, I was sort of planning to go out tonight," Hershel said tentatively.

"Well, yeah, we assumed Roy would be on the prowl," Vince said.

"No. I mean me. Hershel. I want to go to a club tonight."

There was a soft creak of bones as everyone shifted their bodies to gaze at the chair where Hershel was lounging.

"But you don't go out," Vince ventured.

"I don't, because Roy does, and it keeps things much more amiable between us if I give him the weekends. Tonight, though, he isn't feeling like his usual partying self due to Coach George's smack down. So I thought it was a good opportunity to make use of a Friday while I have one," Hershel explained. "Like I said at the party, I don't want all of my college experiences to be secondhand."

"I'm in," Nick nearly shouted.

"You just had your nervous system rewired an hour ago," Mary told him.

"And I'm feeling much better," Nick said. "Hershel on the dance floor, though? No way in hell am I missing this."

"Guess that means I'm in, too," Vince said.

"You want to see Hershel bust a move, too?" Alice asked.

"No, I just don't trust Nick not to try and set him up in some sort of elaborate and embarrassing situation," Vince said.

"Good call," Nick agreed.

"I'll be fine," Hershel told him. "I would love it if you guys came, though. Alex is already in, and I figured we could invite everyone else as well."

"I'm certainly not going to stay home by myself," Alice said, a small chime of happiness echoing through her at being able to truthfully make such a statement.

"I'll call Sasha and Will," Vince volunteered.

"What about you, Mary?" Hershel tried to ask nonchalantly.

Mary waited a moment, savoring the uncertainty as only a girl being courted for the first time is able to do, then let out her answer in a small, reserved voice:

"I think that sounds like fun."

"Awesome," Hershel said, a wide grin breaking through his face's futile restraint attempts.

*   *   *

"No. No. No. No. Dear Lord in heaven, no. No. No. Maybe. No." Alice paused to take a breath and move to another area of Mary's closet. Mary had, much to her almost immediate regret, asked for Alice's input on what to wear out to the club. What she had expected would be a two-minute process to confirm an outfit had turned into an endless critique of Mary's entire wardrobe.

"I thought the yellow shirt looked nice," Mary ventured.

"Nice is for church, class, and dinner with the family," Alice told her. "Going out to the club is about grabbing attention and keeping it there."

"That's not really how I like to dress," Mary told her, not quite able to stop herself from glancing down at her small frame.

Alice stared at her a minute, then realization of what Mary meant clicked into place.

"Oh no no no, I don't mean slutty. That's for costume parties and the like. I just mean attention-grabbing. The right combinations of colors and cuts to draw the eye, highlighting your own look just enough to make sure their gazes stay on you. In that case, less is more. Just trust me, Mary. When it comes to fashion, I've been a Super for years."

"You do always dress nicely," Mary acquiesced.

"Thank you," Alice said, turning her attention back to the closet. "Your clothes aren't bad either. They're just a little . . . eclectic."

"When you're in the woods, function tends to trump fashion relentlessly," Mary said.

"I wouldn't know. The closest we ever really came to roughing it in my family was staying at a hotel that had an indoor garden," Alice said.

"You should go sometime. The air, the smells, the quiet: it's a wholly unique experience," Mary told Alice, her eyes drifting off as she remembered her peaceful trailer in the forest.

285

"I might just do that over the summer," Alice said. "Now that I can, it'd be nice to try."

"Now that you can?"

"Yeah. Now . . . post-procedure. I had to limit my time outdoors before," Alice said.

"Oh, because of the floating," Mary surmised.

"Bingo. When I was really happy, I floated. If there wasn't a ceiling to stop me, that meant a much longer fall to the ground. Being outside was basically taking my life in my hands," Alice explained.

"That seems awful," Mary said. "So, every time you had a rush of joy, it was soon followed by a plummet to the ground? How did you deal with that?"

"Mostly, I stopped doing things that made me too happy," Alice replied. "It wasn't hard in my house. The goal was just to maintain a constant neutral, never have any strong emotions burst through."

"You weren't very good at it," Mary said.

Alice jerked her head up sharply and met Mary's eyes. Mary shook her head. "I wasn't listening. I've just gotten to know you. You took to Lander so easily, accepted this new way of life with almost no problem besides hesitance and fear. Despite how hard you worked to be guarded throughout your life, you even made friends with a telepath. There's no way a girl like that was good at locking down her feelings all the time."

Alice said nothing at first, then placed a shirt on the bed.

"Let's try the purple top with the jeans I picked out earlier," Alice said.

"Sounds good," Mary agreed.

"If the look works, then we can finally get to the real fun."

"Real fun?" Mary asked.

"Oh yeah," Alice confirmed with a gleeful glint in her eye. "Shoes."

80

To say the music was loud would be an understatement of criminal magnitudes. The music here wasn't so much heard as it was felt, the bass quaking through one's bones and forcefully shaking one's brain. It was easily louder than the country-western club they had gone to last semester; however, this one had evidently possessed a designer with a modicum of sense. The club was split up into several different rooms. There was a patio outside, several rooms for lounging, and one wherein dancing was expected. The dance room was where the music reached its tooth-chattering apex, but the others were habitable enough to allow some conversation.

It was in one of the lounging rooms that the Lander students settled down to relax. The final tally had wound up being all of the Melbrook students, along with Jill, Will, and Alex. Sasha had been too sore from the day's class, and they'd had no luck reaching Thomas. They were still a sizable crowd, and as such, grabbed hold of a large, circular booth where they could all sit comfortably.

"So, not to sound like the clubbing newbie here, but now what do we do?" Mary asked after they'd been relaxing in their booth for half an hour.

"Well, normally by this point, Roy would be drinking heavily, dancing on the floor, and trying to figure out which girl to bring home. I think that's pretty much the norm for club activities," Hershel said. "Right?"

"Let's hope not," Vince said. "We've all got marked hands and are under age, so drinking is out. Will and I are in relationships, so we can't chase girls with you, and all that leaves for us is dancing."

"Maybe later on that one," Hershel said. He very much wanted to ask Mary, who was currently sipping cranberry juice through a straw on the other side of the booth, if she would care to dance. Wanting to and having the courage to were proving to be very different things, though. So instead, he was pushing it off, convincing himself it would somehow grow easier as the night progressed.

"Hey, let's not give up on bringing girls home yet," Nick butted in. "Alex and I aren't taken. We can roam the club for young, impressionable women."

"I'm going to leave an impression in your skull," Alice threatened. "Regardless, if we keep sitting here, all we'll do is keep sitting here. Mary, Jill, come with me. We're going to put ourselves near the dance floor and see how many boys come calling."

"Finally, let's move," Jill said.

"Actually, I'm comfortable right here—" Mary tried to object, but Alice took her by the shoulders and began marching her into the next room.

"Read my mind already," Alice urged her. Mary had actually been tuning out thoughts tonight, the ambient sound of music uncomfortably reminding her of the days when she couldn't make the voices stop. Still, she reached into Alice's mind and listened.

It seemed Alice was getting the girls away from the booth in order to force Hershel into making a move. Alice felt that if they stayed, he would dither all night and lose the opportunity, but if he was scared other boys were dancing with Mary, it might push him to action.

By the time Mary had processed it all, they were in the crisp chill of the outdoor area and safely out of earshot from the table. Granted, even in the lounge room, ten feet would put you easily out of earshot from someone.

"I think he would have asked me," Mary said, stopping the progression toward the dance room.

"He thinks so, too, and he would have kept thinking that until we had to leave and it wasn't done," Alice countered.

"Actually, I'm with Alice here," Jill chimed in. "Boys are cowards and morons for the most part. I love my brother, but do you know how he got that girlfriend of his?"

"How?" Mary asked.

"She asked him out. Twice, because the first time, he didn't get that it was a date. You have to give them little pushes here and there, or you'll be waiting forever for them to make a freaking move," Jill told her.

"This is a little push?"

"You're not making out with some dude in the bathroom, you're going with the other single girls to see if anyone will ask you to dance. This is pretty much as gently as we can remind him that other guys find you attractive, too," Alice assured her.

"I guess it can't hurt to go watch the people dancing," Mary caved.

"Atta girl. We'll have him eating out of your hand in no time."

*   *   *

"Is it me, or did this just turn into a total sausage fest?" Nick asked as the girls scampered away.

"No, you're dead on," Alex agreed.

"That seemed . . . odd," Hershel said. "They just sort of all bolted away."

"Alice took Mary away to make you chase after her," Will said simply. "They want you to go ask her to dance before some other guy beats you to it."

"How do you know that?" Vince asked.

"Could be a lot of things. Could be that I have a much higher IQ than you guys. Could be because I grew up with a twin sister, and have a slight insight into how girls think. Could be the bug I slipped onto Jill before we came out tonight," Will said, pointing to his ear. Closer inspection would reveal a small device nestled in one of its cartilage curves.

"You're kidding," Nick declared.

"Not at all," Will said. "My sister has a tendency toward telling very large, very gay men how sexy I think they are when we are out at clubs. She finds it endlessly hilarious, thus, I've begun taking precautions so I can at least be forewarned when she hatches such a scheme."

"Yeesh. Glad I'm an only child," Nick said.

"Wait, so they did that specifically so I would ask Mary to dance? And Mary went along with it, so that means she wants me to ask, right?" Hershel said uncertainly.

"I have no problem betraying my sister's confidence. Mary's is another matter. If you want to find out whether she wants to dance with you or not, then I suggest you ask her," Will told him.

"Why don't we all go in there?" Vince said. "That way, Hershel doesn't seem like he was following them. It's on all of us."

"Works for me," Nick said.

"I'll stay here and hold the booth," Will volunteered.

Vince waved him off. "There are plenty of booths, we can get another. You should come with us."

"Normally, I would agree. However, it seems Jill just located a bodybuilder in that room and is describing her very flexible, very experimental brother," Will explained.

"Oh. Well then . . . see you in a few," Vince said.

"I'll be here," Will cheerfully replied.

81

"Why, hello there, you foxy ladies."

"Get lost, dirt bag," Alice snapped at the poor male uttering such a trite line.

"Dirt bag? Really? I think I have more fastidious hygiene than even you, Princess," Nick shot back, having been the poor line-delivering male in question.

"You drop a sleazy opener, you gotta be prepared for the consequences," Alice said with a shrug. "What brings you boys out here?"

Nick had approached Alice and Mary with Hershel, Vince, and Alex just a few steps behind. The girls were standing by a large door that opened into the dance room. There were ample people huddling in the same area, since it provided an excellent balance. It was outdoors, but the body heat from the physical activity rolled out, creating a pleasant temperature. Plus, it allowed one to see the gyrating and be approached, while still far enough from the eardrum-shattering music to hold a conversation.

"I thought I might grace one of these lucky gals with the pleasure of my company on the dance floor," Nick said.

"And I thought we might be needed to tend to the wounds after he gets slapped silly," Vince joined in.

"One time. One time I got slapped at Halloween, and you punks won't let it go," Nick said.

"She slapped you with a Bible, man. That's the sort of thing that sticks in people's minds," Alex reminded him.

"Fascinating as you boys are, could you proceed with Nick's slapfest elsewhere? No men are going to want to approach us if we're already surrounded by other guys," Alice said, proving just how little she knew about real world courting and the opposite sex.

"I don't mind if they hang out," Mary countered.

"Maybe not, but that hunky guy in the tank top who's been eyeing you will. Priorities, sweetheart, seriously," Alice said, taking Mary's hand and dragging her away from the boys.

"There is no hunky guy in a tank top, is there?" Mary asked as she was pulled.

"Oh no, there is. He's just making eyes at a trampy blonde in the corner," Alice explained.

Mary glanced over and noticed the girl.

"She's dressed like everyone else. What exactly makes her trampy?"

"The fact that the hot guy is looking at her instead of us."

*   *   *

"And again we have sausage fest," Nick said with a sigh.

"It's easy to correct, though. Let's go hit the dance floor and grab us some hotties," Alex pointed out.

"Not a bad idea—"

"Hey guys! Vince! Alex!" The boys turned their heads to find Thomas jogging over to them from the entrance.

"Hey, what's going on? Did you get my message?" Vince asked.

"I didn't know you left one, so no," Thomas said, shaking his head. "Stella took my and her other friends' phones after gym. She said we were all going out tonight to have some fun, or she'd crush them."

"That's certainly . . . aggressive," Hershel said after some hasty vocabulary scrambling.

"That's Stella, she doesn't take no for an answer. It was well-intentioned, though. If she hadn't done it, we'd have all stayed in and licked our wounds instead of going out," Thomas said, a slight defensiveness in his voice.

"You keep referencing 'we,' but you're the only one here," Nick said.

"Oh, yeah, the girls went to go check their purses at the front counter," Thomas explained.

"Thank the gods, you brought more women," Nick said.

"I did, and actually, I think they're coming out now, if my vision serves me well."

Sure enough, Stella's trademark blonde braids appeared around the same corner Thomas had come from, Violet following close behind, and Camille looking around nervously at the end of the line. They spotted Thomas and the others and began making their way over, with the exception of Camille, who suddenly went stock still and had an intense inner debate before finally following suit.

*   *   *

"Don't I know you?"

"Aren't guys the ones who are supposed to use that line?" Alice replied.

"No, I'm serious," said the speaker, a brunette who had been walking past them. She had shoulder-length hair and an infectious smile. "We had poli-sci together last semester. You were the chick with her hand always in the air."

Alice studied the girl for a moment. She did indeed look familiar, and now that Alice was thinking, there had been a similarly cheery voice echoing through the class from time to time.

"I think you're right," Alice admitted. "I'm Alice."

"I'm Natalie," Natalie said. "But everyone calls me Bubbles. So, how've you been?"

"Um, good, I guess," Alice said. "You know, passed the class, now on to new ones. You?"

"I'm doing awesome! I managed to squeak by that one and my math class, and I only barely failed Shakespearean literature, so it's way fewer classes than I thought I'd have to be retaking. Aside from that, I went skiing with my family over break and that was sooooo much fun. Then there was Christmas, and I mean, seriously, who doesn't love Christmas? Plus, I'm out tonight with my new roommate and his best friend and just having a crazy good time. The guys are so cute out here, right? So, who's your friend?"

"I'm Mary, and I think I can see why they call you Bubbles. You certainly have a cheerful attitude."

"Aw, that is so nice, thank you," Bubbles said. "Yeah, that's what everyone thinks at first, but no, that's not why they call me Bubbles. I got my nickname cause I have the cutest ability ever. I can make bubbles appear all over the place. It makes for some awesome foam parties like you wouldn't believe. I mean, last year, my friend Jenny and I went to this kegger and—"

"Wait, I'm sorry to cut you off, but I need clarification," Alice said. "What do you mean you can make bubbles appear?"

"I can make them appear," Bubbles replied. She raised open her hand and sure enough, bubbles began glistening into existence a few inches above it. "I can do all sorts of sizes and numbers of them, too. I'm really good at it."

"So, you're . . . a Super?" Alice said, more out of disbelief than as a genuine question.

"Yup! You should meet my roommate. His ability is even cooler. He's a Powered, though, so he can't really do it on demand, but it's still super neat. Come on, I'll introduce you!" Bubbles declared, virtually bouncing off toward a lounge room.

"I don't think it's the best idea for us to be seen with Supers who are out in the open with their abilities," Mary whispered.

"No, it is definitely a bad idea. But I didn't know there were any Supers here outside of the HCP. And to be honest, I've never met another Powered. Cheery McChatter isn't my first choice for a hanging out companion either, but I'm not sure I can walk away from this without seeing at least a little bit more. Can you?" Alice whispered back.

Mary couldn't.

82

Camille couldn't believe she'd let herself wind up in this situation. She should have just let Stella crush the phone instead of strong-arming her out tonight. It wasn't just Stella and Violet forcing her that had convinced her to leave the dorm, though; it was a desire to get away from the events of the day. She didn't want to sit at home and brood all night, so she thought going out with her friends, even to a place she had zero desire to be, would at least get her mind off the encounter with Vince.

Seeing as Vince was now standing only a few feet away from her, that plan had failed about as horrifically as was conceivably possible. The others were talking and figuring out where to go next, but Camille was just trying to maintain and hold it together. Every now and then, she would catch Vince's eyes darting over to her. She reassured herself it was okay each time. He didn't remember her. She might look familiar, but there was no way he would place her. It had probably just been another day for him, and it was all so long—

"Hey!" Vince said, snapping his fingers and looking at Camille. "I just remembered where I know you from."

Camille let out a very soft, very high-pitched squeak and turned bright red.

*　　　*　　　*

"Freak!"

"Weirdo!"

"Monster!"

"Leave me alone," Camille cried softly, curled up in a ball on the concrete. She'd just wanted to walk down to the pool; the day was so hot. She should have known better. Of course the other kids would be out with the same idea. Of course they would see her. She felt so stupid as she lay there, waiting for them to tire of throwing sticks and insults at her. She hoped it wouldn't be much longer; usually by now, an adult would have come by.

"My daddy says Supers are a menace," Billy yelled at her, hurling a good-sized branch. Thankfully, his small arms hadn't yet learned to aim well.

"They're Heroes," Camille yelled back. She shouldn't have done that; she regretted it the minute she did. She should have just laid there and been quiet while they assaulted her. Now, it would be worse.

"Nuh uh," Rick said, dropping his own stick and walking over to her. Billy might be the leader, but Rick was the enforcer, always willing to walk the extra mile of pain where others would shy off. "Only a few of them are Heroes, and they don't fix everything the others mess up."

"I'm sorry," Camille sobbed.

"You're a freak," Rick said, kicking her once in the back. This was new; they'd never gotten close to hurt her before. It was tentative: Rick was testing the waters. He kicked her once more. A whole new world of possibilities was opening up before his cruel little eyes. It seemed girls weren't immune to being hit the way everybody tried to teach him. There was no magical force stopping him from kicking the freak just like she was a boy. He did it again, just to reinforce the point. She let a cry slip past her lips when he did it this time. A smile began to form on his face. It lingered there for only a moment before a set of knuckles crashed into it, fracturing his jaw and knocking out several teeth in the process.

"Whhhoduhhelllls," Rick gurgled from his bloody mouth, trying to pull himself up from the ground. Camille opened her eyes as well, curiosity at the sudden silence that had fallen over her tormentors. Both the downed torturer and the saved victim looked up and saw the boy who had saved her. It was an image that would stay with both of them for the rest of their lives.

He was long and lean, with clothes that looked like they hadn't been washed in weeks, if ever. There was some dirt on his hands and face, his skin tan from all the time spent outdoors. His eyes were a gleaming blue and his hair was curiously colored a metallic silver.

"You don't hit girls," the boy said simply. He extended a hand to Camille, who gladly took it and was pulled to her feet.

"Hey, you can't just punch our friend," Billy said. The others had been momentarily struck dumb when this strange kid had run across the street of their small suburb and coldcocked Rick, but they were coming round to their senses. One such sense was the ability to realize it was still five of them against one of him.

"He was kicking a girl," the boy replied.

"Well, now, we're going to beat up both of you," Billy said, motioning for the others to begin closing in.

The boy looked at the other children, then at Billy; then his blue eyes stared at Camille for several seconds. He turned back to Billy and shook his head.

"No."

"What do you mean, no?" Billy asked, confused.

"I mean, I can't let you beat us up. I won't let you hurt her," the boy replied with that same, unwavering tone. There was no fear, no uncertainty, just a calm denial of what was about to happen.

"You think you can take us all?"

"Yes."

Billy glanced at the others. They were growing restless. This kid wasn't responding the way others did when confronted with a large group. They were beginning to wonder if something was different here. If he wanted to maintain control, Billy had to act now.

"Fine. Forget the freak. Get him!" Billy yelled, charging at the boy. The others hesitated only a moment before doing the same. Billy ran head on, expecting to sink his shoulder into the boy's gut and drive him to the ground. Instead, he felt a fist bury itself in his ear, destroying his sense of balance and sending him sprawling. By the time he was able to right himself and look up, it was already over. There were bloody noses and faces on his companions, who were scattered around the ground, but the boy was still standing in the same spot, looking unharmed.

"You don't hit girls," the boy said one last time. "Or people like me will stop you." He turned to Camille. "I'll walk you home."

"Thank you," she said, tears still falling down her face, though she wasn't quite sure why anymore.

The two walked in silence for the first block or so, the boy naturally silent and Camille uncertain of what to say. Finally, she decided to begin with the basics.

"What's your name?" she asked the boy.

"Vince," he replied. "Yours?"

"Camy Belden," she said, preferring the nickname her parents had given her to the stuffy one she'd been born with. "It's nice to meet you, Vince . . . what's your last name?"

"I don't have one," he replied. "My dad says he threw his away, so he doesn't have one to pass on to me. He also says if I grow into a good man, he'll help me find one, though."

"Oh. That's . . . cool," Camille said, not sure of what to make of such a thing. "How old are you?"

"Nine. You?"

"I'm nine, too," she said, smiling inwardly. He was the same age as she was. That made her inexplicably happy.

"Neat," Vince said. "You seem pretty nice. I'm sorry those guys were being so mean to you."

Camille shook her head. "It's not about me being nice. They don't like me because I'm a Super. They say it makes me a freak."

"You're a Super?" Vince yelped, his voice full of shock.

"Um, yes," Camille said, kicking herself once more for opening her big mouth. He probably hated them too, and now, he would hate her and be sad he'd even bothered saving her. Why did she say anything?

"That's awesome!" Vince said excitedly. "What's your ability? Is it cool? How long have you known?"

Camille didn't quite know how to respond to this. Everyone said being a Super was great, yet everyone she met seemed to treat her badly because of it. Camille was too young to understand something as complex as that level of jealousy, but she could still feel the hatred from it. Vince wasn't acting that way, though. He really seemed to like it.

"I take away scrapes and bruises by touching someone," Camille explained. "But then, I can also give those scrapes and bruises to other people if I touch them."

"Oh, wow, so you're sort of an absorber then."

"Absorber?"

"It means you kind of take something into yourself, hold it there, then release it when you want to. It's what my father says I am," Vince explained.

"You're a Super, too?" Camille asked.

"No." Vince's face fell immediately, and his pace slowed down a touch. "I'm just a Powered. I can't really control my ability at all. I just make batteries go dead or kill the campfire by accident. When it comes out, it's worse, though. I've set things on fire by accident three times just this year."

"I'm sorry," Camille said.

"It's okay," Vince said, shrugging off the dour mood. "I just have to help people in different ways, like by learning how to fight."

"You sure did that," Camille said, remembering how he'd so easily knocked down the children that had seemed unstoppable to her for so long.

"I still have a long way to go," Vince said. "Besides, I don't like fighting very much. I already hurt people enough by accident with my power. You're lucky you get to make them feel better."

"I don't feel lucky," Camille admitted for the first time. She'd never met anyone else with powers before, never had anyone to talk about this sort of thing with. "I feel like nobody likes me, like I'm always getting picked on just because I can do something they can't. I don't even want to do it. I just want to be normal." Tears once again found their way down her small cheeks.

"You're not using it. Maybe that's why you hate it so much," Vince told her.

"What do you mean?"

"I mean, you're special. You can do something others can't, no matter how hard they work at it. You won't ever be normal. You can be a Super, though. You can use your ability to help people and make a difference."

"But they'll still hate me," Camille said,

"Maybe. Maybe not. Either way, won't you be happier as the one saving people than the one needing saving?"

"I don't know," Camille admitted.

"Might be worth trying. My father always says we have to be the best version of us, instead of trying to be someone else. I really want to be a Super, instead of a Powered.

No amount of wishing will make that happen, though, so instead, I'm just trying to be a better Powered," Vince said.

"I guess that sort of makes sense," Camille said hesitantly. "Um, this white one is my house."

"Oh, okay," Vince said. "It was nice to meet you, Camy."

"It was. We could hang out again sometime," she ventured hopefully. "What street do you live on?"

"I don't," Vince replied. "My father and I are just passing through. I have to go meet him soon, actually. We're catching a train out of town tonight."

"Oh. So I won't see you again?" Camille asked.

"Probably not. The trains don't come through here too often," Vince said.

"Well then . . . thank you again," she said, heartbreak already seeping in. Her hero, the first real friend she'd had, wouldn't even be here for one more night. That hurt more than anything Billy or Rick had ever done. That's when Camille did possibly the first, but by no means the last, brave thing of her life. She whirled around and quickly planted a peck right on Vince's lips. That accomplished, Camille dashed up the sidewalk to the front door of her house, pausing, only briefly, to glance back and see his reaction. Vince's cheeks were bright red, but there was a smile on his face. It nearly matched the one nestled firmly on Camille's.

Neither knew it, but they were both each other's first kiss.

*   *   *

"Hey!" Vince said, snapping his fingers and looking at Camille. "I just remembered where I know you from."

Camille let out a very soft, very high-pitched squeak and turned bright red.

"You were the healer at Jill and Sasha's fight, weren't you?" Vince asked.

Camille slowly nodded her head and prayed the blood would move away from her face sometime soon.

"Ah, great. I knew you looked familiar. That was driving me crazy."

83

"So, Alice and Mary, this is my roommate, Larry, but we all call him L-Ray, and his best friend, Steve. Steve doesn't really have a nickname yet," Bubbles said.

"And I cannot put into words how thankful I am for that," Steve added.

"Just so I'm clear here, it's Bubbles, L-Ray, and Steve?" Alice asked, a part of her very much hoping she would be corrected.

"Unfortunately, yes," L-Ray confirmed for her. "It's nice to meet both of you."

"Ditto," Steve agreed.

While Bubbles looked more or less normal for a girl her age, L-Ray stood out significantly more. He wore a skintight, purple shirt cut in a long V-neck, snug black jeans that left just a bit too little to the imagination, and purple sneakers. All of this was topped off by black hair with the tips dyed purple and a generous smearing of silver makeup all around his eyes. L-Ray looked even stranger when compared to Steve. Steve was wearing a simple polo, khakis, and sensible shoes. His hair was trimmed in a crew cut, and he had the look of a man who definitely knew how to work out and eat right. Neither of the girls would have been surprised to learn he was enrolled in the ROTC program, which he was.

"It's nice to meet you both as well," Alice said. "I had a class with Nata—er . . . Bubbles last semester."

"Forgive me, but I thought Bubbles said she was introducing us to her roommate," Mary said.

"She is. I'm her roommate. Turns out, Lander is pretty laid back about a co-ed arrangement, as long as one of you is gay. I suspect there was a civil suit somewhere along the line," L-Ray speculated.

"Oh, don't be silly," Bubbles said. "I bet they just want everyone to live with the people they have the most fun with. Ooooooh, this year will be so awesome, and we'll have so much fun. I've already got some awesome plans for the next weekend—"

"That sounds wonderful, darling, but first, would you grab us some bottled waters? Just put it on my tab at the bar," L-Ray asked her.

"Sure thing!" With that, Bubbles scampered off to wait in a long line of patrons.

"Lovely girl, but I've found it's best to distract her when meeting new people, or else nothing besides opening pleasantries get exchanged," L-Ray explained once she was gone. "So, what are your majors, what year are you, and Mary, can I just say, I love your contacts? They go so well with your skin tone."

"Thank you," Mary said, not wanting to correct him. Things like her amber eyes or Vince's hair were often hallmarks of people born with powers. The only blessing was that so many people wanted to be perceived as Supers, that such cosmetic versions of these non-human features were almost commonplace, allowing the real ones a bit of room to blend in. There were some who believed this fashion trend had been instigated and kept buoyant by a conspiracy of Supers so they could at least halfway blend in. "I like your eye makeup."

"Really? I felt like it was a bit over the top, but then again, I saw some guy walking around in here with all of his hair done up in silver, so at least I'm not the most garish one in the room," L-ray said. "The truth is, I prefer to dress a bit more subdued normally, but the makeup is the only part of my outfit that's mandatory. Thus, I figure it's better to at least appear as if I was going for a specific look. But listen to me, rambling like Bubbles."

"No, no, it's interesting," Alice said. "Why is the makeup mandatory, though?"

"He's a Powered," Steve answered for his friend. "He has to wear it pretty much all the time."

"I'm afraid I still don't get it," Alice admitted.

"I have spontaneous x-ray vision," L-Ray told her. "It just happens at random intervals. The makeup I wear is specially made with lead in it. That way, when it kicks on, I can just close my eyes."

"Right, because eyelids don't stop x-rays on their own," Alice said, comprehension dawning.

"And, depending on how much you see through, that could be quite a horrifying sight," Mary added.

"Exactly," Steve agreed with them.

"I must say, you're taking this well. A lot of people get uncomfortable when they find out I'm a Powered," L-Ray admitted.

Alice and Mary resisted the urge to exchange tell-tale glances. Barely, but they did.

"I guess we're just open-minded," Alice said with a slightly too-large grin.

"So it seems," L-Ray concurred. "Anyway, I believe you were telling us about yourselves."

*   *   *

"So ladies, which of you wants to take the first sashay around the floor with the dance master?" Nick asked.

"Pass," Violet said.

"No, thank you," Camille replied.

"Lose the shades and maybe we'll talk," Stella shot back.

"No dice, Toots. The shades can be considered welded into my face," Nick said.

"Guess that means you're back to asking some other lady if she wants the pleasure of your company," Vince chuckled. "I'm sure they'll be more receptive to your charms."

"As long as none of them has a Bible on hand," Alex added.

"Wait, what now?" Thomas asked.

"Oh, we haven't told you this story yet?" Alex asked in surprise. "Boy, it's a good one."

"Screw you guys. I'm getting a water at the bar and picking up some girl with self-esteem issues. You'll see, next time your eyes fall on Nick Campbell, it will be as a gorgeous woman swoons into his arms," Nick declared, half walking, half storming off inside.

"You think we were too mean?" Vince said, suddenly concerned.

"Nah, Nick loves having all eyes on him. Hell, sometimes I think he messes up with girls on purpose, just for the stories. Trust me on this one, he's feeling just fine," Alex assured him.

Vince decided to take his word for it, because, while Alex might not have Mary's precision, he was more than capable of picking up on feelings.

"So, what now?" Hershel asked.

"Much as Nick can be a bit peculiar in his methods, I say we take his idea and go dance," Violet said. "Thomas, would you care to start me off, for old times' sake?"

"Of course," Thomas replied with a gentlemanly nod of his head.

"No way I'm sitting that out," Stella declared. "Hershel, your other persona seems to have some moves. Want to do a spin on the floor?"

"Sure, I guess so," Hershel reluctantly agreed. He would have rather been dancing with Mary, but he didn't see the strength of will to make that happen coming anytime soon. Besides, this seemed innocent enough.

"Only one girl left," Alex pointed out. "Vince, if you don't mind, can I steal her away?"

"Sure thing," Vince replied. "I really don't feel right dancing with someone besides my girlfriend, anyway."

"Um . . . well . . . I . . ." Camille said, hesitating. She really didn't have any urge to go gyrate on the dance floor with some man she barely knew. But, then again, the other option was staying here with Vince, possibly alone if Alex decided to search for another partner. As soon as that thought raced into her head, the decision was made.

"That sounds lovely."

*   *   *

"—and that's how I decided to major in geology," L-Ray finished explaining.

"Eeeeeeeee!" Bubbles squealed, dashing up to their cluster and passing out waters.

"Sweet heaven, I think my eardrum just killed itself," Steve complained.

"Calm down, darling, what's got you in such a tizzy?" L-Ray said, working with more patience than Alice believed she could have mustered under such auditory assault.

"OhmygodItotallysawthatguyandhewas—"

300

"Spaces, Bubbles. I need spaces between the words to understand them," L-Ray instructed her.

Bubbles took a few deep, rapid breaths and tried again. "You know that really cute guy I told you about that I see around campus who looks really cool and fun and all well I was up there getting the water and he got in line just a few people behind me and he's still there and what should I do?"

"Well, that was better. No punctuation, but then, I didn't ask for any, so I've only got myself to blame," L-Ray said. "Just go up and talk to him. You're an adorable girl. I'm sure he'd love to meet and hit on you."

"I don't know, he's really cute. I bet girls come up to him all the time, and I bet I'm not as pretty by comparison," Bubbles said uncertainly.

"Which guy is it?" Alice asked, trying to see through the throngs of people at the bar.

"He's wearing a green shirt, jeans, and these awesome sunglasses," Bubbles told her.

"Wait, sunglasses?" Sure enough, Nick was by the bar, a bottle of cold water pressed to his lips and the standard shades still in place. The next words out of Alice's mouth were a prime example of how the tongue can rush forward before the brain's diplomatic instincts have any chance to intervene.

"You have got to be fucking kidding me."

84

"She's surprised at the coincidence," Mary said quickly. "That guy you were talking about is a friend of ours named Nick."

"Oh holy crap, really? You know him? Be honest with me: does he already have a girlfriend, or is he just playing the field?" Bubbles asked.

"Him? Really? Him?" Alice said.

"Yes, she's talking about our *friend*," Mary assured her. "Such coincidences do happen. And Bubbles, he is still single, to the very best of my knowledge."

"That is so awesome! You have to introduce me. Will you please introduce me? Every time I see him on campus, I totally want to say something, but I just think it'd seem so desperate. Pretty please introduce us."

"Every time you see him?" Alice said once more, her mind still not congealing the facts being presented to her.

"I would love to introduce you," Mary said. "Just come with me."

"Cute? Him? *Really?*"

*   *   *

"We don't have to dance much if you don't want to," Alex told Camille once they had put a significant distance between themselves and Vince. "I just thought you might like an exit."

"What are you talking—" Camille began to ask, then basic memory function kicked in. "Right. You're the other telepath in the class."

"I'm not a . . . look, that isn't important," Alex said patiently. "The point is, I had a sense of how uncomfortable you were feeling, and I wanted to help."

"Thank you," Camille said sincerely.

"If you're in the mood, though, I wouldn't mind a little dancing," Alex added.

"I think that would be okay," Camille agreed, oddly more comfortable with this boy despite the fact that her mental privacy had been a bit violated.

"I should also mention that while I don't know what makes you so uneasy around Vince, there's no need to be. I can promise you, he's a really good guy."

Camille wasn't quite able to stop herself from glancing over her shoulder at Vince's silhouette against the too-bright lights of the club.

"I know."

*   *   *

"Hey, Nick, this is my friend, Bubbles," Mary said, approaching him.

"Hey, Mary. Hi, Bubbles. Interesting name. Story I should be aware of?"

"Hi, Nick. Nice to meet you. I really like your sunglasses. Why do you wear them indoors, though? Is it a prescription thing? My mom does that when her contacts fall out, or when she loses her normal pair, or wants to look pretty because she thinks they make her look like Audrey Hepburn even though they don't, but no one tells her 'cause we love her."

"You know what, I think I can put the pieces together myself," Nick said. He looked over this new girl. She was yappy, that was pretty much the definition of evident. She was chipper, though, and that was a plus. Happy people asked fewer questions and demanded less attention, or so he'd found. It didn't hurt that she was cute, too. Tall, with chestnut brown hair and not easily ignorable curves to her body. Not to mention she was clearly at a ridiculous level of into him. This would work.

"Bubbles, I don't mean to be forward, but would you like to dance?" Nick asked casually.

"Yes!" She grabbed his hand and began pulling him toward to the room where the music was blasting.

It wasn't a perfect situation; Nick would freely admit that. She couldn't talk over the music, though, and he had made the boast that he would next be on the floor with a beautiful woman. It could have been worse.

Meanwhile, Mary, having been almost immediately abandoned, made her way back over to the others.

"That went fast," Steve commented.

"What Nick lacks in game, he makes up for in luck," Mary said truthfully. Admittedly, the discrepancy was a much different ratio than those who couldn't read his mind might guess, but the statement was still basically honest.

"She was into Nick," Alice said, still somewhat coming to terms with the idea.

"It was bound to happen eventually," Steve said. "Your friend is pretty good looking."

"I . . . how am I missing this?" Alice asked uncertainly.

"Uh huh. While little miss not-big-on-facing-the-obvious wraps her head around some truth, you ladies want to keep an eye on them on the dance floor?" L-Ray asked. "At least you know we won't try to cop a feel."

"We?" Mary said. "I mean, I know you're gay, but I didn't know Steve was."

"Gay as a Broadway musical ensemble," Steve assured her. "We don't all fit the stereotypes."

Mary blushed. She'd gotten so used to her telepathy that she found herself making serious social blunders without it. "I'm sorry. That was insensitive and stupid of me."

Steve patted her shoulder. "Nothing to worry about. It happens all the time. L-Ray is a little more flamboyant than I am, and that tends to draw the attention of most people's gaydar."

"I'm still sorry," Mary repeated. "But I'd love to take you both up on your offer. Let's go cut a rug."

303

L-Ray laughed. "Oh, you are just precious."

*   *   *

So it was that everyone except Vince, Will, and Jill found themselves on the dance floor. The sweaty, stuffed with people, assaulted by a symphony of screeching, dance floor. Still, it was contact with the opposite sex, albeit only a swiveling of hips and awkward placing of hands. It was a mash of friends, some old and some new, just trying to enjoy themselves in an environment designed for other things. It was even a little fun, too.

Pretty much everyone was terrible at the act of dancing, so no one knew how bad their particular partner was—Nick and Violet being the exceptions. They had natural rhythm and training, so they knew their particular partners sucked, but they pressed on, anyway. There was no conversation to be had on the floor, only meaningful glances and more than one game of poorly-played charades. In a way, this was a blessing, for if any word exchange had been possible, things might have played out differently.

Hershel had been dancing with Stella for a few minutes when Nick and Bubbles wandered in. Hershel had to tip a mental hat to his friend; he'd come through on returning with a hottie in hand. Then he noticed the pair that had followed them in and begun dancing. By luck of the draw, Mary had wound up dancing with Steve, whose broad shoulders and square jaw told the story of a powerful man. A man who was capable and strong, who could get things done. In other words, a man who had all the qualities Hershel only experienced vicariously through Roy.

Hershel's heart sank. He should have asked her when he had the chance. Now, this guy would dance with her all night. After all, who would be stupid enough to let Mary get away? Well, besides him. No, this guy would charm and woo her, then ask her out at the end of the night. They'd start a long-lasting relationship, get married, and Hershel would never see that window of opportunity open again. It was over; he'd missed his shot.

Then, something stirred within Hershel he hadn't felt since he was stranded on the mountain. Sheer, stupid desperation. Roy hadn't been there to help him. His only way out had been to press on no matter what. It was a situation where all he could do was try and move upward, because there was no other option. He didn't know why, but somehow, it was the same now. He had to try.

There was no other option.

Hershel made a polite series of hand gestures to Stella, then began shoving his way through the crowd. It was hard, vaguely disgusting work due to all the sweat. He parted the sea of bodies swimming in sound, step by difficult step. He reached Mary and Steve just as the song was changing. Briefly, he contemplated abandoning this foolishness and running like hell. Instead, he tapped Mary on the shoulder.

She turned around and looked up at him. Mary wasn't even bothering to try and read minds with the noise smashing all around her, but when she looked up at Hershel, she didn't need to. What he wanted couldn't have been any clearer. She looked at Steve, mouthed the words "Thank you for the dance," and then stepped into the arms of her new partner. In the grand scheme of things, it really wasn't very much.

But it was progress.

85

"All right, ladies and gentlemen, today, we take the first steps toward mastering the fine art of battle," Coach George said. It was Monday afternoon, and the combat class was back in the same room they had been in on Friday. The debris had mostly been cleaned up, though a keen eye could still spot a few remaining signs along the ground.

"Not surprisingly, this will start with learning how to fight," Coach George continued. "Now, I'll take a minute here to make sure I'm clear. When I say fight, I don't mean zip around, or turn the ground into fudge, or any other such bullcrap. That's called strategy, and that comes later. When I say fight, what I mean is the ability to get the crap kicked out of you, and the strength to knock the teeth out of someone's head, which, incidentally, will be a test later in the year."

Some of the students exchanged worried glances. A few days ago, they would assumed he was joking, but after Friday . . .

"We're talking about today, though, and this will be the same thing we do for the next several months, so I'd pay attention if I were you. The procedure is simple. I'll call you out in pairs. You'll find one of the many red circles located on the ground in this room. You'll both step in the circle. You'll beat each other senseless until the end of class. You'll go get healed and come back fresh next time. Wash, rinse, repeat."

"What exactly does this teach us?" Stella asked from her place in line.

"Two hundred pushups for speaking without being called on," Coach George snapped at her. "That kind of crap might fly in the dean's class, but I think you'll find me a lecturer much less appreciative of interruption."

Stella looked like she was ready to object for a moment, but her eyes wandered to one of the scorch marks from the last class's brawl. A brawl in which she'd been trounced with ease. She got down and began doing the reps.

"Since Hawkins was smart enough to take her lumps and shut her mouth, I'll answer her question," Coach George resumed. "This is teaching you all the basics of fighting. Not the movements, not the reflexes, not the martial arts, the real basics. Hit and get hit. Be hurt and push through. Feel the painful impact of your knuckles on another person's bones. Those are the lessons you can only learn through experience. Now, I know some of you have had those lessons firsthand already, but these are ones you can never really have too much of. So, for now, you learn to fight. Once you've all got that down pat, we move on to how to win."

Coach George examined the students looking back at him. They were a little worried; most of them seemed to still feel confident, though. After all, they were warriors, and this was sparring. How bad could it be?

"I do have a few rules you should know about, though. First off is that if you get knocked out of the circle, your opponent will get to take a penalty shot at your face, a shot you will not dodge or block. Secondly is that I'm the one who determines your opponent each day, so don't bother me with requests. Sometimes, you'll fight people better than you, sometimes worse, but I'll be keeping careful track of how you all do and making my choices to maximize everyone's education. Third, the fights go on until the end of class. If you're knocked unconscious, we'll grab you a healer, and you'll get back at it. I don't care how much you ache or how tired you are. You fight to the end, no exceptions. Fourth is the last rule, the most important rule, and my personal favorite rule . . ."

A large, unsettling smile crept across Coach George's face.

"No powers."

*　　　*　　　*

"I trust everyone completed the weekend's assignment," Coach Persephone said as the students fell into line.

There was a mumbling to the affirmative that was to be expected. Alice, for once, didn't shoot her hand up to volunteer as an example. For some reason, she'd felt all out of sorts since Friday night, unable to really focus on the assignment and come up with a cool experiment. She'd ultimately settled on trying to levitate just one part of herself— specifically, her hair— Sunday evening. It had been even less successful than it was interesting or impressive.

"Rich Weaver," Coach Persephone called out, pointing to a dark-haired boy with a goatee. "In what new way did you try to use your power?"

"I tried to seal a cat in its own mind," Rich replied promptly. "I've never tried it on animals before."

"Not much in the way of a new technique, but it was an honest attempt," Coach Persephone said. "Did it work?"

"I'm not really sure," Rich admitted. "The cat just sat there and stared at me, but it was doing that beforehand, too. Next time, I think I'll try a more active animal."

"Good idea," Coach Persephone agreed. "Britney Fletcher, what was your attempt?"

"I tried to make a force field," Britney said.

Coach Persephone blinked in surprise. "I was under the impression your power was invisibility."

"It is."

"Then, what would make you think that would, in any way, lend itself to sustaining a maintained field of defensive energy?" Coach Persephone asked.

Britney shrugged in response. "You said to try something really different."

"You overshot the goal a bit there, dear," Coach Persephone told her. "All right, let's move on to Nick Campbell. I trust after our little talk on Friday, you decided to give your homework a try?"

"I did indeed," Nick said. "I tried to use my power in a whole new way."

"Do tell."

"I tried to get laid," Nick stated proudly. The silence that followed his statements lasted several seconds. Seconds that consisted of the others looking at him with a mix of entertainment, curiosity, and disgust from those who suspected the worst. Unfortunately, Coach Persephone's particular expression fell into the last category. Nick at last acknowledged the stares by looking around and raising his hands.

"What'd I say?"

"You attempted to use your power, the thing that makes you a Super and places you in a class of elite beings more capable than any mere human, for sexual gratification?" Coach Persephone asked in a very strained voice.

"Dick's not going to suck itself," Nick replied.

"You used your gift to try and manipulate some unsuspecting girl into intercourse, and you have so little remorse you can make flippant jokes about it? Nick Campbell, I am very close to hurling you out of this class right now," Coach Persephone threatened.

"Do what you have to do," Nick replied. "But let's get something straight. I did the assignment. I didn't do anything illicit or manipulative, though. At our age, sex is eighty percent pure chance of opportunity. I used my luck to heighten the probability of meeting a girl who found me to be a viable and desirable partner. No influence on anything but sheer chance. It was a valid attempt to try my power in a new way. I mean, hell's bells, another term for sex is 'getting lucky.' I did exactly what you told me, lady, so don't go getting too high on your soapbox."

Coach Persephone's lips were pressed into a thin line. The students nearest to Nick began edging away, just in case she let loose with more of the twitching-on-the-floor power. Instead, she released a long, deep breath.

"Were you successful?" Coach Persephone asked.

"Yes and no," Nick said. "I probably could have been, but it turns out just finding someone who wants you doesn't mean you'll want them too."

"True. Good job. And one more thing."

"Yes, ma'am?" Nick asked.

"You were right in that I was jumping to conclusions on what you'd done. You were also right to fully explain yourself before I acted. However, speak to me in a tone that disrespectful again, and I'll leave you a drooling, piss-soaked mess on the floor," Coach Persephone said with surprising evenness to her tone.

"Noted," Nick said.

*   *   *

Coach George could see the desire to speak, to argue, to be contrary in the face of what he'd just told them. Hawkins was still on the floor, pounding out her push-ups,

308

though, and that was an audible reminder that unwarranted comments were not appreciated in his class.

"I know some of you are wondering why I would do this. Others of you have already put it together. For the sake of you dumber students, I'll explain. You're going to fight people who are stronger and faster than you eventually. Right now, I want you learning to fight at a base level. Powers come later, once you've proven you're competent enough to handle them. We'll use them, just not until you're ready. Any questions?"

No one raised their hand. They were learning slowly, but they were learning.

"Good. When I call your names, grab your partner and get in a circle. Once everyone is assigned, the circles will glow red. Start smacking the shit out of each other, and don't stop until those bastards go dark. Clear?"

"Yes, sir!" This was yelled by a large majority of the students, almost instinctually. Coach George loved the sound of that chorus. It meant he was forging order from the chaos.

"Excellent. Castillo and Reid, pair up. Foster and Dixon. Riley and Wells. Reynolds and DeSoto," Coach said, rambling off the names. He read quickly, leaving no doubt in his students' minds that they were expected to move with just as much speed. There was a scramble as the students searched through somewhat familiar faces, trying to find their opponent and get inside a circle as rapidly as their bodies would permit. Before long, Coach George had reached the end.

"Sullivan, grab Hawkins when she's done with her push-ups. Lastly, Daniels and Taylor report to me," Coach George finished. Roy and Chad looked at each other with some confusion, but neither had any more idea of why they'd been singled out than the other.

"Okay everyone, you have five minutes before your circles glow. Shake hands, stretch, pray, or do whatever revs you up before a fight. I'll be here watching when it starts, so make sure you come out swinging," Coach George instructed them. He then turned his attention to Roy and Chad.

"You two follow me. I have a special place for you to fight."

*   *   *

"Here's the deal," Coach George said once they had arrived at an even lower level. This one was as bare as the last, though on the ground were a series of red rings, each one within the last until the final ring that was only five feet across. "You two are now permanent training buddies. Shake hands, make nice, and find peace with it."

"Works for me," Roy said with a grin. "But why am I the only one who gets to pound on Blondie?"

"Because, dumbass, you have to use your powers when you train. It doesn't do Roy any good if Hershel is the one learning the lessons," Coach George explained. "And Taylor here has remodeled his whole body from the ground up. He can't really just turn that shit on and off in the blink of an eye. It works out, though, because you're both strong enough to ring each other's bells."

"I don't feel this will be adequate training for me," Chad said. "He doesn't offer me a significant challenge, or the opportunity for learning."

"Try letting him smash you in the face and work on your pain tolerance," Coach George snapped at him. "It's what we've got to work with, so I suggest you find a way to get some gain from it."

"I'll do my best," Chad replied.

"Goody for you. Now, you two are going to start in the smallest circle. I have to be back upstairs to watch the others, so I'll review tapes of your training at night. When I think the time is right, we'll move you to the bigger circles."

"Aw, why bother with that bullshit?" Roy complained.

"Because, given enough room to move around, Taylor would utterly crush you at your current skill level, like he did a few months ago. At least, in close proximity, you stand a chance of hitting a lucky blow," Coach George told him.

Roy thought about yapping off again, then reconsidered. He really couldn't have asked for better circumstances. He was training against the strongest guy in class every single day. There was no better way for him to improve than this.

"Fine, I guess it'll do," Roy said, walking toward the center circle.

*   *   *

"It's Shane, right?" Vince asked as he and his opponent stared at other from within their circle.

"Right. And you're Vince, the guy who can absorb energy," Shane replied.

"Bingo."

"Nice ability. Not to mention, you must have some exceptional combat skills," Shane continued.

"Thanks, I think. What makes you say that, though?"

"You were beaten in the first round, but you still made eighth rank. You've fended off Michael multiple times, despite his presence in the top three. And then, of course, there's the fact that you're fighting me," Shane explained.

"I take it you're good too, then," Vince said, catching his meaning immediately.

"If not for the experience of fighting Chad, I would have thought myself easily the best in our year," Shane told him.

"I have heard he's pretty talented," Vince said.

"Talent has nothing to do with it. Chad Taylor is a man possessed. I've been working to be a Hero since I was a small child. I've been instructed in various forms of martial arts and had the opportunity to hone my power to a level of refinement it would take the others in this class years to match. And I still cannot match the intensity with which Chad trains for battle," Shane said. "He lives and breathes it. His free time is spent

310

thinking of new strategies and techniques. Even when he's resting, he trains new reflex sequences into his muscles. It is literally his entire life."

"Wow. That's amazing," Vince said. "And kind of sad. I mean, there's more to life than just fighting."

"Perhaps. But he is the best, and we are not. So maybe we're the ones who've taken a wrong turn," Shane pointed out.

Vince would have said more, but the soft hum from behind him was the only warning he got that the circle was beginning to glow.

"Good luck," Vince said.

"Move swiftly and surely," Shane replied.

*   *   *

The first clash lasted only seconds. Before Roy could even blink, Chad had drilled him in the ribs and knocked him on his back. He didn't press the attack, surprisingly. Instead, he took a few steps back and allowed Roy to climb to his feet.

"Thanks," Roy said as he rose. "But you didn't have to do that."

"Kicking you mercilessly while you lie on the ground isn't really a great learning experience for either of us," Chad said.

"True," Roy agreed, rushing him. Chad slid out of the way with ease, catching Roy's shoulder and putting him right back on the ground. Roy pulled himself up again.

"Listen, I don't do this often, but something's been bugging me," Roy said once he was up.

This time, Chad stepped forward and caught Roy in the sternum, sweeping out his legs at the same time.

"What's that?" Chad asked as he looked down.

"I wanted to say I'm sorry," Roy replied, rubbing his chest as he got on his feet. "I'm sorry I insulted your power before. I still think mine is stronger, but I'll admit, yours is a lot more impressive than I would have guessed."

Chad closed the gap between them and punched Roy in the jaw. As Roy's head reeled to the side, Chad grabbed his right arm and hurled him over his shoulder. This time, he didn't just land on the ground, he was slammed there with an impact that left concrete chips on his shirt.

"Apology accepted," Chad said in his usual even tone.

*   *   *

Vince and Shane were both dripping in sweat as they gasped for air, circling one another.

"You're better than I expected," Shane complimented him.

"You, too," Vince agreed.

Each boy was covered in small gashes and bruises. They'd put each other down several times and taken the fight to the concrete more than once, but neither had managed

311

to get so much of an advantage that he could own the day. Plus, they had been unable to drive each other out of the ring even a single time.

"You look tired," Vince told him.

"You look exhausted," Shane replied.

"I think the others are about out of gas," Vince noted, watching the lackluster battles around the room. It might not have been so bad if they hadn't done the usual two hours of hard training before this part of class.

"That your way of asking me if we can softball it 'til the clock runs out?"

"Not in the slightest," Vince replied. He dashed forward, sweeping at Shane's legs. Shane stepped back on his right foot, bringing his left swinging for Vince's head. Vince moved his whole body with the blow, doing a half flip only a few inches above the ground and driving his legs into Shane's chest. Shane stumbled back but managed to drop to his knees before the momentum could send him sailing out of the ring, and both boys scrambled to get to their feet.

"Not bad," Vince said to Shane as they both sucked in air.

"I was thinking the same thing," Shane replied.

*   *   *

"You've gotten better since last time," Chad told Roy as Roy dragged himself from the ground.

"I get better hang time in the air?"

"No, you're thinking when you come at me now. And your reflexes have improved. Not much, but some. You've been learning some martial arts," Chad said.

"Guilty," Roy replied, swaying slightly. "Lot of good it's done me." He hadn't landed a blow on Chad yet, and Chad was hammering away at him every time they came together. Roy was resistant to damage, of course; however, Chad dished out enough to cover that gap and more. In truth, Roy knew the only reason he was still conscious was simply because Chad didn't want to knock him out, and that knowledge made him want to crush the blond bastard even harder.

"It's a process. You should keep that in mind. Steady groundwork is what bears results," Chad told him.

"I'll make sure to remember," Roy replied, stumbling forward. He was too slow; he knew it as soon as he was moving. Chad would capitalize. Sure enough, rather than use a quick series of blows to knock Roy down, Chad instead, took a step forward and smashed him in the forehead with a powerful kick. Roy saw static all around him, and when his vision finally cleared, he was on the ground again. It was beginning to have a familiar, almost homey feel.

"Just stay down already," Chad told him. "I'll go fetch a healer, and we can tell Coach George that this won't work because you can't keep up with me. By this time tomorrow, we'll both have people more appropriate to our skill level."

"Fuck you," Roy spat out, along with a bit of blood.

"I beg your pardon? I was trying to show you mercy."

"You were trying to show me condescension," Roy sneered, getting up for what felt like the billionth agonizing time. "Yeah, you're faster than I am, and more skilled than I am, and a hell of a lot better practiced than I am, but who cares?"

"Off handedly, I'd say your battered body. Don't get the wrong idea here, Roy. I've been going easy on you. This can get much worse."

"Blondie, there's a few things you should know about me," Roy said as he found his shaky footing. "I love whiskey, dumb blondes, and my momma. I don't welch on bets, and I don't cheat at pool. And I never, repeat, *never* give up." Roy locked eyes with Chad and gave him the legendary Daniels' family grin. "Now, bring it the fuck on."

To his credit, Roy stayed conscious for the rest of the fight, even if a part of him truly wished he hadn't.

86

"Yeesh, this guy took one hell of a pounding," said the healer, a female junior. Roy could make out the words dimly over the ringing in his ears.

"That's what she said," snickered a male voice next to her.

"Damn it, Ed, that doesn't even make sense. Try to show a little respect," the girl snapped at him. "Just because he's passed out, doesn't mean you can act like a jackass."

She was wrong; Roy was still awake. He could hear them, after all. It wasn't worth the effort to correct her, though. Not right now.

"Sorry, sorry," Ed apologized. "I just get kind of weirded out being too somber around people this messed up. I don't want to treat them like they're already dead or something."

"No worries on that for this one. He's already healing up on his own. To be this hearty and still be so pummeled . . . it must have been one hell of a beating," the girl commented.

"Maybe he wasn't fighting back," Ed suggested.

"No way," the girl told him. "Didn't you notice all the impact wounds? This guy kept getting up over and over and getting put right back down. He was obviously outclassed, but I'll give him one thing. He did not want to lose."

Roy's head swam, and he finally lost the tenuous grip on consciousness he had been clutching so adamantly.

*   *   *

"Thank you for coming, Mrs. Daniels," the principal said, rising from his desk and shaking her hand. "Will Mr. Daniels be joining us?"

"I'm afraid he's out of town at the moment," Mrs. Daniels said. "His construction company got a job down in Florida that he's overseeing."

"Ah, I understand," the principal said. "In that case, I suppose we can begin. Please, have a seat."

"Not that I'm not eager to find out why you called me down here so urgently, but shouldn't you excuse the student already here before we talk?" Mrs. Daniels asked. She glanced at the small, plastic chair he was sitting in, reclined back and feet swinging freely.

"I'm afraid that boy is actually part of the reason you were called down," the principal said hesitantly.

"Was he in a fight with my son? I know Hershel has been getting bullied since we moved here."

"Not exactly. You see, that boy sitting in that chair *is* your son. Sort of. I'm afraid it's somewhat complicated, Mrs. Daniels. Are you sure you wouldn't rather have a seat?"

Mrs. Daniels didn't take the open chair. Instead, she walked over to the small boy and got on her knees. She looked him in the eye for a long time, long enough that the boy began to squirm uncomfortably.

"What's your name?"

"Dunno," the boy replied.

"Do you know who I am?"

"Mommy," the boy replied.

"Are you Hershel?" she asked.

The boy shook his head. "Hershel was crying 'cause they kept making fun of him. He couldn't make them stop, so I did."

"For the record, 'stopping them' consisted of several children with extensive bruising and an overturned jungle gym," the principal interjected.

"Is that true? Did you hurt the other children?"

The boy looked down at the floor. "It was an accident. They wouldn't stop making Hershel cry. I just wanted to stop them."

"I understand. Well, we'll have to get you some help in learning to stop people without hurting them," Mrs. Daniels said, giving the boy a reassuring squeeze of his hand, then standing up to her full height.

"I must say, Mrs. Daniels, you're taking this all very well," the principal commented.

"My aunt was a Super, so I've always known it might run in our blood," Mrs. Daniels lied.

"I'm afraid you must know that until Hershel can control his powers more effectively, he won't be able to attend our facility anymore," the principal said hesitantly.

"Of course," Mrs. Daniels agreed. "I fully intend to get my son, or perhaps I should say sons, the education they need to become happy, integrated Supers."

"Sons? Mrs. Daniels, that boy is still Hershel. It's just him utilizing his abilities," the principal told her.

This time, it was Mrs. Daniels who shook her head. "That boy isn't Hershel," she said matter-of-factly. "But he is definitely my son." She looked back at the boy and smiled at him. "On that note, I suppose we should find a good name for you."

"Mrs. Daniels, I don't think you—"

*　　　*　　　*

Roy was jerked awake by a coughing fit. He hacked and thundered for several minutes before lying back down on the table.

315

"Sorry about that, big guy," said the girl in a soft, comforting voice. "It's a side effect of when we heal around the lungs."

Roy heard her and understood. He didn't care, though; now that he'd tasted sleep, he wasn't ready to stop gorging on it just yet.

*   *   *

He could hear her crying again through the walls. She would only do it when she thought he was outside, and even then, only into a pillow to muffle the sound. It wasn't muffled quite enough. She was crying so often these days. Because she missed him.

Roy's fists clenched involuntarily. He got so mad whenever he thought about his dad. Mad at him for leaving, and mad at himself for missing him. Last week, Roy had finally managed to lift a pickup truck in the junkyard where he and his dad used to work out. His first instinct had been to run and proudly tell his father of the accomplishment. Then, Roy had remembered.

"He has some things to work out," his mother had told him, choking back her own sadness. "Things he needs space for."

Roy forced himself to let his hands loosen. It didn't make any sense. His dad had always said a man lived up to his responsibilities, he took care of those in need, he helped the weak. But he could walk out on his own family like it was nothing?

Roy steadied himself. She needed him to be strong right now. Besides, Roy already had a plan. He'd find that son-of-a-bitch one day and ask him in person why he'd walked out. And if he didn't have the world's best answer, Roy was going to beat him mercilessly. That was later, though; his dad was still the better fighter between them. For now.

He knocked gently on the door. "Mom," he called. "Are you okay?"

*   *   *

"—looks like he'll be fine," the girl said.

"Glad to hear it," Coach George's gruff voice said, echoing through the room.

"Good thing he's hearty," Ed said. "I can't imagine what he did to deserve a beating like he got."

"He's tenacious," Coach George said. "More so than I was expecting, to be honest. When I paired him with Taylor, I figured it would be his last day in the program."

"Looks like he surprised you," the girl said.

"That he did," Coach George admitted. "But there's always tomorrow."

*   *   *

Roy wasn't sure what to feel. Rage? Betrayal? Mostly, it was just confusion, but the other two were percolating there as well. He sat silently in his bus seat, staring out the window and trying hard not to think. He could feel the stares of some of the other passengers. A thirteen-year-old boy traveling alone tended to attract attention, after all.

316

On the way out here, he'd felt self-conscious about that fact. Now, he didn't give two shits what people were thinking about him.

All these years, he'd dreamed of the day he confronted his father. All these years, he'd trained and worked and sweat for the sake of being better than him. He'd spent days tracking him down, and then, when he finally found him . . .

Roy shook his head. He couldn't deal with it, couldn't see his dad that way. But the image was there, festering in the back of his mind, unwilling to purge itself despite all his efforts.

Roy felt Hershel stirring within him. They'd been switching even more erratically than normal lately. It was possible stress was a factor in their condition. Roy didn't care at the moment. Right now, he just wanted to be alone. Truly alone, not just one half of a whole. He was barely holding it together as it was, and now, he realized he had his little brother to worry about, too. It was just too much.

"Simmer down, Fatso," Roy whispered hotly under his breath. "Nobody fucking wants you here right now."

87

Roy was surprised to open his eyes. He'd thought Hershel would have taken over by now. Slowly, he pulled himself to a sitting position and looked around. He was still in the resting room where the healers worked.

"Careful," Mary cautioned. "You're all patched up, but you might be woozy for a while."

She was sitting in a chair a few feet away. There were several books with her, one cracked open in her lap.

"What are you doing here?" Roy asked, a twinge of harshness in his voice.

"I was keeping watch. I wanted to make sure you were okay," Mary said.

"So kind of you," Roy snapped. "I'll tell Hershel you cared. You can run along now."

"I don't think you understand. I was here checking on you, on Roy. I heard what happened," Mary explained.

"That I got my ass kicked? Come on, I'm not really a delicate flower, and we have healers on call at all times. There was literally nothing to worry about," Roy scoffed, swinging his feet over the edge of the bed and standing up.

Mary shook her head. "Not the fight. I heard what happened after."

"What do you mean?"

"The memories."

Roy felt himself become very still. "You listened to those?"

"Not intentionally, no. They were the psychic equivalent of throat-tearing screams, though. They overwhelmed everything around me. They seemed . . . intense," Mary said.

Roy tried to calm himself, a task made more difficult by the same memory-dreams they were discussing.

"Shit happens," Roy said. "No sense dwelling on it. I'm fine."

"No, you're not," Mary disagreed. "You're harboring a lot of anger inside. I think that's why you lashed out at so much of the world and distanced yourself. It's all anger you feel toward your fath—"

She was cut off by the crashing sound of Roy's bed being slammed to the ground, courtesy of Roy's fist.

"You and I are not friends," Roy said coldly. "You won a bet against me, and I'm honoring the deal. That's it. I do not need, or want, or care about your advice. And if you ever mention my father again, then all bets are off between us. Understood?"

Mary nodded slowly. "That's fair, I suppose. To me, and maybe to you, but certainly not to Hershel. I guess that's between brothers, though." She reached down and began scooping up her books. "One thing I should point out: I don't know what you went through."

"No argument here," Roy said.

"But that doesn't mean nobody here does. If you were to talk to people a little more, you might find others you could share the burden with."

"Please, I talk to more people than any of you social rejects."

"No, you don't. You slap hands, you exchange drinks, you have a few laughs. You don't talk to anyone, you don't bond with anyone, and you don't connect with anyone," Mary told him.

"I'm connecting all over the place," Roy shot back.

Mary finished gathering her books and stood up from the chair.

"Of course you are. That's why this room is so stuffed with people who wanted to make sure you were okay," Mary said, turning on her heel and heading out the door.

Roy looked around at the empty room and the broken bed. He tried to think of a joke he could make about breaking the bed, preferably one that implied he had tremendous genitalia. Nothing really came to mind. Instead, he found his shoes and walked out a different door.

*　　　*　　　*

"Roy!"

Roy was only a few feet down the hallway, headed back to the lifts, when a familiar voice called to him. He looked over his shoulder to see none other than the man who had just beaten him senseless jogging up to him.

"Hello, Chad," Roy greeted hesitantly.

"Hello," Chad replied. "I see you're moving around again."

"I'm a quick heal," Roy replied.

"I'm sure," Chad said. "I wanted to talk to you about today."

"Was there something left unsaid by our fists?"

"Actually, yes, at least on my end," Chad said. "I was thinking about our fight while you were getting healed. Specifically about how hopelessly out of your league you are when you fight me, yet you continued to try."

"Gee, thanks, but I kind of already got the memo that I suck compared to you," Roy said.

"You do, but that isn't the point. The point is that you kept coming at me, you kept trying no matter how hard I put you down. I realized that the kind of man who can withstand the punishment I'm capable of dishing out and then ask for more is a man with a lot of determination."

"Well . . . yeah, actually," Roy agreed.

"I can relate with that sort of mindset," Chad said. "So I came to a conclusion. I won't improve at all by fighting you. You, on the other hand, will improve tremendously if you can continue to fight like you did today. And in the grand scheme of things, one hour per day helping a similar individual reach their goal is something I can tolerate."

"I guess you're saying you want to stay sparring partners," Roy surmised.

"Yes. I'll keep entering the ring with you for as long as Coach George deems necessary. That is, of course, on the condition that your dedication and intensity do not drop," Chad explained.

"That part you don't need to worry about," Roy said. "And . . . um . . . thanks, I guess."

"Glad to help," Chad replied. He turned and began to walk away.

"Hey, Chad," Roy called out.

"Yes?"

"You said you got the same power as your dad. Is he a Hero?"

Chad nodded without looking back. "He was one of the greatest Heroes ever to live. Why?"

"Just curious, I guess," Roy lied. "You're a strong guy. I thought someone else with your power would have been a pretty famous Hero if he was in the business."

"He is still very famous. Just not for the reasons he deserves," Chad said. "I'll see you tomorrow, Roy."

"See you then," Roy told Chad's exiting form. See, he could connect with people. What the hell did Mary know, anyway?

88

As the days slipped by, even something as strange as a daily bare-knuckle brawl became little more than a piece of routine for the combat students. But the alternative training course posed different challenges. It was a mishmash of light sparring, discussion, and "mind exercises." These challenges—presented by Coach Persephone— could be as simple as a riddle, or as complex as an intricate battle scenario where one was expected to provide a step by step plan for victory. The riddles were, on the whole, considered the more popular task.

They, too, settled into a rhythm, and soon, spring was beginning to slip subtle touches onto the landscape. It was a flower here, a green patch of grass there, things that showed winter was losing its stronghold on the terrain. Of course, some signs were less subtle than others.

"Freshman River Trip. March eighteenth to March twenty-second. Final sign up date, February second," Vince read from the flyer posted on the door to Dean Blaine's classroom. He turned and looked at some of the other students who had pooled behind him. "Anyone know what this is?"

"My sister told me about it," Shane volunteered. "It's a big event during spring break for the freshman class. They provide transportation, tents, and tubes for us to float the river on."

Vince shuddered involuntarily. Ever since the mountain, he'd gotten a spike of cold every time he thought about camping.

"Apparently, it's also tradition for the sophomores chaperoning to bring tons of beer and liquor, so that the whole weekend is quite the celebratory event," Shane continued.

"Great," Vince said unenthusiastically. That made it sound even less fun. There was nothing that seemed even remotely appealing about this trip.

"Hells yeah. I'm putting our names at the top of the list," Sasha said, stepping forward and plucking a pen from her bag. "About time we get to have some fun. I'm still kicking myself for missing that sophomore party last semester."

Vince considered trying to stop her, then thought better of it. He wasn't exactly experienced at relationships, but he knew enough not to try and deprive his girlfriend of something she would view as ample fun. Besides, no one was going to force him to drink. He could go and just enjoy the company.

"Rock on!" Nick said, sidling up to him. "Okay, Vince, this is it. This river trip, I am seeing you finally unwind. You, good sir, will try drinking. No arguments, because every time you open your mouth to say no, I'm cramming a shot down it."

Vince supposed a couple would be okay. It was a new experience and all. Besides, they'd be out in nature, along with heaven only knew how many other college kids on spring break. It might be nice to blend in for a bit and get away from all the Lander uniqueness.

"I heard about this thing," Gilbert said, adding his own name to the list. "Don't they have a deal with some landowner, so we're the only ones on that river? No worrying about anyone seeing us use our powers."

Vince was . . . well, Vince was pretty much just thinking "Damn it" over and over and over.

"All right, class, get inside," Dean Blaine said from within the room. "The sheet will be there for at least a week. I assure you, a chance will be had by all to sign up."

There was some grumbling, but they all piled in and took their seats.

"Settle down, class," Dean Blaine told them. "I know you're all excited about this weekend, but try to keep it under control. It's only Tuesday, after all."

There were several exchanged glances of curiosity, followed by a multitude of shrugs admitting ignorance.

Julia raised her hand.

"Yes, Ms. Shaw?"

"What's this weekend?"

"Tsk tsk, Ms. Shaw. I would have expected you to pay at least some attention to the Lander event calendar. Would anyone care to inform Ms. Shaw of what she has forgotten?"

He was met by vacant eyes and silence. The few in the class who did know the weekend's significance didn't dare proclaim it for fear of being judged as looking forward to it. Which they, in truth, were.

"I must say, I'm disappointed. Over thirty of you here and not one person knows what this weekend is? It's Parents' Weekend. I'd have thought you'd all have it marked on your calendars," Dean Blaine said, barely hiding a chuckle. He was significantly older than his students, but not so old that he'd forgotten the stomach-tightening terror of knowing your parents would be visiting you at college.

"Wait . . . you mean our parents . . ." Stella said, slowly circling the answer she didn't want to hear.

"Your parents were all sent invitations inviting them to a weekend of fun and mingling here at Lander. They'll be allowed to tour the facility, join in some parent–child social events, or just wander the campus meeting your friends and professors," Dean Blaine explained.

"And these invitations, these are already sent out?" Rich asked from the front row.

"Indeed. Ever since the year a student attempted to hijack the mail truck, we've made it policy to only remind the students of Parents' Weekend *after* all the invitations are delivered," Dean Blaine said, glossing over the whole of the story. In truth, it had been several students who'd gone after the mail truck, but his class didn't need to know that any more than they needed to know how Dean Blaine had such extensive (one could even say firsthand), knowledge of the event.

"Um . . . what time will they be arriving?" Will asked.

"Friday afternoon. On that note, you should know that gym will start an hour early, during what would usually be your study period. We want you to have extra time so you can all be cleaned up and ready when your parents arrive."

Some of the students looked sullen, a few looked eager, and most looked downright terrified. It gave Dean Blaine a small sense of comfort knowing that, no matter how powerful a child might be, they could still fear the embarrassment of their parents. Then, he noticed a few faces in the crowd that looked nothing like the others. These were the faces of a few who were trying very hard not to look as sad as they felt. Dean Blaine's amusement swiftly passed.

"Enough of that," he said. "It's time to start class."

323

89

"I'm afraid I just don't agree," Mr. Numbers said politely, taking a sip of tea to punctuate his sentence.

"I'm not asking for agreement, merely assistance, even if only by association," Mr. Transport replied.

The two men were taking advantage of the time their charges were occupied in gym to pop out and get lunch at the only place one could find truly delicious Italian food.

"I'll concede that your idea does regain us some of the ground we were forced to sacrifice for the mountain trial. However, I feel it comes off as far too transparent an attempt to do just that," Mr. Numbers said. "If we are seen as actively manipulating their emotions, then it would undermine our efforts, not aid them."

"That argument is only valid if they see it as an act done for the sake of manipulation. If they take it as genuine, then it would do wonders to foster some trust. Trust that would greatly assist us down the line," Mr. Transport countered.

"I think the risk is too great against the potential reward," Mr. Numbers assessed bluntly. "The optimum gain is simply too minimal to justify such an overt gesture."

Mr. Transport slowly cut into his manicotti, considering Mr. Numbers's point. It was true that this could work against them; however, it was also true that Mr. Transport still wanted to proceed with the plan. Not just for the reasons he'd advocated to Mr. Numbers, but because it was an act of decency he wanted to perform. Mr. Numbers wouldn't accept sentiment in place of logic, though. Mr. Transport thought carefully, then voiced an idea.

"We could get some of them to assist us."

Mr. Numbers merely raised an eyebrow, rather than conjure the effort of a vocal reaction.

"It's not without precedent in circumstances such as these. We would need Nick and Mary. The others trust Mary, thanks to her ability, and Nick has been shaping their perceptions since the first day. If they agree to aid us, then we significantly reduce risk," Mr. Transport said.

"Valid," Mr. Numbers said. "However, working with Nick, in itself, generates a risk."

"Then let's begin with Mary. Broach the topic with her over your next chess game. You can gauge her reaction and decide then if the equation is more adequately balanced."

"Very well," Mr. Numbers agreed. "Assuming the risk–reward ratio becomes justifiable, I will agree to help you with your project."

"Thank you," Mr. Transport said.

"Not at all," Mr. Numbers replied. "Shall we get dessert?"

"Sounds delicious. I believe there is an excellent bakery down the street," Mr. Transport suggested.

"Perfect," Mr. Numbers agreed. "One thing I love about New York, variety is always close at hand."

* * *

"Because I'm retired, that's why!" Dean Blaine yelled into the phone. He was in his office and had been attempting to unwind from the day. His attempt was clearly unsuccessful, as his face was flushed, and a small vein near his eye was beginning to throb. Dean Blaine prided himself on his unflappable demeanor in dealing with the students; however, the person currently on the line was not enrolled at Lander. Aside from that, there were just some things that got under his skin.

There was a murmur of words from the phone.

"Save the guilt trip. I've told you people more times than I care to count that I'm done. There are plenty of capable, active Heroes out there who can fix your problem. I know that because I trained them. That's what I do now, since you seem to have forgotten."

Another murmur crackled across the lines.

"Well, if time is such an issue, then quit wasting it with me and find someone who's willing to help. Good day!"

Dean Blaine slammed the receiver down, cracking off a small piece of plastic in the process. He took several deep breaths and got up from his desk. It took him a few moments of rooting through one of the drawers in his file cabinet, but he finally emerged with a small, white bottle. He poured of glass of water, then deposited two tablets from the bottle into the glass and watched as they fizzed enthusiastically. Only after downing the bubbly liquid in a single gulp did he retake his seat.

Dean Blaine knew he should take it as compliment. He'd been retired for nearly a decade and yet, they still called him when things went too far south too fast. No one wanted to accept that he'd retired, even after all this time. Not too shabby for a guy who had barely made it into the HCP to begin with. He had to believe some of the reluctance to let him go was hype, though. After all, he was one of the few graduates still left from his graduating class. The Class of Legends, people had called it.

Globe may have been at the top, but all ten Heroes who came from that class went on to become famous worldwide. Though, admittedly, some gained fame from less than ideal circumstances.

He mentally ticked through the class roster. Globe and Intra were dead, of course. Wisp was in prison. Shimmerpath made herself nearly impossible to find. Bull-Rush had retired and was now in the private sector. Raze was considered wanted and dangerous. His mental accounting stalled on Raze. They had been roommates nearly their whole time at Lander. They'd sparred often, honing their skills against a fellow well-

325

trained opponent. No one had been more surprised than he when word spread about Raze's crimes.

Dean Blaine rose from his chair once again, this time, heading for the door. He would go watch the juniors' class; it would be going on around now. Seeing the students always centered him. It reminded him of his own days at Lander. Years spent fighting, competing, and bonding with fellow Supers. A time when he'd lived and trained with his best friends. Sometimes, when he was watching the young ones work toward their goal, he could almost forget what had happened to the rest of his class, could lose himself in that ignorant memory of decades ago. Only almost, though. Wherever his mind let him wander, reality was always just a step behind, waiting to pounce.

90

"I think you'll like my parents," Sasha said as she and Vince sat on her couch and flipped through the meager offering of television. "They're pretty chill people on the whole. I was thinking we could all do dinner one night."

"That seems nice," Vince said evenly. He'd never actually had a girlfriend before, so meeting the parents was going to be a new experience for him—one that he hadn't heard the nicest things about.

"Yup. So, what else are you going to do with your downtime? I don't want you to be lonely if everyone is occupied with their parents," Sasha said.

"Nothing to worry about," Vince told her. "Alice and Nick both have single parents that work all the time, so apparently, they aren't coming. Hershel's mom is going to be here, though, and so are both of Mary's parents. So, worst case scenario, I'll be part of a trio for the weekend."

"Long as you save Saturday night for me," Sasha said with a smile. "My parents will love you."

"You think so?"

"Sure! What's not to love? You're a Super with an awesome ability, you're smart, you're kind, and pretty darn cute, if I do say so myself," Sasha said.

"That's very sweet," Vince said, squirming a little at his own lack of understanding of how to take so many compliments. Instead, he opted to change the subject. "Your parents wanted you with a Super, I guess?"

"Like you wouldn't believe. They're convinced that two Supers are more likely to pop out Super grandbabies," Sasha said. "Which is great, for when I'm, like, thirty. But I mean, come on, what teenage girl wants to hear her mom rag on the guy she took to the prom for being an inferior genetic supplier?"

"That does seem a bit odd," Vince agreed.

"They mellowed out after senior year, though," Sasha continued, a devilish grin on her face. "I got them to back off by showing them how much worse it could be."

"What'd you do?"

"I let a Powered guy take me out one night. All of a sudden, the normal boys didn't seem so bad," Sasha chuckled. "Since then, they've been way cooler about it all. Sort of a moot point, though, because I wound up with a Super boyfriend, anyway."

"Heh, yeah, you did," Vince said. He squirmed again, but this time, for a very different, uncomfortable reason.

*   *   *

"Good evening, Alice, have I disturbed your studies?"

"No, everything is fine," Alice replied, moving the recently picked up phone to her right ear. She was sitting at her desk, working through some notes, when her father's ringtone had blared out.

"Excellent to hear. I was calling to inform you that my plane will be arriving Friday afternoon. I will be in town until mid-morning on Saturday," Charles Adair told her.

"Wait, you're actually coming in this weekend?"

"Was I unclear? Yes, I will be there for a little under a day. I've already gotten my hotel set up for the stay, but I would like to invite you to dinner during my time there. I could pick you up at six."

"Oh . . . yeah. That sounds great. I'll see you Friday at six."

"Excellent. Dress appropriately. Good night, dear."

"Night, Daddy."

Alice set down the phone, trying to suppress the surprise welling up inside of her. Her dad was actually going to fly in specifically to see her for Parents' Weekend. That was downright flabbergasting.

She glanced over at her poor, already stuffed to its breaking point, closet. When he said to dress appropriately, it meant he was having dinner somewhere extremely high class. This might just call for a whole new outfit.

She shoved aside her notes and fired up her computer. She needed to see what times the local stores were open until tomorrow.

*   *   *

"I need a favor," Mary said, plopping down next to Nick on the common room sofa.

"Wow, you really don't pussy-foot around, do you?" Nick replied, setting down the book he'd been reading.

"Would it do any good?" Mary asked.

"Not even a little. So, what do you need?"

"Alice is going to ask me to go shopping with her tomorrow after class. I'm leading a study group that evening, so I can't," Mary explained.

"Wait, back up a second. Did I miss the part where your power lets you see the future?"

"No, you missed the part where the girl in the room next to me let out a very sharp mental squeal of joy because she found out her father is coming to visit. She started browsing around for stores to buy a dinner outfit at, and then decided she'd prefer to have someone to talk with while she shops," Mary said.

"Okay, see, I think I know where this is going, and I have to tell you, I am really leaning toward no," Nick said. "In fact, it's less of a lean than it is me standing directly on top of no. Like, it's under my feet, the no. I'm saying no, if you didn't get that."

328

"Please, Nick. I think it'll be good for her to have someone to share an excited day with."

"Uh huh, and I'm the natural second choice after you?" Nick asked.

"Well, no, not really. I think I can talk her into it, though," Mary replied.

"Why me?"

"Because you two are actually pretty similar. Besides, you know more about modern fashion trends than any other guy in this house," Mary said.

"Damn, you are just awful at this," Nick told her.

"That's why I try to avoid doing it. I can't come up with a better solution, unfortunately. Trust me, I tried."

Nick thought it over for a moment, turning the situation around in his head. Mary was coming to him with a genuine need. That wasn't a situation he should outright dismiss.

"I don't do favors," Nick said. "I do, however, do deals. So you want me to say yes when you convince Alice to ask me to go shopping with her? Then I want a day."

"A day?"

"Yes. One twenty-four hour period in which you promise to stay the hell out of my thoughts. No peeking, no listening, no popping in. On your honor. One day," Nick said.

"Agreed," Mary said with some slight hesitation.

"Then consider it done," Nick said. "Assuming you really can talk her into asking me, of course."

91

"Pale pink, or off pink?" Alice asked, holding up yet another pair of nearly identical shoes.

"That depends. When you say your father is coming to town, is that slang for your daddy, or your handler, as some girls call them?"

"You're inferring these shoes will make me look like a hooker," Alice replied.

"And they say the blonde ones are all looks," Nick said with an unfazed grin. He wasn't sure how Mary had talked her into it (for that matter, neither was Alice), but Alice had been convinced that Nick would be an acceptable shopping substitute. So instead of spending his evening relaxing and planning for the weekend, Nick was stuck on shopping duty. In truth, he'd been down this road many times with many girls, but he found that if they knew you didn't mind, then they felt encouraged to bring you along more often. That much, at least, he wanted to avoid.

"I know they aren't perfectly high class, but I thought with the dress I picked out, it wouldn't be pushing the envelope too much," Alice said, defending her selection.

"You thought wrong. If we were going out to a bar or with our friends, I would say no problem. If we're talking people with actual fashion, then I think we both know you've gone over the line of class," Nick said.

Alice sighed. "Damn it, you're right. I hate you for being right."

"Long as we're hating me for appropriate reasons, I think I can cope," Nick said.

"You know this means I have to keep looking, though," Alice warned him.

Nick spread out his hands. "I've got all night, Princess. Nobody for me to impress tomorrow, so the room can stay messy, and the clothes piled up." In truth, Nick was only as messy as he needed to be in his Melbrook room. He preferred a meticulously tidy living space; however, such things would draw too much attention in a college freshman, especially when he had roommates keen on stopping by.

"Oh yeah, you, Vince, and I were supposed to be the parentless Lonely Hearts Club this weekend," Alice said. "Sorry I kind of bailed on that."

"You had family come in. If that was a viable option for either of us, we'd easily do the same," Nick assured her. "We'll just have to find a way to soldier on without you."

"Uh huh. Don't do anything too mean to Vince," Alice cautioned him.

"Perish the thought. I was planning on driving him out to have a nice, relaxing dinner off campus, away from the hustle and bustle of those with visiting parents," Nick told her.

Alice raised an eyebrow.

". . . at a strip club," Nick finished with a smirk.

"I'm pretty sure Sasha would punch you if she found out you tricked Vince into going to a strip club. Not like I punch, either. She'd aim right for the dick."

Nick winced visibly. "I hadn't thought of that part. I don't know why she'd react that way, though, it's not like she has anything to worry about. I mean, have you ever known a guy less likely to cheat, on anyone or at anything, than Vince?"

"True, but feelings aren't always so logical," Alice said. "Sometimes, people overreact when the person they care about is ogling tramps."

"I prefer to think of them less as tramps and more as ambitious young ladies paying their way through nursing school," Nick said.

"The nearest nursing school is fifty miles from here," Alice pointed out.

"So they commute. All the more reason to work extra hard—for the gas money."

Alice briefly considered throwing a shoe at him. She stopped herself, though, realizing that wouldn't send the right kind of message. She needed to be calm and rational in her approach to chastising Nick for this type of behavior.

She threw all four shoes instead. It was immensely satisfying.

*   *   *

Mr. Transport stepped through the front door and into the small hallway of the Melbrook foyer. He usually teleported back to his and Mr. Numbers' apartment; however, from time to time, it made sense to do an in-person walk-through. It was a gentle reminder to the students that though they may not be visible, there were authority figures on hand at any given time. Given that it was Thursday night, which was practically a Friday for all college-based purposes, he expected to walk into the common room and find all the students hatching some sort of night-occupying scheme.

What greeted his eyes as he passed from the hallway was significantly less jubilant. Only Vince was there, reading some chemistry book on the couch.

"Good evening, Vince," Mr. Transport greeted.

"Hi, Mr. Transport," Vince said, looking up with a smile. "How's your night going?"

"Very well. And yours?"

"Not bad. Just a few problems left, and I'm done for the night."

"Commendable. Vince, I can't help but wonder where the others are. Some sort of mischief I should be concerned about?" Mr. Transport asked.

Vince laughed. "Nah, nothing that I know of, sir. Everyone is kind of gearing up for Parents' Weekend. Hershel and Mary are both in their rooms cleaning, and Nick went with Alice to shop for some new outfit. Turns out her dad is coming in, and they're going somewhere nice."

"That seems enjoyable," Mr. Transport said, carefully gliding over anything that could be construed as a question as to why Vince's activities weren't in the same vein. Mr. Transport was already quite informed on that answer and tactful enough not to bring it up.

331

"I hope so," Vince replied. "I don't get the feeling Alice sees a whole lot of her dad. She's trying to downplay it, but she seems excited."

"I'm sure it will be fine," Mr. Transport assured him. At the mention of Nick, Mr. Transport recalled that he didn't possess any family likely to visit either. "I assume you and Nick will be up to some merrymaking of your own tomorrow night?"

"He mentioned something about dinner off campus, which seemed like a nice change-up," Vince said. "Say what you want about Nick, he knows how to have fun."

"That he does," Mr. Transport said, feeling a bit relieved. He'd grown a bit fond of Vince and didn't like the idea of the boy stuck alone, surrounded by people with loving families. "Well, I'll leave you to your studies. Have a good night, Vince."

"You, too, Mr. Transport. See you tomorrow when we go to class."

Mr. Transport walked through the common room and into the kitchen. Once there, he made the quick teleportation into the apartment tucked away behind the steel door by the stove.

"You're late," Mr. Numbers chastised him. "You know we have some reports to make tomorrow."

"I stopped to talk with a student," Mr. Transport said defensively.

"That's less of an excuse than you might believe it to be, and more of an explanation on how you wasted the time that made you late," Mr. Numbers snapped. He was often on edge before reports were due, which, given the possible circumstances of a bad one, was not an inexcusable crime.

"I'll remind you of that next time Mary challenges you to a game of chess," Mr. Transport said, joining him at the table where papers were already spread out.

"The chess is different," Mr. Numbers replied. "That is education."

"I'm sure," Mr. Transport said. "Shall we debate this more, or simply acknowledge that I'm here and it's time to get to work?"

"Work," Mr. Numbers said sharply.

"Then work it is," Mr. Transport agreed, concealing something of a grin behind a fit of fake coughing.

92

"Hershel!" yelled an enthusiastic, middle-aged voice.

"Hi, Mom," Hershel said, embarrassment welling up as his mother gave him a tremendous embrace.

The Melbrook students were gathered in the common room, relaxing after gym on Friday. In honor of the weekend's occasion, the dorm's front, steel door had been deactivated, allowing visitors to enter as they pleased. It was a nice way around reminding the parents that their children had been experimented on and were still under careful watch. Plus, it saved anyone from having to get up to welcome people.

Hershel's mother had been the first to arrive, so the remainder of the students got up from their chairs to greet her. All of them were there, though Nick and Vince were present purely to meet the makers of their dormmates.

"These must be your friends I've heard so much about," Mrs. Daniels said after she had thoroughly squeezed Hershel. "I feel like I know them already. The one with the silver hair must be Vince."

"Nice to meet you, Mrs. Daniels," Vince said.

"Good to meet you, too. And I see the other boy is wearing sunglasses indoors and is curiously well-dressed, so that would be Nick."

"Bingo," Nick affirmed. He'd gussied himself up a bit in honor of the night to come. He liked to make the right kind of impression on the ladies of the evening.

"Which leaves these two lovely young ladies as Mary and Alice," Mrs. Daniels concluded.

"Correct," Alice said. "I'm Alice, and this is Mary. It's a pleasure to meet you, Mrs. Daniels. We greatly enjoy our friendship with Hershel."

"Ditto," Mary agreed, somewhat shyly.

"Well, you are such a polite bunch," Mrs. Daniels said. "I'm glad to see Hershel has made such nice friends." She turned back to her son. "All right, let's go see your room, and then we can go out to dinner."

"Sounds great," Hershel said, relieved his mother didn't want to dally too much with the others. He loved his mother very dearly, but there were certain times in a boy's life when a maternal presence is one of pure, unbridled embarrassment. Being around a girl you're trying to work up the nerve to ask out was definitely one of those times.

Hershel took his mother by the hand and walked her into the boys' lounge, the steel door whooshing shut behind them.

"She seemed pleasant," Vince observed once they had gone.

"Yeah. Makes you wonder what kind of nutjob the dad must be to have produced a kid like Roy," Nick added.

Nick felt something kick him sharply in the shin. He glanced down, immediately suspecting Alice, only to see nothing there. On a hunch, he glanced over at Mary. The look in her eyes left no room to wonder about the nature of his invisible assailant.

Before he had a chance to react, though, Mary's focus shifted abruptly.

"Ooh! My parents are here," she cried. "I'm heading out to meet them. See you guys later!"

"Wait, we don't get to meet the folks that spawned our local, wacky telepath? I feel gypped," Nick complained.

"It's nothing personal. They're just normal people, and they're not used to being around Supers," Mary said, making her way to the door. "I need to get them a little adjusted first. I promise I'll bring them around once they can better handle themselves." With that, she was out the door like a shot.

"I still sort of feel like we just got brushed off," Vince said.

"Either we did or they did, and I'm not about to go rooting around the psyche of a telepath trying to figure it out," Nick replied.

"Amen to that," Alice agreed.

There were no new arrivals immediately following Mary's departure, so the other three returned to lounging about. Well, Nick and Vince lounged. Alice sat carefully so as not to wrinkle or upset the outfit she had purchased. The effort was understandable; after all, the girl looked sleek. Her black dress was complimented by a mere whisper of pink trim, along with matching shoes and a handbag. She'd spent more time than she would ever admit on getting her makeup just right, which essentially meant making it look like she wasn't wearing any. Her long, platinum blonde hair was pulled up and styled, with a few key strands hanging down for effect. In short, she was the picture of adolescent elegance, just as she had been taught to be for many, many years.

"I got to go take a wiz," Nick announced, hurling himself up from the chair.

"You are so amazingly crude," Alice sighed.

"That wasn't crude. Crude would be saying I need to go defile the porcelain," Nick countered.

"Touché?" Alice said, not quite certain whether it was a win for Nick or a loss for everyone in the room. Nick didn't stick around to find out; he headed over to the boys' side and swept through the door.

The next man to walk into the room was not a returning Nick with an empty bladder. It was, instead, a gentleman dressed simply, yet spectacularly. He wore black slacks, a white shirt open at the throat, and a black jacket. A simple pair of cufflinks and a watch were all the accessory added to his ensemble. It was a classic look, yet not an impressive one. Unless, of course, one was aware of how much each piece of the outfit cost. At that point, he was a picture of splendor and decadence.

"Good evening," said the tall, suited man.

334

"Hi, Daddy!" Alice said, extracting herself carefully from her chair. It was a difficult task, not only because of the dress, but because of the wave of excitement that crashed against her. She and her father didn't see each other all that often, and this was the first time she could ever remember him making a trip specifically to spend time with her.

"Hi, Mr. Adair," Vince said, pulling himself to his feet and sticking out his hand. "I'm Vince Reynolds."

"A pleasure to meet you, Vince," he said, pumping the hand once and immediately releasing it. "I would love to stay and get to know you better, but unfortunately, Alice and I are shorter on time than I'd intended."

"Oh, no problem," Vince said. "You guys have fun tonight."

"Erm . . . we'll certainly try. Alice, are you ready?"

"Ready," Alice chimed off brightly.

"Then let us make some haste," he said, flashing Vince a million dollar smile. It seemed just a touch familiar to Vince, but it quickly slipped out of his mind.

And just like that, Vince was the only one left in the room. He sat back down and waited for Nick to finish his business so they could go eat. It was only a few seconds of waiting when Nick stepped back in from the boys' side.

"What'd I miss?"

"Alice's dad," Vince told him.

"Damn, I was looking forward to that one," Nick lied. "Oh well, what's done is done. Food?"

"Sounds great," Vince agreed. He hopped to his feet and turned toward the door, just in time to see an unfamiliar man step through it. The man was dressed casually in jeans and a shirt. He was fit without being intimidating, and average looking in nearly every facet. Vince started to ask the man his business here, when Nick's voice from behind to cut him off. It was filled with something odd in Nick's tone, something Vince wasn't certain he'd ever heard there before— surprise.

"Gerry?"

"Wow, you got a big car just to be here for a day," Alice noted as she walked outside and saw the white stretch limousine.

"A necessary evil, unfortunately," her father said.

"I'm confused, though. I thought you hated stretch limos. You said they were tacky, for people who wanted to look impressive, but didn't know how," Alice said.

"And that belief still holds firmly true," her father replied. "Though I'll thank you not to mention it around our guests tonight. The limo was to appeal to their tastes, rather than my own."

"What guests? I thought you flew in to see me," Alice said, slowing down her trot to the car.

"No, dear, I said I was going to be in town and invited you to dinner. I'm here to close a deal with Horatio Vinders for one of his offshoot companies. He insisted on coming into town this weekend to visit his daughter Beth, so I offered to take them out to dinner," he explained, his gait never even considering an idea as indignant as slowing down.

Alice scrambled to catch up. She wasn't sure how she was feeling right now, though she was certain it wasn't pleasant. All the same, she didn't want to be left behind entirely.

"Mr. Adair," called a young girl somewhat older than Alice. She had stepped out from the behind the limo, clearly waiting for them. She had her hair trimmed short and wore a midnight blue dress paired with a few adornments of tasteful jewelry. She looked familiar, and Alice realized she had seen this girl many times before wandering the halls beneath the school. At that time, she'd been wearing a grey uniform, so that made her either a sophomore or a junior. Alice's guess was junior.

"Beth," Charles Adair said, leaning in and giving the girl a respectful kiss on the cheek. "You grow more beautiful every time I see you. Is your father already inside?"

"Oh no, I'm so sorry, but he was caught up momentarily speaking with one of my professors. It was so embarrassing, she wouldn't stop going on and on about how wonderful a student I am. Father sent me ahead to let you know of his delay and to tell you that we certainly don't expect you to wait. You two go ahead to dinner, and we'll catch up later."

Alice felt a bubble of joy rising in her; at least she would have a little time to talk with her dad, just the two of them. It wasn't what she had expected, but it was something.

"Nonsense," Charles Adair said, waving her off. "I wouldn't hear of such a thing, leaving you two to find your own way when I have this enormous vehicle just

336

idling by. Don't even mention it again. Alice and I will wait right here with you until your father arrives."

"Mr. Adair, you are so kind," Beth replied. "And it was Alice, wasn't it? I think I've seen you around. It's a pleasure to meet you."

"The pleasure is all mine," Alice said automatically. She'd been through so many formal greetings it came like second nature to her now.

"Beth's father tells me she's quite accomplished here at Lander," Mr. Adair interjected. "A third year in the same program as yourself, Alice. You would do well to listen to any bits of wisdom she might pass down."

Alice choked herself back from snapping that she already knew what year Beth was just from paying attention below ground. Instead, she lowered her eyes and said, "I am always grateful for the guidance of my seniors."

"Such an excellent attitude to have here at Lander," Beth said, flashing a toothy grin. "You'll find yourself going far with such humility."

Alice said nothing. She'd managed to forget what this was like—the subtle barbs, the plays for power, the dance of the wealthy debutantes. For that's what this was. Beth was from society, too. Her father had less wealth than Alice's, but since Mr. Adair was trying to impress them, it was simple enough for Beth to establish herself as the alpha between the two. It was a tactful duel of concealed attacks and hasty retreats, an art Alice had learned long ago. And now, standing here in the crisp air of a dying winter, she realized how much she loathed it to her very core.

*   *   *

"You look good, Campbell. They already got you whipped back into shape after your month off over Christmas," Gerry said, stepping the rest of the way into the common room.

"Thanks. What brings you to Lander?" Nick asked.

"Well, Ms. Pips couldn't be here herself, of course, you know how busy things get on the weekends, but she thought you might like at least one familiar face on Parents' Weekend," Gerry explained.

"That is . . . surprising," Nick said. He took a moment to recover himself, then turned to Vince. "This is Gerry. He works for Ms. Pips. He was my tutor growing up."

"Nice to meet you, sir," Vince said politely, shaking his hand.

"You too, kid, and that is some grip," Gerry replied. "They making all you kids into ultra-soldiers?"

"Just basic Hero training," Vince said, an unwitting smile coming to his lips.

"Yeah, well, with training like what they're giving you, I'm glad I'm not a criminal. Four years of this, and you'll be able to take on an army," Gerry quipped.

"Maybe, but we'll all hope we never have to," Vince said.

"Damn right, kid. So, Nick, you know any good burger joints around here?"

337

"A couple," Nick replied. "But, Gerry, Vince and I sort of made plans already."

"Well then, Vince can come along," Gerry said with a big grin.

Vince took a step back and raised his hands. "No, no, I really couldn't. You two go enjoy yourselves. I'll call Alex up. His parents aren't coming in 'til tomorrow, so we can have still have unsupervised fun."

"You sure, kid? We got plenty of room in my car," Gerry said.

"Really, Vince, you're more than welcome," Nick reiterated.

"Wouldn't dream of it," Vince said. "You guys have fun. I'll see you when you get back."

"Okay, if you're sure," Nick said hesitantly. Vince nodded emphatically.

"I guess that's that, then. Good to meet you, Vince," Gerry said, stepping over to the door. He and Nick walked wordlessly up the hallway. Only after they had stepped outside, checked to make sure the door was secure, and done a visual sweep did any words pass their lips.

"Good kid," Gerry commented. "He the one without any family?"

"Yup," Nick confirmed.

"You know he was lying about the other friend, right? He's going to sit in there alone all night."

"I know, Gerry. We invited him, though."

"We could have pushed harder."

Nick shook his head. "Wouldn't have done any good. I slipped up and let him see how glad I was to see you. Vince could have never infringed on our time after something like that. He wouldn't have budged, no matter how hard we pushed."

"Huh. Quite a guy you befriended there."

"Whatever you say. Ready to get some food?" Nick asked.

"Sure, my car is over that way," Gerry said, pointing past a garish stretch limousine and a few people dressed to the nines standing around it.

"Crap," Nick said. "Let's circle around. The blonde wearing black is another dormmate of mine, and I'd really rather not get drawn into talking with her or her dad."

Gerry let out a low whistle. "She's quite a looker. Which one is that, the flyer or the telepath?"

"Flyer," Nick replied.

"Alice, then. And the guy with here is her dad. Any idea who the other girl is?"

"Not a clue about her name, but she's one of the few female juniors in the HCP," Nick replied. He had long ago compiled a mental list of every face he saw below ground as well as what class they belonged in.

"She must be some kind of powerful bitch," Gerry observed. "Your friend looks pretty uncomfortable."

"She's fine," Nick said, brushing it off. "Let's go eat."

338

"Campbell, if you think she's fine, we need to go back over how to read body language, and I mean now."

"Fine, so she's miserable and trying to hide it," Nick replied. "That's her problem. I'm off-duty on the friend act."

"Isn't this the girl who saved your life?" Gerry asked.

"Yeah, on the mountain. Why?"

"Heavens above, kid, what do you mean 'why'? The girl you owe your life to is practically biting back tears, and you want to sneak by so she can't see you."

Nick sighed. "You know, for a con man, you sure have a strict moral code."

"The key part of 'con man' is the word 'man.' You have to have empathy with your fellow human beings, or you're just a sociopath, and they make the shittiest con men alive," Gerry pointed out.

"So what do you want me to do? Go slash the tires of the car so they can't go to dinner?"

"Interject yourself, give her someone familiar she can lean on in the middle of a shitty situation," Gerry said.

"How? I wouldn't do that. I mean . . . the me that they know wouldn't do that. Hell, he wouldn't even know how," Nick said.

Gerry shrugged. "You got your license to work solo a long time ago. It's not my job to figure out the angle for you."

"No, it's your job to tell me when to break my cover for no good reason," Nick snapped back.

"Campbell, right now, you'd be dead in the ground if not for that girl. There's your good reason. If you can't see how you owe her at least a little help when she's upset, then maybe basic human empathy is something you've already lost touch with," Gerry said simply.

"Damn it," Nick cursed, taking off his sunglasses and handing them to Gerry. "Give me those back tonight. Lunchie and Munchie's Burgers on 22 and V. One in the morning. And you are so buying after this shit."

"Deal," Gerry agreed as he watched Nick stride off across the grass.

*   *   *

"—so that's why I'm holding myself in seventh place," Beth said, concluding her story. "I could go higher, but right now, I just feel like those other six need the self-esteem from it more. I mean, I'm already so blessed, why be greedy?"

"A very kind gesture," Mr. Adair said. "You're quite the caring girl."

"Indeed," Alice agreed. She wasn't gritting her teeth yet, but it was becoming an effort. It was strange; she'd been the good little daughter for so long without even trying. Yet, after only a few months at Lander, living in this role felt like getting dental surgery without anesthetic. She didn't know what could have changed so much in such a short

339

time. Had Alice been a touch more introspective, it might have occurred to her that the answer was herself. Perhaps she would have arrived there anyway, but at that particular moment, a considerable interruption to her thought process occurred.

Alice felt an arm curl gently around the small of her back. At the same time, a hand cradled her chin and pulled it in close. A pair of lips landed lightly on her cheek before she was released from the silken net of the grip that had held her. She turned her head and found herself looking into a pair of brown, utterly foreign eyes. She was surprised, though not nearly as shocked as when she pulled back her gaze and saw the face that owned those eyes.

"Sorry I'm late, darling," Nick said, giving her a comforting smile. "I got caught up at the study session for physics." Nick turned away from the stunned-into-silence Alice and faced her father.

"You must be Mr. Adair. I must say it's an honor to finally meet you, sir. I'm Nicholas Campbell, Alice's boyfriend."

94

"A pleasure," Mr. Adair said, his eyebrows lifting. "Forgive my surprise, my daughter never mentioned that she had a suitor."

"Yes, we only recently decided to make things official, so there hasn't been much time to tell anyone," Nick said. "It took me quite a bit of work to show your daughter I was worth having."

"Good to hear. A man who won't put in the work is a man who won't stick around when things get hard," Mr. Adair said.

"I couldn't agree more, sir."

It was at this point that Alice's brain finally snapped back from the certainty that she was having a truly awful nightmare and sprang into action. After it entertained a few violent, murderous scenarios for how to deal with Nick, it decided to focus on a more plausible solution instead.

"Honey," Alice said in a voice dripping with sweetness. "Can I speak with you for a minute?"

"Only if your father and his guest will excuse us," Nick said deferentially.

"By all means," Mr. Adair said.

"Um, sure," Beth chimed in.

"So kind of you both," Nick said. He took Alice's arm in his and walked away from the car. When they were about forty feet away, Alice turned to him with a huge smile on her face. From a distance, it was good camouflage, but if you were too close, the murder in her eyes gave away its falsehood.

"Any last words to your testicles before I separate them from your body?"

"Only together for a few minutes, and already you know I love the kinky stuff," Nick replied.

"Nick, what the fuck do you think you're doing?"

"Helping, believe it or not. You looked so helpless dealing with that bitch that I decided to jump in and help."

"I wasn't helpless."

"Fine, miserable then."

That one, Alice had a harder time disputing, so instead, she went after Nick's methods.

"How exactly does you being my boyfriend help?"

"I can be charming when I want to be. Besides, I thought it might just be nice to have a friend along. I mean, you've been looking forward to your dad coming since you found out. From the size of the car and the way that girl is dressed, I'm guessing it isn't the family affair you were expecting. I just figured if I were in your shoes, I'd rather have a friend around than face such a disappointment alone," Nick explained.

"That's . . . surprisingly sweet-intentioned," Alice said. "You're not secretly the shape-shifting kid, are you?"

"Would the shape-shifting kid know you used to have a very well-justified fear of heights?" Nick asked.

"Touché," Alice said. "I still don't know how comfortable I am with you pretending to be my boyfriend, though."

"Look, I've already made the play, and you went with it. So now, we're either together, or you get to explain how your friend took pity on you and pretended to be your beau to your father and that oh-so-lovely young woman."

"Damn it. You've got a point."

"Hence why I made it. Anyway, you got anything else? We need to wrap this up and walk back before it seems like we're up to something," Nick pointed out.

"There is one little flaw in your plan. We're going to a business dinner, and you weren't invited. I appreciate the sentiment, but you won't be able to tag along once Beth's dad gets here."

Nick threw back his head and let out a genuine laugh. "That's nothing to worry about."

"Why not?"

"Trust me, I'll be there at your father's insistence. Just wait and see."

"Okay, wow me, jerk," Alice said with a more sincere smile. "Oh, and one more thing. I like the way you look without your sunglasses."

"Don't get used to it," Nick replied. "But thanks."

*   *   *

"Where is everyone?" Mr. Transport asked as he stepped into the living room and once again found Vince sitting by himself.

"Out with parents, or parental figures," Vince said, mindlessly surfing through channels on the television.

"Ah. I surmise Nick received a surprise visitor?"

"Yeah, a tutor that he's apparently pretty close to," Vince replied. "He was really happy to see him, so they went to spend some time together."

"You didn't tag along?" Mr. Transport asked.

"Nah. It's family, and I got the feeling Nick didn't get to see him much. I wouldn't have felt right intruding."

"Very respectable. What will you do instead?"

"Nothing too exciting. I think I'll go grab dinner at the cafeteria and catch up on some homework," Vince said, standing from the couch and turning off the television.

"I see," Mr. Transport said. Those were productive, responsible activities. They were an excellent way to deal with loneliness or boredom. He should retreat now and leave Vince to his plans. He shouldn't get too involved, after all.

342

"Vince, your comment about eating off campus got me thinking about how long it's been since I dined out myself. I've got a craving for a delicious sandwich shop I know. Would you care to join me?" Mr. Transport asked.

Vince looked wary. "That's okay, Mr. Transport. Campus food is fine."

Of course the boy wouldn't want to accept pity. Mr. Transport tried to adjust his thinking; what would Mr. Numbers do in this situation? He wasn't entirely sure what the answer was, but the thought did lead him down the path to an excellent solution.

"I understand," Mr. Transport said. "It's just that Mr. Numbers is at a meeting, and I do hate eating in restaurants alone. I always feel somehow out of sorts, as if I don't belong as a solo diner. Silly, I know, yet the sentiment remains."

"No, I get that," Vince said. "I guess I can come along. Eating alone does kind of suck."

"Much appreciated," Mr. Transport said. "I'm ready whenever you are."

"I've already got my shoes on, so I guess I'm ready to—" Vince said, then noticed he was standing in the sunshine, white sand beneath his feet and a crystal blue ocean before him.

"—go."

95

"How have things been since the holidays?" Mrs. Daniels asked. She and Hershel were sitting in an Italian restaurant a few miles off campus. It was a quaint place with fair prices, good food, and comfortable chairs.

"Not too bad," Hershel replied. "Roy's actually been working hard in the combat class."

"Roy will tell me all about what he's been up to at length tomorrow, sweetie. I want to know how you've been doing."

"Good, I guess. The classes aren't bad so far, and there's this river trip during spring break that looks like a lot of fun."

"That's nice. How about with girls? You talked a lot about your friend Mary over the break," Mrs. Daniels pried.

"Well . . . we did sort of dance a couple of weeks ago."

"A nice start. Then what happened?"

"Um, nothing. That was it, we danced a few weeks ago," Hershel said, suddenly feeling a bit uncomfortable.

"I see." Mrs. Daniels said. She took a long sip of her white wine. "Darling, you know I don't want to intrude into this new life you've made for yourself, but would you be open to a little motherly advice?"

". . . sure."

"An object at rest will stay at rest. An object in motion will stay in motion, unless it is acted on by an opposing force. Time is a tremendously effective opposing force," Mrs. Daniels said.

"I'm not sure I follow you," Hershel said.

"Son, if you have momentum, then don't let time erode it too much. You danced with Mary, and from the smile when talking about it, you took it to have a romantic connotation. A girl expects a little continuation of courting after moments like those."

"You're saying I should have asked her out?"

"I'm simply letting you know what a woman generally anticipates in the courting process," Mrs. Daniels said with a soft smile.

"Gotcha," Hershel said. He thought about her advice for a moment. "One thing. Roy never really does that. I mean, he'll go for days without calling or even responding to the texts of girls he goes out with."

"What your brother does isn't really courting. It's more . . . well, I can't think of a polite word for it. Just trust me that I know more about nice girls like Mary than Roy does," Mrs. Daniels said.

*　　　*　　　*

344

"Breathtaking, isn't it?" Mr. Transport said, admiring the blue waves crashing against the sand.

"Actually, yeah, it kind of is. Must be really far, though, given the fact that it looks like noon here, and we left at dusk," Vince pointed out.

"Very astute. We are indeed some ways from home. Don't worry, though, I have no intention of leaving you for any type of trial this time," Mr. Transport said.

"Glad to hear it," Vince said, genuinely hoping Mr. Transport was telling the truth.

"I'm sure. The sandwich shop is down the beach a bit. We can walk there in twenty minutes or so."

"Sounds good," Vince said. "Just curious though, you're a teleporter, why not teleport us right to it?"

"Because then, we wouldn't get the experience of walking there," Mr. Transport said.

Vince cast his eyes out at the ocean once more. He had to admit, he could definitely see the appeal of taking the scenic route.

*   *   *

"That was delicious," Mrs. Daniels said, pushing away her plate.

"I told you," Hershel said. "This place is awesome."

"It was. You made an excellent choice, dear. After this, I'll sleep like a baby tonight."

"You'll need it to keep up with Roy tomorrow," Hershel said.

"Of that, I have no doubt," Mrs. Daniels agreed. "Speaking of, you boys worked out a schedule, right?"

"Yup. I'm here tonight and Sunday before you leave in the afternoon. Roy gets all of Saturday. It adds up to around a full day each," Hershel explained.

"Sounds very fair."

"It is. Roy's actually been a lot more amiable lately," Hershel said. "I think the training is giving him a place to take out a lot his . . . energy." Hershel narrowly avoided using the term 'anger.' It seemed closer to badmouthing someone than making a report.

"I'm happy to hear that. I hoped you boys would start getting along again eventually," Mrs. Daniels said. "Most siblings are friendlier in their older years, anyway. I was counting a lot on growing up to help that process."

"Might not have been a bad bet."

"Your mother has her moments," Mrs. Daniels said. "And I know a thing or two about dealing with strong-willed boys."

*   *   *

"You're right, this sandwich is ridiculously delicious," Vince said, the cheese oozing down from his first bite and running along the plate.

345

"I don't often hop across the globe for poor cuisine," Mr. Transport said, tackling his own meal.

"Is going farther harder?" Vince asked.

"Not for me," Mr. Transport said, shrugging his shoulders. "I've heard others say distance creates difficulty for them, but it's all the same to me. A mile or an ocean, I go there in a simple jump."

"That's weird. I never really thought that people with the same power would function differently," Vince said.

"It's a curiosity, I'll give you that," Mr. Transport said. "All I've been able to figure out is that there's no such thing as 'the same power' among Supers. Vast amounts of similarities, but with subtle differences between them. For example, I once knew a large amount of fellow teleporters. One woman left a shower of sparks when she vanished. One man would appear in a large cloud of dark smoke. There was even a fellow who left the smell of sulfur in the air when he jumped. All the same power in a very technical sense, yet each as unique as the Super that wielded it."

"I see what you mean. Sort of like how shifting is the most common ability, but everyone shifts into something different," Vince said.

"And even those who shift into the same basic form have differences between them. Two people who can shift into panther–human hybrids would still look quite different and possess individual strengths and weaknesses."

"So, you're a teleporter who can go any distance with ease," Vince surmised. "That doesn't mean that every teleporter can, though."

"Precisely."

"I guess that makes you one of the better ones, then," Vince said.

"I'm okay," Mr. Transport lied. "There's always someone better."

That last part wasn't a lie, even if Mr. Transport didn't know it.

96

Nick was charming. Alice had never expected that sort of thought to cross her mind, yet, as she watched him schmooze the conversation, she had to admit the boy had his smoothness. It wasn't just that he was knowledgeable on every topic that came up, or that he had an impeccable sense of manners and propriety, or even his effortless likability. It was that he had all those things and understood how to control a conversation. Nick knew the art of not talking.

He spoke infrequently, never interrupting, but only interjecting when a lull occurred. He splashed in a few words or a subtle idea, and then retreated. It was a series of quick, delicate strikes that gave off the impression of a young man with a competent head on his shoulders who still properly respected his elders. Alice sipped her merlot (she'd been allowed a single glass at dinner since she was a young child), pondering just how it was that someone like Nick could so effortlessly become this amazing guy.

They were in a restaurant that catered to upscale clientele. As such, it was done in very dark, muted colors, lit by a soft glow of light that was just bright enough to see that one's food was properly cooked. It was a place that was easily missed, even by the locals, holding only a small placard on the door to indicate a restaurant was there. There were no prices on the menus, and there was ample dust on the bottles. Alice used to love places like this, and while a part of her was always overjoyed at the prospect of food prepared by expert chefs, she found the atmosphere to be a bit drab. Somewhere, amongst the gastrointestinal catastrophes that represented the dorm cafeterias, Alice had grown accustomed to a dining environment that was more . . . lively.

"I must say, Nick," Mr. Vinders's voice blurted, breaking Alice's reverie. "You were quite right about the '62 merlot. I'd never ever heard of that winery before."

"Thank you, sir," Nick said, dipping his head ever so slightly in a gesture of humility. "It was just some knowledge I gleaned from an old teacher. It seems that particular regions of France experienced exceptional flooding about a year before, leaving it unable to grow or produce until 1962. When they finally did, they discovered that the rain had washed new minerals from a nearby village into the soil, leading to exceptional wine."

"That's quite useful knowledge," Mr. Adair said.

"I'm glad I was able to share it with you," Nick said with a smile. He raised his glass and did a small toasting motion before treating himself to a sip.

"That's quite a young man you have there, Alice," Mr. Vinders said. "I wish my Beth could meet one like him."

"*Father!*" Beth hissed. "I'm taking my time in choosing a worthwhile one."

"You've had three years. Alice pulled it off in only one semester," Mr. Vinders countered.

"I suppose Alice got the only good one," Beth said, spreading her mouth into a smile, while her eyes danced with rage at the happy couple.

"Keep trying. The sooner you get married, the sooner you can leave that school. You'll get yourself seriously hurt one of these days. I'd never have allowed you to attend Lander if I'd known they were letting women in the combat classes," Mr. Vinders said. Nick began to suspect the large, mustached man had drunk a little too much of the sumptuous merlot. Fortunately, Mr. Adair was certain of that fact.

"I'm sure she'll meet a kind boy soon," Mr. Adair said. "Be glad she's being choosy, though. After all, a man like you would surely reject ninety-nine percent of the boys who would try to date a girl as lovely as your daughter."

"Quite true," Mr. Vinders agreed.

"Thus, it is both prudent and efficient for her to only bother bringing around the ones who truly have a chance at being worthy of her," Mr. Adair said. "But I think that's enough about our daughters' love lives for the moment. Shall we get down to more immediate matters?"

"I've told you already, Charles, I'm not comfortable selling out my company unless I'm certain you won't go on a firing and outsourcing spree," Mr. Vinders said, his face immediately growing serious.

"I assure you, the headcount will remain unchanged should your company find itself in my employ," Mr. Adair said. He reached out onto the table and plucked up a small, black menu. "However, I find talks like these are best done between two gentlemen in solace, save for a good brandy. The immediate business I was referring to was dessert."

"Ha!" Mr. Vinders let out a chuckle and slapped the table. In a fine-dining restaurant, such a thing would have been unacceptable. In a place like this, acceptability was determined purely by whoever had the most money in the room. "Right you are, Charles. Let's leave business for after we drop off the kiddies. At the moment, I'd rather do some serious damage to a good crème brûlée."

*　　*　　*

Vince and Mr. Transport lounged in the straw chairs, resting their feet in the smooth currents of the ocean.

"This beats the cafeteria," Vince said.

"This beats damn near everything," Mr. Transport said. He took a long drink from the pink liquid in his clay cup. The punch was another specialty of the shop and a feature that made this slice of paradise even more enjoyable.

"Yeah, I'll give you that one," Vince agreed. "I do love the water. Makes me wish I was looking forward to the river trip more."

"What's wrong with the river trip? I've heard it's a highlight of the freshman year at Lander."

348

"There's going to be a lot of drinking," Vince said. "I'm still figuring out how to be part of that whole scene when I don't want to join in."

"Just be," Mr. Transport said. "Contrary to what after-school specials will tell you, people who are drinking don't really care all that much if you're not. It translates to more beer for them, anyway."

"Heh. I suppose that is a good point."

"Why the hang up, though? I mean, most kids your age like to experiment a little."

"Most kids my age haven't spent their whole lives out of control," Vince pointed out. "I'm a little worried that anything that messes with my brain chemistry will send me right back to where I was."

"That's nothing to worry about. We told you, there's no chemical compound that can change you back. You're a Super for life."

"Fear isn't often rational," Vince said.

Mr. Transport took another sip of his drink, mulling over Vince's words. He then extended the cup to his silver-haired charge.

"Fear isn't rational, but facing it can be," he said. "Try a sip."

"I'm . . . um, well I'm underage."

"Actually, in this part of the world, there is no legal drinking age, so no, you aren't," Mr. Transport said. "Aside from which, we're surrounded by a small population, and you've probably only got a little bit of energy stored up. I can easily teleport you somewhere deserted if you start blasting fire at the trees. There is literally no situation I can think of where it's safer for you to take a sip of alcohol."

"But why take the chance?"

"Because hopefully, you'll have a long life ahead of you, and in it, there will be tons of things that might take away control. I'm not saying to get shitfaced or become a drug addict, I'm just saying that I'd rather not see a kid like you spend his life always afraid that fun will automatically be punished by a return to a shittier point in life," Mr. Transport said.

Vince tentatively reached over and accepted the cup, then took a short sip. He handed it back to Mr. Transport, who took a much larger one.

"That was actually pretty good," Vince admitted.

"Yeah," Mr. Transport agreed. "Feeling like you're about to blast the shit out of something accidentally?"

"Not yet," Vince said, settling back in his seat. "I think we better relax by the ocean for a bit longer though, just in case."

"Good idea."

*   *   *

349

"Charles, do you mind if we borrow the limo for a bit, so I can drop my daughter off and say goodbye?" Mr. Vinders asked as they pulled up to the parking lot nearest Melbrook.

"Not at all," Mr. Adair said. "It will give me a chance to say goodnight to Alice as well. Swing back by when you are done."

"Of course," Mr. Vinders agreed. Mr. Adair, Alice, and Nick all departed from the limousine. It puttered off slowly across campus, aimed at a different housing area.

"So good to see you again, dear," Mr. Adair said, hugging Alice lightly.

"You, too, Daddy. Feel free to come visit again."

"I will keep it in mind," Mr. Adair said with a smile. "If it isn't too much trouble, may I ask the chance to speak privately to your boyfriend?"

"I really don't think you need to do that," Alice began.

"It is every father's right to put a touch of fear into his daughter's suitor," Mr. Adair said, turning toward Nick.

"It's fine, Alice," Nick assured her, flashing a confident and relaxed grin. "I'll be inside in a minute or two."

"Nick, you really don't need to—"

"Don't be silly," Nick said, cutting her off. "A gentleman covets the right to speak earnestly with his lady's father."

"Um . . . okay . . . I guess," Alice said. She walked slowly back to Melbrook. Both Nick and her father kept her in their peripheral vision until she was in the door, but neither took their focus off the other. It was only after the door had solidly shut behind her that words were at last spoken.

"You're not actually dating Alice," Mr. Adair said simply.

"You're going to slash the shit out of Mr. Vinders's company," Nick replied.

Mr. Adair raised an eyebrow. "What makes you say that?"

"You called first, you show your hand," Nick said.

"Fine," Mr. Adair agreed. "You're too smart for her; she was too comfortable when you touched her around her father for there to be any legitimate intimacy; you don't particularly care for her, and she was not nearly nervous enough. Shall I continue?"

"No," Nick said. "That was good. You're a smart man, and a good liar."

"That's how you knew I plan to gut the company?"

"Yes. Remove humanity, and it's a simple business decision. I'm sure you'll find a fancy way to word the contract, but it was a simple deduction to make. It's what I would have done," Nick said.

"That might be the first thing you've said all night that I believe," Mr. Adair said. "Your act did cheer my daughter, though, so I suppose I owe you some thanks."

"Consider the meal thanks enough," Nick said. "Are we done here?"

350

"Depends. Are you planning on chatting up the younger Vinders and letting her know about my business intentions?"

"Not even slightly," Nick said. "You played along with my ruse, I'll ignore yours. You were wrong about something, though."

"Do tell."

"I care enough about Alice to tell her father what a bastard he is for baiting and switching the poor girl with a visit like that."

"She loathes business dinners, and I needed her attendance in order to secure the meal," Mr. Adair said unapologetically.

"I didn't expect you to be sorry," Nick said. "Just felt you should know that you're an asshole."

"Nothing new, I assure you," Mr. Adair replied.

"Good. Now, we're done," Nick said. He began walking toward Melbrook. As soon as he opened the door, he saw Alice waiting, pacing along the floor.

"How was it?"

"Standard dad stuff," Nick said, slipping into his usual persona. "Touch my daughter wrong, and I'll have the FBI and the CIA erase you from existence. Nothing new."

"That's good at least. A little surprising from him, but good."

"Yeah. Now, if you don't mind, that heavy meal has me tuckered out. I need to get some sleep," Nick said.

"Oh yeah, no problem," Alice said, stepping out of his way. "But, I just wanted to say thanks."

"Don't worry about it," Nick said, waving her off. "You saved my life. It's the least I could do."

"I know, but . . . still."

"We're cool, Alice," Nick said gently. "Helping each other in rough spots is what friends are for."

Alice smiled. "I'm starting to realize that."

97

"Sounds like you did a real good thing," Gerry commented as he chomped into the greasy, cheese-soaked burger before him.

"Sure, it was a great thing. I showed one of the people I live with that there's more to me than the persona I've been rocking all year, I spent the evening with some truly boring people, and I managed to call one of the richest men on the planet an asshole," Nick summed up. He fiddled with his sunglasses, getting used to them once more. "It was smart choices all around."

"You called him an asshole while sticking up for his kid," Gerry pointed out. "There's thankfully few fathers in the world who can hold a grudge against that."

"He very well could be one of them," Nick said. "What's done is done, though. Alice's night was a lot better than what it would have been without me."

"I'm proud of you, Campbell," Gerry said sincerely.

"Glad to hear it, because I think we both know I didn't do all that for her," Nick said.

Gerry simply nodded his head. "So what else is going on this weekend?"

"Tomorrow . . . well, I guess today, now," Nick said, checking his watch. It was past two in the morning. "Anyway, today, they take the parents down to the underground levels and show them their kids' classrooms. There's a cute speech by the dean, and the opportunity to meet the coaches. For the less trusting of parents, I'm sure they can ask for progress reports as well."

Gerry wrinkled his nose. "Seems more like high school than college."

"Agreed, which is why we won't be attending. Honestly, I think they only do it because it's more palatable for a parent to actually see what their child is going through, than to just know they're being trained in some mysterious program. Giving them a weekend is the path of least annoyance for the school," Nick speculated.

"You're probably dead on with that one," Gerry agreed. "If we're skipping the function, what did you have planned?"

Nick shrugged. "Nothing too exciting. I thought we'd jump in my car, and I'd show you the town."

Gerry laughed. "How about we take mine, instead? I got a real nice one from the rental company."

"You trying to say something about my ride?"

"Not at all, kid, not at all. Did you end up going with the 'won it on a slot machine' lie?"

"Yup," Nick said.

"Why not just tell people you bought it? Tons of kids buy cars. It wouldn't have made you stand out," Gerry said.

Nick shook his head. "Too responsible. I'm trying to capture the image of a guy who is irresponsible and flies by the seat of his pants. Planning and saving for a car doesn't mesh as well as just cheating and winning it."

"Fair point, I suppose," Gerry agreed. "Still not sure why you insisted on a Bug, though."

"I can't win too much. If I'd brought back a Ferrari or something, people would have felt jealousy. Winning a Bug, though, that's a cute anecdote at best."

"I see where you're coming from, but it still makes me chuckle," Gerry said. "I mean, if I told the girls that Nicholas Campbell was driving around in a Bug, they'd bust a gut laughing."

"Which is why it will never leave Lander, right?" Nick asked.

Gerry gave a Nick a big smile. "I'm waiting to see your grades before I go making any promises."

*   *   *

Alice still couldn't sleep. She'd drifted off from time to time, but the rest was always shallow and the dreams too vivid. She had tried a glass of milk, a warm shower, and even counting sheep, yet sleep was still remaining elusive to her. The most troubling part was she knew exactly why: she couldn't sleep because of Nick.

Alice had grown up with her only social interactions taking place in the world of high society. She'd met with diplomats, entrepreneurs, and politicians, and had slowly learned to see through the lies in their smiles. They were all two-faced, and eventually, Alice was able to penetrate their disguises, noticing the small tics and habits that didn't go along with the person they were pretending to be. She'd thought herself quite good at it when she arrived at Lander, ready to classify and manipulate everyone in sight. She hadn't been prepared for what greeted her, though—an entire mass of people her age who didn't bother with such pretense. Most of whom couldn't, actually. It seemed like people were more occupied with finding out who they were, than in deciding who they wanted everyone to see them as.

Maybe that was why she had missed it; she'd eventually stopped looking after weeks of seeing no double faces. No, that wasn't it. Blaming her lax observations didn't give enough credit where it was due. Sure, she'd stopped trying to see through people, but even if she'd been on top of her game all the time, Alice was certain Nick still would have slipped by her.

He'd always been the same guy. Smarting off, acting up, making stupid comments and organizing waste-of-time events. Even the stupid glasses were just him wanting to be noticed. Yet tonight, he'd taken them off and effortlessly been someone else. Someone charming, smart, sophisticated, and amiable. There had been no trace of the old Nick, from the way he moved to something as simple as opening a car door. Everything he did had suited this new persona of his. Had she met him for the first time

353

tonight, she would have never imagined the version she'd known for the last several months could exist.

So now, Alice was lying in her bed, staring up at the ceiling, unable to find sleep. Was she that much worse at seeing through people than she thought, or was Nick that much better than she was? Either way, it was curious. Under any other circumstance, she would have banged on Mary's door to compare notes and try and put things together. It didn't feel quite right, though, not when he had shown Alice this part of himself in order to help her. She wouldn't go around stirring up trouble for him in response to his kindness. She would keep her curiosity and observations to herself.

One thing was certain, though: Alice was definitely paying attention again.

98

"Thank you again for taking the time out of your lives to come and visit us here at Lander University," Dean Blaine said, circling the group back to the lifts, where they had entered an hour and a half ago. "This concludes our tour of the facility, and I hope you all now have a greater understanding and appreciation for the education being taught to your children."

The tour had gone off pretty well; they almost always did. The gyms were closed, no classes were held, and every non-freshmen student had their ability to use the lifts disconnected for two hours when the parents were wandering around. It was always officially billed as "technical difficulties." The older students, however, had long ago reached the obvious conclusion: nobody wanted a problem to occur when outsiders were around.

This crop had been well-behaved, and Dean Blaine was letting out mental sighs of relief that he would soon be passing the buck to George and Persephone.

"Now, we've reserved a dining hall just for you folks today, where you can eat with Coach George and Coach Persephone," Dean Blaine explained. "You can talk with them about your children, or just relax and meet the other parents. The whole area will be secure, so there's no need to worry about spilling the beans on any student's secret identity. Though I would remind you that outside of there and here, utilizing the utmost discretion is advised."

The parents nodded appreciatively and began filing toward the elevators. As they moved past, Dean Blaine made an effort to see which group of adults was with which student. A dean should be able to recognize his charges' families, after all.

It was clear not all of the students had come, though more had turned out than usual. Dean Blaine noticed Shane DeSoto walking to the lifts with his older sister and their parents, as well as an older gentleman. There was something slightly familiar about the older man, but Dean Blaine couldn't place it before he was out of sight. It seemed Roy Daniels was here with his mother, a dowdy woman with a persistent smile. Looking at her, it was hard to believe she'd raised a child as rambunctious as Roy, though it explained quite a bit about Hershel. Sasha Foster had both parents with her: a middle-aged couple that had been particularly wide-eyed during the tour.

"Blaine," said a soft, familiar voice next to him, stealing him from his thoughts.

"Miriam," Dean Blaine said warmly. "I was hoping you'd stop to chat before you left." He clasped the woman's hand briefly and squeezed, only for a moment.

Miriam was middle-aged and holding up well under her years. She had shoulder-length, blonde hair and tan skin from a life spent living near the ocean.

"Of course," she said, returning the smile Dean Blaine hadn't realized he was giving. "I know we can talk to the coaches, but I wanted to speak with you directly and see how things were going."

Dean Blaine glanced at the platforms carrying parents and students back to the surface. It was slowly thinning the crowd. There were clearly several trips left, though.

"I'd love to, Miriam. This is probably not the best place, though. Would you like to join me in my office?"

"That would be fine. Thank you, Blaine."

"Will he be all right?" Dean Blaine asked.

"Certainly. I'll let him know I'll be meeting him a bit later for lunch," Miriam assured the dean.

"Excellent. Well then, let us away," Dean Blaine told her.

The trip was short. Dean Blaine's office was relatively close to the lifts, just in case he needed to get out in a hurry. That feature seemed to smack more of the "abandon ship" mentality than Blaine preferred, but he hadn't been around when they designed the place, and it would be an enormous hassle to fix now.

They entered the office door and Dean Blaine poured them both a drink. He already knew how Miriam took her scotch, so he didn't bother asking. Many things about people might change as the years wear on, but that feature seemed to remain constant.

"Thank you," Miriam said, accepting the glass. She glanced inside. "Halfway full with three cubes. Impressive."

"The important things tend to stick in my head," Dean Blaine said as he settled into his high-backed leather chair. "Tell me how you've been."

"As good as can be expected," she said. "I went back to school and started my nursing degree a few months back. Now that I'm alone in the house, I'm thinking about downgrading to a condo. I haven't told my son yet. I'm not sure how he'd take his childhood home being swept out from under him."

Dean Blaine smirked. "You managed to steer us on topic remarkably quickly. Okay, let's talk about your son." He reached into his desk drawer and rummaged around briefly. Within a few minutes, he extracted a manila envelope. Dean Blaine set it on the table and skimmed the contents. He already knew most of them off the top of his head.

"Chad Taylor," Dean Blaine said, reading off the front page. "Currently ranked top of his class in combat. Tested exceptionally well during the first semester finals. Expected to easily stay at the top of the class when the next trials are held at year's end. As for above ground, he's pulling straight A's. All in all, he's a model student."

"I knew all of that, Blaine," Miriam said. "I was more talking about how he's adjusting to being here. You know, seeing his father's alma mater, walking the same halls, taking the same classes. I wasn't sure how he'd acclimate."

"I think he's doing fine," Dean Blaine assured her.

"Define 'doing fine' for me, please. Does he have any friends?"

"Certainly. He spends most of his time with Shane DeSoto and Michael Clark," Dean Blaine said.

"I see. And what are the ranks of these boys?" Miriam asked.

"Um . . . well, two and three, respectively."

"So he has training partners," Miriam assessed with a sigh. "I suppose asking about a girlfriend is out of the question, then."

"To my knowledge, he hasn't become intimate with any of the female students yet," Dean Blaine admitted.

"How about male? I'll take what I can get here."

"Miriam . . ."

"Oh, I know, I know," she said. "It's just frustrating. He's such a good boy, yet all he does is think about training and getting stronger and being like his dad. You know he didn't apply to any other schools? Only Lander."

"We do have a very prestigious reputation."

"Come on, Blaine, Lander is great, but the other four schools give out Hero Certifications just as valid as yours. Everyone hedges their bets."

"Perhaps Chad simply knew he would be able to take his pick," Dean Blaine suggested.

Miriam shook her head. "No, it was because he wanted to go to the same place. If you'd turned him down, he would have just kept applying, year after year until you let him in. He is stubborn as a drunken mule."

"I suppose that makes his path toward emulating his father at least a little bit shorter, then," Dean Blaine said.

Miriam let out a short, barking laugh. "You may have a point at that." She set her glass down and glanced at her watch. "I really should be getting to that lunch now."

"Of course. I've got some things to do as well," Dean Blaine said, shuffling papers that were previously arranged quite correctly.

"I appreciate you humoring me checking up on him," Miriam Taylor said, rising from her seat. "I just worry. You know how it is."

"Indeed I do," Dean Blaine agreed.

"I hope to see you again before I leave. If not, at least you'll be coming around for Easter."

"About that," Dean Blaine said haltingly. "Now that I'm an authority figure over your son, I'm not sure if that's such a good idea."

"Nonsense," Miriam said. "You got off the winter holidays with that excuse, and I've been kicking myself for letting you ever since. You'll come to Easter at our house in a few months, and you'll bring your famous chocolate pies. Not one argument about it."

357

Dean Blaine contemplated protesting, then thought better of it. "You win as usual, Miriam. Have fun at lunch."

Miriam wrinkled her nose. "Blaine, have you forgotten I went to Lander, too? I know what to expect from the food."

99

"This is certainly . . . colorful cuisine they serve," Mrs. Daniels said, working her way through the plate. "Do you happen to know if anyone horribly offended the cooks in some way?"

"Nope, that's just dorm food," Roy said. "We don't have to eat here, though. We can go anywhere you want."

"Don't be silly, this is fine," Mrs. Daniels said. "Besides, I want to talk to your coach and see how things are going."

"There's no need, they're going great."

"Then you must be anxious to hear him tell me that himself," Mrs. Daniels said knowingly. "It looks like the crowd is thinning out. You stay here while I go speak with him."

"Yes, ma'am," Roy said. He stayed put as his mother got up and stood in line with the other parents. His stomach twisted a bit. Yeah, he'd been able to keep up with the poundings Chad had been delivering for the past few weeks, but he still hadn't gotten a hit off yet. That had to reflect badly on his overall performance. Not to mention the fact that he'd only participated in one challenge battle last semester and had gotten his ass kicked. Sure, his grades had been all A's; but that had been all Hershel's doing. Much as he would deny it if anyone asked, Roy wanted to make his mother proud, too. Now, he had to trust in a progress report that would be delivered by Coach George of all people: the man who seemed least impressed by Roy's substantial abilities out of anyone. This was going to be a bad day.

*   *   *

"Mrs. Daniels," Coach George greeted, shaking her hand carefully. "Pleasure to meet you."

"You too, Mr. George, but how did you know who I was?"

"Just George is fine, and I make it a point to know the names and faces of all of my students' parents," Coach George explained. "In case one of them tries to jump me."

"That seems a bit paranoid," Mrs. Daniels said.

"It would be paranoid if I was doing it before any such situation had occurred. After that, it's called learning," Coach George countered.

"I . . . see. At any rate, if you know who I am, then you know who I'm asking about. How is Roy doing in class?"

"How can I put this?" Coach George said, pressing his thumb to his jaw as he pondered. "Your son is arrogant, pig-headed, vastly overestimates his abilities, and spends too much time chasing tail instead of training. I've been expecting him to wash out since the first week, and at the beginning of this semester, I even put him up against the strongest kid in the class to see if he would flush down the drain once and for all."

"I'm not sure how to—" Mrs. Daniels began. Coach George cut her off with a quick raise of his finger.

"*But*, he is also incredibly resilient, unrelentingly determined, and has shown a tremendous amount of humility in accepting lessons from those who have proven themselves his better. When I challenged the combat class to take me on, he was the first one to step up, and that takes some courage. He's been getting the stuffing knocked out of him five days a week since the spring semester began and every day, he shows up asking for more, and he does it because he understands that each day makes him a little bit better."

"So what are you trying to say here?" Mrs. Daniels asked.

"I'm saying your boy has plenty of flaws, and very well might not make it all the way to being a Hero because of them. He also has steel in his spine, fire in his gut, and balls the size of watermelons. Those might take him to the top. Honestly, it's just like the rest of this program: it will depend on the work he puts in," Coach George explained.

"Thank you, George," Mrs. Daniels said. "That was enlightening."

"Glad to keep you in the loop," Coach George said with a smile.

"It was appreciated," Mrs. Daniels said, turning to leave. "Have a nice day. I hope none of the parents jump you."

"That will be seen," Coach George said. "Not everyone got such kind reviews of their kids as you."

*   *   *

Roy's nervous waiting came to an end as he saw his mother leave Coach George's side. He clamored to his feet as she walked back over.

"What'd he say?" Roy asked, poorly hiding the nerves in his voice.

"About what I expected," Mrs. Daniels replied. "That you're good, but if you want to be the best, you still have a long road ahead of you. Although, he said it in an exceptionally vulgar way."

"Yeah. That's Coach George," Roy said.

"He also mentioned you seemed to be dating a lot of nice young girls. Do I get to meet any of them today?"

Roy (yes, Roy Daniels) blushed. "Nah, Mom, it's nothing like that. I just have a lot of female friends."

"Mmmhmm. If that's what you want to go with . . ." Mrs. Daniels said.

"It really is."

". . . then I suppose we can skip over it for now. Besides, I think we're done here. Now, how about you show me the town?"

Roy let a big grin break across his face. "It would be my pleasure."

100

"That bad, huh?" Nick asked.

"Yeah. I spilled my tea, accidently tripped the waiter, and briefly set the table on fire when I knocked over the centerpiece candle," Vince said. "So, her family is not all that fond of me."

"I never thought of you as all that klutzy," Nick said.

Vince shrugged. "I'm not normally, but I was so nervous about meeting my girlfriend's parents for the first time, I just got flustered."

Nick and Vince sat in the common room, the Sunday afternoon light shining on them through the windows. All the parents but Hershel's had departed; he was saying goodbye to her in the parking lot currently. Alice was catching up on homework in her room, and Mary sat in a chair nearby, reading.

"You're still a nice guy, though," Nick pointed out. "I'm sure her parents were just glad she was spending time with a quality fellow."

"They kept mentioning a nice young Super her uncle knew with coordination and exceptional powers. They were adamant she meet up with him for coffee next time she is in town."

"Wow, they are not fans of fumbling," Nick said.

"Yeah. Apparently, they're all about powerful Supers good enough to breed with their daughter. Weird thing, though, as bad as last night went, Sasha was exceptionally affectionate when we kissed goodnight later on," Vince said.

"You really are clueless, buddy. Think real hard about why a girl with dyed-pink hair might actually be happy to find out the guy she's with was not well-liked by her parents. When you come up with a theory, get back to me," Nick instructed him.

"I don't see why the hair is important, but okay," Vince agreed.

The sound of the front door opening interrupted them as Hershel walked in.

"See your mom off?" Vince asked.

"Yup," Hershel confirmed. "It was nice to see her, but it's sort of weird having her around in this environment."

"Tell me about it," Nick agreed. "Gerry's a good guy, but he was all sorts of cramping my style. Didn't want to hit strip clubs or cock fights or anything."

"The visits all passed without any terrible incidents or blown secret identities, though, so I think we can chalk this weekend up as a win," Hershel said.

"I'd wait to hear Vince's story about dinner with Sasha's parents before I made that statement," Nick said.

"Bad?" Hershel asked.

"I'm seventy percent sure they tried to sneak out and ditch me when I went to the bathroom," Vince said.

361

"That's pretty bad," Hershel surmised.

"What about you? Roy didn't get your mom into a biker brawl or tossed in jail or something?" Nick asked.

Hershel laughed. "Roy? Roy loves our mother. They spent the afternoon touring little niche shops downtown. He's a model son when she's around."

"Huh, and there you go," Nick said. "Well fellows, we only have a little bit of weekend left. Anyone up for video games in the boys' lounge?"

"Normally, I'd say no, but with everyone gone, I was able to catch up on my all homework already, so why not?" Vince agreed.

"Sweet. Hershel?"

"I'll join up with you guys in a few minutes," Hershel said. "I have to take care of something really quick."

"Cool deal," Nick said, pulling himself from the couch. He and Vince headed into the boys' area, the steel door locking firmly shut behind them.

Hershel took a deep breath. He wasn't good at these sorts of things; that is to say, brave things. He preferred to let Roy handle that. Hershel was the brain and the heart, Roy was the brawn and the guts. It wasn't a perfect arrangement, but it had sufficed for many years. There was a flaw in that system, though. It didn't account for when Hershel needed bravery for something only he could do. Admittedly, such a scenario hadn't really come up before now.

Personally, Hershel blamed his mother. She'd put the thought in his head, and it had stewed about all weekend. By the time he'd kissed her cheek goodbye, he had come to the undeniable realization that she was right. Admitting that was unfortunate, because it demanded action. He had to make a choice, and even if he did nothing, he now knew that was a choice in itself. Hershel no longer had the convenience of self-deception. The only question left was if he had enough courage of his own to take the risk. Well, to be fair, that wasn't the *only* question left.

"Mary?" Hershel said shakily, walking over to the chair where she was sitting.

"Yes?" She looked up at him and set the book on her lap.

"I was wondering if you would like to go out sometime, to do something with me if you wanted."

Mary arched an eyebrow. "Could you elaborate?"

Hershel's stomach began gurgling. He sent it a mental note that it could complain and vomit in stress all in wanted in five minutes, but for now, it should please shut the fuck up.

"I want to take you on a date." Hershel's eyes widened slightly: that was more straightforward than he'd been shooting for. Still, it was out there now.

A slow smile crept across Mary's face. "I'd like that. What did you have in mind?"

362

"Um, just dinner on Friday. Off campus, of course. Around seven?"

"Works for me," Mary said, straining to keep her own voice even and calm. "It's a date."

"Awesome," Hershel said. "I mean, cool. It'll be fun. Yeah . . . I'm going to go play video games with Nick and Vince now. But I'll see you on Friday."

"We live in the same dorm. I'll see you before then," Mary pointed out. "I get what you mean, though. See you then."

"Right," Hershel said. He then, in an act of wisdom well beyond his years, immediately retreated to the boys' lounge before he could say anything stupid and mess things up.

For her own part, Mary waited until she was sure Hershel was staying behind in the other room before bolting out of her chair and dashing into the girl's side, banging on Alice's door.

Interestingly enough, both sides had similar reactions to the news:

"About freaking time."

101.

"So you finally did it," Nick said, slapping Hershel on the back. "What gave you the kick in the pants?"

"Something my mom said, actually," Hershel admitted.

"Make me grandbabies or don't bother coming home?" Nick asked.

"A touch more tactful than that. She just pointed out that it wasn't going to get easier at this point, and the longer I waited, the worse my chances got."

"Good for you," Vince said. "I bet you two have a great time. What are you planning?"

"Just dinner," Hershel said. "Someplace kind of nice, probably."

"Classic start," Nick said. "Then what?"

"I don't know . . . digesting?"

"Right. Let me get this straight. You've been trying to ask this girl out for over six months, you finally got up the courage and she agreed to be your date for an evening, and you don't plan to do anything besides go to dinner and come back?" Nick asked.

"It sounds really lame when you say it."

"I can't imagine why," Nick said, shaking his head. "Hershel, my boy, I don't know a lot of things about women. I know they like chocolate, shoes, and movies that induce crying. I know they get offended if you ask if their behavior is due to a regular monthly occurrence. I know that some of them get a little violent if you try to give them an innocent nickname."

"Sugartits isn't what I'd call innocent," Vince interjected.

"Stay on subject, Silver. My point is that I know precious few things, but one of those is that a woman expects a little woo to be pitched on a first date," Nick said. "Assuming you want there to be a second one."

"I would very much like there to be a second one," Hershel said.

"Then we better get brainstorming, because a girl like Mary is going to take more than a chicken parmesan and some kind words to win over," Nick said.

*   *   *

"So where do you think he'll take you?"

"I'm not sure. Someplace nice, I'm sure, but hopefully not too fancy. I'm a simple girl, and I think Hershel knows that," Mary said.

Alice nodded her head in agreement. "He seems to be slightly less thick-headed than the other men we're surrounded by."

Mary laughed. "They might surprise you. Some of them are actually quite sharp."

"I'm sure," Alice said. Before, she would have brushed off the comment as Mary being good-natured. Now, though, she once again found herself thinking about

364

Nick's little transformation. Even if he could lie that well, there was no way he could keep it from Mary's telepathy. She had to have some inkling of what was going on in the head behind those sunglasses. Sadly, this wasn't the time to ask her about it. Right now was about Mary . . . and Hershel, to a similar extent.

"Any clues on where he'll take you after dinner?" Alice asked.

Mary blinked. "After?"

"Yeah. I mean, he asked you on a date. You don't think he's planning on just driving to get food, then coming back and saying bye do you?"

"Sort of. Yeah," Mary admitted.

"Ah. Dates usually consist of more than just food. At least first ones do, anyway. It's the guy's chance to really show you how awesome he is, so they love doing it up big," Alice explained.

"I see. I suppose that doesn't seem so bad," Mary said. "You know a lot about dates."

"Only second-hand. The few times I ever 'went out' with a guy were formal dinners where my dad wanted me to charm the son of some CEO or royalty," Alice said. "They were pre-arranged events with chaperones, and the guys were always boring as hell."

"That bites," Mary said.

"It did, but who cares? Those days are long since past. Now, let's focus on you, little missy. Have you picked out an outfit yet?"

"I was thinking . . . the peach-colored dress?" Mary ventured very tentatively.

"Hmm. You know, that would work nicely," Alice said.

Mary let out a sigh of relief.

". . . as a start," Alice continued.

"A start?"

"Sure. It's a base layer. Dressing up is all about picking a base, then building tasteful accessorization on top of it," Alice explained. "Don't worry. We've got nearly a week to play around with all kinds of combinations. By the time Friday night gets here, we'll have gone through every conceivable variety of outfit and picked the absolute best one."

"Oh, joy."

*　　　*　　　*

"We've ruled out comedy clubs, movies, miniature golf, and strip clubs, though the last was under extreme protest," Vince surmised.

"It's a touch of daring and adventure!" Nick proclaimed. "Plus, it puts the sex issue right on the table. It's perfect!"

"It's done, Nick, let it go," Vince said. "We're on to new suggestions now."

"I'm running dry," Hershel said. "You and Sasha have been together for a while now, what kind of first date did you take her on?"

"I just did dinner," Vince said. "This whole woo-pitching thing is news to me, too."

"Wait, you did just dinner?" Hershel turned to Nick. "If he got away with it, why can't I?"

"Several reasons," Nick said. "For one, the whole lovably clueless thing works for Vince."

"I'm not clueless," Vince protested.

"Whatever you say, Cupcake. You don't have that type of charm. You're a smart, good-hearted guy. That means you're expected to do your research and put out some real effort," Nick said.

"I guess I can see that," Hershel agreed.

"Secondly, ask yourself something. This is your first date with a girl you really like. Do you want to 'get away' with half-assing it, or do you want to leave her speechless?"

"Okay, okay. Point taken. I have to do more than just dinner. But we still haven't answered the question of what," Hershel said.

"I keep telling you guys, there is a gentleman's club south of town with exceptionally reasonable steak prices on Friday nights."

"Still no on that one."

"I think you have to ask yourself less of what you'd like to do, and more of what Mary would enjoy," Vince said. "It's about impressing her, so it needs to be something she'd have fun doing."

"Carnival?" Hershel ventured.

"That would actually work . . . if there were any going on right now," Nick said.

"Damn. This is a lot harder than I thought it would be. Roy always made dating seem effortless," Hershel said.

"That's because Roy didn't care, so he didn't put in effort," Nick pointed out. "That's another type of charm, though, once again, a type you don't have."

"Relax, Hershel, you've got most of a week 'til Friday. I'm sure you'll think of something," Vince assured him.

"And if you don't, there's always steak and tits," Nick tossed out. "Just saying."

102

Mary returned home from class on Tuesday to find Mr. Numbers setting up the chess board in the common room.

"Is it Saturday already?" Mary asked.

Mr. Numbers shook his head. "We missed our weekend game. I thought we might play today, instead."

Mary paused for a moment, then walked over and set down her bag. "Why not?"

Mary made the opening move, followed by Mr. Numbers. In the time they had been playing, she'd been slowly growing better. She was lasting a move or two longer each game so far, though Mr. Numbers anticipated her progress would reach a plateau within another five games.

"So, what's on your mind?" Mary asked as she shifted her knight's position.

"Just the game."

"Now, I think we both know that's a lie," Mary said.

"Listening in?"

"Not during our games, no. But I've heard you long enough to know you're a creature of habit, and you'd rather miss a game than reschedule it," Mary said.

"True," Mr. Numbers said. "Mr. Transport and I have been entertaining the idea of another project, one that would require the assistance of you and Nick."

"I should warn you, I'm still putting extra blankets on my bed and drinking my tea hot as symptoms from the last 'project' you two hatched."

"It's nothing like that," Mr. Numbers assured her. "This one would be both harmless in nature and universally beneficial."

"I'm sure."

"Are you willing to hear me out?"

"Yes," Mary said. "If for no other reason than I'd rather be forewarned and forearmed."

Mr. Numbers carefully ran through the plan Mr. Transport had presented him some days before. He was careful to include every detail he had currently determined and to be absolutely truthful. Even if Mary really wasn't listening in right now, that didn't mean she wouldn't be checking in on him in time to come.

"I like it," Mary said. "And I'm on board for it. I can't speak for Nick, though."

"I daresay no one could claim such an ability," Mr. Numbers remarked.

"Maybe, maybe not. Either way, you'll need him," Mary said.

"I was, unfortunately, certain you would say that."

"You're good at what you do. Anything else I should know?" Mary asked.

"Indeed. Checkmate," Mr. Numbers said, moving his bishop and springing the trap he'd laid.

Mary blinked. "Did you distract me with this just to beat me?"

"Don't be silly," Mr. Numbers said. "It was a necessary conversation. And I don't need cheap ploys to beat you."

"Yet," Mary said.

Mr. Numbers looked down at the small, unassuming girl and the confident look in her eyes. His brain buzzed, assessing the multiple factors he'd gleaned about her. Her ambition, her determination, her aptitude, and her focus.

"Yet," Mr. Numbers agreed, sweeping up the board and heading into his room.

* * *

Nick was relaxing in the common room later that night, flipping through television stations, when a flash of blonde hair and pink dress dropped into the seat next to him.

Nick raised an eyebrow. "Can I help you?"

"What?" Alice said. "Can't a girl sit down and watch some TV with her friend?"

"That depends," Nick said. "Is there a reason she needs to do it right next to him, as opposed to one of the many other scenic locations?" He gestured at the empty common room and the abundance of seats contained within it.

"Oh no, I think proximity is very important. It fosters deep, intellectual conversations. Conversations about new developments, and what those new developments might be doing this weekend," Alice said.

"You want to know where Hershel is taking Mary on Friday."

"See, I always told people how smart you were," Alice said.

"Liar."

"Admitted," Alice said. "But I still want to know, so spill it."

Nick laughed. "And why would I betray the secrecy of my dear friend for the curiosity of a girl who repeatedly hits me?"

"Well," Alice said, leaning forward slightly. "Maybe because a gesture of that sort would make her feel better disposed toward you. Maybe she'd show you a softer, kinder side."

"Yeah, not buying it."

"Fine. Then how about maybe because she's right next to you with her hand in punching range of your crotch?"

"Now, see, that, that I believe," Nick said, shifting his legs slightly to provide cover. "Even if I wanted to tell you though, I can't. As of when I last checked, Hershel doesn't even know what he's going to do with Mary after dinner."

"That sucks," Alice said. "He better think of something soon. Mary's looking forward to a good night out."

368

"I'm sure our little nerd boy will come through in the clutch," Nick assured her. "He can be tenacious when the mood strikes him. Plus, Vince and I offered up a veritable plethora of helpful suggestions."

"Please. You probably suggested something moronic, like taking her to a strip club."

"I would never!" Nick cried in a hurt tone. "I can't believe you think so little of me."

"Uh huh. Whatever you say, stud. Let me know if he tells you anything," Alice said, getting off the couch.

"No promises, but if it's exceptionally interesting, I might seek you out," Nick said.

"That's probably as good as I'm getting out of you," Alice sighed. "I'm going to go work on some chemistry. Night, Nick."

"Night, Alice," Nick said, giving her a perfunctory wave. Once the door was closed, though, worry descended on his face. She'd been much more comfortable and familiar around him than normal. The whole mock-flirting thing had demonstrated that amply well. Such an attitude could be problematic. The last thing he needed was her to grow so at ease around him their friendship developed into romance. No, it was best to nip this in the bud right away.

Nick flipped out his cell phone and selected a number from its directory. That was the good thing about catching these situations early, they could often be resolved in a single phone call.

103

The concrete crunched under the forceful impact of Roy's substantial form crashing against it.

"Getting tired?" Roy croaked from his prone position on the ground. "That last one lacked your usual flair."

"Did it?" Chad asked. "I'll be sure to make up the difference on this one."

"I appreciate it," Roy said, pulling himself vertical. "I'm not here for the B course, after all."

Chad did something then that Roy hadn't seen from him so far, something that, to his knowledge, no one had witnessed:

Chad laughed.

"You know, for all of your flaws, you've got tenacity," Chad said, chuckling to himself. "It's refreshing, even after all these weeks. I'd started thinking there was no one who could take my strength and keep coming."

"And all this from the guy who wasn't even worthy to fight you," Roy said, smiling as he tried to get his feet steady.

"Indeed," Chad said. "It almost makes me wish you were on my level. I think fighting someone with your resolve at a higher talent level would benefit me greatly."

"Then you take this as a Roy Daniels promise: when I'm stronger than you, I'll still be your sparring partner."

"I appreciate the intent," Chad said, taking a stance as he prepared to bring Roy down again. "You do know that you'll never be better than I am, though, don't you?"

"I know that you think that," Roy said. He charged forward, left arm swinging around at Chad's head. Chad easily stepped to the side, caught Roy's arm, and wrenched it around to his back.

"With moves like that, you'll be lucky to even land a blow on me before the year's end," Chad said. He expected Roy to make another witty comment before Chad swept his legs out from under him and deposited him on the ground. What met his ears was something entirely different.

"AAAAAAAAAAAAH!" Roy released a gut-wrenching scream, one that tore at his very vocal chords. Chad was taken by surprise. He was behind Roy, pulling Roy's left arm to his back against Roy's considerable struggling, ready to send him sprawling. It should have hurt him, yes, but not nearly enough for a reaction like that. Fleetingly, Chad wondered if his continuous beatings had somehow left lasting nerve damage that the healers hadn't gotten. It was only a half second of doubt and confusion, yet almost instantly, Chad realized what it had cost him.

The fingers of Roy's right hand wrapped around Chad's left bicep. Chad felt the arm in his grip dangle weightlessly, his hold no longer effective as Roy turned around to face him.

"You . . . ripped your entire left arm out of its socket?"

"And screamed loud enough to distract you while I did it," Roy said. "See, for guys with our kind of strength, it's hard to tell the difference between regular struggling and bone-shattering effort. It all feels the same weighed against our power."

He was right. Chad had felt him bucking against his grip, but Chad had assumed it was merely his usual, boisterous escape attempts.

"A good point," Chad said. "Now what, though? Your left arm is useless, and you know I'll break that grip you have on me in no time. You still can't win."

"Newsflash, Blondie," Roy said, gritting his teeth through the pain that his left arm was broadcasting. "I'm not trying to win." In one motion, Roy jerked Chad forward, digging his hand deep into the arm and pulling forward with all his weight. Chad braced himself for a throw, reaching out for Roy's shoulder to reverse it before he was airborne. That was to his detriment, because too late, he realized the meaning of Roy's words.

"Dodge, fucker," Roy said, slamming his head directly into Chad's temple. The world dissolved into static and Chad's head swam in pain. He wasn't so far gone that he forgot his years of experience, though, and by the time his vision cleared, he had placed Roy back onto the concrete with considerable force.

"You lose, yet again," Chad said, his vision clearing to reveal a badly-battered Roy coughing up blood from the ground.

"Yeah, I do," Roy said, his voice ragged. "But I hit you."

Chad felt a soft trickle of blood run down his cheek. He sealed the cut on the side of his head immediately, but there was no denying the damage that had been dealt.

"You tore your arm out of its socket and sacrificed every advantage in our confrontation just to land one blow?"

"Damn right," Roy said, pushing himself up with his right arm. It took him a moment to get standing, but he made it eventually. He faced Chad once more, right arm pulled into a fighting position, left arm dangling uselessly at his side.

"That was an insane gamble," Chad remarked.

"It wasn't just some gamble. I've paid attention to your favorite moves in response to how I come at you. I've watched your style all these weeks, and I knew if I ran at you dumbly, you'd put me in a lock before dropping me. I had a feeling you'd defend against a throw over a headbutt, too."

"What made you assume that?"

"Because you fight with polish and tactics, and you always go for the win. People like you defend like the other guy has the same thing in mind. It would never occur to you that I'd be going for a headbutt instead of trying to toss you out of the circle and win," Roy explained.

"Because it's ludicrous," Chad pointed out.

It was Roy's turn to laugh. "Yeah, yeah it is. But it worked."

Chad shook his head. "I suppose it did. So, you finally hit me, Roy. Now what?"

"Now, I go for two," Roy said, flexing his right hand and cracking the knuckles.

One minute ago, Chad would have dismissed such a notion as sheer foolishness. Now, he merely nodded and took his own stance. Roy Daniels was lacking in training, refinement, and overall skill, but he had determination in spades. Chad knew firsthand how dangerous that particular quality could be. He wouldn't be underestimating his opponent again.

"Whenever you're ready," Chad said.

104

"How do I look?" Hershel asked.

Nick made a twirling motion with his hand, which Hershel obliged by slowly spinning around in place. He was wearing a hunter green, button-down shirt, khaki pants and loafers. It wasn't the most fashionable outfit possible, but for a guy who wore shirts with dice on them, it was one hell of a step up.

"You look great," Vince assured him.

"Almost perfect," Nick agreed. He stepped forward and slightly adjusted the angle at which Hershel's shirt was tucked in. Neither Hershel nor Vince could see any difference when Nick stepped back; however, he seemed quite pleased with himself. "And there we go. You're ready for a night on the town, you ladykiller."

"Heaven deliver us from such nicknames," Vince said. "Let's go over the list again. You have your wallet? Your cell phone? Nick's keys?"

"Check, check, and check," Hershel confirmed. "And thanks again for the loan."

Nick shrugged. "I can't let you take out a girl like Mary on Roy's motorcycle. She deserves more class than that."

"Agreed," Hershel said.

"Just be safe with my car. I don't fancy going back to walking my happy ass everywhere."

"Will do."

"So, did you ever think of a good place to take Mary after dinner?" Vince asked.

"Sort of," Hershel said. "I have no idea if she'll like it. It's all I could think of, though, so I guess it has to work."

"Any hints on what the brave act of desperation is?" Nick asked.

Hershel shook his head. "Nothing personal, but I want it to be a surprise. Mary doesn't read my thoughts, but she hasn't made any such claim about you guys."

"A fair point," Vince said. "And I think that's everything. Are you ready to pick up your date?"

"Dear God, no," Hershel said, clasping his hands to keep them from trembling. "But let's go ahead, anyway."

"Atta boy," Nick said, throwing his arm around Hershel's shoulders as they left the boys' lounge and entered the common room. "By the way," he whispered, "I left a box of condoms in the glove box. Just tossing it out there if you need to know."

"What happened to treating a classy lady right?" Hershel whispered back.

"Hey, I'm not making judgments or assumptions. I'm merely of the mind that it's better to be safe than sorry."

"Thanks, Nick. I think."

With that, they were in the common room, walking in on the sight of Alice standing in a very guard-like way by the girls' side. She examined Hershel critically, her expert eyes assessing his ensemble and demeanor. Whatever test was being performed in that blonde head evidently culminated in Hershel passing, because she knocked twice on the steel door next to her and said, "He's here."

A moment later, the door swung open and revealed a girl none of the boys could have immediately placed, if not for process of basic deduction. Gone was the wild-haired girl who often wore outfits consisting of capris and combat boots. In her place was a petite young lady wearing a peach dress with her hair styled carefully. Her face was lightly dusted with makeup, gently accentuating the features her tussled locks often hid. She was a little bit taller, thanks in no small part to wearing heels for once, and the smile on her face was absolutely entrancing.

"Hi," she said, fidgeting slightly as she stepped into the room.

"Hi," Hershel echoed, his tone saturated in the same sense of sheer wonder that the rest of him was feeling. "You look really nice." The boy had a talent at understatements.

"You, too," Mary said. They continued looking at each other awkwardly for a few moments more, though it in no way compared to the awkwardness the other three felt at standing around observing this haphazard attempt at romance. Eventually, something in Hershel's head snapped into place, and he extended his arm.

"Shall we head out?"

"Sounds great," Mary said, taking his arm. The other two boys would have had to stoop slightly to link arms with Mary, but for once, Hershel's vertical disparity was working in his favor. The well-dressed couple walked out the door, though it was a slightly more complicated task than normal since they were now linked together.

"That was just plain adorable," Alice said once they'd left the room.

"I feel like I just watched a pair of kittens wrestling playfully," Nick said. "I'm not sure I like this warm feeling creeping up inside."

Alice swatted his arm half-heartedly. "You know you're just as happy as we are that they're finally going out."

"He talks a tough game, but he ran Hershel through the ringer getting his outfit right," Vince said.

Had Mary been there, she would have slammed Vince into the ceiling and proceeded to detail all the different fashion combinations Alice had forced upon her during the last five days, showing no mercy until he had a whole new appreciation for what "going through the ringer" was really like. Since she was otherwise happily occupied, the comment went unpunished.

"You got me, I'm a big ole softy," Nick said.

"I don't know about that. But I'll give you points for loaning your car to Hershel," Alice admitted.

"Why not? He's a careful guy, and it's not like I'll be using it tonight, anyway. My date is driving. Oh, that reminds me, I need to go change before she gets here," Nick said, glancing at his watch and dashing off into the boys' lounge once more.

"Ugh, that is so like him," Alice said. "He does one nice thing, but he puts off getting himself ready and now, some girl will have to . . . wait—HIS WHAT?"

"His date," Vince replied helpfully. "Didn't he tell you? I guess Hershel's bold move finally put the right spring in his step."

"Right. Just so we're clear here, this is Nick we're talking about, right? *Nick* has a date?"

"He sure does," Vince said.

Alice's next words were careful, measured, and calm. That should have tipped off Vince that this news was not being nearly as cheerfully received as he might have imagined. Vince being . . . well, Vince, the verbal cue went unnoticed.

Alice let out a deep breath. "With whom?"

105

So far, Hershel was surprised at how easily his date was going. The conversation was flowing now that they'd gotten past their initial awkward hurdle, and Mary seemed to be genuinely enjoying herself. This put the part of him that had been secretly wondering if she had accepted his invitation out of pity at ease. The small boost in confidence helped him return the volley of words, and thus increased the fun Mary was having. It was a self-perpetuating cycle, but an exceptionally enjoyable one.

"Hmm. The steak looks really good," Mary said, glancing over the menu for the first time since they'd arrived.

"It's what they're known for," Hershel told her.

"Well then, I think I'll give it a try," she said, setting the menu back down. "It's been too long since I had a well-cooked haunch of meat."

"Got a carnivore streak?"

"I did live in the woods for several years. Canned food can only get you so far, and a girl has to eat," Mary said.

"I bet you throw one hell of a barbeque."

"You would not be disappointed," she confirmed. "Once it warms up again, that might be a fun activity one weekend."

"Yeah, it would. Maybe they'll organize one for us. The school seems to be on top of it, what with the river trip and all," Hershel pointed out.

Mary wrinkled her nose. "I'm not sure if I'll be going on that. Much as I miss the outdoors, the things I enjoyed were the peace and serenity. I don't think I'm likely to find those things with thirty alcohol-saturated freshman splashing around."

Hershel nodded. "It's really not my scene either, but Roy is beyond-words excited about it."

"He has been good lately," Mary said with a sigh. "I suppose he deserves a break here and there."

Hershel winced involuntarily at the word "break."

"I'd say he definitely deserves a little time to cut loose," he said.

"And you're not just saying that because you get to share in the memories of those loose times, huh?" Mary asked.

"Not at all," Hershel replied. "Roy has some fun, but I much prefer my own memories. Especially on nights like this."

"Very smooth answer, Mr. Daniels," Mary said. "Roy might have some competition for the role of charmer."

*   *   *

"Wow, this place is really nice," Bubbles observed as Nick pulled out her chair for her. The restaurant wasn't actually all that high class, at least, not by Nick's standards, but as he walked over to his own seat, he decided he might as well roll with it.

"Just my way of saying thank you for your willingness to drive tonight," Nick said.

"Oh, it's no problem! I mean, if you'd already promised your friend he could use your car, then that's how it is and you should keep your promises. Even when it's super inconvenient. 'That's a promise' means you'll do it no matter what."

"Indeed," Nick said, wishing dearly he had a fake ID and could order some wine.

"Besides, it's totally worth a few minutes behind the wheel to come out to an awesome place like this with you," Bubbles said, a rosy blush tinting her cheeks.

"You're sweet," Nick replied. "But I consider myself the lucky one. After all, I'm out with the most beautiful girl in the whole restaurant. And she's a Super at that."

"No way, I'm barely a Super at all. I mean, yeah, I love my power and it's really cool and fun, but let's be honest here: I'm not going to be saving any babies trapped in a fire or knocking out bank robbers. When I was little, I kept thinking my power would bloom into something really cool, and then it never happened and I was bummed for a while, but then I kind of figured it's easier to be a normal girl than a Hero anyway, and that's when I got okay with it."

"That's a very mature attitude," Nick said. "And, for the record, I think it's an amazing ability. It must be a tremendous feeling to conjure something out of nothingness."

"It's pretty cool," Bubbles agreed. "I didn't use it too much first semester though, 'cause I was really scared of showing it to someone in the HCP and getting laughed at."

"HCP? Oh, that's right, Lander has a program for Supers, doesn't it?"

"Oh yeah, it's a big deal in the Super community. The ones who are in it keep themselves a secret, though, so it could totally be anyone you meet on campus," Bubbles explained.

Nick raised an eyebrow. "Anyone, huh? So, you're telling me I could very well be sitting with a bona fide Hero in training right now."

"As if. I hear that thing is crazy hard, anyway. I'm much happier being a regular girl with something extra special about her," Bubbles said chipperly.

Nick smiled. "I can see the appeal there. We normal people just have to find our specialness in other places."

"So what makes you special, then?"

"I am spectacular at blackjack," Nick replied.

"I've heard of that. It's the game that's like Go Fish, right?"

"My dear girl, I have so very much to teach you."

*   *   *

"You know, I'm really not used to surprises," Mary said as Hershel piloted them around town in Nick's car. "I'd be perfectly okay with you telling me where we're going."

"No way," Hershel said. "I get to be possibly the first boy to surprise a telepath. You think there's any way I'm passing on that honor?"

"Honor, huh? Someone is feeling confident."

"Well, it has been a good night so far," Hershel pointed out. It had been, too. The longer he'd been out with Mary, the more they'd fallen into the comfortable rhythm of friends. There was still a romantic element to the evening, but the thing about knowing someone for several months is that changing one aspect of being with them doesn't affect the entire existing dynamic. People who are friends don't shift to entirely different individuals when they date; they merely become friends who are involved.

"Besides," Hershel continued, "I could either be upbeat or worried, and worried seemed like it would have kind of dragged down the night."

Mary giggled. "You make a good point. I still want to know where we're going, though."

"And you will. Just as soon as we arrive," Hershel assured her.

Mary stuck out her tongue at Hershel, an act made all the more humorous by her prim and proper appearance. She really did want to know, but it bears mentioning that at no point did she ever consider reading his mind to find out. Well . . . not seriously consider, anyway. As far as Mary was concerned, tonight, she was a normal girl on a normal date.

106

"We're here," Hershel said, pulling Nick's car to a stop.

Mary peered out the window; a small twinkle of lights set against rolling waves of darkness greeted her.

"The docks?"

"The docks," Hershel confirmed. He opened the door and stepped out, the salted air washing over him. It was a familiar, comfortable feeling. He'd thought all week about what to do with Mary after dinner, and on Thursday, he'd decided to engage in a favorite activity to clear his head. The thought right on the heels of that decision was why not kill two birds with one stone and bring Mary along? After all, it was a fun activity, outdoorsy, and something Hershel had a bit of talent in.

"I'd like to point out that you specifically requested I not read your mind, refused to tell me where we were going, and then drove me out to the docks at night," Mary said as she left the car and joined him. "Just saying, this looks a lot like the start to one of those horror movies Nick loves."

Hershel laughed. "Mary, you're the strongest girl in our class. If Roy couldn't beat you, what chance do I have of pulling off something underhanded?"

"A fair point. I would still like to know what we're doing here, though," Mary said.

Hershel held out his hand. "By all means."

Mary slipped her smaller digits into Hershel's and the two began walking toward the water.

*   *   *

"This place is so pretty. It reminds me a lot of the woods near where I grew up, but I mean, obviously smaller, and not as woodsy, but I still like it," Bubbles said. She and Nick had finished dinner and were walking through a local park. Unlike Hershel, Nick hadn't put a tremendous amount of effort or thought into his post-dinner activity.

"I'm glad you enjoy it," Nick said. "I come here when I'm feeling particularly far from home or thoughtful. The sounds of nature always makes me feel centered." Nick deftly avoided tripping over a small bump in the worn dirt path. Between the unfamiliar terrain and those stupid sunglasses. he was having a hell of a time not tumbling all over the place. In retrospect, he was glad he'd made a trip here the day before to ensure the park was well lit and fit within the desired aesthetic parameters. If it were any darker, he'd have had to shed his shades.

"Oh my gosh, that is so deep. I wish I did stuff like that, but when I get bored, I just go out to the club with L-Ray or play racquetball or make pasta or watch TV or—"

"We all have our own ways of dealing with stress," Nick assured her. He had already learned the same lesson many had before: when it came to Bubbles, one had to own the conversation, or it turned into a monologue. "There's not a better or worse. It's like people, we're all unique, but that doesn't make anyone superior. Just different."

"I can see that," Bubbles agreed. "Talking about different, though, can I ask you something?"

"Of course."

"Not to pry, and if it's something serious like a scar or something, I am sooooo sorry, but I'm really curious and I want to know and not that they don't look great on you 'cause they totally do, but why do you wear sunglasses all the time?"

Nick weighed his options. He had a few standard lies he used depending on the person asking. For Bubbles, one of the less complex answers was likely the best route to take.

"My eyes have a photosensitivity condition," Nick told her. "It's not a big deal, but it means I get some pretty bad migraines if the light isn't dimmed and filtered. My lenses stop that from happening."

"That totally sucks. Were you born with that or did something happen?"

"Born that way," Nick explained. "Like I said, it isn't really that big of a deal. I can take them off if the occasion demands, I just leave them on as a general rule for my own comfort. Besides, after all these years, my glasses feel like a part of me."

"I totally get that. I mean, I wore the same shoes for three years and they were just, like, a part of my life, and when they finally fell apart, I didn't know what to do and I went barefoot for like a week before I could finally feel comfy in new ones. They look good on you, though."

"Well then, it's a win all around," Nick replied. He hopped at the last second to dodge a dip beneath his foot. Maybe he should have picked a slightly easier-to-navigate terrain.

*   *   *

The sea sprayed upward, leaving a fine mist in the air that lingered on Hershel and Mary's skin.

Mary let out a delighted squeal as the winter water touched her face. Her body was wrapped in a protective poncho that Hershel had stashed in Nick's trunk, keeping her clothes safe from soaking. She'd left the hood down, though, preferring to feel the air run through her locks, absolutely wrecking the style Alice had worked so hard to craft.

Hershel adjusted their course slightly, moving toward a calmer patch of water.

"I still can't believe I never knew you sailed," Mary said, adjusting her grip on the bow of the small boat Hershel had procured.

"My mom taught us when we were younger. Lake Michigan was nearby, and we'd spend our summers out on the water," Hershel explained. "It always made me feel great, so the first week we were here, I looked up a place I could get out on the water if I needed to."

"And this is the first time you've used it?"

"Second," Hershel said. "I came out here around our third week in, when things were getting really stressful. After you put Roy in line, life got a lot more manageable, though, so I haven't needed it."

"I think I'd be out here quite a bit, need it or not," Mary said, a wave knocking against the side and shifting her balance.

"Yeah, I thought the same. But things get busy, and time slips away from you," Hershel sighed.

"I'm glad you took me out here tonight," Mary said, looking over at him.

Hershel knew a goofy grin was splitting his face, and he sincerely did not care. He looked back into the amber eyes that he'd been unable to get out of his mind since his first day at Lander.

"I wanted it to be a special night," he said.

"Mission accomplished," Mary replied, an equally silly smile on her own face.

107

Hershel and Mary were the first ones back. They still smelled of salt and were lost in a conversation that had been uninterrupted for the past hour when they stepped into the Melbrook common room.

"So, I guess this is good night," Hershel said, realizing there wasn't much of a dropping off at the door opportunity.

"Looks that way," Mary agreed. "I had a really good time."

"Me, too. Would you be interested in doing it again sometime?"

"I think you'll find me receptive to the idea," Mary said.

"How's next weekend work for you?" Hershel asked.

"Not great," Mary said.

"Oh. What's wrong with it?"

"Just seems like an awfully long time to avoid you," Mary pointed out.

Hershel chuckled. "Okay, okay, you got me. Guess we'll be seeing each other tomorrow and Sunday. I'm not sure how to really proceed from here. I'm sort of new at this."

"I wasn't exactly prom queen myself," Mary said. "I think we should try to do more nights like this, where it's just us and we have the romance and all, and then the rest of our time together is just that. Time spent together."

"Sounds good," Hershel said. "I think this might be one of those things we're supposed to figure out as we go along."

"It's to my understanding that that's supposed to be part of the fun," Mary said.

"Then I'll look forward to it."

"That makes two of us. Good night, Hershel."

"Good night, Mary," Hershel replied. He very much wanted to kiss her in that moment, standing there in their dorm common room, the memory of the ocean still fresh in their minds. Instead, he pulled her in closer and squeezed her tightly into a hug. Roy would have gone for the kiss, of that Hershel had no doubt. But Hershel wasn't Roy, and tonight, for the first time in a very long time, Hershel was happy about that fact.

They released each other and parted, going back to their respective sides of Melbrook and into their rooms. Mary was surprised not to find Alice waiting to hear all about her night out. Had she been less preoccupied through the week and kept better tabs on Nick, then Alice's absence might have been anticipated. As it was, Mary went into her room and reluctantly headed for the shower. Much as she loved the smell of the night ocean on her, it was hardly hygienic to go to sleep with so much salt on the skin.

*   *   *

Nick and Bubbles arrived about an hour after Hershel and Mary.

"This place is really nice!" Bubbles remarked as they entered the common room. "And there's only, like, five of you? That is so cool. How did you swing getting into a dorm like this?"

"Just good luck," Nick told her. "I've heard it was originally built for faculty, but they weren't so receptive to living on campus with students, and, well . . . waste not, want not."

"Still, it's super nice. I mean, I love living with L-Ray and all, but you guys actually have a kitchen. Plus, it's so secure and off on its own, it's, like, a totally different world and ugh, now I am so jealous."

"This is just the central area. Maybe next time, I'll show you what the rooms look like," Nick said.

"Next time?"

"Assuming you want to see me again, yes."

"Oh yeah, I totally want to see you again. What are you doing tomorrow?"

Nick laughed. "The rest of my weekend is, sadly, already spoken for by homework. I'll call you later in the week, and we can work out the best time for us to go out."

"Sounds awesome!" Bubbles said. She then realized the level of her volume and the lateness of the hour, and dialed it down a few degrees before she spoke again. "Tonight was really nice. Thank you for taking me out."

"Thank you for being my company. And driving," Nick added.

"I guess I should be getting back then."

"Indeed, but we'll talk soon." Nick assured her. They walked back out to the front door, which Nick graciously held open for Bubbles. Once they were in the brisk night air, she turned around to thank him one last time. Before she had the chance, Nick's hand ran lightly up her cheek and behind her ear, drawing her face close to his. The kiss caught her by surprise for a moment, then she melted into it.

They broke apart eventually, Nick planting a final kiss on her cheek, as if he was signing his name.

"See you soon," Nick said, pulling away.

"Mmmhmmm," Bubbles replied, her tongue still adamant about staying in make-out mode and not surrendering itself back to the mundane task of talking. In this, Nick had accomplished something a multitude of teachers, parents, and friends had failed to accomplish— he'd rendered Bubbles speechless.

Nick stepped back into Melbrook and shook himself a bit mentally. It'd been a while since he'd had physical contact with a beautiful woman, and the first time he'd ever done so in his current persona. He should have held back a bit more. This Nick shouldn't be quite so adept a kisser. He made a mental note for next time. It would likely be all right. If his skill level decreased, Bubbles would almost certainly just assume her memory of their first kiss was rosily remembered due to the hormone cocktail most people knew as romance.

He walked down the hall and stepped into the empty common room once more. All in all, the night had gone well. The girl never stopped talking, but Nick had excellent selective attention, so he'd manage to stave off annoyance most of the evening. She provided excellent visual stimulation as well, to which he was never averse. Most importantly, Alice was nowhere to be seen, meaning she had either gone to bed or was talking with Mary. Either way, she wasn't concerned with Nick Campbell, which was precisely how he wanted it.

Nick opened the boys' side door and stepped in, greeted by Hershel and Vince, who were already discussing Hershel's date. The door swung shut behind him on the common room, now empty once more.

*   *   *

On this particular occasion (and countless other, less relevant, ones before it), Nicholas Campbell was wrong. Alice Adair was neither asleep, nor talking with Mary, nor even in Melbrook at all. She was currently floating high above the Lander campus, clad in an enormous jacket, ski pants, and face mask to protect against the cold and the wind.

She'd dipped down momentarily when he and Bubbles had come home, not enough to make out words, but enough to see the show. She'd also seen Mary and Hershel arrive earlier. She thought about how she should probably be down there, talking with Mary and making sure everything had gone okay. She would do all that, too. She would just do it tomorrow. For right now, Alice was floating through the air, truly enjoying her power for the first time since she'd gained control of it.

In a way, it was a surreal experience. When she was Powered, happiness had always been what sent Alice airborne. Tonight, though, she was melancholy. Everyone was hooking up and becoming romantically involved, yet she was lagging behind. There was a fear snaking through her heart, one that said, at this pace, she'd find herself alone once more. She tried to calm it away, but it was persistent. It reminded her that even Nick had met someone. If he could get a date, then it was only a matter of time until everyone was caught up in their budding romances. So she'd decided to get out of the house. Normally, this would involve a drive down the highway. Tonight, though . . .

Alice rotated slowly in the air, staring up at the nighttime sky. It was breathtaking, the vastness of space made all the more real by the empty air beneath her. It was both humbling and inspiring. Alice drank it in, letting the wonder suffuse her. She knew she had to go in eventually, and she would. She'd shower to warm herself up, sleep late in the morning, then take Mary out for a girls' breakfast to hear all about the night. She'd face her slowly-growing fear of solitude by strengthening the bonds with those she found herself caring for. She would tackle everything facing her.

Just not this moment.

108

Monday, as the freshmen finished their first two hours of gym, the combat class began heading toward the stairs, while the alternative class moved to the empty side of the room. This had been their pattern since the new system began, so it was a surprise when Coach George moved between himself and the doorway to the stairwell, waving the students back, instead.

"Not today, you eager little beavers," Coach George said. "Line up with the alternative class."

The students exchanged a few confused glances, but by this point, Coach George's most important lesson (do what you're freaking told and shut up) was starting to stick. They jogged over and lined up alongside the rest of the class.

"Today, we'll be introducing you to another kind of training. This one is useful to Supers of all types," Coach Persephone said once everyone was in place. "We're going to work on ranged techniques. Expect to do this about once a week, though the exact day will be changed as George and I deem necessary."

"Now," Coach George said, stepping forward and taking over. "Some of you have powers that lend themselves to ranged attacks, some of you have powers that will lend themselves to it with a little teaching, and some of you have jack shit in that department. We'll be splitting you into three-man teams based on which of these groups you fall into and getting you going in shooting range rooms. We won't be supervising much, because this part is really simple. There will be targets. You will shoot said targets. New targets will lower. Rinse and repeat until we come for you. Get into your teams as I call your names."

The class barely had time to glance at their friends before Coach George's barking voice filled the air.

"Smith, Griffen, Riley!"

Mary, Alex, and Adam all hustled toward the area and stood in a trio.

"Reynolds, Dixon, Wells!"

"Campbell, Reid, Weaver!"

And so it went until everyone had been crammed into a three-man unit, after which, the coaches led them down the stairwell to a new level. This one looked like nothing so much as a honeycomb of rooms. At each room, a team was deposited with the same instruction: "Find the weapon that works best for you, shoot as many targets as you can, don't stop until we come get you. You're being watched."

The rooms were stocked like a riot control officer's wet dream: all variety of pistols loaded with rubber bullets, shotguns equipped with beanbag rounds, and even a net cannon leaning in the corner. There were weapons of more lethal force as well—everything from throwing knives to hatchets. Most curious were the items that seemed to have no place in these rooms at all, like the sack of steel ball bearings or the roll of cloth bandages.

As for the targets, they amounted to what seemed like a very in-depth, well-funded carnie game. The targets popped out periodically from a shifting spectrum of cardboard buildings that acted as cover. The lights would pulse when a shooting session had commenced, alternating between blinding flashes and utter darkness. There would be minute-long breaks between these periods when reloading was expected to occur. The situation as a whole was frustrating, annoying, and left most of the students with a headache that would persist for the remainder of the day. The exercise bore fruit, though, as some discovered they had talent in this new form of battle, while others were finally able to showcase the skills they'd already developed.

*   *   *

"Booyah!" Allen yelled, a bolt of green energy leaping forth from his hand and exploding against the cardboard cutout of a shadowy villain. Small, burning chunks rained down on where the poor target had once stood, the only remnants of an inanimate object taken before its time.

"Not bad," Amber admitted, stepping up to the front. "But still amateur hour. Watch how it's done." Amber closed her eyes and raised both hands, her middle fingers pressed against her thumbs. Her lips pursed, and a low, almost undetectable whistle leaked out. The lights could flash all they wanted; Amber didn't need her eyes to make these shots.

From Vince's perspective, what happened next was inexplicable. Amber was still for a moment, then she began snapping her fingers on both hands. With each snap, another target, often barely emerged from its cover, would explode into pieces. The lights stopped flashing after a mere twenty seconds of this, presumably because the system had to load more cutouts for them to shoot at.

"Wow," Vince said. He'd assumed he would be paired with other Supers sporting ranged abilities, but he hadn't imagined he'd see anything like that.

"Respectable," Allen said grudgingly.

"Thank you, thank you," Amber said, opening her eyes and taking a few bows. She then glanced back at the wreckage that remained from her assault. "Sorry about that, Vince, didn't mean to hog your turn."

"I think it'll be okay," Vince said. "I'm sure there's plenty more where that came from. I have to ask, though, how did you do that?"

"Ranged is sort of my thing," Amber said excitedly. "I control sound waves, and those can be deadly, even over a distance."

"Hang on," Allen said, stepping up. "You're telling us you did all that with sound? I call bullshit, I didn't even hear anything."

"Of course you didn't hear anything, Dumb-dumb," Amber said. "When I snapped my fingers, it generated a sound wave. I amplified and focused that wave on whatever target I wanted to blow up."

"Then we should have a really loud noise if you were amplifying it," Allen pointed out.

This time, it was Vince who corrected him.

"Sounds don't work that way. What we perceive as 'hearing' is a wave coming in contact with our eardrum. If she was sending the whole wave to an individual spot, then there wouldn't have been anything left to reach us."

"Very good, Vince," Amber said. "You hit it right on the head."

"I still don't think I get it," Allen said.

The lights began to flash once more.

"I can explain after class," Amber offered graciously. "Right now, I think it's Vince's turn to blow some shit up."

"Um, thanks," Vince said uncertainly. He had drained quite a few lighters recently, but he had a suspicion that if he didn't finally use the electricity Coach George had mandated, he would be lectured about it at very loud volumes. Besides, this actually was a good learning opportunity. Up until now, he'd just been absorbing from the battery, then recharging it at the end of class, since powers had been off limits during close combat. Vince already knew how to shoot fire; today, he could see how good he was with lightning.

Vince stepped up to the center area where the others had shot from. The lights started pulsing and shadowy targets began to emerge and retract. Vince took a deep breath. Fire was wild, always aching to be let out. Shooting it wasn't hard, all you really had to do was take aim and let it run free. He figured electricity was pretty similar in a lot of ways, so his best bet was to try the same methods he'd developed for fire.

Vince focused on one of the center targets and raised his right hand. What happened next was pieced together by the remaining film footage, accounts from Amber and Allen, and analysis of what remained from the shooting area.

The consensus was that Vince raised his hand, and what sprang from it was something that resembled a tree made of light. The initial bolt of lightning got halfway to its target before several other bolts arced off it, heading in different directions. From those, more bolts arced off, and so on and so on. This all happened in less than half a second, so, to the mundane eye, it merely appeared as if Vince had conjured a massive blast of lightning going in nearly all forward directions (it was exceptionally fortunate that Amber and Allen were behind him) that struck simultaneously the target, the cardboard buildings, the walls, and nearly every instrument that moved the cutouts, arcing through their wiring and into the power grid for the room.

In the localized power outage that followed, dimly lit by the burning remains of a few cardboard husks, it was agreed on all accounts that only a single word was spoken in response, and that it was spoken by Vincent Reynolds:

"Oops."

109

"I'm really not sure how comfortable I am with this," Mary said.

"I'll tell you, if I were in your shoes, I'd feel the same," Coach George agreed with her. "But this is the guy's power, and we're here to train everyone."

"I'll be right here the whole time," Adam pointed out. "And I'll turn back before we leave, so you can see everything I do and make sure it's all on the up and up."

"Still . . ." Mary said once more. She wasn't just dragging her feet on this one out of concern for what Adam would do while occupying a duplicate of her body. It also scared her because she didn't know entirely how his ability worked, and if he would duplicate her as she was now, or how she was before the procedure. Not to mention the fact that giving him access to her telepathy, even briefly, could easily unravel the secret of herself and the other Melbrook students. In short, there were just too many ways this could go wrong.

"Here's the deal: he's a boy and you're a girl, so legally, I can't force you to allow him to mimic you," Coach George said. "This is part of training mimics and absorbers, though, so try not to let your squeamishness have a negative effect on the learning opportunities of another student."

"He could mimic me first," Alex offered. "It doesn't bother me."

"Appreciated, Griffen, but we want to start him off learning how to control a . . . more traditional form of telekinesis," Coach George said, skirting the issue. Griffen was a fine Super: George wasn't going to go telling the kid he was a few macaroons short of cookie bouquet just because he needed to perceive his ability in a different light. Coach George was a results man, not one to get bogged down in the details.

"No, it's okay," Mary said with a sigh. Yes, it would be taking some significant risks, but she and the others had never really expected their secret would endure all four years. It had simply been nice to enjoy being like everyone else while it lasted. She couldn't start letting it affect the training of others. They were here to learn how to be Heroes, after all. Every little piece of knowledge furthered that goal, and it wasn't her place to withhold such a thing from another student.

Mary extended her arm slowly. Adam gently took her hand in his and focused for a moment. There was a soft tingle where his skin touched hers, and then Adam began to ripple as his bones and skin shifted. In mere moments, Mary was looking at an exact duplicate of herself, albeit with an oversized uniform, since Adam normally had several inches on her.

Adam-Mary's eyes popped open, revealing identical amber irises, and gave Mary a smile. "I won't take too long," Adam-Mary promised.

Hearing her own voice out loud was such an unnerving experience that Mary almost hopped backward. Instead, she marshaled herself and regained control. She placed some vacant, training-based thoughts at the forefront of her mind and returned the smile.

"Good luck," Mary wished her doppelganger.

"With power like yours, I doubt I'll need it," replied Adam-Mary.

*   *   *

"That . . . that was just awful," Coach Persephone said as Nick lowered his pistol. "You actually managed to miss everything. By sheer chance alone, you should have at least hit a building."

"Yes, thank you, we get the point. I'm a bad shot," Nick said, trudging back to the side and tossing his pistol in the pile.

"Bad shot? No, you are beyond a bad shot. You are a statistical anomaly of awful," Coach Persephone said.

"Maybe he was just nervous," Rich suggested generously. Gilbert, on the other hand, just beamed a giant smile as Nick was read the riot act. It wasn't very nice, he'd freely admit that, but Gilbert was still a bit sore at being punched and eliminated by Nick in the mid-term exam.

Coach Persephone raised her eyebrows. "Is that it? Would you like to blame your nerves, Nick?"

Nick shook his head. "Just a bad shot. We can't all be good at everything."

Coach Persephone stared at him for a moment longer, then turned her attention to the other two. "Right then. Well, I can only spend so much time with your team before I move on to the next one. Gilbert, wipe that grin off your face and let's see what you can do."

"No prob," Gilbert said. He pulled a revolver from the pile and comfortably twirled it down the length of his finger. "I've been shooting since I was ten."

"I'm far less concerned with how long you've been shooting than I am with how much you've been hitting," Coach Persephone said.

*   *   *

"Not too shabby," Coach George said as Adam-Mary sent ball bearings through the center of yet another target. "You're getting the hang of it."

Adam-Mary had been going for around ten minutes and was getting a healthy competence with telekinesis. He had nowhere near the subtlety or precision a real user could produce, of course, but mentally hurling objects at high speeds was proving to be within his wheelhouse.

"That will do it on the girl," Coach George announced as the flashing lights stabilized. "Time to try Alex."

Adam-Mary nodded understanding and shifted back into just Adam.

"That does not stop being creepy, does it?" Alex asked.

"I've been told that no, it does not," Adam admitted.

"At least you're honest," Alex said with a sigh, holding out his hand.

While Adam took Alex's hand and began to shift into another person's form, Mary let out the breath she'd been holding for several minutes. It looked like everything had gone over fine. She'd kept any shocking, secret thoughts out of her head and Adam had turned into a perfectly-functioning version of her. As Mary relaxed, she realized just how much effort it was to be on mental guard around someone constantly. She'd experienced this secondhand while listening in on people's thoughts, but living it for one's self was a whole other story.

Adam-Alex had finished his new shift and was back in front of the target range. The lights began to pulse, the targets began to move, and then . . . nothing happened. Adam-Alex looked confused at first, then frustrated, and after a few more seconds, a vein began to bulge in his forehead as his face grew redder. The lights eventually stabilized once more to find Adam-Alex staring intently at one of the hatchets, concentrating with all of his might, and finding absolutely zero success in moving it.

"I don't get it," Adam-Alex said at last, turning away from the instrument. "I was able to use her power fine. What's wrong with yours?"

Rather than answer outright, Alex stepped over to Adam-Alex and began whispering in his ear. The words were hurried and soft, but Mary was positive she made out the word "force" somewhere in there.

"You're joking," Adam-Alex said, staring at Alex.

Alex shook his head.

Adam-Alex looked over at Coach George, who did nothing more than shrug. The lights began to flicker once more, and Alex stepped away from the central area.

"What do you have to lose?" Alex asked as he resumed his former position.

Adam-Alex kept his eyes trained on Alex for a moment, then, with a 'what the fuck' roll of his shoulders, placed his attention back on the hatchet.

Seconds later, it whirled through the air, slicing neatly through a nearby target and wedging itself in the wall.

"I'll be damned," Adam-Alex said to no one in particular.

*　　　*　　　*

"Again? You missed everything again? At this point, I'm forced to assume that you are doing this on purpose," Coach Persephone said.

"Oh yeah, because you railing on me for sucking is just my idea of an awesome day. Maybe next, we can do the thing where you nerve stun me. You know, really put some icing on this cake," Nick snapped back.

Gilbert and Rich stepped back involuntarily. They'd both done fine on their firing rounds; however, they weren't entirely convinced that Nick's poor aim and back talk wouldn't result in a burst of ass-kicking that would find them twitching as collateral damage.

Coach Persephone felt a great temptation to oblige Nick's request; however, she had been at this job for a long time and acquired many useful teaching tools. One of those was not beating the students unconscious every time she was provoked. Another was knowing when to take away an actor's audience.

"Gilbert and Rich, go take a walk. Come back in ten minutes. I want to have a private discussion with Nick about the importance of a positive attitude," Coach Persephone said.

The words were barely out of her mouth when the other two boys finished bolting through the door. She couldn't help but smile a bit inwardly. After all these years, she could still put the fear of God in her students when needed. Most of them, anyway.

"Okay, Nick," she said, softening her tone. "Let's talk, you and I. I understand that you aren't an exceptional shot, but why aren't you even trying?"

Nick raised an eyebrow. "How do you know I'm not?"

"Nick, your power is luck. Even if you were to do nothing more than shut your eyes, use your ability, and pull the trigger, you'd likely have at least a decent hit ratio. For you to miss every shot means you're not even putting forth that minimal amount of effort."

"Look, and I say this as respectfully as possible, I'm here to learn. And I mean that: I'm here to become as skilled and powerful as I can be. I'm not here to learn how to shoot people, though," Nick said sincerely.

Coach Persephone found herself genuinely surprised. She'd dealt with all kinds of attitude from Nick since she'd begun working with him, yet she hadn't found anything like this. The boy didn't want to hurt people; so much so, that he was refusing to learn a skill that could be turned toward lethal ends. It was a poor hang-up for a prospective Hero to have, yet it was one she respected all the same.

"Listen, I understand where you're coming from. There's a lot of pain and needless death in the world already. It can seem wrong that we're teaching those of you who are supposed to lessen those things how to kill. It bothered me when I first joined the HCP. What you need to come to terms with is that Heroes are defenders of the innocent from the wicked, and much as we wish otherwise, sometimes, the bad guys just refuse to stop until they're dead. It's a harsh reality, I know. It's one you'll have to deal with eventually, though," Coach Persephone said, funneling as much understanding as she was capable of into her voice.

Nick cocked his head for a second, then let out something between a sigh and a snort.

"I think we just had a misunderstanding," he said.

"Oh?" Coach Persephone asked.

The lights began to pulse once more, indicating another firing round was nearly upon them.

Rather than stand with her, Nick walked over to the shooting area. From a nearby bin, he drew a pair of medium-sized pistols, one in each hand. He sized up the weapons, testing their weight and balance in the time it took to raise them. What followed next was, unbeknownst to anyone in the room, a near repeat of Amber's stunt minutes prior. While Nick's shots didn't take every target, they did hit most of them dead center. The sounds of gunshots echoed off the small wall in a nearly continuous report until both clips were spent.

With a cold detachment and movements slick as an ice cube left on the kitchen counter, Nick finished off the last of his bullets and slid the guns back onto the table. He strode back over to Coach Persephone, whose mouth was slightly ajar.

"I'm not here to learn how to shoot, because I've been doing it since I was three. I was taught to be ambidextrous, to fire on the run, and to draw at speeds that made sure mine was the first shot off. Add in the fact that I can dose my rounds with a healthy burst of good luck, and you understand why my bullets so often find their target. I was missing because I don't particularly like to broadcast that fact. It raises too many questions, and I hope you'll respect my privacy," Nick said simply. "If you have anything you think you can impart to me on being a better shot, I'll be glad to listen. Otherwise, I'm going to go work on an area where I actually need improvement."

"Dismissed, for now," Coach Persephone said, her voice still recovering a bit from the surprise. "For next week's ranged training session, we'll be graduating you to a more advanced shooting range."

Nick gave a nod of understanding and stepped out the door.

394

110

Nick walked into the Melbrook dorm a few minutes later, thankful that the lift system could take him back to the top without involving Mr. Transport. He didn't expect anyone to be back yet, since they would actually be using this time for training, so it was a surprise when a voice called to him before he could get over to the boys' side.

"Nick, may I have a moment?" Mr. Numbers asked, stepping out from the kitchen.

Nick sighed loudly, and his shoulders slumped. He was only a few inches from the door. So close, and yet so far.

"Look, I know I should have just used the time and faked a few shots, but they were talking about doing this for an hour a week. That kind of time really adds up, and I feel like it's only fair for me to spend it actually improving myself," Nick said preemptively as he turned toward Mr. Numbers.

Mr. Numbers blinked twice. "I'm not sure what you're talking about, though I can assure you I will be before the end of the day."

"Awesome," Nick said.

"At any rate, I had something else I wanted to discuss with you. Something I'd like you to keep private from the rest of the group, excluding Mary," Mr. Numbers said.

"Oooh, now my curiosity is piqued," Nick said, a small grin growing on his face. Maybe this day would take a turn for the better, after all.

*　　　*　　　*

Vince was mortified. He sat in Coach George's office, waiting for the man to come in and let him know what the consequences from his accidental electrical outburst would be. There had been quite a bit of commotion after Vince had destroyed the power grid to the room, what with the small fires and people rushing in and what not. Vince had been hustled into this office and told to sit tight. He wished they'd skip the formality and tell him to just pack his bags now.

The door slapped open as Coach George walked in. He was reading over a manila folder and collapsed into his chair without so much as sparing a glance for Vince.

"My goodness," Coach George said. "You did quite a little number on that room. The whole thing is going to have to be rewired and rebuilt. Not too shabby."

"Not too shabby?"

"Well, you didn't blow a hole through the concrete, so I'm not going to go calling it great or anything. It was respectable, though. You earned that."

"I'm . . . confused," Vince admitted. "I thought I would be getting yelled at or kicked out right now."

"Kicked out? For what? You did what I told you: you tried to use a new type of energy in an environment specifically designed for learning to use your powers," Coach George said.

"But I messed up. I wrecked the whole room," Vince pointed out.

"Oh, yeah, you did screw up, no one's fighting you there," Coach George said. "But that's part of learning. I mean, if we drummed out everyone who ever had a slip up, the only thing battling evil would be an overinflated sense of ideals."

"I guess. But, I just thought, I mean, there were all those other students who got dropped last semester . . ."

"Look, let me lay it out for you here. If you get lazy, or overconfident, or careless, then I'll have you out of my gym with a fresh bootprint on your ass. No one is going to kick you to the curb for making an honest mistake in the pursuit of learning, though. That's how you get better at something: you screw up until you've learned not to screw up anymore. Let me ask you this, you going to try and shoot lightning the same way again?"

"God no."

"Then lesson learned," Coach George said, spreading his arms.

"So, if I'm not in trouble, then why was I brought here to wait for you?" Vince asked.

"We wanted to make sure you were okay. Things like this can really shake some people up, so we try to be proactive and talk to you about it as soon as it's happened. Put things in the right perspective and all," Coach George explained.

"Oh. I guess that does sort of make sense," Vince said.

"That it does," Coach George agreed. "To that effect, though, do you know what went wrong today? I mean, you nailed Castillo no problem during the exam, but this time, it seemed to get out of control."

"I'm not sure," Vince admitted. "It could be a lot of things. Thomas was closer, so maybe it never had the chance to split. I had less power to use in the first place. Maybe even my state of mind. I wasn't focusing on how to release the energy when I used it in the exam, I was just concentrating on getting the timing right. I can't sincerely say where it went wrong."

"That's okay," Coach George assured him. "It just means you've got a few more mistakes coming before you know how to handle this."

"Oh dear," Vince said.

"Don't worry so much. Next time, we'll have you in a room where a mistake won't be quite as alarming," Coach George said. "Insulated walls, detached grid, grounded floors. Trust me, we've been doing this for a long time with a lot of Supers."

"That might be okay then," Vince said.

"Nice to hear you're on board. Any other questions, or things you want to talk about?"

"No, I think I'm all right for now," Vince said.

"Excellent, then get your butt out of my office and back above ground," Coach George said. "I've got paperwork to do."

"Yes, sir," Vince said immediately, scampering up from his chair and dashing out of the office.

*   *   *

"It's certainly contrived, and I can see why you'd want me and Mary helping," Nick said after Mr. Numbers finished his proposal. "It could go over all right, though. Possibly even well."

"Happy to hear you're on board," Mr. Numbers said.

"I haven't actually said that yet," Nick pointed out. "I've only said it's logically sound in premise."

"Then, what's stopping you?"

"As I told Mary, I don't do favors. You want me to help steer things positively for you, then there's something I want in repayment," Nick replied.

"Dare I ask what?"

"Actually, nothing too complicated," Nick said. "I want you to agree that, at some point in the future, you will submit to my request that you refrain from interfering in whatever I am doing at the time."

"I see. And if I don't?" Mr. Numbers asked.

"Then neither do I," Nick said. "That is the give and take of favors, after all. I would like to point out that I'm not asking for you to participate or intervene in any way with whatever activities I might be perpetuating: merely to do nothing. It's even possible you would have done nothing anyway, and I will have burned my favor pointlessly."

Mr. Numbers carefully weighed his options. Making an open-ended deal with someone like Nick was far from desirable; however, the terms were slightly in his favor. It only required him to feign ignorance, turning a blind eye at some future point. Even if it was at a critical juncture, Mr. Numbers was confident he could stick to the letter of the deal while still circumventing Nick's plans if needed. And worst case scenario, he could always just break his promise.

"Deal," Mr. Numbers said.

Nick spread a wide grin across his face. "Then it looks like we're good to go."

111

Michael Clark was drinking again. He was alone in his dorm room, having paid the extra money to live without a roommate. He knew it was a bad habit for someone like him to have, and he sincerely had been trying to cut back, but days like this invariably seemed to find him at the bottom of a bottle. It was strange: he'd never had a drink before college, yet ever since some seniors had procured hooch for Welcome Weekend, he'd been hitting the sauce with regularity. Had Michael known a bit more about alcoholism, he would have known he was genetically predisposed to it by way of his mother, but that was one of the many subjects Michael had never bothered studying.

He poured another glass of cheap scotch. Michael knew whose fault it was that he was here tonight; it was the same as always. Vince Reynolds. Michael could feel the alcohol curdle in his mouth at just the thought of that name. That little son-of-a-bitch had shown him up on the first day, and even though Michael had emerged triumphant, it seemed like Vince was always nipping at his heels. Vince was ranked eighth, even though he'd lost in the first round. Vince was dating the hottest girl in the freshman class. Vince lived in some fancy, high-class, private dorm with only four other students. Even today, Michael had been showing off his tremendous skill at ranged fighting. Everyone was impressed, and then, what happens? They finish up and find out Vince had nearly wiped out an entire room, without even trying. Oh sure, he'd said it was an accident, but who would buy something like that?

No, Vince had wanted to show up Michael once again. To show, one more time, that even though Michael was clearly better, Vince was the one who would get the attention.

Michael noticed his glass was empty and swiftly remedied that problem. Ever since that first day, when Vince had thought so little of Michael's abilities that he'd shown up with barely any energy to fight with, Michael had known what kind of prick that silver-haired douche really was.

And sooner or later, everyone else would, too. Michael fully intended to see to that.

*   *   *

Julia Shaw was painting her toenails a candy-apple red, watching television. She wasn't sure why she was bothering: boys never paid enough attention to feet, and she didn't have any capable female competition to notice the cute little details. She shrugged and kept on with it, anyway. Even if no one else noticed, she still knew, and it made her feel pretty.

She glanced absent-mindedly at the clock. Ten until nine. If Roy was going to come over, he wouldn't do so until ten thirty at the earliest. Hershel liked to study in the evenings, and Roy wasn't going to pick up the academic slack, so they usually didn't switch over until ten. Julia felt a slight tingle of frustration that she knew so much about the schedule of a boy she wasn't even dating. Not that she wanted to date a hound like Roy, anyway . . . okay, maybe a little.

He was just so much fun; it felt like every minute spent with him was energized and entertaining. Not to mention the things he could do in bed . . . Julia shivered involuntarily. She didn't think she could ever go back to boys that weren't Supers after so many months intermittently rolling through the sheets with Roy.

Julia smiled as she switched to the next foot. Hershel had told her recently that their situation was the longest Roy had consistently maintained a booty call. It wasn't the nicest compliment, she could freely admit that, but it was something. Julia felt she was far and wide the most capable virgin out there. She shared memories, sensations, and experiences with her clones, but she'd never known a man with her own body. That, she was saving until marriage, just as the Lord intended. Besides, when she could feel everything the clones felt, anyway, what was the point in soiling her purity?

Julia finished the other foot and blew on it. They should be done by the time Roy might roll through. Even if they weren't, though, no harm done. It wasn't like it would actually be her own feet hiked over his muscular shoulders, anyway. That was clone work.

*   *   *

Will yawned loudly and set down the book he'd been flipping through. He slid his glasses down to the edge of his nose and massaged the bridge. Will had hit a wall earlier in the night and was trying to slowly bore through it.

Sitting in front of him was what might appear to the layman as a falconer's glove with wires running across and through it. In fairness to the layman, that's exactly what it was. Will stared at his glove-shaped obstacle, and then turned his eyes away. Today's class had brought to his attention that while he'd created several devices for Jill to use, he was still lacking anything dependable in his own ranged arsenal. Sure, he could use one of the guns or throwing weapons they provided him, but that would be as good as stamping his own pass home.

Will was under no illusions. He was here because of his gift with technology. If he couldn't deliver in that department every time, then there was no point for him to be enrolled at Lander. Not in the HCP, at least. So if he wanted to stay, he needed to show up to the next training session with a weapon all his own.

Will pushed his glasses back into their normal position and picked up the book once more. He wasn't going to sleep until he'd gotten at least three shots out of this thing. No compromises. No excuses. If Will failed out, then Jill would be here all alone, and he'd promised a very long time ago to make sure that never happened to her.

Not again, anyway.

Will's resolve strengthened, and he began tweaking one of the circuitry systems. It sparked and sizzled in less than four seconds.

It was going to be a long night.

112

Friday afternoon, as she trudged home from class, Alice had to admit she'd had better birthdays. She'd had worse ones, too, but those had been the ones spent at home. Since her father was usually off doing his own thing, Alice would take her birthday as an opportunity to go on a trip, seeing Tuscany or Paris or Venice, sometimes all of them in the span of a few days. She'd had to take precautions, of course—a Powered girl can't very well travel without some assistance in case of floating—but on the whole, she'd still enjoyed herself immensely.

This one had been bleh so far. She'd been in a bit of a funk all week, ever since date night last Friday. The ranged training on Monday hadn't made things any better, reminding her once again how useless she was compared to her peers. She would have hung out with Mary to make herself feel better, but the small girl had been occupied with something all week long. Vince and Hershel had become swept up in papers for different classes, and in a fit of desperation, Alice had even tried to waste time with Nick. Sadly, even he was busy with other things, leaving Alice to her own devices.

When she'd come down from floating last Friday, Alice had convinced herself that she was overreacting to her friends going out on dates. It didn't mean they were going to abandon her or neglect their friendship. It just meant they had something new and awesome in their lives. Making her way slowly back to Melbrook, she was wondering if she had been right the first time. They weren't even walking with her today: they'd been off like shots as soon as gym had ended. She wasn't sure how they'd gotten out of there so quickly; Alice was almost certain she'd been in the first group up a lift.

She let out a breath, hoping to see it hang in the air. That time of year was done, though; the days were warmer with each sunrise. Too bad: Alice sort of liked the cold.

Perhaps she was taking this all too personally. It was college, people were bound to be busy from time to time. Besides, she hadn't even told anyone it was her birthday today. She could hardly blame everyone for not making a fuss, when she'd never clued them in to why they should. They probably would have, too. Alice understood that, rationally. Somewhere in the back her head was a small voice that repeated the same question whenever she tried to cheer herself, though.

"What if they didn't?"

That's why Alice hadn't told anyone it was her birthday. Because right now, there was an excuse for no one caring. If she'd said something and they still hadn't . . . well, then she might have had to face an unfortunate truth or two.

It was better this way, she assured herself as she neared Melbrook. Better to play it safe and maintain a medium level of happiness. Contentment had worked for her all her life, it would certainly suffice for today.

Alice opened the Melbrook front door and walked down the hallway. It seemed too silent for after class on a Friday. They should be on the other side of the door, watching television and making a ruckus. Hershel savoring the last few hours before he handed off the weekend to Roy, Vince and Nick debating how to spend the evening before eventually settling on something ridiculous, and Mary sitting quietly and laughing at them all. Alice had gotten used to it. She supposed they were busy; even on a Friday, they all had their own things to do. Alice wondered if it was too late to book dinner and a massage in town. That would certainly be a combination to lift her spirits. She reached the end of the hallway and pressed her thumb against the pad. It beeped and Alice stepped into the common room.

"Surprise!" The lights flashed on (though why they had been off was anyone's guess, since the room didn't have any windows to the outside), and the Melbrook students leapt out from behind various pieces of furniture. Once again, one could speculate on why they'd been hiding in the first place; however, one might conjecture that a surprise party has some conventions so inherent to it that they are obeyed even when non-applicable.

"Hubuwahnow?" Alice sputtered, trying to regain her composure.

"It's a surprise party," Mary said, stepping forward. "Hence us yelling 'surprise.' You know, for your birthday."

"I . . . um . . . wait, how did you know it was my birthday?"

"Mr. Numbers and Mr. Transport told us," Mary replied. "They actually helped us organize the whole thing."

"That's suspiciously nice of them," Alice remarked.

"Nah, they're actually pretty good guys," Vince chimed in. "Otherwise, we wouldn't have known about your special day, since someone didn't bother to tell us."

"Oh, well, um, birthdays aren't such a big deal in my family. I guess it slipped my mind," Alice said lamely.

"Happens to the best of us," Nick said. "Luckily for you, it certainly didn't slip ours. Now, I hope you're prepared for a night of collegiate celebration."

Alice let out a smile she wouldn't have believed possible earlier in the week.

"I think that might be okay."

"Your words say okay, but your height says awesome," Nick said.

"My what?"

Mary tugged on her sleeve and pointed down. Alice glanced at the floor and realized she was nearly a foot above it. With as much grace as she could manage, Alice lowered herself back to a gravitationally compliant position.

"Old habits," she said by way of explanation.

"At least we can always tell when you're happy," Hershel pointed out.

"She's like a buoyancy mood ring," Nick agreed.

402

For her own part, Alice just kept on grinning like an idiot. As for that questioning voice in the back of her head, it wasn't entirely gone, of course; such things just don't happen overnight.

It did shut the hell up for the evening, though. There was a certain amount of triumph in that fact alone.

113

Alice was exhausted, but filled with the soft glow of genuine delight. She was sprawled on the couch in the common room, the last (wo)man standing from the night's festivities. And festive they had been.

It turned out, the reason everyone was so busy this week was that they'd each been putting things together for her party. Vince had scoured cookbooks and local grocery stores in an effort to make a five-star dinner. He'd actually done pretty well too, starting with scallops, then rack of lamb, and finishing up with a tiramisu, all of which were Alice's favorites. She wasn't entirely sure how he'd worked that out, but then again, she'd gone dining with Mary several times, so maybe the small girl had just paid a lot of attention.

Mary had gone above and beyond, too. After dinner, they'd gone to a section out in the forest that had been completely overhauled. There were stands, barriers, and even some small bunkers. Hershel had designed an entire paintball course, and Mary had built it, all in the span of a week. Here, they met up with Thomas, Will, Jill, Sasha, and Alex to participate in a paint-based battle that can only be described as truly epic. Turns out nine Supers in the woods makes for quite a tournament. Alice still wasn't certain who had won, since, after a certain point, it seemed to degenerate more into a brawl than any regulated system of scoring. She just knew it had been fun.

After a return to Melbrook, everyone had showered, then had a slice of the fudge cake Vince had somehow cobbled together when no one was looking. Songs were sung, candles were blown out, and more processed sugar was ingested. Eventually, the others had grown tired and headed off to their respective dorms. Then, her own dormmates had begun succumbing to the demands of biology and gone to bed.

Alice had been too wired; even now, as she sat alone in the common room, she felt jazzed up. She'd be sleeping late tomorrow, no doubt, but that's what Saturdays were for. She readjusted her pose and a white envelope fell to the floor. Ah yes, she'd nearly forgotten. Hershel had given that to her before going to bed, emphasizing quite clearly that it was from Roy, and Roy alone.

At the time, she'd been hugging Mary goodnight, but now, her curiosity was tickled. She slid a manicured nail beneath the envelope's lip, breaking the seal. Inside was a slip of paper with only a few lines written on it:
"Redeemable for one night of sex.

—Roy Daniels"
Alice couldn't stop herself, she began laughing with her whole body. The best part was that she knew, in Roy's mind, this was probably a very thoughtful gift. That notion redoubled her chuckles. Finally, the fits subsided down to giggles as she wiped a few tears from her eyes and carefully placed Roy's coupon back in the envelope.

"Still in the party spirit, I see."

Alice whipped her head around. Nick was standing by the boys' side door, holding a small book at his side and dressed in sweatpants and a t-shirt.

"I didn't hear you come in," Alice said.

"That tends to happen when your eyes are shut and your ears are ringing with laughter. Plus, I'm actually twenty percent ninja, so there's that, too," Nick said. He walked over and sat down on the couch with her.

"Twenty percent? How does that work?"

"Oh, a great grandparent who was a full ninja, and then an uncle who was a fifth or something. I've never been great with fractions, so who can tell."

"We all have our failings," Alice replied. "Why are you still awake?"

"Aside from the cackling emanating from the common room? I wanted to give you your present," Nick said.

"And here I assumed you being civil all night was my gift," Alice said.

"Nope, just happenstance. It's hard to be snarky when looking down the barrel of a gun stuffed with paint."

"I can see your point," Alice agreed.

"Any guesses on what you're getting?"

"I wouldn't mind another night out with that guy I introduced to my dad. He was pretty enjoyable company," Alice said.

"Sorry, he was sort of conjured on the spot. I don't know if I could do that again, even if I wanted to," Nick lied.

"Ah, well," Alice said. "I suppose you'll do for now."

"So happy to hear it. Anyway, here," Nick said, handing her the book. "Happy birthday."

Alice opened the diminutive tome and saw a young blonde girl staring back at her. It took a few seconds before Alice realized why the girl seemed so familiar. She turned the page and found the same face staring up at her, a winning grin on its face and a trophy hoisted overhead. More pages, same girl, slowly growing into a more recognizable woman.

She didn't speak. She literally couldn't think of any words. Instead, she simply looked up at Nick for explanation.

"You once told me you didn't have many pictures of your mom. You'd be surprised how many times we all end up in pictures on public record. Anyway, I know a guy who knows a guy who specializes in this sort of—ooof!"

Nick's sentence was cut off by Alice spearing him in the chest as she engulfed him in a hug. Her arms knit around him and squeezed, her head resting on his chest. She held him like that for some time before either spoke.

"Thank you."

"My pleasure," Nick said, quite honestly for once.

They stayed in place for a moment more before Nick disturbed the quiet peace.

"If you're going to keep cuddling me like this, then I demand either sex or dinner. I've got my principles as a man, after all."

Alice laughed and released her grip on him. "Sorry, I just got a little . . ."

"Don't worry about it. I had a similar reaction when Ms. Pips gave me my book."

"Your book?"

"Well, yeah. How do you think I know a guy who specializes in this sort of thing? I wanted to see my parents, too," Nick explained.

"Of course, I . . . sometimes I forget there's a real guy behind the smart-assery and sunglasses," Alice said.

"Oh, he's real all right. Real freaking tired. I'm off to bed, and if you're smart, you'll do the same," Nick said, rising from the couch.

"I'll go to bed soon," Alice assured him.

"Sure, sure," Nick said. He walked over to the boys' side and opened the door. "It's your night, stay up as late you want. I hope you had a good birthday, though."

"I did," Alice said. Nick nodded and stepped through the door, leaving Alice alone once again. She flipped through the book some more, savoring each new image in every detail, right down to the sound of the pages flipping.

"I really did."

"Today," Dean Blaine said as the class settled into their seats, "I want to talk about categorization."

Dean Blaine began walking along the front of the classroom, stepping out of his usual center area.

"Controllers, generators, absorbers, healers, enchanters, shifters, speeders, teleporters, advanced minds, and illusionists," Dean Blaine said, ticking off each term on his hands as he rattled them out. "And that's just a few off the top of my head. The full list of all the classified types of Supers goes on for several pages and is constantly evolving. Just from that statement, what can you tell me about the nature of this categorization? Mr. Murray?"

Will's head snapped up. He hadn't raised his hand, nor had anyone else. Dean Blaine had called on him before even Stella had the chance to bark her answer.

"A cursory analysis would suggest that if we're still adapting something as general as the categories for different Super types, then it means we're still in a state of discovery regarding them," Will said.

"Very good, Mr. Murray," Dean Blaine complimented. "Will is correct. We are still learning more and more about Supers every day. Not just how certain powers function, either, but learning more about the broad spectrum different abilities can fall under. That isn't the whole story, though. Anyone else? Mr. Matthews, perhaps."

A long, lean boy in the front row snapped to attention.

"I guess it implies that there is still active research ongoing in the field of Supers," he ventured.

"True, but a restatement of Will's previous conjecture. Please pay more attention, Terrance," Dean Blaine told him. "Let me add this nugget to the discussion. Did anyone else know that, until seven years ago, Mr. Murray's ability was not actually recognized as a power? Show of hands."

Will and Jill slowly put their hands up. The rest of the class's remained down.

"Thank you, you may put them down now," Dean Blaine said. "So, until seven years ago, Mr. Murray would not have been considered for the HCP. He would have been classified human by all metrics of the time. Yet here we are, seven years later, and he is doing exceptionally well, posting excellent marks on a consistent basis. So, what changed seven years ago that altered Mr. Murray from a mere human to a Super, and a Hero candidate at that?"

"Duh," Stella said, voicing her opinion at last. "You already told us. Extreme technological genius was classified as a power."

"I did, Miss Hawkins, I did indeed. But that's merely what I said. I'm looking to see if anyone noticed what I told you. There's a conclusion here that I want you to reach," Dean Blaine said.

It was a soft, unfamiliar voice to most of the class that piped up at last.

"The labels don't mean anything," Camille said, barely breaking over a whisper.

"And why is that?" Dean Blaine probed.

"Because nothing significant really changed. Will can invent things that make him a candidate to be a Hero. That's true whether you call him a Super or not. He'll always have that capability."

"That is correct, Camille," Dean Blaine said. "No change in terminology can take away the actual talent Mr. Murray has, nor any of your abilities. There was a time when telepaths were all thought to be charlatans, and illusionists nothing more than skilled stage magicians. It's only over time, as these respective groups have consistently demonstrated their abilities, that they have been reclassified. Which brings us to the most important thing you need to know about categorization."

It was Vince who raised his hand this time, and Dean Blaine gave him the nod.

"They're reactionary. The terms, the categories, everything in that area is created in response to new Supers or Powereds showing up and changing what they thought they knew."

"Very good, Vince," Dean Blaine agreed. "And that is the heart of the matter. Some of you are classified as shifters, or healers, or absorbers, and while the terms are comforting in that they make us feel like someone higher up the chain knows what is going on, it is critical that you all recognize them for what they are: words. It is human nature to put words to things, to file and sort even the ineffable. We do this because it makes us feel like we can control that chaos."

Dean Blaine stepped back into the center of the room and gazed at the faces of his charges.

"Chaos is not here to be controlled. It cannot and it will not bend to the will of something as fleeting as an ancillary term ascribed to it. You are not controllers, or teleporters, or even Supers. You are individual people with individual skills. Never forget that. And never, ever forget that the same can be said for anyone you face out in the field. Grouping is a lovely tool for paperwork and mental accounting. Assuming you know what a person is capable of because you know the general shape of his power is dangerous, though. Often, it's downright deadly."

"Deadly?" Stella snickered.

"Yes, Miss Hawkins, deadly. Because seven years ago, if you had run across a predecessor of Mr. Murray who lacked his moral code committing a crime, you would have undoubtedly assumed him to be nothing more than another frail, powerless human," Dean Blaine said.

"Yeah," Stella agreed.

"And when he pulled out a device capable of liquefying steel, then utilized it, what would you have thought of him then?"

"Well—"

"That is incorrect, Miss Hawkins. You would have thought nothing, because, with all due respect to everyone's individual beliefs about the afterlife, dead people do not think."

"Okay, fine. But obviously, someone realized Will has a real ability and took notice of it," Stella said. "So that's a bad example."

Dean Blaine raised an eyebrow. "Yes, Miss Hawkins, 'someone' took notice. I want you all to think about something, though. Which seems more likely: that there was a long certification process through which ample evidence and documentation was provided, making the case for technological brilliance to be considered a power, or that a scenario very similar to the one I just described occurred, and a Hero's corpse was all the proof that was needed?"

"Oh," Stella said, sliding down a few inches in her chair.

"Yes. Oh." Dean Blaine realized he'd been addressing Stella directly and turned back to the rest of the class. "Please remember, a story like that is applicable to almost all of your powers."

Some of the more astute students noticed a sliver of sadness in his voice at his next words. Luckily, they were also astute enough to gather the reason and keep it to their damn selves.

"So keep your wits about you, and never make assumptions. Because I'd very much prefer it if the next power to be added to the list was done so through the boring paperwork route. It would be a very welcome change of pace."

115

Sasha's lips pressed firmly against Vince's neck, slowly trailing down to his collar bone. She kissed that more delicately, then gently nipped a bit of the skin between her teeth. The first time she'd tried this trick, things had gone poorly, but Sasha was an older, more practiced girl now.

Her hands worked her way under his shirt, her nails slowly etching their way up his back. He'd always been lean, but with each month, the body she touched was growing stronger and more muscular. He'd been cute when they first met; now, the boy was bordering on hot.

She reversed the direction of her hands, circling around and leaving scratches down his front. She paused when she reached his belt line and took a moment to lightly run a finger across the implied border. She ran her left hand from one hip to the other, marking the line in the skin, then she pressed onward, downward. Her thumb popped the button on his pants before Vince reacted.

"That's okay," he said, taking her adventurous digits and clasping them caringly in his own conservative ones. "I'm fine with just kissing."

Sasha sighed and sat back. They were on the couch in her common room, making out, yet again, at the end of one of their dates. Most of the other girls were off having fun (naked fun at that, Sasha knew all too well), so she and Vince were free to pursue their hanky-panky right here in the open. Unfortunately, it was, once more, turning out to be all hanky and no panky.

"I know you're fine with just kissing," Sasha said, exasperation settling in and making itself quite at home in her voice. "You've been fine with just kissing me, your girlfriend, for months now. And while I appreciate the gentlemanly care that entails, I have to tell you, I'm starting to wonder if there's something bigger here. I mean, you find me attractive, right?"

Sasha leaned forward a bit at the word "attractive," treating Vince to a panoramic view down the front of her low-cut shirt. She was wearing tight, denim shorts as well, and (although Vince didn't know it) lingerie designed to plump and pull in all the right directions. She'd put in a lot of work to look sexy tonight, in the exceptionally frustrating exercise of trying to seduce her own boyfriend, and it had paid off. She was beautiful in a way that conveyed accessibility, rather than intimidation.

Vince swallowed. "You're gorgeous. I find you incredibly attractive. That's not it."

"Then, what is it? I know you don't want to push me or anything, but in case you've missed the signals, you aren't pushing anything. I'm ready. I have been in a continual state of readiness for some time now, so where are we hitting the snag?"

"I'm not," Vince said.

"You're not what?"

"Not ready," Vince took a breath and glanced away from Sasha, trying to get some of his blood flowing in the proper directions.

"You're eighteen and male. A sweet male, but yeah, pretty sure there's a biological mandate that you guys are always ready at this age," Sasha pointed out. "If you aren't, then I'm guessing there's a deeper reason than just being nervous about your first time."

Vince thought very carefully before his next answer. He'd never lied to Sasha about this, or even hinted in that direction. He had noticed that she'd never asked him the question, though, and somewhere along the line, he suspected the assumption she'd made. That was going to make this awkward, but he'd made that choice of non-action and now, he had to face the consequences for it.

"It wouldn't be my first time," Vince admitted. "I'm not a virgin."

Sasha's eyes widened. "Wait, what?"

"I'm not a virgin," Vince repeated.

"Look, I understand you might have messed around with a girl a little and accidently finished, but that doesn't count as losing your—"

"Sasha," Vince said taking her hand. "I've had sex. Full-on, real-deal sex."

"Wow . . . um . . . when? I mean, was it a girl you met in the program before me?"

"We met on the first day," Vince reminded her. "And no, it's no one here. It was years ago."

"Years? How many years are we talking?" Sasha asked. "I mean, you're eighteen now, so . . ."

"I was sixteen," Vince told her.

*   *   *

"Stop! Thief!"

Vince's breath was ragged as he pounded through the dense forest. A rogue branch scratched at his face, but he didn't so much as break stride. He needed to keep—

*   *   *

"I was seventeen," Sasha said, snapping Vince back to the moment at hand. "I guess we never really talked about it, but I mean, I figured you would assume after knowing me this long. And, of course, I assumed from the way you kept holding off that . . . anyway, I was wrong."

"It's my fault, too," Vince said. "I thought you might be under that impression, and I didn't correct you. That was wrong of me, and I am so very, deeply sorry. I understand if you want me to leave."

Sasha barked out a laugh, then subsided into a fit of giggles. "Wow," she said once she'd regained her composure, "I can't believe you sometimes. I mean, here I am

411

wondering if this semi-secret means there's some hidden darker side to you, and then you go and apologize because you thought I might have made a wrong guess about you and you didn't immediately correct me."

"But I really am sorry," Vince repeated.

"I know you are, sweetie," Sasha said, her posture relaxing. "That's part of what makes you so you. It's not your fault I assumed you were a virgin. If I wanted to know, I should have just asked. You wouldn't have lied to me."

"Of course not," Vince said.

"Of course not," Sasha echoed, leaning in and kissing him. This wasn't a kiss like earlier, meant to seduce. This was one driven by so much emotional connection that it burst forth and had to manifest in a physical form. This was her kissing him because, in that moment, she simply had to. It was as unstoppable as an airborne object's eventual descent.

They eventually parted, but their faces stayed close, almost touching, yet not quite, as they picked up their conversation.

"So, if you've already lost it, and you keep putting me off, and it's not because I'm unattractive to you, then I can only guess that the first time didn't go so hot," Sasha speculated.

"It was fine during," Vince said. "It was the after that was problematic."

"That can happen," she said. "And you're not ready to try it again?"

"If it matters that much to you, then maybe I can—"

"No." This time, it was Sasha's turn to cut off Vince. "You wouldn't ask me to do something I wasn't ready for to make you happy, I'm not going to do that to you. Take your time. I'll be here when you're ready."

"Thank you."

"No problem, cutie," Sasha assured him. "That said, when you are ready, I expect to be told immediately. I don't care if we're knocking people senseless in the middle of gym and a rogue blow puts it in your head. Immediately. No delays. Zip. Deal?"

Vince laughed. "Deal."

"Good," Sasha said, kissing him lightly once more. "For now, though, let's go hit the video store."

116

In the course of any given year, there are certain periods which elicit expectation in their arrival among different demographics. In most of America, the season of football is met with widespread anticipation. In Seattle, there is a constant hope for a period called "two days in a row when it doesn't fucking rain." The deeper south looks forward year-round to its three days of winter, or "Christmas," when they are able to wear long-sleeved shirts and pants without bursting into sweaty messes. Some seasons, however, are enjoyed less by a geographical demographic and more by a gender-based one.

"God I love mini-skirt season," Alex said as he, Hershel, and Vince trekked their way across campus to the cafeteria. His comment was sparked by the bevy of co-eds currently crossing their paths, many of whom were employing the aforementioned fashion device.

"Pretty sure they call that 'spring' nowadays," Vince said.

"'They' can call it what they want," Alex replied. "I know what I look forward to, and it is not the increase in heat."

Despite debate about its proper term, spring had undoubtedly sprung. Gone at last were the occasional snow flurries, the chilling wind, and desolate landscape. In their place was a bounty of foliage and endless warming sunshine.

"Call it whatever," Hershel chimed in. "I'm just glad I don't have to wear a jacket anymore. I've been ready for this ever since the beginning of Christmas break."

"That far back?" Alex asked.

"Uhh, Chicago is really cold," Hershel said lamely. In truth, it had been their trip up the mountain that had soured him on winter weather, but he could hardly explain that to Alex without going into why the Melbrook students had taken an extra mid-term. That was a conversation Hershel hoped to put off until an appropriate time. Like, say, on his death bed.

"So I've heard," Alex said, not sounding too convinced. "But who cares, it's over now. And just in time for spring break!" Alex actually yelled the last two words, leaping up and punching the air. On a coolness scale of one to ten, it looked ridiculous. None the less, there were other calls of "Spring Break!" and some generic "Wooos!" that met Alex's enthusiastic outcry.

"Plus, we get the best spring break out of anyone," Alex said. "Next week at this time, we'll be floating down the river, surrounded by friends and girls in swimsuits and no fear about getting busted if someone sees us using our talents. It will be heaven."

"I'm not sure how some people would feel about heaven including young women in skimpy clothing, but I see where you're going," Vince said. "And it will be fun to get away from it all for a while."

"Glad you finally got on board," Alex said. "How about you, Hershel? Excited?"

"What, are you joking? That trip is going to be all Roy," Hershel said. "He's been excited about it since January, and it is definitely more his scene than mine."

"Aw, that sucks," Alex said. "You don't even want to hang out for a while?"

"Nope," Hershel said. "Roy's been pretty accommodating about letting me have some weekend time to spend with Mary. I owe him this."

"I guess I can see your point," Alex admitted. "Still, won't be as fun without you. I'm sure Mary will feel the same."

"I doubt it," Hershel replied. "She isn't going."

"Seriously?"

"Have you met her? Yeah, the wild, drunken river trip isn't her idea of a good time," Hershel said.

"Wait, people are staying?" Vince asked.

"Don't even think about it," Alex snapped. "If Hershel's not going to be there, then you have no way out. Besides, we both know how much Sasha is looking forward to it."

"I almost forgot that," Vince said. He shrugged his shoulders. "Oh well, I already signed up anyway, and I'm sure it will be plenty of fun."

"That's better," Alex said. "So, Hershel is out, Mary is out, any other friends skipping the class trip?"

"Not that I know of," Hershel said. "Nick and Alice are both gung-ho."

"Same for Will, Jill, Thomas, and his friends," Vince added.

"Good good," Alex said. "Then we can still have an awesome time."

"That is the goal," Hershel agreed. "Any word on who they got to chaperone us yet?"

"Not sure who it will be, but someone told me they always get the top-ranked people from sophomore year to fill the role. It's a reward to them, since they get to spend their time on a free trip, and it lets us know from the get-go that these are chaperones we can't mess with," Alex said.

"Some of the top-ranked sophomores, huh? I wonder if it will be anyone we've met," Vince said.

"I doubt it," Alex replied. "I mean, the only ones we really talked to were the beer-pong douches, and I'm not thinking either of them qualifies as a heavy hitter."

"People can surprise you," Vince said. "Besides, you're forgetting someone. The hostess."

"Oh yeah," Alex said. "Man, she did have some badass mojo about her. Sort of cute, too, in a scary way. I don't remember her name, though."

"I do," Vince said. "It was—"

414

"Angela," Shane DeSoto mumbled as he neared the blonde girl in the hallway. He gave her a brief nod and hoped she would continue walking. He was not so lucky.

"Shane," she replied. "Have you heard the news?" She pulled herself to a stop, and he was expected to do the same. He complied. They were in their HCP uniforms, walking along the corridors below campus. He'd just wanted to squeeze in some quick training. Of course he'd run into her, though. It was that kind of a day.

"I have not," he said stiffly.

"It looks like they selected Ben and me to supervise the freshman river trip this year," she said.

"I expected as much," Shane said. "You are the number one in your class, after all. That's why I don't plan on going."

"Don't be silly, your name was on the sign-up sheet," Angela said.

"I must inform you that you are mistaken. I certainly did not sign up for this trip."

"And yet your name is on the sheet all the same. I suspect you'll have to buck up and have some fun, anyway," Angela said.

Shane stared at her. Of course, she had put his name on the sheet. She undoubtedly had some other plan should he try to cancel his place as well. Likely several others for different contingencies.

"Why is it mandatory I attend?"

"Because it's one of the best parts of being a freshman. One of the few good ones, actually. Plus, it is tons of fun, and I think you could use that," Angela explained.

"There is training to do," Shane countered.

"With whom? Nearly everyone worth fighting will be on the river. Even your sparring buddy Chad signed up," Angela said.

"Did he sign up, or is his name on the sheet?"

"Does it matter?"

"Yes. You might find him less receptive to your machinations than I am," Shane pointed out.

"Nope, he agreed to go willingly," Angela said. "I just had to motivate him."

"Threats?"

"Promised I would give him a match if he went."

"Ah," Shane said. "That would do it. I suppose you have me over a barrel then."

"I always do," Angela replied. "Try to just go with it and enjoy yourself."

"I'll do my best."

"Uh huh. I'll believe it when I see it," Angela said.

"That is probably the best strategy."

Angela patted him on the shoulder. "That much I already know."

415

"Was there anything else?" Shane asked.

"Just that."

"So I can go now?"

Angela waved him off. "Go, train, be boring. But come next weekend, you better be prepared for some relaxation, little brother."

"I'm bigger than you," Shane replied instinctively.

"But not better," she countered with a wicked grin. "Remember, fun is not the enemy." With that, she sauntered off toward her own class.

Shane continued drudging forward, a foul mood descending over him. If he was losing spring break, that meant he needed to work extra hard this week. It was all well and good to preach the benefits of having fun and enjoying one's self, but those speeches could only be made by the one standing at the top of the hill.

Shane looked dearly forward to tossing down a few himself.

Eventually.

117

"Come on, be brutal," Alice said, turning around slowly.

"Honest opinion?" Mary asked.

"Absolutely."

"It seems to show an awful lot of skin," Mary replied.

"That's the point. But does it cross the line between 'Look at this hot body' skin and 'I have no self-respect and gain all my sense of value through your ogling stares' skin?"

"You might be leaning a little bit toward the latter," Mary said.

"Hmm, I'll put it in the maybe pile then," Alice said. She stepped into her bathroom and shut the door. A moment later, she emerged in sweat pants and a t-shirt with a small amount of pink fabric between her hands. "Next, I'll try the green one."

It was the night before the river trip, and Alice had more or less (more) bullied Mary into helping her choose some appropriate swimwear. It was far from the way Mary wanted to spend her first night of vacation, but she knew Alice was feeling a bit insecure about being the only girl from their group going on the trip.

"I still can't believe you're skipping this," Alice said as she rifled through her dresser. "It's going to be the event of the year."

"I'll hear all about it secondhand," Mary said. "I'm sure people's heads will be swimming with memories of this for weeks to come. As for actually experiencing it, I think I would enjoy that significantly less."

"I know, I know. The party thing isn't your scene. Still, it won't be as much fun without you."

Mary laughed. "I sincerely doubt many people will notice my absence. In fact, if the levels of alcohol provided are anywhere close to what I've heard, I doubt they'll notice much of anything."

"I don't think it will be that bad. I mean, it's not like most of us have much practice drinking. My money says everyone talks a big game and then only has, like, a beer each," Alice said.

To this, Mary could only nod. It would have taken her far too long to explain to Alice the extent to which hormone-driven youths in scanty clothing would leap upon a social lubricant as effective as alcohol. Instead, she changed the subject.

"This seems like an awful lot of effort just to decide what swimsuit to wear while floating motionless in a tube," Mary pointed out. "Someone specific you're hoping to impress?"

"Don't be silly," Alice lied. Out of courtesy, Mary pretended not to be aware of the man who dashed through her mind at that question. "It's just our first time in a really relaxed, social setting. You never know who you might hit it off with."

"I see. You're trying to look good just in case you strike up an enjoyable connection with a boy," Mary said.

"I was looking at it more as chumming the waters and seeing who comes for a bite, but your version sounds much nicer," Alice said.

"Yours does have an almost predatory tinge to it," Mary said.

"Maybe mine was better, then," Alice chuckled. "Still can't believe you're not at least curious to see all the boys in their swim trunks. Don't you want to see who's a hottie, and who's a nottie?"

"I have faith I will receive a diligent report on that information once you have returned," Mary said.

"That is an excellent point," Alice yielded. "Aha!"

Alice's hands emerged victorious from the dresser with a swath of dark green fabric. She promptly walked back into the bathroom and shut the door. She stepped back out a few minutes later.

"So?" Alice asked tentatively.

"You look like you're one fast movement away from tumbling out of it," Mary assessed quite accurately.

"Really?"

"The adjective I think best describes it is 'bursting,'" Mary said.

Alice looked down at herself. "Bursting, huh? I can work with that. Another for the maybe pile."

*   *   *

"All right boys, from the top," Nick announced. "Swimsuits?"

"Check," said Hershel, glancing in his bag for visual confirmation.

"Check," Vince echoed.

"Towels?" Nick asked.

"Check," Hershel and Vince popped off in unison.

"Sunscreen?"

"Check," Vince said.

"Roy doesn't really burn, so I didn't bother picking up any. Plus, he likes to tan," Hershel said.

"Fair enough, power-based immunity invalidates need," Nick judged. "Flip-flops?"

"Check," Vince said.

"In multiple styles," Hershel added.

"Good stuff," Nick said. "Novelty beer drinking helmets?"

"Check," Hershel said.

"Yeah, it's in there, but I still don't see why I need to bring one when I don't even drink," Vince protested.

"Vince, your objections were heard, considered, and overruled earlier in the night. Let's not revisit old business," Nick said.

Vince looked over to Hershel for backup.

"In all fairness, they were," Hershel pointed out.

"Fine," Vince mumbled. "Check."

"Good man. Sleeping bags?"

"Check," Vince and Hershel sounded off together.

"Tents?"

"Check."

"Flashlights?"

"Check."

"Case of condoms?"

"Check," Hershel snapped off in rhythm.

"Wait, what?" Vince yelped.

"Case of condoms. Come on Vince, try and keep up," Nick chastised him.

"Why would I need condoms for a river trip? And why a case of them?"

"Vince, be logical. We're spending a few days with beautiful, fit women who've had little outlet for all their pent-up frustrations over the course of the year. Add into that the remote setting, not to mention the tremendous amount of booze being bussed in, and can you really not imagine how it might be better to be prepared and have a condom, rather than to make a mistake in the heat of the moment?" Nick asked him.

"I guess I can see some logic behind that," Vince admitted. "But again, why a case?"

Nick shrugged. "Aim for the stars?"

Vince glanced over at Hershel.

"What? You think I'm arguing with him? Remember, I'm packing all this stuff for Roy. The last thing I want is to explain to people how my alter ego knocked someone up, and that's why I, technically, have a kid," Hershel said. "I packed two cases, just in case."

Vince sighed. "Okay, okay, points have been made. Let's just keep going."

"Fine by me," Nick said. He glanced at the sheet of paper in his and ran a pen down it. "Where was I? Ah, there we go, after the condoms. Insect spray?"

"Check."

"First aid kits?"

"Check."

"Chocolate-flavored body spread?"

"Oh, come on!"

And so the night went.

118

The parking lot was a celebration in itself. Freshmen were gathering to obtain directions for driving out to the trip's starting point, then lingering around to greet friends as they joined the commotion. What began as a few cars stocked with students clutching maps, soon escalated to nearly the entire first-year population of the HCP. Thankfully, most of them were carpooling; otherwise, there never would have been enough room for everyone.

"I think that's everything," Vince said, surveying Nick's trunk.

"Your stuff, my stuff, Alice's stuff, Alex's stuff, and Will's sister's stuff?" Nick asked.

"Yup, we've got a full house," Vince confirmed.

"Also, my name is Jill," Jill added in.

"Just ignore him," Alice advised her. "He remembers. He just likes being difficult."

Jill shrugged. "Whatever. He's driving us all down. That makes up for a little annoyance."

"The day is young," Alice mumbled under her breath.

Vince turned away from the trunk and faced his girlfriend. "Sure you don't want to ride with us? We could have someone sit on a lap to make room."

"Thanks, but no thanks," Sasha replied, patting him on the chest. "I have, like, zero patience for sitting in cars. It bugs me to spend hours doing something I can do in minutes."

"It won't be as fun without you," Vince said.

"Damn straight it won't," she agreed. "I'll be waiting when you guys arrive, though. So drive fast."

"That's more up to Nick than me," Vince pointed out.

"I assure you, I'm properly motivated to make haste," Nick chimed in. "It's time spent cramped in my car on the highway, versus time spent floating down a river with a cold drink in my hand."

"Hear, hear," Alex echoed.

"Sounds like the matter is well in hand," Vince told Sasha.

"Then, I'll see you there," Sasha said, planting a peck on his lips. There was a blur and a blast of wind, and she was gone.

"I still think there's a bit of room left," Vince said after he'd recovered from Sasha's speedy exit. "Jill, are you sure Will doesn't want to come?"

"Positive," Jill assured him. "That's really not his scene. Besides, he says he has some project he wants to work on during the break. Trust me. My brother is way happier with his nose in a book, than with his body in a swimsuit."

"To each his own," Alex surmised. "I take it Her—I mean, Roy is making his own way there?"

"Took off on his motorcycle this morning," Vince supplied. "Said he would have someone text him the directions when they were handed out."

"At least he showed a little forethought in that regard," Alice said. "I suppose progress is progress."

"On that note, I suggest we 'progress' our butts into the car, so we can get on the road," Nick said. "I don't know about you, but I'm not really feeling spending my day in the parking lot when there's an aquatic option just a few hours down the road."

*   *   *

Roy fed his steel pony some gas and picked up the gallop. He was racing down the highway, sunglasses on his face, duffel bag slung across his back, and helmet nowhere to be seen. Sure, some cop might bust his balls, but one quick demonstration would show that, in a battle between Roy and concrete, concrete was going to get its shit wrecked.

His phone vibrated against his side, and Roy whipped it into view. It was a text from Julia, letting him know the exact location they were starting at today, along with flowery language about looking forward to seeing him. He supposed he did owe her a good deep-dicking for sending him the directions. Plus, she wasn't boring in bed, even after all these months. There was something to be said for that.

Fast as Roy was going (and, to be honest, the speed limit was a distant, arbitrary marker for him at this point), he was still utterly smoked a few moments later, as something that registered as no more than a blur tore past him and kicked up a tremendous gust of wind.

Roy coughed on the dust that had been stirred up before choking out the word "Bitch." He pulled back harder on his throttle and ripped further past the speed limit, aware that he had zero chance of beating the girl who'd dashed past him, and equally aware that he was going to try anyway.

*   *   *

"I think we're ready to go," Dean Blaine said as the last of the freshmen drove out of the parking lot.

"About time," Angela said, walking over and stretching her back, resulting in a series of popping sounds. "You'd think, when your choices are cruising the water and sitting in a parking lot, people wouldn't lag so much in the latter."

"They were relaxing with their friends," Ben pointed out. "We did the same last year."

"Speak for yourself," Angela countered. "By this time, I was already three beers deep and topless."

"There's no way you were already on the river by this time last year," Ben said.

421

"I don't think I claimed I was," Angela replied with a coy smile.

"Such a wonderful thing for the dean to hear about the female half of his chaperones," Dean Blaine sighed.

"Look at it this way, I know all the stupid crap they're likely to try," Angela said.

"I suppose we'll call that a silver lining and just breeze past it," Dean Blaine said. "Now, you two remember how this works?"

"Sure," Ben said. "We meet them at the start point, unload the river cruising gear, and pile all their stuff on the bus in its place. Then, we give them tubes and outfit them with copious amounts of alcohol. One of the local staff drives the bus to the campsite, and we cruise the river with them to make sure everything is okay. That night, we camp and feed them. The next day is pretty much rinse and repeat, and so on until we come home."

"Glad to hear at least one of you is up on procedure," Dean Blaine said. "But I would appreciate it if you would at least go to the trouble of lying to me about the presence of underage youths and alcohol. We try to look the other way during this trip so they can let loose from stress, but there are limits. Now, off you two go. We don't want to make our students wait."

"Psh, with all the tech this bus is outfitted with, I bet we beat the super-speed kid there," Angela said. "We'll be fine."

"Drive carefully," Dean Blaine said, handing the blonde girl the keys. He watched warily as she hopped into the cab and fired up the engine, almost immediately stomping on the gas. Inwardly, he wondered if it was such a good idea to choose chaperones purely by rank, instead of by those with high levels of empathy and responsibility. Then he remembered some of the antics from his own trip so many years ago and resolved that it was better to have someone who was able to handle the big problems, rather than someone with a talent for handling little ones.

He hoped.

119

"Okay people, grab a tube, a cooler for those who want them, a few friends, and hit the water," Angela yelled to the crowd. "We're on the buddy system, so no one floats alone. Leave your crap in the bus. It'll be waiting at the campsite when we finish today."

"Don't have to tell me twice," Nick said, slinging off his duffel bag and tossing it into the rapidly accumulating pile by the bus. In its place, he scooped up a bright yellow tube and a Styrofoam cooler. A cursory inspection showed it to be filled with ice, beer, box-wine bladders sans their boxes, and Jell-O shots. There also may have been a bottle of water or two, if there was room. Nick let out a low whistle. "Wow, they really do things right on these trips."

Vince glanced over Nick's shoulder. "Is that all for one person?"

"It is now," Nick said, slipping the lid back on.

Alice grabbed a tube and a cooler as well, with Alex and Sasha following suit. Vince tried to stick with just the tube, but he was informed in no uncertain terms that he was getting a cooler too. They assured him that even if he didn't drink the contents, someone would.

The group trekked down the worn, dirt path, some admiring the forest around them, while other's' eyes were focused on the co-eds already splashing around in the river. They reached the edge of the water, running into Thomas, Stella, and Violet, who were already setting down their tubes. Thomas and Vince noted that each was carrying a cooler and exchanged knowing glances. It seemed those chosen to be mules for extra booze could recognize others of their kind. The crew from Nick's car, as well as Sasha, placed their tubes delicately in the river and hooked the floating drink repositories to them using attached lines of rope. Then came the stripping.

It was a quick affair—one person from each group piling all the clothes into a cloth sack, while another bagged the shoes. It was a matter of efficiency and quickness as most hurried to get water covering up these newly-exposed parts of their body. Some were less self-conscious than others, though. Nick and Stella both moved slowly in disrobing down to their swimsuits, giving ample show to anyone who cared to watch. As Alice settled into her own tube, she was glad she had gone with the pink suit over the green one. Bursting was all well and good for show, but for a long day of relaxation, she didn't feel like worrying about things slipping out the whole time.

The group finished bagging the clothes and cast off from the shore, joining the slow-moving convoy of fellow students drifting down the river. They were in their own clusters, with little more than a few tens of feet between each grouping.

"Now this is the life," Alex said, plucking out a beer and cracking it open.

"A man after my own heart," Nick said, pulling out a beer of his own.

The others, with the exceptions of Vince and Thomas, joined in as the current began pulling them forward.

*   *   *

"Here at last, I see," Angela said, handing tubes to Shane, Michael, and Chad.

"We took the scenic route," Shane said.

"Did you now?" Angela looked over at Chad, who shook his head.

"He tried to hijack the car and steer us in a different direction," Chad said. If it had been an interesting experience, one would never have guessed it from his tone.

"Ah, and what stopped him?" Angela asked.

"Me." Chad took the tube and glanced down at the coolers. He reached into one and procured a lone bottle of water, then began heading toward the river. Michael, on the other hand, scooped up a cooler for himself, as well as the one Chad had poorly pilfered, and quickly began stepping after the blond leader.

"So, tried to run, huh?"

"I somehow find it difficult to believe you're genuinely surprised," Shane sighed, accepting a tube.

"I'm not surprised. More disappointed, really," Angela said. She reached down and grabbed a cooler, holding it out to her little brother. He stared at her, making no motion to accept it.

"So sorry to disappoint," Shane said, turning away to follow his friends.

"Ahem." Angela cleared her throat.

"Must we do this?"

"You're going to enjoy yourself," she declared.

"And the only way to achieve such a lofty goal is with the use of underage drinking?" Shane asked.

"For you, probably. Otherwise, you'll spend the day moping in your tube, stuck on the fact that you were forced to be here, rather than just enjoying how awesome it is," Angela said.

"And your solution is to force me to do even more things I don't want to?"

"In for a dime, in for a dollar," Angela said, beaming a shameless smile.

Shane considered resisting, then surveyed his surroundings. It was still morning, and while the trees cast plenty of shadows, there was no denying the sun was out in full strength. Beating Angela would be hard enough if he'd had an environmental advantage. Without it, he was as good as wrecked.

Shane trudged back over and snapped the cooler out of Angela's hands.

"Good boy. Now, catch up with your friends. We're strict about the buddy system here," Angela said.

"Then where's yours?"

424

"Up ahead, minding the flock," Angela said. "I insisted on waiting behind to make sure my dear little brother arrived safely."

Shane's eyes narrowed. "You know I'm going to beat you one day."

"Maybe, maybe not. But unless you think that day is today, I'd recommend getting your hustle on."

Shane hesitated a moment longer, then took a brisk pace down the path after Michael and Chad.

Angela gave him a few minutes' head start, then grabbed a tube and cooler for herself and began heading down. She hummed to herself, enjoying the sunshine and the beautiful day before her. She briefly wondered if today would be the day Shane earnestly tried to kill her. She doubted it; he was a strong kid, he could take a little more.

She'd be on guard, though, just in case.

120

"Dare," Stella said confidently.

"Fine, I dare you to shotgun a beer," Violet challenged.

Stella dipped her hand into the cooler and produced a fresh can of low-proof alcohol. Her hand turned metallic as she slammed her index finger into the can's side while popping open the top. Without coming up once for breath, Stella drained her drink and cast the can back into the cooler.

"See, this is why games played with your roommate are always more fun," Stella declared, exchanging a high-five with Violet.

"Your turn to pick someone," Thomas reminded her.

"Oh, believe me, I'm aware," Stella said, her voice bordering on predatory. "I'm looking at you, Nick. Truth, or dare?"

"Truth," Nick replied immediately. It was the obvious choice. Actions were undeniable; however, he could always lie with words.

"What in the hell is up with the glasses? I mean, seriously," Stella said.

Nick took a draw from his own drink. He'd found that answering too quickly put up people's defenses that it might be a deception. Going slow, however, and pretending as though the act of answering required alcohol-based fortification, those things sold listeners on the legitimacy of an answer. Of course, it also helped to make it something that was either slightly revealing or embarrassing.

"They're a social mechanism," Nick said. "They keep me a little bit different, a little bit separated from everyone else. Back home, I was so used to being special because of my powers, that when I came up here, I guess I was scared of blending in. So I made sure everyone would notice me."

"Huh," Stella said. "That was more honesty than I was expecting. Kudos, kid. Your turn."

"I'm picking Vince," Nick said. "Truth, or dare?"

"Um, truth," Vince said.

"Psh, that's a waste," Sasha chimed in. "Vince always tells the truth anyway."

"A valid point, but how else am I going to get the boy to drink if I don't try to catch him in a dare?" Nick pointed out.

"Fair enough," Sasha conceded.

"Anyway, here's my question for you, buddy. I noticed something odd when you took your shirt off. You have no scars, like, at all. Now, since you've been at Lander, you've had healers on hand to patch you on the fly, but for a guy with your level of martial arts experience, it seems odd that you never sustained any injury. What's the deal?" Nick asked.

"That's a pretty invasive question," Alice noted.

"I'm pretty set on making him pick dare next time," Nick said. "So, Silver, how's about it?"

"I used to have scars," Vince said. "I got into an accident when I was sixteen, though. I was taken care of by a healer."

"Oookay, so what happened to all the injuries your body had sustained in the years prior?" Nick prodded.

"He was a very good healer," Vince said, glancing away.

"Damn," Stella said. "That's an intense power."

"No kidding," Alex agreed.

"Question well answered, though I feel like there's more story than I'm getting," Nick said. "Your turn."

"Hmm. I pick Jill. Truth, or dare?"

"Dare!" Jill announced enthusiastically.

"Oh," Vince said. "I suppose I dare you to put more sunscreen on your nose, so you don't burn."

"Seriously?" Jill asked, her excitement deflating.

"Sure," Vince said.

"Wow, okay. You guys are awful at this game," Jill sighed, pulling out her sunscreen and briskly reapplying it to her face. "It's not supposed to be these deep ass questions. It's supposed to be embarrassing and at least vaguely sexual. For example, it's now my turn, and I pick Alice. Truth, or dare?"

"After that lead in? I'm going with truth," Alice said.

"Works for me. I've wanted to ask for a while, anyway. Are those things fake or natural?"

Alice began blushing as soon as the meaning of Jill's words registered. Still, she was playing the game, and that's how these things went sometimes.

"Natural," Alice said. "Apparently, it runs in my family."

"Ugh, and with that tiny waist, too. You're such a bitch," Jill said, her tone full of more friendliness than her words.

"I do what I can," Alice said, taking a drink from the chilled wine-bladder that had been one of the features of her cooler. It was awful, awful stuff, made even worse if the consumer knew anything about wine. Her father would have died to see his daughter consuming such swill. Which might have been a significant factor in why Alice was chugging away on it.

"Okay, so my turn. I choose our tan stoic," Alice said. "Thomas, truth or dare?"

"Truth," Thomas said.

"Let's see," Alice said, drumming her fingers on the side of the tube. "Oh, I know! In terms of bases, just how far did you get with our little Violet back when you two dated?"

427

"I'm not sure that's appropriate for a gentleman to disclose," Thomas began.

"Oh, it's fine. That's the whole point of the game," Violet interrupted. "Tell away, I'm not ashamed."

"I believe the term is 'Home,'" Thomas said, keeping his eyes firmly away from everyone else in the group.

There was a series of catcalls and whistling, as well as grumbling from Alex about even the ones who didn't want it getting more play than him.

"That's right, that's right," Violet said, lifting her arms in pride. "I nailed me a good boy. I know, I'm your hero."

"Moving on," Thomas said. "I select Jill. Truth, or dare?"

"Dare!" Jill said, once more yelping with enthusiasm.

"Very well. I dare you to lay a kiss on Alex that renders him incapable of coherent thought," Thomas said.

"Woo, Thomas. Taking it up a notch," Sasha cheered.

"She did advocate a more risqué theme in the game," Thomas justified. "Besides, I find it permissible to look out for my friends."

Jill began paddling over to Alex, who threw up his hands.

"There's no need for that," Alex said. "I'm not into girls kissing me out of obligation."

"Oh, shut up," Jill said as she reached him. She grabbed his tube and pulled herself close. Without pause, she latched onto Alex's shoulders and lifted her body up to his level. The kiss lasted for nearly a minute, long enough to become mildly uncomfortable for those watching. At last, Jill released Alex's narrow form and dropped back into her own tube, the force of her landing setting her drifting back toward Alice.

"I don't know about coherent thought," Jill said as she paddled to steady herself, "but I guarantee he won't be able to stand without embarrassment for at least five minutes. That work?"

"That works," Thomas confirmed. "Your turn."

121

If you'd asked Alex, he would have told you he was buzzed. If you'd asked someone with a bit more drinking experience, they would have told you he was past buzzed, nearing snockered, and well on the road to wasted. Regardless of his level of intoxication, though, he was happy and floating along.

He'd drifted away somewhat from his original group, but he was hardly concerned. There were students all around him, some still clustered, some floating freely as they found their concerns subdued by the rocking of the current and the chemical effects of alcohol.

Every now and then, he caught sight of the chaperones, moving up and down through the crowds, keeping an eye on them to ensure everything was all right. For all their talk about the buddy system, they seemed content to let the free-floaters be, so long as they were at least in eye and earshot of everyone else.

So lost in lack of thought was Alex, that he didn't even notice he was coming up on another tube until he bumped softly into it.

"Whoops," Alex said. "Sorry."

"Eh, no worries," came a lilting, somewhat familiar voice.

Alex blinked and lifted his head, focusing on the inhabitant of the tube he'd just smacked into. She had long, dark hair and the bikini she wore exposed plenty of her caramel-colored skin.

"Hey. I know you. You're the chick that beat me and Vince in the finals," Alex declared.

The girl laughed lightly. "In fairness, I beat a lot of people in the finals."

"Oh, yeah. You had the really pretty voice."

"Well, thank you. Always nice to meet a fan."

"Don't know if I'd call it that," Alex said. "But I respect the talent. I'm Alex, by the way."

"Selena," she said. "You're the other telekinetic, right?"

"For the love of . . . fuck it. Sure, why not?" Alex said, a measure of defeat in his voice.

"Did I say something offensive?" Selena asked.

"No, no. Not your fault. Forget it. Let's focus on you, instead. What exactly is your power?"

"You mean my merry harmonies don't qualify?"

"You had a pretty voice," Alex admitted. "Not pretty enough to make us just up and lose without a fight, though."

"I've had better compliments, but I'll take it," Selena said. "The truth is, I'm classified as an enchanter. I cause certain effects in people when I sing."

"Like making everyone who hears it your love slave?" Alex asked.

"That's one example, yes. It's one of my more limited techniques, however. To influence someone that profoundly requires constant stimulus," Selena said.

"You, uh, you sort of lost me there," Alex said.

"Sorry, how can I put this? A person's mind is resilient. It tends to buck against outside influences. So, to take you over like I did in the finals, I had to keep singing the whole time. If I'd stopped, you would have come back to your senses pretty quickly," Selena explained.

"There's another option?" Alex asked.

"Sure. I can influence people in more subtle ways. Ways that don't throw up the same mental red-flags and can persist even after my voice stops."

"Huh. Don't suppose you could provide an example?"

"I can do better than that," Selena said. She tilted back her head and took a deep breath. What next emerged from her was a throaty, fast-paced melody. It emanated outward, rippling through the air and into the ear drums of those on the river. As it spread, so did a wave of calm. Backs unstraightened, knotted muscles began to loosen, and worries slipped out of minds, splashing, abandoned, into the water below.

As the last of Selena's notes faded, she lowered her head and looked back at Alex.

"What did that do?" Alex asked.

"I helped people chill out a little," Selena explained. "Made them feel happy and more at ease with the world."

"I see," Alex said. "Any potential side effects from messing with their heads like that?"

"Nah," Selena assured him. "I didn't do anything bad, just made them all feel a little bit better. I mean, worst case scenario, some people's inhibitions might go down a bit, but that's just a side effect of feeling good. You tend to worry less."

Alex barked out a laugh. "You make people feel relaxed and possibly lower their inhibitions? You're like alcohol without the liver disease!"

Selena's well-featured face creased with concern. "Oh, yeah . . . everyone is drinking, aren't they?"

"Not everyone," Alex said. "But a lot of us." To prove the point, he produced his beer and downed another swig.

Selena bit gently on her lower lip. "I forgot about that."

"Why does it matter?"

"It probably doesn't," Selena said, though which of them she was trying to assure was up for debate. "It's just that alcohol has a significant effect on the brain chemistry, and what I did will have an effect for at least a few more hours. And sometimes, two separate influences can . . . compound on one another."

"So people will be super relaxed and happy. Doesn't sound like such a bad thing," Alex said.

"Yeah . . . yeah, I'm sure you're right," Selena said. She reached over into her own cooler and produced a beer. Normally, she wasn't much of a drinker, but suddenly, she found a strong craving for something to settle her nerves. Pity her own ability didn't work on her.

"Wow, you worry too much," Alex said. "I can feel your stress from here. Chill out a little, pretty lady. It's the river trip!"

She stared at Alex for a moment. She'd nearly forgotten he was also a telepath. The only one here, since the short girl had skipped. That might come in handy. If people got unbalanced, he should at least be able to provide some sort of a heads up. Selena made a mental resolution not to let this boy out of her sight until she was certain there wasn't going to be any trouble.

It would be fine, though. She'd only used a little bit of power, and people certainly hadn't had all that much to drink. Besides, she'd just sung them into a more peaceful, happier frame of mind. There was no way that could backfire.

Probably.

122

Mary snapped her book shut with a sigh. Everyone had been gone since the morning and she was finding herself uncharacteristically bored. Sure, she was used to being alone, but the thing about living in the woods as a teenager was that there was always something to do. Wood to chop, food to hunt, water to gather, even traps to set. On a college campus, life was much easier. That was a good thing most of the time, but on days like this, it was a solid pain in the butt.

Mary was in the library, the one under Lander's surface, accessible only to those in the HCP, reading up on some historical Supers. At least, that had been her plan. Unfortunately, only a few minutes into the book and the words began slipping around the page, freed from their positions by the reality-shifting power of her boredom. Or at least, that's what it felt like. Admittedly, she could have had Mr. Transport pop her home just as easily as to the library, but her parents were swinging by tomorrow to grab her for a spring road trip and she doubted they wanted to be disturbed a day early. They were big on taking time out to keep the romance in their marriage alive. Which left her a day to kill.

Mary noticed some movement from the corner of her eye. When she turned and faced the source, she fleetingly wondered if she really had gone insane. Standing on the side of the table, waving for her attention, was a small, orange paper cutout of a human shape. From the size and color, Mary guessed it had been made from a sticky-note, and from the way it was jumping around trying to grab her attention, she assumed that sticky-note had come from an ancient tome of great and unspeakable power.

The paper man seemed to realize she was looking at him, because he pointed his arm at her, then toward the rows of books off to the left.

"You want me to go into the stacks?" Mary asked. She was taking it pretty well, but then again, when you're a telepath in a school for people who bend (and occasionally break) the rules of matter and physics, your threshold for weird tends to be higher than most.

The paper man nodded, then began scampering over on all fours toward her. It wasn't particularly dignified; however, it was more efficient than trying to balance on a pair of two-dimensional feet. He reached her side of the table in seconds and pulled himself back to a standing position. He pointed once more—this time, at the hand she had resting on the table.

"What?" There's nothing in it," Mary said, holding her palm face-up to prove the point. In a flash, the paper man had scampered into her upturned hand and perched himself there. Once situated, he pointed toward the same area of the stacks once more.

"I see. You still want me to go, you just want to come with me."

The paper man nodded and gestured once more. Mary stared at him a bit longer, then shrugged and got up from her seat. Sure, this was eyes-meltingly weird, but it wasn't boring. That was enough to keep her entertained for now.

They entered the stacks on the row her guide had indicated. She began walking down them, eyes alert for anything out of the ordinary. They'd only gone down a few rows when the paper man patted her hand and pointed her to the right.

Mary made sure she had the correct row, then turned and kept advancing forward. They went on like this for a few minutes, the paper man leading her deeper into the twists and turns that the library stacks offered. Mary was impressed at the sheer volume of books these different sections could hold. She hadn't spent much time in the library, though that was likely to change after gaining firsthand knowledge of how comprehensive their collection was. The paper man pointed her down one last turn, and the purpose of their adventure became abundantly clear.

"Hi there," squeaked a girl hanging on the very top row of books by her fingers. "I don't suppose you'd mind helping me down from up here?"

"Not at all," Mary said. "You're only about five feet off the ground, though. Why not just let go?"

"I'm scared of heights," the girl said. "I climbed up here to get a book, and then I made the mistake of looking down, and . . . I sort of freaked out, and now I can't look down to find my footing or let go, and my hands are really starting to hurt."

"Right," Mary said. "Just close your eyes and try and relax your hands. I've got a good grip on you."

"But you're standing over . . . right, you're the telekinetic girl. Okay, okay. Just give me second while I try to loosen my grip." The dangling girl took a series of deep breaths. Mary wasn't sure how long she'd been up there, though from the way her forearms were twitching, it was clear she wouldn't have been for much longer.

"I'm letting go," the girl announced. Mary pulled her away carefully, focusing on keeping the girl steady without squeezing too hard. Mary lowered her gently to the ground, the girl blasting out a groan of relief when her feet touched the floor.

"You're safe," Mary said. The girl wobbled at first, then leaned against the wall of books as she got her bearings back.

"Thank you so so so so much," the girl said, her eyes still squeezed shut. "I just wanted a stupid book about the first animator, and I've been stuck up there for twenty minutes."

"No problem," Mary said. "We freshmen have to stick together. You're Agatha, right?"

"Yeah," Agatha confirmed. "And you're Mary, the number one ranked girl."

"Eh, that was over half a year ago. I'm certain things will change when we get reevaluated," Mary deflected.

"That's not what everyone else thinks," Agatha said, her eyelids slowly parting.

"Thank you," Mary said. She noticed the paper man in her palm was pointing toward Agatha. Mary obliged by mentally air-lifting him over to the still-recovering girl, depositing him on her shoulder.

"What is he, exactly?" Mary asked.

"Oh, this little guy? Just an animation," Agatha said, picking up the paper guide. There was a small flash of turquoise and the paper hung limply in her hand. "There were some sticky-notes on the shelf. I juiced them up and sent them out to find help."

"I see," Mary said. "I've heard about that power. You can control inanimate objects, right?"

"Sort of," Agatha said. "It's more like I put a little piece of myself into them, my own energy if you will, and then they follow my commands."

"That's kind of cool," Mary observed.

"Yeah," Agatha agreed. "That's just the first level for animators, though. Those of us who are really good can sense the location of our objects, see and hear through them, even control them like an extension of our body, rather than just as a henchman."

"Wow," Mary said. "Can you do any of that?"

"The sensing, yes. The seeing and hearing, sort of. The extension part is still miles beyond me, though," Agatha said. "Otherwise, I would have juiced up the entire shelf and had it lean down to lower me to the ground."

"You couldn't give it an order to do that?"

"I could, but it might have interpreted 'help me down' as 'collapse totally' since that was the fastest way to comply," Agatha explained. "Anyway, thank you again for the help. I'm going to go back to my dorm room and lie down until my hands stop shaking."

"Understandable," Mary said. "Nice meeting you, Agatha."

"You, too, Mary," Agatha said. She headed off toward the exit, her steps still cautious, as though she expected to be swept into the air at any moment. Mary, for her part, turned her attention to the tomes surrounding her. Now that she knew about all the information here, it seemed her day might not be so boring, after all.

123

The initial plan was for the tubes to be stacked up carefully in a designated area by the riverbank. That way they could be accounted for and easily dispersed the next day. Unfortunately, that plan failed to take into account the effect of several hours' drinking (and one Super's relaxation melody) on the mind of the average adolescent. The result was that, as the Lander students emerged from the river at the designated point, a veritable clusterfuck of rubber tubes formed. They were tossed, dropped, or sometimes left to drift down the stream, forgotten entirely. Angela and Ben had prepared for this, having been contributors to the mess last year, and were managing to at least stop the ones breaking for freedom down the blue aquatic road.

As a result, they were of little help as the predominantly intoxicated teens began the arduous task of setting up their tents. Coupled with the fact that many of the students possessed very destructive capabilities, it was thanks only to the few who had remained sober that the campsite didn't wind up as a smoking crater in the ground.

"Okay," Vince said, wiping the sweat from his brow. He'd need to take a dip in the river again when this was all done just to feel clean. "I've got mine, Sasha's, and Alex's all done."

"I've completed tents for myself, Jill, Stella, and Violet," Thomas replied. His power made the set up a much faster process, since he could use his energy to grasp multiple tools simultaneously.

"Meanwhile, I've barely managed to put up my own and Alice's, thanks to her insistence on helping," Nick grunted from the ground where he was tying off a stake.

"You needed my help," Alice protested, her words clearly slurred. "You're drunk."

"Quite right. What would I have done without you tripping into the fabric, uprooting the entire structure and forcing me to start all over?" Nick said.

"Damn skippy," Alice said, crossing her arms.

"Besides, you're drunk. I've only managed to get a buzz, since someone keeps stealing my beers," Nick said.

"At least we know where this one is," Vince said, pointing at Alice. "Has anyone seen the rest of the girls?"

"I've kept an eye on them," Thomas assured him. "They're over near the bus, milling with the rest of the group."

"That seems safe enough. And Alex?" Vince asked.

"Last I saw, he was still hanging around that Selena girl," Thomas said.

"Good for him," Nick said. "That girl is hot with a capital sex."

"Pffft. That doesn't even make sense. And you can't say stuff like that, anyway. You're a bound man now—you and Bubbles keep going out together," Alice said. Normally, she would have done a much better job keeping the spite out of her voice.

"Bubbles is great, but the day I stop appreciating the female form in all its splendor is the day they're laying me in the ground. And even then, I'm not making any promises," Nick shot back, ignoring her tone.

"You're such a goddamned asshole." Alice swayed herself to a standing position and began wobbling off into the woods at a brisk pace.

The boys stood uncertain for a few seconds, trying to comprehend her reaction.

"Huh, I didn't think it was that bad," Nick said. "I figured, at most, she'd punch me in the arm."

"That did seem to be a bit of an overreaction," Vince agreed. "I mean, in comparison to the stuff you normally say, that was pretty tame."

"I think, perhaps, both of you missed the crux of that situation," Thomas said. "Regardless, she seems to be getting away from camp without slowing, so it might be a good idea to go after her."

"You guys have fun with that," Nick said. "If I chase her down today, I'll be filling out a domestic abuse complaint tomorrow. Not sure why she only hits me."

"You do the most to provoke it," Vince said. "But that's fine. You get some food working. It will be dark pretty soon, and everyone will be hungry. Thomas and I will go make sure Alice is okay."

"Oh, it is fucking *go* time!" That declaration was launched in the audible tenor of Stella Hawkins. Her voice was thick with fury, and emanating from the collective area near the bus.

"Or, we'll go find out what's going on before Stella seriously hurts someone," Thomas amended, immediately dashing over to the area.

"Crap, there are a lot of people milling around. This might be bad," Vince noticed. "I should go help Thomas. Nick, do you mind?"

Nick was already on his feet, producing a flashlight and a compass from his bag. "No, I get it. If there's a Super throwdown, you and Thomas can help keep the peace. That means the 'calm down the drunken princess' mission falls to the guy without astounding powers."

"Your powers are very astounding," Vince told him. "Just not in this particular venue. I think they're well-suited to your task, though. Talking down Alice will require a little bit of luck."

"Saints preserve us," Nick said. The two boys parted in separate directions, Nick heading north and Vince, just over to the buses.

The crowd at the buses was thick and difficult to cut through. Their intoxication and fascination with any altercation made the situation even more troublesome. Thomas had handled this hurdle by conjuring a wedge out of orange energy and plowing right through. Vince, on the other hand, was left with slipping through slowly, apologizing as he went. Finally, he made it to the front. The sight that met his eyes was one of Roy Daniels and Stella Hawkins, both a foot or so off the ground, cocooned in a familiar orange glow. Thomas stood in the center, sweat beginning to materialize on his face. This had to be a heavy burden for him, especially as both captives struggled violently.

"You two . . . need to calm down," Thomas said, his breath broken by effort. It wouldn't have been so bad if Stella hadn't shifted, but a girl made entirely of steel was considerably heavier than one made of flesh.

"Fuck that. Put me down, Thomas!" Stella yelled.

"Let the lady come get her licking," Roy agreed, flexing against his own bands.

The next voice that pierced the fray was neither of the three. It came from the back of the crowd and parted it like a 1950's haircut.

"I agree, let them both down," said Angela. She stepped forward effortlessly, a peaceful air surrounding her as she entered the chaotic fray. "They won't be attacking one another until I find out what happened."

"You . . . sure?" Thomas grunted.

A wide, gentle smile slid across Angela's face.

"They will behave. That is a promise."

124

Nick clicked on his flashlight and grumbled to himself. The girl had been less than a minute ahead of him, and yet, he'd already lost sight of Alice. It wouldn't have been so bad if not for the quickly diminishing rays of sun and Nick's lack of wilderness knowledge. He'd had extensive training in so many areas, but not surprisingly, they'd skimped a bit on what to do in the woods. For a syndicate in Vegas, it was assumed that if you were getting dumped in the forest, you were no longer in a position to navigate your way home, or anywhere else, for that matter.

The trees were doing a marvelous job obscuring what little light was left, their long shadows and thick foliage darkening the path at every step. Nick was aware that the farther he went, the harder it would be to find his way back, to the point where another search party might be formed to find him. Still, the fear of being hopelessly turned around in the woods was not at the forefront of worry on Nick Campbell's mind.

Something was wrong in his head. He couldn't put a finger on it, but he knew something was amiss. He'd watched his alcohol intake carefully, and over this amount of time, he knew how he should be feeling: a slight mellow with no impairment of judgment. Instead, he was feeling increasingly relaxed, despite the danger of his situation. There was something else ticking through his synapses, too. It was difficult to describe; however, if he had to take a guess, Nick would have called it giddiness. It was an unwelcome guest in his cranial space, yet the longer it remained, the harder it was to remember why he disliked it.

Something was amiss in his brain, and that fact terrified Nick Campbell far more than the dark forest he was presently getting lost in.

*   *   *

Thomas carefully lowered the would-be combatants to the ground and released his energy grip. To their credit, neither dashed forward and began assaulting the other, though anyone looking at their eyes could see it was only a hair's breadth from happening. In this case, the hair holding it back was the smiling blonde stepping between them.

"Why don't you explain why you two were headed for blows?" Angela said calmly.

"I'm sick of his shit!" Stella yelled. "He was running his mouth again about how women have no place in the battlefield, and I decided to shut it for good."

"To be fair, my exact words were 'the only useful power for a woman is one that conjures up food or babies,'" Roy corrected. "And I was joking around. Someone must be leaking steel blood today."

"I'll show you blood," Stella said, taking a step forward.

Angela whipped her head around and met Stella's eyes. They stayed like that for only a moment before Stella pulled her foot back to its previous position.

"To make sure I understand, Roy made a misogynist comment about women being weak, and Stella opted to give him an objective lesson in the incorrectness of his assumptions. Right?" Angela asked.

"They also bickered for a while before it came to blows," a random voice in the crowd volunteered.

"I'd assumed about as much," Angela said. "Okay then, have at it." She moved backward.

"Wait, what?" Thomas squawked.

"They're having a legitimate disagreement, and neither of them is going to get seriously injured from duking it out. All I ask is that you take it to the woods, so you don't mess up the bus or anyone's tents," Angela said. "And by ask, I hope you can infer what I mean."

They inferred quite well.

"Truce until we're a few minutes out in the woods," Roy proposed.

"Fine by me," Stella agreed. "I can wait a bit to mess up those pretty-boy looks."

Roy snickered, but began heading south into the forest. Stella followed suit a few steps behind. Silence fell upon the remaining students as the two fighters crossed the tree line and faded from view. Fortunately, it was quickly broken by a cheery tone.

"Okey doke, folks, I think it's time for roasting hot dogs," Angela declared.

*   *   *

Vince walked away from the crowd once he was certain the Roy and Stella situation was handled. He had to admit, Angela's solution made sense. They were both hard-headed and weren't likely to give up on the idea of fighting once it had been planted in their brains. That might have been fine, if they weren't too strong to stop once they got going. No, the best course of action was to just have them work out their aggression at a safe distance from the campsite.

A part of Vince felt like he should have followed along, just to keep an eye on them. Another part felt that he should go after Nick and Alice to make sure they got back safely. The part that won, though, was the piece of Vince's brain that advocated jumping back in the river before either course of action. Putting up the tents had left him sweaty and stained with dirt. He decided he would take a quick dip to cool off, then see which of the situations was the most pressing.

Vince walked carefully out toward the river, enjoying the slight serenity of being at least close to alone on the forest path. There was still plenty of noise coming from the campsite; enough that Vince didn't notice the footsteps following his own. Instead, he tried to block it all out and draw in deep breaths of clean air. He'd almost forgotten how much he enjoyed being outdoors on his own. Sleeping under the stars,

439

cooking over an open fire, even rinsing off in a river were all little joys he'd once savored. Joys he was looking forward to indulging in again this weekend.

Vince reached the water's edge and splashed forward. He dove under a few times, letting the cool liquid soak his silver hair and run down his back. He waded back up to waist-deep level and turned to watch the sun dip down below the horizon. He took a deep breath and felt several knots of tension flow gently down the river. There was a light splash behind him, and this time, Vince heard it. He would have turned around to investigate it, too.

The only thing that stopped him was the pair of arms that snaked around his body, locking him in place and squeezing hard on his torso.

125

Nick was lost. He'd come to terms with this fact several minutes ago, and was now in the recovery stage of dealing with such a realization. His first attempt was to retrace his steps back toward camp; however, the sun had slipped away completely and Nick's tracking ability was already poor. His tracking ability by flashlight was at a level of failure on par with the combination of moonshine mixed with chocolate milk. Had Nick been in this predicament a year ago, his only remaining recourse would have been to start a forest fire and hope someone came to investigate. This was not the Nick of a year ago, though, and he had another option available to him.

Nick stopped trying to find his way and focused his luck. He closed his eyes, spun around, and began walking in a random direction, using his flashlight to see, but making no attempts to track his course. Whichever way the trees seemed to break, that was the path he took. It was slow going, navigating the shrubbery in the night wearing only a swimsuit, sunglasses, and flip-flops, but step by step, progress was made. Nick just wasn't sure about progress toward what.

That was the thing no one seemed to get about luck. In a confined sense, it was very predictable, like a dice or card game. Under those circumstances, there were defined outcomes that were positive and negative. Good luck yielded the good results, and vice versa. The larger the scale of the task, the more variables were present, and the more potential outcomes were at hand. Good luck would yield a desirable outcome, of course; however, that didn't guarantee it would be the one he wanted. He was hoping to find his way back to camp, but he could just as easily fall into an undiscovered gold mine, or get chased by a bear into the arms of a beautiful woman. Luck, even when you could control the direction it flowed, was unpredictable. That was why he so rarely used his power outside of tightly controlled circumstances.

As the sound of a familiar sniffling reached his ears, Nick let out a sigh. Once again, Lady Fortune had heard his plea and then decided to do whatever she damn well pleased to him. Nothing to do but make the best of it.

"Alice," Nick called. "Are you okay?"

Her response came from higher than he'd expected. "Nick?"

"You got it," he said, waving his flashlight around so she could see him.

"It would be you," Alice muttered from the darkness. As Nick squinted into the night, he made out a bikini-clad shape slowly descending toward him. Alice floated down from the tree she'd been perched in and settled at his side.

"How you feeling, Drunky?" Nick asked.

"A little scared," Alice admitted. "And a lot lost. I didn't mean to walk so far, and then the sun set, and I wasn't sure what to do."

"Fifteen beers will do that," Nick said, patting her shoulder. "My bet says our friends have lit a fire to cook on by now. Why don't you float over the tree line and see which direction they're in?"

"Okay. That makes sense," Alice agreed. She flew carefully upward, trying to dodge tree branches with only a moderate success rate. Once she crested the tops, she could feel the night wind lapping against her skin. It took only a moment to spot the orange glow of her camp. They were a little bit to the north, maybe a five minute walk away. Alice let out a sigh of relief and lowered herself back into the trees. She took a few more scratches as she flew toward the beacon of Nick's flashlight, however, she ultimately reached the ground safely.

"Did you see it?" Nick asked.

"I sure did," Alice replied.

"Whew. Okay, Princess, you point the way, and we can get out of these damn woods," Nick said.

Alice opened her mouth to tell him the appropriate direction, but before she could, something else entirely leapt out.

"No."

"No?" Nick asked.

"No," Alice confirmed, her brain, boozy as it was, catching up to her mouth. "I have you trapped in the woods with information you need, and no audience. You and I are going to have a talk."

"A talk?"

"A talk," Alice repeated.

"Okay, what are we going to talk about?" Nick asked.

"You," she said.

"I guess that works. My favorite food is sushi, favorite color is gold, big fan of horror movies, fifteen inch penis, love long walks on the beach, just tell me when you've heard enough," Nick rambled.

"No," Alice said, waving him off. "I mean we're going to talk about just what your damn problem is."

"Wow, drunk Alice really doesn't pull any punches," Nick observed.

"Enough deflecting. I mean it. You act like this intolerable jackass with a never-ending stream of snarky comments and bad jokes. Then, with the flip of a switch, you can become this charming, knowledgeable, really sweet guy," Alice said, her voice raising a few octaves. "I mean, what the fuck?"

"'Intolerable jackass.' You sure know how to sweet talk," Nick spat back. "I explained before, the thing with your dad was just an act. I pulled together some crap I saw from movies about high society and did my best. I'm glad it worked, but that doesn't mean there's some super deceptive side to me."

442

"I don't believe you!" Alice's voice crescendoed higher, passing the line of stern talking and entering the realm of the yell. "I know there's more to you than that. Yes, that was the first time I saw it, but I'm not blind, Nick. I've been watching since then, and I keep seeing little snippets of that guy. You can lie all you want, but I'm done being a sucker. I know there's more to you than this."

Nick took a deep breath and steadied himself. He could feel that strange tickle in his brain still, clouding his judgment. Only slightly, but it was growing stronger. He needed to end this discussion, quickly. Unfortunately for Alice, that meant going for the throat.

"Alice, I'm sorry," Nick said.

"So, you finally admit it?"

"No," Nick said. "I'm saying that I'm sorry you have a crush on the guy I pretended to be. That wasn't what I meant to happen, and I hope you know that."

"You think I have a crush on you?"

Nick shook his head. "No, not on me. On who I pretended to be to impress your dad. You obviously liked him. That's why you think you keep seeing glimpses of him in me. That's why you've developed this radical idea that I've been faking who I am the entire year, instead of just that evening. I mean, really think about it, Alice, which seems more likely?"

Alice stared at him, her wide eyes gleaming in the glow of the flashlight. "You . . . you're lying. You're lying again."

"I wish I was, Alice. Things would be a lot easier. But the truth is that you got enamored with a fictional character."

"That's bullshit, Nick. I'm not falling for this!"

"Falling for what? The fact that you only like a version of me you saw for a few hours at a dinner—a dinner where you knew I was lying the whole time? Or facing the fact that the lie version of me is the only version you've ever been attracted to, a fact I'm trying really hard not to let hurt my feelings, by the way."

"Why would that hurt your feelings?"

"I don't know, maybe because someone I've spent half a year living alongside, who knows what it's like to grow up with the same defect, and climbed a fucking mountain with, had to invent a complex delusion just to find me the least bit bearable," Nick shot back, raising his own voice in turn. "You don't see how that might be the least bit shitty for me?"

"But . . . I know he's you," Alice said weakly. Nick smiled inwardly; her hesitation was the sign that he'd successfully sown doubt. He was home free now. All he had to do was wrap things up carefully and he would put both Alice's affections and suspicions to bed for good. And then, as Nick felt the genuine joy of a well-played altercation mingle with the giddiness from Selena's song, something slipped.

443

"Please, Alice, you don't even know the real me," Nick said. He slammed his mouth closed so hard that his teeth clicked. That hadn't been how he'd meant to phrase it. That said far, far more than he wanted to. Briefly, Nick hoped that in her still-addled state of mind, Alice would miss the meaning in those words.

One glance in her eyes dispelled all traces of that dream, like a broom sweeping through cobwebs.

"'I don't even know the real you,'" Alice said, some of the conviction returning to her voice.

"That's not what I meant," Nick said, backpedaling quickly.

"Now that, I believe," Alice said, a smirk twitching at the corners of her mouth. "Maybe you're right, Nick. Maybe I've been seeing that version of you because I wanted to. And maybe he's as fake as you claim. That doesn't automatically make this version of you real, though."

"Alice, you're sounding deluded again."

Alice silenced Nick with a finger to his lips. "You just said something honest to me. Possibly one of the very few things that has crossed your lips that falls into that category. Please don't taint it by lying again already. Just give me a few minutes."

Nick looked at her green eyes. The jig wasn't necessarily up, but if he pushed her any harder on this, it very well could be. It was more logical to wait, to let her sober up and hope she had poor drunken-recall. And, if Nick were being brutally honest with himself, perhaps a part of him enjoyed someone looking at him and actually seeing even a piece of what was really there.

Nick simply nodded, unable to trust his tongue not to twist any words that might start with the best of intentions.

"Thank you," Alice said softly. "We can go back to camp now." She took his hand and began leading him north. Alice came to a halt after only a few steps, though.

"Oh, what the hell," Nick heard Alice say, and that was his only warning before a soft, warm body and a clumsy pair of lips crashed against his own.

Alice was an awkward kisser, but what she lacked in experience she was not missing in passion. Nick had spent the entire year trying hard not to notice just how shapely Alice was, and as she wrapped her body around him, his efforts came crashing down. He kissed her back, a flurry of resistance and indulgence as he warred with himself inside. At last, one part pulled ahead of the other, and he pushed her back.

"Alice," he said carefully. "You're a beautiful girl, but this isn't right. You're intoxicated, and I'm seeing someone. We shouldn't do this."

"I agree," Alice said, her voice steady, but her breath panting. "That kiss wasn't for you, tonight. It was for the real you."

"The kiss was for the real me?"

444

"Yup. In case I like him. Because I hope you know that I *will* meet him one day."

Nick forced out a laugh. "Whatever you say there, Drunky. Let's head back to camp and get some food to sober you up."

Alice let his comments pass and instead, took his hand once more. She led him swiftly to the camp, though not so swiftly that she didn't get to savor leading him around for once.

126

Vince reacted immediately, his mind racing to analyze the situation. He had no electricity and little fire in his arsenal at the moment, which meant he could flare up quickly and drive off the attacker, but have nothing left for afterward. He was waist deep in water, so any fast movements to break the hold were going to be extra difficult to execute in the way of legwork. That left relying on a swift blow, coupled with his flexibility.

Vince twisted his right elbow around with all the force he could muster, intent on driving it into the temple of his attacker. It would hurt his shoulder, but unless the assailant had enhanced durability, it would disorient them enough for Vince to slip free. That was the plan, anyway.

What actually happened was Vince's well-thought-out attack connected with nothing. All at once, the arms holding him were gone and Vince was jerking through the water, knocked off balance by the momentum of his failed blow.

"Geez, somebody doesn't like surprise hugs," Sasha said from the shore. The wake dispersing through the water made it pretty clear just where she'd been standing when Vince was grabbed.

"I . . . sorry," Vince said, finding his footing in the water. "I thought you were attacking me."

Sasha tilted her head. "That's an interesting assumption to jump to. Got a reason to suspect someone might be out to harm you?"

Vince hadn't told her about Michael's Halloween attack, or the constant aggression the boy showed him at every turn. It just hadn't seemed like something she needed to worry about.

"Not really. Not today, anyway," Vince said. He hadn't had an altercation with Michael in months, so there really was no good reason for him to be so jumpy.

"Mmhmmm," Sasha said, walking back toward Vince at a slow pace. "You know, you're lucky your girlfriend has speedy reflexes, or this would be really awkward right now."

Vince paled. He hadn't even thought about that. If he'd slugged Sasha, he would feel absolutely abominable.

Sasha laughed. "Oh, relax, I'm kidding around. It was a good elbow, but it wasn't a secret death shot. Worst case scenario, I'd have a bump and some static in my vision for a few minutes." She reached Vince, the water coming up to her navel, rather than her hips. Vince was a few inches taller than she, and as she leaned against his chest, Sasha reflected, for the umpteenth time, on how much she enjoyed that feature.

"There wouldn't have been words to say how sorry I was," Vince said, curling his arms around her.

"I know that, silly," Sasha assured him. "You're all about keeping the people you care about safe. And you do a great job of it. I never feel safer than when you're holding me tight."

*   *   *

"Tights," she said, leaning over him. "What am I going to do with you?" As she moved, her curly, dark hair tumbled down, dangling only a few inches from his body.

"You could start by not calling me that," Vince suggested. His voice seemed to be caught somewhere in his throat, causing it to come out rougher and lower.

"I could, but I won't," she said. She smiled down at him, and for the first time, the smile could be seen in her emerald eyes as well as on her face.

"Worth a shot," Vince said, returning her grin from his own prone position.

*   *   *

"Woo, this water is starting to cool down," Sasha said, breaking their embrace. "What's say we go get toweled off and warmed up?"

"Why, Sasha Foster, are you asking me to put more clothes on?"

"I am, though, if you have a better warming method, I am quite open to suggestions," Sasha replied.

Vince pulled her back into his embrace and kissed her, running his hand through her hair and holding it tightly. He didn't pull, he just held her there, locking her lips and body against his own. He released her a few seconds later, pulling his face mere inches away.

"That do it?" Vince asked. He'd meant to sound casual, making light of the intense kiss they'd just shared. His throat felt thicker than normal, and the voice that emerged from it sounded like someone had poured molasses on his usual tenor.

Sasha didn't respond verbally. Instead, she leapt up onto Vince's long frame and wrapped her legs around his waist, burying her lips against his. The movement would have knocked most men down, but then, most men weren't undergoing daily physical training in the Lander HCP. The affection assault did rock him backward, though, carrying him toward the shore opposite the camp full of other students. Sasha fully expected to get another good kiss, then be set down by her boyfriend as he reminded her that wasn't the type of relationship they had. He took her by surprise instead, scooping his arms under her to get a grip, then carrying her the rest of the way to the shore.

They came down at last, falling onto the soft ground a few feet away from the river's edge. They rolled even further inland, bit by bit, a constant rotation of top to bottom positioning as they tried to stay comfortable on wet grass. When they finally broke apart, they were far enough from the water to have it obscured from view, but not so far that they couldn't hear its gentle lapping against the shore.

"Whoa," Sasha said, catching her breath. Her skin was tingling, and her body was quite far from cold. She tried to steady her mind and trembling hands. She'd

447

promised to be a good girlfriend and wait for when Vince was ready. And she'd meant it, too: he was too good of a guy for her to trade his mental comfort for some fleeting physical fun. That being said, if he kissed her again, there was a good chance she would tear off his swimsuit and tie him to a tree until he found his willingness.

"Yeah," Vince agreed. He felt like his whole body had been short-circuited somewhere along the line. Everything seemed sharp and enhanced; even the wind on his skin was noticeable. At the same time, his brain felt half-fried. All his thoughts seem to show up simultaneously, then evaporate into silence.

"Sorry about that," Sasha said, pulling herself to a standing position. She wanted to rest her head on Vince's shoulder again; however, she didn't trust herself to touch him right now. Not even lovingly.

"No, no, it's my fault," Vince said, remaining in a sitting position for certain logistically-embarrassing reasons. "I started it."

Sasha let out a small chuckle. "Man, how sad is it that we have a crazy good make-out session, and our first response is to apologize to each other for it?"

"Pretty sad," Vince agreed.

"So, let's agree: no more of the 'I'm sorry' stuff. We're boyfriend and girlfriend, we get to make-out guilt free. That's one of the many perks of being together," Sasha said.

"Along with movie and dinner partners," Vince pointed out.

"Not to mention someone to cuddle with," Sasha said. "And of course, best of all is that we each get a great friend."

"A very great friend," Vince said.

"All right, then: nice, logical perks of being a platonic couple. This helping you calm down at all?"

"Not really," Vince admitted.

"Me, neither," Sasha said. "But we'll get there. Maybe the cold water will help."

"You seem pretty determined."

"Damn skippy," Sasha said. "I want to be able to get kissy with my boyfriend, even if that means devising all sorts of self-control methods to stop it from going any further."

"Or . . . we could let it go further," Vince said.

Sasha's skin froze and her blood turned to fire simultaneously.

"What are you trying to say, Vince?"

Vince brought himself to a standing position, deciding eye contact was more important than modesty for a moment like this.

"I'm saying that you're my girlfriend, and I care a lot about you, and I trust you," Vince said, cradling her face as he spoke. "And that I'm ready."

"You sure about that?"

448

"No," Vince admitted. "But I don't think I'll get to be totally sure. There's some inherent risk in connecting with someone deeply. So, I'm not sure that it will all end well, and I won't get hurt. But I am sure that I consider being with you worth the risk, though."

Sasha stretched herself upward and kissed him gently on the bottom lip.

"I'll be gentle," she said with a slight smirk.

"Liar," he replied, kissing her lightly on the nose.

"Perceptive boy," she said. She leapt atop him once more. This time, Vince made no effort at all to stay standing.

127

Roy's punch caught Stella in the sternum, lifting her off the ground and sending her hurtling back several feet. So far, they'd just been dancing, a few light taps here and there. This hit, though, this signaled the beginning of the real match.

Stella rolled with the blow as she landed, doing a few spins across the hard, dirt floor of the forest and flipping up onto her feet. Roy idly noted that if she'd weighed the same amount as a normal person, his punch would have easily sent her all the way to the tree line. They were in a clearing about forty feet across, so that wasn't saying a whole lot, but Roy felt he would have at least appreciated the satisfaction of such a sight.

"That all you got?" Stella taunted as she got her footing. Roy's punch had taken some of the breath from her, a fact she was trying to hide by stalling. She'd been caught off guard; last time she'd seen him fight was at the beginning of the year. Back then, he'd swung wide and blocked minimally. Things had clearly changed in the last few months.

"Not even close," Roy replied with a smile. She was buying time to recover, and he was well aware. Hell, he'd gotten more experience at that than any other aspect of fighting in the time he'd been sparring Chad. Roy had no qualms with letting her catch her breath. He wasn't going to let her win, but that didn't mean he felt the need to utterly crush her.

Stella steadied herself and regained control of her breathing. She also took the opportunity to fix the top of her suit slightly. Admittedly, challenging someone to a fight while wearing only a bikini might not have been the smartest move; however, Stella Hawkins had never been one for a tremendous amount of forethought.

"Thank God, I was scared I'd get bored," Stella shot back, moving toward him carefully. Roy began advancing as well, a series of small, careful steps with his eyes never swerving from her body.

In a flash of sunset glinting off steel, Stella dashed forward, faking a right before throwing her momentum into a slide. It carried her through Roy's initial punching range before he could adjust to the shift. Taking advantage of the low position and the opportunity, Stella swept her legs around, striking the side of Roy's knees. They immediately buckled and sent him tumbling forward. Stella readied herself to nail Roy in the torso when he moved to catch himself. Instead, she was caught off guard as Roy threw his right leg in front of him, stopping the descent in a move that would have easily broken the ankle of a normal combatant. Roy pushed off on his heel, reeling against the fall and spinning his body around in time to take a swing at Stella. The punch was too short, but it forced her on the defensive as she scrambled back to her feet. Seconds later, they were circling each other once more.

"I make it a personal goal never to bore a lady," Roy said, flashing Stella his patented smile.

"No, just to infer that we're weaker, softer, and don't belong on the battlefield," Stella replied.

"Am I still inferring? I thought after a certain point it was considered speaking what you were thinking," Roy said.

"That is fucking *it*," Stella said, charging forward. This time, she didn't even bother with a fake blow, she just reared back and swung with a hard right. She was positive he'd be able to block it, she just wanted to make sure it would hurt. Roy caught her by surprise once more, though. Rather than try and stop her blow, he lowered his head and met it dead on. With his skull.

Stella winced at the unexpected pain, a movement that cost her the chance to see Roy's next move. This was unfortunate, because Roy used his lowered frame and her open right side to catch her dead under the chin with an upward blow. Her eyes flashed with sparks as she was sent sprawling. There was no fancy roll this time, just coughing and clawing at the ground as she tried to regroup. To his credit, Roy made no move to come after her as she recovered, though this only served to agitate her more.

"So, what?" Stella said, spitting on the ground and checking to see if she was bleeding. "You don't press the attack if the opponent is a girl?"

"Could be, or maybe I'm just admiring how nice your ass looks when you're crouched like that," Roy responded.

Stella slammed her fist into the ground and pulled herself up. "You are one dead motherfucker."

"Says the girl who has only landed glancing blows so far."

"I'm warming up," Stella lied.

"Sure you are, Sugar Dumpling," Roy said. He spread his feet apart and readied for another charge. Stella wasn't the type of opponent one wanted to let catch them off guard.

"Geez, your parents must have really done on a number on you," she remarked as she looked for the best angle to attack from.

"That a fact?"

"Yeah. I mean, for you to hate girls as much as you do, there must be some really messed up shit in your past," Stella sniped.

Roy blinked in genuine surprise. "You think I hate girls?"

"Of course you do. You just see us as holes to fuck, not equals," Stella said, her own rage boiling over and culminating in another charge. There was no good angle to come at, she could see that clearly. No matter what she did, he'd be able to counter. His headbutt to her fist had inspired her, though. This wasn't a fight in the gym, this was a brawl. She didn't care if he got in some good licks, as long as she gave them right back.

Stella slammed her shoulder into Roy's abs, ignoring the two punches he landed on her shoulder when she came in range. She used her superior weight to drive him back,

451

slamming him against a tree before dragging him to the ground. They crashed into the dirt together, immediately rolling around to get on top. Stella had more experience at groundwork, but the previous blows were muddling her head, and Roy's non-metallic frame gave him an advantage in speed. As a result, they soon came to a rest with Roy perched on top of Stella, his knees pinning her chest to the ground.

"For the record," Roy said, leaning back to avoid her hand that was clawing at his face, "I don't hate women."

"Sure, you're a goddamn patriot of feminism," Stella huffed from her prone position.

"Probably not," Roy admitted. "But I don't hate them."

Stella stopped struggling for a moment to look up at him. The boy was interrupting a good fight to make this point, so it was clearly pretty important in his eyes. And speaking of his eyes, they actually looked sincere at this particular moment. Stella didn't think she could have ever guessed what sincerity would look like on Roy Daniels, but there it was, plain as day.

"Fine, I'll concede that you don't hate women. You don't think of us as equals ,though."

"Agreed. I think you're kinder, smarter, and gentler than men can ever hope to be. And yes, physically weaker and softer. Paint me as an asshole all you want, but that's just how I see it. So I prefer to see woman away from the battlefield, safe where they won't get hurt. Because the world outside of combat needs them far more than it needs men, especially men like me," Roy explained.

"You realize that's still misogyny, right?" Stella asked.

"Realize it? I don't even know what it means," Roy said.

"And all the random sex?"

"I'm an adult, so are they. Everybody likes fucking. I'm not apologizing for that one." With that he stood up, taking Stella's hand and jerking her to her feet as well.

Stella accepted his help and brushed herself off. Much as she hated to admit it, her anger had all but completely ebbed away. Yeah, he was six feet and a few hundred pounds of pure dickbrain, but his motivations weren't quite as pigheaded as she'd thought.

Roy was feeling about the same way. "Guess we're done with the fight, huh?"

Stella replied by socking him in the ribs. Roy doubled over and began coughing.

"Hell no," she said. "I' might not be mad, but I'm still all worked up. Besides, I haven't had a fight this good in a long time. So there is no way I'm letting you go already."

"Fine by me," Roy said, coming back up and rubbing his side tenderly. "I'm good to go all night long."

"Boys and their empty promises," Stella said, taking another swing at him as he stepped backward.

The remainder of the fight lasted about five minutes. The sex that followed lasted considerably longer.

128

"So, day one was, as you've described it here, a 'hookup bonanza,' correct?"

"Yes, sir," Angela replied.

"I can certainly see how that would happen," Dean Blaine said. He turned the page in the packet of documents he was holding. "Now, the forest fire on the second day, that one will require a bit more explanation."

Ben squirmed around in his chair. The dean's office was plush and comfortable, but having to answer for the actions of a class of drunken Supers was worse than sitting on pins made of lava.

"It's really quite simple, sir. You see, some of the students decided to make a campfire at the end of the day. Unfortunately, we were still collecting the tubes, and we had the matches, so one of the students chose to do the job himself."

Dean Blaine cocked an eyebrow. "Would that have been Mr. Reynolds?"

"No, sir, he actually helped us quell it before it got out of hand. The one who started the fire was Allen Wells," Ben said.

"Ah yes, the young man who can throw explosive balls of energy."

"Yeah, the idiot figured it would be combustive enough to ignite the nearby wood," Angela scoffed. "And he was right."

"Indeed he was. The park service is none too happy with me about the damage left behind," Dean Blaine said.

"In our defense, we did manage to get it contained very quickly," Ben pointed out.

"You did, I'll give you that," Dean Blaine said. "Though you were somewhat slower in response to the glacier that now occupies a chunk of the river."

Ben swallowed hard. This was not the way he wanted to spend the first afternoon back from vacation.

*   *   *

Nick sat on the couch, watching television and applying lotion to the side of his nose. He'd miscalculated the necessary SPF to defend him all weekend and was now paying the price. The boy knew a lot about sunshine and desert heat, but less about the sunscreen-washing-off properties of a river. Alice walked over from the girls' side, clad in tank top, flip flops, and shorts.

"Sun got you, too?" Nick asked perfunctorily

"Like I owed him money," Alice said. She sat down next to him and pulled out her own bottle of lotion, one that was both more expensive and more effective. "Where is everyone? We've had all morning to rest up. I figured they'd have swung back to life by now."

454

"They have," Nick said. "Vince left with Sasha a few hours ago. And Mary came in a little after lunch, so she and Hershel took off to catch up and be all couple-like."

"Well, they are sort of a couple," Alice noted.

"Thus the word choice."

"Ah," Alice said. "Not to be forward, but would you mind getting the backs of my shoulders?"

Nick hesitated for a moment, then said, "Okay." Alice realigned her couch position so her back was facing Nick, then handed him her lotion. She slid the straps of her tank top down to the sides of her arms and pulled her long, blonde hair around front, revealing the bare upper half of her back.

"So, when are you going to see Bubbles next?" Alice asked as Nick's hands worked the soothing cream into her skin.

"Probably in a couple of days," Nick said blandly. "I've got stuff to do and what not."

"We didn't have any homework over the break. What kind of stuff do you have?"

"You know, just stuff," Nick reiterated lamely. He was having trouble conjuring up his usual silver tongue, mostly because he was focusing on keeping his physical tells under control. Ever since that kiss in the woods, he'd lost his ability to deny that he was physically attracted to Alice. He'd coped with this new development by keeping his distance, but now, he was kneading her flesh with his hands and things were getting more difficult. If Nicholas Campbell had any weakness, it was women.

"'Just stuff.' Okay," Alice said, letting it go. "You know, Nick, about the first night of the river trip, there was something I wanted to say."

A lesser man would have let his hand stiffen in fearful anticipation of what was coming next. Nick may not have been a better man; however, he was a better liar. His fingers never paused, and his voice betrayed nothing.

"And what's that?"

"Just that I wanted to say thanks for coming after me. I don't remember if I ever expressed gratitude. I was pretty drunk, after all. I just wanted to make sure I thanked you," Alice said.

Nick relaxed a bit internally and got back to the task at hand. So, she didn't remember things too clearly. That would make proceeding from here much easier.

Had Nick been sitting a few inches to the left, he would have been able to see Alice's face in a mirror that hung on the wall. And had he been gifted with that vantage point, he surely would have noticed the wry, cunning smile on her face.

*   *   *

455

Jill was sitting in the central area of their dorm room, reading a magazine. She flipped casually to the next page, ears working hard to ignore the sounds seeping through the walls around her. She zeroed her attention in on an article about toning one's thighs. For a second, she thought she had obtained a Zen level of focus, because the sounds ceased. This theory was disproven moments later when Sasha emerged from her and Julia's room clad in a pink robe.

"Hey," Sasha said, making a beeline for the fridge.

"Hey," Jill said back, turning to another page.

Sasha reached in the fridge and grabbed two bottles of water, then stood at the door for a moment, staring into its depths. She reached back in and grabbed four more, juggling the six vessels as she made her way back into her room and firmly shut the door.

Jill sighed. She would get maybe ten or fifteen minutes before the noise would start again. Maybe she would go to the library and read for a while. Or just go for a walk around campus. Or go see what Will was up to.

Jill was still contemplating her options when the ruckus began once more. She needed to have a talk with Sasha about turning on the radio or something during boyfriend time. Really, though, Jill realized she needed to start freaking meeting men. This was just getting insufferable.

*   *   *

"All things totaled, you had approximately five thousand dollars' worth of damage caused by the students under your watch, destroyed a small patch of a national forest, and caused ecological damages to no less than nine different species' habitats," Dean Blaine surmised.

"Yes, sir," Ben said weakly.

"Looks like it," Angela agreed.

"Well then, good job, you two," Dean Blaine said, setting down the packet of papers.

"Beg your pardon?" Ben asked.

"That's one of the least destructive river trips in the last decade. You did your jobs very well. You have my thanks, and the thanks of your school."

"Sweet," Angela said, hopping up. "We done here?"

"Yes, Ms. DeSoto, you are free to go," Dean Blaine replied.

"Cool. Come on, Ben, let's go grab a late lunch," she said, tugging on her fellow chaperone's arm.

"Okay, I guess," Ben said unsurely, getting out of the chair and allowing himself to be pulled from the room.

Once the door was shut, Dean Blaine turned his attention back to the paperwork required for the cleanup. Even with such minimal damage, there were still a lot of forms to file and sign. He briefly wondered how many documents had to be filled out by the dean after his class went on the river trip.

He couldn't be certain without the hard numbers, but he suspected it was enough that he would quit by way of setting the building on fire should such a pile ever be presented to him.

129

"You all look nice and rested," Coach George said as he walked in front of the line of students in the combat class. "That's good. I'm glad you all got time to heal up and re-energize, because we have now entered the last mile of your freshman year. And does everyone remember what happens at the end of your freshman year?"

There was no response; he'd long ago drilled out the habit of speaking without being called on. There was fear, though—fear and uncertainty dancing behind nearly all of their eyes. He'd have preferred to see it in every last set of orbs, but some of them were just too stupid to face the possibility that they wouldn't make the cut. There were also a few too smart not to know they were a shoe-in.

"That's right: at the end of the year, we have ourselves another set of matches. These won't just be fighting this time, though. They'll test every aspect a Hero needs to bring to the table. Strength, intelligence, cunning, resourcefulness, and yes, even a bit of battle prowess. So keep those memories of your time off tucked away in a nice, safe spot in your mind. You'll need them to keep you sane every night when you crawl into bed, your bones creaking and your spirit crumbling. These next two months will be hell on you, because I am going to be personally applying the pitchfork. You see, this is my last chance to get you pansies strong enough to actually survive the second year's training, and I take that responsibility very seriously. So, do we have any questions?"

Not one person's hand even dared to entertain a thought about ascending.

"Glad to hear it," Coach George declared. "Pair up as I call your names and get into your fighting circles. Oh, and we're changing something up today."

The students looked at him with an uneven mix of anticipation and trepidation.

Coach George gave them a winning smile. "Today, my little charges, I declare that you have had you asses whipped in mortal ways long enough. As of now, you may begin using your powers."

There was a physical mumbling, if not a verbal one. It was the sound of backs cinching up in fear, knuckles cracking in excitement, and eyeballs roving in their sockets as they sized up their opponents in a whole new way. If Coach George could, he would record that sound, put in on a loop, and play it continuously as he nodded off to sleep every night.

Instead, he began hollering out the pairs.

*   *   *

"As you all know by now, not every member of this class will make the cut into the sophomore program," Coach Persephone said, walking in a nearly identical fashion to her male counterpart. "Now, while George likes to take this time to deaden the nerves of his students, I prefer to sharpen the minds of mine."

Curiosity danced in the eyes of the Supers lined up before her. That was good. Curiosity meant listening and listening meant thinking. Thinking was what would make the difference between success and failure for her charges. That, along with creativity and determination.

"Some of the tests you'll endure will be combat-based. I won't sugarcoat it for you: with precious few exceptions, most of you will come out the loser in these encounters."

The gazes of several faces turned toward the floor.

"That is an acceptable loss, though, because it does not comprise the entirety of these evaluations. Think of it as giving away a pawn in order to take their king. They will hone their bodies and battle instincts over the coming months. We will be honing our minds and adaptability instead. We will double down on our strategic lessons. Your minds will ache with effort, and you will tear out your hair in frustration, but you will improve. And, at the end of May, when you go into your trials, you will emerge as victorious sophomores."

It wasn't the best inspirational speech in the history of the school, but it did seem to bestow her kids with a bit of hope. At this point, that was really the best Coach Persephone could shoot for. These Supers were fighting an uphill battle, proving that they were useful even without the ability to fend off an army. When they crested that hill, they would understand just how powerful they really were. Until that point, all she could do was keep them working hard in hopes of achieving what most of them saw as impossible.

Persephone at least had the advantage of knowing something they didn't:

Sometimes, attaining the impossible was simply a matter of continuously putting one foot in front of the other, no matter what.

*   *   *

Dean Blaine and four other figures stood in a small room lined with television screens. Normally, these screens would show a variety of rooms with different teams from different classes on each one. Today, however, they showed different angles of the two rooms where the freshman class was being addressed.

"Interesting crop," said the smallest figure, a woman' whose voice had seen its share of days.

"That's what you say every year," Dean Blaine pointed out.

"It's true every year," she countered.

Dean Blaine had no rebuttal to this—he never did—so instead, he moved on to the task at hand.

"You've seen their files, you've watched the tapes, and you know their names. Today, we divvy them up, and you have one and a half months to devise their test, then half a month to get it all set up," Dean Blaine explained.

459

"George and Persephone already made their picks?" This time, the voice came from a tall, male figure.

"Turned them in to me before Spring Break," Dean Blaine said.

"Such a prompt pair," said a new female voice, this one young and lilting.

"Would that I could see such efficiency from the rest of you," Dean Blaine said.

"Let's be fair, you don't keep us around because we adhere so well to the red tape," said the old voice.

"No, but I still expect you to take tasks like this seriously. You have the room for the next two hours. Make your selections and have them on my desk by the end of the day," Dean Blaine instructed them. He walked briskly out the door before any other snide comments could be made.

"Now then," said the fourth figure, a voice like silk being torn thread by thread, "I think it's time to get down to business."

130

"Shit!" Coach George yelled, diving for cover. The errant bolt of electricity sizzled by his head, narrowly missing him. Instead, it struck a hard, concrete outcropping a few feet behind him as other bolts followed different paths to similar results.

"Sorry," Vince said sheepishly. The first time, he'd been tripping over himself in concern that he'd wounded his teacher, but truthfully, after so many near misses, the initial panic had become notably subdued.

"No harm done," Coach George assured him. "Refuel and try again."

Vince and Coach George were having a one-on-one session for ranged training. They were in a room with exceptional insulation and no electrical conduits or metal. Coach George hadn't been exaggerating about the variety of resources at Lander. They really did have a room for nearly every conceivable training necessity. That was proving to be a very good thing, because, by George's calculations, the kid would have caused hundreds of thousands of dollars in wiring damage by now if they'd been outside this room.

"Yes, sir," Vince said, jogging back over to the car battery at the edge of the room. In the weeks they'd been training, he hadn't been having much luck, so they were now trying a new tactic. Instead of draining the battery at once, Vince only took a little bit of electricity at a time, used it in an attack, then drained a little more. This had two benefits in that it allowed a single battery to fuel him for a long training session, and it kept the damage from being too spectacular when his blasts went off course, which, to date, was pretty much every time he threw one.

"Let's decrease the distance again," Coach George suggested once Vince had, in a sense, reloaded.

Vince nodded and approached a small pile of concrete on the ground. So far, they'd tried breathing techniques, aiming techniques, and even rubber gloves with the fingers cut out. None of it had kept the electricity from splintering. Now, they had gone back to basics. The only time Vince had successfully used electricity was against Thomas, with a very small gap between them. The new set of tests were to see if there was a distance which was small enough that it didn't allow time for the energy to slip out of control. If such a measurement did exist, then the next step would be to increase it.

"How far this time?" Vince asked.

"Last time, we did forty feet. This time, let's take it to thirty," Coach George told him. He repositioned himself carefully behind his student. While a shot of lightning certainly wasn't going to kill someone like George, that didn't mean it was something he was chomping at the bit to experience. Especially not in his human form.

Vince narrowed his focus and slowed his breathing. He concentrated on the pile of rocks in front of him, on the spot just at the very top. He raised his hand carefully, his fingers tentatively outstretched. Vince imagined the electricity, bright blue and white hot, arcing from his palm to the rocks in a single, brilliant beam. He held that vision firmly in his mind, drowning out the rest of the world. Nothing existed outside the room. There was no coach standing behind him. Even he didn't exist. Nothing permeated this world save the rocks, his hand, and the arc that would connect them. Vince expelled a breath outward and let the energy fly.

It struck seven different spots; though, to give appropriate credit, one of them was fairly close to the rock clump.

"Crap," Vince swore.

"Chin up, Reynolds," Coach George said, walking forward. "Believe it or not, this is progress. It didn't split up as much this time."

"Yeah," Vince agreed, dejection slithering in his voice. "That means if I get really close, it probably won't splinter at all."

"And that's a good thing," Coach George reminded him.

"It is and it isn't. To be honest, I was holding out hope that the reason I was able to use electricity against Thomas was something to do with my mindset, or my technique. That way, I could learn it, master it, and begin relying on a new form of energy in combat."

"Which is what we're doing."

"Not exactly. What we're really doing is finding at what distance the lightning separates. That isn't me affecting anything, except how close I can be when I use it. I suppose I would just prefer overcoming a personal limitation to a physical one."

"Heh, that in itself makes you an oddball," Coach George said. "Listen, Reynolds, this kind of thing is a process with any power. First, you get the concept of it, then you find its flaws and limits, and then you figure out how to circumvent as many as you can. It's something all Heroes have to go through, and it can take a long-ass time. Hell, why do you think we put you through four years of this before you're even allowed to work under an existing Hero in the field?"

"I just wish I had better control," Vince said.

Coach George patted him on the back. "That's the hardest part of all this. Throwing cars, bouncing off bullets, jumping between continents, all that shit is easy if you've got the gift. But knowing how to do it safely, and, even more importantly, when to do it—those are the real skills a Hero needs to master."

"I guess that means I won't be adding lightning to my arsenal anytime soon," Vince noted.

"Maybe, maybe not," Coach George said. "The best arsenals are versatile ones. If we find out you can't use electricity safely from more than ten feet, then yeah, you won't be including it in your ranged repertoire. On the other hand, it could be a devastating technique to whip out in close combat. Even if it was down to a few inches, you could make it so that every punch you throw is an over-clocked taser."

Vince considered the idea and thought back to his first fight of the year with Michael. If his one punch had carried just a little extra juice, the whole thing could have turned out differently.

"That might not be a bad idea," Vince admitted.

"Glad to hear an eighteen-year-old believes I can actually do my job," Coach George said. "Go refuel."

"Yes, sir," Vince repeated, jogging back to the battery. If nothing else, this training was giving him a lot of experience in controlling how much energy he took from a source, rather than draining it dry. That was one skill he was exceptionally happy to master. It was a constant, daily reminder that no matter how much trouble he might be having, at least he wasn't Powered anymore.

That was usually enough to lift his spirits quite effectively.

131

"As our year begins drawing closer to its end, I would like to move our conversations to more summary topics," Dean Blaine said. He'd been taking it a little easier on them in the past few weeks, well aware that George and Persephone would be turning up the heat and stressing them out. Add that to the demands from their regular classes, and it could be argued that the real point of this semester was training in how to handle eye-gouging levels of stress. An argument, by the way, that would not be entirely off point.

"Today, I wanted to talk about the HCP as a whole. We take people with extraordinary abilities and a desire to help, and we refine them into nigh-unstoppable warriors of justice. Yet, at the same time, we take others with equally amazing talents and cast them out, telling them they are forbidden from getting involved when they see innocents in distress. The question I pose to you is why? Why do we insist so emphatically that the only person worthy of wearing the title of Hero is someone who has been given this course's full education?"

"Everyone knows that," Stella said. "Insurance."

"If you're going to speak out of turn, you could at least present a fully-formed argument," Dean Blaine chastised her.

"Okay," Stella said. "I mean, it's really obvious. People with abilities can cause a whole lot of collateral damage, even more so when they are fighting someone else with powers. That means people filing insurance claims for their homes and businesses. The companies really hate paying out all that money, though. They'd make us quit getting into fights, but regular law enforcement agencies aren't able to restrain people with strong powers. At least, not as effectively as we can. So since they can't tell us not to stop Supers who are killing and stealing, and they can't refuse to pay out every time one of us causes damage, the only other option is to demand that the people stopping them, the people we call Heroes, have been properly trained to minimize that collateral damage. That's why the training and certification started. It was so Supers could do their job without being held financially liable for every flipped truck and melted mailbox that wound up in their wake."

Dean Blaine blinked in surprise, as did a large amount of the class. Stella, while forceful, was rarely so well-informed on a topic.

"That was an excellent, well-reasoned theory," Dean Blaine said.

"My dad is an insurance adjuster," Stella said by way of explanation.

"I see. That sheds a little light on it," Dean Blaine said. "And Ms. Hawkins is correct. The roots of the HCP are most certainly in the goal of allowing those with special talents to use them to help people without being afraid of fiscal reprisal. That was the beginning, though, designed to suit a program far less expansive than our current HCP. Who else can tell me why we hold our defenders to such rigorous standards?"

This time, several hands went up. Dean Blaine called on the fastest to get it out of the way.

"Yes, Ms. Adair?"

"Because we have to know more than just how to do the least damage to a city block. We need to know how to avoid, or least limit, civilian casualties. We need to know how to deal with hostage situations, and how to cope with the political implications of chasing someone across international lines. Being a Hero means people are trusting you with their lives. We need to be as best prepared to live up to that trust as possible," Alice said.

"Very good," Dean Blaine said. "However, as with the insurance, these are things that are already widely known and accepted as reasons for the HCP. I'm more looking for things that you, as participants, can appreciate that an outsider wouldn't understand the necessity of."

Most of the hands went down at this stipulation. A few stayed raised, though, and Dean Blaine perused his pickings, selecting one after a few seconds of analysis.

"Mr. DeSoto."

"We're learning humility," Shane said. "Most of us came from towns where, if we weren't the only Super, we were one of very few. We grew up feeling like we were untouchable. We aren't, and some people needed to experience that firsthand to believe it."

"Now, that is an excellent one," Dean Blaine complimented. "Few people not in the program would understand just how important losing is. Mr. Wells, what is another example?"

"We're learning what to really expect," Allen said. "Before this class, it had never occurred to me how many hard choices would come with being a Hero. I thought of it as just blasting away at bad guys. Knowing what I do now, I'm approaching this potential future with a lot more caution. I still want to do it, but I have a better idea of what I'm in for. If I'd had to face some tough situations in the field, with no mental preparation, it could have ranged from problematic to traumatic, depending on how bad things got."

"Quite true," Dean Blaine agreed. "The preparation of the mind is, in my opinion, one of the most undervalued necessities we instill here at Lander. Mr. Campbell, do you have another point you'd like to add?"

Nick's hand hadn't been up, but he rolled with the question, anyway. Dean Blaine had made it clear long ago that the hand system was ancillary: he would call on whomever he pleased to answer him.

"The physical training," Nick replied. "I mean, yeah, most people get that a Hero needs to be strong, but how many understand that he needs to have stamina, flexibility, and pain endurance even when he isn't a front-line fighter? I think outsiders picture us just lifting buses and chewing on nails. They don't appreciate the full range of effort we have to put in just to be adequate in a support capacity, let alone a front-line one."

"A bit obvious, but valid, I'll give you that," Dean Blaine said. "Now, that's all focusing on the positive, what you get out of being here. That isn't the entirety of the process, however. For every student who graduates, there are tens to hundreds that tried for that spot. Putting aside obvious concerns about physical capability, why do we keep them out? Wouldn't it make more sense to allow everyone to help who wants to do so?"

"No," Vince said, speaking up. "Because not everyone should be a Hero."

"Would you like to elaborate, Vince?"

"I just mean that being looked up to, and exalted, that comes with a lot of prestige. A lot of power. That's going to attract plenty of Supers, not just the ones who genuinely want to help. It's not a bad idea to have some sort of filter before we just hand out a title that tells everyone this is a person they can trust and rely on," Vince explained.

"You're quite right," Dean Blaine said. "Heroes are trusted by civilians and governments alike. We have to be very careful who we give such responsibility to, and not just in case they have less-than-pure intentions. Who can tell me another danger of letting anyone through the HCP?"

"Because the worst-case scenario is that someone starts as a genuine Hero and then turns," said Chad, face staring down at his desk.

"Go on," Dean Blaine said softly.

"A Super who commits crimes is a pain for the regular people to deal with, but Heroes can handle most of them in relatively short order. When a Hero turns, on the other hand, he doesn't just bring his abilities to the table. He brings all the training he received in the HCP, all the combat experience he acquired on the job, all the secrets he was made privy to, and all the trust that other Heroes have in him. When a Hero turns away from the law, entire towns get destroyed and other Heroes almost always die."

"There is a very unfortunate amount of truth in that statement," Dean Blaine said. "It is one of the key reasons we screen so thoroughly before admitting someone to the HCP. We seek to determine not only who they are, but also who they will become over time. It is a difficult task, and one we put tremendous effort and resources into. However, we are not, I'm sad to say, always successful."

132

The class looked like life had come after them in a dark alley wielding a sock full of quarters. They were haggard, tired, and worn. Since the return from break, George and Persephone had kept their promise, treating each gym session as though it were their final chance to enact some sort of long-festering revenge on the students in their charge.

The battles were brutal, the mental exercises exhausting, and there was constant drilling of strategies historically used by different Heroes. The end result was that, as the class gathered on Friday afternoon, they didn't fall into line so much as gradually limp there. Some of them were suffering from literal physical pains: the class had just ended and they hadn't had a chance to meet with the healer yet. Others were simply laboring under a weary spirit, demonstrating physical distress as an outlet for what they were coping with internally.

"You all look like utter shit," Coach George said as they finished lining up. "And with only three weeks left until finals. I don't think most of you could take on a sack full of terminal kittens right now, let alone a trained warrior wielding superhuman abilities."

The class stood stoically, most of them in healthy agreement of his assessment.

"A mind is like a knife," Coach Persephone said, taking her turn to walk down the line. "It must be kept sharp, bright, and always at the ready. Look at you all. Half of you haven't even been able to hear this whole speech, that's how much your brains are glossing over."

Again, the coaches were met with a weathered, beaten silence.

"It is for these reasons that things will be changing a bit," Coach George said. "Persephone and I feel that we have taken you as far as you are capable of going in the time allotted to us. That isn't to say we couldn't whip your squishy asses into beasts if we had a decade to play with, but all we were given was a single school year. So, rather than drive you into the ground one by one over the remaining time before your exam, we're taking a different approach."

"As of Monday," Coach Persephone announced, "you are all ordered to be on rest for one week."

There was a ripple through the students, certain their feeble minds had snapped and full-blown delusion had set in.

"The gym, the training rooms, and all the facilities will be completely off limits to you during those seven days," Coach Persephone continued. "Once that time has passed, you will spend the remaining two weeks undergoing a personalized training regimen. By that, we mean you will work out in the ways that you find most effective. This can occur during your formerly scheduled gym time, or whenever you have free time. We are legally obligated to remind you that staying in the HCP requires the maintaining of a C average or better, so budget your time between training and study wisely."

Looks were now being exchanged, each seeking clarification from the others that this was really happening.

"During these two weeks, Coach Persephone and I will be on hand, should any of you wish to schedule time with us for personal tutorials. That will be the limit of our involvement from now until your exam, though," Coach George said.

"And one last piece of business," Coach Persephone said. "Many of you have noticed that there is a day between the last finals at Lander University and the commencement of your test here in the HCP. This day is used as a dead day for final preparations and recovery. It is something of a tradition, however, for the staff to put on a small festival for the students on the night testing is over. It will occur in the gym, and there will be food, some dancing, and games. This is done as a stress-relieving outlet, and to buffer between the sets of finals. We hope to see you all here."

With that, she and Coach George turned and made a swift exit. They never turned back once, yet the students still didn't begin to mill about until several moments after the doors had swung shut.

*   *   *

"Can anyone else not believe that just freaking happened?" Nick said as the group walked briskly toward Melbrook.

"It makes a lot of sense, if you really think about it," Mary pointed out. "We're supposed to be at our peak for the exam. That's hard to pull off when we're getting pummeled every week."

"No kidding," Roy agreed. "Even I'm starting to feel it after these past few months. Three more weeks and I think Chad would be the only man able to still stay standing on test day."

"Roy Daniels, did you just admit you think someone is stronger than you?" Mary gasped.

"Only for now," Roy replied with a smarmy grin.

"Yeah, well, this is a boon none of us expected, and I say we celebrate," Nick tossed out. "I'll go to the video store—"

The group groaned collectively.

"Not another bad movie night," Alice protested. "Literally, anything but that."

"Literally? Okay then, how about a rousing game of strip Twister?" Nick asked.

"One day, some lucky girl is going to castrate you, and I sincerely hope I'm around to see it," Alice replied.

"All dong mangling aside, I'm with the chicks on this one," Roy agreed. "Even Hershel is tired of those things."

"You guys are nuts. My choice in horrific cinema is the stuff of legend. Back me up here, Vince," Nick said.

"Yeah, whatever you guys want," Vince said, his eyes shifting about. "I've got something to take care of real quick. I'll see you back at the dorm."

With that, Vince was jogging off hastily, backpack bouncing against him as he dashed.

"That was odd," Nick observed.

"Let him be," Mary said. "He'll be back soon."

Nick glanced at her momentarily, then shrugged it off.

"Whatever. I say we start with the *Death Couch II* and *Death Couch IV* just to set the mood—"

This time, the group groan was louder and held for a full thirty seconds.

133

There was a timid knock on George's door.

"Come in, Reynolds," Coach George called out, not even glancing up from his work.

Vince stepped in slowly, working his way forward and standing in front of the desk.

"How did you know it was me?"

"Because my superiors and colleagues don't knock, and you're the only frequent student visitor who hits the door like he's scared it will hit back."

"Oh. Sorry, I guess," Vince said.

"Don't worry about it, kid. On my list of stuff to watch out for, someone who knocks softly isn't exactly on top. So, what can I do for you?"

"I wanted to schedule some one-on-one time to work on my electricity techniques."

Coach George let out a sigh. "I was afraid you were going to say that. Take a seat, Reynolds."

Vince complied and plopped down in the available chair.

"We've been at this for months now, and what we've discovered is that, at a distance of more than a few inches, your electricity arcs wild every time. When it does, it's impossible to determine which direction it's going. Hell, half the time, it doesn't even include the initial target in the spray of places it strikes," Coach George pointed out.

"Yes, sir," Vince agreed. "That's why I'm here to schedule time. So I can get better."

"And I applaud that kind of spirit, that a problem is only a problem until you work through it. That said, you've got three weeks until we put you through one of the hardest tests of your life. You're going to need to be in peak form. Do you think there might be a better way to spend your time?"

"I'm confused. Are you telling me to give up on using electricity?"

"Absolutely not," Coach George said emphatically. "I've known Supers who would kill for the level of versatility your power gives you. What I'm saying is that sometimes, it's all about time management. You have two weeks of allowed training time. Now, what do you think will pay off more for your test: struggling to invent a way to utilize electricity, or polishing up and refining what you can do with fire?"

"I guess that would depend on if I succeeded with the electricity or not," Vince said honestly.

"Not really," Coach George disagreed. "It's two weeks, not two months. Even if you do neglect other parts of your training and manage to find a way to control the bolts, you're not going to have time to master it. The best-case scenario is you walk out there with an unrefined technique that may or may not play out well, as opposed to being fresh and ready with an element you know how to use."

"I suppose there's logic in that," Vince admitted. "I still want to learn better electrical control, though."

"I'm one hundred percent behind you on that, kid. All I'm saying is pick your timing. Playing with new stuff is for down time. This is crunch time. Crunch time is for focusing on what you've got."

"Yes, sir. I think I'll do that," Vince agreed. He stood from the chair. "Thank you for your time, and for the advice."

"That's why they pay me the big bucks," Coach George said. "And, for what it's worth, kid, I hope to see you back here next year."

"Thank you," Vince said, stepping out of the office. He wasn't certain, but he was pretty sure he'd just experienced the closest thing to a compliment Coach George was capable of imparting.

* * *

A manila envelope fell out of Michael Clark's locker as he pulled the door open. He had just finished doing some extra Friday training before the ban went into effect and was going to grab his clothes to change back. This envelope was a new addition to his items, one he hadn't added. Michael reached down and scooped up the envelope, cursorily noting it seemed to be moderately thick with contents.

He glanced around, almost more out of obligation than expectation. If someone had slipped an envelope into his locker like this, it was highly unlikely they were going to stick around to be seen. He'd been training for three hours, so that left an enormous window of time for anyone to come in here and squeeze in it through an opening in the door. No, the only viable clue to the envelope's origins was the envelope itself.

Michael carefully undid the metal clasp and pulled out the first few pages. Some were newspaper clippings, some were police reports, some were just random photographs. There didn't seem to be any theme throughout them; not one that Michael could discern, anyway.

Michael was about to toss the mystery back into his locker when something in one of the photographs caught his eye. Michael's breath froze in his throat, an electrical burst of wonder jolting through his system. He looked through the documents again, this time, with a better sense of what to check for. He scoured them for five solid minutes before he realized he was still standing in the gym locker room. The cold air and blazing excitement swirled in contrast as he sprang into action. Hurriedly, he threw his street clothes on, tucked the envelope carefully into his gym bag, and made a bolt for the lifts that would take him to his dorm.

As soon as he arrived, Michael locked the door tight. His eyes danced briefly to a bottle of scotch in the corner. Michael brushed the thought away immediately. He could, and would, drink later to celebrate.

Right now, he had work to do.

134

"It's official," Hershel said as the credits began to roll. "We never let Nick pick another movie. All in favor?"

A reverberating chorus of "Aye!" momentarily deafened everyone in the room.

"You guys just don't appreciate good cinematography," Nick defended.

"By all means, please explain to me the cinematographic brilliance of *Blood Fountain 3: The Bloodening*," Sasha dared.

"For starters, there was the way the splatter patterns always caught the light in just the right way to maximize the sensation of gore," Nick said. In response, he was struck in the face by a pillow, hurled from across the room by Alice. Nick turned his head and glared in response, only to be met by an innocent smile and a covert point toward Alex. Nick wasn't buying it, partially because he wasn't stupid, and partially because he had seen her do the tossing in his peripheral vision. Nick snatched the pillow from the ground, reared back, and let fly at his blonde target.

The pillow ceased its trajectory in mid-air, floating slowly into Mary's lap. She was nestled on the couch with Hershel, and while his arm wasn't wrapped around her, their proximity was far closer than that of platonic friends.

"No pillow fighting in the living room," Mary said. "That's how things get broken."

Nick stuck out his tongue. "You suck, Mom."

Vince laughed. "You know, if anyone in this dorm had the authority to play the mother role, it would be Mary."

"I don't think that's true," Mary began, though her speech faltered when she noticed the entire population of the room, which consisted of the Melbrook residents along with Will, Jill, Alex, and Sasha, all nodding in agreement.

"It's a good thing," Alice assured her. "It just means you're the only one who can put everyone in their place. Also, I mean, you are kind of the mom."

"How am I the mom?"

"You stop us from throwing pillows in the house," Nick pointed out.

"You make us all get salads at dinner," Vince added.

"You make sure everyone has done their homework each night," Alice said.

"You've said before that if you could have a car, it would be a mini-van," Hershel said delicately.

"Oh, don't you start," Mary said, thrusting a finger into Hershel's chest.

"Sorry," Hershel said, a very unapologetic smile visible on his face.

"Oh!" Jill said, sitting up excitedly. "I've got one. You always seem to have Kleenex or tissue on hand."

"Okay, okay, I get it!" Mary tossed up her hands in mock frustration. "I'm the mom. You got me. Yeesh, part of me is glad I've only got three more weeks of you people."

"Three weeks to cram with as much vintage cinema as possible," Nick said. This time, he ducked the pillow Alice chucked at him. He was not so lucky, however, with the one thrown by Mary.

"I thought you said no pillow throwing," Nick coughed as he dislodged the pillow from his chest.

"Who's your mommy now?" Mary retuned with a Cheshire grin.

Nick reared back to return fire, but Vince leaned forward and deftly plucked the projectile from his hand.

"I'll be the mom. No throwing pillows indoors. Besides, you know she'll just catch it halfway there and send it back at you," Vince said.

"True. You combat types and your ranged deflecting capabilities," Nick said.

"Part of it is that, part of it is that she's planning on spending her next three weeks training instead of watching movies. Funny how much that can add to one's skill level," Vince pointed out.

"Three weeks? You've got to be kidding me. I think at this point, if we aren't good to go, we might as well just pack our crap," Nick replied.

"Have any of you guys thought about that?" Alex asked tentatively.

"Thought about the test? Sure, it's been a worry for me and an excitement for Roy ever since they announced it," Hershel said.

"No, I mean have you thought about what happens if you fail the test? About what it would be like to not come back next year," Alex clarified.

"Oh," Hershel said as the meaning set in. "A little bit. To be honest, I haven't worried about it a whole lot. Roy has gotten amazingly better throughout the year, especially since he started sparring with Chad. I don't think he's going to be top of the class, but I'm pretty sure we won't get sent home."

"I might," Alice said, her voice lightly tremoring with fear. "I mean, I do well at some of the puzzle and strategy exercises, but I haven't made any progress in finding new ways to use my power. I just fly. That's all I've ever done, and I'm not sure if that's going to cut it."

"Flying is a useful ability," Vince assured her. "The first rule in every battle is 'Capture the High Ground.' Elevation is important for a lot of different strategies."

"Useful? Sure, I'll agree with that. But we're not talking about just being useful, we're talking about becoming a Hero."

"By that logic, several of us are at high risk," Will chimed in. "My talents are most often assessed in a support role, rather than a primary one. Your power is somewhat

474

limited in its applications. Alex is little more than a weaker form of Mary, and Nick's power is nebulous and ill-defined at its best."

"Wow, way to cheer everyone up," Jill said, noting the downcast faces throughout the room.

"I wasn't finished yet," Will said. "My point was that failure is a constant possibility for us. We can't alter the abilities we were given, so the only thing within our control is to press forward with all we possess. We must train relentlessly, fight unyieldingly, and refuse to surrender in spite of all odds. These are qualities needed not just to make it through another round of the HCP, but ones we must absolutely have if we truly wish to be Heroes."

"That was surprisingly eloquent," Sasha said.

"I have my moments," Will replied.

"Much as I agree with Will, I feel obligated to point out that we have been banned from training for the next week," Nick said. "So, I think it is our duty as both students and as potential fail-outs from the HCP to try and enjoy ourselves a bit. You know, just in case."

"I can't believe I'm saying this, but I agree with Nick," Mary admitted.

"It only burns the first time," Vince told her. He glanced at Sasha, who gave a shrug and kissed him on the cheek. "I guess we're in for whatever."

The others nodded in a noncommittal fashion, which Nick chose to interpret as an unflinching, complete adherence to any word he spoke.

"Awesome," Nick said. "Now, to start us off right, the multiplex downtown is doing a blood and gore marathon tomorrow night—"

It was at this point that he was forced to vault behind the chair to escape the spontaneous, coordinated barrage of pillows directed at his body.

135

Alice leaned back in her chair and let out a groan.

"Ugh. I'm sick of this. What asshole created calculus in the first place?"

Mary glanced up from her own pile of books. "I think Isaac Newton is credited with a lot of it."

Alice arched an eyebrow. "The gravity guy? I can see why the apple took a swing at him."

"That's actually just a story," Mary said, her eyes going back to her work. "Like Einstein failing math as a kid. I think they circulate them to make geniuses seem more human."

"After spending a week reading over this crap, people who comprehend calculus seem less human to me than the coffee maker," Alice replied. She stretched her back with a series of audible pops and settled back down to her own tasks.

The duo was sitting in the library, the above-ground one for all Lander students, along with several hundred of their peers. With finals pressing down on them, the Lander populace was hitting the books with the determination available only to the truly committed and the incredibly desperate. Oddly, the two categories were often one and the same. Every table in the place was occupied, with an abundance of students prowling along the walls, eyes darting about for any seat about to become open. The instant it did, there was a mad flurry of movement, concluding in triumph for one lucky soul and bitter failure for the others. If any of them paused to reflect on just how much study time they were wasting by trying to study alongside everyone else, the thought had as much effect as pointing out to an amateur writer how much time and money they wasted each day by insisting they commute to Starbucks to pound out their masterpieces in view of apathetic patrons.

Alice and Mary had set up shop earlier in the day, staking out a table and leaving only in shifts while the remaining girl gave death glares to anyone approaching the empty chair. They'd been working together as finals drew closer, keeping the other accountable for the amount of effort they had to put in for each class. It was, of course, tempting to slack off, but with the other always at hand, giving the guilt eyes, they'd managed to stay on track for all their tests so far.

"Shouldn't we be devoting more time to training?" Alice asked a few minutes later.

"Think it will make a difference?" Mary asked.

"Honestly . . . no. Not really. I think I'll just need to warm up for a few days before. I don't see me getting much better than where I'm at, though," Alice admitted.

"Same here. Think another few hours figuring out this math will help?"

"Eeeeeerrrrrmmmmmmmm . . . probably," Alice yielded.

"Then back to it," Mary replied. "Only another two hours, and we can break for dinner."

"That'll be nice," Alice said.

"Yeah. Plus we can use flash cards to drill each other while we eat," Mary pointed out.

The thump of Alice's head slamming into her books was loud enough to draw a chorus of shushes from the nearby tables.

*   *   *

Alex turned the page in his book and let out a deep breath. Unlike the girls, he was doing his study time alone in his dorm room. His roommate was off training his body for the exam, so Alex had the place to himself. That was a good thing; he functioned best in peace and quiet.

Alex sat cross-legged on his bed, a biology book resting comfortably in his lap. All around the small room various objects were floating in the air. Pencils, books, toothpaste, and a pillow were just some of the levitated furnishings. About once an hour, Alex would add another object to the fray, splitting his concentration into yet another new direction. He'd been at this for a few days, and he'd successfully raised the maximum he could handle while studying from fourteen to nineteen. His goal was to hit twenty-five before the exam.

On that note, Alex realized it had been an hour. He mentally scooped up his alarm clock a few feet from the ground and turned the page in his book. Alex felt really bad for the people who had to pick between working on their academics and their HCP material. For his money, there was no strategy quite like multi-tasking.

*   *   *

To the untrained eye, it would look like Nick was watching television in the middle of the afternoon, when he should have been studying. To the trained eye, it would look the same, except they might notice the depression on the couch and the lines on his face that indicated he had been there all day. Nick let out a yawn and switched the channel.

He'd have to go out with Bubbles tonight—she was proving to be too excellent an excuse and shield to let go of anytime soon—but for now, he was just relaxing. He'd browsed through his class materials on the first day off and decided he had an A- to C-grade understanding of everything he would be tested on. That meant he was free to use his study time to sit in front of the television while mind-numbing schlock flickered across the screen. It would have been a terrible strategy to employ . . . if he'd actually been watching it.

The problem with both the trained and untrained eye is that they wouldn't see the cogs whizzing about in Nick's brain. They wouldn't know that he was going back through his entire year, day by day, interaction by interaction, and scanning each minute for information about the people he'd be coming up against. No set of eyes, regardless of training, could discern that the boy lounging lazily was, in fact, readying himself for his upcoming trials by searching out every weak point and emotional lever he could find in his opponents.

Which, of course, was exactly the reason Nick's body told the story of a boy blowing off his academic responsibilities.

* * *

Thomas fought the urge to vomit while struggling to gulp down some air. His entire body was slick with sweat as he pressed his hand against the cold concrete of the training cell for support. He'd been down here for hours, and he would be here for hours more.

Thomas had used his week off of training to think long and hard about new ways to apply his power in combat. He'd been unable to think of anything entirely new, but he had recalled a technique he'd tried and failed at when he was younger. Deciding to give it the old college try, Thomas had spent his first several days back in the gym making it work. He'd eventually succeeded, leaving him less than a week and a half to get this new strategy to a point where it was viable in combat.

Coach George would have undoubtedly encouraged him to use his time more wisely, and Thomas would in no way have listened. He'd been beaten in the first trials of the year by being ill-prepared for what his fellow students would bring to bear. Now, things were different. Now, they'd had months upon months to see the capabilities of each person's power. Now, there were no surprises left.

No surprises, except for what one could conjure in the scant two weeks afforded to them. Thomas finished catching his breath and stood up straight. A vibrant, orange glow emanated from his hands. His days were short.

It was time to train.

136

Roy caught the fist aimed at his head and twisted it to the right. Stella let out a muffled groan of pain as her shoulder was jerked and her body sent sprawling. Roy turned to intercept the next attacker and received a kick in the ribs from a highly-dense foot. The only sound he could manage was a muffled cough as he doubled over, trying to catch his breath.

"Gotta be quicker than that," Violet scolded as she stepped back so he could recover.

"And here . . . I thought . . . chicks . . . dug . . . lasting power," Roy wheezed out as his lungs did their best to recuperate.

"Real women need speed *and* longevity," Violet said, flashing him a smarmy grin of her own. "Speaking of, how you holding up, Stella?"

"Arm is sore," Stella growled. "No worries, though, I'll get him back."

"Good," Violet said. "Because, in twenty minutes, it's your turn."

"Fuck to the yes," Stella said, stretching her limbs as she finished standing.

The three of them had been going for a few days like this, doing one-on-one fights at first, then progressing to two against one. They were each doing some exercises in their own time as well. At the end of the day, however, they all subscribed to the same mentality: the only way to prep for a fight is to fight. A lot.

"That's enough girl talk," Roy said, rearing up to his full height. "I've still got twenty minutes left, and I want to see just how well you two can double team a man."

"I swear, it's like he wants us to aim for the balls," Violet sighed, taking a stance and bracing herself.

"Well, let's be honest," Roy said. "With ones as big as mine, it's harder not to hit them."

Stella and Violet exchanged glances. After several days of Roy's banter, they were getting used to his thinly-veiled attempts to rile them up so they'd come at him harder. That said, they were also very much beginning to enjoy when it was his turn to get attacked.

*   *   *

Camille exhaled and shifted her position. The sun was just cresting over the horizon as she sat on the hill, knees situated on a soft, yet durable, blue mat. She was doing yoga, as she did most mornings, though this time, she was doing it outside. She was near the edge of the campus, away from where most people traveled, but still within range of being discovered. That was the real point of today: to risk people seeing her.

She wasn't indecent; she wore a baggy shirt over a sports bra and some cloth pants. She was just making strange motions with her body and that was a little embarrassing. Camille didn't particularly like to be watched; she didn't like to stand out in the crowd. It was undoubtedly a survival mechanism left over from her years of abuse at the hands of neighborhood bullies who had hated her for being different.

Camille inhaled and rotated her legs. None of that mattered anymore. She wasn't the weirdo of her school, she wasn't the outcast cowering behind the bushes, willing her pursuers to not find her. She wasn't helpless. Camille was a Super. She'd owned that term for years now, and if she wanted to take it to the next level, that meant keeping her concentration in the face of distractions.

A set of voices reached her ears from some distance away. They were getting closer; soon, they'd come upon her doing her morning exercise. Her breath tried to catch in her throat, but Camille refused to let it. It was fine if people saw her. It was okay to be noticed. There was nothing wrong with being seen. She had to come to terms with that, because, if it came to a point where she had to use her full potential in this test, people were going to notice the living crap out of her. And she had to push through that. She had to be strong. No matter what, she had to advance to the next year.

She knew that *he* would advance. He would undoubtedly be here next year, fighting and training and laughing and growing. He would be one step closer to being a Hero. And he would need someone to heal him.

Camille exhaled as she lowered her hips and raised her shoulders. She heard the people walking by her, felt their eyes as they noticed the small, pale-haired girl stretching in the sunrise. She felt the blood rise in her cheeks, but otherwise, showed no response. Soon, the voices passed and Camille changed position again.

He would be here next year, and he would unavoidably get himself into trouble. He would get hurt. So Camille and her power would be here, too. That's all there was to it.

137

Shane knocked on Michael's door again. He and Chad waited patiently for a few moments before Shane turned around.

"Still no answer."

"I'm aware," Chad said.

"That's weird, though, right? Michael has his crap, but the guy never flakes on training."

Chad shrugged with the casual apathy Shane had grown accustomed to. "Pressure makes some people better, and it makes some people break. Maybe he couldn't take it."

"I guess. That just doesn't seem like him," Shane said.

"Yes, because Michael has shown such excellent coping mechanisms throughout the year," Chad replied.

"Never this bad, though," Shane pointed out.

"That's why it is called escalation," Chad told him. "Look, he isn't picking up his cell, and I can hear through the walls that he isn't in there. Let's give him the benefit of the doubt and assume he's off doing some special training on his own. In the meantime, you and I have only a few days left."

Shane started to protest, then thought better of it. Michael had barely shown up for three days of training throughout the two weeks, and he'd been distracted each time. Shane considered Michael a friend, but whatever was going on, it was apparent Michael wasn't going to share. So Shane needed to focus on making sure he was at his peak when test time came.

"Okay," Shane agreed. "We'll try again tomorrow."

*   *   *

Vince released a blast of heat into the concrete wall, creating a focused pillar of flame between himself and the boundary. In the corner of the training room was an ever growing pile of Sterno cans, adding an even more decrepit ambiance to the seared room. Vince had been training down here for most of his two weeks, stopping only for study, tests, food, and more fire. He'd worked hard with his heat, trying new blast patterns and ranged techniques. He'd focused on close combat as well, driving up the temperature around him to near intolerable levels for any human who passed through it. His body was sore, sweat poured from him constantly, and some of his muscles felt like a bat had been taken to them.

Vince couldn't remember a time he'd felt better. He released the bolt of flame from the wall and cupped his hands. Between his palms a fireball formed, swirling about until he threw his arms forward. The fireball launched into the wall and spread across it, leaving a swath of fresh scorches in its path.

Vince paused to pick a new target area and realized that he was more or less out of clean space to hit. They were going to have to do a hell of a job fixing up this combat room. Then again, Vince had faith there was an efficient process in place for such things; otherwise, there was no way this school could function with people like himself in it. He picked up a water bottle at his feet and took a deep drink.

Tomorrow was his down day, the night of the festivities. The day after that was the exam. He still didn't feel ready, not completely, but Vince had been around the block enough times to know that he never would. He would do the best he could to prepare and then things would just play out. He wouldn't know if he was ready or not until it was all over, because that's when the results would dictate the answer.

In the meantime, Vince still had a few hours before dinner with Sasha. The air around him seemed to be rippling as the temperature was strong-armed upward. The water bottle at his feet began to melt into the grey stone floor. Vince trained his eyes on a heavily scorched section of wall. Well, if he couldn't measure his progress by marking, he'd have to measure it by melting.

Vince stepped forward and let fly with everything he had.

138

Vince wandered into the common room to find Hershel and Alice already watching television on the couch. All three were clad in pajamas, though Alice's were a pink, silk set and Vince's were composed of a tank top and sweats. Hershel, on the other hand, was sporting an enormous t-shirt and a pair of work-out shorts. It was definitely dead day, a day in which lounging was not only encouraged, it was downright mandatory.

"Morning," Vince said.

"Hey," Hershel replied.

"Hi, Vince," Alice said.

"Anything good on the tube?"

"Nah," Hershel said, changing the channel. "Just some wildfires out in western California that they're trying to get under control. Interesting story, but once you've seen one clip of trees on fire, you've kind of seen them all."

"Too bad," Vince said. "I know the HCP carnival thing doesn't start until around six tonight. I've been spending so much time training, I'm not sure how to kill a day off."

"Ooooh, we could go into town and do some shopping," Alice suggested.

Vince and Hershel stared at her, their eyes unblinking.

"Screw you both. I'm a girl, I'm allowed to like shopping."

"I'll give you that," Vince agreed. "But we're boys. We're allowed to really not like it."

"Would you rather we let Nick organize another movie gore-a-thon?"

"The lady makes a point," Hershel conceded. "I'm scared we'll be seeing more than enough gore for my tastes tomorrow."

"It won't be that bad. We had to fight each other at the beginning of the year, and there were matches all through the first semester. Not to mention, we also had our daily sparring. I think the coaches have a good sense of what they're doing and won't let anyone get seriously hurt," Vince assured him.

"That's easy for you to say, you're smart enough to quit when you can't win. That's a trait my alter ego lacks," Hershel said.

"I think you give me too much credit," Vince said.

"Oh, you'll both be fine," Alice snipped. "Remember, you two have actual powers. I just float."

"It served you pretty well in the semester final. You outlasted both of us," Vince pointed out.

"Not to mention, it saved Nick's life on the mountain."

"Ah yes, what on earth was I thinking with that one?" Alice asked aloud.

"That we had a friend in need," Vince said, giving her a smile and plopping down in a chair near the couch. "It's kind of weird, though, you know?"

"That I saved Nick?"

"No, I mean being here, at the end of the year," Vince said. "Thinking back to how things were at the beginning, it feels like so much has changed."

"True," Alice said. "I was terrified of living next to a telepath. Now, Mary is a dear friend."

"Roy was completely unmanageable. Now, he's . . . well, still pretty unmanageable, but at least he's motivated to put in effort," Hershel said.

"I was so scared of my power, I went into the initial test with nothing more than a single lighter's worth of energy," Vince said.

"How much do you have now?" Hershel asked.

"About two and a half," Vince replied.

"Oh yeah, the world is completely flipped on its head," Hershel chuckled.

Vince shrugged. "I'm just not one to take unnecessary risks."

"So some things haven't changed," Alice said. "That's a bit reassuring."

"Just weird to imagine, if this is how different things are after one year, imagine what it will be like after four," Vince mused.

"I think that's the entire point of the HCP. Bringing us from the Supers we started as and radically changing us into Heroes," Hershel said.

"Yeah, except for the whole 'starting as Supers' part of it," Alice said.

"We were Supers when the school year started. It counts," Hershel replied.

"Very true. And given how many years of practice everyone else had on us, it's amazing we've all hung on this long," Vince said.

"I don't know. I think being Powered for so long gave us an edge over the rest of them," Hershel said.

"And that is?" Alice asked.

"We know what it's like to lose. We know what it's like to not be the cream of the crop, the top of the class. We've spent most of our lives considered pariahs, while they were hailed as demigods. Long story short, we had vastly more motivation to work for the Hero title than the rest of them."

"I can see that," Vince agreed. "With a few exceptions. Shane is certainly one determined Super."

"Credit where it's due, Chad is a pretty relentless guy as well," Hershel admitted.

"Yeah, what is that guy's deal?" Alice asked. "I mean, I rarely ever see him smile, or laugh, or do anything besides train."

484

"He and Roy trained together for a while. I can't say for sure, but I got a strong impression that whatever his motivation is, it had something to do with his father," Hershel said.

"Eh, who isn't at least a little messed up from their parents?" Alice said. "Anyway, gents, we've strayed from the main point of this conversation."

"How different things are?" Vince asked.

"No, figuring out what the shit we're going to do until tonight," Alice said.

"I have all my Dungeons and Dragons books," Hershel volunteered softly.

"Let's table that as Plan B," Alice said.

"You have a Plan A?" Vince asked.

"Did you miss the whole 'let's go shopping' thing?"

Vince and Hershel groaned together.

"We could get some of the others together and see what they think," Hershel said.

Alice shook her head. "They're as bad at this as we are. By then, Nick will be up and we'll all just go along with whatever asinine activity he pitches."

"Someone call?" Nick said, walking in to the room.

"We were just going over our plans for the dead day," Vince said.

"Oh, don't worry about that," Nick said. "It turns out there is a *Skull Splitter* marathon at the Cineplex downtown. They start with the original *Skull Splitter* and go all the way through *Skull Splitter 5: Daughter of Son of Skull Splitter*."

Vince and Hershel cast glances at Alice, hoping against hope she had come up with some idea in the last ten seconds that would deliver them from this terrible fate.

"As much fun as that sounds, we've already come up with a way to burn the day," Alice said.

"Oh, did you?" Nick asked.

"Yup," Alice confirmed. "Hershel, go get your books."

"Really?"

Alice looked at his excited face, then at Nick's cocky grin, then back at Hershel. "Really."

139

"Holy crap," Alice said, her eyes taking in the full array of festivities. Mr. Transport had just dropped off the five Melbrook students in the central area underground, which wore a significantly different look than its usual cold, stone veneer. Instead, there were bright colors hanging from the ceiling in the form of streamers. Large pictures of famous Heroes had been hung along the walls, and several oversized signs directed the students to different locales within the area.

"A midway?" Nick said, skeptically reading one such sign aloud. "I thought they were kidding about the games."

"Evidently not," Hershel said. He was dressed more nicely than usual, a collar on his shirt and slacks rather than jeans. The lovely girl whose hand he was holding (Mary, obviously), was also adorned in a slightly fancier fashion. The two of them had decided to treat this evening like a date night, since it was quite possibly the last one they would have before summer break. That was, of course, ignoring the possibility that one of them might not be invited back after the semester's end.

"I don't know about you guys, but I'm supposed to meet Sasha in the dancing area," Vince said. He was also wearing a collared shirt, though his pants were still of the blue jean persuasion.

"Dancing, and I'm sure with a DJ no less," Nick sighed. "So much for life after high school."

"Actually, I think it's kind of nice," Mary said. "A lot of us didn't get very normal high school experiences, being Supers in a school full of humans. This is a good fill-in for some of the things we missed."

"That's one way to look at it," Nick said. "You go find your girl, Vince. I'm off to check out the games."

"Count me in with you," Alice said. "I'd be more comfortable throwing ping pong balls at fish, than huddling around a punch table."

"What about you guys?" Vince turned to Hershel and Mary.

"I think we'll take the punch table," Hershel said, not quite controlling his idiotic grin. He couldn't help himself; it was impossible not to be smile-happy when he had such a wonderful girl on his arm. Had Mary been listening to his thoughts, she would have blushed. Then again, had Mary been listening to many people's thoughts, things certainly would have played out very differently that night.

"Okay then, we'll catch up to you later," Vince said. He gave Alice and Nick a perfunctory wave and headed off toward the gym, where the dance area was set up. Hershel and Mary followed suit, though not before Mary shot a sly, knowing look at Alice.

*　　　*　　　*

The gym hardly seemed to be the same place as the temple of sweat and pain the students had toiled in throughout the year. Instead, there were a series of refreshment tables, paper lanterns hanging from the ceiling, and an impressive sound system woofing from the walls. This controlled noise was directed from a small booth near the corner, currently manned by a junior in a grey uniform. The occasional authority figure, be it Dean Blaine, Coach George, or an adult none of the freshmen recognized, dotted the landscape. They were experts at blending in, making their presence known only in the capacity that they existed, not in that they intended to interfere in the night's revelry. It was, in truth, a little overly high school for the maturity level of the attendees, but it resonated with many just the same, and the overall spirit could be described as boisterous.

One such cheerful soul was Vince as he scooped Sasha up into a spinning hug, the outer layer of her bright pink skirt (it matched the tips of her hair) sent twirling about behind her. They kissed briefly, and Vince set her back to the ground. The music was loud enough that talking was possible, if a bit uncomfortable. Fortunately, Vince and Sasha had little to say that required words. They looked into each other's eyes as her feet made contact with the floor, and she kissed him again. This one was less brief.

It didn't take long before the rest of their friends had clustered around them. Will, Jill, Stella, Violet, and Thomas seemed to have all come as a singular unit. Alex surprised everyone, introducing them to his date for the evening: Selena. Her caramel skin looked all the deeper against the deep green of her dress, and her long hair had been styled up expertly with just a few wisps left hanging down. Vince gave his friend a questioning look, which was met with a shrug and a smile, as if to say, "Beats me how I pulled it off." Vince laughed and squeezed the hand of his own date. The group stayed clustered for only a short while before giving in to the inevitable expression of high spirits and close friends.

They found their way to the dance floor and began to make utter fools of themselves. Limbs thrashed about, rhythm became a poor, downtrodden concept, and endorphins surged through their veins. In the shadows, their supervisors smiled. Despite the harsh nature of the program, those selected to teach the HCP genuinely enjoyed the education process. One perk of that process was this time every year, when they got to see the young, happy sides of their charges, not the hardened warriors they were sculpting them into. It was both rewarding and heartbreaking, because each teacher knew that most would lose the ability to act so carefree. Probably by this time next year.

Another set of eyes watched the dancers, though these were not filled with such kind-hearted sentiments. No, these eyes were calculating and hard, but nearly brimming over with excitement. These eyes told the story of retribution long denied that was on the cusp of being unfurled. For the moment, all they did was watch. This moment had been so long in the making that there was no need to rush. It needed to be perfect, because the owner of those eyes had a feeling he would be savoring it for years to come.

140

The various classrooms that dotted the underground area had been filled with carnival-style games of chance for the delight of those who considered themselves too refined for such frivolity as dancing. The music from the gym could still be heard, thanks to a well-connected (but thankfully low in volume) PA system with speakers at each corner. Grey-uniformed middle classmen were tasked with manning the various booths, serving as free labor as well as a control should some of the youngsters get rowdy.

"This is ultra-lame," Nick complained as he and Alice meandered the halls. "I mean, seriously, dart throwing? Haven't we all spent, like, the past couple of months training in ranged combat?"

"I think it's quaint," Alice disagreed. "It's a reminder of the normal world. It's easy to get so caught up in all this that you forget what it's like for the rest of the humans. Or the rest of the Supers, for that matter. I have trouble remembering a time when the HCP didn't seem to dominate a majority of my life. This is a pleasant break."

"Yeah, except that, for some people, that break might be a bit more permanent than they'd like," Nick said.

Alice looked at him, trying in vain to see past the sunglasses into the eyes that lurked behind them. "Worried?"

"Just aware. Not everyone makes the cut, and I'm not exactly a ranked combatant. There's nothing wrong with a little focus."

"Pfft, a little focus, my butt," Alice said. "This from the guy who spent the entire two weeks of training watching television on the couch."

"It was part of my training regiment," Nick replied.

"Only if you're training for a bad-sitcom trivia game show."

"And the lady has uncovered my backup plan if the HCP doesn't work out."

"Uh huh, whatever you say there, slick," Alice huffed. "I'm sure you have some secret scheme to slide through these tests with a passing grade. In the meantime, there's a more pressing matter facing you."

"What's that?"

Alice pointed at a game some yards down the hall.

"They have giant bears, and you are going to win one for me."

"Why would I do that?"

"Because I'm not above guilting you into dancing with me, and then stomping on your feet all night."

Nick sighed. "A bear for the lady it is then."

*　　　*　　　*

As time slipped by, the group dancing gave way to the inevitable coupling up of partners. Vince and Sasha were the first to slip off, followed not long after by Alex and

Selena, then Hershel and Mary. Thomas did double duty, switching between Violet and Stella as dance partner at their whims. Stella would never admit it, but she, along with several other girls, wished it was Roy making an appearance tonight, instead of Hershel. They were hard out of luck, though, because, with all the training and prep work Roy had been putting in for the test, it had been no contest giving this night over to Hershel. Besides, Mary had been very adamant that she get to spend the night with the boy she was actually dating, and the wagers of their bet still held effect for the next two days.

Hershel noticed Alice and Nick wandering into the gym area (Alice clutching an oversized, plush bear), as he and Mary stepped into the hallway to get a little space. This is where several of the games had been set up; however, there were also several classrooms left open, presumably for the purpose of those who wanted to get away from the racket for a while. It was in one of these that the duo found themselves resting after the better part of the hour they had spent kicking up the dance floor.

"Woo," Mary said as she plopped down. "I have no idea how some girls do that in heels."

"Practice?" Hershel ventured.

"I'd rather do a Coach George workout than practice that," Mary said, shaking her head. "No question about it, I'm a flats girl."

"I didn't know that point had ever come up for debate," Hershel said.

"It hasn't. I'm just putting it out there preemptively, lest you expect me to start donning pumps on special occasions."

"So, you see us celebrating special occasions together then, I take it?"

"Well, yeah," Mary said. Her eyes fluttered downward and an unfamiliar blush crept into her cheeks. "I mean, you and I are sort of . . . well, I mean, you're my boyfriend, aren't you?"

"I'd hoped so, but I never really wanted to press the issue," Hershel admitted, a tomato coloration rising in his own face.

Mary tittered nervously. "You and I aren't very good at this, are we?"

"Doesn't look that way," Hershel agreed. "I mean, we've been dating for a few months now, and I'm really enjoying it."

"As am I."

"And there isn't really anyone else I want to be dating."

"I'll second that motion as well," Mary said.

"Then, yes, I think we are, in fact, in a relationship."

"You certain? I bet we can get a second opinion," Mary offered.

"Nope, no need. I'm calling it officially. I am your boyfriend and vice versa," Hershel declared.

"Well, when you say it with so much confidence, I don't know how I can refuse." The two had scooted closer during the conversation. Now, they were locked into each other's eyes, idiotic smiles splitting their faces and a slow twitch of nerves jerking through their skin.

"We are ridiculous," Hershel said.

"But adorable," Mary tacked on.

They leaned in and kissed, their first one since taking the next step forward in their relationship. It was familiar, scary, awkward, and overrun with joy.

It, along with the sharp crackle of electricity, was also their last conscious memory for the next several hours.

*   *   *

"Where'd the happy couple go to?" Nick asked as the music dimmed in volume. The DJ could be seen evacuating his booth in pursuit of a bathroom and a fresh water bottle, so dancing was tabled for the duration of his break.

"Off, away from all these prying eyes," Sasha theorized. "A sentiment I can get behind, if you know what I mean." In case anyone didn't know what she meant, Sasha took the opportunity to slap Vince firmly on the ass.

"I'm sure they just wanted to talk in private," Vince said, eyes darting about as he searched inwardly for any strategy to hide his fresh embarrassment. Sadly, he found no such method: Vince had always been cursed with wearing the truth on his face.

"On that note, though, Alex and Selena seem to have left, too," Thomas pointed out.

"I saw her slip out with him a few songs ago," Violet said. "I'm going to go out on a limb and say they were definitely not just heading out to talk."

"Alex and Selena, huh? When, and more importantly how, did that happen?" Nick asked.

There was a collective shrug. "They hung out a lot during the river trip," Stella said. "I guess they found a connection."

"Huh. Kudos to him. That girl is crazy hot. A toast to our buddy scoring some out-of-his-league tail," Nick said, snatching up a few punch glasses from the table and handing them out.

"How about we just cheers to a great year, instead?" Vince offered.

"Whatever," Nick said by way of agreement. The friends clinked glasses and downed the cherry-flavored drink. A crackle from overhead indicated the DJ booth speaker was about to be used.

"I'm sorry to interrupt your fun," said a new voice, half-strangled with its own excitement. "However, I've recently discovered some information that the entire HCP needs to be alerted to."

Nick felt the muscles in lower back tense immediately.

490

"I just thought it should be known that, despite what they have told us, the entire Melbrook populace—Nicholas Campbell, Alice Adair, Hershel Daniels, Mary Smith, and Vince Reynolds—are not Supers. They're all Powereds. And I have proof."

141

"Sounds like somebody spiked their own punch," Nick quipped, attitude cavalier and brain slammed into overdrive. His eyes swept the room at a fevered pace, thankfully hidden by the tinted frames as he assessed their situation. Despite what years of television had conditioned one to believe, the shocking announcement was not met with immediate riots. It was instead greeted with confusion as uncertainty rippled through the crowd. Some of the students were looking at the DJ booth, trying to figure out who had broken in to make such a strange declaration. Others were talking amongst themselves, likely trying to figure out who all those names belonged to. The Melbrook students did, after all, only account for a small segment of the freshmen class, so they were not household names. It seemed some of the adults were making beelines for the booth, no doubt in an attempt to find out exactly what was going on and regain control of it. All of which were factors Nick could have handled. The problem was, as it often is, with the people they had counted as friends. Thomas, Stella, Violet, Will, and Jill were all staring at him, Alice, and Vince. Sasha was still holding her boyfriend's hand, though her body language made it clear she was uncertain how to feel about such a strange declaration.

"No kidding," Alice said. "I mean, I know stress is high, but that seems like a strange prank to try and pull."

Nick could have kissed that girl. She might not have been the world's best liar, but growing up around businessmen and diplomats had given her some acumen. Not to mention, she was smart enough to follow the leader when the time was right.

"That does seem strange," Sasha said. "Right, Vince?"

"Twelve years ago a Vegas paper called *The Strip Beat* ran a story about the collapse of a local restaurant, the cause of which was ultimately determined to be a young Powered boy by the name of Nicholas Campbell," the voice said over the crackling PA system.

"Sure, he can claim a fake news story, but did he go to the trouble of making a fake paper as well? You know that's where the quality of a prank is determined: in the details," Nick said.

"Aren't you from Vegas, though?" Thomas asked.

"A fact that is readily available to anyone in our class," Nick replied.

"This is really stupid, isn't it, Vince?" Sasha asked again.

"Three years ago, there was a police report filed against a Powered named Roy Daniels for underage drinking and destruction of property," the voice continued. "Eight years ago, there was a search ordered for a Powered named Alice Adair who floated out of her home's garden on a spring afternoon. And then, there are the literally dozens of reports of a young, silver-haired homeless child shorting out and inadvertently destroying thousands of dollars in property across the country. All of which I have documentation of, along with locations of the original sources, in the booth with me."

The tide of the crowd was turning. While initially, they'd been waiting for a punch line to the gag, it was becoming evident that whoever had hijacked the booth intended to be taken seriously. That shifted the tone of the announcement greatly. Nick noticed more and more stares turning toward him and his dormmates as identification was made and skepticism gave way to suspicion.

"While I enjoy a good witch hunt as much as the next guy, it is a lot less fun when you're the one with a wart on your nose. Maybe we'd best take our leave until they settle that joker down," Nick said, scanning the room for the nearest exit back to the lifts.

"No, there's no need for you guys to go," Thomas said. "Just because someone is making baseless accusations, doesn't mean it should ruin our night."

"That's right. Some guy is just being an asshole. There's no way you guys could have lied to us all year. Right, Vince?" This time, Sasha was practically pleading, her months spent with Vince allowing her to see the truth in his face and his silence, before the others noticed. While Nick and Alice might be playing it off well, the guilt of having lived a falsehood for so long had suddenly crashed down upon Vince's shoulders. His face was a tapestry of shame. As Nick looked at his friend, the strategy immediately changed. There was no chance for damage control. The only course of action now was an immediate exit.

"I'm sorry," Vince said softly, his eyes drawn to the floor, rather than face Sasha.

"Alice, get the hell out of here," Nick whispered.

"What about Hershel and Mary?"

"The whole place is wired for sound, I'm sure they heard our outing. Plus, Mary is a telepath, so if she's listening to any of us, she'll know we're making tracks," Nick assured her. "Now, hurry your ass up. Vince and I will be right behind you."

Without another word, Alice slunk off through the crowd, the giant, stuffed bear acting as a buoy to mark her location.

Nick stepped forward and wrapped his hand around Vince's arm. "Come on, buddy. I think we should get out of here while the air gets cleared. We don't want anything bad to happen over some silly misunderstanding."

"What do you mean you're sorry?" Sasha asked, pulling her hand free of Vince's clasp.

"I mean . . . I never meant to lie to you, Sasha," Vince said. Though the words were meant only for her, the meaning was not lost on the rest of their friends. Nick saw shock, then uncertainty ripple through their faces. He knew it was only a short jump before that turned into anger and betrayal, so he dug his fingernails into Vince's arm and pulled him close.

493

"Vince, if you have ever trusted in me or our friendship at all, then, for the love of shit, come with me right fucking now," Nick said, abandoning all pretense and dragging his friend toward the exit.

"What about the others?"

"All taken care of. They'll meet us at the dorm," Nick told him.

"I meant our friends and classmates."

Nick sucked in a tight breath through his teeth. "Vince, if we stay here, I can just about promise you we won't have any of those left when they're done with us. We need to regroup in a safe place. Now, stop dragging your fucking feet and hustle."

"You're sure this is the right move?" Vince's big blues were wide and scared. The kid might be hell in a fight, but he didn't know to deal with things like subterfuge and discovery. He needed guidance, and he was trusting Nick to provide it to him. To put him on the right path in this time of tribulation.

"Absolutely. Things will be fine," Nick lied. "But we can't be here when they find out that guy is telling the truth, and the room hits a fever pitch. We get safe, we let things cool off, and we fix whatever is still broken when the dust settles."

"Okay," Vince said with a nod, finally picking up the pace as he and Nick cleared an exit at the south end of the room. Once they were out of the gym, they broke into a flat-out sprint down the halls until they hit the lifts. Alice was already in place, and as soon as they crossed the threshold, she flipped the switch, sending them slowly back upward to the real world.

142

Mr. Numbers and Mr. Transport were enjoying a quiet cup of tea in the kitchen when they heard the front door slam open loudly. They exchanged a wary glance, and Mr. Numbers tensed momentarily as a flood of possible attack scenarios played out in his head. Their concern was (briefly) alleviated when the voices of their charges reached their location. That reprieve lasted only until they ascertained the context of said discussion.

"Didn't you see their faces? They aren't going to forgive us," Alice's voice declared from the living room.

"They're our friends. They'll understand why we had to keep it a secret," Vince disagreed.

"Forgive us? Are you two joking, or just playing dumb?" Nick berated. "Do you not realize the full scope of what this outing means? Forget feelings of betrayal from our friends, that shit is nothing. We're Powereds that have become and functioned as Supers in the HCP for an entire school year. Our existence challenges everything they know about the distinction between Supers and Powereds. Trust me, when that realization really sets in, we're looking at a lot of trouble. I'll be amazed if they don't have this house burned down by morning."

Mr. Transport's eyes had grown larger throughout Nick's tirade. By the time it ended, his eyes could have passed as twins to the saucer currently resting under his teacup. He and Mr. Numbers exchanged another look, this time, fully aware of the situation and taking up their respective roles for how to deal with it. Mr. Numbers made an immediate exit into their room, shutting the door firmly behind him. Mr. Transport took one last sip of his tea and stepped out into the living room.

"It won't be that bad," Alice said. "I mean, what do they care if Powereds can get control of their abilities? It doesn't stop all the Supers from having theirs."

"Alice, there are about nearly double the number of Powereds in the world as there are Supers. Powereds who have spent their whole lives being looked down on, belittled, and treated as second-class citizens. Powereds who, for all they know, will be turning into Supers with a pretty justified grudge by year's end. How do you see that playing out? Because I promise you, they're assuming the worst-case scenario," Nick said.

"But that's not going to happen," Vince pointed out. "We're the only ones."

"What's true doesn't matter. Only what they're afraid of is relevant," Nick replied.

"I'm afraid Nick has a point," Mr. Transport said.

"They're going to burn the house down?" Vince asked.

"Not necessarily. But he is correct in that things will be getting worse before they get better," Mr. Transport clarified. "This revelation will need to be handled carefully, and the public delicately managed. They will make peace with it, though. Eventually."

"What can we do to help?" Vince asked, taking a step forward.

"At the moment, with things as uncertain as they are, the only thing we need from you is to stay safe. I'll be extracting you all to a safe location once Mr. Numbers determines the optimum place for us to use," Mr. Transport said.

"Wait, you don't already know where we're going?" Alice asked, a new flavor of fear pungent in her voice.

"No, but I assure you, it will only take us a short while to make the determination," Mr. Transport said.

"Yeah, that's great, but if you don't know where you're taking us, then I'm guessing you didn't already take Hershel and Mary there," Alice said.

"That would be a correct guess," Mr. Transport agreed.

"Then where are they?" Alice asked. "We got slowed down by worming through all the people out celebrating the end of finals on campus, crowds Mary could detect and avoid with her telepathy. They should have easily beaten us here, but they didn't. So, where are they?"

"Excuse me," said a new voice, one soft and female. "The door was open so I . . ."

Mr. Transport and the three students whirled on their feet at the intruder, only to find one of the HCP freshmen girls looking awkward in the doorway.

"I'm sorry, young lady, but this is not an opportune time for visiting," Mr. Transport said briskly.

"I know. I mean, obviously. I mean, I was underground and everything, and heard the announcement," she said. "But there's something I really need to tell you guys."

Nick gave her a brief nod.

"Then you better say it quick, because I think this place is going to empty pretty soon."

"Right, um, so, my name is Agatha, and I'm in class with you guys," Agatha said. "But I mean, you knew that, I'm the only animator in our year. Anyway, I know none of us really hang out or talk or anything, but over spring break Mary helped me out when I was stuck in the library, so I know she's a really nice girl, and I guess we're kind of friends. Tonight, I was using my power to just sort of eavesdrop on everyone with some folded paper figures."

"Not to be rude, but I trust there's a point coming around the bend," Nick said.

"There is. I had one hanging out in an empty classroom when Hershel and Mary walked in. I was going to have him leave, but then they started talking and it was really sweet, so I kept listening in. And that's why my creation was still around to see what happened," Agatha said. She took in a deep breath and stared miserably at the floor. She wasn't one for speaking to groups of people, and this was going to be hardest part to tell.

"They were knocked out and taken."

"They were *what*?" Vince yelled, his back jerking straight as a flagpole and his hands curling into fists.

"What? No, no, no, that's crazy," Alice said, aggressive denial setting in. "I don't believe it. This is a horrible joke to play, on tonight of all nights."

"Both of you shut up," Nick said, not quite raising his voice to a yell, but projecting loud enough to overwhelm them both. He stepped toward Agatha, taking in every last detail about the girl. The angle of her eyes, the position of her feet, the wrinkling around her eyebrow, not one piece of it escaped Nick's focus. This was unfortunate, because it all pointed to a single conclusion.

"She's telling the truth," Nick announced. "But there's something I don't understand. Hershel might be powerless in his normal form, but Mary is a juggernaut. Who could have subdued both of them without causing a ruckus, and then slipped them out of the gym?"

Agatha somehow managed to look even more uncomfortable as she squirmed in place.

"That's why I came to tell you all, instead of getting a professor or the dean," she said. "I'm really hoping there's a logical explanation for this, but just in case there isn't, I thought you should know."

"Tell us who took them," Vince said. The initial panic had passed from his voice; what remained was a tone that was flat as a blade and just as sharp.

Agatha licked her lips and tried to remember the kind act of the girl she was worried about. There probably was a good reason for what she had seen, but as she remembered Mary's unconscious body being tossed over that man's shoulder so unceremoniously, she couldn't think of a single one that would fully explain the situation.

"The people who took them . . . it was the coaches. George and Persephone."

143

"This is ridiculous," Alice said, shaking her head. "We're really going to believe a crazy story given to us by some girl we've never even talked to?"

"She was telling the truth," Nick reiterated. He used the past tense, because after her revelation, Agatha had quickly excused herself. In her defense, the room had reacted somewhat less than calmly to such an accusation and only now, was reason reasserting its dominance. "That doesn't mean she really saw what she thinks she saw, it just means she believes it."

"The maybe she made a mistake," Alice said hopefully. "Maybe Hershel and Mary just went somewhere on their own."

"And turned off their phones?" Vince asked.

"I don't know. Maybe they didn't want to be interrupted," Alice said, clinging desperately to the hope of her fantasy.

"I'm afraid we have to assume the girl was right," Mr. Numbers said, walking into the room and joining the conversation.

"You heard what happened?" Vince asked.

Before Mr. Numbers could bother coming up with an explanation, Nick beat him to it with the truth.

"They constructed this whole place to monitor us, Vince. Obviously, the room is bugged."

"Correct, but hardly the most pressing matter at the moment," Mr. Numbers said, ending the conversation on ethics before it could even begin. Though normally, such a discovery would undoubtedly hurt the goodwill his charges held toward him and Mr. Transport, at present, Mr. Numbers would rank that as a "non-concern."

"Hershel and Mary's phones were both dumped in a trash can near the edge of campus," Mr. Numbers said. "There are also tracking chips in some of their pieces of clothing, and in their bodies, all of which I've confirmed seem to have been disabled. Whoever orchestrated this abduction had a tremendous level of skill, and a high level of knowledge regarding the safety procedures we put in place to deal with situations just like this one. I'm afraid both of the coaches fall into that category."

"Wait, you bugged our bodies?"

"Priorities, Miss Adair. There will be ample time for you to mourn your violated privacy at a later date. Right now, we have two of your group confirmed as abducted, and no idea if the rest of you are being targeted for a similar attempt," Mr. Numbers chastised her. He turned his attention to Mr. Transport. "I've spoken with our home office, and we are going into an immediate lockdown. They will be sending an enforcer as additional protection until a safe extraction point is determined. He will arrive within the hour."

"And what about Hershel and Mary?" Vince asked. "What's the plan to help them?"

"We have been tasked with ensuring the safety of you, our remaining charges," Mr. Numbers said, several degrees of cold forced into his voice. "I'm not certain what efforts will be undertaken to reclaim your friends, but I do know that we are not going to be part of it."

Mr. Numbers and Mr. Transport looked at each other. They both knew their role in the company. If home office wasn't sending their team after the abductees, then it meant no one was going after them. The company had decided to protect the three it had, rather than chase the two it lost, and it was sending down a representative to make certain the orders were complied with.

"No," Vince said, shaking his head. "We're going after them."

"Don't be ridiculous," Mr. Numbers said. "You have no idea how to find them."

"There has to be a way," Vince replied with a shrug. "I'll find it."

"That is not a plan. That is a slapdash idea that will culminate in nothing more than putting yourself at risk by leaving a safe environment," Mr. Numbers countered.

"I don't care. I won't sit around while my friends are in trouble," Vince said. "Though, I'll admit, I'm out of my depth and welcome your help."

"Ludicrous. We have our orders, and we are complying with them," Mr. Numbers said.

Mr. Transport, on the other hand, stepped toward Vince and softened his voice to a kinder tone, as if in hopes of reasoning with the boy.

"Vince, you need to think about what you're saying. Even if you could find them, what would you do when you caught up? Coach George is much stronger than you, and Persephone has ample cunning to go with her power."

"No question about it," Vince agreed. "But I won't be alone. I'll have Alice and Nick. Besides, I don't have to beat them. I just have to keep them busy long enough to make sure everyone gets away."

"What does that accomplish? You'd just be trading in your own freedom for theirs," Mr. Transport pointed out.

"Yes. I would," Vince agreed. "Though I doubt it would come to that. The coaches could have taken any of us. If they took those two, then it's because they're the ones they wanted."

Mr. Transport stared at the boy for a long moment. He'd been in charge of these kids for nearly a year now, and he'd seen them change and grow so much in that short time. Mr. Transport still remembered Vince on that first day, so awkward and uncertain in how to handle himself. The boy had gotten comfortable here, but the one thing he'd never truly overcome was that lingering fear about his power. It tainted everything he did, colored his own confidence and how he carried himself through life. There was no fear in

499

his eyes right now, though, only a relentless drive to act. Looking at those eyes, Mr. Transport realized the only way he was going to stop Vince was to knock him unconscious, and even then, he wasn't one hundred percent sure the boy's body wouldn't keep crawling toward the door.

"We'll help you," Mr. Transport said.

"We most certainly will not," Mr. Numbers disagreed. "Mr. Transport, do I need to remind you that—"

"Enough, Luke!" Mr. Transport said, whipping his head toward his partner and raising his voice. "They took our fucking kids. Mary and Hershel, the students we've watched over and we've said we were responsible for. We were supposed to protect them and that rat son-of-a-bitch snatched them right out from under us."

"While I understand your attachment, there is no need to let emotion cloud our judgment," Mr. Numbers said, his voice remaining perfectly even. "We have our orders, and we will comply with them."

Mr. Transport scooped something off the coffee table in a fluid motion and strode over to his partner. When he next spoke, his voice was no longer raised; instead, it was a whisper with the intensity of a deathbed confession.

"They took our kids. I'm not the company, and I'm not some stranger. Don't pull the automaton act with me. I know you aren't unfeeling. I know you're pissed off. I know you're aware that no one else is going to help them."

"They are not 'our kids,' Mr. Transport. They are just our latest assignment. An assignment that has been altered."

"Sure they aren't," Mr. Transport said. He slapped his right hand into Mr. Numbers's own palm, pressing the object he'd nabbed from the table into the shorter man's flesh.

Mr. Numbers turned his hand up slowly, revealing the white king from the chess set resting between his fingers.

"They took Mary and Hershel. And the company is just going to let them go."

"We have spent our lives as loyal employees. How do you recommend we even go about the act of committing treason against our handlers?" Mr. Numbers asked.

"Easy. With a whole lot of lying," Mr. Transport replied.

"You're sure you want to do this?" Mr. Numbers asked.

"I am."

"We don't have long before the enforcer arrives."

"Then we'll move fast."

Mr. Numbers curled his fingers around the chess piece, grasping it tightly in the ball of his fist.

"I'll go talk to the other half," Mr. Numbers said.

"I'll drop you off in a moment," Mr. Transport said, giving his partner a brief smile. He turned to address the others, who had been watching their hushed exchange with growing trepidation.

"We can't do much, but we'll help," Mr. Transport announced.

"Thank you," Vince said. "With all of us working together, I know we can help our friends."

"Yeah, just one problem with that," Nick chimed in, taking a few steps away from the other two. "You guys can have fun riding up and playing cowboy, but my ass is out of here."

144

"That's not funny, Nick," Alice chided him.

"I'm not joking," Nick told her. Gone was his usual smirk and taunting tone. Instead, his face was pinched and serious, coated with more gravity than any of the dorm's residents could remember seeing before. "I'll stay until we get the all clear, and then I'm going back to Vegas."

"But our friends are in trouble," Vince said.

"Your friends, Vince," Nick corrected. "In case you missed the big reveal downstairs, our cover just got blown. Now, while you and Mary and probably Roy can all still get by after being outed, my only shot was to fly under the radar. The blowing of the whistle on us signaled the end of my career at Lander."

"That doesn't change the fact that Mary and Hershel need us, though," Alice jumped in.

Nick laughed, a hard and bitter sound, instead of his usual robust chuckles.

"What part of this aren't you getting? I'm leaving. That means I'm done with this whole facade. I'm not risking my neck to save those two, because it's not my problem. They mean nothing to me, and I no longer have to pretend otherwise."

"I don't understand," Vince said slowly. "You're our friend, a fellow former Powered. You're one of us."

"No, Vince. I'm just a great liar who wanted to learn as much about his abilities as he could," Nick told him, something that might have been gentleness leaking into his voice. "Nothing personal. The day our secret came out was always going to be my exit. I just needed a group of allies to use during my time here."

"I don't believe you," Vince said simply.

"I didn't expect you to," Nick said, half a smile twitching across his face.

"You'll come help us. I know you will," Vince told him, patting him on the shoulder. "I have to go get ready for the fight, but I have faith you'll reach the right decision. There's more to you than you think."

Without another word, Vince walked away, past Mr. Numbers and Mr. Transport, who were furtively whispering in their own corner, content to let the students resolve their own problems while the duo tackled logistics of the rescue effort.

"Same old Vince," Nick said, shaking his head. He turned to Alice. "Are you going to give a cute little speech, too?"

"No," Alice said softly. "I just want to know something. You're saying you were lying this entire time? About everything?"

"Sorry, Alice, but yes. I guess, on the plus side, I can finally admit your suspicions of my duplicitous nature were right. Kudos. You're the only non-telepath one who caught on."

"I guess I was," Alice said. Nick expected a lot of things to follow. He was braced for tears, accusations, pleas, or even yelling. Unfortunately, he was not braced for the right hook Alice deftly slammed into his face. There was an audible CRACK and a muffled thudding as Nick fell to the floor, his hands racing up to cover the eye Alice had punched. Nearby, his sunglasses tumbled to the ground as well, cleaved neatly in two by the blow, the left eye's lens spinning to a stop some feet away.

"What the *fuck*?" Nick demanded from his prone position on the floor.

"You lied to us, you manipulated us, you want to abandon us, and you're surprised I hit you? I thought you were supposed to be smart!" Alice shook her hand in pain with as much subtlety as she could muster, trying not to let her eyes tear up from a potent mixture of injury, outrage, and betrayal.

"I did what I had to in order to get by," Nick spat at her.

"Bullshit. You could have gotten by on your own if you were so determined to stay alone. You didn't have to be the bastard who makes people trust him, only to bail when things get hard. You didn't have to let us think we could . . . care." Alice stared down at the boy she had spent so much of the year fighting with, pining after, verbally sparring with, and finding comfort in. And much as she hated herself for it, a part of her still wanted to offer him a hand up from the ground.

"You know what really turns my stomach, though? That night I kissed you, I did it hoping that under the slick veneer there was actually this decent guy with good reasons for hiding himself. I thought that the man behind the mask had to be better. And now I find out that the real you is nothing but a selfish coward who won't risk anything for people who would put it all on the line for him if things were reversed."

"Are you done yet?" Nick asked, glaring up at her unabashedly.

"Only with you," Alice said, spinning on her heel and walking away.

*   *   *

Hershel's eyes began to flutter as he came around. His first thought was wondering who had stuffed his head full of cotton. His second was to realize that probably wasn't the case, but he was working through one hell of a groggy headache.

"I still wish we could have used the teleporter," said a female voice, though it sounded vaguely muffled, like it was coming through a wall.

"Wish in one hand, shit in the other," barked back a harsh, male voice. This one, Hershel took only seconds to place; he'd heard far more of it, after all.

Hershel opened his eyes to see what was going on. He didn't remember anything after kissing Mary, so he had no idea why his head hurt so bad. Or why he was apparently riding in the back of a moving truck. Or why he was handcuffed and shackled to the floor. What had been mere curiosity was quickly transitioning to apprehension.

"Looks like Sleeping Beauty is coming around," Coach George said, giving him a smile. Hershel noticed that Mary was sitting next to him, not handcuffed, but also not conscious. She had a silver mechanism wrapped around her head that he was certain hadn't been there previously.

"Was goin ahn?" Hershel asked, his tongue feeling thick and slow in his mouth.

"Whew, seems like that slumber Persephone induced did a doozy on you, Daniels," Coach George said. "I think she might have used too much. Sorry about that."

Hershel wasn't sure how well he could communicate verbally, so instead of trying again, he looked around, then raised his metal ensnared hands with a questioning look on his face.

"Ah, you want me to explain, I take it?"

Hershel nodded emphatically.

"Well, Daniels, the short answer is actually pretty simple," Coach George said with a reassuring smile. "You're being kidnapped."

145

"Klidnrapped?" Hershel mumbled, his mind comprehending, but his mouth still refusing its usual duties.

"Close enough," Coach George agreed. "Though, to be honest, you're more being brought along because you were there. Wrong place, wrong time sort of thing. There was only one of you we actually wanted."

Hershel's eyes flicked to Mary.

"Obviously. Process of elimination when there are only two of you isn't that tough," Coach George confirmed.

"Wats on hler hlead?"

"Oh, you like? It's a subsonic neutralization . . . aw fuck, this thing has a really technical name, but I can never remember it all. It's a gizmo that keeps people unconscious. Very useful, but very controlled and hard to come by. Hence why you aren't sporting one. I mean, why bother?"

"Caush I wash jusht there," Hershel managed to spit out.

"Yes, that," Coach George agreed. "And the more obvious reason. Mary is one of the most powerful advanced minds in recorded history, let alone at her age. Containing her awake would be hellacious, to say the least. You, on the other hand, are a fat smart-kid with self-esteem issues."

"Roy," was all Hershel managed to get out before Coach George laughed.

"Roy? I'm sorry, do you think I'm going to be giving you any whiskey? You can't access Roy, and that means you're of no more concern to me, than any other regular human."

Coach George paused for a moment and regarded his conscious captive.

"It's kind of funny, you know; back when you were just Powered, you almost certainly would have shifted by now. But without a specific trigger, you're stuck there, utterly helpless. In a way, you were actually stronger back before you had any control. Ain't that a bitch?"

Hershel made a valiant effort to spit at Coach George, but his slippery tongue and untrustworthy mouth betrayed him once more, leading to little more than a stream of drool falling from his lips. Though his cheeks burned on instinct, his eyes continued to send daggers at Coach George's rugged, unbearably smiling face.

* * *

"We have fifteen minutes," Mr. Transport announced as he returned to the room. He had left with Mr. Numbers only seconds prior, but was returning as a solo act. "At that point, we will go, pick up Mr. Numbers, find out Mary and Hershel's location, drop you off, and return to meet the man coming to stop us from doing those very things."

"You won't stay and help?" Alice asked, a new dimension of fear entering her voice. Losing Nick had been worrying; losing the only two adults left in their party was an altogether terrifying development.

Mr. Transport shook his head. "Alice, try to understand. If Mr. Numbers and I are believed to have gone against company orders, then come next year, not only is there zero chance of us still being here, but there will be vast repercussions for him and me both. If they just think you all got the drop on us, we might still be able to swing the same post here next year. Additionally, we will be here to distract our . . . associate from finding you all too soon."

"Why does that matter?"

"Because his order will only be to recover you three. It won't bear regard to your friends. And he will execute his orders. Trust me," Mr. Transport said, a bit of the color slipping out of his face.

"We understand," Vince said, standing up from the sofa where he'd been resting. "We have fifteen minutes?"

"Fourteen and a half now," Mr. Transport corrected. "Gather any tools or weapons you might favor, get dressed for combat, gather whatever you think will give you the best edge." His eyes flicked briefly to the boys' side door, which Nick had slammed ceremoniously behind himself directly after his and Alice's altercation. Alice pretended not to notice.

"Guess I'm getting out of my dress, then," she said, turning on a stiletto heel and gliding through the girls' side door.

"Vince, I assume you'll want to change out of slacks and a button-down," Mr. Transport urged.

"Of course. There's something else I need, though; something very important," Vince said slowly.

"Then go get it! This deadline is non-negotiable."

"I'll need your help," Vince explained. "It isn't exactly close at hand."

"Fine, fine. As long as we can get it in time to get back here for Alice's pick up, I'll take you wherever you need to go," Mr. Transport agreed.

Vince told him the location. Mr. Transport's already pallid coloration whitened another shade.

* * *

Nick sat on his bed, staring off into space. Every now and then, he would reach to adjust the sunglasses that were no longer there. Instead, they rested on his desk as a pile of debris. It was no great loss; in truth, he'd planned on smashing them himself once his time here at Lander had ended. He was still a bit miffed that it was that girl who'd had the pleasure of their destruction instead of him, though. Nick's hand almost tightened in reflex at the thought of Alice and her sucker punch. He was slipping; he couldn't believe

506

he nearly allowed an emotion to manifest itself as a physical gesture. He'd have to put himself in some intense retraining when he got back to Vegas.

At least his planning wasn't slipping. Nick had kept a go bag under his bed since his first day in Melbrook, a bag that was now propped up against his door. He could grab it when the rest left to go on their suicide mission and make his escape. He'd purchased and parked two vehicles other than the Bug in key locations on the Lander campus, vehicles with no record of being owned or driven by Nicholas Campbell, just in case. The windows were tinted to minimize recognition. There were toll passes to accommodate any route he might take stashed in his glove boxes.

Nick reran his mental checklist and confirmed what he already knew. That he was forethinking, that he was intelligent, and that he had planned for every possibility.

Almost.

146

"Are you certain this is a good idea?" Mr. Transport asked, his voice slightly raised to be heard over the roar and crackle of the blaze.

"Honestly? Not really," Vince admitted, his own tone at an equal volume.

The two stood about a mile away from the perimeter of a tremendous inferno—the forest fire that was currently assaulting southern California. Since that morning's report, the ravaging flames had grown in intensity, defying the valiant attempts of local officials to bring it under control. The area had been evacuated hours ago, so Mr. Transport and Vince stood alone as they stared into the flickering heat steadily creeping toward them. Even from this distance, Mr. Transport's face was warm, and his breath felt a touch smoky.

"Then perhaps we should conceive of a different plan," Mr. Transport proposed.

Vince glanced down at his wrist watch. "We have ten minutes left. Any ideas for something we can put together and execute in that much time?"

"We could raid a camping store. You could pop the Sterno cans one by one to absorb their heat in more manageable chunks."

Vince shook his head. "I somehow don't think it would be quite the same effect."

"And why, exactly, do you need this effect?" Mr. Transport asked. "I realize you are facing a significant challenge, but doesn't this seem a bit like overkill?"

"None of us landed a single hit on Coach George when we fought him," Vince told Mr. Transport. "Not even Mary or Chad. With only Alice, Nick, and me coming at him, we have zero chance of winning, or even stalling long enough for one of us to recover our friends and escape."

"I was beginning to wonder if you were aware of the realistic odds."

"I am. I am also aware that I'm the only one of us left who was enrolled in the combat training. That means, I'll have to handle George on my own and trust the others to retrieve Mary and Hershel. As it stands, I have minimal ability to battle against Coach George and no defense against Persephone. That only leaves me one viable option."

"Do tell," Mr. Transport encouraged.

A slow, half-mad smile spread across Vince's face. The firelight's reflection danced in his blue eyes as they seemed to drift off to some long ago place and time.

"Pure offense."

"That seems like a poor strategy to win," Mr. Transport told him. "Assuming you can even handle this much energy. I've read the reports on your activities, you know. You've spent all year focusing on minimizing how little you took into your body. You haven't tried to find your limits in the slightest. For all we know, this exceeds what you can contain."

"It very well might," Vince agreed.

"So, again I must ask, why are you so set on this course of action?"

"Because even if this has a ninety nine percent chance of killing me or not being enough, at least it gives us a shot. I'll take one percent over zero any day."

Mr. Transport let out a short laugh in spite of himself. "I think that's more the mindset of a fool, than a Hero."

"My father once told me the best Heroes were the ones too stupid to care about the odds," Vince replied. "So, thank you." Vince drew in several deep breaths, saturating his lungs with oxygen. He knew once he entered the blaze, he would have little time and less air to act with. A few moments lost choking on the smoke could break his concentration and cost him everything. He glanced down at his watch. Eight minutes left.

For all his brave words, the truth was Vince was scared to step forward. He wasn't at all sure he could do this. And even if he did, he wasn't sure he would be able to take back Hershel and Mary. He was afraid he would die in the process, of course, but that didn't scare him nearly as much as the knowledge that there was only one chance to get them back. He, Alice, and Nick were that chance. Vince was terrified he wouldn't be strong enough, and he would let his friends down. But despite all that fear, he never questioned the fact that he had to try.

"I'm ready," Vince said softly. Mr. Transport gave a curt nod and moved them through space. They reappeared at a central point in the fire, Mr. Transport lingering long enough only to be sure the heat didn't render Vince unconscious. The boy stood stalwart, so Mr. Transport retreated to their previous position. Vince could survive such temperature through his ability, but Mr. Transport had no such protection. All he could do now was wait and try to have faith in the strange, silver-haired boy.

Vince didn't breathe once he was dropped off. He'd had more than enough experience to know that, in this environment, the air would burn his lungs as it was already doing to his skin. Normally, when he was absorbing, Vince had to reach out to connect to the energy, finding it amidst the ambient sources permeating the world around him. This time was different; from the moment he appeared, the heat was overpowering him, trying to choke and claw its way inside his fragile, fleshy form. The heat wasn't just knocking at the door, it was slamming its shoulder against it and screaming profanities in an effort to force its way in. Vince didn't have to reach out this time. Instead, he closed his eyes, steeled his nerves, and flung the door wide open, demanding every ounce of energy this fire could give.

For a sliver of an instant, nothing happened.

What followed next was captured on satellite imagery. The cause of it was debated for several years to come, with a wide variety of conspiracy theories centering around it and entire doctoral theses being written on the phenomenon. It wasn't until

Vince's story was told and the dots were connected that the curious event finally made sense.

From the images, it initially seemed as though a glitch occurred in the system tracking the wildfire. It went from moving in a standard pattern to turning inward, the direction of every path becoming a single uniform spot. The fire then began flowing in the direction of this spot. It moved at similar speeds to earlier at first, then steadily sped up in ever-increasing intervals. An image near the very end showed a circular pattern, as though the fire was swirling about like a hurricane as it was funneled down into a singularity. After that are two progressively smaller images of the fire before the final photo showing nothing.

Nothing except for miles of earth that had been scorched to the ground in mere minutes, instead of the days it should have taken.

The man's skin was like coal dipped in midnight, his muscular body scarcely contained in his black suit. The lady across the table was quite the opposite, a middle-aged woman of small stature with just a few grey hairs woven amongst her blonde ones. She, too, wore a black suit, though she had eschewed the tie in favor of a more casual appearance.

"Numbers," said the woman, her tone measured and even. "What a surprise. You must join us for tea."

"I appreciate the offer, Mrs. Tracking, but I'm afraid my time constraints are somewhat pressing," Mr. Numbers declined. He took a seat at their table, suppressing his urge to marvel at the glorious scenery their penthouse suite afforded them. Japan was always such a lovely place; Mr. Numbers intended to come back for a proper visit one day, just as he had intended for the better part of a decade.

"So I gathered. Transport did little more than a pop and drop. Quite rude," Mrs. Tracking commented.

"I'm afraid it will be much the same when he picks me up. We have a lot to talk about and little time to work in," Mr. Numbers replied. He glanced at the man, who sat so still one might believe he was little more than an exquisitely lifelike carving.

"I suppose I'll take the cue," the man said in a low, powerful baritone. He touched the hands of both Mr. Numbers and Mrs. Tracking. The world around them slowed to a crawl, then ceased to move at all from what they could discern.

"Thank you, Mr. Stop," Mr. Numbers said. "What I need to discuss with you is off the record, off the books, and will most likely label me as off the reservation."

"Oooh, sounds exciting," Mrs. Tracking said, a bubble of vivaciousness welling up in her. "I do enjoy the occasional black bag operation."

"What do you need?" Mr. Stop asked, vastly more stoic than his partner.

"Just a location," Mr. Numbers replied. "Two of our current charges have been taken, and they've disabled all the methods we had to pinpoint them."

"That is hardly off the books. You're doing your job," Mrs. Tracking said, her voice rich in disappointment.

"No," Mr. Numbers admitted. "I was given a direct order not to pursue."

"I see," Mrs. Tracking said. "That does change things."

"I'm aware," Mr. Numbers agreed.

"I believe I can fulfill your request, Numbers. All that's left to determine is the price." Mrs. Tracking flashed a grin that had signaled the end of many a man. "Let us negotiate."

*　　　*　　　*

Alice stepped into the common room wearing jeans and a t-shirt. She wished she had an outfit that better screamed "Warrior," but the only thing that came close was her Lander uniform. She didn't want to face the coaches dressed like a student; something about that just felt wrong.

Vince was already waiting, his own outfit similar to hers. He glanced up at her as she entered, giving her a quick nod. If he was feeling anything like her, then his stomach would be twisting in knots of worry.

"Mr. Transport went to pick up Mr. Numbers," Vince told her. "He'll be back in a second."

"Okay," Alice said, sitting down next to him.

"Nervous?" Vince asked.

"God, yes."

"Good," Vince said. "We're taking on a near-impossible task. It's going to be hard enough with just the three of us."

"Two of us, Vince. Nick isn't coming."

"He'll come," Vince said.

"He won't. It's just the two of us."

"Three," Vince corrected.

"Two."

"Three."

"Two."

"Three," Nick said, the door to the boys' side whispering shut behind him. He was dressed in a pinstriped suit, and a deep purple shirt left open at the collar. His shoes were black, well-fitted to the foot and competent for all forms of movement. His jacket was buttoned only on its top button, holding the shape together without pulling it taut to his frame.

"You're coming?" Alice asked.

"Of course he's coming," Vince said, standing from the couch. "Though, I'm not sure why he's dressed like that."

Nick shrugged. "Up until this year, I've always dressed this way. When we do this thing, I don't want to be dressed like the ineffectual smart ass. I want to feel like the version of me that can get things done."

"Whatever works," Vince said, patting his friend on the back.

Nick stared at Vince for a moment. "You never waver, do you, Silver?"

"Why would I waver on the things I know?"

"Heaven save me from honest men and lunatics," Nick replied. He looked at Alice, who had risen to her feet and was staring him down.

"What changed your mind?"

"Honestly? I'm not sure," Nick admitted. "Let's just chalk it up to the fact that I haven't gotten to really cut loose in a while, and this seems like a good outlet."

"You expect me to believe that?"

"Nope, which is why I didn't bother with the truth. No sense in wasting it when you won't trust anything I say," Nick replied.

"She'll trust you to help our friends," Vince assured him.

Mr. Transport and Mr. Numbers reappeared in the room, looking at the Melbrook residents.

"I have the place. Are you ready?"

The three looked at each other.

"Now or never," Nick said.

"Then I pick now," Alice said, forcing more courage than she felt into her voice.

"We're ready," Vince said. They gathered around Mr. Transport and Mr. Numbers.

An instant later, there was only an empty room, the echoes of voices still gently reverberating off the walls.

148

The night was strangely bright as Nick, Alice, and Vince stood on the dusty road. It was still used by the locals during the day, but by this time of night, the only ones traveling its worn lengths were the local wildlife and the occasional tourist who got lost. There were some lights scattered about; however, if not for the moonlight, the visibility would have been greatly reduced. Nick wasn't sure if that suited their purposes well or hurt them. He suspected he wouldn't know for sure until this whole affair had concluded.

"We're sure they're coming down this route?" Alice asked, yet again.

Nick nodded. "Mr. Numbers said his coworker could tell they were moving fifty miles an hour down this highway. It's off the beaten path, so if we'd launched a manhunt, they wouldn't easily be spotted, but the inverse is that there aren't exits to the highway between where they were and us. They're coming this way, presumably doing the speed limit so as not to get pulled over, which means we have a couple more minutes, by my calculations."

"I know, I just . . . what if they stop for the night? Or get a teleporter to help them? Or if wherever they're going is on this road, and they've already reached it?"

"Relax," Nick ordered her. "If they had a teleporter they could use, then they wouldn't be taking a truck. As for stopping, Mr. Numbers will contact us if his source senses any dramatic change in their movement. They're coming, Alice."

"Okay," Alice said, vainly willing her heart to cease its mad pounding. "Okay."

"You'll be fine," Vince assured her. "Just stick to the plan."

"Right. Get Hershel whiskey, and get Mary away," Alice said.

"Bingo," Nick said. "I'll help you if I can, but my main goal is to provide Vince with cover while he fights the coaches. Hopefully, however they're holding Hershel is something Roy can easily overcome. Mary will definitely be unconscious, though."

"Why are you so sure about that?" Alice asked.

"Because if she was awake, there'd be no way to stop her from trashing the vehicle. Even Persephone's nerve twitch pheromone didn't stop me from thinking. If she can think, then she can kick ass."

"All you have to do is get her clear," Vince reiterated. "We'll meet up with you down the road. If, for any reason, we're delayed, call Mr. Transport after five minutes for pickup."

"But you won't be delayed, right? You're going to get away."

"Of course we will," Vince assured her. "But it never hurts to have a backup plan."

Alice looked away from him, staring down the dark road instead. She didn't think Vince was lying: just believing in the happiest possible scenario. Alice didn't quite feel the optimism welling up in herself; her mind kept dwelling on all the ways this could go to shit.

"Heh." A nervous giggle escaped Alice's lips. "This sort of feels wrong, doing it at night. Shouldn't we be having our showdown at high noon?"

"Personally speaking, I prefer poor lighting and shadow when facing overwhelming forces," Nick replied.

"Don't count on a whole lot of that," Vince said.

Nick shot his friend a curious glance. The boy had obviously done something to prep for this fight, but he hadn't shared it with his comrades. In fact, Vince hadn't contributed much to any of their hurried planning process. His eyes had been sharp and focused, but not on anything the others could see. For as lunatic a situation as they were in, Vince had been calm and detached nearly the entire time. This was another variable that Nick wasn't sure if he found comforting or terrifying.

As it would ultimately turn out, the answer was both.

*   *   *

The man wore a grey, silk shirt, black pants, and an expression of extreme derision as he paced in front of Mr. Numbers and Mr. Transport.

"I'm expected to believe that two of our top operatives were surprised and overpowered by a group of children?"

"Teens, actually, all of them old enough to be counted as adults. Except for drinking," Mr. Transport pointed out.

The man stopped and delivered a withering glare. "This is not the time for semantics or splitting hairs. What you are telling me indicates tremendous incompetence at best, and full-out betrayal at worst. I trust I don't need to explain to you what happens if it's determined to be the latter?"

Both men would have gulped if they'd had more control over their bodies. However, Mr. Move was not notorious for his mercy or kindness, so as soon as he'd heard the bad news, Mr. Move had taken over control of everything in their bodies, except for speech.

"I have to tell you, I've very disappointed in you two," Mr. Move said, taking a seat on the table in front of them.

"I am certain that our supervisors will find our actions both understandable and non-traitorous. We were taken by surprise and bested. No one is perfect, after all," Mr. Numbers defended.

"Maybe they will," Mr. Move agreed. "But we'll be finding out soon. Mr. Transport is going to take us to the home office, so that you two can explain things in person."

Mr. Transport and Mr. Numbers would have shared a look of concern, had they been capable. They'd known this reaction was within the realm of possibility and had

515

tried to take action to mitigate it. Unfortunately, they had yet to see the results they were hoping for, which could prove detrimental to the plan. If they went to the head office, they wouldn't have their phones, and that would result in no one being on hand to retrieve their charges once the mission was complete.

"An excellent idea," Mr. Transport said. "Won't you need to give them advanced notice, though? It is a late hour, after all."

"No need," Mr. Move replied. "They were already assembled to decide how to react to the initial kidnapping. I was given full authorization to move personnel to their location should a need arise."

"Well then . . . excellent," Mr. Transport said, unable to think of an alternative argument. He could refuse to use his power: Mr. Move only overtook their bodies, not the abilities that they wielded. That move would end the game, though, labeling him and Mr. Numbers as traitors and moving their own safety far higher on their immediate concerns list. Still, it was a viable strategy, and one he might have to employ.

Mr. Transport was saved from his decision by a loud, authoritative knock on the door. Mr. Numbers and Mr. Transport couldn't see one another from the way their heads were positioned. If they had been able to, they would have known they were both smiling quite unprofessionally.

Mitigating factors had arrived.

149

The three would-be ambushers saw the distant headlights long before they heard the steady thrum of the truck's engine. The pinpoints of light were too high off the road for a sedan and too widely-spaced for a standard pickup. That left eighteen wheeler, or large transport vehicle.

Nick glanced down at his watch. Estimating from the truck's speed, it would be here in another three minutes, a time which fit neatly into the expected window.

"It's them," Nick announced, shooting a quick look at his compatriots. "Everyone ready?"

Vince nodded. Alice did as well, though more hesitantly.

"Good. As soon as they stop, everybody stick to the plan," Nick instructed one last time. He'd tried to keep things general, rather than bogging them down in details, but it was crucial that each one stick to their roles. Their chances of success were already disgustingly slim. If a single person broke rank, then all hope would be lost.

"About that. I have a question," Alice said.

Nick glanced again at the approaching lights, now increasing in size and brightness. "Make it a quick one."

"It's about stopping the truck. How do we know standing in the road will get them to brake? What if they just mow us down?"

"Alice, did you really think I would build an entire plan that depended on basic human decency? Give me a little credit."

"Then, how are you stopping the truck?"

Nick gauged the truck's speed once more. It would be here very soon, so he might as well get started.

"With a whole lot of bad luck." Nick clenched his fist and drew in a deep breath. He realized the futility of exercising fake tells when he could no longer hide his real one, but Nick Campbell was nothing if not committed to his role. Nick focused on the truck bearing down on them, on the front part of the cab, on the engine, and specifically, on the driver. He wasn't sure who would be at the wheel, but he certainly knew who he was hoping for. He kept his mind aimed at the vehicle, and then he began to gather the bad luck. Normally, he could use a simple burst; however, for a project this big, he was going to need one doozy of a wallop.

Alice gasped and took a step back in surprise. Vince was more stoic, merely commenting, "Well, that explains the glasses."

As the luck built up in Nick, the irises of his eyes began to glow with a golden light. It was dim at first, slowly growing brighter as the power accumulated. Nick kept those radiant eyes trained on his speeding metal adversary. He needed to act when the machine was far enough away not to catch them in whatever catastrophe occurred, but close enough to be quickly reachable by Alice. Optimum timing would come down to a difference of mere seconds. The right corner of Nick's mouth tugged upward ever so slightly. He hadn't had a challenge like this in years.

The truck grew nearer, and the time was at hand. Nick hardened his focus, shifted just a touch more bad luck in the driver's direction, and then let fly.

What happened next was an orchestra of malfunction. The engine caught fire and began billowing smoke, all four tires blew out simultaneously, and both axles snapped as the truck came careening to the ground. It dove forward in a headfirst motion, smashing the grill into the ground and severely crumpling the front compartment. It skidded across the cement, coming to the verge of tipping before slamming back onto its base. Dust flew freely into the air, and a sea of shrapnel lay in the truck's wake. Though it was a tremendous amount of action, it occurred in mere seconds. By the time Nick's eyes had dulled to their normal brown, the only sound remaining on the dark, country road was the soft crackling of flames coming out of the engine.

"Holy shit," Alice said, her voice dumbstruck.

"Worship me later," Nick chided her. "Right now, we've got to get over there before they can recover."

He and Vince began dashing down the road at top speed. Alice lifted off the ground and accelerated, quickly passing them in the race to save their friends.

*   *   *

"Well, that was a shitwreck," Coach George commented calmly as he tossed Mary over his shoulder. The tall man had switched to his robotic form at the first wobble they'd felt from the floor. The crash had been predominantly absorbed by the front of the vehicle, but Hershel still found himself sore, pitched to the side, and with blood trickling from where his handcuffs had pulled against his skin. It seemed Coach George had lifted Mary up during the worst of it, otherwise, she would have been tossed about, since she wasn't restrained to the floor.

"What was that?" Hershel asked, his head finally clearing up with the input of these new injuries.

"Hey, Persephone, report. Did you hit a squirrel or something?" Coach George demanded.

No response came from the smoking front cab.

"Fuck. Guess this just became a one-man job." Coach George kicked open the back door, sending it sprawling off its hinges. He turned back to regard Hershel. "Kid, it's been fun, but my job is delivery of your friend, not to deal with whatever the hell just smashed my truck. Looks like at least you're off the hook. I can only fly with one passenger."

A series of flaps on Coach George's back opened and his legs began pulse with a green energy. Of course; of course he could fly. Hershel cursed inwardly. Someone had

518

come to save them, and now Coach George was going to soar off before they could reach Mary. Coach George was going to get away, and Hershel was going to be just sitting here. Useless as always. It was amazing Coach George had even bothered chaining him to the ground. Hershel blinked and looked at his restraints. His hands were still bound by a long length of chain, but the bolt that held him to the floor had been ripped off in the crash. Hershel sucked in a long breath that made his ribs ache. He made a snap decision.

Coach George was still powering up his legs when over two hundred pounds of husky student slammed into his back. Before he could bring himself to believe what was happening, a chain had been thrown around his neck, then wrapped over again. Hershel managed three more layers before George reached up and snared his right arm.

"It has occurred to you that, in this mode, I don't need oxygen, right?"

"I pretty much assumed it," Hershel wheezed. Holding himself onto George's back was already proving a difficult task to maintain. That had been the true purpose of looping his chains: it bound him to the metallic man with something more than his poor arm strength.

"So what are you doing?"

"You can't fly with two people," Hershel replied.

"Really, kid? You've spent your whole life living in the shadow of your better alter ego, and now you decide you want to play Hero? I've got an idea. Let's skip to the part where you realize you can't cut it and just let go. Otherwise, things might get . . . troublesome." On his last word, Coach George tightened his grip on Hershel's arm. Hershel managed to bite back a cry. George's fingers felt like they were already gripping him on the bone, and Hershel was under no illusions that this was the strongest he could clutch.

"Roy isn't the only son of Titan. Do your worst. I won't let you take Mary," Hershel spat back, his voice low as he tried to keep it from quivering.

"Have it your way," Coach George replied.

Hershel wasn't able to stop the next scream that rose, or any of the many that followed.

150

George—he had ceased to think of himself as a coach since this night's inception—was both surprised and aggravated. The tear-stained butterball now panting on the truck's cock-eyed floor had held on longer than he'd expected. It had taken no less than seven breaks in his arm to finally force Hershel to let go. Of course, George could have just ripped the damn thing off in the first place; however, he knew that wouldn't have sat well with the man at the top of the ladder.

George turned his back on the softly weeping boy and readjusted his grip on Mary. It didn't matter that he'd been slowed down. All that mattered was the girl. That was his job, and that was what he would deliver. George was a singularly focused man. He took care of the mission at all costs. That was what had made him a great Hero, and, ironically, what had knocked him down to the point of teaching snot-based brats how to fight.

George stepped out into the crisp, late-spring night. He flexed his rudders and checked his energy levels. Flying took some extensive warming up of his leg thrusters, but he was nearly there, even with Hershel's delay. He'd be ready to take off in less than a minute.

George made it fewer than five steps away from the battered vehicle when a pillar of flame thick as a fist came rocketing past him, missing only by a few inches. It struck the ground several feet away, the tar immediately bubbling at the sudden influx of heat. It was a bold move, one that gave away both position and tactical advantage in favor of declaring one's intentions. George knew plenty of fire users, but only one stupid enough to make an opening gambit like that. He turned around to greet his opponent.

"Reynolds," George acknowledged, his voice tinged with an electronic variable.

Vince stood down the road, illuminated by the still smoldering spot at George's back. The air around him shimmered as its temperature was forced upward. He was practically leaking energy; the guy must have absorbed a house fire or something. Gone were any traces of the happiness and optimism that usually peppered his expression. In their place was a vicious stare and eyes that said quite clearly that the only way one of them would come away from this was in a broken, bloody mess. It was a shame things had to go this way; George felt like he could have sculpted the kid into a real warrior.

"Let Mary go," Vince demanded. His tone wasn't angry or impatient. It was calm and flat as the waters of an abandoned bath tub.

"Sorry, Reynolds, not going to happen," George replied.

"What if we say pretty please?" Nick Campbell stepped into view from behind the front of the truck. He must have been making sure Persephone was down for the count. Smart kid. He edged slightly closer to his friend, though the emanating heat forced a healthy distance between the two. In his hands were a pair of guns, one a standard black pistol, but the other, a long-barreled, silver six-shooter.

"Campbell, I thought you were one of the bright ones. What are you doing out here?" George just needed a little more time to charge up and he could get away without having to risk his unconscious package in a throwdown with these kids.

"Friendship can make us do some spectacularly stupid things," Nick replied. He squeezed the trigger with his right hand and sparks flashed off George's torso as the bullet ricocheted.

"Whoa, kid, not even a warning shot?"

"That was the warning shot," Nick replied evenly.

George assessed the situation and weighed his options. Reynolds was pissed off enough to actually fight worth a damn and clearly hopped up on more energy than usual. Campbell was practically worthless if all he had was a pair of guns, but he could be surprisingly clever and behaved like he had ice-water in his veins. Adair was floating overhead, trying to stay unnoticed as she clutched a huge rock. Whatever their plan was, it couldn't be that sophisticated. Still, he was under strict orders to deliver the girl undamaged, and with kids this inexperienced, they could easily make a mistake and injure their friend.

"Last chance," Vince said, taking a step forward. Flames began swirling in his hands as he prepared to release a dual barrage of fireballs. "Let Mary go."

At long last, George's thrusters came online and showed a 'Ready' status.

"Thanks, but no thanks," George replied. His robotic face wasn't really equipped to smile, though it did put forth an impressive level of effort. He activated the thrusters and began to lift off the ground.

It was only because of his enhanced hearing that George was able to make out the gunshot over the roar of his leg engines. He did see the barrel of the six-shooter in Nick's left hand flash, and that was the last thing he saw for several seconds. A white-hot explosion of light erupted in front of his eyes, blinding his sensors and forcing him back to the ground. He heard another sound, the soft whistle of an object in free fall and put two and two together. The idiots had shot something to blind him so Adair could drop that stupid rock on him. It was a completely brainless plan, and the only person it might genuinely hurt was Mary. George threw up both his arms, gauging the rock's strike point on sound alone. He managed to deflect it with his forearms, shattering it into a dozen pieces that scattered along the ground.

It was only after George had lowered his arms and shaken his head in a vain attempt to get his visual sensors back to full functionality that he realized his left shoulder was considerably lighter. A quick glance to the rear confirmed his suspicions as a blonde figure holding a brunette one sped across the sky.

"You little shits," he cursed.

521

"Come on, did you really think we'd be stupid enough to fight you with Mary in danger?" Nick taunted. "A little misdirection is the key ingredient in any theft."

"I suppose it is," George agreed. "What was that thing you shot at me?" His vision was finally clearing up as his system compensated for the damaged lenses.

"Phosphorous bullet: a little something one of my *real* teachers whipped up years ago," Nick replied, his own face having no trouble displaying its cocky grin.

"Nice job there, kid, sincerely. Though, I'm curious how you expected the rest of this to play out. You do realize I can easily catch that girl, right?"

"Actually, we didn't even know you could fly," Nick replied. "But it doesn't really matter."

"And why is that?" George asked.

"Because Mary isn't here to get hurt anymore," Vince answered.

The silver-haired boy took three steps forward, and the inferno broke loose.

151

Alice rocketed through the air as fast as she dared move with Mary's (thankfully light) frame clutched in her grasp. She didn't know how the small girl was still asleep, though she was smart enough to guess it had something to do with the metal headband wrapped around her skull. Alice glanced behind her to see if Coach George was somehow following her. She'd been so shocked when he'd lifted off the ground that the rock had slipped from her grasp. It was fortunate Nick had fired in time for the plan to work, so she could steal Mary away in the confusion. Still, she had no idea how they were going to keep him busy long enough for her and Mary to get away.

Alice slowed the pace at which she was cutting through the air. She needed to get Mary awake, which meant stopping to take off the headband. It was a risk, because Coach George might catch up to her in the time it took. Alice thought it was even riskier to continue through all this without Mary's help, though. Vince had assured her they could handle Coach George. Alice slowed to a hover and lightly descended to the ground.

She would trust in her friends.

*   *   *

George skirted another fireball and nearly stepped into a column of focused flames. George wasn't someone who normally feared a little heat; however, the flames that Reynolds was pumping out were intense enough to make him concerned for his inner circuitry. He pulled back and raised his arm to take aim, but the burning road made getting a precise bead on his target quite difficult. It certainly didn't help that Vince's attacks didn't need to be precise to be troublesome, as the boy had clearly spent his two weeks crafting the art of the area blast. Before George could get a shot off, a blazing wall rose up in front of him, obscuring his vision entirely.

Vince soon burst through it, reabsorbing the energy around him while doling out new bursts of power. So far, the dance of these two warriors had been one of distance by necessity. Vince was keeping the area around him at high enough temperatures that George would sustain damage to enter it. This kept the older combatant's exceptional strength and skill restrained, while giving Vince a temporary advantage. George knew the kid never absorbed too much power, so sooner or later he would run dry and George could put a swift end to this foolishness. Vince released another flurry, and George hurried to get out of the way.

From a safe distance, Nick watched calmly as the world burned around him. Most people probably would have been surprised to see Vince fare so well against his former coach, given his performance all year. Nick was not one of those people. He had long ago noticed the pattern that indicated Vince was an "all on the line" kind of fighter. He was good most of the time, yet he could never tap into his true potential. That was, of course, unless his back was to the wall. Then, the guy could come out of his corner swinging. And if it was his friends in danger, instead of himself . . . well, that was when you saw what good ole Silver was really made of.

Still, he couldn't keep this pace up forever, and they both knew it. Even if the fire's energy didn't run out, his own eventually would. He was using a lot of movement to try and keep George on the defensive and that would take its toll. Nick had originally planned to get to the truck and slip Hershel some whiskey; however, a series of poorly timed fireballs had cut him off from access to it. That was okay; Nick knew he would get the chance to play his role soon enough. He just hoped it was at a point before all hope of victory was lost.

*   *   *

"Come on, come on, wake up already," Alice said, bobbing through the air. She'd peeled the band off of Mary and taken back to the skies; however, the telepath had remained unresponsive.

"They need you, Mary. We need you. I need you. I don't know what to do without you," Alice pleaded to the unconscious form cradled in her arms. "I don't know if I should even be running away right now. I know I can't help, and I'd only be a distraction, but . . . I'm tired of only being good at running away."

Alice moved upward in the air, hoping the chilly breeze would snap Mary into the waking world.

"You know when you fought Chad in the midterms, and I ran away? I hated that, and I almost came back. Nick convinced me that sometimes being a Hero means knowing when to retreat, though. Knowing how to apply your assets so that they don't get in each other's way. Looking back at that moment now, I can't believe I fell for that bullshit. Then again, I fell for a lot of his bullshit. God, Mary, please wake up already. I want to talk to you, to tell about everything that's happened, to get your opinion on what I should do. But most of all, I want to save our damn friends. And I can't do that. We need you."

Alice began flying faster, causing the wind to tear at her eyes and whip her hair about violently.

"We need you, Mary. So please wake up."

*   *   *

George got off a series of shots, driving Reynolds back as he rolled away. It was bad luck that George's projectiles were bolts of energy, but good luck that Reynolds had never experimented with his repertoire enough to see if he could absorb them. Now was not the time to try and find out, so the kid had to dodge. Finally given a bit of breathing room, George decided he had wasted enough time with this grudge match. There was no doubt he could still outfly the Adair girl, but every minute this went on meant finding her would be more difficult. Since Reynolds seemed to still have gas in the tank, George decided on an alternate method for victory.

524

He dashed toward the truck, able to leap past the surrounding flames that had deterred Nick, and hopped in the back. He emerged moments later, right arm holding Hershel's battered body and left arm wrapped around his throat, choking off any protests Hershel might have been voicing. For good measure, George finally used his thrusters and rose several feet into the air.

"*Enough!*" George screamed at his top volume. "Unless you're in the mood for barbecued hostage, I'd refrain from any more pyrotechnics."

Vince stopped in his tracks, a half-formed fireball reabsorbing into the hand that held it.

"There's a good student, finally doing as you're told," George said from his airborne perch. "I swear, kid, if you'd shown that much spirit throughout the year, you could have been second in the class."

Vince returned his verbal volley with only a vicious stare.

"No demands that I release your friend? Good, glad we're past that phase. Now, here is what is going to happen. I'm going to fly off with your buddy in my possession. When I catch up with Alice, I'm going to trade him out for Mary. I'm then going to fly away, and you all are never going to see me again. Clear?"

Vince only glowered at the metallic man hovering in the air.

"Don't be such a sore loser, kid. Maybe you should have paid more attention in the dean's boring class. I mean, didn't it ever occur to you that I might use the one of you without powers as a human shield?"

"As a matter of fact, it did," Nick quipped from twenty feet away on George's right.

Nick's revolver barked its second shot, and Hershel forced out a strangled scream of pain.

152

George didn't really have the capacity to blink in his current form, but if he could, he certainly would have done so in surprise. Blood flowed from the fresh bullet wound in Hershel's right shoulder onto the dirty, grey metal of George's arm.

"Shit, Campbell, are you fucking blind? Not only did you try and shoot me with a bullet we both know wouldn't hurt, but you missed and hit your friend."

Hershel twitched violently for a few seconds before becoming still. George had just enough time to wonder if the boy had gone into shock when Hershel's head flung forward and then smashed back into George's face. The world morphed into static as George was sent reeling through the sky and crashed to the ground, his grip and direction lost as he struggled to understand how his hostage had mustered enough strength to hurt him.

Had George been able to pay more attention, he would have gotten an immediate answer to his question, for while it was Hershel Daniels that slipped from George's grasp, it was Roy Daniels who crashed into the ground. Nick and Vince dashed to his side.

"Are you okay?" Vince asked.

Nick didn't bother with a verbal query; he didn't know how long this transformation would last without supplementation. He pulled a silver flask from his pocket and slapped it into Roy's left hand. The right arm was dangling uselessly, Hershel's significant injuries all the more apparent on Roy's muscular form.

Roy tore the top off the flask with his teeth and hurriedly gulped down the contents. He tossed it to his side and pulled himself up to a standing position. Glancing at the bullet wound in his arm, only then did he finally speak.

"You coated a bullet in whiskey?"

"Seemed like the fastest way to get it into your bloodstream," Nick replied.

Roy gave him a curt nod, then looked at the metallic figure that was moving toward them once more. "I rang his bell pretty good, but we need to hurry if we want to keep him from flying off."

Vince gestured to Roy's arm. "What happened? Are you sure you can fight with that?"

A dark look passed over Roy's face. "I'm dead fucking sure. If Hershel can be man enough to hold on to that psycho's neck while he snaps his bones, then there's no way I'm backing down."

"The girls should be far enough away now, it might be prudent to retreat and heal," Nick pointed out.

"To hell with that. Do you know what Hershel's last thought was before I took over?" Roy asked, his eyes unwavering from his formerly airborne opponent.

"Do tell," Nick sighed, already seeing where this was going.

"His last thought after being kidnapped, beaten, and taken hostage by someone he trusted was 'Sorry about the arm.'" The knuckles on Roy's left hand cracked with a thunder that left lightning envious. "No way I'm letting my little brother show me up like that. I owe that tin man son-of-a-bitch. I owe him hard."

"I'll fight with you," Vince said, stepping next to him. Roy stayed focused on the steadily approaching target, but Vince spared a glance over at Nick.

"In for a dime, in for a dollar," Nick replied, taking a few steps back, but raising his weapons. He was under no impression that he'd be able to make any more difference in wounding George, but perhaps a well-timed shot could prove a distraction. At this point, it was all he had left.

"Just for reference, how resistant to fire are you?" Vince asked Roy with the little time that remained.

"No idea," Roy replied. "But I bet we're about to find out."

*   *   *

The knock on the Melbrook door was quickly followed by its forceful opening. Seconds later, Dean Blaine, along with a petite, elderly woman and a medium-sized man with jet-black hair, entered the living room.

"You two had better have a damned good explanation," Dean Blaine ranted. "First, your students get outed by one of their classmates, then you contact me that two of them are missing and point me toward another student, who assures me the perpetrators were two of my staff. An accusation that would have been laughable if not for the fact that I am now unable to find either one of them. Now I come in here and find you both just sitting there, seemingly without a care in the world. So, you'd both better tell me what is going on and where my students are, and I mean now!"

Mr. Numbers and Mr. Transport both sat still as early morning in response. Mr. Move, however, stepped forward to meet the dean.

"Dean Blaine, I can assure you that everything is well under control, and you have nothing to worry about."

Dean Blaine strode directly by Mr. Move and leaned in to yell more at the sitting men. "Are you two deaf? I said I want to know what's going on."

"Perhaps you would feel more at ease if you sat down and relaxed," Mr. Move commanded. He was going to take hell for using his power on the dean, but it seemed unavoidable at the moment. However, things did not go as Mr. Move expected. Rather than hunkering down with the other two, Dean Blaine spun around and drove his fist into Mr. Move's temple with a single fluid motion. Mr. Move tumbled to the floor, not accustomed to taking blows and certainly not from someone as experienced as Dean Blaine.

527

"I wasn't talking to you, whoever you are," Dean Blaine said to the now unconscious man. "I was talking to these two."

"These two" were experiencing a tingle across their skin as they regained authority over their appendages. They exchanged a quick glance to confer that they were on the same page about coming clean with the dean and found that they, in fact, adamantly were. Before they could rise to a standing position, however, Dean Blain leaned in and placed a hand on each of their shoulders.

"Last chance, gentlemen. Where. Are. My. Students?"

153.

Roy threw a vicious haymaker that George sidestepped with ease. George capitalized on Roy's open side by delivering two quick jabs to the boy's ribs and then kneeing him in the diaphragm. Roy coughed as the wind left his body and he sank to a knee. George moved in to put him down for good when a horizontal pillar of fire smashed into his head, momentarily blinding him and sending his temperature to dangerous levels. George was forced to roll away and regroup, a consequence of which was that Roy was afforded the same privilege.

George had to admit it: Daniels had gotten a lot better since the start of the year. He was thinking his movements through, recovering well from hits, and fighting with a brain, instead of all brawn. All those weeks slugging it out with the number one rank had done him a world of good. Not so much that he could pose an actual challenge to George, though. This fight would have been over in minutes if not for Reynolds doling out those flame-based blasts. Every time George went to return fire, Roy came at him in close range. The two were focusing on their specialties and keeping him off balance enough that he couldn't permanently remove either one from the fray. It was a terrible strategy if they wanted to win, but for buying time, he had to concede it was pretty functional. Somewhere deep down inside his metallic system, George felt a sensation akin to pride. The little dipshits had actually learned.

George activated his thrusters and began rising into the air. Unlike his opponents, he had no compelling reason to try and win this fight. All he had to do was get away and recapture the Smith girl for delivery. Unfortunately, Roy had already recovered and was ready for this. He leapt several feet in the air, grabbing George by the leg and getting a face full of thruster fire for his trouble. Roy didn't even seem to notice; he pulled himself out of its range and tightened his grip.

"I'd think between you and your brother, one of you boys would think of a different strategy than just clinging on to me," George said.

"If it ain't broke, don't fix it," Roy snapped back. He tested his right arm and found it still unresponsive. He knew it would heal eventually, probably within the half hour. That just wasn't much help at the moment, though. It was a shame, if he'd had both appendages, he could have been hammering away on George while in this position; instead, he was leaving himself wide open. Roy steeled himself for whatever was about to come. If Hershel could take it, so could he.

For his part, George wasn't feeling particularly creative. He raised his own arm and fired off several bolts of energy into Roy's torso. The boy's grip was shaken as pain rippled through him, but he held on. George readied himself for another volley; however, he was forced to sweep through the air instead, to dodge a flurry of fire from Vince on the ground.

"You little pains in the ass," George swore. "How long do you think you can keep this up? Two more minutes? Maybe five? It doesn't matter! I'll catch that girl before the sun is up, no matter what you do. I'm a trained, experienced, veteran Hero, and you are just three Powereds who got a little control. The three of you alone could never beat me."

George's arms suddenly shot out to his sides and his legs snapped together, locking his whole form into a rigid lower case "t" shape. Though his face was capable of only showing the barest emotion, Roy still recognized the look that swept through his eyes. It was the same one he'd worn on a fall night only a few weeks into the school year. Roy turned his face to George and gave him the biggest smile he could muster.

"Guess it's a good thing they made five of us, then." Roy released his grip and fell away as George was sent violently slamming into the ground. The concrete exploded upward at the force of his impact and cracks sprawled outward all the way to the road's edge. Before the dust could settle, George was airborne again, being lifted up and driven back into roughly the same spot with ever increasing force.

It was on his third trip up that George finally saw her, the five-foot-tall Valkyrie being lowered to the ground by her blonde escort. Their eyes locked for a moment before he slammed into the earth once more. The next time up he used his thrusters to try and break free, but all that earned him was a faster return to the earth. George was impressed; he'd fought telekinetic Supers before and knew holding on to someone as strong as he was took a whole lot of power.

The others were impressed as well, though that emotion was being steadily passed by fear for the prime position. In all the time they'd known Mary, she had always been calm and composed. A bit eccentric at times, certainly; however, her cheerful demeanor had faithfully shone through whatever other fleeting emotions were clouding the surface. That wasn't the Mary that strode across the concrete, though, moving steadily closer to man who had taken her. This Mary wasn't cheerful, or kind, or motherly in the slightest.

This Mary was pissed off.

At long last, she reached the crater that bore a plethora of George shaped dents in it. She stood over the edge and glared down, increasing the pressure on him so that moving even a finger would require tremendous effort.

"You kidnapped me," she accused.

"Only attempted to kidnap at this point," George pointed out. He was feeling all those drops—not even he was immune to that kind of assault—but he'd been through worse attacks and survived. He'd get free eventually; Mary couldn't keep up this level of power indefinitely. Even if she held him down and the others beat him up, George was confident nothing they had could truly put him down for the count.

"You hurt my friends," Mary continued.

530

"Now, that one I'll give you. But, in fairness, they started it."

"Do you feel even the slightest remorse for what you've done today?"

"Of course," George replied. "I regret that your friend interrupted me, otherwise, I could have been done with this whole mess by now."

"I suppose asking why you did it is a waste of time," Mary surmised.

"Why don't you try reading my mind and see?"

Mary shook her head. "I can't read you when you're in that form. Maybe that's how you hid this from me until it happened. I don't know, and I don't care. If you're not going to talk, then I won't bother asking."

"Is this the part where you try to kill me?"

"No, this is the part where I make you what you made me: helpless. Vince, drain him."

"What?" Vince asked.

"What?" George near-yelped.

"He's not just metallic like Stella. He's a functional, robotic life form. He was quite clear about that during our class. That means he's running on some kind of energy. Let's see what happens when that tap runs dry."

"But what if it kills him?" Vince asked.

"Then stop before he dies," Mary instructed.

Vince thought about questioning her more, but then he saw the look in her amber eyes. Not just the rage, but also the fear. She'd been taken from a place she thought was secure by someone she thought she could trust. Now, she was just trying to hold it together until it was safe to break down. Vince looked at the face of the man who had done that to her, and he could swear there was a smirk on his robotic face. Vince set his resolve.

He hopped down into the crater and pressed his hand against George's chest. He was surprised to feel electricity flow up his arm; Vince had half expected some super New Age form of power. Instead, it was a good old, familiar current; familiar only thanks to the man he was currently depleting. Vince wasn't sure if that was ironic or not; he'd never been good at figuring out what fit that definition. He knew it made him smile, though.

"Wait, stop," George said, the first real hint of worry entering his voice. "You don't understand what you're doing."

"I'm stopping you," Vince replied. "I think I've got a good handle on it."

"I'm saying there's more to this than you think. You don't understand the implications."

Vince increased the rate he was pulling the energy. George had quite a bit, but sooner or later, every well ran dry. He knew he was making progress, though, because George's voice was growing weaker.

531

"You stupid kids . . . you have . . . no . . . idea . . ."

There was a ripple across his body and suddenly, the students were staring at their former teacher's human visage. George looked tired, but awake as he stared up at the five faces peering down upon him. He'd been too cocky, too sure they couldn't hurt him. Now, he'd have to wait, recover, and then ambush them when they weren't expecting it. George was still plotting his next move when a pair of well-manicured hands lifted his head from the rubble and slipped a silver band around it. After that, it was some time before he was allowed another conscious thought.

Alice clapped the dirt off her hands and floated back up to the road level. "That should take care of him. Now, who is calling Mr. Transport?"

"If no one objects," Nick said, plucking his phone from his pocket. "I think Alice and I are the only ones with non-smashed or melted phones, and since she made it last time, I believe it is my turn."

The others signaled their agreement, and Nick punched in the number.

"We're ready to be picked up," he said. For the first time that year, an emotion Nick didn't intend crept into his next words, happiness bounding free and plain for anyone with sense to discern.

"All of us."

*   *   *

Dean Blaine handed Mr. Transport back his phone. The tall man took it and looked at the dean with uncertain eyes.

"It was Mr. Campbell. It seems they're all safe and are requesting to be picked up," Dean Blaine informed him. "This adds only more to the heap of explanations you gentlemen owe me."

Mr. Transport and Mr. Numbers both nodded. The last few minutes had been . . . unpleasant. Dean Blaine had been significantly displeased with their story so far, and it was only going to get worse as they continued. They'd been fortunate he had consented to picking up Mr. Transport's phone, on the possibility it could be the students in question.

"A heap of explanations, by the way, that you will be providing me. Tonight. But, after you've retrieved your charges," Dean Blaine said. He certainly wasn't going to make the children wait any longer than they had to. They'd surely had a hard enough night; it was time for things to get easier for them. As for their caretakers, on the other hand, their evening was only just beginning.

154

Morning found the Melbrook quintet clustered in their living room, a firm lockdown being adamantly enforced. The television was on, but none of those sitting in the room were paying attention. Every now and then, Hershel would touch his shoulder, expecting pain to stab through his arm. A healer had been called during the night, so the physical damage had been completely negated. The other kinds were still unwelcomely present. Mary reached over and took his hand in hers, squeezing it to both give and receive some comfort.

"How do you think they'll take it?" Vince asked, breaking the silence that had descended on them since being left alone. After a quick night's sleep, Dean Blaine had met them at dawn to ask a few questions and outline what was going to happen next for them.

"Badly," Nick replied. "He's going to confirm the truth about us, and then tell them we're not having to take the final with them. That's not going to help the situation."

"That's not our fault, though," Alice said. "We didn't ask for our friends to get kidnapped."

"No, but we did choose to go after them," Nick pointed out. "I'm not trying to say we should be taking it. We're all beat to hell in every way, but the literal one. I'm just saying they won't take that news well coupled with what they learned last night."

"I wonder who dropped that bomb," Mary said quietly. "I was already out by then, so I didn't get to hear."

"It was some person from the DJ booth," Alice said.

"It was Michael," Vince corrected. The others turned to look at him. He merely shrugged. "I know what his crazy, screaming voice sounds like. I heard it when he attacked me on Halloween."

"He attacked you on Halloween?" Hershel asked.

"Why didn't you tell me you knew who it was?" Nick tossed out as well.

"Yes, and it didn't seem important at the time," Vince answered in order.

"Not important? How is that not important?" Nick demanded.

"The secret was already out. What mattered at the time was getting us together and safe. Then, when the whole . . . thing happened, it sort of slipped my mind," Vince explained.

"Michael, huh? I wonder how he found out. Or why he bothered to out us like that," Alice speculated.

"He had something against me. Even though he won our first match, he felt like I made him look bad. That's the only motivation I ever knew about," Vince replied.

"We'll make sure to give him a special thank you some time," Nick said. "On the subject, though, why didn't any of us know about the Halloween attack?"

Vince shrugged again. "I got out of it fine. I guess I just didn't want to worry anyone."

"Given the events of the past twenty-four hours, I fear we're going to need to adopt a policy of more information and worry, rather than less," Hershel noted.

"Agreed. On the plus side, we're all okay. And we all get to come back next year," Alice pointed out.

"I'd feel a lot safer if we knew what all it was about, though," Mary said. "Or where Persephone snuck off to."

The collection process of the students and the former Coach George had turned up a passenger cab coated in blood, but absent the blonde kidnapper. Given all the distractions of dealing with George, there was no way to estimate when she'd made her escape, though all five said a silent prayer of thanks she'd chosen flight rather than fight. They'd barely coped with just one coach to subdue. Two would have annihilated them.

"She'll turn up eventually," Nick assured her. "Even the wiliest rat has to come out for food."

"I'll feel better when she does," Mary said. "My telepathy will give me a heads up if she's approaching me, now that I'm on guard, but I still don't know how safe I'll feel in my woods all summer."

"Good thing you're not going off to the woods alone, then," Alice told her. "You're spending the summer with me."

"Am I?"

"Mary, you were the target of this whole debacle. The last one of us to be off on their own should be you," Vince said.

"I don't think endangering Alice is the right way to address that problem," Mary replied.

"Endangering me? Mary, did you forget the whole 'my dad is worth more than some countries' thing? We don't have a security guard in my home, we have security battalions. Several of them. My father might be an ass, but he takes safety seriously. If Persephone wants to take you from my home, she'd better bring an entire army of Supers, or it will be an insult," Alice said firmly.

"I'll . . . um . . . I'll have to check with my parents," Mary said lamely as she struggled to find another excuse.

"Be persuasive," Nick instructed her. "I don't particularly feel like repeating tonight's performance anytime soon."

"All of you are welcome, too," Alice added. "I have a whole wing of the house to myself, so you won't be imposing."

"It's a generous offer," Hershel said. "But I think I'll be okay at home. I'm looking forward to getting back to Chicago for a little while."

"Any of us could be targets, though. You should take her offer seriously," Vince said.

"I am. And trust me when I say, I'm perfectly safe at home. My dad wasn't a billionaire, but he was a renowned Hero. Lots of his old partners and friends live on the same street as us and keep an eye out for his family. The neighborhood might look like Sunday picnics and barbeques, but it's got more spandex and laser vision than anyone would suspect."

"I suppose that's a pretty safe place then," Vince conceded.

"Agreed," Nick said. "And while I appreciate the offer, I'll be declining as well. This year produced an ending I really wasn't expecting. I need to go home and figure out what that means for me, as well as my future at Lander."

"You are coming back, though," Vince said.

"It's sad that I know you well enough to assume that wasn't a question," Nick sighed. "I'll probably be back, if for no other reason than this little nuthouse has proven to be excellent training for expecting the unexpected. I'll also add that my place is quite safe in its own regard. Can we take me at my word on that one?"

"We can," Vince said before anyone else could raise the fact of just how questionable Nick's word was these days. "I'm going to say no as well. I don't have a fortress to return to, but no one will be able to catch what they can't find."

"You're going back on the road?" Alice asked.

"I am. It's where I feel at home. Well, that and here."

"Touching," Nick said. "I guess that handles our plan to survive the summer. That just leaves how we'll get through next year, now that everyone knows what we really are. Anybody got a bright suggestion for that one?"

The room was silent, save for the perplexed weather man on the television reporting the strange phenomenon to strike the California wildfires.

155

The reactions from most of the student body had been shocked and dismayed, but it was the freshman class filing down the hall to their exams where anger budded most prominently.

"This is utter horse shit," Allen Wells complained, his hands itching to dole out some explosions to demonstrate his outrage. "First, we find out they're fucking Powereds, then they don't even have to take the test. I wonder who I have to blow to get on the special treatment train?"

"Were," said Thomas's flat voice.

"Were what?" Allen asked.

"They were Powereds. Now, they're Supers," Thomas corrected. "Did you not pay attention at all to the dean's announcement?"

"Oh, I heard him loud and clear. We're all stuck with the standard test to fight for spots, while they've just been waved on through," Allen snapped back.

"They weren't waved through," Will said, joining the discussion. "Two of them were kidnapped, and then the five of them subdued Coach George. Do you think your test will be harder than that?"

"What the fuck ever, there's no way the coaches would actually do something like that. I'm sure they just objected to the Powereds being let into the program at all, so now, they're being tossed under the bus, just like Michael," Allen said.

"I'm with him on this one," Terrance stepped forward to add. "It is sort of crap that they've put Michael under 'judicial review' just for telling everyone the truth."

"He 'told the truth' by breaking into a sound booth and endangering those five," Thomas shot back. "I'm amazed they didn't flat out drop him from the program all together."

"They didn't do it because they knew we would have rioted if they'd taken it that far," Allen said, his voice raising a few octaves. The steady march toward the exam room had slowed as the discussion grew; now, it was grinding to a halt. One partly pink-haired individual never broke stride, though, moving up to the debate from her position in the rear.

"Sasha," Thomas called out. "Would you please help me explain to this imbecile that our friends are not the amoral monsters that current opinion seems to paint them as?"

Sasha never looked at him, never slowed down, never even moved her eyes. Her only response was a single pair of words delivered with such venom that clarification wasn't needed in the slightest:

"Fuck them."

"See, even one of their girlfriends knows they don't belong here," Allen declared triumphantly.

Thomas considered pushing the issue further; however, Sasha's comment had taken most of the wind from his sails, and he wasn't sure how to recover the lost ground. Instead, he retook his place in line and shook his head.

It was a good thing all five of the Melbrook students had been outed simultaneously, because Thomas had a firm suspicion they were going to be leaning on each other a lot come next year.

*   *   *

Dean Blaine poured himself two fingers of scotch, then stepped back. After a moment's consideration, he filled up the rest of the glass. He stared at it for a few more seconds, then went to his cabinet. He emerged holding a much bigger glass, dumped the original glass's contents into it, and then filled it up the rest of the way.

The announcement had gone over about as well as he'd expected. It wasn't the initial reaction one had to watch out for in situations like this. No one ever really grasped the full implication of big announcements immediately. No, the part he had to be on guard for was in the weeks to come, when the simmering thoughts would lead people down all the rabbit holes of possibility that he'd pursued himself nearly a year ago. They'd find the same conclusions, too. That this procedure, if evaluated and approved as successful, would significantly alter the landscape of Supers and Powereds, permanently. And, while it was a good thing, overall, it also meant taking the group that had been seen as secondary and elevating them to the status of equals. Dean Blaine might have slept through his college history courses, but even he knew you didn't have to dig hard to find all the examples of that being a tumultuous process at best. At worst . . . well, he was going to have to keep an eye on those five next year. He was certain there were plenty of people who would like to see their little experiment declared to be a failure.

It was a shame, too; they were good kids. Under different circumstances, a few of them might have even gone all the way, with the right guidance. Dean Blaine took a big gulp of his scotch at that thought. George and Persephone . . . they'd been teaching here for over ten years, longer than he'd even been at Lander. For them to have stolen away with students in the middle of the night . . . Dean Blaine didn't think he would have truly believed it if he hadn't been present to retrieve George's unconscious body. When he was thoroughly secured, Dean Blaine intended to have a very long, very in-depth chat about exactly what the point of their little stunt had been.

For right now, though, their absence created a more pressing dilemma. Dean Blaine had only two and a half months to find adequate replacements for their roles. That included background checks, board approval, negotiations, and training—a process that usually took at least a year to complete. Dean Blaine let out a sigh and drummed his fingers on the desk.

He was going to need more scotch.

156

Nick slammed down the hatch on his car and looked up into the bright sky. It figured: the first time all year he genuinely needed sunglasses, and they were lying in a broken heap at the bottom of the trash can. He'd have to pick up a pair of cheapos at the first gas station he passed. The drive from Lander to Vegas wasn't a particularly long one, but it was sunny as a son-of-a-bitch.

Alice was nearly done loading her own car as well, Mary's bags packed alongside hers as they struggled to fit Alice's ever-expanding wardrobe into the limited space a trunk had to offer. Mary was thankful she'd managed to talk Alice out of bringing everything home. They were coming back in a few months, after all. Mary took a step back and popped her back after the labor of packing the bags down. A part of her was sad that she wouldn't be going home for the summer, back to the peace and quiet of her woods. She was a pragmatic girl, though; she understood what her friends had risked by coming after her. To not take her safety seriously after such a gesture would be an insult to all of them, even if they didn't take it that way.

Hershel was tossing his final parcel into the car, while his mother spoke in hushed tones with Dean Blaine.

"Again, I'm sorry you had to drive all the way out to pick up Hershel," Dean Blaine apologized. "We're just short-staffed of teleporters at the moment."

"It's fine," Mrs. Daniels assured him. "What about their caretakers? After what you've told me, I'd like to have a little discussion with both of them, especially Mr. Transport."

"I'm not clear on much about them at the moment," Dean Blaine replied. "They're currently being debriefed by the company they work for. I haven't received any definitive word on if they'll be replaced next year or not."

"Please keep me in the loop," Mrs. Daniels said as Hershel walked up to the two.

"All done," Hershel said, patting the station wagon proudly.

"Such a strong young man," Mrs. Daniels said. "Why don't you go say goodbye to your girlfriend? We'll be leaving as soon as I take care of something."

Hershel took the hint and set off to give Mary an emphatic, but publicly-appropriate farewell.

"Was there something else?" Dean Blaine asked uncertainly.

"Yes, but not from you," Mrs. Daniels replied. "You've been wonderfully helpful. Thank you for coming out to explain things in person."

"Ma'am, it is quite literally the very least I can do," Dean Blaine said.

Mrs. Daniels walked across the parking lot, eventually stepping off the concrete and onto the grassy area that surrounded it. Sitting beneath a tree, making some adjustments to the straps on his backpack, was a silver-haired boy, thoroughly absorbed in the task at hand.

"You're Vince, if I remember correctly."

Vince looked up and gave his friend's mother a polite smile. "Yes, ma'am."

"I wanted to let you know how much I appreciate you going after my son. All three of you. It must have been terrifying, and I'm so very amazed you all had the courage to do something like that."

"It's not a big deal. Hershel would have done the same for any one of us. We're friends."

"You're good friends to have. Still, handling someone as strong as George, you must be one amazing Super."

"Only eighth in my class," Vince told her.

"I'm sure that will change soon," she assured him. "I have a question for you, though. As strong as you are, do you think you could beat me in a fight?"

"I beg your pardon?"

"I'm asking you if you think you have it in you to physically render me unconscious, should we engage in an altercation."

Vince squirmed slightly, searching her face for a snicker or smile to show that she was joking. He found nothing.

"I suppose I probably could," Vince answered at last. "But I'd really much rather never find out."

"That is a shame, because the only way I'm letting the young man who helped save my son wander off on his own with no food or shelter is when I have been knocked stone cold out," Mrs. Daniels informed him.

"I'm a little confused, ma'am."

"You will be coming home with Hershel and me, where you will be subjected to proper meals and a roof over your head all summer long," Mrs. Daniels explained. "Along with adequate safety, should anyone else make an attempt on one of you."

"Thank you very much, but I couldn't impose," Vince said.

"I feel I was quite clear about this already, young man. Either go put your bag in the car, or put up your fists, because there are only two possible endings to this discussion."

"I . . . yes, ma'am," Vince said, looking deep into her eyes and realizing this woman was one hundred percent not fucking around. He headed over to the station wagon where Hershel was already waiting.

"She strong-armed you into coming home with us, didn't she?"

"How'd you know?"

"I know my mom," Hershel replied with a shrug. "If it makes you feel better, you never stood a chance."

"Not particularly," Vince said. "But, I suppose, there are worse things than spending a summer with a friend."

"It's not excitement, but I'll take it," Hershel said. He slapped Vince heartily on the back. "Try and enjoy yourself, man. Next year is going to be one hell of an uphill battle. Speaking of, there's this group I hang out with back in Chicago, sort of a simulated attack-strategy group. I think you'll fit in really well with them."

"Is this that LARPing thing you told me about?"

"Exactly. Now, let me ask, what mythical creature do you see yourself as? Because, while your hair and cheekbones lend themselves to elf, I personally think you've got the fighting spirit of an orc."

Vince tossed his bag in the back of the car and then buckled himself in. It seemed that summer would, at the very least, not be boring.

Epilogue

For what it was, the warehouse was actually quite well-maintained. One often expected places such as this to be leaky and derelict; however, this particular enclosure was about as homey as it could be with concrete floors and walls. The lack of windows and the single entrance certainly didn't add to the domestic appeal, though the sprawled out rugs and series of sofas did bring several degrees of comfort to the equation. It only went to show, good or evil, human or Super, at the end of the day, everyone needed a soft place to sit.

Persephone limped through the entrance and approached the center area where the others sat. She'd been in too much of a hurry to look for a healer, only pausing to make a quick call from a payphone, so they knew the operation had failed. It had been a hellish several hours getting here, and she'd only made this good of time thanks to a car stolen outside a dusty gas station.

Persephone had made it halfway across the room when she felt her body lift from the ground and be pulled to a red chair. She was set down gently in the soft, leather surface, facing three of her cohorts.

The oldest was the one who had relocated her, a powerful figure wearing a tattered and patched, red coat that hung to his knees. To his right was a pale, blonde woman as beautiful as she was silent, which is to say very. On his left was a young boy, barely over the age of ten, who looked at her with a gaze so furtively curious, she couldn't stand to be around him for more than a few minutes at a time.

"The mission failed, and what's more, George was taken," the man said, his voice dark, deep, and calm as a mile below the ocean's surface.

Persephone nodded. She didn't need to bother with excuses. He was a seasoned warrior. He understood that sometimes, things didn't go as planned.

"That is unfortunate," the man said, drawing out the word as if he was considering the appropriateness of its use. "Of all possibilities, it didn't occur to me that our efforts would result in losing George."

"Me, either," Persephone admitted.

"Still, you two drew enough attention for our other agent to complete his job, so on the whole, we'll have to consider this as a success," the man added. "And I'm glad you were able to make it back to us, Persephone. There is still so much work to do. Even more, now that we've lost George."

Persephone glanced at her feet, ashamed she hadn't been able to help save George. The mission directives were clear, though: if they were compromised, she was to make escape the first priority. George could hide out in his robot form, where he had no fear of telepaths. She would only have her discipline to rely on, discipline that could be broken by a professional with enough time. As her eyes stared at her worn and dirty

541

shoes, she noticed something. The wound on her leg had closed, and the aches she'd been carrying since the wreck were no longer present. She turned her eyes upward and was greeted by a comforting smile from the man she'd once so greatly feared.

"You don't need to worry, Persephone. I'm not mad at you. You did as you were instructed along every step of the way. And yes, while this operation certainly hit a snag, I find myself hard pressed to be too upset about it. After all, if he was able to help take down one as strong as George, then I can only conclude my son has flourished quite well in my absence. I'm a bit too topped off with pride to feel anything negative at the moment. So rest well. You've earned it."

The man reached over and patted her on the knee. "I mean it. Enjoy this down time, because when we move next, it will be a long while before we stop again."

Persephone understood. She had an area that was hers to stay in within the warehouse, but she didn't want to leave the comfort of his presence. Instead, she lay down on the couch she was already sitting upon and placed her head against the cushy arm in place of a pillow.

The future held terrible battles and nightmarish tasks, there was no question of that. For today, though, for just this moment, there was time to rest.

About the Author

Drew Hayes is an author from Texas who has now found time and gumption to publish a few books. He graduated from Texas Tech with a B.A. in English, because evidently he's not familiar with what the term "employable" means. Drew has been called one of the most profound, prolific, and talented authors of his generation, but a table full of drunks will say almost anything when offered a round of free shots. Drew feels kind of like a D-bag writing about himself in the third person like this. He does appreciate that you're still reading, though.

Drew would like to sit down and have a beer with you. Or a cocktail. He's not here to judge your preferences. Drew is terrible at being serious, and has no real idea what a snippet biography is meant to convey anyway. Drew thinks you are awesome just the way you are. That part, he meant. You can reach Drew with questions or movie offers at NovelistDrew@gmail.com Drew is off to go high-five random people, because who doesn't love a good high-five? No one, that's who.

Read or purchase more of his work at his site: DrewHayesNovels.com

Printed in the USA
CPSIA information can be obtained
at www.ICGtesting.com
LVHW091259211123
764544LV00003B/5

9 780986 396878